Other Deathstalker Books

Twilight of the Empire
Deathstalker
Deathstalker War
Deathstalker Honor
Deathstalker Destiny
Deathstalker Legacy
Deathstalker Return
Deathstalker Coda

The Adventures of Hawk & Fisher

Swords of Haven
Guards of Haven

Also by Simon R. Green

Blue Moon Rising
Beyond the Blue Moon
Blood and Honor
Down Among the Dead Men
Shadows Fall
The Man with the Golden Torc

Ace Books

The Nightside Series

Something from the Nightside
Agents of Light and Darkness
Nightingale's Lament
Hex and the City
Paths Not Taken
Sharper Than a Serpent's Tooth
Hell to Pay

SIMON R. GREEN

DEATHSTALKER REBELLION

——◦◉◦——

Being the Second Part of the Life and Times of Owen Deathstalker

A ROC BOOK

ROC
Published by New American Library, a division of
Penguin Group (USA) Inc., 375 Hudson Street,
New York, New York 10014, USA
Penguin Group (Canada), 90 Eglinton Avenue East, Suite 700, Toronto,
Ontario M4P 2Y3, Canada (a division of Pearson Penguin Canada Inc.)
Penguin Books Ltd., 80 Strand, London WC2R 0RL, England
Penguin Ireland, 25 St. Stephen's Green, Dublin 2,
Ireland (a division of Penguin Books Ltd.)
Penguin Group (Australia), 250 Camberwell Road, Camberwell, Victoria 3124,
Australia (a division of Pearson Australia Group Pty. Ltd.)
Penguin Books India Pvt. Ltd., 11 Community Centre, Panchsheel Park,
New Delhi - 110 017, India
Penguin Group (NZ), 67 Apollo Drive, Rosedale, North Shore 0632,
New Zealand (a division of Pearson New Zealand Ltd.)
Penguin Books (South Africa) (Pty.) Ltd., 24 Sturdee Avenue,
Rosebank, Johannesburg 2196, South Africa

Penguin Books Ltd., Registered Offices:
80 Strand, London WC2R 0RL, England

First published by Roc, an imprint of New American Library,
a division of Penguin Group (USA) Inc.

First Printing, July 1996
20 19 18 17 16 15 14

PUBLISHER'S NOTE
This is a work of fiction. Names, characters, places, and incidents either are the product of the author's imagination or are used fictitiously, and any resemblance to actual persons, living or dead, business establishments, events, or locales is entirely coincidental.

The publisher does not have any control over and does not assume any responsibility for author or third-party Web sites or their content.

Deathstalker.
It's not just a name. It's a destiny.

PROLOGUE

In the beginning was the Empire, and all was well. It was the great adventure of humanity, springing out from its homeworld, pressing on into the endless dark in search of new worlds and wonders. It was a time of heroes and marvelous deeds, as humanity spread from world to world, and the frontier pressed remorselessly outward. A thousand worlds, with a thousand civilizations, blazing so brightly against the dark. The Empire.

It took four hundred years for the rot to set in.

Parliament became corrupt, the Company of Lords grew increasingly powerful on the profits from plundered worlds, and the Emperor ruled over all with an iron fist from his Iron Throne. Technology produced human clones and espers, declared them nothing but property, and institutionalized slavery. It was still a great Empire, but only if you were rich, or of noble birth, or had connections in the right places. Everyone else worked hard, kept their heads down, and tried not to be noticed.

And so it went for nine hundred years.

By the time of Owen Deathstalker, the Empire was ripe for rebellion. Owen never wanted to be a hero. Despite his Family's martial history, he always saw himself as a scholar rather than a warrior. But when the Empress Lionstone XIV had him outlawed and put a price on his head that had his own people scrabbling to kill him, he had no choice but to run for his life and reluctantly grasp his destiny. He fell in with fellow outlaw Hazel d'Ark, pirate, bon vivant and ex-clonelegger, and together they fled to the rebel planet Mistworld, where they encountered Jack Random, the legendary professional rebel, Ruby Journey, the female bounty hunter, and Tobias Moon, an augmented man from lost Haden. Together they traveled to the planet Shandrakor, with its boiling jungles and endless carnage, and at the Last Standing of the Deathstalker Clan they discovered Owen's ancestor of some nine hundred years earlier: the man

called Giles, first Warrior Prime of the Empire and creator of
the terrible Darkvoid Device. He took them to the Wolfling
World, where they met the last Wolfling, sole survivor of his genetically engineered kind. They passed through the Madness
Maze and were changed, emerging much more than they had
been.

Together they would inspire and lead the greatest rebellion the Empire would ever know.

In her palace of brass and steel, set within a massive steel
bunker deep below the surface of the planet Golgotha, the Empress Lionstone XIV, the beautiful and adored, whose word
was law and at whose whim blood flowed and people died horribly. At her side, the Lord High Dram, Warrior Prime and
Consort, called by some Widowmaker, though never to his
face. At her command, loyal subjects like Captain Silence and
Investigator Frost of the starship *Dauntless*. At her feet, the
Families jostled and conspired to win her favor, and hunted
down her enemies without mercy. Lionstone had strengths and
surprises of her own and would not easily be brought down.

And watching from the sidelines, waiting to see which
way the wind might blow, many who might be swayed one
way or the other. Valentine, head of Clan Wolfe, favored and
powerful, a dandy and drug user of legendary proportions.
Kit SummerIsle, head of his Clan, called by some Kid
Death, the smiling killer. Cardinal James Kassar, fanatic and
rising star of the Church of Christ the Warrior.

In the shadows, the clone and esper underground fought
their losing battles and dared to dream of freedom. They had
allies in the cyberats, computer hackers and non-people by
choice, and also in restless younger sons who knew they
would never inherit the Family name and riches. And just
occasionally a hero would come to them, such as Finlay
Campbell, once known as the Masked Gladiator, uncon-
quered champion of the Arena; and Mater Mundi, Our
Mother Of All Souls, uber-esper and unfathomable mystery,
powerful beyond hope or sanity.

All the players were in place. The stage was set. All that
was necessary now was for someone to strike the first blow.
Owen Deathstalker, that reluctant hero, headed for Golgotha
in the company of Hazel d'Ark, on a strange golden ship run
by augmented men once known as the Enemies of Humanity; and though posterity has no access to his thoughts, they
were probably "Why me?"

CHAPTER ONE

Golgotha, Opening Gambit

Why me? thought Owen Deathstalker as he headed for the toilet yet again. He knew he wouldn't really need to do anything once he got there, but his bladder wasn't listening to reason. Not for the first time, it had ideas of its own. He was always like this when the pressure was on, and he had too much time to think. The afternoon before he'd made his first major speech at the Imperial Historians' Convention, he'd spent so long in their toilets that they actually sent someone in to ask if he was all right.

Owen sniffed, stepped inside the starship's single toilet, and pulled the door shut behind him. It wasn't much; just a small steel cubicle with a gleaming steel bowl. Owen unzipped and aimed carefully. He didn't want the others to think he was incredibly nervous. It was the waiting that got to him. He was hardly nervous at all during a fight. Usually, because he was too busy trying to keep himself from being killed to have time to worry. But beforehand, his imagination always insisted on picturing all the ways things could go horribly wrong in a hurry. And his current mission of heading for Golgotha, the most closely guarded planet in the Empire, in a golden ship built by inhuman beings who were once officially known as the Enemies of Humanity, had never struck him as being that sane an idea in the first place.

Even if it had been his idea.

But it had to be said the Hadenman ship was the best choice open to the nascent rebellion. His own ship, the marvelous *Sunstrider,* had been one of the fastest in the Empire, but he'd had to leave it where it crashed, deep in the deadly jungles of Shandrakor. And his ancestor Giles's vessel, the Last Standing, had been ruled out very early on. A huge stone castle with a built-in stardrive was many things, but inconspicuous wasn't one of them. The sleek golden ships of the Hadenmen, however, were everything the rebels needed, and more. Incredibly fast, powerfully armed, and so tightly cloaked there wasn't a sensor display in the Empire sensitive enough to pick them up. In theory, anyway. The Hadenmen had been out of things for a while.

The one thing the starship hadn't had was a toilet. Apparently, augmented men didn't need such things. Owen hadn't inquired further. He didn't think he really wanted to know. When Owen had discovered he and Hazel d'Ark had been volunteered to represent the rebellion on this mission, he had argued long and loudly against the decision. And when he lost, as he'd always known he would, even before he opened his mouth, he had stated flatly that he wasn't going anywhere with the Hadenmen until they installed a toilet. The Hadenman craft might be incredibly fast and powerful, but it was still a long trip to Golgotha, and Owen knew only too well what his nerves were going to be like.

So they'd added this cramped little cubicle especially for him and his nerves. There was no washbasin, rug around the base, or even a seat to lift. There was no toilet paper, either, but Owen had already decided very firmly that he wasn't going to think about that eventuality. He looked at his reflection in the steel wall before him; a man in his mid twenties, tall and rangy with dark hair and darker eyes. Not exactly soft, but not the kind of person you'd be scared of meeting in a back alley, either. Owen sighed deeply, finished what he was doing, zipped up again, and left the toilet with as much dignity as he could muster.

Minimalist though it was, he preferred the look of the toilet to the interior of the Hadenman ship. Its layout had not been designed with human comforts in mind, like sense or logic, and some of its aspects were positively disturbing. Owen concentrated on getting back to Hazel, who was sitting cross-legged on the deck between two enigmatic protrusions of Hadenman machinery. She was busy dismantling and cleaning her new projectile weapon, and she spared Owen only a scornful glance as he approached. Hazel d'Ark was never bothered by nerves. Give her something destructive to play with, and she was happy as a pig in muck. Owen sank down beside her, being very careful not to touch anything.

There were no seats or rest stations anywhere in the ship. Instead unfamiliar inhuman technology filled the interior from stem to stern, with Hadenmen plugged into it here and there as needed. The augmented men were part of the ship, or it was part of them, and they ran it with their thoughts. Owen and Hazel fitted in where they could, and tried not to look too directly at the incomprehensible machinery. It made their eyes hurt. Lights came and went, of painful brightness and unfamiliar hues, and the angles of the larger shapes were disturbing, as though trying to lead the human eye somewhere it couldn't or wouldn't follow. Owen settled himself as comfortably as he could on the unyielding steel deck, and hugged his knees to his chest. The ship intimidated the hell out of him, and he didn't care who knew it. He looked at Hazel, who was completely absorbed in what she was doing.

A tall, lithely muscular woman in her early twenties, Hazel always looked as though she was about to explode into action at any moment. Green eyes peered challengingly out at the world from under a mane of long ratty red hair, and her rare smiles came and went so quickly they were often missed.

As usual, she'd loaded herself down with weapons. Her disrupter hung in its usual place on her right hip, in its well-worn leather holster. Standard energy pistol, powerful enough to blast through steel plate as long as the gun's energy crystal was fully charged. And provided you didn't mind waiting the two minutes it took for the crystal to recharge between shots. Her sword hung on her left hip, the chased metal scabbard stretched out across the deck. Standard sword, heavy enough to do real damage, without being so long it became unwieldy. Scattered across the desk before her were the component parts of her projectile weapon. Actually, there looked to be enough parts to make several weapons. Owen had no idea the things were so damn complicated.

He had ambivalent feelings about the antiquated projectile weapons his ancestor Giles had provided from the Last Standing's armory. They weren't nearly as powerful or as accurate as energy weapons, but when they were pumping out several hundred bullets a minute on full auto, they didn't really need to be. There was none of that waiting for two minutes between each shot nonsense with them, either. Hazel had all but fallen in love with the new (or more strictly speaking old) type of weapons, and sang their praises at every opportunity. She'd taken to carrying several of the guns and enough ammunition to bulge every pocket she had.

Owen remained unconvinced, as yet. He carried a projectile weapon of his own as well as his disrupter, but he thought he'd wait and see how the gun performed in a continuous firefight before he made up his mind. Personally, he thought Hazel liked her new toys so much only because they had lots of separate pieces she could play with.

And finally, when push came to shove, he still believed in cold steel as the answer to most problems. A sword had no parts to go wrong, never ran out of ammo, and didn't need to recharge for two minutes between use.

"You keep squeezing it dry like that, you're going to flatten it," Hazel said casually. "Never known anyone spend so much time in a toilet. Check your guns again. It's very comforting."

"No it isn't," said Owen. "There isn't a single comforting thing anywhere in this unnatural ship, and that very definitely includes you."

"You never cease to amaze me, aristo. I've seen you fight appalling odds and go charging into situations I wouldn't tackle for all the credits in Golgotha's Treasury. You come from one of the greatest warrior Families in the Empire, but every time we have to wait around for a bit, you get jumpier than a nun at a dating agency."

"I am not a warrior," said Owen determinedly, not looking at her. "I am an historian who is temporarily—and under extreme duress—being forced to act as a soldier of the rebellion. Personally, I can't wait for the rebellion to be over so I can go back to being a minor scholar again, of no importance to anyone but myself and with no pressures apart from the occasional symposium. I still don't see why I was volunteered for this mission."

"Because it was your idea in the first place," said Hazel. "Serves you right for being a smart-ass. If anyone shouldn't be here, it's me. I'm still not convinced any of this is going to work."

"Then, what are you doing here?"

"Someone's got to watch your back. Besides, I was getting bored just sitting around back there. A complete lack of human comforts, far too much talking, and no action of any kind. I need to be doing something, or I get cranky."

"I had noticed," Owen said dryly. "Trust me; the plan will work. It's been discussed from every angle and subjected to intense analysis. Even the Hadenmen liked it. This mission is just what we need to start the rebellion with a bang. Something to make the whole Empire sit up and take notice."

"Oh, sure. They can all tune in their holos and watch us getting our ass kicked in living color. Probably repeat it at prime time, with extra slow motion for the gooey bits."

"I thought I was the nervous one?"

"You are. I'm just practical."

"So am I. That's why this plan is the best way to announce the rebellion's presence. We can't hope to win a head-on fight. They've got far more men and guns and ships than we have. So instead, we launch a lightning attack and hit them where it really hurts. In their pockets. With the Hadenmen's help, we'll slip right past Golgotha's defenses unobserved, sneak our way into the main Income Tax and Tithe Headquarters, perform our little act of economic sabotage, and be gone before anyone even knows we were there. It's really very elegant when you think about it. We transfer a whole bunch of credits to our preprepared rebel accounts, and then erase and scramble everything else.

"Thus, we not only kick the Empire and Church where it really hurts, and give a major boost to rebel funds, but we also make a lot of friends among the general populace when they realize the Empire won't be able to tax them again until they've got all the records sorted out and reestablished. Which could take years. Hazel, could you at least try and look interested in what I'm telling you? You managed to avoid most of the strategy sessions, but you need to understand what we're going to be doing down there."

"No I don't. Just point me in the right direction and turn me loose. If it even looks like an Imperial Guard, it's dead meat. I was good in a fight before we went through the Maze, but I'm hell on wheels now. I've got all kinds of abilities I never had before, and I can't wait to try them out."

Owen sighed quietly. "We're not just fighters anymore, Hazel. Like it or not, we've become important figures in the rebellion. If we can pull this off, we'll become heroes, even legends. People will look to us for inspiration on how to strike back against the Empire, and they'll join the rebellion in droves. The underground on Golgotha are committing a lot of their people and resources to help us in this, just because they believe in us. By surviving everything the Empire sent after us, we've become the hope of everyone who ever dreamed of being free."

"If we're their only hope, they're in big trouble."

"Maybe," said Owen. "But whatever the truth of the matter, we have responsibilities now. If we do pull this off, it'll be a sign that this rebellion has a realistic chance of succeeding. The people might believe in us, but the cold facts are that rebellions are extremely expensive to mount. Starships and rebel bases don't come cheap. Remember how Jack Random had to deal and concede and make questionable promises to questionable people, to get funding for his wars? And he was the legendary professional rebel. He had to compromise; with the credit we'll be lifting, we won't have to."

"All right," said Hazel. "Assuming, for the sake of argument, that we do bring this off without being killed in horrible ways, what then? Turn pirate, and pick off Empire ships between planets? Last I heard, the Empire was handing out some really nasty deaths for piracy."

"Didn't stop you being one."

"I'm not exactly noted for my career choices. So what's the plan, Deathstalker? I can tell you're just bursting to tell me."

"That's because it's such a good plan. As you'd know if you'd attended the strategy sessions like you were supposed to."

"Nag, nag, nag. Get on with it."

"We start small, picking our fights carefully, and build success on success until we're a viable force within the Empire. Then we call on the people to rise up against Lionstone. They've never dared in the past. Quite rightly, they fear reprisals. They also value their comforts too much. They think they have too much to lose. Unless their noses are rubbed in it, they don't like to think about where those comforts come from, and who suffers to produce them. Our task is to change the way people think, the way they see the Empire. First we educate them, then we encourage them to rise up, and then we help liberate them. Classic strategy. If the Empire really understood the lessons to be learned from studying history, they'd ban it."

"You're really getting into this, aren't you, Deathstalker? You've come a long way from the amateur scholar who just wanted the world to leave him alone."

Owen smiled briefly. "The world insisted on being heard. I can't go back to being what I was, much as I might like to. I've seen too much, done too much. But don't ever see me as some kind of warrior or hero. I might have to play the part for the rebellion, but it's not me. I'll fight when I have to, and that's it. And when it's all over, and the fighting's done, I'll be only too happy to climb back up into my ivory tower and kick the ladder away. I've spent most of my life trying to be the scholar I wanted to be rather than the warrior my Family expected. Circumstances may compel me to act the hero, but circumstances change, and the moment I'm no longer needed, I'll become an historian again so fast it'll make your head spin. People watching will suffer from whiplash."

Hazel sniffed, fitting her gun back together with calm, practiced fingers. "It's fighters, not dreamers, who make things change."

"I know what you want," said Owen, just a little testily. "You think all of us who went through the Maze should use our special abilities to cut a bloody path straight through the Empire to Golgotha, so that you could strut right into the Imperial Palace and take on the Empress head to head. Well, you can forget that. The moment we step out into the open, Lionstone will step on us, hard, even if it takes half her fleet to do it. We're not gods or superhumans. We've been given a few extra abilities, that's all. Very useful abilities, but only if used in the right ways at the right times."

"You're no fun," said Hazel. "What did the others think? I suppose they all wanted to pussyfoot around, too?"

Owen frowned. "Giles wanted to spend the next few years gathering data from a distance and develop hidden power bases throughout the Empire, before risking catching Lionstone's attention. If we'd listened to him, we'd still have been sitting on our ass twenty years from now, wondering if it was the right time yet. He hasn't been the same since he killed Dram. He's gone all cautious and noncommittal. Jack Random wanted to raise an army on the strength of his name and fight the Empire world by world, like he used to. He had to be reminded rather forcibly that his old way hadn't worked then and wouldn't work now. Ruby Journey just wanted to kill someone as soon as possible. And the Wolfling . . . wanted to be left alone. So I've been making most of the decisions, of late, because everyone else was too busy sulking."

"Maybe I should have got more involved, after all," said Hazel.

"We all asked you at one time or another. You didn't want to know. You were always off on your own somewhere, preoccupied with your own business. Whatever that might have been. Target shooting with your new toys, or trying to seduce a Hadenman, probably."

"I was busy experimenting with the new abilities the Maze gave us," Hazel said hotly. "You might be afraid of the changes it made in us, but I'm not. We're all stronger, faster, fitter than we were, but there's more to it than that. There's a connection between us now, a mental link on some deep, basic level. It's not esp. I can't read your mind or anyone else's. But we're . . . joined now, in some new, primal way. Mind to mind, body to body, soul to soul. Anything you can do, I can do, and vice versa. For example, I can boost now, just like you."

Owen looked at her sharply. Boost was both the gift and the curse of the Deathstalker Clan. For short periods he could become all but superhuman; inhumanly fast and strong, unbeatable with a weapon in his hand. A combination of mental training, engineered glands, and secret chemical caches deep within his body, boost was a jealously guarded Clan secret. It was also more seductive and addictive than any drug could ever be. Owen had learned to use it only sparingly. The candle that burns twice as brightly lasts half as long. Too much use of the boost would quite literally burn him up. Hazel knew some of that, but not all, and not nearly as much as she thought she did. Owen kept his voice carefully calm and even as he spoke:

"You must be mistaken, Hazel. The boost isn't some esper phenomenon; it's the result of inherited characteristics, physical changes in the body, and a hell of a lot of training."

"And I've got it." Hazel smiled triumphantly. "I've been practicing with it. You never told me it would feel so good, Owen. I hadn't thought about physical changes being involved, but you're probably right. So what? It just means my body has adapted itself as necessary. Interesting. I wonder what other changes I could make in myself, just by thinking about it . . ."

Owen leaned closer, so he could look her right in the eye.

"You're heading into dangerous waters, Hazel. We don't understand enough about what's been done to us to just experiment wildly. You're jumping off the edge with no idea of how deep the drop is. We need to take this one step at a time, under carefully controlled conditions."

"You're just frightened of the possibilities!"

"Damn right I am! So should you! The Maze was an alien artifact, remember? Designed by alien minds for alien purposes. The last people to go through it ended up creating the Hadenmen. Every time you experiment blindly, you're risking your very humanity. It's important we take this very slowly, very carefully."

"There isn't time! The rebellion needs us now. You're the one who said we had responsibilities, who keeps going on about how important this mission is. If we're going to survive this mission and the ones that follow, we're going to need every advantage we can get our hands on. If you're not prepared to lead the way, stand aside for someone who is. Don't you worry, aristo; once I've reached my full potential and I'm the superhuman you're so afraid of becoming, I'll take over the rebellion and you can go back to your books. You're too soft to be a real warrior, Deathstalker. You always were. You still dream about that kid you crippled on Mistworld, don't you? Let it go. She would have killed you without a second thought."

"That doesn't matter," said Owen, still meeting her gaze with his. "She was a child, and I cut her down without thinking, without caring, because I was caught up in the thrill of battle. I won't do that again. If I have to be a fighter, I'll be the kind of fighter I choose to be, not the kind my Family or you might prefer. And I won't give up my humanity in the name of necessity.

"I'm making the decisions in this rebellion because I'm the only one who's studied wars and insurrections from the past, and how they're won and lost. We'll fight the Empire through sabotage and subterfuge, and by winning the hearts of the people. No innocents will ever die by our hand. And if you think people will flock to follow some strange, superhuman leader, you're wrong. They'd scream for the Empire to hunt you down and kill you, just so they wouldn't have to be afraid of what you might do. We're going to attack the Income Tax and Tithe Headquarters as planned. It'll be the signal for a new kind of war, a new kind of rebellion, where no one has to die unnecessarily."

"Like I said. Soft. And still far too prone to lecturing people. I was hoping the Maze might have cured you of that, but apparently not."

"Then why are you here, Hazel?"

"Damned if I know, Deathstalker. I was hoping I was in for a little excitement, but it seems I was wrong about that, too. Doesn't matter. This is the start of the rebellion, and I'm not missing out on it. And if things do go wrong in your carefully worked-out plan, I'll be there to save your ass with my inhuman powers. Fair enough?"

"You don't understand, Hazel. I'm not afraid of the abilities themselves, just the price we might have to pay for them farther down the road."

Hazel looked at him expressionlessly. "You're a fine one to talk. You took that new metal hand of yours from the Hadenmen fast enough. They could have built all kinds of hidden surprises into it, and you'd never know till they activated them."

Owen looked down at the gleaming golden artifact that had replaced the left hand he lost fighting a killer alien the Empire had brought to the Wolfling World. The new hand was perfect in every detail and responded to him just as readily as his real hand had. Though it always felt subtly cold. He looked back at Hazel and shrugged uncomfortably.

"It's not like I had a choice. I needed a new hand, and I can't trust regeneration machines anymore. Not after my treacherous personal AI programmed the last one with control words the Empire could use against you and me."

"Ozymandius is gone, Owen. You destroyed him."

"Doesn't make any difference. Who knows what other surprises might be lying in wait for us in any other Empire machine we trusted our bodies to? I don't trust the Hadenmen completely, I'm not a fool, but right now they're the lesser of two evils. They can only mess with my hand, not my mind. Besides, they did a really good job on this hand. Full sensory analogues, and far more powerful than the original. And I don't have to trim the nails on this one."

"It's still a product of the Hadenman laboratories," said Hazel. "And I don't trust anything that comes out of them further than I could spit into a hurricane. The last time the Hadenmen took on the Empire, it was as Gods of the Ge-

netic Church, bringing transformation or death. Become a
Hadenman or become extinct. Remember? You must have
read about it in one of your precious books. And now here
they are again, born again, and so polite and helpful and reasonable it's downright spooky. I want to jump out of my skin
every time one of them approaches me. I keep waiting for
the other shoe to drop."

Owen nodded. He knew what she meant. They both
looked silently at the augmented men running the golden
ship. There were twenty of them, connected to their strange
machinery by thick lengths of cable plunging into their bodies or immersed in gleaming technology like a man half sub-
merged in water, their inhuman minds communing directly
with their unfathomable technology on a level no human
mind could understand or appreciate. Each Hadenman had a
specific function aboard the ship and performed it perfectly,
for as long as required. They did not suffer from boredom or
fatigue, from inspiration or original thought. At least not
while they were working. Perhaps off duty they were real
party animals, but Owen rather doubted it. From what he'd
seen of the Hadenmen as they went calmly about rebuilding
their strange and unsettling city deep below the frozen surface of the Wolfling World, the augmented men had no attributes that were not strictly logical and functional.

The only Hadenman Owen and Hazel had known at all
well was Tobias Moon, who'd traveled with them for a
while, but he'd spent so long among humans that he'd acquired a surface gloss of humanity—or at least a very good
copy of it. He'd worn out most of his energy crystals down
the years, losing many abilities and functions along the way,
and freely admitted he was only a pale weak version of the
real thing. Still, it had to be said that even on his good days
he'd been a disturbing son of a bitch. The glowing eyes and
inhuman buzzing voice hadn't helped, but it was in his mind
that the real differences lay. Tobias Moon thought differently, even when he tried not to.

The augmented men who'd emerged from the Tomb of the
Hadenmen, after Owen released them from their long restor-
ative sleep, had moved like living gods. Their eyes blazed
like the sun, their movements perfect and graceful. They still
scared the shit out of Owen, even after the past few months
of getting used to them. They called him their Redeemer and
were always quiet and deferential to him, but Owen knew

better than to warm to them. He'd studied the old records of their attacks on humanity. Seen the sleek golden ships running rings around the slower, clumsier human ships, blowing them apart with perfectly aimed weapons. Seen the tall shining figures stalking through blazing cities, killing everything that lived. Seen what happened to the humans they experimented on, the living and the dead, in the name of their Code of the Genetic Church. When you no longer have to worry about human emotions or restraints, you can do anything; and the Hadenmen had. They created abominations, seeking always an inhuman perfection of man and machine, a whole that would be greater than the sum of its parts.

They would have won the war if there had been more of them and less of humanity, but in the end they were thrown back, their golden ships outnumbered and blown apart, and the few survivors had fled back to the safety of their Tomb, hidden deep within the endless night of the Darkvoid, beyond the Rim of Empire. But they had come very close to wiping out humanity and replacing it with something altogether horrible. Owen remembered what he'd seen in the records, and all the politeness in the world wouldn't make him forget what they had done—and might yet do again.

But none of that mattered a damn for the moment. He needed them. The rebellion needed them. And if he was to go up against the Empire, there were going to be times when he'd need an army of trained fighters to meet Lionstone's armies. And that was where the Hadenmen would come in. Assuming they could be controlled or at least pursuaded to follow orders. Owen was under no illusions about the danger he'd reintroduced to the Empire. Given time, the Hadenmen might become a worse threat than Lionstone could ever be. Owen tried not to think about that too much, for the time being. It helped that he had so many other problems to worry about.

"Let's talk of more cheerful things," he said determinedly to Hazel. "Assuming we get past Golgotha's defenses as easily as the Hadenmen have promised, this will be our first chance to make real contact with the underground. They're practically the only organized rebellion left in the Empire. Mostly clones and espers, as I understand it, but with a great many useful fellow travelers; some of them quite influential. We need them on our side. Hopefully, kicking the crap out

of the Tax and Tithe HQ will make a good first impression
and convince them we're a force to be recognized. Jack Random's name should open a few doors. He's given me the
names of a few people he swears we can trust, but they
could be years out of date. Or dead. He betrayed a lot of
people when the Empire mind techs were working on him in
their interrogation center. Which is not going to make him
very popular in some quarters. His name could work *against*
us as much as *for* us. Same with my ancestor Giles, the original Deathstalker. Having a living legend on your side is
very useful in recruiting people, but there's always the
chance those same people will be disappointed with the reality rather than the perfect legend."

"Assuming he really is the original Deathstalker," said
Hazel.

"There is that, yes," said Owen unhappily. "He does seem
to know a hell of a lot about what's been going on recently,
for someone who's supposed to have been in stasis for the
last nine hundred years."

"So if he isn't who he says he is, who is he? An Empire
plant? A clone? Some madman with delusions of grandeur?"

"That's certainly some of the possibilities," said Owen.
"But I had something rather more disturbing in mind.
There's always the chance he could be a Fury."

Hazel looked at him speechlessly for a long moment,
struck dumb by the very thought. The Furies were terror
weapons created by the rogue AIs on Shub to act as their
agents in the world of men. Creations of living metal within
cloned flesh envelopes; identical to humans as far as the naked eye could tell, but capable of appalling havoc and destruction if detected. Unstoppable killers and merciless
opponents. Luckily, the Empire hadn't encountered too
many of them down the years. An esper could spot them
easily, and disrupters didn't care how strong the Furies were.
But there was always the possibility there were still some
around, undetected, living their fake human lives, reporting
back to Shub, and waiting for the order to destroy humanity
from within.

"Do you have a reason for thinking Giles might be a
Fury?" Hazel said finally.

"Nothing specific. It just seemed a little odd to me that
with so many factions appearing to take part in the rebellion,
Shub is the only one we haven't heard from. Not that I'd

give them the time of day if they had, but if I was them, I'd have an agent or two planted in the Court and the underground. Shub has a vested interest in knowing when the Empire is weak."

"You're right," said Hazel. "That is a disturbing thought. If you have any more like that, feel free to keep them to yourself. I have enough to be paranoid about as it is. If you're that worried, why haven't you said anything before?"

"I haven't any proof. And besides I wasn't entirely sure of who might be listening. Or who I could trust. Personally, I think Giles is exactly who he says he is."

"Why?"

"Because you have to trust someone."

"Yeah," said Hazel. "That's what's been bothering me."

Owen sighed. "Life never used to be this complicated. There was a time when my most arduous decision of the day was which wine to have with my meal."

Hazel smiled suddenly. "And you want to give up all this excitement, just to go back to that, and your dusty books?"

"Damn right I do. I want my old life back. I was perfectly happy being a minor historian, of no importance to anyone but myself. The best wines, first-class meals, every whim indulged and waited on hand and foot every minute of the day and night. No worries, no responsibilities I couldn't safely delegate to somebody else, and absolutely no chance of being suddenly and nastily killed. I'd go back like a shot, if I could."

"And leave behind all your friends? And what about me?" Hazel batted her eyes at him coquettishly. Owen winced.

"Please don't do that. It looks almost unnatural when you do it. You needn't worry that I'll abandon you, or the others. I've seen too much of the suffering and injustice the Empire is built on to be able to turn a blind eye to it anymore. Millions of people bled and died and were enslaved, so that I and a few others like me could have our lives of comfort. I have sworn upon my blood and upon my honor to put an end to that, and I will see it through or die trying. I just don't have any illusions about myself or how I came to be doing this. I'm nobody's hero, Hazel. Just another poor soul caught between a rock and a hard place. Let us change the subject yet again. Was there anything new from Mistworld before we left?"

"Nothing helpful. Ruby and I knew a few useful people in

Mistport, and Jack Random came up with a few more names, but they're all still very suspicious of us. We didn't make any friends on our last visit, and they've learned the hard way down the years to trust no one but themselves. They're waiting for us to commit ourselves first. They want a sign; something bold and audacious, and above all, successful."

"Fair enough," said Owen. "This first strike against Golgotha should impress the hell out of them. Assuming nothing goes wrong and we don't foul up. We only have one chance at this, and we've had no chance to practice. I have done my best to stop thinking about all the things that could go wrong; it just makes my head hurt and does terrible things to my bladder. I was never meant to be a warrior, no matter what my father wanted."

Hazel looked at him for a moment. "Owen, you think about your father too much. You've told me how he tried to manipulate you all your life, through his schemes and intrigues and hidden agendas, but he's dead now. It's all over now. Let it go. You're your own man these days."

"Am I? He's still pulling my strings, even from the grave! This is just the kind of magnificent heroic gesture he always believed in! I'm becoming exactly the kind of man he wanted, the kind of man I've struggled all my life not to be: a bully with a sword."

Hazel sighed inwardly and wondered how many times they were going to have to change the subject before they could find something they could both safely talk about. There had to be something. "This Stevie Blue, who's supposed to be meeting us dirtside; know anything about him?"

"You read the same reports I did. Apparently, he's an esper clone, in fairly high standing in the Golgotha underground. Assuming we manage to get together, he'll come back with us to be the underground's voice in our planning sessions. Reading between the lines, I get the feeling he's a bit of an anarchist, but it takes all sorts to make an Empire. Or a rebellion."

"What do you expect to happen after we've won, and it's all over?" Hazel said suddenly. "We've never really discussed this, any of us. We've spent a lot of time talking about bringing Lionstone down, but none at all discussing what we're going to replace her with."

"It's all rather moot at the moment," said Owen. "The

odds are stacked against us surviving, let alone winning. But if we do depose her ... Well, I suppose Parliament and the Company of Lords will put forward suitable candidates, and together we'll choose someone new to become Emperor and begin a program of reforms. Clean up the corruption, work in a little more democracy here and there, and of course a pardon for all rebels past and present. Then we can all get back to leading normal lives again."

"To hell with that!" Hazel said hotly. "We're not going through all this just to settle for the same old same old, with some pretty new window dressing! The whole system is corrupt from top to bottom, and our only chance for real justice is to tear it all down and start again. No more Emperor, no more Lords, liberation for all clones and espers, full democracy and freedom for everyone!"

"Everyone?" said Owen aghast. "Clones, aliens, espers . . . everyone?"

"Damn right. It has to be for everyone. That's what freedom means."

"Sounds more like anarchy to me. Not to mention total bloody chaos. If no one knows their place, how can you achieve anything?"

"I have never known my place, and I've achieved quite a lot. You'd be surprised what people can do, given a chance."

Owen looked at her thoughtfully. "Hazel d'Ark. The d'Arks used to be nobility, not all that long ago. Do I detect just a little overreaction here? By someone just a little ashamed of their aristocratic roots? Surely, Hazel, you must feel some loyalty to the Iron Throne?"

"Not one damned bit. The only soft spot I've got for the nobility would be a massive quicksand big enough to swallow the whole lot of them. I was never an aristo. I wasn't born a d'Ark; I stole the name when I was on the run and needed some false papers in a hurry. Mainly, because I liked the sound of it. I didn't want to risk my family finding me again or being sent back to them if I was rounded up."

"You never talk about your family," said Owen. "Don't you ever miss them?"

"No I bloody don't," said Hazel. "If I never hear from them again, that will suit me just fine."

Owen chose his words carefully. "Did they ... abuse you in any way?"

"Oh, no. Nothing like that. They were just so bloody boring and nice I couldn't stand them. Their idea of a wild party was a wine and cheese tasting where you spit the wine out. I had to get away, see the universe, taste some life before I got old and gray like them. You know how it is."

"Yes," said Owen. "I suppose I do. But I never had a chance to leave my Family. Too many duties and responsibilities. In the end they all left me, dying one after the other while I just stood by helplessly and watched it happen. There was never anything I could have done, but it didn't stop me feeling I should have done something.

"The boost killed a lot of them while they were still children. Only a few in every generation survive its first onslaught. The price of our genetic gift. Which is why I am all the sons and daughters of my father's line. I'm pretty much all that's left of the Clan now. Apparently, they found some distant cousin to take over the Lordship in my place, but I'm the last of the direct line. When I die, my line dies with me. I'm not sure whether that's a good thing or a bad thing. Seems to me we did as much harm as good down the years, but then I suppose that's true of most of the Families. And above it all, my father, sacrificing me and everyone else in his endless schemes and intrigues ... I never had a life of my own, ever since I was a small child. This mission is the nearest I've come to running away, to doing what I want to do instead of what my father planned. It feels very ... liberating."

He smiled suddenly. "You're right. I do tend to lecture people, don't I? One of the more socially acceptable vices of the scholar, I'm afraid. What were we talking about? Oh, yes, universal suffrage, even for the non-people. I really don't think you've been thinking this through, Hazel. If all the clones and espers were to be freed and enfranchised, the Empire itself would collapse. Its whole economy is based on the exploitation of clones and espers. They turn the wheels that keep things moving. Without them, everything would just fall apart. Food and power distribution would be disrupted, businesses would be in chaos ... Civilization itself could be threatened. Billions of innocents would suffer."

"No one's really innocent, if their lives of comfort are based on the suffering of others. If we have to tear civilization apart in order to put it back together again in a more just form, then that's what we'll do. Remember how horrified you were at how people lived on Mistworld? The appalling conditions and short brutal lives? Think how bad the lives of clones and espers in the Empire must be, if they're prepared to risk their lives just for a chance to flee to Mistworld. They're not second-class citizens, they're not even slaves. They're just property. Worked till they dropped, because there are always more to replace them. When I said tear it all down, I wasn't kidding. Anything would be better than what we've got now."

"I can't argue with that," said Owen. "I spent most of my life ignoring things I didn't want to see; I won't do that anymore. But there's still the problem of the aliens. There are at least two new alien species Out There somewhere, not counting whatever created the Madness Maze, all of them at least equal to our own level of technology. Weaken the Empire too much, and they might just walk in and wipe us out."

Hazel shrugged. "We can't afford to think about all the possibilities, or we'd go mad. There'd always be some good reason why we should put things off. Lionstone has to fall if the people are to be free, and if you and I are to live in safety. All we can do is take things one step at a time. We'll worry about the aliens as and when they make an appearance. They don't have to be enemies, you know. And anyway, you're a fine one to talk; you're the one who woke a whole army of Hadenmen from their Tomb. The only reason the Hadenmen aren't still the official Enemies of Humanity is because the AIs on Shub are worse. I suppose you'll be suggesting we team up with them next."

"I would rather cut off my head with a rusty saw," Owen said firmly. "The Hadenmen are a calculated risk. Shub, on the other hand, will settle for nothing less than the extermination of the human species. I may be reckless, but I am not stupid."

They both looked up sharply as one of the augmented men approached them. Hazel surreptitiously turned her reassembled projectile weapon so that it tracked the Hadenman's progress. Owen let his hand drift casually closer to his disrupter. The augmented man loomed over them, his movements inhumanly graceful, his eyes blazing so brightly Owen and Hazel couldn't look at them directly. His face held nothing that could be recognized as a human emotion, and when he spoke his voice was a harsh, grotesque buzzing.

"We have left hyperspace and are currently in orbit over

Golgotha. The ship's computers have made contact with the orbiting security satellites and persuaded them that our presence here is entirely natural and unthreatening. Our cloaking device will conceal us from passing ships and planet-based sensors as we descend toward the surface. There will be no difficulties. You may prepare yourselves for the drop."

"Thank you," said Owen politely, but the Hadenman was already walking away. They weren't much for small talk. Hazel pulled a face at the Hadenman's departing back and then looked at Owen.

"So, are you ready for the drop or do you need to disappear into the toilet again?"

"I don't think you could get another drop out of me if you used a siphon. Let's get down to the cargo bay. It's time to get this show on the road."

"Damn right," said Hazel.

They made their way back through the hulking alien machinery, climbing carefully over it when there was no clear path around it. The gleaming metals felt uncomfortably cold, and some of it shimmered uncertainly, as though it wasn't always there. Owen and Hazel gave the machinery as much room as they could, kept their hands strictly to themselves, and descended floor by floor to the empty cargo bay. The vast steel cavern was lined with thick-ribbed cables that curled around and over each other in eye-numbing confusion, but the only equipment set out in all the empty space were two standard gravity sleds and a small package of carefully prepared code discs to be fed into the Tax and Tithe computers. Owen and Hazel checked the sleds over thoroughly, just in case, and then settled down to wait. It wouldn't be long now.

The sleds were really nothing more than a flat surface disturbingly like a coffin lid with an antigrav motor, a set of controls, two built-in disrupters, and a force shield to protect the rider from the wind. Pretty basic, but all they'd need. If nothing went wrong.

Owen hefted the computer codes in his hand. A very small package to do so much potential damage. Rather like Hazel, in fact. He smiled at the thought and looked across at her. She had her sword out and was polishing the blade with a filthy piece of rag. Owen was never entirely sure how he felt about her at any given time. He respected her, certainly, and admired her skill with weapons . . . She was one of the finest fighters he'd ever fought beside. And he certainly respected the fire in her voice when she spoke of freedom and justice, even if he didn't always agree with her solutions. She'd come barging into his life like a runaway horse, saving him from almost certain death, and then proceeded to shake up and question everything he thought he believed in. And somewhere along the line, quite against his will, he'd fallen in love with her.

He hadn't told her and wondered if he ever would. He was everything she claimed to despise, a naive aristo with more ancestors than sense. He liked to think she respected him as a fighter, but beyond that he had no idea how she felt about him. Besides, he was a Deathstalker. He had a duty to marry someone of his own station. Except . . . he wasn't an aristocrat anymore. Lionstone had publicly declared him an outlaw and stripped him of every rank and privilege. Which meant he was free to do as he liked. And Hazel was brave and true, with a great smile and eyes to die for. Pity about her hair . . . She was smart and quick, and determined not to take any shit from anyone, least of all him.

He loved her, in a way that made him realize he'd never really loved anybody else. Cathy had been his lover for several years, but she was his mistress, which was really just another kind of servant. She'd been an Empire spy, and had tried to kill him when he was outlawed. He'd killed her without hesitating. There'd never been much love in his Family, particularly from his father, who was always busy somewhere else, so he'd learned to live without love. And then Hazel burst into his life, and everything changed. Sometimes he couldn't look at her without catching his breath, and his heart quickened when she spoke to him. Her infrequent smiles could put him in a good mood that lasted for hours.

To be honest, he could have done without love. It complicated their relationship and distracted him from more important things. But, he didn't seem to have any choice in the matter. He loved her, despite all her many faults, or even perhaps because of them. Even if he could never tell her. At best she'd laugh at him or tell him to go to hell. At worst, she might be kind and understanding as she said no, and he didn't think he could stand that. He knew nothing of love or

lovers, but even he knew hope was better than disillusion-
ment.

An alarm sounded quietly through his comm implant, and
he saw Hazel's head snap up as she heard it, too. She put her
sword away and climbed aboard her gravity sled, ready for
business as always. Owen slipped the computer discs into an
inside pocket, zipped it shut, and powered up his sled. A
view from the ship's sensors appeared before his eyes,
patched in through his implant, showing the main landing
pads stretched out below. There were ships everywhere, of
all shapes and sizes, growing steadily larger as the
Hadenman ship descended at speed. There wasn't room anywhere for the Hadenman ship to set down, but that was all
right. It wasn't intending to land. Owen grinned. The plans
called for the Hadenman ship to drop the cloaking about
now. Then things should get really interesting.

They were almost on top of the starport control tower
when the cloaking device shut off. People stopped believing
their sensors, took one look at the huge sleek golden craft
hovering right above them, and launched straight into a mass
panic. There was a lot of screaming and shouting, and a
great deal of running around and around in circles. Owen
didn't blame them. The last time Golgotha had seen a
Hadenman ship this close, they'd come in force as the Enemies of Humanity, to wipe out the homeworld's defenses.
They'd come uncomfortably close, too, according to some
suppressed records that Owen had happened across while
looking for something else.

The visual feed cut off, and Owen smiled across at Hazel,
who grinned back. In that much chaos and confusion, no one
was going to notice two small gravity sleds. Owen gripped
the controls of his sled firmly. Only a few more moments
and he wouldn't have time to feel nervous anymore. He
hoped Hazel was feeling as confident as she looked. It
would be nice if one of them was. The alarm sounded briefly
in his ear again, and the great cargo bay doors cracked open
below them. The temperature in the hold dropped sharply,
and Owen could see bright sunlight through the widening
crack. He raised his sled slightly so that it was hovering just
above the floor. Hazel lifted hers, too, and moved in close
beside him. The cargo bay doors opened wider, and now
they could see the landing pads below. It looked a long way
down. Owen took a deep breath and directed his sled down

and through the opening doors. Hazel followed close behind. Together they dropped out of the belly of the great golden ship, and plummeted down toward the landing field.

The bay doors slammed shut behind them, and the Hadenman ship shot away, already pursued by half a dozen Imperial attack ships, firing everything they'd got. The golden ship's force shields flared briefly here and there, but never even looked like going down. No one noticed two tiny figures heading silently for the ground, too small for the heavy-duty port sensors, too fast for the naked eye. The plan was very simple. The Hadenman ship would hang around, drawing attention to itself, while Hazel and Owen got on with their mission. It would take some time for the starport to come up with anything big enough to worry the golden ship. By that time the mission should be over, and the ship would return to pick Owen and Hazel up again. They would then depart at great speed, drop back into hyperspace, and be gone before the Empire could get its act together.

A very simple plan. Owen believed in simple plans. The more complicated a plan was, the more chances there were of something going wrong. He wasn't worried about anything happening to the Hadenman ship. The strength of Hadenman force shields was legendary, and the ship itself was bulging with all kinds of weapons, some of which Owen didn't even recognize. He'd made the augmented men promise to use their weapons sparingly and only in self-defense. It wouldn't do to start the rebellion with a bloody Hadenman massacre. It would give entirely the wrong impression, and first impressions were important. The augmented men had nodded very politely and said yes and no and of course in all the right places. Owen had crossed his fingers and hoped for the best.

The sled's force shield snapped on automatically as he dropped like a stone, protecting him from the rushing wind. Speed was all that mattered for the moment, to get out of the starport and disappear into the crowded city before either he or Hazel could be spotted. The pastel towers of the city loomed up before him, and he slowed a little so he could duck and dodge around them. The force shield snapped off, to conserve power. The wind whistled past Owen, cold and bracing, blowing tears from his eyes. He narrowed his gaze and concentrated on the map he'd memorized earlier. It wasn't that far, but the route was tricky, particularly if you weren't intending to follow the established traffic paths. Owen flashed past a floating red light and tucked in close beside a tower to avoid an oncoming tour bus. He had a brief glimpse of openmouthed faces from windows on both sides, and then he was through and in the clear again. He grinned and activated his comm unit on the shielded channel.

"Still with me, Hazel?"

"Damn right I am. You'll have to do better than that to shake me."

"I thought you said you hadn't had much practice on a gravity sled before?"

"I haven't. Half the time I feel like I'm riding a crashing elevator. But I can follow anywhere you lead, Deathstalker."

"Wouldn't doubt it for a minute, Hazel. We're almost there, so stand ready to guard my back. Remember, they stripped these sleds down to basics for extra speed, which means we have only minimum shields. One good hit from a disrupter, and they'll go down faster than a backstreet whore. So I'm counting on you not to let anyone hit us. On the other hand, please also remember we're supposed to be the good guys here, so try not to kill anyone except the Imperial Guards. It's important we make the right impression here."

"Details, details," Hazel said airily. "You concentrate on your map and leave the fighting to me. That's how we work best."

Owen felt a strong answer to that rising up in him, but he forced it down. He was going to learn to be polite and charming to Hazel if it killed him. He pressed on through the city, whipping back and forth between the towers and fighting the sudden updrafts. The city was only just waking up, still wrapped in early-morning light. The sky was a bloody red, painting the pastel towers with crimsoned shadows. There was hardly any air traffic yet, but that would change in a hurry once the sun was up and the business day began. The plan called for Owen and Hazel to get into the Tax and Tithe HQ, do the dirty, and get the hell out while the skies were still comparatively uncrowded. Owen piled on the speed, and the force shield snapped on again, giving his tearing eyes and numbed face a break. He and Hazel were on their own till they could land and make contact with the underground, and right now he felt very alone and extremely vulnerable.

He could feel Hazel crowding close behind him. He didn't look back to make sure. He didn't need to. All of those who'd passed through the Madness Maze were linked to each other now, in some deep fundamental way that none of them understood yet, but none of them doubted. It was a kind of low-level esp, an unquestioning certainty as to where the others were at any given moment. They couldn't read each other's thoughts, for which Owen for one was very grateful, but as Hazel had already proved, whatever gifts or talents one possessed, the others now had, too, as though they'd always had them. Owen could feel Hazel's presence at his back. It felt reassuring. He whipped around a tower, so close he could have reached out and trailed his fingertips across the windows flashing past, and then, right before him, dead bang where it was supposed to be, was the Tax and Tithe Headquarters, in Tower Chojiro. Owen grinned fiercely and opened his secure comm channel again.

"Almost there, so brace yourself. And, Hazel, don't use the boost unless you have to. There are things about it you don't know. It's ... unwise to use it too often."

"Nag, nag. You always were a bit of an old woman, Deathstalker."

Owen decided he wasn't going to answer that one, either, and made himself concentrate on Tower Chojiro as it loomed up before him. He cut his power and slowed steadily, but kept the force shield up. The sled's built-in cloaking device was supposed to be keeping him invisible, as far as the tower's sensors were concerned, but he didn't feel like taking chances now he'd got this close to the objective. Tower Chojiro was the tallest and ugliest of the immediate towers, a gleaming monument of glass and steel, the Clan colors and signals clearly marked. It was also undoubtably bristling with hidden weapons and other nasty surprises. The Hadenmen had assured Owen on more than one occasion that his and Hazel's sleds had been carefully adjusted so that they would slip past the tower's defenses unmolested. But of necessity, there had been no way to test this in advance.

Owen shrugged mentally. It was a bit late to be worried now. Either it would work, or he and Hazel would end up spread across the tower's energy fields like flies on a windscreen, and the rebellion would have to start somewhere else. Oddly, Owen discovered that he didn't feel particularly nervous. The Hadenmen had assured him their devices would work, and he had no reason to distrust them. Not over that, anyway. Everything else, maybe. He took a firm hold on the controls, braced himself, and headed the sled straight for the top floor of the tower. The windows came flying toward him at incredible speed. Owen just had time to realize he must have passed safely through the tower's force shields before the sled slammed through the toughened steelglass window, as though it wasn't there.

The gravity sled screeched to a halt some twenty feet past the shattered window, and its force shield snapped off. Owen released his death grip from the controls and stepped down, just a little shakily. He looked quickly about him but the top floor of Tower Chojiro was deserted, just as it was supposed to be. There was a little furniture scattered here and there on the thick carpeting, all of it designed within an inch of its life, and just the occasional small painting on the walls. Originals, of course. Clan Chojiro were famed for their minimalist approach. Owen hoped it applied to their interior security systems as well, but he rather doubted it. His and Hazel's entrance had to have set off all kinds of alarms, and since the interior weaponry hadn't finished them off any more than the exterior force shields, the odds were that a large number of heavily armed men were currently on their way up to find out why. Of course, they'd have to start at the bottom and work their way up floor by floor, to make sure everything was secure. Which should take them some time. More than enough for him to deal with the computers and leave. Theoretically. He drew his disrupter and activated the force shield on his wrist. The oblong of glowing force formed instantly on his arm, its familiar low hum distinctly comforting. Hazel moved in beside him, a gun in each hand.

"Tax and Tithe is four floors down, right? Elevator or stairs?"

"Stairs, of course. The elevators can be overridden by the tower's central computers. Didn't you attend any of the briefings?"

"I leave all the heavy thinking to you, stud. Just find me something I can shoot at, and I'll be happy."

Owen decided there was nothing to be gained in answering that, and led the way out of the empty room and on to the stairwell. It was well posted and exactly where it was

supposed to be, which cheered Owen up a bit. At least the
intelligence reports seemed to be accurate. The stairwell was
narrow, brightly lit, and looked as though it had last been
whitewashed sometime in the previous century. After all,
who used stairs anymore, except in emergencies? It was all
deathly quiet, apart from the racket Owen and Hazel made
clattering down the bare steel steps. No doubt the tower defenses were sounding all kinds of alarms, but that would be
on the tower's private security channel, and Owen didn't
have the time to search out which particular channel they
were using that day. No doubt security changed it regularly.
He would have. Hazel checked the lock at the bottom of the
stairs, a simple combination mechanism, and sniffed disparagingly.

"This wouldn't stop a ten-year-old on Mistworld. I'll have
it open in a few minutes."

"No," said Owen. "Let me try." He bent over the lock,
studied it carefully, and then entered a short series of numbers. The lock clicked open. Owen straightened up and
smiled at Hazel. "You got the boost from me; I got breaking
and entering from you. Somewhat improved by the Maze's
changes. Wonder what else we've got that we don't know
about?"

"This is getting spooky," said Hazel. "At this rate, we'll
end up with more augmentations than a Hadenman."

"Now, that is a disturbing thought. But it'll have to wait.
When I open this door, everyone in the room beyond is a target. We don't have the time to deal with prisoners."

"Suits me," said Hazel. "Never did like tax collectors."

Owen put his shoulder to the heavy steel door, and it
swung open inward with surprising speed. Five technicians
looked up, startled, and barely had the time to draw breath
to cry out before Hazel picked them all off with separate
shots from her projectile weapon. Owen quickly swung the
door shut behind them, and everything was quiet in the computer room. He was glad he hadn't had to use his disrupter
to back Hazel up. Using an energy weapon in a confined
space full of delicate equipment was rarely a good idea. He
holstered his gun and leaned over the nearest body to make
sure it was dead. He grimaced in spite of himself. Projectile
weapons got the job done, but they were extremely messy.
There was blood all over the floor and holes in the bodies

big enough to stick his fist into. Disrupters tended to be much neater and cauterized their own wounds.

"Marvelous weapons," Hazel said happily, studying the wounds she'd made. "Don't you just love them?"

"Check they're all dead," said Owen flatly. "I don't want any surprises while we're working."

"Oh, sure," said Hazel. "You have a bash at the machines, and I'll guard your back. What I know about reprogramming computers could be engraved on my left thumbnail."

"It shouldn't be that complicated," Owen said hopefully, studying the terminals before him. "Jack Random and the Hadenmen worked out the programming between them. All I have to do is load the discs and let them run. If you'd like to cross your fingers at this point, feel free to do so."

He pulled up a chair and sat down before the massive bank of computers that covered the whole wall before him. Together with the machinery scattered throughout the room, these computers were responsible for setting and collecting the many taxes of the entire Empire. Trillions of credits came and went at these computers' commands every day. Decisions made here could be questioned by no one lower than the Empress Lionstone herself. That the Church of Christ the Warrior, quite possible the most paranoid religion of the time, trusted these computers to run its Tithing system as well, spoke volumes for the machinery's efficiency and security. They distributed the wealth of the Empire, with contributions from the lowest to the highest. Even the Families paid taxes through their business interests. It took a lot of money to run the Empire and keep Lionstone in the manner to which she'd become accustomed. Everyone trusted the computers implicitly. Of course, they'd never come up against Hadenman technology before. Few had. Owen grinned broadly. The entire financial base of the Empire ran through this room, and he, a despised outlaw, was about to bring it all crashing down in ruins.

He entered the necessary codes, removed the package of software discs from his hidden pocket, and slotted them into place. He paused, just to savor the moment, and then hit the final entry key. Nothing obvious happened. The machines hummed on as before. But deep within the database, changes were being made. First, extremely large sums were being diverted from the Empire coffers into previously prepared rebel accounts. Billions of credits, soon to be chasing from one short-lived bolt-hole to another, until their provenance was hopelessly lost and confused. It seemed only fair and right to Owen that the Empire should fund its own destruction.

And once it had completed that little task, the program would then set about erasing or at the very least hopelessly scrambling every scrap of data in the computers. No record would remain of who paid what, or when. In short, utter chaos. There was no copy of the records anywhere else, for security reasons. Lionstone believed very firmly in centralization. Having things in one place made them easier to control. And who would ever have thought that the mighty Clan Chojiro's extensive security systems could be defeated by two lowly individuals on gravity sleds, backed by Hadenman technology?

So once the news got out—and it would get out eventually—whatever the Empire did, a great many lesser people would suddenly find they were a great deal better off than they had been, courtesy of the rebellion. The Empire, on the other hand, would not only find itself suddenly short of working funds, it would also have to spend even more credits and man hours just trying to put together a picture of how badly off they were. It would be years before Lionstone could raise taxes again. And while the Empire was so preoccupied, the rebellion could get on with more serious projects.

"How long is this going to take?" said Hazel.

Owen looked back at her and shrugged. "Beats me. I did ask, but since no one's ever done this before, no one knows for sure. Basically, we just hang around here till the computer spits out the discs, and that should be it. Let's just hope it doesn't take too long. Clan Chojiro's security forces are undoubtably following standard procedure and working their way up the tower floor by floor even as we speak. They'll stop to secure each floor as they go, but even so it won't be that long before they come hammering on our door. Hopefully, the discs will be finished, and the underground representative Stevie Blue will have already made contact with us. Otherwise, we are in deep shit."

"I love it when you talk technical," said Hazel. She stopped and frowned suddenly. "What's the password for Stevie Blue? I can never remember things like that."

Owen paused, frowning. "Now, I knew it, until you asked me. What the hell is it? Oh, well, it'll come back to me."

And then they both stopped and looked sharply at the closed metal door. They hadn't heard anything yet, but they both sensed something. Another gift from the Madness Maze. Owen moved quickly over to the door, eased it open a crack, and listened intently. From not all that far away came the sound of massed booted feet crashing on steel steps, drawing steadily closer. Owen let the door close silently and backed away from it.

"Company's coming," he said flatly, not looking at Hazel. "Lots of them. Either they're not bothering to secure every floor, the cheats, or there's a hell of a lot more of them than we were led to believe."

"I knew this was going too smoothly," said Hazel. "Well, let them come. I could use a little exercise."

"Not for the first time, you're missing the point," said Owen. "If the security forces are already this close, how is Stevie Blue supposed to make contact with us?"

"Tricky," Hazel agreed. "I suppose we'll just have to kill all the security people, won't we?"

Owen looked at her. "You've become altogether too cocky since we survived the Maze. We're a lot more than we used to be, but we're not unbeatable."

"Speak for yourself, Deathstalker. We're stronger, faster, and sharper than any damn security guards. We can take them. It doesn't matter how many of them there are. You worry too much, Owen."

He shook his head sadly. "Cocky. Definitely cocky. Unfortunately, since we can't leave here yet, we have no choice but to let them come to us. Try not to get yourself killed, Hazel. I'd hate to have to start training another partner."

Hazel glared at him. "First, we are not partners, and second, if there's any training going on here, I'm the one that's doing it. If it weren't for me, you'd have been killed a dozen times over. I'll do the fighting, you watch for those discs to reappear. Once they're out we are gone."

"And Stevie Blue?"

"Can save his own ass. Serves him right for being late."

The sound of approaching feet was very close now. Owen hefted her two guns and stood facing the closed door. Owen hauled the dead technicians to one side, so he and Hazel would have room to maneuver, if they needed it. He got blood on his hands and sleeves, and wiped them thoroughly on the front of his jacket. He didn't want his hands to be slippery if he had to use his sword. Feet crashed on the floor outside, and the door swung inward as three guards put their shoulders to it. They paused a moment in the doorway as they took in Owen and Hazel and the blood on the floor, and that moment was all Owen needed to aim his disrupter and fire. The energy beam blasted a hole right through the first guard's chest and took out the man standing behind him as well. Hazel got the other one, her disrupter beam neatly separating the man's head from his body. And that was when the rest of the guards came crashing in, convinced their opponents' energy weapons could be useless now for the next two minutes. Owen and Hazel ducked down behind their personal force shields, and energy beams ricocheted around the room. Various pieces of equipment exploded and burst into flames. The guards put away their exhausted guns and pressed forward with drawn swords. And that was when Hazel lowered her force shield and opened up with her projectile weapon.

Explosive bullets tore through the men in the room, ripping them apart and throwing their lifeless bodies aside. Blood flew in the air, and the roar of the gun was deafening in the confined space. The guards could get through the door only a half dozen at a time, and the projectile weapon cut them to shreds while they were still struggling to get into the room. It had been designed that way, to make the room easier to defend against mass rebel attacks. The guards had no force shields—too expensive. They relied on numbers. And all too soon Hazel's gun ran out of bullets and fell silent. Hazel swore briefly and holstered the gun. The guards came crashing in again, and Owen and Hazel went to meet them with cold steel in their hands.

Swords rang on swords, but though the guards outnumbered the outlaws a dozen to one, it was still no contest. The guards were already confused and demoralized, with so many of them already dead, and Owen and Hazel both had the boost. Owen's smile stretched into a death's-head grin as blood roared in his veins and thundered in his head. His enemies seemed to be moving in slow motion, and he cut them down easily and gloried in their deaths. He'd always been fast when boosting, but the Maze had made him inhumanly fast. The guards fell quickly, butchered like so many helpless animals in the slaughterhouse. And then there were no more targets, only unmoving bodies on the bloody floor.

Owen checked that the room was empty—apart from him and Hazel and the lifeless bodies—peered out the door into the empty corridor, and then dropped out of boost. He shuddered helplessly as the reaction hit him. For a few fleeting moments he had been almost a god, and now he was only human again, and it hurt. His muscles ached from the strain he'd put them through, and his movements seemed unbearably slow and sluggish. He breathed deeply, concentrating as he'd been taught, and his senses quickly returned. The Deathstalker Family had spent generations perfecting the surge of strength and speed that was boost, but even so the human body could stand it only for short periods. It burned up the nervous system with a remorseless appetite, and there was always a price to be paid afterward. And even above that, there was the terrible joy of the boost, wild and over-powering, more tempting and addictive than any drug could ever be. The boost: pride and curse of the Deathstalker Clan. And Hazel was caught up in it and burning so very, very brightly.

She hacked and cut at the dead bodies before her, laughing breathlessly, her face slick with sweat. Her eyes were wide and feral, fixed on some inner private Valhalla. Owen called to her, but she didn't hear him. He moved toward her and she spun on him, sword at the ready, her grin terribly eager. He sheathed his sword, switched off his shield, and held out his hands to her, so she could see they were empty. Her head cocked a little to one side as he spoke to her soothingly. He took another step closer, and she lunged forward, her sword flying toward his gut. Owen tapped his boost, just for a second. Just long enough for him to sidestep so that her sword flashed past him, missing his side by less than an inch. He clamped his arm down hard so that the sword was held in place and hugged Hazel to him. She fought him fiercely, and Owen knew he couldn't hold her for more than a few moments.

He held her blazing eyes with his and reached out to her through the mental link they shared, the Maze-given connection of the undermind. He couldn't reach her with words, or thoughts, only the simple truth of his presence, who and what he was, and how he felt about her. Her mind was bright and dazzling, darting like quicksilver, sharp and deadly.

Owen reached out to her, and slowly she responded calmly, inch by inch. Her eyes slowly cleared, and he felt the first faint stirrings of her own feelings before a barrier slammed down between them as Hazel cut off the link and dropped out of boost. She almost collapsed as her legs shook, and Owen held her trembling body close to him, until she had enough strength and control to push him away and stand alone. She took a deep, shuddering breath and nodded to him brusquely. He knew that was the only acknowledgment he'd ever get of what they'd felt and shared for a moment. Hazel's hands were almost steady as she wiped the sweat from her face with the same filthy rag she'd used earlier to clean her sword.

"That . . . was something else," she said finally. "I've never felt anything like it, and I've tried a lot of things in my time. I was so alive . . . I would have killed you, if you hadn't stopped me. Is the boost always like that?"

"Mostly," said Owen. "You never really ever get used to it. That's why I only ever use it when I have to. Take it easy for a few minutes. It takes time for your body to replace the energy the boost burns up."

"And you've lived with this most of your life?" Hazel looked at Owen with new respect. "You're a harder man than you look, Deathstalker. I was once a plasma baby, addicted to Wampyr Blood. And the boost is stronger than any drug I've ever known. How do you stand it?"

"By using it only when I absolutely have to," said Owen. "And I have had training you haven't. It gets a little easier in time, but not much. I did try to warn you."

"Yeah, you did." Hazel turned away and looked at the dead bodies scattered and piled across the room. The floor was awash with blood, and she shuddered briefly before she was back in control. "You suppose that's all of them?"

"I very much doubt it. This was just the first wave, sent in to check out the situation. Look at the bodies; they're all wearing short-range sensors. Their superiors know exactly what happened here. Which means not only can we forget about having the advantage of surprise, we can also expect a heavily armed, much larger second wave. The experienced fighters. Things are about to get really interesting."

He broke off, and they both looked at the closed door again. Someone was coming. They could feel it. Owen pulled the door open and stepped out into the corridor, his guns at the ready. Behind him, Hazel was quickly reloading her main projectile weapon. Owen moved slowly toward the stairwell. Someone was coming up the stairs, his unhurried footsteps loud and echoing in the quiet. Hazel moved in beside Owen, nudged him to get his attention, and mouthed *One man?* Owen shrugged, and they both moved forward to look down the stairs. The newcomer took his time climbing the last flight of stairs, and then came to a halt at the last corner, looking impassively up at Owen and Hazel. He was a tall, blocky man, with thick slabs of muscle and a patient, brooding face. His skin was dark, his close-cropped hair was white, and his cold eyes were a startling green. He wore no armor, only a long green kimono of the Chojiro Clan, decorated with stylized dragons, and he carried a long curving sword in each hand.

"Oh, shit," said Owen.

Hazel looked at him. "You know this guy?"

"Unfortunately, yes. This is ex-Investigator Razor. Used to work for Clan Wolfe as their pet killer and intimidator, but given the Wolfes' downfall and that extremely tacky dress he's wearing, I can only assume he's taken up a similar position with Clan Chojiro. If you know any good religions, now would be a really good time to start praying."

"He doesn't appear to have any guns. Why can't we just shoot him from a safe distance?"

"One, he undoubtably has a personal force shield, and two, it might annoy him."

Hazel put away her guns and drew her sword. "So we get our hands dirty."

"Hazel, Investigators are killing machines; the best there is with any weapon you care to name."

"So what do you suggest we do?"

"Anybody else, I'd suggest surrendering, but Investigators don't take prisoners. So we're going to have to fight him. *Oh, shit.*"

"Will you stop saying that! He's just one man. I'll take first crack at him."

"No you won't. I will. You still haven't recovered from boosting."

"I can take him! Really!"

"Excuse me," said the Investigator.

"You be quiet," said Owen. "We'll get to you in a minute. Hazel, I am taking first crack, and that's all there is to it."

"Since when were you in charge of this mission? If I want to take him, I'll take him!"

"Hazel, this is really not a good idea!"

"Excuse me," said the Investigator firmly.

"Shut up!" said Owen and Hazel, glaring at each other.

Investigator Razor shrugged, and surged up the last few stairs impossibly quickly, his two swords swinging in shimmering blurs. Owen and Hazel stood their ground, swords at the ready, and dropped into boost. Blood pounded in their heads, and strength burned in their arms like living flames. Razor hit them like a thunderstorm, his swords like lightning. The air was full of the ring of steel on steel as Owen and Hazel were driven back, step by step, unable to meet the sheer ferocity of his attack.

Razor left the stairwell behind him, moving implacably forward, until Owen and Hazel bumped up against the corridor wall behind them, and there was nowhere else to go. Owen and Hazel separated, and attacked him from two sides at once. Razor held his ground and stood them both off, his blades moving too fast to be seen. Owen ducked at the last moment, and a flashing sword cut a groove right into the wall where his head had been. Hazel lunged forward, hoping to catch Razor momentarily off balance, and then had to hurl herself to one side as a waiting sword leaped out to meet her. She hit the floor rolling and was quickly back on her feet, breathing hard. Blood soaked her left sleeve, but she ignored it, cushioned from pain and shock by the boost.

Owen had already realized they couldn't beat Razor on their own. The Investigator had been trained to the peak of perfection in all the killing arts, and Owen didn't have the expertise to match him. Neither did Hazel. But they did have the boost, and what the Maze had done to them. He reached out to Hazel through the mental link, the undermind they didn't have to understand to use, and their minds touched. They threw themselves at Razor, attacking in perfect synchronization, two swords wielded by one concerted will. Razor fell back a step, and then another, but that was as far as he would go. Even joined, Owen and Hazel could only ever be his equal.

And there was no saying which way the fight might have gone, if Razor's kimono hadn't suddenly burst into roaring flames. He threw himself to one side, rolling on the carpeted floor to try and crush the flames, but they just blazed the brighter. The flames were already licking up around his face as he lurched to his feet and ran off down the corridor, but he never once made a sound. He disappeared around a corner, still burning, and was gone, and all they could hear was the departing echo of his feet.

Owen and Hazel dropped out of the boost and the mental link, and clung to each other as they waited for the reaction to pass. Hazel's cut on her arm had been messy but minor and was already healing itself. It still took a while for the trembling to stop and their breathing to return to something like normal. When they finally let go of each other and looked around, they found themselves facing three women with the same face, smiling sardonically at them from the top of the stairs. *Clones,* Owen thought immediately. Presumably from the underground. They looked tough enough.

All three women were wearing battered leathers adorned with brightly polished lengths of steel chain, over T-shirts bearing the legend "BORN TO BURN." They looked to be in their mid twenties, but their faces were somehow older, more harshly used. They were all short and stocky, with bare muscular arms, and their long dark hair was full of colorful knotted ribbons. There were splashes of color on their faces, too, perhaps to disguise how pretty they might have been if it weren't for their cold eyes and determined mouths.

"Can we help you?" said Owen politely, not lowering his sword. He had a suspicion he was smelling strongly of sweat, but decided he wouldn't bring it up if they didn't.

"The seagulls are flying low tonight," said the woman in the middle, meaningfully.

Owen looked at her and then turned and looked at Hazel, who looked back at him.

"The seagulls are flying low tonight," said the woman in the middle with extra emphasis.

"Sorry," said Owen. "Didn't quite catch that. The seagulls are what?"

"Hold everything," said Hazel. "Seagulls. That was part of the contact phrase, wasn't it?"

"I don't know," said Owen helplessly. "I can't remember. It's gone right out of my head."

"If I don't start hearing an answer sometime soon, I am going to start shooting," said the woman on the left.

"Angels!" Owen said quickly. "Something about angels!"

"Something something angels in the moonlight," said Hazel. "I think."

"Oh, hell," said the woman in the middle. "That's close enough. Be here all day otherwise."

"We're your contact," said the woman on the left. "Sorry it took us a while to get here, but there are security guards all over the place, and we didn't want to kill them all. It would only have attracted attention."

"Fair enough," said Hazel. "What happened to Stevie Blue?"

"We're right here," said the one in the middle.

"Right," said the one on the right.

"All of you?" said Owen.

"Got it in one,' said the Stevie Blue on the left. "I'm Stevie One, this is Two and Three. Don't get us mixed up. We're touchy about it."

"I take it you're also espers," said Owen, putting his sword away. Hazel reluctantly sheathed hers, but kept her hands near her guns. Owen gave the Stevie Blues his best diplomatic smile, and vowed silently to do something really unpleasant to the divot who'd got Stevie Blue's personal details wrong. "Nice work on the Investigator. I think he was prepared for everything except a sudden flash fire. Next time, feel free to reduce him to a pile of smoldering ashes. All right, let's get down to business. The program's in the machine and running. All we have to do is keep the hostile natives at bay until it's finished, and then we can leg it. We've got a ship coming back to pick us up. It's a Hadenman ship, but don't let that panic you. They've been very reasonable. So far."

The three Stevie Blues smiled in unison. "Anyone annoys us, they're toast," said Stevie One. "We're pyros. Elfs; Esper Liberation Front. We kick ass."

"And you're the underground's idea of diplomats," said Hazel. "You're going to be very popular at strategy planning sessions. I might just start attending them again."

"The cyberats are running interference to keep this tower isolated," said Stevie Two. "No one from outside will know anything's happened till it's all over."

Owen frowned. "Computer hackers aren't exactly noted for their reliability."

"You can trust these," said Stevie One. "If only because they know we'll kick their ass if they screw up."

"Right," said Stevie Three.

Owen and Hazel suddenly turned away and looked thoughtfully at the stairs. Hazel drew her guns, and Owen turned back to the clones.

"Visitors are on their way."

"You espers or something?" said Stevie One.

"Something," said Owen. "The Investigator must have put himself out and alerted his people. Any minute now we're going to be hip deep in security guards."

"That's not all," said Stevie Two. "They've got an esp-blocker with them. I can feel my powers fading as it gets closer."

"Wonderful," said Hazel. "Can anything else go wrong?"

"Quite a lot, if we just stand around here waiting for them," said Owen. "May I suggest we get the hell back to the computer room?"

"Too late," said Stevie Three. "They're here."

The three clones drew their swords with the same quick, professional motion and moved to block the head of the stairwell. Owen and Hazel moved in beside them, guns at the ready, just in time to see a single tall figure step into sight at the final corner of the stairs below. He was dressed in jet-black robes and battle armor, looked to be in his early thirties, and was handsome in an unspectacular way. His dark eyes and slight smile were utterly cold, and just standing there with empty hands, he looked calm and confident and very dangerous. Stevie Two whistled softly.

"The Lord High Dram his own bad self. We should be honored. He normally only murders espers from a safe distance."

"He can't just blast and burn the tower this time," said Stevie One. "The Empress would have his nuts if he let the Tax computers be destroyed."

Owen and Hazel looked at each other thoughtfully. "That man is quite definitely dead," said Owen. "I saw the body."

"So who's this?" said Hazel. "A clone? Does anyone at Court know? Or was the one we saw die a clone?"

"Are we supposed to understand any of that?" said Stevie One.

"I'll explain later," said Owen. "Assuming there is a later. "For the moment, just believe me when I say things just got a lot more complicated. The Widowmaker will be a major rallying point for the Empire that we hadn't counted on. We have to get this information back to Rebel HQ."

"I've got a better idea," said Hazel. She raised her projectile weapon and let Dram have it point-blank. The stairwell echoed to the roar of the gun as bullets hammered into the steel walls over and over, but Dram's cold smile never wavered. His holo image shimmered slightly, but was otherwise unaffected.

"You didn't really think someone of my quality would come in person to deal with rebel trash, did you?" said Dram calmly. "The lower floors of this tower are now blocked off and occupied by my troops. There's no way out, and nowhere for you to go. Surrender, and at least you'll live long enough to stand trial."

The Stevie Blues glared at him fiercely. Stevie One spat on the floor. "What makes you think we'd trust treacherous scum like you? You came to us pretending to be a man called Hood, and we trusted you. In return, you betrayed us to the Empire forces. Hundreds of good men and women died that day, just because they happened to be espers or clones. We'll all die before we surrender to you."

"Suit yourselves," said Dram, and his holo image disappeared like a popping soap bubble. The steel stairs shuddered as a large body of armed men came crashing up them. Owen fired his disrupter down the stairwell, but the energy beam ricocheted away from an advancing force shield wall. The espers concentrated and boiling flames filled the stairwell. The force wall just kept coming, pushing back the flames, which were already beginning to die out as the esp-blocker drew nearer. The Stevie Blues looked at Owen and Hazel.

"Don't look at me," said Hazel. "I'm right out of ideas. How much longer does the program have to run, Owen?"

"Can't be long now. A few minutes at most. But we can't afford to be cornered in the computer room with it."

"And we don't have a few minutes, anyway. How about setting up a barricade?"

"Couldn't hurt," said Owen. "See, you can come up with ideas when you have to. Stevies, if you'd care to lend a hand . . ."

They dashed back into the computer room, grabbed everything blocky that wasn't actually welded in place, and manhandled it out into the corridor. Between them they maneuvered the heavy equipment over to the top of the stairwell, and launched it down the stairs. The way was immediately blocked, and the enemy advance came to a sudden halt. Force shields were excellent at stopping energy blasts or bullets, but they had real problems coping with three hundred pounds of assorted wedged office equipment. The security guards stopped to discuss the matter, while Dram snarled at them acidly from below. Owen and Hazel grinned at each other, and at the esper clones, and then they all spun around at an unexpected sound behind them. It was the bell that signaled the approach of the elevator.

"That shouldn't be possible," said Stevie One. "The cyberats were supposed to have cut off the elevators."

"Never trust anyone who has an unnatural relationship with his softdrive," said Stevie Two.

"Right," said Stevie Three.

They spread out before the elevator door, guns and blades at the ready. It was very quiet in the corridor. Owen's hands were sweaty, and he wished he had time to dry them. The elevator chimed again, and the doors slid open to reveal a medium height impeccably dressed man with a heavily lined face and long, carefully styled white hair. He smiled at them all engagingly, and the Stevie Blues let out their breath and lowered their weapons.

"We should have known," said Stevie Two. "If anyone could slip past an entire army of guards and just waltz in here, it would have to be you."

"You know how it is," said the newcomer, in a deep, resonant voice. "I do so love to make an entrance. Now, be a dear and introduce me to your friends. Guns make me nervous."

"This aging reprobate is Alexander Storm," said Stevie One. "Longtime rebel, adventurer, and gadfly by appointment. Hero of the rebellion, professional clotheshorse, and a general pain in the ass. We only put up with him because he's so good at making the Empire forces look like pratts."

"Right," said Stevie Three.

"Couldn't have put it better myself," said Alexander Storm. He stepped out of the elevator and clapped Owen firmly on the shoulder. "I'm an old friend and comrade in arms of Jack Random. I've been semiretired for a while, you know how it is, but once I heard Jack was back in the thick of things, I knew I had to join him. It'll be just like old times, fighting shoulder to shoulder again. I haven't seen the dear fellow since Cold Rock. Not one of our better showings, I'm afraid. Still, it's the thought that counts. Anyway, I contacted the underground, pulled a few strings, and here I am. The Stevie Blues will represent the clones and espers, and I shall speak for the other parts of the underground. Delighted to meet you at last, Deathstalker. Word of your exploits has spread far and wide. Everyone in the rebellion is delighted to see you following in your father's footsteps. He'd be so proud of you. But then, Deathstalker has always been an honorable name. Great things are expected of you, my boy. You are the hope of humanity."

Owen became aware of a dangerously quiet, fuming figure at his side. "This is Hazel d'Ark," he said quickly. "I'm sure you've heard of her, too."

Storm smiled at her dazzlingly. "Of course. The rebellion can always use another canny fighter. Tell me, Owen, how is Jack Random these days? Last I'd heard, he'd taken a hell of a beating at the Empire's hands."

"He's ... better than he was," Owen said carefully. "Try not to look too shocked when you see him. He's been through a lot."

"Are we going to stand around here chatting all day?" said Hazel ominously. "Or is someone going to check whether the program's finished running yet?"

The barricade filling the top of the stairs shifted suddenly, as someone underneath tried to move it, but it just settled itself more comfortably. And then an energy beam tore right through the mass of equipment, scattering fragments of molten metal in the air. The rebels ducked back and covered their heads with their arms. The security forces began dismantling what was left of the barricade.

"Let's save the official getting-to-know-each-other session for a better time," said Owen hastily. "I'll check the program. You shoot at anything that moves till I get back."

He sprinted down the corridor and into the computer room, and saw with relief that the program discs had finished their task and ejected themselves. He grabbed them, pressed the attached self-destruct, and watched with satisfaction as the discs were consumed in smoke flames. He wrinkled his nose at the smell and dropped the burning discs to the floor. Now, even if he or any of the rebels were to be captured, there would still be no way the Empire could reconstruct what the program had been. He ran back to the stairwell, where Hazel was spraying the disappearing barricade with bullets, to no obvious effect.

"Time to go," Owen said briskly. "The program's taken care of, and we have more than outstayed our welcome. Grab anything that's yours or might be useful, and head for the roof. There are gravity sleds waiting there."

"We can use the elevator," said Storm. "The cyberats have control of it."

"We'll use the stairs," said Hazel. "The cyberats' commands could get overridden, and it'd be a damn silly way to get trapped."

She headed for the stairs, without looking back to see if the others were following. Storm raised an eyebrow at Owen, as though surprised he wasn't taking charge. He was the hope of humanity, after all. Owen shrugged sheepishly and hurried after Hazel. Storm and the Stevie Blues followed behind. Owen kept his gun trained ahead of him, just in case, but there was no one lying in wait on the stairs, and they reached the top floor without incident. The gravity sleds were waiting where they'd been left, for which Owen was very grateful. This would not be a good time to have to walk home. Hazel was already aboard her sled and powering it up. Owen took Storm on his sled, while the three clones insisted upon crowding onto Hazel's.

The two sleds rose into the air and headed for the shattered windows they'd originally entered by. Energy beams stabbed the air around them as Dram and his people burst into the top floor, firing wildly. Owen and Hazel pushed the gravity sleds to full speed and shot away between the pastel towers, dodging and diving erratically to throw off the guards' aim. The sleds had force shields, but the power needed to sustain them would quickly drain the sleds' energy crystals of power they needed more urgently for speed. The Stevie Blues hung on grimly to the bucking gravity sled and fired back at their attackers. More guards appeared at the windows of other towers and opened fire on the sleds. Dram must have got the word out. Owen and Hazel darted in and out of the towers, fighting updrafts and dodging unexpected protrusions, and the energy beams came at them from every side.

A disrupter beam hit the front of Owen's sled a glancing blow, blasting it off course. White-hot metal spattered across

his hastily flung-up cloak as he struggled to regain control.
The cloak burst into flames. Storm pulled it free from
Owen's shoulders and threw it overboard. It fell away, burning brightly, finally disappearing into the long drop. Owen
fought the sled back under control, but its speed had
dropped by half. Hazel dropped back to keep pace with him.
Owen gestured for her to go on, but she shook her head
stubbornly. Owen activated his comm implant.

"Hazel, will you please get the hell out of here! Dram will
be putting sleds into the air anytime now."

"Exactly," Hazel said calmly. "You're going to need
someone to watch your back. We can't let you die. You're
the hope of humanity, remember?"

He would have argued more, but they whipped around the
side of a tower to find themselves facing rows of armed
guards waiting for them on top of the next tower. Owen and
Hazel cursed simultaneously and threw the sleds into a dive.
Energy beams slashed past them, and one hit Stevie Two
squarely in the back. The force of the blast threw her over
the side of the sled. The other two Stevies screamed in unison as the burning body plummeted toward the distant
ground. Owen sent his sled plunging after her, pushing its
speed well past its recommended safety limits. The engine
whined protestingly, but he ignored it. He overtook the falling body, swept the sled underneath, and then surged up to
catch her. The burning body slammed onto the deck. Storm
wrapped his cloak around her, to smother the flames. Red
warning lights glared all across the sled's controls, and
Owen snarled back at them. He'd saved a life from the Empire's venom, and that was all that mattered.

Hazel's sled swept in beside him. Stevies One and Three
were firing Hazel's projectile weapons at the guards, driving
them back under cover. Hazel gestured back over her shoulder, and Owen glanced back briefly. Imperial gravity sleds
were coming up behind and closing the gap fast. Energy
beams flashed past the rebels' sleds, from behind and ahead.
Warning shots fired, to show they'd got the range. Owen
caught Hazel's eye and pointed upwards. She nodded, and
the two sleds darted straight up, leaving the sheltering towers behind. Owen activated his comm unit again.

"This is Rebel One to Golden Boy. I can't come to you,
so you'll have to come to me. Lock on to my signal and get
your ass here fast."

There was no answer, but he hadn't expected on. The two Stevie Blues were firing down at the pursuing Empire sleds, tears for their fallen sister streaming down their cold, set faces. Their guns ran out of ammo, and the espers dropped the projectile weapons to the deck and grabbed two more from Hazel's belt. They opened up again, and one of the pursuing sleds suddenly erupted into flames and fell spiraling between the towers like a burning leaf. Owen and Hazel sent their sleds whipping back and forth over the towers, their Maze-amplified speed and reflexes enabling them to make decisions and pull off evasions their pursuers couldn't hope to match, but still the Empire sleds came on, remorselessly closing the gap with their superior speed.

And then the great golden ship of the Hadenmen appeared out of nowhere right before them as it dropped its cloaking shields, filling the sky, gleaming brighter than the sun. The pursuing sleds took one look and did everything but throw themselves into reverse. A few fired off useless shots at the huge ship, but most just settled for shuddering to an unruly halt in midair. Owen glanced back over his shoulder and saw Storm looking up at the ship with his mouth open. Even the Stevie Blues had stopped firing at their pursuers. Owen grinned and flew up into the open cargo bay doors in the ship's belly, Hazel right behind him.

"Get the hell out of here right now!" yelled Owen. "Go, go, go!"

The belly doors slammed shut, and Owen and Hazel landed their sleds. Owen slumped over the controls, exhausted, but made himself turn around as Stevie One and Stevie Three ran over to the sled. Storm was bending over the unmoving body of Stevie Two. He looked up as the esper clones reached him and shook his head sadly.

"I'm sorry. She must have been dead from the moment the beam hit her."

Owen wanted to say something, but couldn't. Stevie One nodded stiffly to him. "You risked your life to save her, even though she was just a clone. It's not your fault she didn't make it. We'll never forget what you did, Owen Deathstalker. Wherever you lead, we'll follow."

"But now there are only two of us," said Stevie Three quietly.

Stevie One put her arms around her and hugged her hard. After a while she let go, and the two Stevie Blues walked off a way to be by themselves for a while. Hazel came over to join Owen and Storm.

"Nice flying, Deathstalker. Maybe you are the hope of humanity after all."

"You're never going to let me forget that, are you?" said Owen.

"Listen, aristo," said Hazel. "You need me to keep you honest. If you're the hope, we are in deep shit. Hey, Hadenmen! Any chance of showing us what's happening outside?"

A viewscreen appeared, hovering on the air before them. The planet was falling away below them, but a dozen starcruisers were coming after them. They were unusually large, bulky ships of a kind Owen didn't recognize. He looked at Storm, who was biting his lower lip and frowning.

"The Empress's new fleet," he said quietly. "E class, all with the new stardrive. Reputedly even faster than the legendary Hadenman ships. It would appear we're about to find out whether that's the case."

The Empire ships opened fire. Disrupter cannon fired in sequence, one after the other, so that the starcruisers could maintain a constant fire. The golden ship fired back, but the Empire ships were rapidly closing the gap. Owen assumed the Hadenmen's shields were still holding—on the grounds everyone on board would have been breathing vacuum by now if they weren't. And then the ship's engines roared, and the viewscreen disappeared as the Hadenman craft dropped into hyperspace and was gone. Owen let out a long slow sigh of relief, and Hazel slapped him on the back.

"Told you we'd make it, aristo. Personally, I was never worried. Not for a minute."

"Then, you should have been," said Owen. "If those new ships are typical of the E class, we are all in real trouble. Think of a fleet of ships as fast as my old *Sunstrider*. We'd been relying on the Hadenman ships to give us an edge, but it would appear they're not number one anymore. Which means, if we're going to go head-to-head with the Empire, we've got to have ships with the new stardrive, too."

"What the hell," said Hazel. "We can worry about that later. The mission was a success. The Tax and Tithe computers are toast, and we got most of the contacts out alive."

"We still lost one," said Owen.

"It wasn't your fault," said Storm. "You tried. These

things happen. I'll go and have a word with Stevie One and Three. Offer them some comfort and a friendly shoulder to lean on."

He bowed formally and moved away. Hazel watched him go. "These things happen! He's going to be a real comfort, he is."

"I think we could both use a drink and some rest," said Owen. "Perhaps you'd care to join me, Hazel? Or we could have a meal together. Would you like that?"

"Not really, no," said Hazel. "No offense, Deathstalker, but let's keep our relationship professional, okay?"

She smiled at him briefly, then strode over to Storm and the two esper clones, gesturing for them to follow her. Owen watched them go. He was sure he must have been turned down faster than that at some time in his past, but he was damned if he could think when. Things like that weren't supposed to happen. He was a Lord, after all. And the hope of humanity.

"Nice try, though," said the AI Ozymandius through his comm implant.

"Shut up, Oz," said Owen. "You're dead."

CHAPTER TWO

Up to Gehenna and Down to Golgotha

Captain John Silence of the Empire starcruiser *Dauntless* was going home to die, and was trying hard not to give a damn. After all, he'd only failed in his mission and got most of his people killed. He looked at the brimming glass in his hand and pulled a face. The trouble with sustained heavy drinking was that after a while your tongue went numb, and you couldn't tell what you were drinking. Though given exactly what he was pouring down his throat in great quantity, that wasn't necessarily a bad thing. The food synthesizers could produce alcohol and flavorings, but the combinations, like the quality, were strictly limited. It was supposed to be red wine, but all the red part did was turn his teeth pink. Still, for a wine whose vintage was under ten minutes, it wasn't that bad. Not that it made any difference. He would have drunk it anyway.

His head hurt, his hands were shaking, and his stomach lurched this way and that when he moved. He'd been drinking steadily for almost three days now, taking time out to eat and sleep when he absolutely had to. He didn't drink much normally, and he was finding getting drunk and staying drunk harder work than he'd expected. But he kept at it. Nothing else to do. He was a failure, going home to report that failure to an Empress who'd kill him for it.

And all those good men lost . . .

He was heading back to Golgotha with bad news and worse, and while the Empress Lionstone might have pardoned him once for screwing up, she wouldn't put up with it a second time. He'd been sent to the Wolfling World on a straightforward mission. Accompanied by a contingent of trained adjusted men, the Wampyr, and the Empress's lover and right-hand man, the Lord High Dram, he'd been commanded to arrest and execute that most renowned traitor Owen Deathstalker, and all with him, and then return to Golgotha with the rebels' heads and the secrets of the legendary Wolfling World. They'd even given him the single Grendel alien ever to be subdued and controlled. An extraordinary and so far unique specimen. The mission should have been a walkover.

Instead Dram's body was down in the cargo hold, the Grendel alien had been killed, which was supposed to be impossible, and the three Wampyr who hadn't died fighting the rebels had been detained by the newly risen Hadenmen. Silence didn't want to think what for. He took another drink. The Hadenmen. Once the Enemies of Humanity. Defeated long ago in a fierce and bloody war, they were supposed to be extinct, or at best sleeping endlessly in the hidden Tomb of the Hadenmen. But Owen Deathstalker had found and woken them, and now they sided with the rebels. And God help the Empire. The walls were falling, and the wolves were running loose among the flock.

He downed another drink and another. He really wasn't looking forward to explaining to the Empress that the Wolfling World was in fact also Haden, home of the Hadenmen. Which meant the rebels now had access to the legendary laboratories of Haden, and all the wonders and horrors they had produced in the past. Science beyond reason, weapons beyond hope of stopping, and all of it aimed at the Empire. By his failure he'd signed the death warrant of civilization and quite possibly all of humanity as well.

No, he had nothing but bad news to lay before his Empress, and she would kill him for it. If his own men didn't do it first. All the men he'd taken down into the caverns deep below the frozen surface of the Wolfling World had died there, facing weapons and horrors they could not have anticipated. And instead of avenging them, Silence had been forced to take his ship and run. His crew didn't understand what he'd seen down there. Why it was vital he abandon everything and flee, to be sure the Empire would get advance warning of the threats to come.

So now his crew despised him. Many hated him. If the Investigator Frost hadn't stood by him and made it very clear she would personally avenge him if he died, he wouldn't have had to worry about facing Lionstone. There would have been a sudden, regrettable accident, and it would all have been over. Which might have been kinder, really, but you couldn't expect an Investigator to understand that. They

were trained from childhood to hunt and kill aliens, and the
subtleties of human behavior often escaped them. So he left
the running of what used to be his ship to his second in command and sat alone in his cabin, drinking. To pass the time,
as much as anything else.

There was a knock at his door, and he looked up, just a
little blearily. He knew who it was, who it had to be. Only
one person ever came to see him these days. He thought
about getting up to open the door himself, but decided
against it. He didn't trust his legs that much. So he worked
his numbed tongue around his slightly slack mouth and said,
"Door: open," with as much authority and clarity as he could
manage. The door slid open, and Investigator Frost stepped
into his cabin. She nodded to Silence, and looked unhurriedly about her as the door closed behind her. Silence didn't
look. He knew the place was a mess. He'd never been particularly tidy, but normally his batman took care of things
like that. He hadn't seen his batman in five days, and he
found it faintly surprising just how bad things could get in
five days, when you didn't give a damn anymore.

He did sneak a quick look at himself in the mirror on the
wall opposite, and winced. A tall, lean man in his late forties
looked back at him, with a pale lined face that could use a
shave topped by a distinctly receding hairline. He looked
rumpled and badly used, like the unmade bed he was sitting
on. His uniform was a disgrace. He'd been sick down it
twice, and the left sleeve had never really recovered.

The Investigator, on the other hand, looked utterly immac-
ulate in a tight starched uniform with brightly polished buttons, as though she was just about to step out onto a parade
ground. She was tall and lithely muscular, in her late twenties, though her eyes were much older. They were cold and
blue, burning fiercely in a pale controlled face topped by au-
burn hair cropped close to the skull. She wore a gun on her
hip, despite shipboard regulations, and a long sword hung
down her back. Just standing there at her ease she looked
ready and willing to take on a fair-sized army all by herself.
And it was a brave man who would have bet on the army.
She was handsome rather than pretty, and it was a brave man
indeed who'd even smile at her without a direct invitation.
In advance, in writing. Frost smiled only when she was killing something. She pulled up a chair, removed and discarded
a dirty shirt with thumb and forefinger, and sat down facing

Silence. He raised an eyebrow. Frost was usually impeccably formal, even in private.

"What are you doing here, Investigator?" he said tiredly, pleased his voice was still steady, if a little slurred.

Frost sniffed. "I thought we'd agreed you were going to stop drinking."

"You agreed. I just got tired of arguing."

"It won't help, Captain."

"It can't hurt, either," Silence said reasonably. "Things are already as bad as they can get."

"There's always the chance they might improve unexpectedly. We have to keep our wits about us, Captain. Be ready to take advantage of any opportunities that might arise."

"You take advantage, Investigator. I'm too tired, and I really don't care that much anymore. No matter what happens our mission is still a mess. Civilization is doomed, and my men are still dead. They were good men. They followed me into the Madness Maze because I ordered them to. Because I told them it was safe. And not content with that, I ended up sending the survivors head-to-head with Hadenmen. It would have been kinder to shoot them all in the back. Except, that's what I did, really." He sighed, as the familiar guilt and pain washed over him again. He'd lost men before, but never like this. Failed before, but never like this. "Now, if you'll excuse me, Investigator, I have some serious drinking to attend to."

He looked down at his glass, to give her a chance to leave with dignity, but when he looked up again she was still there, staring at him coldly.

"I can feel your distress," she said evenly. "No matter where I am. Ever since our experiences on the ghostworld Unseeli, you and I have been ... linked, in some strange way. Not quite telepathy, but close. I chose to disregard it, as did you. We didn't want to be taken for espers. But then we entered the Madness Maze on the Wolfling World, and the link has become stronger. Unavoidable. If I concentrate, I can feel what you're feeling, sense what you're thinking. And sometimes it comes whether I concentrate or not. It's really very annoying. For an Imperial officer, your mind is extremely disorganized. Your feelings are as undisciplined as your thoughts, and my mouth is currently full of the taste of whatever garbage that is you're drinking. It has to stop."

"I can't feel you," said Silence. "But then I wouldn't,

would I? You're an Investigator. You don't have any feelings."

"My mind is disciplined," Frost said calmly. "Unlike
yours. Is that why you're trying so hard to climb into a
bottle and drown?"

Silence glared at her. "In case it has escaped your attention, Investigator, the *Dauntless* is carrying us back to inform the Empress that not only was our mission shot to hell,
not only is her lover and Warrior Prime dead and cold, but
also a major rebellion complete with an army of reawakened
augmented men is in the offing. She is not going to be
pleased with us. Not at all. If we're lucky, she'll just kill us
both on the spot. But we haven't been particularly lucky so
far, have we, Investigator?"

"So why are we going back?" said Frost.

The words hung in the air between them, refusing to let
Silence ignore them. He looked into his glass, but it had no
answer for him. He sighed heavily, and made himself meet
the Investigator's cold blue eyes.

"Because it's my duty. I may have screwed up everything
else in my life, but I still know my duty. The Empress must
be warned. I swore an oath upon my honor to serve and protect the Empire to the last drop of my blood, and I still believe in that, irrespective of whoever happens to be sitting
on the Iron Throne. The Empire is worth preserving, for all
its many faults. All the alternatives are worse; from barbarism and mass starvation on a thousand worlds if the system
breaks down, to all kinds of petty dictatorships if the Empress's authority is broken. The rebellion is a threat to civilization itself. I don't even want to think of what might
happen if those damned AIs on Shub seized the opportunity
to attack while we were preoccupied with a rebellion. And
what about the aliens? You saw that thing on Unseeli, with
its half-living ship. Lionstone must be warned and made to
understand the urgency of the threat. She won't want to believe me, so she'll order a mind probe; and she'll believe
that. Whether she wants to or not. So I'm going back because I have to. But you don't have to, Investigator."

He took a long drink. His throat was dry. Frost shook her
head. "I have to go back, too. The Empire trained me to be
an Investigator, and I don't know how to be anything else.
And I wouldn't want to, even if I could. I like being what I
am. It's direct and uncomplicated. But only the Empire has

any use for an Investigator. So I'm going back, and hope that between now and then something happens to get us off the hook."

"And if nothing does?" said Silence. "If I did run, afterward . . . would you come with me, Frost?"

"No. I can't. I have to be what they made me." She looked at him for a long moment. "I can warn the Empress. It doesn't need both of us. And it certainly doesn't make any sense for both of us to die."

"I can't do that, Frost. I couldn't leave you to face the storm alone."

"I'd leave you, if I could."

"I know that." Silence smiled at her and wasn't bothered that she didn't smile back. She was an Investigator. And though she was supposed to be nothing more than a cold, calculating killing machine, Silence thought he understood her, even in the things she didn't—or couldn't—say. He didn't need the link for that.

"How's Stelmach?" he said finally. It was as good a way to change the subject as any. Frost snorted.

"Still sulking, because we had to leave his precious alien pet behind on the Wolfling World. Apparently, he only learned to control the Grendel alien by accident and isn't at all sure he can re-create his success again with another subject. Still, you can be sure he's already got some story worked out, to make him look good and us very bad."

"Undoubtably," said Silence. "I swear he was closer to that bloody alien than he ever was to anything human. Mind you, if I'd been christened with the name Valiant and only ended up as a Security Officer, I'd be hard to get along with, too. Whatever report he turns in, you can be sure his main motive will be to stab us in the back."

"Of course. That's what Security Officers are for."

"The point being, that he'll be more interested in looking out for his own interests than in convincing Lionstone of the rebel threat. Just another reason why I have to go back. Dammit."

"We could always kill him," said Frost. "Hard to stab anybody in the back from inside a coffin."

Silence thought about it. "No. It would only complicate things further. He doesn't know enough to really hurt us. He doesn't know about the link."

They'd never told anyone. The link wasn't esp, as far as

they could tell, but it wouldn't prevent the Empire treating them as espers, if word ever got out. And espers were second-class citizens, little better than a clone. Certainly it would be the end of their careers as Captain and Investigator. They'd end up as lab animals, specimens to be quarantined, studied, and quite probably vivisected. So they never told anyone.

"Have you heard anything from your daughter recently?" said Frost.

Silence shook his head. His daughter Diana was an esper. She'd been with them when everything went to hell on Unseeli. She'd gone through a lot—enough to break anyone else. But she was his daughter, after all. Diana survived and emerged stronger than she had been before. Strong enough that when they returned to Golgotha from the Unseeli mission, she jumped ship and disappeared into the clone and esper underground. Silence hadn't seen her since or received any word from her. He was glad of that. He would have hated having to turn her in. Diana was his daughter, his only child, and he loved her deeply; but he knew his duty. Which was probably why she'd had the sense not to contact him.

He hoped she was well and happy.

"What's happening with the crew?" he said finally, changing the subject yet again. "Anyone giving you any trouble?"

"They wouldn't dare," said Frost. "A few of them tried giving me the cold shoulder, so I slapped them around a bit, to teach them some manners. They'll be fine, once they get out of the Infirmary. In the meantime everyone else is being very polite and obedient, as long as I'm around. I don't know what they're griping about. So we lost a few people. Sometimes that's part of the job."

"But we lost an entire away team," said Silence. "And all the Wampyr."

"Trust me, Captain. No one gives a damn about the Wampyr."

"But they were the last battle-trained adjusted men in the Empire."

"That's like saying they were the last cockroaches. Everyone on this ship is glad they're gone."

"They were still my men," said Silence. "I was responsible for them. And I just stood there and watched as the Hadenmen led them away."

"There was nothing you could have done. We were out-numbered."

"They'll be dead by now. Cut apart to see what makes them tick; pieces in neatly labeled jars in some Hadenman laboratory."

"Best place for them," said Frost. "I never trusted them."

"They fought beside us," said Silence. "And most of them died doing it. Doesn't that mean anything to you? No, of course it doesn't. I was forgetting. You're an Investigator. All you've ever cared about is killing the enemy. And God I wish I was like you."

He lifted his glass, but it was empty. He reached for the bottle, and Frost put a hand on his arm.

"Please. Don't."

They looked at each other for a long moment, and then a chime sounded suddenly in their ears. Silence raised an eye-brow. It had been some time since anyone had contacted him on the command channel. He activated his comm implant and paused a moment to be sure his voice was calm and steady.

"This is the Captain."

"Bridge here, Captain. Communications Officer. I think you and the Investigator had better come up to the bridge immediately."

Silence frowned. There was something in the man's voice. Something more than concern. "What's the problem?"

"We've had a signal come in, Captain. I think you're go-ing to want to hear this for yourself."

Definitely something in the voice. Something had shaken the Comm Officer right down to his socks. Which was why he'd come running to his Captain. Silence smiled grimly. "All right, I'm on my way. Go to Yellow Alert and prepare all battle stations. Captain out." He broke contact and looked thoughtfully at the Investigator. "Must be something really unusual, or dangerous, if they want both of us on the bridge. Could be an alien contact."

Frost stood up and pulled at her uniform here and there, to ensure everything was as it should be. "I told you some-thing would come up, Captain. Something always does."

"That's what worries me," said Silence. "The way my luck's been going, this could turn out to be something really nasty."

"Good," said Frost. "Maybe I'll get the chance to kill something."

Some twenty minutes later, Captain Silence and the Investigator strode onto the bridge of the *Dauntless*, and headed straight for the Communications station. Silence had taken an emergency purge and was feeling very sober. He also felt like he'd just run a twenty-mile marathon. His legs were shaking, and so were his hands when he forgot to clench them into fists. He'd shaved and climbed into a fresh uniform, but he still felt like death warmed up and allowed to congeal. He bent over the Communications station and studied the board. Nothing seemed obviously wrong. The Comm Officer leaned away a little, and Silence realized his breath must still be really foul. Tough. He made himself concentrate on what the Communications Officer was saying.

"We dropped out of hyperspace just inside the Rim, so we could reestablish contact with the Empire. Our signals still won't cross the Darkvoid. Since comm signals travel through hyperspace it shouldn't be possible for anything to interfere with them, but that's the Darkvoid for you. Anyway, the minute we reappeared in normal space, my station began operating normally again. And the first thing we picked up was a signal in emergency code. No visual, just a voice. It's from the Empire Base on Gehenna. I looked it up. It's an unpopulated world, right out on the far edge of the Empire. Nasty place, by all accounts. The single Base is a scientific research lab, with 107 personnel. They're calling for help. The emergency code they're using is top priority. I think we actually have to be at war with something to use a higher code. Officially, standing orders say we're supposed to head straight back to Golgotha, to report in person on the outcome of our mission, but I thought you ought to hear this, in case you wanted to override."

"Quite right," said Silence. "Let me hear the signal."

He listened intently to the whispering voice coming from the Comm station. It was barely audible, despite everything the Comm Officer could do to boost the signal. Silence looked at Frost, who was frowning thoughtfully, but she just shook her head. Silence turned back to the Comm Officer. "What do the computers make of it?"

"Not a lot, Captain. It's a beacon, repeating a recorded message over and over. The only clear parts are the origin of the signal and the plea for help. We've tried contacting the Base directly, but there's no reply."

"If it's a beacon, how long has it been sending?" said Frost. "And why hasn't anyone else picked it up?"

"Unknown, Investigator. But the signal is very weak, and this is the Rim, after all. Strange things happen out here. Perhaps we only picked it up because we're right out on the Rim, too. What are your orders, Captain?"

Silence looked at Frost again. "We should ignore this. Go straight to Golgotha. The beacon could have been repeating its message for ages. Whatever happened on Gehenna, it's probably over by now."

"Of course, Captain," Frost said solemnly. "But those people could still need our help, and we are the only ship out here."

"Precisely," said Silence. "Our duty is clear. Helmsman, set a course for Gehenna. Investigator, we'll discuss this further in private. Second in Command, let me know when we get there. Otherwise, I don't wish to be disturbed."

His Second sniffed audibly, contempt clear in the sound. Frost spun on him, her hand dropping to her sword, but Silence stopped her with a hand on her arm. He strode over to the command chair, gripped the Second by the throat with one hand, and lifted him effortlessly out of the chair. The Second's eyes bulged, and his tongue protruded from his mouth. He scrabbled at Silence's hold with both hands, but couldn't budge it. He drew his disrupter, and Silence slapped it out of his hand. The gun skidded across the floor until Frost stepped on it. The rest of the bridge crew took in the look on her face, and sat very still at their stations. Silence let go of his Second's throat, and he dropped back into the command chair, gasping for breath. Silence leaned forward so his face was right before the Second's, and locked eyes with him.

"You show disrespect for my rank again, boy, and I'll fire you out of one of the torpedo tubes in your underwear. Now, get on with your business and leave me to mine. Is that clear? Good. I'm glad we had this little talk. Feel free to come to me again if you need anything else explained to you."

He turned and left the bridge, Frost falling in beside him. As he passed the Communications station, the Comm Officer murmured, "Good to have you back, Captain." Silence had to hide a smile. The door slid shut behind him, and Silence let out his breath in a long sigh. He stopped and leaned back against the corridor bulkhead. His head ached sickly, and his hands were shaking again.

"I need a drink," he said tiredly.

"No you don't," said Frost.

"Look, who's hangover is this, anyway?"

"You didn't need any help hauling the Second out of his chair," said Frost calmly. "And with only one hand, too. I'm impressed."

"So am I," said Silence. He pushed himself away from the bulkhead and strode off down the corridor. Frost fell in beside him again, and they didn't say any more until they were safely back in the Captain's quarters. It was no secret that the Security Officer had the whole ship bugged from stem to stern. Silence debugged his quarters on a regular basis, and since he had access to better tech than Stelmach, he was just about keeping ahead. Silence sank into his favorite seat, and Frost pulled up a chair opposite. Silence looked thoughtfully at the half-empty wine bottle and then looked away. Maybe later.

"So, Investigator, it would seem our short time in the Madness Maze changed us more than we realized. For a moment there, the Second seemed to weigh nothing at all. I could have ripped him apart with my bare hands. And part of me wanted to."

"I wonder if I'll get stronger, too," said Frost. "Or perhaps there are other surprises in store for me. I wonder what we might have become, if we'd made it all the way through the Maze ..."

"You can always ask the rebels, if we ever get another bash at them. They made it all the way through."

"Either way, I think this is something else we should keep strictly to ourselves, Captain."

"I couldn't agree more, Investigator. Let us talk of safer things. What do you think could have happened on Gehenna, that their only call for help was a voice in an automated beacon? Under normal conditions, all they had to do was call on an open channel, and an Empire starcruiser would have been there within hours. That's standard, no matter where in the Empire you are. Of course, we are right out on the Rim, but even so ... Could it be the first rebel attack?"

"I doubt it, Captain. First, they don't look anywhere near

organized enough to mount a major attack. Secondly, I don't think they've got the resources to mount anything major yet. And thirdly . . . I've got a bad feeling about this. To take out a planetary Base so quickly and so thoroughly that they only had time to fire off a beacon would require weaponry of immense power. Perhaps greater power than either the rebels or the Empire could muster."

"So what are we talking about here? The Hadenmen? Shub?"

"Perhaps. But I can't help thinking the last time a Base fell silent, we ended up on Unseeli."

"Where we discovered a crashed alien starship of a technology unknown to the Empire and quite possibly superior to anything we have, and a Base full of dead people." Silence scowled thoughtfully. "You think it could be those aliens again?"

"Could be," said Frost. She smiled briefly. "And I'm just in the mood to kick some alien ass."

"I've never known you when you weren't, Investigator. Personally, I'm just glad of a good excuse to put off our return to Golgotha. Possible alien attack is one of the few acceptable excuses we could come up with. But I have to say, I don't like the idea of our losing another planetary Base. It leaves us vulnerable to all kinds of things. And there's always the chance this is some kind of trap, designed to pull in unsuspecting ships."

"Then, we'd better get there first," said Frost. "We are, after all, expendable."

"You speak for yourself," said Silence.

The *Dauntless* dropped out of hyperspace and settled into orbit around the planet Gehenna, the world of eternal fires. It burned like a blazing coal in the dark; continent-wide flames leaping and flaring but never dying down. Long ago something set light to the surface of the planet, and through some kind of chain reaction the fire had spread till it covered all the world. The poles had melted and the oceans had evaporated, and all that remained was the flames. The surface burned, consuming itself slowly but inexorably. There was evidence that Gehenna had once been inhabited by an alien civilization, but no trace remained of the aliens or their works. Only a handful of strange stone bunkers, huge and impressive but utterly empty, buried deep in the bedrock, away from the all-consuming fires. If they had any secrets, they remained a mystery. No one knew what had happened to the alien civilization: whether they were destroyed by some outside force, or whether they did it to themselves. Whether the fire came first, or was just an aftereffect of whatever destroyed an entire species so thoroughly that not even a hint remained of what they might have been.

The Empire was of course very interested in something that could set an entire planet alight. It would make one hell of a weapon, and Lionstone wanted it. So she gave orders for a Base to be established there, right in the heart of the flames, protected by the strongest force Screen the Empire scientists could provide. According to the *Dauntless*'s records, the scientists in the Base had been working there for nine years and were still no nearer to finding any answers.

Silence led the away team himself. Partly because if the Base had been compromised, he needed to be right there on the spot making decisions, but mostly because he didn't want to go. He still felt like shit, his crew were still sneaking sidelong glances at him when they thought he wasn't looking, and he wasn't at all sure he was up to making command decisions when people's lives might be on the line. But that was why, in the end, he had to go. If he didn't, he might as well resign his Captaincy, and he wasn't ready to do that just yet. So he led the away team. And prayed he was up to it. Frost accompanied him, of course, as the ship's Investigator. More surprisingly, Security Officer Stelmach insisted on coming along, too. Probably because he didn't trust the other two out of his sight. The rest of the team consisted of six marines chosen by lot, and Communications Officer Eden Cross. He'd worked at Gehenna Base briefly, two years ago. He didn't seem at all happy to be paying the place a return visit.

Cross was average height, average weight, dark-skinned and tight-lipped. He hadn't been one of those who conspicuously ostracized the Captain, but he rarely had much to say outside his duties anyway. Though he'd become almost eloquent when it came to trying to find reasons he couldn't or shouldn't be part of the away team. Silence approved of that. He didn't want mindlessly loyal people with him in dangerous situations. He wanted people who were scared, on their toes. Survivors. Interestingly enough, Cross hadn't been a Communications Officer all that long. He'd been passed from one position to another, usually at his own request, apparently because he just got bored after a while, no matter what he was doing. He was an overachiever, in a Service where uniformity was prized above all. He'd either make Captain before he was thirty, or burn out early. As it was, Silence made him pilot of the pinnace that would take them down to Gehenna's surface. Cross would get them down safely or die trying. It wasn't in his nature to do any less.

Silence gripped the arms of his seat tightly as the pinnace dropped like a stone toward the planet below. He accessed the pinnace's sensors through his comm implant, and temperature readings sprang into life before his eyes. He watched blankly as the figures rose in sudden spurts, starting high and moving rapidly from incredible to unbelievable. Silence cut off the figures. They made him nervous. The long slender ship slammed through the overheated atmosphere, rocking and bucking as it plunged into the roaring flames that leapt miles above the endlessly burning surface. Silence made himself let go of the seat's arms. The pinnace's outer hull would protect them against any temperature to be found on a solid world, and there was always the force Screen. The pinnace could handle anything Gehenna could throw at it.

Theoretically.

Silence wasn't convinced. There were already too many unanswered questions about Gehenna, of which the emergency beacon was only the latest. He tried to stir uncomfortably in his seat, but the hard suit wouldn't let him. He'd put on the protective suit before he got into the pinnace, like everyone else. He wouldn't need it till the pinnace landed, but getting into a hard suit was difficult enough at the best of times, when you had plenty of room to move around in. It would have been impossible for a crew of ten to manage in the cramped confines of a pinnace.

A hard suit was part space suit, part armor, and part weapons. It was designed to keep the bearer alive, no matter how inimical conditions got. Once all the systems were connected, the suit guaranteed to keep the wearer cool and calm, no matter what was happening outside it. They tended to be low and awkward and about as subtle as a flying half brick, but they got the job done. They'd been pretty much superseded by portable force shields and Screens, but they still had no equal for where someone needed to make hands-on investigations. Radiation-proof, environmentally secure, harder than steel, and able to withstand practically anything except a point-blank energy beam, they'd originally been intended as combat armor for extreme field conditions. However, they were too clumsy and slow for that, so the fleet inherited them as go anywhere, do anything suits. Everyone else on the pinnace seemed to be moving easily and confidently within the suits' limits. Silence felt as though he'd been dripped in congealing tar.

Sweat was beading on his face, but he couldn't lift his armored arm high enough to wipe at it. He shouldn't be feeling so hot. The pinnace's life-support systems automatically maintained a comfortable interior temperature. But you couldn't think about the impossible heat outside and not feel something, even if it was only in the mind. The six marines were trying to pass a bottle of something back and forth, and spilling most of it as they overcompensated for the suits' servomechanisms. Silence couldn't help wishing they'd pass the damn thing his way, but he couldn't ask. It would look bad. Weak. It was important he appear strong and confident before his men. Particularly, after what happened the last time he led an away team down to a planet.

He made himself look away. Stelmach was sitting by himself, a quiet, nondescript man, anonymous as any civil servant, staring straight ahead, clearly wishing he was somewhere else. Anywhere else. Frost was frowning slightly, her eyes far away. Times like this were what she lived for. This and the promise of a little mayhem. Gehenna Base promised a fascinating deductive problem and the possibility of killing something. Any happier, and she'd probably explode. It occurred to Silence that she might be studying what was going on outside the pinnace. Therefore, he patched into the ship's exterior sensors through his comm implant, so he could see, too.

His eyes were immediately filled with roaring flames as the pinnace bulkheads appeared to become transparent where he looked. And no matter where he looked, there was always fire. Now and again he thought he caught a glimpse of the dark, hard-baked surface far below, always burning, somehow never completely consumed. There was nothing else. Nothing lived there anymore, as far as anyone knew, and the only surviving structures were deep underground. That would have been the most sensible place for the

Base, too, but Lionstone had insisted it be constructed above ground. It was a matter of principle; to show the Empire could build and preserve a Base right there in the heart of hell, where no one else could. The Base should still be intact, behind its force Screen. And if the Screen was still up, the Base personnel ought to be intact, too. The Screen could stand up to anything this world could throw at it. And even if the Screen had fallen, for whatever reason, the Base had been constructed specifically to withstand Gehenna's heat. Silence tried to feel optimistic, but it was hard work. Gehenna was an unforgiving world, waiting always for the smallest mistake or oversight.

"Coming in for landing, Captain," said Cross. "Hold on to your seat belt. It's been a while since I had to land a ship here."

Silence cut off the sensor input, and the pinnace's walls snapped back into being around him. He felt hotter than ever. He realized the others had turned as far in their seats as their suits would allow to look at him, waiting for some last and hopefully reassuring word from him. He took a deep breath, and when he spoke his voice was calm and casual as usual.

"We are landing, people. Power up all systems, and get ready to put on your helmets. Remember, a hard suit can keep you alive for up to a week down here if necessary, but even so take things carefully. Keep your eyes open and watch everyone else's back as well as your own. This place will kill you if you give it the slightest opening. And watch the readings on your energy crystals; hard suits soak up a lot of power, even when you're standing still.

"The moment we're down, the Investigator will exit the craft first. She'll make an immediate assessment of the situation and decide whether the mission can proceed. Assuming we haven't dropped into an actual war zone, the marines will disembark next and set up a defensive perimeter. Then Cross, Stelmach, and I will bring up the rear. Remember, people, this is a rescue mission, not an invasion. You shoot anyone you don't absolutely have to, and I am going to be really annoyed with you. I want survivors with answers, not bodies with holes in. All right, that's it. Secure helmets. Cross, take us in."

He picked up his helmet from his lap, a featureless steel helm that fitted perfectly onto his shoulder yoke. There was a moment of utter darkness as the suit's connections linked up, and then the helmet's sensors kicked in, patching into his comm implant to give his eyes a 360 degree view. It was as though his helmet had suddenly disappeared, though he could still feel its weight on his shoulders. The rest of his team looked blind in their blank helmets, which made Cross at the controls look particularly worrying. And then the pinnace slammed down onto the planet's surface and skidded along, barely slowing. Silence and the others clung desperately to the arms of their seats, only their heavy-duty seat harnesses keeping them from being flung into the aisle or smashed against the walls. The ship shook them back and forth and then lurched to a sudden halt as though it had hit something.

Silence hit his seat harness release with a steel fist and rose jerkily to his feet, the whine of servomechanisms loud in his ears as they translated his body movements into suit responses. He stomped down the aisle to the inner air-lock door, where Frost was already waiting for him. Her suit bore the colors of her uniform, just as his did, but he would have known it was her anyway. Only Frost could have got to the door that fast. Most of the marines were still trying to get out of their seats. Silence waited for Cross's raised hand and then hit the inner door release. The door hissed open, Frost stepped inside the air lock, and the door closed behind her. There was a pause, and then Frost's voice sounded calmly in his ear.

"Outer door open, stepping out onto the surface." Another pause. "No problems, all clear. No sign of anything but dirt and flames. Not unlike walking into a crematorium, actually. Come on in; the inferno's lovely this time of year."

Silence smiled despite himself, opened the inner air-lock door, and waved the marines past him. It didn't take long for everyone to cycle through, and Silence stepped out onto the surface of Gehenna with only the slightest of hesitations. At first, all he could see was the flames. A blazing sea of scarlet and gold, leaping high up into the air. Vague shadows moved in the fire around him, and then the hard suit's computer enhancements kicked in, boosting the helm's sensor images until the shadows came into sharper focus as members of his team. He looked down and could only just make out the ground he was standing on. It was baked black, broken apart here and there with deep crevices from which flames belched forth in sudden jets, mixing with the constant glow around him. The temperature readings were unbelievable.

Welcome to hell, thought Silence. *Welcome to the broken lands, and the fire that never dies. When the Empress finally has me executed, at least I'll know where I'm going.*

"Captain, this is Cross." The Comm Officer's voice sounded loudly in his ear. "If you're ready, I'll get us moving. I've locked onto the beacon; the Base is only a few minutes' walk from here."

"Of course," said Silence. "Good piloting, Cross. Lead the way. Everyone else, power up your weapon systems; but remember what I said about unnecessary firing. I'm all for making a dramatic entrance, but I don't want to end up accidentally killing the very people we're here to rescue. Are you listening to me, Investigator?"

"Relax," said Frost. "I only kill people who need killing."

"I'm sure we're all very relieved to hear that, Investigator," said Cross dryly. "Pay attention please, everyone. Follow me in single file, your hand on the shoulder of the person in front of you. Take your time and don't get distracted. It's only too easy to get lost here. If you do lose contact with the team, your suit will automatically lock onto the pinnace's beacon. Go back there and stay put till we get back. Have I forgotten anything, Captain?"

"No," said Silence. "You're doing fine. Carry on."

He waited patiently while the team formed itself into a single line, and then he put his hand on Stelmach's shoulder in front of him. He could see his steel gauntlet resting on Stelmach's shoulder, but he couldn't feel it. As the line moved off, he realized what Cross had meant about how easy it would be to get lost. Inside the hard suit, the only sense he had left was his sight. The only sound on Gehenna was the constant roar of the flames. He'd automatically turned that down to protect his ears and hear his teammates over the comm. The hard suit cut him off completely from the world. It had to, to protect him.

He trudged on after Stelmach, and the fires raged impotently around him. Sweat was dripping off him again, despite the cool air circulating inside the armor. Time passed slowly, with no landmarks to show any progress. Cross had said the Base was only a few minutes away. Surely, it had been that much already? Or had Cross lost his bearings and begun to lead them in a huge blind circle? He hadn't thought to check the time before they started. The answer suggested itself almost immediately, and Silence was glad the others couldn't see him blushing. He switched the comm to the emergency channel, and the Base's beacon sounded out, loud and reassuring. His sensors placed the Base straight ahead, in what would have been plain sight on any other world. He stared hard into the flames, pushing the computer enhancements to their limits, and a huge dark shape slowly formed before him.

It seemed to leap into being as he drew nearer, and its image grew sharper on the inside of his helmet. It was only then that he realized he shouldn't have been able to see it that close. The shimmer of the Base's raised Screen should have stopped them before this. He called for Cross to stop and then walked himself carefully down the line, shoulder by shoulder, till he was standing next to Cross and the Investigator. At this range he could clearly see the cracked and broken walls of the Base. The outer wall had been designed and built to withstand a sustained barrage from disrupter cannon and everything from earthquakes to a nuclear firestorm, but something had cracked the Base open like an eggshell. Wide jagged rents crawled up the walls from top to bottom. The main doors were open, with only darkness beyond. Silence bit his lower lip. One thing at least he could be sure of. This wasn't the result of any earthquake or natural force. The odds were that something had hit the outer walls again and again until they broke apart, and whatever was responsible for the attack could get in.

"This isn't supposed to be possible," said Cross's voice in his ear. "I saw the specifications for the outer walls. This Base was designed to survive intact even if the Screen went down. It was ten times tougher than any Base has ever been. And why would they lower the Screen anyway?"

"You're missing the point," Frost said calmly. "Something did this. Something unknown. And to be able to do this, this unknown force must have had a technology not only equal to our own, but quite possibly superior. So where is this unknown force? Still inside the Base? Or if it's not inside, where has it gone and is it coming back anytime soon?"

"Good questions," said Silence. "But you're missing something, too, Investigator. The force Screen is down, and the walls are broken in so many places they might as well not be there. So why hasn't the whole Base gone up in flames along with everything else on this infernal planet?"

"Only one way to find out," said Frost, and Silence didn't need to see past her featureless steel helm to know that she was smiling.

"Lead the way, Investigator," Silence said calmly. "But remember, answers not bodies."

"Of course, Captain. Of course."

She moved past Cross and strode forward into the open doors. Silence moved after her, with Cross's hand on his shoulder, and the marines and Stelmach followed. The Security Officer was being very quiet, but Silence doubted that would last long once they got inside. A place like this was bound to be full of sensitive material that lowly Captains and lesser ranks weren't supposed to know about. Silence didn't give a damn. If there were answers here he was going to find them, no matter where he had to look.

He stepped carefully through the gaping doors, his gaze sweeping back and forth, but everything seemed quiet. It was dark, and Silence turned on his suit's exterior lights, mounted on his shoulders. More light pushed back the darkness as the rest of the away team turned on their lights, and the foyer slowly formed around them. The first thing Silence noticed was that it was raining. It took him a moment to realize that it was the sprinkler system, still somehow operating. Except the water should have evaporated in this heat. He checked the exterior temperature from his suit's sensors, and the figure appeared immediately low, down on the inside of his helmet. It was only a few degrees above standard temperature, despite the broken walls and open doors. Which should be impossible. With the Screen down and the walls breached, there was no way the Base could be maintaining a standard temperature.

"Investigator, check your sensors. What temperature do you have?"

"Same as you, Captain. Standard, near as damn it. I'd swear there was an energy Screen still protecting us, but nothing registers on my sensors. What we do have here is standard gravity, and a breathable atmosphere, but don't ask me what's maintaining them. We could survive here without our suits, if we had to."

"Don't even think it," Silence said quickly. "Don't even take your helmet off. Since we don't know what's maintaining these conditions, we can't be sure they won't cut off at any moment. Also, I want full quarantine procedures followed. Suit integrity is to be preserved at all times. Is that clear, everyone?" Quick affirmatives came back to him from the rest of the team. Frost just grunted, but that was to be expected. Silence glared about the deserted foyer. "Marines, move out and set up a defensive perimeter. Investigator, don't wander too far away just yet. Stelmach, don't touch *anything*. Cross, you've been here before. First impressions?"

"The place is a mess," said Cross. "Whoever came through here really wrecked the place. I can't tell anything from this."

Silence had to agree that the Communications Officer had a point. The foyer looked as though a grenade had gone off in it. Maybe several grenades. Furniture had been overturned and scattered everywhere, much of it wrecked or reduced to little more than kindling. The main reception desk, a huge slab of ironwood, had collapsed in the middle, as though something extremely heavy had sat on it. None of its built-in instruments were functioning. There was no trace of life anywhere. There were wide cracks in the walls through which could be seen the hellish glow of the fires outside. But strangely, the bronze light didn't penetrate far into the darkness. The sprinkler rain had touched and soaked everything, forming pools and little lakes here and there.

"No blood and no bodies," said Frost from the far end of the foyer. "But somebody put up a fight. There's damage to the walls and ceiling from discharged energy weapons. No sign they actually hit anything, though."

Silence looked up at the jagged holes in the ceiling. Trust Frost to spot something everyone else would have missed.

"Why the ceiling?" said Stelmach suddenly. "How big were their attackers?"

"Let's try and keep an open mind," said Silence. "We don't have any hard evidence yet that there were any attackers. This could turn out to be just another really bad case of cabin fever. Unlikely, I'll admit, but we have to consider all possibilities. Frost, run an energy scan on these disrupter holes. See how old they are. Stelmach, see if you can find a working terminal somewhere in this mess that'll let you access the Base computers. The Commander's log might give us a few clues. And Cross, how come the sprinklers are still working? Surely, they should have run out of water long ago?"

"The sprinkler systems feed off the underground lake," said Cross. "It's a long way down, but there are millions of gallons down there. It could rain forever in here, on a planet of eternal fires. It's like a miracle."

"Don't start getting religious on us," said Frost. "I'd hate to have to puke inside this helmet."

"Over here," Stelmach said suddenly. "I've found someone."

"Stay put," said Silence sharply. "Don't touch anything. Investigator, check it out."

The Security Officer was crouching beside the collapsed main desk. Frost moved quickly in beside him and studied the situation for a long moment. "It's a hand, Captain. Human. Unprotected. No obvious booby traps attached, according to my sensors. Help me move the desk, Stelmach."

They moved awkwardly around the desk in their clumsy suits, and Cross and Silence moved forward to help them. A pale colorless hand protruded from under one side of the desk. Working together, the four of them used the power of their suits' servomechanisms to lift the massive ironwood desk and put it carefully to one side. And then they all stopped and looked at what they'd uncovered. It had been a woman once, but most of her was missing. The bones were still there, piled loosely together, but picked so clean of flesh they seemed almost polished. The only flesh left was on the face and part of the arm attached to the hand they'd found. Most of her long hair was still there, but something had cracked open the back of the skull and removed the brains. Sprinkler water pattered down on the head and ran down the staring face like tears.

"Picked clean," said Frost. "And judging by the ragged end of the remaining arm, I'd have to say this was brought about by teeth, rather than any blade or sharp instrument. Same with the back of the skull; brute force did that, not a cutting tool. I wonder why they left the face and the arm . . ."

"Perhaps it, or they, were interrupted," said Cross.

"What could have done this?" said Stelmach, his voice thick with nausea. "What kind of creature . . ."

"Move away and take some deep breaths," said Silence. "Vomiting inside a hard suit is not a good idea."

"I'm all right," said Stelmach angrily. "I can handle it."

"It was a good question," said Cross. "What kind of creature would feed like this?"

"Practically anything," said Frost. "If it was hungry enough. The thoroughness is interesting, though. They didn't just go for the fat and the muscle; they took everything. That's unusual. More commonly, different species feed off different parts of the body . . . Maybe the attackers killed her first, and then something else came along afterward, and fed off the body."

"There are no living things anywhere on this planet," said Cross. "Unless the attackers brought something with them."

"Still think this was cabin fever, Captain?" said Stelmach.

"I'm not ruling anything out yet," said Silence calmly. "This is looking more and more like an alien attack, I agree, but we still have no hard evidence that anything other than humans were ever here. Remember, the Hadenmen are loose again. And there's always Shub and its Furies. Investigator, could the tissues taken from this body have been intended for study, rather than food?"

"Quite possibly, Captain. It would explain the thoroughness."

"This can wait," Silence decided. "I want this whole Base checked out, floor by floor. There'll be time for questions and hypotheses after we're sure this place is secure."

He gestured sharply to the marines. With Frost in the lead the party moved on deeper into the Base, weapons at the ready. Things grew worse the further in they got. There was destruction everywhere, and more partial bodies. Doors had been torn out of door frames, holes punched through walls, instruments wrecked, the pieces scattered to no apparent purpose or pattern. Every room had been torn apart and wrecked, but nothing obvious had been taken. The number of bodies mounted steadily. The amount consumed or taken varied, but the heads were always left intact apart from the brains, leaving so many silently screaming faces. Silence felt a slow core of cold anger building within him. This wasn't an attack, it was a slaughter; and he swore silently to every new dead face that he would take a bloody revenge for them all.

Frost just seemed increasingly interested, but she was an Investigator, after all. Cross said very little, except to comment on the increasing destruction and identify the occa-

sional face in a choked voice. Stelmach had nothing to say,
but kept very close to the others. The six marines maintained
their defensive perimeter, checking every open doorway and
turn of the corridor with trained weapons. Tension built inexorably as the away team moved on through the darkness,
their only light what they had brought with them. Shadows
loomed and danced; the only sound was the dull thuds of
steel boots on the floor and their own increasingly harsh
breathing. No one felt like talking much. There was still no
trace of any actual alien, but broken swords lay discarded
here and there, shattered on something harder than steel, and
there was more damage to walls and floor and ceiling from
discharged energy weapons. Here and there great holes had
been punched through the thick steel walls, as though by
some incredible force. Silence couldn't have done it, even
with all the strength of his powered armor. The last creature
he'd seen capable of such a feat had been the genetically engineered aliens he'd discovered sleeping in the vaults on
Grendel. The thought disturbed him, so he kept it to himself,
for later. And everywhere they went, the water came down
in an endless rain, as though trying to wash away what had
happened.

On the second floor Frost stopped suddenly and knelt
down, shining her lights onto something on the floor. The
others crowded around her, adding their lights to hers. The
Investigator studied the pool of dark liquid thoughtfully and
then stirred it slowly with a steel finger. It was a thick,
sticky liquid that tried to cling to her finger when she pulled
it away. She had to shake her hand hard to get it free.

"What is it, Investigator?" said Silence finally.

"Too early to say, Captain. I've seen smaller splashes of
it here and there, but with nothing to suggest what it is or
where it came from. But it looks organic."

"Alien blood?" said Cross.

"Maybe," said Frost uncommittedly. "I'll take some samples, and the *Dauntless* labs can run tests on it."

"Follow full quarantine procedures," said Silence. "Just in
case."

"Of course, Captain."

*Of course. She knows what she's doing. Let her get on
with her job.* Silence took a deep breath and let it out slowly
as he straightened up. He looked about him and scowled inside the safety of his helm. It wouldn't do any good for the

others to see how frustrated he was getting. They'd ended up in one of the main control centers on the second floor, and it was even more of a mess than anywhere else, if that was possible. Most of the instrumentation had been ripped out of its settings and partially dismantled. As though the dismantlers had never seen anything like it before. Perhaps they hadn't. Not for the first time, Silence remembered the alien ship he and Frost had found crash-landed on Unseeli, with its strange and unnatural biomechanical systems. A ship that had been grown as much as made. The single alien from that ship had killed every human being in Unseeli's Base Seven and transformed the Base itself in horrid alien ways. Hopefully, that wasn't what they had here. The signs were different.

"Stelmach, try and find a computer terminal you can access. I need the Commander's log."

"I'm doing my best, Captain. There are some working systems still on-line, but reaching them's the problem. Whatever came through here really trashed the place."

I want results, not excuses! Silence nearly snapped, but kept it to himself. "Do your best, Stelmach. We won't leave here till you've exhausted every possibility." He looked around as Cross came over to join him. "Anything new?"

"Not exactly, Captain. There's something wrong here. Apart from the obvious. There aren't enough bodies."

"Explain."

"Given the size of the contingent running this Base, we should have encountered far more bodies than we have. Unless they're all piled up somewhere we haven't found yet, I'd have to say as many as seventy to eighty per cent of the Base personnel are missing. Which suggests to me that the invaders may have taken the surviving personnel with them when they left."

"As hostages."

"Or specimens."

"But there is a chance they could still be alive?"

"Unknown, Captain. They could have been taken to the alien craft for . . . study."

And that was an interesting choice of word, Silence thought unhappily. It could mean anything from observation to vivisection. Either way, it was a complication Silence could have done without. He came to Gehenna to investigate what had happened at its Base, not go chasing blindly off after missing personnel. But he couldn't just ignore them. Not if there was a chance, however small, that some of them might still be alive. He scowled, torn over what to do for the best. His duty was clear; discovering what had happened in the Base had to have top priority. Whatever had trashed the Base so thoroughly could be a threat to the Empire itself. Just at the time when the last thing it needed was another threat. But he couldn't abandon people to death or worse. He couldn't. He made himself stop frowning. His head was beginning to ache again. Facts. He needed hard facts to help him make his decision.

"Stelmach . . ."

"All right, all right! I think I've got something . . ."

Silence and Frost moved over to join Stelmach and Cross beside a comm panel that didn't look quite as wrecked as the others. It still looked pretty bad, and from the way Stelmach and Cross were fiddling about with its innards, there was clearly still a lot wrong with it.

"Bear with us for a moment, Captain," said Stelmach without looking up from what he was doing. "I've cobbled together parts from a dozen panels, and if we're very lucky, it might just condescend to work for us."

"I helped," said Cross.

"All right, I was going to tell them. This man's wasted in Communications, Captain. He knows more about the inside of comm tech than I do, and I thought I knew everything. Ever thought about a career in security work, Cross?"

"Save the recruiting speeches for later," said Frost. "What have you got?"

"If we're extremely lucky, access to the security systems. There are surveillance cameras throughout the Base, and their files are kept separate from the rest, hidden away for obvious reasons. Apparently, the aliens didn't dig deep enough to find them."

"Yeah," said Silence. "Right. That sounds like Security."

"You'd better hope I'm right, Captain," Stelmach said stiffly. "Whatever happened here, it's over. The attackers are long gone. These security files could be the only records of what actually happened here."

"We'll applaud later," said Frost. "Get on with it."

Stelmach sniffed loudly, just to let them know his feelings were hurt, and then he and Cross made the last few connections. The information in the security files downloaded directly through their comm implants so that visions from the past played directly on the inside of their helmets. They were patchy and incomplete, flashes of sight and sound, a swift succession of scenes from throughout the Base, but taken together the story they told was clear enough. Of what happened the day the aliens came to Gehenna Base.

They were insects, of all shapes and sizes. Spiders and bugs and praying mantises and yard-long centipedes, scuttling and crawling in an endless tide. They varied in size from less than an inch to bigger than human, and everything in between. Horrid combinations of dull carapaces and shimmering wings, too many legs and eyes, and all of them moving incredibly quickly in sudden darting movements. They snapped and stung and tore at human victims with clawed limbs. Some had clacking mandibles big and strong enough to rip a man's head from his shoulders with an ease that was almost obscene.

Silence's skin crawled with instinctive reaction. There was something awful and unnatural about insects that big. That organized. He watched with mounting horror as the insects swarmed through the Base, crawling over all the surfaces, running along the walls and ceiling, jumping up and dropping down on the Base personnel, biting and tearing without pause or mercy. Blood splashed everywhere, and the smaller insects licked it up. Disrupters and cold steel took their toll on the invaders, but there were so many insects, thousands of them, and they never stopped coming. And men and women died from poisoned bites and stings or lay shuddering on the floor while smaller insects burrowed in their flesh. Huge bugs like living armor tore human limbs away with horrid ease and waved them like dripping banners. People screamed and fought and died, and still the insects pressed on.

"Interesting," said Frost quietly. "I've never seen so many apparently different and unconnected species acting together. Could be a mass consciousness, a gestalt or group mind. Or maybe they're all drones, following orders from some hidden and protected queen. I can't be more certain without specimens to examine. But I'll tell you one thing for sure, Captain. Those big bugs aren't natural. Insects don't get that large. Body structure won't allow it. Which implies they were genetically engineered, constructed and adapted for various functions. Maybe all of them were. Which in turn suggests a level of biotechnology well in advance of anything we have."

"How can you be so calm?" said Cross angrily. "Those bastards slaughtered men and women and tore them apart, and you sound as though this was nothing more than a training session!"

"All part of the job," said Frost.

"Damn you, those were real men and women!"

"She knows that," said Silence. "But she's an Investigator. She's seen worse. Now, be quiet and watch the records."

"I think this new file shows the beginning," said Stelmach. "It's the last intact one."

The Base's force Screen shut down suddenly, for no reason anyone in the Base could understand. Which was supposed to be impossible. The personnel weren't too worried—at first. The Base had been designed to protect them from the heat of the fires, even without the Screen. And then the insects came, cracking the Base open like an eggshell to get at the unprotected flesh within. The Base called for help with increasing desperation, but the comm systems were useless. Jammed. Which was also supposed to be impossible.

Finally, one by one, the cameras stopped recording as the insects discovered and destroyed them. And after that, there was only darkness.

The control room surroundings reappeared on the insides of everyone's helmets as the security file came to an end, and they all stood quietly for a long moment.

"There was a pattern to the invasion," said Frost. "The larger insects broke things, the medium range attacked people and investigated human tech, and the smaller ones cleaned up after them, sucking up blood, carrying away machinery, and eating the fallen, whether human or insect."

Silence closed his eyes, but he could still see the images of men and women screaming, struggling helplessly, or crying out for help that never came. He was glad he'd seen only glimpses of the carnage. He didn't think he could have stood seeing the horror of it in real time. He opened his eyes and breathed deeply to clear his head. He had to be cool and centered if he was to have his revenge on the bugs.

"They were specialized by function." Frost was still speaking, and Silence made himself pay attention. "Designed for specific purposes. But what did they want here?"

"What aliens always want," said Stelmach. "To destroy humanity."

Silence swallowed hard, his mouth dry. "It isn't usually that simple, Stelmach. We know what happened here, but not why. And without the why, we can't hope to predict what they'll do next. They could be anywhere inside the Empire by now. There has to be a reason for all this destruction and slaughter. Investigator, you said the insects appeared to have been designed for specific tasks in this assault. That implies there was an aim to be achieved, an end to be reached."

"Yes," said Frost. "Almost certainly. I get the impression they were after information, as much as anything. They certainly seemed to pay special attention to the computer records. People were mostly killed or attacked when they got in the way or tried to interfere with the search. I think they were looking for something."

"What could they have wanted here?" said Cross. "Gehenna is the farthest planet in this sector of the Empire. There's nothing beyond here but the Darkvoid."

"And they couldn't have come this far through the Empire without being noticed," said Stelmach. "So they must have come from . . . outside the Empire."

"Nothing lives in the Darkvoid," said Frost. "Apart from the traitors on Haden."

"Then, maybe they came from the other side of the Darkvoid," said Silence slowly. "And this was the first human outpost they discovered. But why just attack? We always try to communicate first. If only to find out what we're getting into. Did the Base have something the aliens wanted? Something they knew the Base personnel wouldn't give up voluntarily?"

"I think we're reaching a bit here," said Cross.

"Of course we are," said Frost. "It's all we've got. Now, unless you've got something useful to say, shut the hell up. We're thinking. So they took tech apart, killed people in search of something. Information. What did they want to know that we wouldn't tell them?"

"Weaknesses," said Stelmach. "Defense stations, weaponry, secrets . . ."

"The location of homeworld!" said Silence. "Destroy Golgotha, and the whole Empire would be crippled!" A shudder ran through Silence as his thoughts raced ahead of him.

"You thought this was a trap, Investigator, but it isn't. It's a decoy intended to keep us occupied here while the aliens head for Golgotha! Heads up, everyone. We're leaving."

"Oh, come on," said Cross. "This is really reaching."

"No," said Frost. "It feels right. It's what I'd do."

"But what about the missing personnel?" said Cross. "What if they're being kept somewhere here on Gehenna? If we go chasing off after a theory, they could die here! What if we're wrong about this?"

"Then, we're wrong," said Frost. "Now, shut up and move. Homeworld must be protected, at all costs. No wonder you keep being transferred, Cross. You talk too much."

"We are leaving, people!" said Silence. "Investigator, lead the way. Cross and Stelmach, stick with me. Marines, bring up the rear. If anything moves, shoot it. We don't have any friends here anymore."

And so they made their way back out of the Base, breasting the endless sprinkler rain like swimmers in a race. It was hard to run in the heavy, clumsy hard suits, but they did it anyway. There was no telling what kind of advance the aliens had on them. The attack on the Base couldn't have happened long ago. What was left of the human bodies hadn't had time to corrupt much. That meant a few days at most. So everything depended now on what kind of stardrive the alien ship had, and whether it was the equal of the *Dauntless*'s new drive. The *Dauntless* was supposed to be the fastest thing in the Empire, but Silence and Frost knew something the others didn't. The amazing new stardrive was based on a drive Silence and Frost found in the alien ship crash-landed on the planet Unseeli. Which meant there was no telling how fast the new alien ship might be. Especially, one that had apparently crossed the Darkvoid from one side to the other; something no Empire ship had ever dared attempt.

Usually, the Empire found aliens and made decisions about their future. The aliens could join the Empire, be subjugated, or die. No other choices were available. This time, something had found the Empire. And all Silence could do was hope the *Dauntless* got back to Golgotha in time to give a warning. Before the aliens arrived and started making decisions about humanity.

* * *

The *Dauntless* dropped out of hyperspace and plunged into orbit around Golgotha, all weapons systems charged and ready, and immediately began broadcasting warnings on all channels. Sensors raked the darkness for signs of the alien ship, and only then discovered that the homeworld's defenses were in a complete shambles. The *Dauntless* homed in on the main starport, only to find everyone was shouting at everyone else, and no one was listening. Cross ran through all the comm channels, but the chaos had spread even to the most restricted emergency channels.

"What the hell is going on down there?" said Silence. "Did the alien ship beat us here?"

"No sign of anything on the sensors," said Frost immediately. "But that's not all that's missing. There are supposed to be six starcruisers constantly on patrol, orbiting Golgotha, as the Empire's last line of defense. I can't find a trace of any of them."

Silence looked across at the comm station. "Cross, are our warnings getting through?"

"Impossible to say, Captain. The channels are such a mess that priority's a joke."

"Let me try," said Stelmach, moving in beside Cross. "I have access to security channels that most people don't know about."

"Go ahead," said Silence. "Frost, use the long-range sensors. Get me some pictures of what's going on down there."

Frost grunted something, preoccupied with her instruments, but after a moment the viewscreen suddenly flickered into life. The starport and its landing pads had been systematically destroyed. Smoke rose up from blazing buildings, and broken starships lay scattered across the broken pads like so much shattered crockery. The steelglass control tower was cracked like a jigsaw, and everywhere fires blazed out of control. Emergency services were doing what they could, but things had obviously got out of their control long ago. There were bodies everywhere, and Silence had no doubt there were many more he couldn't see.

"The alien ship got here about six hours ago," said Stelmach. "Launched an attack while the control tower was still trying to identify it. It blew up the ships on the pads and then made dozens of strafing runs, raking the port and the city with energy weapons of an unfamiliar type. Force fields and Screens were no protection. They either failed or the energy weapons blew them aside. Known casualties are in the hundreds of thousands. As yet the Empress is in no danger; she's safe in the Imperial Palace, deep below the surface. We can only hope the aliens don't know she's there."

"This is insane!" said Silence. "How could one ship have done so much damage unchallenged?"

"It appears the aliens got a lucky break," said Cross. "As far as I can make out, the rebel underground launched some kind of sabotage attack only a few hours before the alien ship arrived. They then made their escape on a Hadenman ship. The six starcruisers took off after it. Security were busy chasing their own tails trying to sort out the extent of the sabotage, and got caught napping."

"It wasn't security's fault!" Stelmach said quickly. "The rebels crashed nearly all of the computer defenses. We were helpless."

"Forget about laying the blame and get me some information I can use," said Silence. "Where's the alien ship now?"

"On the far side of the planet," said Frost. "It's on its way back here. Two, three minutes tops, depending on whether it stops to blow something else up."

"What are you going to do, Captain?" said Cross.

"Blow it to shit," said Silence.

"No," said Frost immediately. "Normally, I'd agree with you, Captain, but for now we need answers more than revenge. We have to know more about them, where they come from. If this ship really did cross the Darkvoid to find us, who knows what else might be following them? We need prisoners to interrogate and the ship as intact as possible, to study."

"Any other restrictions you want to lay on me?" said Silence.

"There's also the case of the missing Base personnel," said Cross stubbornly. "If they're being held on the alien ship . . ."

"Then they're expendable," said Silence. "I'll save them if I can, but I'm not making any promises. Same to you, Investigator. Stopping the attack comes first. Homeworld must be protected. And if it comes to blowing the alien ship apart rather than letting it escape, that ship is dead."

"Understood," said Frost. "You'd have made a good Investigator, Captain."

"Thanks a whole bunch," said Silence. "Cross, where is it?"

"It's coming," said Cross. "Should be in visual range any time now."

"Red Alert," said Silence. "All shields up, everyone to their battle stations. Power up all weapons and tie in fire-control systems. Cross, download our log so far, along with any other useful information concerning the aliens and what happened at Gehenna Base, and launch the files in an emergency buoy. If anything should happen to us, the information can be retrieved later by whoever survives this mess."

"It's coming," said Cross. "I have it in my sensors. Its speed is incredible."

"Put it on the viewscreen," said Silence.

The scene on the viewscreen changed to show the great glowing curve of Golgotha, and the darkness and the stars beyond. One of the stars was moving rapidly toward them, jumping in size as Cross increased magnification. The alien ship finally sprang into view, and Silence leaned forward in his command chair. The alien craft appeared to be a huge ball of sickly white webbing, tied and tangled together. It reminded Silence of a wasp's nest or a cocoon. Insect imagery. The ball had no details of shape or structure and no identifiable technology.

"How big is it?" Silence said finally.

"About two miles in diameter," said Cross. "I'm listening on all channels, but I'm not picking up anything from the alien craft."

"Sensors indicate mainly organic material," said Frost. "Presumably protected by some kind of force shield, but the few energy readings I'm picking up make no sense at all. No identifiable drive, or weapons, or . . . anything, really."

"Try talking to them," said Stelmach. "Maybe we can negotiate."

"Unlikely," said Frost. "Even the best computer translators take months to produce a working language. Besides, I'd say they've already made their intentions clear."

"Damn right," said Silence. "I don't negotiate with butchers. Anything else on the sensors?"

"Getting some high-energy readings as we get closer, nothing familiar. Wait a minute. Something's happening. The energy readings are building . . ."

Flaring energy leapt out from the alien ship, crossing

the intervening miles in a moment, and crackled across the *Dauntless*'s force shields. It seethed and hissed all over the shields, testing, searching for weak spots. Alarms went off all over the *Dauntless* as slowly, inexorably, the crackling energy tore through the force shields, seeped through the outer hull, and burst into the ship's interior. Blazing light leapt out of workstations on that side of the ship, incinerating crew members where they stood. More alarms sounded every minute, and fires burned unattended in a chaos of screams and shouted orders. Emergency systems were bypassed, and the energy spread.

"Evacuate that section!" said Silence. "Get out as many as you can, and then isolate the section and seal it off. Set up a series of force shields in the corridors. See if you can slow it down at least. Frost, talk to me. What is that stuff? What is it doing to my ship?"

"Sensors indicate pure energy, Captain," said Frost calmly. "But it also has definite physical properties. Possibly some form of plasma energy in suspension, but don't quote me. It's ignoring everything we throw at it. And if these readings are to be believed, the energy has begun to infiltrate our instrumentation in that section, subverting it and taking it over."

"We just lost sectors H through K," said Cross. "They're no longer responding to central control, or auxiliary backups. Life-support systems are shutting down in those sectors."

"Is everyone out?" said Silence.

"Most of them," said Cross. "Those that didn't get out won't last long."

"Evacuate the adjoining sectors," said Silence. "Seal them off with as many interior force shields as we can generate. Any injured are to get themselves to the Infirmary. Everyone else is to stay at their posts. Investigator, any recommendations?"

"Our shields won't hold back the energy for long, Captain. Defensive measures are strictly temporary. This would seem to indicate the need to take the offensive. If the alien ship has any force shields, my sensors can't find them. It's looking more and more like our best bet is to hit them with everything we've got and see what happens."

"I was hoping we'd have something else we could try first," said Silence. "I don't like playing our main hand this early. But needs must prevail when the devil drives. Gunnery Officer, target the alien ship. Hit it till its shields go down and we start inflicting actual damage, and then break off and stand by for new orders."

The *Dauntless*'s disrupter cannon opened fire in sequence, one after another, maintaining a constant barrage of destructive power. Strange energy fields suddenly flared into being around the alien ship, shimmering fiercely. The disrupter cannon pounded away at them, but they held firm. Within the *Dauntless,* the strange crackling energy spread slowly but inexorably from one section to the next, infiltrating and subverting essential systems as it went. Life support was going down sector by sector. Crew members died at their posts, or running for their lives.

A workstation on the bridge exploded suddenly, throwing its operator lifeless to the floor, his clothes and hair burning fiercely. Strange energies danced on the bridge air like heat lightning. Silence yelled for people to back away from the blazing workstation, but for everyone else to hold their posts. Fires licked along one wall, hot and blazing.

The disrupter cannon fired and fired, and suddenly the alien ship's fields went down. Chunks of the sickly white webbing were blown away into space. And as suddenly as that, the strange energies infesting the *Dauntless* disappeared. Workstations returned to normal, emergency systems began taking care of fires, life support was reestablished, and the attack was over. Silence ordered the disrupter cannon to break off firing, but to stand ready to resume the attack as necessary. The fires went out, the injured were helped, and the dead were dragged away. When the last alarm went off, it was eerily quiet on the bridge.

"All right," said Stelmach. "What do we do now?"

"We board the alien ship," said Frost. "We've done them some damage, but we have no way of telling how much, or how long it'll take them to make repairs. So we'd better strike now while they're still weakened."

"Agreed," said Silence. "I want that ship taken intact, so our people can take it apart and see what makes it tick. Especially, the shields and the weapons. We might have to face them again. But even so, given the state of the *Dauntless,* I can't authorize more than a small boarding party. You, Investigator, myself, and a dozen marines."

"Sounds good to me," said Frost.

"You can't leave the ship now, Captain," said Stelmach. "There are damage reports coming in from all over."

"Then, you deal with them. I'm needed on the boarding party. If only because I'm one of the few people here to have faced aliens and lived to tell of it. Cross, you work with the Security Officer. See he has all the support he needs."

"Yes, Captain," said Cross. "But I do feel I should point out that Regulations clearly state . . ."

"All right, you've pointed it out. Now, forget it. With all the trouble I'm in, a few more broken Regs are the least of my worries. You don't need me, Cross. This ship is dead in the water. Just watch over her, and don't let Stelmach get too carried away with his new responsibilities. Anyone calls, you know where to find me. Let's go, Investigator. I want a close-up look at the kind of ship that can trash an entire city and starport and almost took out an Imperial starcruiser."

"Right," said Frost. "And with a bit of luck, we'll get to kill some aliens, too."

"There's always the chance they're playing possum," said Stelmach.

"Then, they'll soon be dead possums," said Silence.

The *Dauntless* maneuvered carefully with the little power she had left to set herself alongside the alien craft, which made no move to acknowledge her presence. Sensors picked up no energy readings or life signs. Silence lay quietly in his hard suit inside the torpedo tube, listening to the reports over his comm implant. He didn't place too much reliance in the sensors. He had a strong feeling the alien ship was still perfectly capable of keeping its secrets to itself. He stirred uncomfortably, as best he could. He was lying facedown in one of his own torpedo tubes, the shoulders of his hard suit brushing against the steel walls, and he barely had room to twitch his fingers, never mind attend to the itch that was building with slow malevolent intensity between his shoulder blades. Normally, he'd only have to wear a hard suit maybe half a dozen times in a year, and this was the second time in one mission. He sighed deeply and ran through his suit's built-in diagnostics again. Anything to keep his mind occupied. As soon as the *Dauntless* got close enough, he was going to be fired out of the torpedo tube toward the alien ship, and he wasn't looking forward to it one bit. Even if it was his idea. There was no entry port he could fly a pinnace to, and blowing a hole in the alien craft big enough to dock a pinnace might have all kinds of unpleasant consequences. That just left climbing into a hard suit and knocking on the door the hard way.

Silence sighed again and wished he'd made time to visit the toilet first. The suit's facilities were efficient but primitive. The inside of his helmet had nothing to show him but the inside of the torpedo tube, and whatever displays he felt like calling up. It felt like he'd been stuck in the tube for hours, but the suit's timer, blinking officiously low on his left, insisted it had been barely twenty minutes. Silence wondered idly if this was what the inside of a coffin looked like, and then rather wished he hadn't.

"Captain, *Dauntless* is in position," said the Second in Command's voice suddenly in his ear. "Launching now."

Silence had an almost overpowering urge to say *No, stop, I've changed my mind*, and then pressure exploded around him, and he was shot out of the torpedo tube and into space. It was very dark, but the stars were very bright. They whirled around him in dizzy arcs, and then settled down as the hard suit orientated itself and its built-in computers locked onto the alien ship. The rocket pack on his back kicked in and nudged him toward the alien craft with a series of carefully considered bursts. The huge white ball hung silently before him, blank and ominous. This close, the tangled strands of webbing looked more like thick twisting cables. It also looked disturbingly organic. Alive. And quite possibly not nearly as damaged as it was pretending to be.

He could see the damaged areas increasingly clearly as he drifted closer. They were deep, ragged pits in the sickly white surface, sinking deeper than even his suit's augmented vision could follow. The ragged edges of the broken cables hung limply, unmoving. Silence frowned and studied them closely. He kept thinking he saw some of them twitching just on the edge of his vision, but when he looked at them straight, they were still.

He could see Frost, coming into view beside him, and his sensors told him the dozen marines were spread out around him in a narrow curve. Their presence was immediately reassuring, and he began to breathe a little more easily. He hadn't spent much time in actual space since his cadet days at the Academy, and he'd forgotten how cold and lonely it could be. Golgotha lay below him, great and golden and giv-

ing him at least a sense of up and down, but the sheer size
of space was horribly intimidating. And lovely though the
stars were, they were a hell of a long way off. It was also a
hell of a long way down, but he was trying very hard not to
think about that. If anything were to go wrong with his suit,
he could end up dying in a variety of really unpleasant ways.
But nothing was going to go wrong. The suit's diagnostics
were fine, and its computers would get him to the alien ship
far more safely than he could have managed on his own. At
which point he would no doubt encounter some really disgusting alien life forms, more than ready to kill him in even
worse ways. Join the Imperial Navy and see the universe. He
smiled despite himself. He'd still rather be here than stuck
helplessly back on the bridge, worrying about what Frost
and the marines were getting into.

He concentrated on the alien ship growing steadily larger
all the time. It filled space before him, expanding like a
small planet as he drifted toward its surface. The white cables were now thicker than a landing craft, impossibly long
as they stretched away in each direction, and pocked with
small and large holes, as though something had been gnawing on them. Silence found that thought disturbing. What the
hell could the alien craft have encountered in its long travels
through the Darkvoid that had actually tried to eat it? He put
the thought out of his mind and concentrated on his landing.

Silence and the Investigator and the marines drifted down
onto the surface of the alien ship, like so many settling seeds
on a forest floor, and collected on the edge of one of the
holes the *Dauntless* had blasted in the outer surface of
the ship. It was a good thirty feet across and went down at
least a hundred feet. There was no telling how much deeper
it went. The hard suits' sensors couldn't follow that far.
Even though they should have been able to. Silence checked
his other instruments. No ambient heat from the hole, no ra-
dioactivity, no magnetic fields, and only low traces of gravity. Maybe one-tenth human level. Whatever secrets the
alien ship had left, it was keeping them jealously to itself.
Silence activated his comm implant.

"*Dauntless*, this is the Captain. Do you hear me?"

"Loud and clear, Captain," said Cross immediately. "Sensors are locked on your position, and we have full telemetry
on your hard suits. Wherever you go once you're inside the

alien craft, we'll be able to follow your movements and advise you."

"I feel safer already," said Frost. "Keep your guns trained, Cross. Whatever happens, this ship is not to be allowed to escape. You will prevent such an escape with all means necessary, whatever the cost. Is that clear?"

"Captain?" said Cross uncertainly.

"Do as the Investigator says," Silence said flatly. "She's the expert here. If it comes down to the bottom line, we're all expendable. The Investigator and I perhaps a little more so than others. We're going in now. Let's all stick together, people. And whatever we find inside this ship, don't get distracted. I want information, not dead heroes. Investigator, if you'd care to lead the way, we can get this show on the road."

"Of course, Captain."

Frost stepped off the edge of the pit and began to fall slowly down into the great hole the *Dauntless* had made, helped on her way by short bursts from her backpack. Silence followed her, and one by one the marines came after him, in a long line of slowly falling bodies. The shoulder lights on their hard suits pushed back the darkness as they fell, but there wasn't much to see. The inside walls of the pit were composed of the same thick white cables, pressed and twisted together. The controlled fall seemed to go on for ages, and then the floor of the pit loomed suddenly up beneath them. Frost touched down first, got her balance in a moment, and looked quickly about her, built-in weapons at the ready. Silence joined her a moment later. The massive cables beneath his feet didn't give at all, bulging around him like waves in a frozen sea. The marines drifted down around him, dropping out of the gloom into the light like great silver snowflakes. They landed easily, with casual skill, and moved out to form a defensive circle around Silence and the Investigator, who was thoughtfully studying the floor of the pit.

"Interesting," she said finally. "We hit this ship with everything we had. When its shields went down, the outer skin of the hull, or whatever the hell this stuff is, took the full brunt of disrupter cannon firing at virtually point-blank range. Solid steel would have melted and run like water, where it didn't immediately evaporate. But I can't find any trace of heat or structural damage."

"Self-regenerating?" said Silence, and the Investigator shrugged.

"Maybe. If it is, it's far beyond anything we've got. And why just repair the walls? Why not seal over the hole?"

"Because they knew we'd be coming, and they wanted to control where we landed," said Silence. "The word trap suggests itself to me. Suggestions?"

"Blast a way through to the interior," said Frost. "I brought enough shaped charges to blow a path through a small moon. Once we're inside, we'll see if anyone comes to complain about the noise."

"If you're going to start messing about with explosives, I am getting myself and my men out of here," Silence said firmly. "I never met an Investigator yet who understood the concept of subtlety when it came to explosives."

And then he broke off and looked sharply at the wall beside them. Two of the thick white cables were twisting slowly apart to form a tunnel leading deeper into the ship. Frost leaned in cautiously, her suit lights illuminating the tunnel as far as they could. It seemed entirely empty. Silence tried his suit's sensors, but they weren't picking up anything. As far as they were concerned, the tunnel might not even have been there.

"Silence to *Dauntless*. You picking up anything on your end?"

"We're patched into your suits' comm signals, Captain," Cross murmured in his ear. "We can see everything you can. But long-range sensors have nothing to add. I can say we're not picking up any life signs yet. We've heard from Golgotha starport; they're still too busy putting themselves back together to be able to offer us any help. The good news is that the six starcruisers who went chasing off after the Hadenman ship apparently lost contact with it. They're on their way back. Should be here in just under an hour."

"Well, that's something, I suppose." Silence turned to Frost. "Your call, Investigator. Do we go in?"

"Into a possible trap, possibly crammed with murderous aliens? Of course, Captain. Nothing to be gained standing around here."

"I had a feeling you were going to say that. All right, lead the way. Marines, stay close behind us. Be ready to fire at a moment's notice, but exercise caution. There's always the chance we might find the missing personnel from Gehenna

Base in here somewhere. I'd like to get them out of here
alive if at all possible. Lead on, Investigator."

Frost stepped carefully into the tunnel and moved in step
by step. Silence and the marines moved after her. The cables
making up the tunnel's inner walls were smoother, thinner,
but just as unyielding to the touch. Their white color had
thin blue traces in it, like veins. Silence increased the magnification of what he was seeing, and the wall seemed to
leap toward him. The cables were pulsing slightly in a regular rhythm. He stepped the view back to normal and
touched the wall with the tips of his steel fingers. The
built-in sensors detected no warmth of life, only a faint
stickiness. The walls were rounded, like the floor and the
ceiling, as though he and his team were walking through the
bowels of some enormous beast. And maybe they were at
that. Silence glanced back over his shoulder, to see how the
marines were coping, and only then realized that the tunnel
had closed itself off behind them. The cables had fitted together again, thick and impenetrable. Silence quickly alerted
the others and then spun around to see for themselves. Frost
was all for going back and blasting it with her disrupters, but
Silence stopped her.

"Let's follow the tunnel first. See where it leads. We can
always come back and blast it later. *Dauntless,* have you followed what's happened here?" There was nothing but quiet
in his ears. "Hello, *Dauntless*? Do you hear me?" He listened hard, but all he could hear was his own harsh breathing. "Investigator, see if you can raise them."

Frost tried, and then the marines, to no avail. Frost
growled something under her breath and then turned to Silence. "It's not the suits. All the diagnostics check out.
Something's blocking the signal. We're on our own, Captain."

"Not for the first time. Press on, Investigator. I don't think
the occupants of this ship let us in just to hold us here. I
think . . . they're expecting us."

Frost sniffed loudly and led the way on. And as they pen-
etrated farther into the ship, the cables continued to open before them, creating more tunnel, and closing off behind
them, to prevent turning back, so that Silence and his people
moved constantly in a traveling pocket within the webbing.

The cables varied even more in size now, and there were
other changes, too. The corpse-white cables swirled around

and over each other, tangled together beyond sense or meaning, some little more than a finger's width. The floor was no
different, and more than ever Silence felt like he was walking on a spider's web, sending out rhythmic signals of where
he was and where he was going. The impression grew stronger as all the strands grew increasingly sticky to the touch.
It got harder to pull their boots free from the floor, and soon
only the power of the hard suits' servomechanisms kept
them going. Strange lights pulsed within the rounded tunnel
walls, come and gone so quickly it was difficult to decide
what color they might have been. Sometimes Silence
thought they weren't any color he'd ever seen before. But
still there was no sign of any construction or device, or any
sign at all of whatever crewed the alien ship.

The tunnel puckered in suddenly from all sides, so that the
away team had to crawl through on their hands and knees,
one after the other. And on the other side they rose to their
feet as they found themselves in a great, egg-shaped chamber, with a high ceiling and smooth polished walls. Dark
shapes and oddities budded out from the floor and walls,
carefully formed but enigmatic in meaning. Frost snapped
out a warning not to touch them, which Silence for one
found completely superfluous. He wouldn't have touched
any of them on a bet. For no reason he could put a finger on,
his mind kept throwing up an image of himself stuck helplessly to one of the dark shapes, while the chamber filled
slowly with digestive juices. He was sweating inside the
hard suit, despite the cool air it was circulating.

They moved on through the vast chamber, stepping slowly
and carefully, touching nothing, and finally left the chamber
through another of the puckered holes. Beyond lay more tunnels, opening before them and closing after them, and more
chambers studded with various shapes, none of them immediately comprehensible to the human mind. Until finally the
away team encountered another, smaller chamber, and discovered what had happened to the missing Gehenna Base
personnel.

The chamber was some hundred feet in diameter, the
walls pockmarked in rows both vertical and horizontal, and
a thin layer of vapor covered the floor, beading wetly on the
hard suits' armor. There was light of a kind, a harsh unforgiving blue-white glare that seemed to come from everywhere and nowhere at once. Long flat slabs of some

unfamiliar metal were scattered across the floor, held just
above the vapor, and on those slabs, held firmly by some unseen force, were the remains of the Base personnel. Some
were only parts: organs and limbs and faces. A dozen complete torsos had been messily vivisected, and from the few
with heads attached and the expression on their faces, Silence had no doubt at all that these men and women had
been alive and aware when the vivisection began. Anywhere
else he might have felt sick, for all his experience, but right
then he was too full of rage and fury to feel anything else.

"They'll die for this," said Frost in a calm, cold voice.
"Every living thing on this ship shall pay in blood and suffering."

The marines stirred restlessly, looking this way and that
for something to aim their weapons at. Silence knew how
they felt, but kept an icy firm control on his anger. "You can
kill the aliens only after the specialists have squeezed every
drop of information out of them, Investigator. Until then, I
want captives, not corpses. Marines, remember your orders.
Minimum force only, unless in life-threatening situations.
Use your own judgment, but you'd better be prepared to
back it up later. There will be a time for vengeance, but we
must have the information this ship holds. We might have to
face more of its kind in the future."

"Don't lecture me," said Frost. "I know my duty."

"Sorry, Investigator. Just speaking for the record. There's
nothing more we can do here. Mark this chamber's location
on your suits' maps, and we'll move on. We can send people
in to retrieve the bodies later. Right now we have to find the
control section. I want this ship immobilized and helpless
before it can finish its repairs. I also want a good look at the
crew, and more and more it seems the only place we can be
sure of finding them is at the control center. They wouldn't
dare abandon that."

He led the way across the chamber, moving carefully between the crimson spread-eagled bodies on the slabs, trying
hard not to look at them. It was easier to control his anger
that way. It seemed to take forever to reach the opening on
the far wall, but as he drew near it puckered shut in a mass
of solid, tightly packed cables. Silence prodded it here and
there with his steel fingers, but it didn't give anywhere. He
hadn't thought it would. He hit it once with his fist, and then
turned back to the others. They stared at him silently with

their featureless steel helmets. Slowly, and without any fuss, the light was going out. The slabs with their grisly specimens began to disappear into rising vapor. It didn't take much imagination on Silence's part to picture the alien crew massing on the other side of the closed portal.

"Marines, I feel we are quite definitely now in a life-threatening situation. Feel free to shoot anything that moves that isn't us. I'd like a few specimens left alive, just a few, so if anything runs, let it. Investigator, make an opening here."

Frost aimed her armored right hand at the closed opening, and the disrupter built into the glove blasted a hole right through the tightly packed webbing. A sickly green light spilled into the chamber through a ten-foot-wide hole, and everyone braced themselves for an attack that never came. Silence and Frost edged forward and peered through the new opening. Hanging ends of ruptured cables hung twitching and jumping from every side, but showed no signs of knitting themselves together. They pattered weakly against the hard suits, but did no harm. Beyond the opening lay a narrow milky-white tunnel with smooth, faintly glowing walls. It was barely eight feet in diameter, only just big enough to take the away team in their hard suits, and Silence couldn't help wondering if that was deliberate. There was no sign of any enemy.

"I'll take the lead," said Frost. "This is Investigator business now."

"Couldn't agree more," said Silence. "After you."

Frost stepped through into the narrow tunnel, the gauntlets with built-in guns held out before her. Silence followed, and the marines brought up the rear. The floor of the tunnel gave disturbingly under their weight, as though it might rupture at any moment and spill them into whatever lay waiting below. But somehow it held. Silence pressed on and tried hard not to think about it. He'd lost all track of where he was in relation to the ship's exterior. He wasn't actually lost. The suit had kept track of all his twists and turns, and could easily lead him back. But he still didn't know where he was precisely; he just had a strong feeling he was getting deep and deeper in, being lured remorselessly toward the dark heart of the alien craft. He checked his air supply, but he'd barely touched it so far. Theoretically the re-breather could keep him alive for up to a week. Under normal conditions.

He deliberately didn't finish that thought and instead studied the tunnel walls to either side of him. They were flat and smooth, not cabled, more like membranes. They pulsed and fluctuated to no apparent purpose, and waves of pale color briefly tinged the milky white like passing thoughts or dreams. The passage was also narrowing, slowly but inexorably. Silence used his suit's sensors to measure the diameter of the tunnel and compared it to the size it had been when they entered it. He frowned at the answer and calculated how long it would be before the tunnel grew too small for his team to continue on. He liked that answer even less. Four minutes, thirty-seven seconds. No buts or maybes.

"Investigator, marines, stop right where you are."

They did so. Frost didn't look back, but he knew she was watching him quite clearly on the inside of her helmet. Silence measured the tunnel behind him with his suit's sensors and wasn't at all surprised to discover that the tunnel had already narrowed beyond the point where they could pass through it.

"I was wondering when you'd notice," said Frost. "It would appear the aliens have us where they want us. Shall I blast it?"

"What the hell," said Silence. "When in doubt, make a loud noise. Let someone know we're here, and we're not at all happy about it."

Frost aimed her built-in disrupters at the narrowing tunnel before her, and the milky-white walls split apart in a hundred places as insects beyond counting burst in on the away team. The bugs ranged in size from many-legged things the size of a fist, which swarmed all over the hard suits looking for weak spots and entry points, to huge bulky things with their own armor and vicious pincer claws. The tunnel was briefly full of flashing disrupter bolts, and insects fried as the tunnel walls blew apart, but once the guns fell silent the away team disappeared beneath a writhing mass of silent insect life. Tiny things swarmed over the suits' sensors, and Silence was suddenly blind and deaf. He tried to brush the insects away with his powerful steel hands, but there were just too many of them. Warnings flashed up before his eyes as acid began to eat into his armored joints, threatening the hard suit's integrity. Screams sounded in his ears as the insects invaded a marine's armor and began to eat him alive. More screams followed.

"Frost!" said Silence. "You still have those explosives?"

"Enough to blow us all to hell, if that's what you want."

"I was thinking more of just enough to blow the insects to shit without rupturing our suits. Think you can manage that?"

"No problem. Brace yourself."

When it came, the explosion was powerful enough to briefly fill the inner screen of Silence's helmet with a dozen warnings, but they faded out one by one as the suit held. He brushed vaguely at himself, and sight and sound returned as dead insects fell away and the sensors cleared. The tunnel hung in tatters around them, and beyond and around them lay the secret of the alien ship; the vast, imposing shape of the Queen of the alien hive.

She filled the space beyond the tunnel, a great bloated sac of living tissue, hundreds of yards across, living walls of pale pulsating flesh, studded here and there with black lidless eyes. Ridiculously small atrophied limbs protruded in places, remnants of a forgotten earlier life. Metal instruments and gleaming cables plunged into her great flesh from all around, as though she was built into the ship or it had been grown around her.

Silence tore his gaze away and looked around him. The swarming insects had been blasted away by the force of the explosion. Dead and injured alien forms lay everywhere, some twitching feebly. But Silence had no doubt more were already on their way., Eight of the marines were still standing, looking numbly to him for instructions. The Investigator only had eyes for the Queen. Silence checked the four fallen marines for life signs, but he already knew what he'd find. Their suits had ruptured from the combination of the explosion and insect damage. Four more good men lost to the aliens. Silence looked up sharply as his suit's sensors picked up scrabbling sounds, drawing nearer.

"Investigator, more insects on the way. Recommendations?"

"Hit the Queen. She's the heart and mind of them all."

"You heard the Investigator, marines. Hit the Queen with everything you've got."

Vivid light seared from the away team's disrupters and blasted away great chunks of the Queen's body. The pale flesh boiled and vaporized and blew apart, only to seal itself together again in moments. The Queen was just too big for them, too huge even for energy weapons to do any real damage. She towered over them, vast and monolithic, and from everywhere at once lesser aliens came suddenly swarming into what was left of the tunnel. There seemed no end to the living wave, and Silence knew that this time no weapon he had would be enough to stop them. They would just keep coming until their sheer numbers overwhelmed the away team. If he was lucky he'd die then.

Damn. More good men lost. Frost. I wish . . .

And then everything changed. The enigmatic gift he'd acquired from the Madness Maze blazed brightly in his mind and Frost's, and they were linked again, mind to mind, soul to soul. A vast, incomprehensible roar filled their heads: the alien thoughts of a million insects, and thundering through it like a great heartbeat, the commands of the Queen.

It took Silence and Frost only a moment to patch into the roar of the mass mind, seize control, and impose their own commands upon it. The insect tide turned away from their human prey and fell upon the Queen. They swarmed all over her gigantic body and began to eat her alive. The last thing Silence and Frost heard before the link broke and they fell back into their own heads again was the Queen, screaming. They both grinned savagely.

Only human again, Frost and Silence looked at each other. They couldn't see each other's faces, but they didn't need to. Silence glanced briefly at the stunned marines watching the insects devour their own Queen, and decided explanations could wait. He activated his comm implant and accessed Frost on the command channel.

"It's not the same as the creature we found on Unseeli," Frost said calmly. "And it's nothing like what those poor bastards found on Wolf IV. So what exactly have we got here? The creators of those killer aliens in the vaults on Grendel? Or the ancient enemy the Grendel Sleepers were created to fight? Or something else entirely?"

"Beats the hell out of me," said Silence. "Let the specialists worry about it. We need to talk, Frost. This . . . link of ours. It's getting stronger. I don't know how much longer we can keep it hidden."

"We have to," said Frost. "They mustn't know what really happened here. They'd reclassify us as espers. Strip us of our rank. Turn us into lab rats. I'd rather die than live like that."

"There's always the underground."

"Not for us."

"No," said Silence. "Not for us. Aliens like these could return at any time, and only a strong and undivided Empire can hope to stand against them. So we'll keep quiet about what happened here. Act like it's a mystery to us, too. Lionstone doesn't need to know."

"On the other hand," Frost said thoughtfully, "Lionstone was actually really quite lucky here today. With the fleet gone and the planet's defenses in disarray, Golgotha was practically defenseless. If we hadn't turned up when we did, this ship could have trashed half the damn planet. We saved her Imperial ass. Could be she'll be grateful. Grateful enough to overlook our recent failures. What do you think?"

"Not a chance," said Silence.

CHAPTER THREE

Drowning Men

Finlay Campbell, outlaw and terrorist, once the most fabled fop and dandy of his age, and under another name secretly the Masked Gladiator, darling of the bloodthirsty Arena fans, hung upside down on the end of his rope and wondered if perhaps he was getting a little too old for heroics. Spread out below him lay the wide streets and bristling avenues of Golgotha's main city, the Parade of the Endless. It took its name from the endless supply of would-be heroes who came thronging every year to try their strength and courage in the Arena the city hosted. The aristocracy lived in the city, too, in their tightly guarded pastel towers, because after all this was the very best place to be, to see and be seen, in all the Empire. Apart from Lionstone's Court in the Imperial Palace, but you went there only when summoned. And if you were wise, you made out your will before you went. Just in case.

Finlay decided that his thoughts were drifting in unnecessary directions. Hanging upside down with the blood rushing to your head will do that to you. He sighed once, reached up and took a firm grip on his line, and hauled himself back up, hand over hand, till he reached a convenient resting place on the side of Tower Silvestri. Luckily, the Silvestri Family went in for rococo design, so that the sides of their tower were crusted with hundreds of niches and unexpected curves, full of ugly little statues with exaggerated genitals and faces only a mother could love. Finlay squeezed in beside a particularly well-endowed gargoyle with dyspepsia and got his breath back. All this time and trouble just to climb a nine hundred–foot tower. Definitely getting past it. Be taking milk in his coffee next.

If it hadn't been for his safely line, he'd have made a really nasty sploch on the ground below. That was what you got for hurrying. Normally, he'd have known better, but he'd fallen behind schedule. His own fault. He'd stopped off on the way to the tower to indulge himself with a good meal at a decent restaurant. Nowhere fashionable. He couldn't afford to be recognized. But since his Clan had fallen prey to an extremely hostile takeover by Clan Wolfe, he'd been forced to flee for his life. And the only people he could flee to were the clone and esper underground, who were fine when it came to courage and ideals and sticking it to authority, but rather lacking in the comforts department. In particular, Finlay missed the fine cuisine his position entitled him to. While never exactly an epicure, he knew what he liked. Soup so clear you could swim in it. Meat served very rare. In fact, just kill the beast, dismember it, wave the meat in the direction of the fireplace, and then slap it down in front of him, that was all he asked. A few out-of-season vegetables, just for bulk and fiber, and finally, a disgustingly sticky sweet to finish on. Heaven. Absolute heaven.

He'd been denied it for so long, and the smells wafting out of the little tucked-away bistro he passed proved just too tempting. A quick glance at the watch face embedded in his wrist had assured him he was well ahead of schedule, so . . . he allowed himself to be weak. He hadn't looked at his watch again till after his third helping of dessert and was horrified to see how much time had flown while he indulged himself. He dropped a handful of coins on the table and ran out the door like a man ashamed of the tip he was leaving. He'd got to the base of Tower Silvestri with aching lungs, a stitch in his side, and his recent meal rumbling rebelliously in his stomach. It was a wonder the guards hadn't heard him. He followed the agreed-upon approach, slipping between patrols, and threw himself at the side of the tower like a sailor fresh home from the sea visiting his wife. He was still very late, and he'd hurried the climb. Which was how he nearly came to be decorating half the pavement with his insides.

He checked his watch again. He was cutting it very fine. He worked on his breathing, slowing it determinedly back to normal as he stared out over the city. The pastel towers stretched away in all directions, a forest of metal and glass and alien stone, gleaming prettily in the sunlight. He glanced at his reflection in the mirrored steel behind him. He needn't have worried about anyone recognizing him in the bistro. He didn't look at all like he had used to. In his glory days he'd looked like nothing so much as a multicolored bird of paradise, dressed always in the brightest silks and graces current styles allowed. Tall and graceful and fashionable to the very moment, from his polished leather thigh boots to his velvet cap. On his last visit to Court, with his florescent face and metallized hair, he had worn a long cutaway frock coat that showed off his exquisite figure, and a pair of jeweled pince-nez spectacles he didn't need, and everyone there had bowed to him as one of the not-so-secret masters of fashion. Now look at him.

The face in the reflection could have been anyone. No cosmetics to camouflage a minor defect or bring out the bone structure. No bright colors to loudly announce status and rank, or attract the attention of other proud peacocks. Finlay's face these days was thin and drawn, with deep lines accentuating the mouth and eyes. He was just twenty-five and looked at least ten years older. His long hair was a yellow so pale it was almost colorless. At Court it had shone a bright metallic bronze, curled and bouncing over his shoulders. Now it hung limp and lifeless, and he didn't give a damn. He wore a simple leather headband to keep it out of his eyes. He knew he should cut it short. It would have been much more practical. But somehow he couldn't bring himself to do that. It would have been too much like cutting his last link with the person he used to be.

Once his clothes had been the peak of fashionable excess. Now he wore a loose-fitting thermal suit with a chameleon circuit that took on the colors of his surroundings. Finlay smiled briefly, and the man in the reflection smiled back, but Finlay still didn't recognize him. That man looked rough and hard-used, and very, very dangerous. His eyes were cold and careful, and his smile had only a sad humor in it. He could have been an ex-soldier or a mercenary, hired muscle for sale to anyone with the right price. He had the look of that most dangerous of men: someone with nothing left to lose.

No, he thought firmly, and made himself look away. He still had his love for Evangeline, and the new cause he'd embraced. As a noble, he'd never thought about the lot of those beneath him, let alone the non-people, the clones and espers at the very bottom of the heap. Then he came face-to-face with the horrors of Silo Nine, also known as Wormboy Hell, where rogue espers were imprisoned, tortured, and eventually executed, and what he saw there changed him

forever. Now he fought for justice for all, and if he couldn't
have that, he'd settle for revenge.

Which was what had brought him to Tower Silvestri in the
first place. He forced himself to his feet and began climbing
again. His arms and legs trembled from the strain, but they'd
get him where he had to go. The underground had offered
him a choice of stimulants, chemical miracles to put a little
pep in a tired man's muscles, but he'd turned them down.
He'd never needed chemical courage in the Arena, and if he
wasn't quite the man he used to be, he was still the best the
underground had. He laughed breathlessly as he flung himself on, clambering over jutting gargoyles and howling stone
faces like a swift-moving shadow, his chameleon suit blending him seamlessly into his surroundings.

Maybe after this the Silvestri Family would take the time
to rethink their image. Gothic rococo was all very well and
picturesque, but it made sneak missions like this a breeze.
On a high-tech building like Tower Shreck, with its featureless walls of steel and glass, he would have been spotted in
a minute. But like everyone else, both Clans put their faith
in extensive high-tech security systems, which to be fair
were all you really needed, most of the time. They were
more than enough to see off your average thief, spy, or industrial saboteur. They were enough to keep out anyone, unless you happened to have the backing of those cunning
cybernetic anarchists: the cyberats, bless their dark little
hacking hearts, who were currently feeding Tower Silvestri's
systems a bunch of comforting lies, with no mention at all
of the silent figure darting up the defenseless exterior.

He reached the end of his line and stopped to lean companionably on the forbidding stone statue of some noted
Silvestri ancestor. He pulled up the line and wound it securely around his waist. He'd come as far as he needed. Just
as well, given the state of his aching arms and legs and the
cold sheen of sweat on his face. He scowled, breathing
deeply. He'd built his muscles as a gladiator in the Arena,
and despite his recent enforced absence from the killing
sands, he prided himself he was still in damned good shape.
The climb alone would have killed a lesser man. He flexed
the muscles in his arms and legs, blocking out the pain. He
was almost there. Just a little farther. He swung carefully out
and around the stone statue and made his way slowly across
the face of the tower, finding hand and footholds where he

could. Forget the pain building in his muscles and back. Forget the precarious holds, the gusting wind, and the long drop down. Just climb, foot by careful foot, and concentrate on his mission and the kill at the end.

For most of his adult life, the world had known Finlay Campbell only as a fop and a dandy, highly visible at Court, and a constant disappointment to his renowned warrior father. No one knew of his secret second life as the Masked Gladiator, undefeated champion of the Golgotha Arena, except for the man who trained him and the woman who loved him. When circumstances forced him to flee for his life, Finlay had been forced to reveal his prowess as a fighter to the underground. It was the only coin he had to buy their acceptance. There was no room among them for passengers; particularly, if you were neither clone nor esper but merely only human. They sent him on a mission, alone and unsupported, to prove himself or die, and when he came back trailing blood and victory, they shrugged and allowed him his place among them. But though they knew him as a fighter, he never told them about the Masked Gladiator. They didn't need to know that.

He also hadn't told them about his need, the constant burning need for action, violence, and sudden death that had driven him to the Arena in the first place. There were times when it seemed to him that he felt really alive only when he was killing someone. Evangeline Shreck had silenced or at least pacified the need when she was with him. Their love had been all he needed or desired, but their time together had only ever been one of snatched moments. Their Families had been at daggers drawn for generations, and both young lovers had always known that they could never hope for a future together. Somehow that foreknowledge fanned the flames of their love rather than diminished it, and the man who once lived only to kill lived instead for the moments of peace he found in her arms.

But now he lived down below, in the underground, and she had returned to the world above, to Tower Shreck and her awful father. Her position and connections among the occupants of the pastel towers made her too valuable for her to be excused for long. So they held each other one last time and tried not to cry, and said good-bye in choked voices. He went with her as far as he could, and then stopped and watched her walk away until she disappeared into the distance. They'd promised each other they'd be together again, but neither of them really believed it. Happy endings were for other people. Finlay Campbell walked back to the underground alone, and if a part of him died that day, he kept it to himself. It didn't interfere with his being the killer the underground needed for their ongoing struggle.

He'd never thought of himself as a rebel. Never thought about the society he moved in, any more than a fish considers the water it swims in. He took its delights and perquisites for granted, and never knew or cared whose work and suffering provided them. He had been an aristocrat other aristocrats bowed to, heir to one of the most powerful Families in the Empire, possessed of power and wealth beyond counting.

Then the Wolfes slaughtered and scattered the Campbells, and he was suddenly just another face on the run, with any number of Wolfes and their hired swords snapping at his heels, ready to kill him on sight. His only safety now lay with the underground, whose rationale he distrusted and whose ideologies mostly left him cold. He understood their hatred for the way things were. What had been done to the espers and clones in Wormboy Hell was indefensible, for any reason. The torture and suffering he'd seen had turned even his hardened stomach. It took him a little longer to realize that espers and clones faced similar, smaller horrors every day of their lives, in or out of Silo Nine. They were non-people. Property. Their owners could do anything with them they wanted. Finlay always had.

He'd never been much interested in politics, and never would, but he had developed a grudging respect for the rebels, and a willingness to fight on their behalf. Apart from that he didn't have anything much in common with them. He had nothing to say to them and didn't understand or care about what interested them. They thought he was naive, and he thought they were boring. He also spent a lot of time sulking because he no longer had access to the pretty clothes and sparkling parties that had so distracted him when he wasn't in the Arena. The underground didn't have time for nonessentials like fashion or parties. When he wasn't sulking, Finlay tended to brood about the destruction of his Clan, the triumph of his enemies the Wolfes, and what Evangeline was doing without him. All in all, he was a pain in the ass most of the time, knew it, and didn't give a damn. So the un-

derground did their best to keep him busy with missions, for
both their sakes. It wasn't difficult. The underground had a
lot of enemies, and Finlay had an endless need for a little action.

So he volunteered for all the high-risk missions. The underground accepted, and they were both happy. It was hard
to tell which of them was the more surprised that he kept
coming back alive.

This mission was pretty typical. The underground had
marked a powerful and particularly vocal opponent for
death, and Finlay was to be their instrument. Only this time
the target and intended victim was the notorious Lord William St. John, Second in Command to the Lord High Dram
himself, and therefore constantly surrounded by a small
army of well-armed guards and high-tech security. Never
moved in public without his people covering the ground for
miles around in advance. A portable force Screen for emergencies and his own personal flyer to carry him everywhere.
Completely untouchable. Unless you were mad, desperate,
or supremely skilled. Like Finlay, who was all three at various times, according to his needs. Which was why he was
currently crawling up the side of Tower Silvestri like a tiny
gray spider, hopefully overlooked by all.

He finally reached the relatively deep recess he'd noted
earlier on the architectural plans the cyberats had dug up for
him, and he pulled himself into it. There was just room for
him to curl up into a ball and still keep a weather eye on the
scene below. He was about a hundred and twenty feet up,
and snug as a bug in a rug. Waiting. Lord William St. John
would be here soon, according to the underground. Billy boy
the bully boy, whose word was death for clones and espers
and anyone else who got in his way. Billy the Butcher, hated
and reviled by practically everyone, but entirely untouchable
because of his position. The Empress was said to be quite
fond of him.

And he was coming here to Tower Silvestri, stopping off
with his armored entourage to pay his compliments to his
friend and ally Lord Silvestri, on his way to officially open
a new orphanage nearby. Appropriate really, given how
many orphans St. John and his people had created over the
last few years. Since Dram became the Empress's official
Consort, as well as Warrior Prime, he'd had to delegate most
of his duties in the field to his Second in Command, St.

John. Billy boy had taken over the pursuit and persecution of potential rebels, and the execution of rogue clones and espers, and did it all with great efficiency and even greater gusto. Blood and death followed in his wake, and he was never known to bring in his prey alive. Cruelty and slaughter were his pastimes; mercy was not in him. The underground had voted unanimously for his death. St. John's execution would send a message to the Imperial Palace that could not be ignored.

No one would weep for his passing, not even his own kind. Of late, St. John had taken to playing politics, seeking to improve his position to something more than just the Lord High Dram's shadow. He went about it with his usual vim and venom, and made enemies among his rivals with sneering abandon. Opening a new orphanage was safe and uncontroversial, and bound to get St. John good publicity. The man of action with a soft spot for big-eyed children. Couldn't fail. All the big holo networks would be there. Finlay grinned. They didn't know it, but they were in for some of their best ever ratings.

Finlay hadn't missed the similarities between himself and St. John. They were both men with a need for blood and death, and a willingness to get their hands dirty in the process. As soldiers in a war they'd have been heroes, feted by all, with medals and commendations. They'd have been comrades, perhaps even friends. Sitting around a roaring fire in winter, with drinks in their hands, toasting old campaigns and lost comrades. But if there was a war, Finlay and St. John were on different sides. And the similarities between Finlay and St. John just made it that much more of a challenge.

Finlay looked up sharply. He could hear the publicity circus approaching. A brass band led the way, marching down the street in full ceremonial uniforms, playing something pointedly martial and patriotic. After them came a full company of St. John's private guards, conditioned by mind techs to be loyal unto death, surrounding a small personal flyer on which St. John stood tall and proud, smiling and waving to the crowds that packed the street. Finlay sniffed, unimpressed. The crowds had appeared with suspicious speed. One might almost think they'd been paid to gather in just the right place to impress the holo cameras.

St. John was looking good in his everyday uniform with

no decorations. Nice touch, that. Meant to suggest that at heart he was just one of the boys, just another soldier doing his job. He was tall and broad-shouldered, with a barrel chest and a handsome face—the best the body shops could supply. And if his smile was a little practiced and his eyes a little cold, well, people were used to that in the politicians.

Finlay ignored the man, concentrating instead on his flyer. It was really nothing more than a large personalized gravity sled with extra armor, decorated so lavishly with precious metalwork and studded jewels that even Finlay's taste was faintly appalled. You needed style to bring off that kind of excess, and Finlay had a strong suspicion St. John wouldn't know style if it walked up to him on the street and bit his nose. Just another reason to kill him, and put him out of everyone else's misery. The air was shimmering slightly around the flyer; force Screens generated by the craft to ensure the onlookers kept a respectful distance. Strong enough to turn aside an energy beam or the blast from an explosion. St. John's security people knew their business. However, force shields kept out everything. Including air. So the force shields covered only the sides of the craft, leaving the top open so St. John could breathe. It wasn't much of a risk. At the first sight of a flyer or gravity sled approaching from above, the top would be sealed instantly and maintained for as long as it took the potential threat to pass. No problem. Unless of course there was no flyer, no gravity sled. Just one man crouching precariously in a recess in the wall of the tower above St. John.

Finlay grinned. He'd spotted the opening the moment the underground had explained St. John's security setup to him. Attack from above was thought to be impossible, given the surrounding towers' security systems, but even the most sophisticated instruments could be fooled or bypassed by a man willing to take risks; a man who didn't care whether he lived or died. The openness of that thought shocked Finlay for a moment, mostly because it was true. He could live without a Family or his place in society, but he couldn't go on without Evangeline. Events were conspiring to keep them apart, possibly forever, and a life without Evangeline wasn't worth a damn to him. He looked down at the entourage moving into place below him, and his smile widened into a death's-head grin. Someone was going to die soon. St. John stopped his flyer before the tower's main entrance, directly below Finlay, and was preparing to begin his speech. All Finlay had to do was draw his gun and shoot the little toad through the head.

Except, of course, that would have been far too easy. Finlay Campbell had a reputation to uphold.

And he liked to get his hands dirty.

A flick of his hand was all it took to send his rope darting down the side of the tower till it hung unsuspected over St. John's head. It had the same elusive qualities as his chameleon suit, and was for all intents and purposes invisible, even to security systems. Finlay eased himself out of his concealing niche, clinging tightly to his rope, and leaned out over the long drop. He paused, savoring the moment, and then pushed himself away from the side of the tower, sliding down the rope with gathering speed. Leather gloves protected his hands from the growing friction. Wisps of heated smoke escaped between his fingers as he hurtled down, but he waited till the very last moment to clasp his hands shut, slowing his descent. He freed one hand and drew the dagger from his belt. At the last moment St. John must have heard or sensed something. He looked up, and it was the simplest thing in the world for Finlay to let go of the rope, drop down, and stab St. John neatly through the eye.

The Lord convulsed, his arms flying wide, but he was already dead. Finlay's feet hit the deck of the flyer hard, his leg muscles absorbing the impact. He jerked the dagger out of St. John's ruined eye in a gush of blood, and the Lord slumped bonelessly to the deck, twitching and shuddering. The flyer was still rocking sickly from the impact of Finlay's sudden arrival, and the handful of guards on the flyer with St. John were too busy trying to regain their balance to put up much of a defense when Finlay tore into them with his sword and his dagger and his death's-head grin. He swung his sword in short, chopping arcs, doing the most damage possible without risking the blade getting caught in flesh or clothing. He laughed breathlessly, cutting down the disorientated guards with brutal professionalism, and if sometimes their blades came too close for comfort, he didn't give a damn. He was in his element, doing what he was born to do, and loving it.

His sword slammed into a guard's gut and out again in a flurry of blood, and the blade rose quickly to parry a blow from another guard that would have taken his head off. Finlay was glad someone was making a fight of it. He threw himself at the guard, and for a moment they stood head-to-head, neither giving ground. And then something in the guard's eyes gave him away, and Finlay flung himself to one side, just as the other guard behind him lunged forward. Finlay laughed nastily as the other guard ran through his previous opponent, and cut the man down from behind while his sword was still trapped in his comrade's body. There were only three guards left now, and Finlay disposed of them quickly. He didn't have the time to savor it.

He ran the last guard through with a flourish, jerked the sword out in a welter of blood, and looked about him, taking in the situation. He wasn't even breathing hard. Only a few minutes had passed since he'd struck St. John down, and outside the flyer most of the dead Lord's security people were still trying to figure out some way of getting into the flyer so they could get at his assassin. The force shields were still keeping everyone well back, as they'd been designed to, and as yet it hadn't occurred to any of them to try climbing Tower Silvestri, as Finlay had. One poor fool fired his disrupter at the flyer, and they all had to duck and dodge as the energy beam ricocheted back. Someone with his wits about him was yelling for extra flyers, and Finlay took that as a sign it was time for him to leave.

He moved quickly over to the flyer's controls, stepping carefully over the bodies, and lifted the flyer up into the air. A quick glance around showed him more flyers approaching at speed from the south, and he sent his flyer weaving quickly in and out of the pastel towers, accelerating rapidly to a speed his pursuers would be hard-pressed to match if they had any sense of self-preservation. He laughed aloud and stamped his boots on the deck for the simple pleasure of hearing his boots squelch in the pooled blood of his enemies. He'd done it again, made the kill that everyone said was impossible, and got away with it. He'd shake off the flyers behind him and make his escape. He always did. He glanced back at the dead Lord William St. John, lying very still with a surprised look on his bloody face, and Finlay laughed again. It sounded loud and confident; and if it was a crazy kind of laugh, too, well, Finlay could live with that.

Adrienne Campbell, wife of Finlay, once the scourge of polite company and owner of the biggest, loudest, and foulest mouth in all society, sat fuming before her blank viewscreen and wondered whom to call next. She'd tried practically everyone she could think of, including some she would have sworn she wasn't talking to, but no one would talk to her. Some made excuses, some were rude, but most just instructed their servants to say that they were not at home, the liars. Adrienne had fallen from grace when the Campbell Clan went down in flames, and she was taking it hard. She was now banned and ostracized from the very society she once dominated through the sheer strength of her personality. But that was when she had the power and position of Clan Campbell behind her. Now she was just one of the very few survivors of a broken Clan, and isolated as she'd never been before. No one would talk to her. They were afraid that what happened to her might be catching.

Her cousin by marriage, Robert Campbell, had been protected from the fall by his position in the military. The fleet looked after its own. It was only through his influence and protection that Adrienne had survived the vendetta pursued so viciously and methodically by the triumphant Wolfe Family. Blood had flowed in the streets, with no one to answer the begging and the screams, but she had been left strictly alone. As long as she didn't interfere. So she hardened her heart and locked her door, and didn't answer the desperate knocking that came again and again. They begged and threatened and called her name, and some of them cried; but she sat as far away from the door as she could, with her hands over her ears. It didn't help. She could still hear when the Wolfes came to drag the screaming voices away. Sometimes they stopped screaming suddenly, and the silence that followed was worse.

Finally, the voices stopped coming, and no one knocked at her door anymore. Adrienne Campbell was alone. The Wolfes now owned everything the Campbells had, leaving her nothing but a few scraps of personal jewelry. Her credit rating had been revoked. A few very minor Campbell cousins escaped the bloodbath, usually because they had connections or protection, like Robert, but they wanted nothing to do with her. She didn't blame them. The reign of the House of Campbell was over in every way that mattered.

Adrienne was of average height and a little less than average weight. Nothing like fear and desperation to back up a restricted diet. She'd lost pounds in the past few months she would have sworn would be with her till the day she died. She couldn't go out to buy food or even order it through her viewscreen. She had no money. She was dependent on Robert for everything now, and he had his own problems. He still did what he could, bless him. When he could. And whereas previously she'd proudly worn the latest and most garish outfits society had ever seen, outside of her husband, she now made do with a wrinkled housecoat of plain, subdued colors. She'd had to leave her wardrobe behind when she fled for her life. She didn't really miss her clothes. She'd worn most of them only to annoy and upstage her fashion-obsessed husband. But it was the principle of the thing. She couldn't bear to think she looked boring. Robert provided her with clothes now, when he thought of it, just as he'd provided this bolt-hole. Like most men he had no taste at all.

She scowled at her reflection in the viewscreen. Adrienne had a sharp face: all planes and sudden angles, her scarlet mouth currently compressed into a flat angry line. She had dark, determined eyes, and a ridiculously turned-up nose that had seemed like a good idea at the time. She still had her great mop of curling golden hair, though it looked more than a little distressed at the moment. All in all, she'd looked better.

She sighed and leaned back in her chair. She was too tired and dispirited even to stay angry for long. How far had she fallen to end up here like this. A bedraggled wreck in a dingy apartment, trying to wheedle invitations and support from boring acquaintances and lesser Families she would have disdained only a few months previously. Not that Adrienne was a snob. It had always been a point of pride with her that she despised everyone equally.

Now here she was, trying to improve her position by playing politics with the only card she had left: Finlay. He'd managed to disappear very thoroughly, which surprised Adrienne. The Finlay she'd known had never been that good at anything. Still, a lot of people wanted him, for reasons they mostly preferred not to discuss, and thought perhaps they could get to him through her. Either through bribes or threats. Adrienne knew nothing, but took their money anyway, and spun them out as long as she could with hints and promises before they finally wised up. She ignored the threats. Robert and his friends in the military were protecting her, and everyone knew it. No one was ready to go head-to-head with the fleet over knowledge they weren't even sure she had. The fleet had a long memory for insults, and it bore grudges. So Adrienne played her little games, a small fish in a big pond, and tried to avoid being eaten by the sharks.

She assumed she was currently ahead of the game. She was still alive, after all. If you called this living. She sniffed angrily and glared at her reflection in the viewscreen. She'd spent a lot of time with her thoughts lately and had come to the uncomfortable conclusion that she didn't like herself much. She was too busy being negative about everything to be positive about anything, even herself. But she knew she was right about this one thing. Adrienne had built her personality quite carefully and deliberately, being hard and harsh and uncompromising, because that was the only way she knew to get things done. Being soft just got you hurt, or even killed. High society had always believed in the survival of the fittest. Besides, she'd enjoyed being rude and obnoxious and loud. If only because she was so very good at it. But all her strength and all her hardness and all her clever, vicious words hadn't been enough to save her when the House of Campbell fell.

Her children were safe, at least, in a military school. Not quite the future she'd intended for them, but a safe haven, none the less. Robert had arranged it for her. Strange to think that that young man with the naive background and the vague smile was now the Campbell, head of the Family. There was no one else with a better claim but Finlay, and he had given up all claims to power and position when he chose to disappear into the underground. Now only a few very minor cousins remained with any legitimate claim to the title, and they were mostly still in hiding—keeping their heads well down till the storm passed and the waters calmed. The rest were mostly dead, or missing and presumed dead. A few had married hastily into lesser Houses, giving up their name in return for protection. Some of those had gone missing, too. The Wolfes had a long reach and endless malice.

Adrienne knew that if she had any pride, she should give up on society, as it had given up on her. But she couldn't. It was all she knew. The great game of influence and intrigue was the only game worth playing, and it was infinitely addictive. She'd do anything, promise anything, to get a foot in the door again. It was either that, or retreat into the underground, which she despised. She had no taste for rebellion. Full of thugs and non-people and the lower classes. And she'd never been one to hide her light behind a bushel. On the whole, apart from her present circumstances, Adrienne liked things as they were. If she could only find just the right leverage, she had no doubt she'd be accepted back into society again. They had to take her back. She was one of them. She might have verbally attacked society on occasion, but she was lost outside it. All she knew was how to be an aristocrat and play the game.

Which was why she'd been reduced to making more and more desperate calls to fringe elements, lesser Houses, and those "personalities" who lived on the edge of events for whatever crumbs they could pick up from the greater players. Renowned for taste and repartee and knowing all the latest gossip, they passed in and out of fashion according to a season's taste or whim.

But one figure was always there, raising laughter and eyebrows with barbed bons mots and the perfect put-down. Chantelle. Not so much a friend, more an honored rival, but Adrienne had known her for years. Chantelle had no aristocratic blood or political power, but somehow still commanded everyone's attention at those soirees she deigned to attend. She decided fashion, chic, and everything else that mattered with a gorgeous smile or a flared nostril, and never gave a pretender an even break. You could break fingernails on her charm, but she never forgave a slight. She and Adrienne had always had a lot in common. Including several ex-lovers, who kept their mouths firmly shut on certain matters, if they knew what was good for them. If Adrienne could get Chantelle's backing, no one would dare insult her, or refuse to take her calls. If Chantelle accepted you, so did society. If society knew what was good for it.

Adrienne braced herself and made the call. There was always the chance Chantelle would see her own possible future in Adrienne's fall and feel sympathetic. Adrienne jumped despite herself as the viewscreen cleared to show Chantelle's frowning face. The doyen of fashion was wearing last night's rather lived-in gown and makeup, suggesting she'd only just got in from a late night, or more accurately, an early morning. Her long hair gleamed a lustrous bronze with silver highlights, and her heart-shaped face glowed florescent. And only the truly picky would have pointed out that the sheen on her hair was looking rather dull in places, and that the makeup around her mouth was smeared. Adrienne bore it in mind in case she needed ammunition later on. She smiled bravely into the viewscreen, but before she could speak Chantelle sniffed loudly.

"I wondered when you'd get around to me. Yes I do know why you're calling, and no I can't help you. You are out, Adrienne dear, so far out I can't even see you from where I am, and nothing short of a major miracle or direct divine intervention will get you back in. Your Clan is scattered, your influence broken, and your credit rating has sunk so low you'd need an earthmover to find it. Personally, I don't think it could have happened to a more deserving person. You were never really one of us, Adrienne, with your big mouth and bullying ways. You never understood decorum or proper behavior. The right way of doing things. You aspired to be a scandal, but truth be told, you were always too boring for that. If I were you, I'd run to your friends for protection. But then you don't have any friends, do you? Good-bye, Adrienne. Don't call this number again."

Chantelle's face disappeared from the viewscreen. "Good-bye, Chantelle," said Adrienne. "I do hope you have dysentery soon."

She was debating whether to call Chantelle again, just to remind her that her choices in dress had always inspired projectile vomiting in anyone with a smattering of taste, when her viewscreen chimed, alerting her of an incoming call. For a moment Adrienne just sat there. No one had called her since she arrived here. Not least because most people weren't supposed to know where she was, and those who did were careful to contact her only in person. Adrienne drew herself up and accepted the call. Maybe she'd won the lottery. The viewscreen cleared to show Lord Gregor Shreck, head of Clan Shreck. A short, fat butterball of a man, with a bulging fleshy face and deep-set eyes, the Shreck was one of the most dangerous men in society, mostly because he never cared what his actions cost him as long as he got what he wanted.

"Dear Adrienne," said Gregor, his voice oozing a charm that didn't reach his eyes. "I have a proposition for you. A little give-and-take to our mutual advantage. Are you interested?"

"Depends," said Adrienne in her most frosted voice. It didn't do to get chummy with Gregor. He took advantage. "What do you want from me? As if I didn't know."

"You never liked him, Adrienne, even if he was your husband. And you really haven't got anything else to bargain with that anyone wants. You don't have to do anything difficult. Just contact Finlay and persuade him to emerge from the underground at an agreed time and place, so we can be waiting for him. We'll take him away, and you can return to society, as though nothing had ever happened."

"You don't have that much influence."

"I will have once I have Finlay."

"What makes him so important?"

"You don't need to know, dear."

"What will happen to him?"

"What do you care? I'd suggest you make good use of this offer while it still stands. Finlay is currently very hot, and a lot of people want him. He's just killed Lord William St. John and has made a rather amazing escape."

"Wait a minute," said Adrienne. "Hold everything. Finlay's killed someone?"

"Yes. I wouldn't have believed it myself if I hadn't seen the holo recordings. He's really quite an excellent swordsman. I can only assume he's been taking lessons in the underground. But not to worry. I'll have more than enough men standing by to handle him."

"St. John's dead? The Empress's own personal attack dog?" Adrienne shrugged. "Can't say I ever liked the man. Thought he was God's gift to women, and he had clammy hands. I had to hit him around the ear with a candlestick once."

"That's as may be, Adrienne. Will you help us, or do I have to apply a little pressure? You have two very lovely children. Quite charming. Be a shame if anything were to happen to them."

"You touch my babies, and I'll rip your balls off with my bare hands," said Adrienne. Gregor continued as though she hadn't spoken.

"Robert isn't the only one with friends in the military. Think about it. And call me when you've made your decision. Don't take too long. If all else fails, I might decide to do terrible things to you, in the hope Finlay would come to rescue you. Rather a distant hope, I'll admit, but we could do all kinds of interesting and inventive things to you while we were waiting for your husband to show up."

"I'd smack you right in the mouth, Shreck, if I wasn't afraid of catching something disgusting from you," said Adrienne in a voice so cold she barely recognized it. "Now, remove your loathsome presence from my viewscreen. My neighbors will think I've got a toilet overflowing in here. If I change my mind, I'll contact you. But don't hold your breath."

Gregor Shreck just laughed. Adrienne hit the off switch, and a sudden echoing silence filled the room. She sniffed and stretched slowly to get the tensions out of her body. She must be losing her touch. She should have been able to handle a creep like the Shreck. There was a time she could goad a man into an impotent homicidal fury with just a few well-placed barbs. But this time Gregor held all the major cards, and he knew it. Worst of all, she was considering his offer. Finlay had never meant much to her, and she couldn't risk anything happening to her children. Robert had sworn he'd protect them, but when all was said and done, he was only a junior officer in the fleet. And if Finlay really was going around killing people . . . She bit her lip. If she allied herself with the Shreck, and Robert found out . . . Robert had been due to marry the Shreck's niece, Letitia, in an arranged marriage. They'd almost completed their wedding vows when Gregor killed her, rather than have her dishonor him. He'd strangled her with his bare hands while the Campbells held Robert back. He'd never forgiven the Shreck for that.

Adrienne's scowl deepened. if she was going to do this, Robert must never know. Which meant she'd have to shake off the people Robert had protecting her, before she could start making arrangements to contact the underground. She'd be putting herself at risk. Gregor wouldn't be the only one to think of using her as bait in a trap to catch Finlay. Not that he'd come anyway, the bastard. Finlay had never made any secret of his feelings, or rather lack of them, for her. They had absolutely nothing in common except the children, and on the few occasions they absolutely had to meet, they could hardly exchange a dozen words without sniping at each other. After a dozen words they tended to escalate rapidly to shouting invectives and throwing things.

It had been an arranged marriage, of course. Neither of them had had any say in the matter. Personally, she'd always thought Finlay was mentally disturbed, with his obsession over clothes and fashions, and his recent exploits only seemed to confirm that. But would he really stand by and do nothing while his wife was tortured to death? Would she, if the situation was reversed? Well, yes, probably. Adrienne had always known she was a hard bitch at heart. But Finlay had put his own life at risk to save hers when she was mortally wounded during the Wolfe hostile takeover. If he hadn't got her to the regeneration machine in time, she would have died. She could still feel the sword punching through her belly and out her back. Sometimes she dreamed about lying helpless on the gravity sled's desk, awash in her own blood, while Finlay strove desperately to shake off the pursuing Wolfe craft. She woke drenched in sweat and couldn't sleep again until the morning brought comforting light. Finlay had saved her life, when he didn't have to. But typical of the man, he had to do it in a way that insulted and humiliated her.

She hadn't known about Evangeline Shreck then. She'd known there was someone in his life, some other woman who mattered to him in a way she never had. But she hadn't known who till she woke up in the regeneration machine in Evangeline's apartment in Tower Shreck. Robert and his people were standing guard over her, but Finlay and Evangeline were long gone. Robert had got her to safety. Evangeline finally resurfaced, free of guilt or any connection to Finlay, and returned to her apartment. But Adrienne had never found the courage to call her.

Adrienne sighed and looked around her at her cramped quarters. It had started out life as Robert's bachelor pad, somewhere for him to crash and burn on his infrequent leaves, and hadn't improved since. It might almost be worth making a deal with Gregor, just to get out of this dump. She'd had Jacuzzis that were bigger. And it was strictly masculine territory, with no frills or fancies or real comforts. She itched to transform the place according to her tastes. But one, she didn't have the money, and two, Robert would have a fit. He actually liked it this way. Men. Probably washed his underwear in the hand basin, and clipped his toenails in the bidet. He let her have what money he could, but it wasn't much. Clan Wolfe now possessed all the old Campbell assets, bad cess to the bastards. She'd been selling what personal jewelry she'd been wearing on the day, piece by piece, to keep her head above water, but it was nearly all gone now. She hadn't got much for them. She was limited in where she could go. Old friends didn't want to know her, and businesses were afraid to make enemies of those in society who openly gloated over Adrienne's downfall. It appeared her big mouth had offended practically everyone at one time or another. Adrienne sniffed. Hell with them if they couldn't take a joke.

If she were to work with the Shreck and betray Finlay, he'd probably let her name her own price. She could be rich again and part of society and laugh in the faces of all those who'd ostracized her . . .

There was a knock at the door, and she spun around sharply, face flushed as though she'd been caught doing something wrong. As though whoever it was had known what she was thinking, she made herself breathe steadily and glared at the door. Two callers in one day. She was getting popular. She forced her voice to be calm even as she asked who it was, and then tensed again as Robert Campbell identified himself. He'd made it clear right from the beginning that he wouldn't be visiting her often. There was a limit to how much he could be seen helping her. He had his career to think of. And his own safety. Adrienne understood. If he was here now, it must be important. She flushed again. He couldn't know about the Shreck's offer already. He couldn't. She made herself open the door, and Robert came breezing in, wearing full fleet uniform with a kit bag over his shoulder. He nodded and smiled at her, dropped the kit bag on the floor, and looked around his apartment.

"Just a flying visit, I'm afraid, Adrienne. My orders came through this morning. I've been posted to one of the new E-class ships, the *Endurance*. Massive bloody craft, with twice the usual weaponry, as well as the new stardrive. She takes off tomorrow, two weeks of tests and shakedowns, and then we're off to patrol the Rim for six months. Which means not only will I not be able to protect you anymore, but the fleet is going to want these quarters back for someone else. Sorry to spring this on you, but I wasn't given any warning myself. I've got some friends here in the city who'll try and look out for you, but I can't speak for their loyalty if anyone starts putting the pressure on."

"I understand," said Adrienne, and she did. The Shrecks' contacts in the military were already at work, arranging things. Removing her options one by one till she had no one left to turn to but Gregor Shreck.

"There is someone who might be prepared to help you," said Robert. "But you're really not going to like it. I've contacted Evangeline Shreck. She was, and is, Finlay's love, but she's a good sort, for a Shreck. She'll do anything for Finlay. Even protect you. Go and see her, Addie. You might find you have more in common than you think. Now, I've got to go. They're expecting me on the *Endurance*. I'll try and keep in touch. Good-bye. Good luck."

He grabbed up his kit bag, pecked her quickly on the cheek, and left, closing the door quietly behind him. Adrienne scowled, her hands clenched into fists at her sides. She'd always known her residence here was only temporary, but it still came as something of a shock to be thrown to the sharks so suddenly. The question was, did Evangeline know about her father's plans for Finlay? Was she, perhaps unwittingly, a part of them? If so and Adrienne warned her, that would put Evangeline in her debt. Adrienne nodded, smiling coldly. She always felt more comfortable when dealing with people from a position of power. She would go and see Evangeline Shreck. If only so she could hear about a side of Finlay she'd never known herself.

Evangeline Shreck stood before the single great window in her apartment in Tower Shreck, looking out at the world beyond, a prisoner in her own home. The door wasn't locked, of course. Nothing as obvious as that. But if she were to try and leave the tower without getting her father's permission first, polite guards would calmly but firmly insist that she return to her apartment while they waited for instructions from the Shreck. And they'd walk back with her, just to make sure she didn't get lost along the way. The Shreck wanted her going outside as little as possible. Officially, he was concerned that the Empress might try and seize her, to become one of her maids—a mentally conditioned slave with no will of her own. Lionstone had already done it once with the Shreck's niece. No one had done anything. No one had said anything. No one dared, not even the Shreck.

But mostly Gregor was concerned that Evangeline would be revealed as a clone, in these very anti-clone days. If it were ever revealed that the Shreck had cloned his daughter after she died suddenly, and then passed the clone off as the real thing, there would be outrage in the Court and in society. Being replaced by a clone of oneself was an aristocrat's worst nightmare. Gregor would be punished and ostracized, and the clone Evangeline would be destroyed—mostly for the crime of having fooled them all for so long.

But even that wasn't the whole truth. The Shreck kept her a prisoner because he could. He wanted to love, cherish, and own her completely, as he had his real daughter. For the Shreck had loved his daughter not as a father, but as a lover. Which might have been why he killed her. Evangeline didn't know the true story. The Shreck insisted it had been an accident, but he liked to drop hints, now and again, that no one ever defied him and lived to boast of it. Evangeline kept her head bowed and did as she was bid. For though she hated her father and would have killed him in a moment if she could, she had no choice. By playing the loving, dutiful daughter, she bought the Shreck's protection for her true love Finlay's wife and children, as she had promised Finlay she would. He never knew the price she paid. He must never know, or he would come storming up out of the underground to take a terrible revenge, not caring if he died as a result. Evangeline cared, so she never told him. She loved him so much she played a role that was destroying her, and never once allowed herself to think how unfair that was.

Evangeline was cracking up, though she hadn't realized that yet. She had too many commitments to too many people. To her father for his protection. To Finlay and his family for his love. To the clone and esper underground for the Cause. They all wanted something from her, and sometimes their needs clashed. It was getting harder to keep them separated. Different lies for different people, until the truth got lost in the smoke. She still loved Finlay with all her heart, though she saw him less and less. The underground kept him busy with missions he never explained to her. She had been the underground's contact with the Court and society, but since she got out so rarely now, she was of less and less use to them. She couldn't explain. They might tell Finlay. And, of course, she couldn't ever tell her father about Finlay or the underground. He'd kill her for what she'd done—for defying him, for daring to love someone else.

After all, he could always clone another Evangeline. He'd done it before.

And so she walked up and down in her apartment, thinking furiously, beating at the shifting walls of her various personas, getting nowhere, going quietly insane. She hardly opened her mouth to anyone, for fear of saying the wrong thing to the wrong person. And always worried that the next person at her door would be from security, with a warrant to drag her away to the interrogation cells. They'd make her talk. Everyone depended on her silence—lover, father, and Cause—and she felt less and less dependable with every day that passed. So far she had kept herself from cracking up through sheer force of will. Partly, because of her love for Finlay, and partly, because of all those who would suffer if she was weak. If she allowed herself to be weak.

And so the weight she carried grew ever heavier, and she could not, would not, put it down. Poor Evangeline.

She jumped despite herself as her comm unit chimed politely, alerting her to an incoming call. She knew who it was, who it had to be, but she went to answer it anyway. She sat down before her dressing table, and the mirror cleared to become a viewscreen, showing her the fat smiling face of her father. A cold hand clutched at her heart. She had to fight to get her breath, and she clenched her teeth together to keep her mouth from trembling.

"Just called to let you know I'm on my way," said Gregor Shreck. "Think loving thoughts till I get there, my precious. And wear the pink nightgown. The one I like. I won't be long. And then we can have some fun, just you and I. Won't that be nice?"

The fat smiling face disappeared, and the mirror returned, showing Evangeline her own face again. For a moment she didn't recognize it. Her face was thinner than it had been, the pale skin stretched taut over the protruding cheekbones. Her eyes had a trapped, hunted, haunted look. She tried a smile, rehearsing for her father, but it looked more like a grimace. She had a feeling the Shreck preferred it that way. And then there was a knock at the door, and she nearly jumped out of her skin. She stared blankly at the door, her heart hammering in her chest. It couldn't be him already. Had they come at last to drag her away, screaming and kicking, to the torture of the mind techs, where neither lover nor father nor Cause could save or succor her? She snatched up a heavy pair of scissors from the dressing table. Not as good as a knife, but close. She'd make them kill her. She'd be safe then. Somehow she backed away from hysteria and got a grip on herself, precarious though it was. She moved slowly to the door, still clutching the scissors. It seemed to take forever to get there. When she opened the door with a hand that hardly trembled at all, Adrienne Campbell was standing there waiting for her. Evangeline stared blankly at Finlay's wife, and all she could think was *Oh, great. Another complication.*

"Well?" said Adrienne. "Aren't you going to invite me in? We have so much to talk about."

"Oh, hell," said Evangeline. "I haven't got time for this."

"We need to talk."

"This isn't a good time. I'm ... expecting someone. Could you come back again?"

"I doubt it," said Adrienne, smiling slightly. "Your security people didn't want to let me in at all. I had to speak to them very firmly. Even so, they were still going to turn me away until I demanded a strip search. That slowed them down. I may have fallen from grace, but I am still a Campbell and noble born. Let them try to explain to their superiors that they'd strip-searched an aristocrat, and their next job would be delivering bad news to the Empress. I understand there are always vacancies. They were falling all over themselves to apologize as they let me in, poor bastards."

"What do we have to say to each other?" said Evangeline.

"I don't know," said Adrienne. "But we do have at least one thing in common. Or rather, one person. Have you heard from Finlay lately?"

"Oh, hell. You'd better come in. But you can't stay."

She stepped back to open the door wide, and Adrienne Campbell strode in like she owned the place. She always did. It was practically a trademark. Evangeline realized she was still holding the scissors and tossed them onto a nearby chair. She didn't want to be tempted. Adrienne looked around Evangeline's apartment with a slightly arched eyebrow, implying with a glance that she'd seen much better, but was too well-bred to mention it. She picked out the most comfortable chair with infallible instinct, and sank into its embrace with a single graceful movement. She smiled graciously and waited patiently while Evangeline pulled up a chair and sat opposite her. There was something of the Empress visiting one of her lesser subjects in Adrienne's manner, but Evangeline didn't take it personally. That was just

Adrienne for you. She might have fallen from favor, but she hadn't fallen far. Evangeline still felt like slapping her face, on general principles. A giggle almost escaped her, but she forced it back. She didn't have the time for hysterics. She settled herself opposite Adrienne and met her gaze with a cool calm look.

"Finlay never loved you," she said flatly. "You must know that."

"Oh, of course. I never loved him. Our marriage was arranged for various business and Family reasons that no doubt seemed good at the time. We might have made a go of it, but we quarreled walking out of the church, and it all went downhill after that. He had his lovers, and I had mine, and we were both very civilized about it. You look shocked, dear. Surely, you didn't think you were his first?"

"No. He never talked about his other women. But I knew. It didn't matter. He never loved them. Not the way he loved me. I'm just surprised you admit to having lovers, too. I wouldn't have thought love was your style."

"Oh, I've had my moments, dear. You'd be surprised how many men have a secret yen for a good tongue-lashing. In more ways than one."

"Why have you come here, Adrienne?"

"I . . . need to talk to you. About Finlay. Before the Wolfes declared vendetta and ambushed us at a Family meeting, I would have sworn Finlay cared no more for me than I did for him. But when I was injured and near to death, he put his own life at risk to save mine. He even brought me here, to you, to find the protection I needed. I just wondered . . . if you knew why."

Evangeline nodded slowly. "He said you were very brave. That you were wounded fighting to protect the Clan. He admired that."

"The Finlay I knew was a fop and a dandy," said Adrienne. "He wore a sword, but I never once saw him draw it. He never took me to the Arena. Said the sight of blood made him feel faint. But when the Wolfes came howling into Tower Campbell, he tore into them with sword and gun like he'd been doing it all his life. To save me, he outran and outfought a dozen pursuers, all trained fighting men. And now I hear he's on the run, after killing the notorious Lord St. John, despite all the Lord's guards. I can't help feeling there must be another Finlay, one I never knew."

"You're right. There was."

"Can you tell me about him?"

"I don't think it's my secret to tell. You'd have to ask Finlay yourself. But I will say he was the bravest, finest man I ever knew. The fop and the dandy were just masks he wore, to keep people like you at bay. To keep you from seeing the real him."

"Married all these years, and I never knew the real him." Adrienne smiled briefly. "But, then, I never looked."

"You never cared."

"That, too. I care now."

Evangeline looked at her steadily. "Why? What's changed? What's happened to bring you here, to me, asking questions about Finlay?"

For the first time Adrienne looked away, but her voice remained steady. "I need help, and there's nowhere else to go. Do you really think I'd be here if I didn't have to be? Robert was protecting me and the children, but he's being sent offplanet. Your father helped arrange it. He's been putting the pressure on. Threats to me, to my children. I can look after myself, but the children must be protected. I need help; some weapon I can use to defend me and mine. That I ended up here should give you some idea of how desperate I am. You loved Finlay, and I married him. He's been a part of both our lives and put us both through a lot, one way and another. Perhaps we can find something in common. I'm sorry you had to hear about your father's part in this. I know you and he are close, but ..."

"No," said Evangeline abruptly. "We're not ... close."

Adrienne raised an eyebrow. There had been something in Evangeline's voice ... "In public and at Court, you're always together. You certainly give the appearance ..."

"Appearances can be deceptive. Please, you must go now. He'll be here soon, and he mustn't find you here. I want you to leave now."

"Why? What's so important about a father visiting his daughter?" Adrienne's eyes narrowed. "There's a secret here. I can smell it, like I can smell your fear. What is it? Has he been hurting you? The Shreck's a bully and a bastard, like most men, but I never knew he was violent to his own Family," Adrienne stopped, silenced for a moment by the sudden rush of misery suffusing Evangeline's face. Tears ran down her jerking cheeks as she gasped for breath. Adrienne leaned forward and took Evangeline's hands in hers. "Now, now, don't take on so, pet. Whatever it is, I'll fix it. I'm good at fixing things. And there never was a man born that was worth tears like this. Is it your father? Has he been beating you? I can talk to some people at Court . . ."

"No. He's not . . . violent. He . . ." Evangeline's throat clamped shut suddenly, cutting off her words. She could feel the heat in her cheeks as her face flushed with shame. Her father's words thundered in her head. *You can't tell anyone. Ever. Or they'll find out you're a clone. And you know what they'll do to you, then. And you know what I'll do to you if you ever so much as hint to anyone else. They wouldn't believe you, anyway. But if you ever do, I'll hurt you, Evie, little Evie. I'll hurt you till your throat goes raw from screaming. Don't you ever dare tell!*

She held Adrienne's hands tightly, as though trying to draw strength from them. She was sitting with the one woman she'd hated the most, and was closer than ever before to telling her secret, the one thing she'd never told anyone, even Finlay. Because perhaps only a woman like Adrienne could hear it and not judge. Hear the pain and the horror and not the shame. And, surely, only a woman like Adrienne wouldn't give a damn that she was only a clone . . .

"Tell me what it is, dear," said Adrienne, keeping her voice calm and steady so that Evangeline wouldn't realize how much her grip was hurting her hands. "We girls have to stick together. It's a man's Empire, even with an Empress on the Iron Throne, but we don't have to take any shit from anyone. Men may have the power, but we're smarter than they are. Whatever it is, I'll find a way around it. He's been locking you up here, hasn't he? That's why we only ever see you together, right? Take out an action against him. Divorce the bastard. Society would stand with you. They don't have any time for that kind of petty bullying."

"You don't understand. He doesn't . . . hurt me. Not like that."

"What way, then? What has he done to you, to put you in such a state?" And then Adrienne stopped and looked at her. Evangeline braced herself for a look of pity, or even disgust, but instead she saw only shock, giving way to anger. "My God. He's been bedding you, hasn't he? Shitty little *bastard*.

He's been forcing you, hasn't he? Don't you worry, pet. Society will crucify him for this!"

"No!" said Evangeline sharply, fighting back the tears so she could speak clearly. "No one must ever know. If Finlay ever found out, it would kill him. Or he'd try to kill Daddy and be killed anyway. I've kept the secret this long. I can keep it a little longer. To keep Finlay safe. I can't help you, Adrienne. I can't even help myself."

"Now, stop that," Adrienne said briskly. "All right, we can't go to society, but there are other ways. I never met a man yet who couldn't be outthought and outmaneuvered by a woman who put her mind to it. Let me think for a moment. I'll find a way out of this that won't involve Finlay. You're quite right. He mustn't know. He'd only overreact. Men are like that, bless them."

"And if you help me, I have to help you," said Evangeline. "Is that the deal?"

"No deals," said Adrienne. "Not this time. I'd help anyone in your situation. Now, let me have my hands back and dry your tears; then we'll figure out how best to stick it to the Shreck."

"Will you, my dear?" said Gregor Shreck, standing in the open door of the apartment. "How very intriguing."

Both women looked around, startled. Evangeline jumped to her feet, her hands rising to her mouth. Her skin was white as a sheet, and her eyes were very wide. Adrienne took her time getting to her feet. She didn't want the Shreck thinking he could fluster her. She gave Gregor her best icy glare.

"Haven't you ever heard of knocking?"

"In my own home?" said the Shreck, smiling widely. "Now, why should I do that? The tower is mine, along with everything and everyone in it. I own them. Isn't that right, Evangeline? Now, be a dear, and tell your new friend to run along. I have so much to say to you."

"No," mumbled Evangeline, staring at her shoes.

"What was that?" said Gregor. "I don't think I can have heard you correctly, my dear."

"No," said Evangeline, lifting her head to stare at him defiantly. "I'm tired of being scared. You lied to me, Daddy. You swore to me you were protecting Adrienne and her children and all the other surviving Campbells. Now I find out from Adrienne that you've been threatening them, to get at Finlay. You lied to me."

"It's politics, dear. Things change. I don't expect you to understand. All you need to know is that I'm doing what's best for the Family."

"If your Clan found out that you've been screwing your daughter, they'd disown you," said Adrienne calmly. "Such a tacky crime, Gregor. And backed up with a coward's threats and lies. I'm disappointed in you, Gregor. I never thought you were much of a man, but I never suspected you had to bully women into your bed. Now, turn around and get out of here. You ever lay a hand on this poor dear again, and I'll see everyone in your Family knows your dirty little secret. They'll remove you as head and throw you out of the Clan. They can do that if enough of them agree, and I can't see any of them disagreeing over a nasty little mess like this. Without a Clan, no one will talk to you, or politic with you, or do business with you. You'd be an outcast, just like me. Only I can handle it. You couldn't. Don't slam the door when you leave."

"And you'd agree to this?" said the Shreck to his daughter. "You'd turn against your own father, who loves you so dearly?"

"What you do to me isn't love, Daddy. And you lied to me. I'd like you to leave now, please. And don't ever come in without knocking again."

"Think you're so clever, don't you, both of you," said the Shreck, his broad glistening face flushing red with rage. "Think you're smarter than me. But you should know, dear Adrienne, that you don't know everything. You see, Evie hasn't told you her real secret. She wouldn't dare. So you tell this Campbell bitch to leave, Evie, or I'll tell her what you really are."

"No need to put yourself out, Daddy. I'll tell her." Evangeline drew herself up and threw Adrienne a look that was part defiance and part plea. "I'm a clone. Daddy had me made to replace the daughter he murdered. That's how he's controlled me all this time. Or so he thinks. You never knew I was part of the clone underground, did you, Daddy dear? No, I can see from your face that you didn't. You threaten me, and the underground will have you killed. You tell anyone about me, and I'll disappear into the underground. I only stayed because Finlay made me promise I'd protect his Family. You don't have a hold over me anymore. You never did, really, apart from my own fear. You told me you owned me, and I believed you. I don't believe that anymore."

"Good for you, girl," said Adrienne. She looked triumphantly at the Shreck. "Get out of our sight, you nasty little toad."

Gregor Shreck looked from one woman to the other, struggling for words, then turned abruptly and left, slamming the door behind him. Adrienne let out her breath in an explosive sigh and collapsed back into her chair. Evangeline remained where she was.

"Well?" she said quietly. "How do you feel about me now, now that you know I'm just a clone?"

"My dear, after everything you and I have been through, your being a clone is the least of it. I'm actually rather fascinated. I've never known anyone in the underground before. Apart from Finlay, of course, but I think we've established I never really knew him."

"How do you feel about me being a rebel, then?"

"Damned if I know. This is all happening a little fast, even for me. I suppose I should be shocked and outraged, but I haven't been shocked since I was fourteen, and I'm too emotionally exhausted to be outraged. You're a clone and I'm a bitch, and the Empire doesn't have much use for either of us. So to hell with them, and long live the underground. Do you have a battle hymn? I feel like singing something loud and defiant."

The viewscreen on the dressing table chimed suddenly, and they both jumped. They smiled at each other, and Evangeline moved over to answer it. Adrienne got up and moved quickly out of sight. "Better if no one knows I'm here for the moment, Evie."

Evangeline nodded, sat down before the dressing table, and accepted the call. The mirror cleared, and she nodded as she recognized a familiar face. It was Klaus Griffin, her immediate contact in the underground. As far as the outside world was concerned, he was her costumier. For once he wasn't smiling, and Evangeline sat up a little straighter.

"Are you alone, Evangeline?"

"Of course. Is there a problem?"

"This call is being shielded. We can talk freely. We need you to come below, to talk to Finlay. It's urgent. Can you get away?"

"If I have to. What's wrong with Finlay? Is he hurt?"

"No. But it's imperative he undertake a particular mission and we need you down here to convince him to go."

"Why wouldn't he want to?"

"Because this one will almost certainly get him killed."

"And you expect me to talk him into it? Are you crazy?"

"We need you, Evangeline. We need him. The safety of the entire underground is at risk. He's our only hope. Will you come?"

"I'll come, but I'm not promising anything. Finlay's gone on enough missions for you. You've no right to expect this of him. And don't you dare try and talk him into this before I get there. He's not going anywhere until I've talked to him, and maybe not even then. Damn it, Klaus, we've done so much for the underground already. Find somebody else."

"It has to be him. How long before you can get here?"

"Give me an hour." She broke contact and glared into the mirror. "Bastards. Do they really think I'd betray Finlay, even for the Cause?"

"This gets more fascinating by the minute," said Adrienne, coming over to join her. "Dear Finlay, the last best hope of the underground? I'm beginning to think you're right, and I never did really know him. Since you apparently know him better than I, what do you think? Would he go on a suicide mission if it was important enough?"

"Oh, yes. That's what worries me. Most of his recent missions would have been suicide runs for anyone else. He never was very strong in the commonsense department, and since he lost his Family, he's become increasingly reckless. He feels guilty for having survived, when so many died. If this mission is so dangerous that even Finlay would hesitate, it must be really bad. I've got to go, Adrienne. Thank you for all your help; I wish there was something I could do for you."

"There is," Adrienne said briskly. "Take me with you. There's no place safe here for me anymore now that I've made an enemy of your father. If I'm to find protection for my children, the only people left to turn to are the underground. Though, God knows what I've got to buy their protection with. Gossip, maybe. I know more secrets about more people than half the Court put together. Some of it has got to be prime blackmail material. Besides, whatever you eventually decide, you're going to need my help to convince

Finlay. I always could talk him into anything. I think I'm going to enjoy being part of the underground."

"What makes you so sure they'll accept you?"

"What makes you think they'll have any choice? I can be very determined when I put my mind to something. Besides, I really can't wait to see this whole new Finlay I've never known. I have a feeling I might like him a lot more than the old one. Shall we go?"

Julian Skye, rogue esper and agent of the underworld, had been handsome once, but that was before the Empire interrogators got their hands on him. They'd started with a vicious beating, not because they expected him to talk, but just to soften him up. They didn't even ask any questions. Two of them took it in turns holding him up, while the third worked him over in brutal, efficient ways, until every part of him moaned with pain. Then they hurt him some more. They paid special attention to his face. Damage there was psychologically damaging as well. Eventually they left, and he sat naked and alone in the interrogation cell, held upright by the thick straps holding him to the bare metal chair, waiting for them to come back and start again. One eye was swollen shut, his nose had been broken, and dried blood crusted his face. They'd left his mouth pretty much untouched. He was expected to be able to answer questions when they finally got around to asking him any.

He'd been left alone to consider his position and worry about what was to come. And Julian Skye, who'd always thought he was a hero, was ashamed to find he couldn't stop crying. He was a young man, with a young man's courage and ideals, but he'd had the courage systematically beaten out of him. All he had left now were his ideals, and they didn't seem as strong and convincing as they once had. He finally managed to sniff back his tears, though the occasional harsh sob still took him by surprise, and looked around him as best he could. He was in a bare, featureless room, deep below the surface, in the dark metal bowels beneath the Imperial Palace. The walls were bright shining steel, without windows or details, showing vague distortions of himself in the painfully bright light from the single unit directly above him. He could feel the heat from the unit beating on the top of his head, as though his brains were on fire. The door was a dull black metal, right in front of him,

sealed electronically. It could be opened only by someone
from the outside with the correct access codes.

Julian Skye sat naked in his metal chair, stripped of everything that might give him physical or psychological comfort.
They'd even taken away his suicide option; a hollow tooth
with poison in it. They ripped it right out of his jaw with a
pair of pliers. He probed the gaping hole with his tongue
now and again, as though hoping it might be there this time.
It had been a small hurt compared to what came afterward,
but he still cried when he thought of it. The tooth had been
his last hope. He'd pissed on himself, and he couldn't clean
it off his legs. Just more of the softening-up process.

He knew he had no one but himself to blame for his capture. Julian Skye had always been too wild for the slow and
steady underground, too bold and impetuous even for the
esper terrorists of the Esper Libereration Front, the elves. So
he'd been left alone to run his own operations with his own
people—attached to the underground, but not a part of it.
Which was how he'd come to be in the middle of everything
when the raid on Silo Nine went to hell in a hurry, and the
underground had to scatter. He'd been the only one at a safe
enough distance to take charge. He ran things for as long as
he could, setting up safe houses and new names and passwords, until he, too, was compromised by the treachery of
the man called Hood, and he had to run for his life. He'd got
away, as he always did, leaving the security guards nothing
but the echo of his mocking laughter. Julian Skye was an old
hand at the great game of intrigue, after all, despite his
young years. He thought he was unbeatable, untouchable.
He was wrong. Truth was, he'd just been lucky. And his
luck finally ran out when he made the mistake of trusting the
wrong person.

At least he wasn't in Silo Nine, with one of Wormboy's
engineered worms burrowing in his brain, controlling his
thoughts. If nothing else, the underground had made a thorough job of trashing the detention center and destroying
Wormboy, before the raiding force was betrayed and routed.
It would be years before the Empire could get it up and running again, even if they could create another artificial esper
like Wormboy to be their perfect gaoler again. And the
worms wouldn't work without him. Which was why Skye
was being held in a detention cell, mentally neutered by an
esp-blocker. He smiled slightly for the first time. He might

be prevented from using his esper abilities, but at least his thoughts were still his own. His smile quickly disappeared. The mind techs would get his thoughts out of him, along with anything else they wanted.

He wondered what would happen to him in the end, when they'd got everything they wanted from him and he had nothing left to tell them. Wipe his mind clean, probably, and replace it with a new personality more suited to the Empire's needs. They'd send it back to the underground with his face in front of it, and a convincing story to cover his escape; and what little he hadn't already betrayed would be wiped out in quick order, long before the espers could crack his new persona. Or perhaps he'd do such a good job betraying the underground right here in this cell that they wouldn't need him anymore. He'd heard they saved some of the monsters from Silo Nine. The espers and clones they'd experimented on, stirring their sticky fingers in their subjects' DNA, shaping their flesh and their minds into new, monstrous shapes. Maybe that was his destiny. To be no longer human, except on the genetic level. To be a living weapon, unleashed as needed on the Empire's many enemies.

He didn't care. He just wanted it to be over. The pain and the fear and the horror. He wasn't a hero anymore, if he ever had been. Just a man, waiting to be broken. A small gush of rebellion surged within him at the thought. He wasn't broken yet. Don't think about what they want. Keep it out of his mind. Bury it deep. Make the mind techs work for it. Buy time. Don't think at all. Be a blank page. Give them nothing to work with or on.

But he couldn't stop thinking. His body hurt too much to be ignored, and held helpless and naked in his chair by a dozen thick straps that cut painfully tight into his flesh, he had nothing else to do but think. He was safe for the time being. Underground espers had gone deep into his head long ago and constructed a series of mental blocks there, impervious shields that would keep out all but the most powerful Empire espers. He'd activated the safeguard with a conditioned code word the moment he realized he was trapped, and the shields had come slamming down in his brain. Now he no longer had the information his torturers wanted. It was locked away where he couldn't get at it. Can't tell what you don't know. Push the blocks too hard and his mind would self-destruct, taking the information with it.

So for the moment they were being very careful what they said to him. When they chose to speak to him. Between the beatings. They couldn't use an esper on him without first removing the esp-blocker from the cell, and the moment they did that he'd have access to his own esper abilities again. He'd rip this place apart with a psistorm like they'd never seen. The only way into his head now was through the mind techs. The Empire's specialists in pain and truth and mental conditioning. They'd use drugs and technology and all the psychological tricks they'd spent centuries perfecting. Until finally the shields went down, and he had nothing to hide behind anymore. Then he'd break and tell them anything they wanted to know. He'd beg to do it.

He knew it had to happen. Everyone broke eventually. All he could hope to do was hold on for as long as possible, to buy the underground time to rescue or kill him. He wasn't putting much hope in a rescue. He wasn't afraid to die anymore, not after what his tormentors had done to him and what he knew they planned to do, but he was afraid of being made to betray the underground. Once he was safely dead, his secrets would die with him. He couldn't do it himself. After pulling out his poison tooth, the interrogator had put a full spinal block on him. He could still feel everything, but all he had left were involuntary movements, and the straps took care of them. He could hear himself whimpering, but couldn't stop it. He'd never been so scared. But then, he'd never thought he'd end up here. Getting caught was something that happened to other people. He was crying now. He could feel the tears trickling down his cheeks. He would have screamed if he could. It didn't matter. He'd scream enough later.

There was the sudden sound of electronic locks disengaging, and the sealed door swung slowly open. Julian would have cringed away, but even that was denied to him. His chief interrogator strode in, a tall slender man dressed all in white, so the bloodstains would show up dramatically. So much of pain is in the mind. He nodded briskly to Julian and moved around the chair, taking his time, checking the straps were still tight and the spinal block on the back of his neck was still in place. He was always polite and never raised his voice. He didn't need to. His movements were sharp and precise and very efficient. Julian didn't know the man's name. He didn't need to know, so nobody told him. The interrogator moved around to stand before Julian.

"You have a visitor, Julian. I've adjusted the spinal block so you can talk freely. Make the most of your time together. When you've finished, it'll be my turn to talk to you."

The interrogator left, while Julian tried to get his thoughts in order. Who the hell could it be, that the mind techs would allow the visit to a man they were in the middle of softening up? Some other poor bastard from his team, perhaps. Someone else they'd caught, that they thought he cared about. Someone they could hurt or kill in front of him. He moved his head slowly back and forth, partly in denial, partly just to feel it move after being still for so long. He licked his lips and tasted dried blood and salt from his tears. He heard footsteps approaching and braced himself as best he could.

And then BB Chojiro stepped through the door and into the cell, and Julian thought his heart would stop. She looked beautiful, as always, a petite little doll of a woman, with long dark hair and sharp Oriental features. She wore a bright scarlet kimono, to match her lips, and looked at him steadily with dark lustrous eyes. She stopped before him, and the door swung shut behind her. Julian looked at her and felt the horror rise in him again. They knew about BB. If they hurt her . . . he thought he'd go out of his mind, just at the thought. She stepped forward, moving even here with the perfect grace of all her Clan, and produced a small metal box from inside her sleeve. She pressed the single stud on the top, and the spinal block released the rest of its hold on him. He slumped forward, held up only by the restraining straps. His fingers spasmed helplessly. BB Chojiro knelt before him, so she could look right into his face. Julian tried to smile for her, but it felt more like a grimace. She put away the metal box and produced a silk handkerchief to wipe some of the blood and tears from his face. Her touch was very gentle.

"My poor Julian, what have they done to you? You used to be so strong, so sure. Now they've broken your wings, and you'll never fly again."

"BB," he said hoarsely, forcing his mouth to obey him. "Have they hurt you? What . . ."

"Don't try to speak. Just listen. I can't stay long. I want you to tell them everything, Julian. I want you to tell them everything you know. It's for the best, really. You know they'll get it out of you anyway. They always do. Only what will be left of you then won't even know who I am. If you cooperate, they'll let you go eventually, and then we can be together again, just like we were before. You'd like that, wouldn't you, Julian?"

He looked at her and didn't say a word. He'd known her less than a year. She'd been his younger brother's lover originally. Auric Skye had tried to get a position in Clan Chojiro, so that he could be with her. To impress the Clan, he fought the Masked Gladiator in the Arena. The Gladiator killed him. Auric never stood a chance against that legendary butcher of men. Julian had told him that, but Auric wouldn't listen, and Julian had watched in silence as they dragged his brother's body away across the bloody sands. Julian would have avenged Auric if he could, but he at least had the sense to know he couldn't beat the Masked Gladiator in a fair or unfair fight.

So he put it behind him, as just another evil episode in an evil Empire, and went to see BB Chojiro, to comfort and console her over Auric's death. They talked about Auric all through the evening and on into the night, and at the end she cried in his arms. They met again, and again, and fell in love. Julian felt guilty about that for a while, but BB talked him out of it. She made him see that Auric would have been glad for both of them. He cried in her arms then, finally saying good-bye to his brother. After that, Julian and BB were together as often as they could be. It wasn't very often. It was vital that the Clan Chojiro didn't find out. They were very strict and wouldn't have approved at all. And Julian had his obligations to the underground. It was a long time before he told her about that. She was surprised at first, but then she hugged him and kissed him and told him he'd done the right thing in telling her. It wasn't long after that they came for him. Not long at all.

Julian Skye looked at his love, kneeling before him, and knew for the first time who it was who had betrayed him.

"I thought you loved me," he said finally. "How could you do it?"

"It wasn't difficult, darling. My duty has always been to my Clan, first and foremost. Auric knew that. That's why he died trying to be a part of Clan Chojiro. You never did ask me what my real name is. What the BB stands for."

"You told me not to."

"Yes. And you always did what you were told. But the fact that I kept something as basic as that from you should have told you something. BB isn't my name, darling. It's my designation. I'm from Blue Block."

The words hit Julian like blows. He'd heard of Blue Block, but only in whispers. Blue Block was the Company of Lords' deepest secret: a hidden private army of lesser cousins, to be the Families' final defense against the Empress and her people. Every Family provided a number of candidates, willing or unwilling, and sent them to Blue Block, where they were trained and conditioned to be totally loyal to their Clans. Even to the death. They were everywhere, unknown and unsuspected, programmed to get as close as possible to people who mattered. In the last resort, they would be the Lords' last poisoned weapon to throw at Lionstone, or anyone else who tried to take away their power and position. Or so it was said. Blue Block was only a whisper, less than a rumor. Lionstone didn't take it seriously. If she had, she wouldn't have rested until every graduate of Blue Block had been tracked down and executed. She would never have allowed such a threat to her power to exist.

BB Chojiro. Blue Block. Bound to her Clan beyond hope or honor, life or death.

"Our love meant nothing to you, did it?" he said finally.

"There's no room in my life for what you think of as love. I was very fond of you. I still am. That's why I want you to tell the interrogators what they want to know, and get it over with. The interrogator's one of us. He's Blue Block, too. Once he's got everything out of you, he'll put you back together, as much as he can, and you can come back to me. You can be part of Clan Chojiro, just like your brother wanted. You'll have to go through Blue Block, of course, but it's really not so bad. And then you won't care anything about who you used to be or what you used to be."

"If I talk," Julian said hoarsely, "hundreds will die. Thousands will be endangered. The underground would have to scatter again. It might never recover. I can't do that. I won't."

"You will. You know you will. Talk to the interrogator, darling. Do it for me."

"Do it for you?" Julian would have laughed, but his throat was too dry. "Who are you? I don't know your real name. I don't know the real you. I loved you, you bitch. I would have done anything for you, even die for you. Now just looking at you makes me feel sick."

"Don't be like that, Julian; we had some good times together, just the two of us. Remember flying out over the Ravenscar mountains, and chasing each other on gravity sleds in and out of the great waterfalls as they came thundering down? Remember watching the double stars burning brightly over the Tannhouser Gate? Remember us dancing around a fire on the Dust Plains of Memory, dancing and singing as though the night would never end? Those were real times, Julian. Times we shared. We could share them again. We could still have a life together. It's up to you. You'll forget all about the underground, with me."

"BB. Will you do something for me?"

"Of course, darling. Would you like some water?"

"No. Just lean closer."

BB Chojiro smiled and brought her face in close to his. He could smell her familiar perfume. She pursed her mouth for a kiss. And Julian called up all the strength he had left and head-butted her in the face. He couldn't get much force behind it, but the impact was enough to knock her right back on her ass. Shock and surprise filled her face, and then pain as she brought her hands up to her nose. Blood streamed from her nostrils. Julian chuckled harshly, even though it hurt his throat. BB blinked at him uncertainly over her hands, and then rose jerkily to her feet. She wiped at her nose with a silken scarlet arm, but just succeeded in smearing more blood across her face. She gave up on it and drew herself up, perfectly composed, ignoring the blood. She smiled at him in a brittle, satisfied way.

"Thank you, Julian. I was beginning to feel a little sorry for you. For what you're about to undergo. You've helped remind me why I turned you in. You're scum, the lowest of the low, so far beneath the Families we can't even see you from where we are. And to think I nearly made you one of us. Talk about the Blue Block all you like. Only the interrogator will hear you, and he will see it doesn't go any further, even if he has to edit the security tapes. Think of me while he's working on you. I'll be thinking of you."

She rapped imperiously on the door, and it swung open. BB Chojiro blew Julian a kiss and strode out of the cell, every inch the perfect little aristocrat. Julian seethed inwardly

against the restraining straps, but they held him securely.
Still, she'd made a mistake in not reactivating the spinal
block. He could find some way to kill himself now and escape his interrogators. But he was too angry to think about
that. He had to live now, so he could escape and kill BB
Chojiro. He would survive everything they could throw at
him, waiting for the slightest slip, the smallest mistake that
would let him break free. And then he'd kill the interrogators and anyone else who got between him and BB Chojiro.
He'd loved her so much, but all he could think of now was
his hands around her perfect throat, her mocking smile replaced by a scream of terror. He laughed suddenly, a harsh
brutal sound of the darkest humor, and the interrogator
paused in the doorway of the cell, as though suddenly aware
he was about to enter a small enclosed space with a dangerous animal. But the moment passed, and the interrogator
strode in, smiling avuncularly at his prospective victim. He
shut the door firmly behind him, so that Julian's screams
wouldn't bother anyone walking down the corridor outside.

Finlay Campbell returned from his mission on a limping
flyer, bloody and battered and just a little out of breath. The
flyers dogging his trail had proved determined, if not particularly skillful, and it had taken every trick he knew to shake
them off. He landed the flyer with a defiant thud, and
slumped over the controls a moment. Members of the underground came running up to drag the flyer out of sight before
it could be spotted, and Finlay straightened up with a jerk.
It wouldn't do for word to get around that he was getting
soft. He stepped down from the flyer, enjoying the expressions on their faces as they saw what he'd left in the flyer
for them. He'd brought St. John's body with him, partly as
proof that he'd done his job, partly to upset the Lords over
the missing body, and partly as a trophy. He'd had a vague
idea about having St. John stuffed and mounted, and stood
somewhere prominent so that everyone could enjoy it. But
for the moment he couldn't be bothered.
  He left the body in the stolen flyer for someone else to
take care of, and trudged unwillingly toward the waiting elevators. Blood squelched noisily in one of his boots, from a
wound he'd taken in his leg. He'd taken hurts in other
places, too, but he kept his back straight. He had a reputation to maintain. He waited impatiently in front of the eleva-

tor doors, his hand on the pommel of his sword, drawing strength from it. The doors finally opened, and he strode in. They closed behind him, and he immediately slumped in a corner, held up only by the steel wall. He'd felt better. Getting old, and past it. Be playing checkers next. All he really wanted right now was a bed and several days' uninterrupted sleep, but the underground leaders were waiting for him to make his report. He couldn't make it in writing, of course; that would be far too easy. No, he had to stand there before them and tell them every detail, like a schoolboy in a classroom. He thought fondly of his quarters and a large glass of the good brandy. During the last stages of his trip back, it had only been thoughts of the brandy that had kept him going. That, and memories of Evangeline. She was never that far from his thoughts, whatever he was doing.

He straightened up slowly, pushing himself away from the supporting wall, and sniffed disparagingly at the various aches and pains that bothered him. He didn't really know why he was bothering with this report. All the esper leaders had to do was go take a look at the body in his flyer to know his mission had been a success. But they'd want details. They always did. It gave them the illusion that they were in charge. And since he was dependent on the underground for his few remaining comforts, not to mention further missions, he played along. Grudgingly.

The elevator doors finally opened on a floor that didn't exist on any official plans, and Finlay lurched out into the gloomy corridor. There never seemed to be enough lights in the underground. They probably did it deliberately, just to make the place look mysterious. Either that, or they were saving energy again. Finlay realized his thoughts were drifting again, and made himself concentrate on where he was going. Down here in the subsystems, far below the surface of Golgotha, one abandoned steel corridor looked much like any other. There were a few people about, and he found the energy to grunt a greeting to them as they passed. They all nodded politely to him, and quite right, too. He was Finlay Campbell, damn it.

He finally stomped into the main meeting area, an abandoned workstation that the cyberats had wiped from official memory. It was a large open space bounded with sharp-edged steel plates, and cables dangled everywhere, giving the place an unfinished, transient look. Quite suitably, really, for an underground that might have to pick up its belongings and run at any moment. After the debacle of the attempted storming of Silo Nine and the purges that followed, what remained of the underground lived from moment to moment, and tended to be even more paranoid than it used to. Finlay strode up to the esper leaders waiting for him in the center of the open space, and nodded to them briskly. There were three of them today, powerful espers hidden behind telepathically projected images to protect their identities. At least that was their story. Finlay liked to think they did it to hide really bad skin conditions or unsuccessful hair transplants. Finlay Campbell didn't believe in being in awe of anyone.

The leader, usually referred to as Mr. Perfect, was a tall naked Adonis, his impossibly defined musculature gleaming with sweat, though he never actually did anything but stand there. He had harsh, forbidding features that were just a little too classically handsome. He even had a dimple in his chin, the bastard. Finlay carefully refrained from looking at Mr. Perfect's genitals. It would only depress him. Next to Mr. Perfect, a mandala of ever-shifting shapes and colors hung unsupported in midair, a spinning wheel of interlocking patterns. Finlay didn't like to look at that too much, either. The sudden changes in color and brightness, and the way they swirled away into nothingness, made his head ache. The third leader presented his or her self as a twenty-foot dragon wrapped around the branches of a tall tree. It didn't speak much, as a rule, but its great golden eyes rarely blinked, and it gave the impression of listening very carefully. Finlay also had a lurking suspicion that just maybe the tree might be more than it seemed, too.

To put off making his report, Finlay looked around at the medium-size crowd attending the meeting. Finlay's reports always drew a crowd. He smiled at them pleasantly, and they smiled back and bowed their heads in respect. A few even applauded. There was the usual mixture of elves in their leathers and chains, clones with the same face, and assorted hangers-on, like him, tolerated by the powers that be because they were useful. Apart from the expectant crowd, people were also darting in and out—carrying messages, making their own reports to lesser officials, or just earwigging in the hope of picking up something useful. The underground thrived on gossip.

And then Finlay's roving gaze juddered to a halt, and his jaw dropped as he recognized two faces at the front of the crowd. Two faces he'd never expected to see together, let alone in the underground. Adrienne Campbell and Evangeline Shreck. His wife and his lover, chatting happily together and apparently getting on like a house on fire. His first thought was that it had to be some kind of esper illusion, some extremely nasty joke or trick to throw him off balance, but no one apart from him knew about the two women in his life. So it had to be them. Here. Together. Finlay looked quickly around for the nearest exit. Stuff his report, he had to get out of here. There were some things no man could face. Maybe if he just turned and ran very quickly . . .

"Finlay Campbell, attend us," said the mandala in a loud and piercing voice that echoed painfully inside his head, and that was that. Apparently, the voice hadn't just been aimed at him, as everyone else was now looking in his direction. Finlay sighed resignedly and strode forward to nod briefly to the esper leaders. He didn't get too close. There was something about the projected illusions that put his mental teeth on edge. He gave them a brisk salute, as much for the crowd as anything, but didn't bother with standing to attention. If they wanted a soldier, they could get one. He was just a troublemaker on a grand scale, with a reputation to live down to.

"Can you slow your colors down a bit?" he said sharply to the mandala. "I'm starting to get seasick. I don't know why you three are bothering with the illusions anyway. I've given up being impressed for Lent. Don't you trust me, after all I've done for you?"

"It's not a matter of trust," said Mr. Perfect in his pleasant, charismatic voice. "What you don't know, someone else can't make you tell them. Security is vital, now more than ever."

Finlay sniffed loudly, carefully not looking in Adrienne and Evangeline's direction. He could feel cold beads of sweat forming on his forehead. "I take it you want a report. All right. I killed Lord William St. John and a lot of his people, stole his personal flyer and got clean away. End of report. Can I go now please? Back in my quarters, a large brandy is calling for me with growing impatience."

He ignored the disappointed murmurs from the crowd, his

gaze fixed on Mr. Perfect as the least disturbing of the three leaders. The mandala's colors flowed suddenly in a direction his eyes tried to follow in spite of himself, but couldn't, and then its voice echoed loudly in the wide chamber.

"Normally, we would press you for a more detailed report, but there is no time. We need you to go out on another mission. Immediately."

Finlay stared at the leaders, for a moment almost lost for words. "You want *what*? I've only just got back, damn it! I've been cut at, shot at, chased halfway to hell and back while dodging in and out the pastel towers on a glorified gravity sled, and only just got away in one piece, and you want me to go out again? Does the phrase *Stick it where the sun don't shine* sound at all familiar? Have you all gone crazy, or are you just harboring a death wish? On the ground that if you don't change your minds about this new mission in one hell of a hurry, I am going to find what's behind these over-rehearsed mirages of yours and slice and dice all three of you into pie fillings! I am tired, hurt, and completely lacking in the sense of humor department. And no I don't have any sense of loyalty or honor. I'm an aristocrat, remember? I'm not going anywhere till I've had a good long soak in a hot tub, three or four good meals on the same plate, and an extremely long and uninterrupted nap. I am like a disrupter. I need to recharge my batteries between jobs. Right now my batteries are sitting in a corner crying their eyes out, and my get-up-and-go has got up and gone without leaving a forwarding address. In other words, no I'm not bloody going!"

The crowd applauded. This was what they liked to hear. Finlay looked hopefully at the esper leaders, but they'd heard it all from him before, and it hadn't impressed them then. Mr. Perfect rippled his muscles impressively and looked sternly at Finlay.

"This mission is vital. The security of the whole underground is at stake. During your absence, a previously unheard of band of rebels attacked the city. They invaded the Income Tax and Tithes Headquarters, disrupted the computer systems with great efficiency and thoroughness, and made their escape in a Hadenman starship. Our previous contacts with this group had been somewhat tentative, but their actions have established our new allies as a force of great power, if not subtlety. They also brought us news of great importance. Jack Random has returned to lead them."

The crowd burst into applause and scattered cheering. Finlay didn't join in. He'd heard of the professional rebel, everyone had, but the man had to be getting on in years now. And he didn't trust legends anymore. Not since he found he'd become one himself.

"What's all this got to do with the new mission I'm not going on?" he said loudly, and the applause died away as everyone looked interestedly at the esper leaders and waited for their reply. This was why they enjoyed Finlay's reports. He always gave a great performance. Mr. Perfect looked steadily at Finlay.

"Thanks to our new friends' attack, Golgotha's defenses and security systems are currently in tatters. Things are now possible that were not before. You will remember Julian Skye. It was only thanks to him that the underground was able to reform itself after Silo Nine. Skye has been captured. They haven't had him long, but it is imperative that he doesn't talk. He alone knows all the locations, names, and passwords that made our reforming possible. There are blocks and defenses in his mind, but they won't last long once the Empire mind techs really get to work on him. Any other time, we would have been helpless to retrieve the situation, but in the current chaos, who knows what might be achieved by one determined man?"

"Who knows what might be achieved by a small army with lots of weapons?" said Finlay doggedly. "Think of all the other prisoners you could rescue."

"We can't risk losing any more of our people," said the mandala. "Skye is being held in the maximum security area. Even with the present disruption, he will undoubtably be very well guarded, by both human and inhuman guards. One man might sneak in and out, where an army could not hope to. You will be that one man."

"Because I'm brave, talented, and entirely expendable?"

"Exactly. It helps that you are also the most likely to succeed in such a desperate mission, despite the odds. What's the matter, Finlay? I thought you liked a challenge?"

"This isn't a challenge, it's a death sentence. And contrary to popular impressions, I don't do suicide missions. Find another sucker."

"You will this time. Skye must be rescued or silenced before he talks. You will decide which option is the most practical, under the cirumstances."

"Hello? Are you listening to me? I'm not going!"

"We have a trace on Skye. All espers in the underground have a telepathic beacon, buried deep in their minds. The Empire hasn't silenced it yet, so we have his exact location. Which means we can teleport you right to him."

"All right," said Finlay. "I'll bite. What's the snag?"

"The Empire must know about the beacon. They've captured enough espers before and silenced their beacons quite efficiently. If Skye hasn't been blocked, it can only be because he is being set up as bait in a trap. They know how badly we need his silence. They're expecting a small army. They won't expect you. However, we feel it only fair to warn you that while we can teleport you in, we will almost certainly not be able to teleport you out again. The Empire will no doubt have taken measures to prevent that."

"Let me get this straight," said Finlay. "You're going to drop me right in the middle of the Golgotha interrogation center, surrounded by legions of armed guards, both human and inhuman, and it's up to me to free Skye and fight my way out?"

"That's right," said Mr. Perfect. "A walk in the park. We have every confidence in you. After all, since it's so obviously a trap, there's always the chance they won't be expecting anyone to actually walk into it. Let alone one man on his own. You should take them entirely by surprise."

"I can't help thinking *should* is the operative word there," said Finlay. "I told you, I don't do suicide missions. And I haven't heard one thing so far that's going to change my mind."

"That's why they wanted me to be here," said Evangeline. She walked slowly forward to join him, their eyes holding contact all the way. She put out her arms to hold him, but he stopped her with an upraised hand.

"Don't. I'm covered in muck and blood. I'll get your dress dirty."

Evangeline looked him over, trying not to wince at the sight of his wounds, and shook her head sadly. "More blood. More pain and suffering, on my behalf. I've always known you only do this for me. You've never given a damn for the rebellion or the underground, have you?"

"I needed something to do down here," said Finlay uncomfortably. "Something to keep me busy. And I do care, in my way. I still remember what I saw in Silo Nine, down in Wormboy Hell. I will not allow that kind of suffering and horror to continue. I have sworn a death oath, upon my blood and my honor, to fight to put an end to Silo Nine and the system that produced it. The underground's the best way for me to do that. But I'm still not going on this mission, Evie. Not even for you. I know my limitations."

"So do I. You're quite right. It probably will get you killed. But we need you to do this mission. I could come with you, if you like. Fight at your side, die beside you."

"No! I don't want that. I nearly lost you in Silo Nine. I won't risk that again. I need to know you're safe. I wouldn't want to live without you. Is this Skye bastard really so important?"

"If he talks, the underground will have to scatter again. Thousands of clones and espers and their supporters would risk capture or death all over again. It could take anything from ten to twenty years before we could pull ourselves back together again, and that's being optimistic. The underground might not survive at all. Certainly the rebellion would be set back indefinitely. It's the timing that's so ironic. Things are finally going our way, Finlay. These new rebels, with Jack Random to lead them, could be the final spark we need to blow the whole corrupt Empire apart."

"What do you want me to do, Evie?"

"I want what you want: for us to be here, safe, together. But what we want doesn't matter anymore. If Skye talks, what little we have will be taken from us. You have to go, Finlay. You're the only one who stands a chance of bringing this off and coming back alive."

"And if I don't? If I get myself killed, fighting for the damn Cause?"

"Then part of me will die with you," said Evangeline, looking at him steadily. "I know what we're asking of you. What I'm asking. It's tearing me apart. But . . ."

"But you're still asking."

"Yes. I know my duty. To every esper and clone who suffered in Silo Nine, or suffers every day as non-people in the Empire."

Finlay smiled briefly. "You always did fight dirty."

"I love you, Finlay. If you say no, I'll still love you."

"I love you, Evie. Even though you're asking."

They looked at each other for a long time, seeing nothing but each other, their love so strong and fierce it filled the chamber. The crowd was silent, holding its breath. So Adrienne cleared her throat and stepped forward.

"Don't do it, Finlay. You'd have to be crazy to take on a mission like this. Everyone's been telling me what a great fighter you are, but no one could face these odds and come back in one piece."

Finlay smiled coldly at her. "You never did believe in me, Adrienne."

"That's not the point. Let them find somebody else. There's always somebody else."

"There isn't time," said Finlay. "Weren't you listening?"

"Damn it, stop fighting me! I'm worried about you!"

"Really? What brought that on?"

"Damned if I know. I don't even know what I'm doing here. But Evangeline and I have become rather close just recently, much to our mutual surprise, and since she's clearly not stupid or easily impressed, I'm forced to the opinion that you must be something of the hero and fighter she says you are. Though if you're that good an actor, you should be on the stage. But this assignment has suicide mission written all over it. You might as well walk into the Arena with no weapons and one leg tied behind your back. Don't go, Finlay. I don't want you dying before I've had a chance to finally get to know you. Tell them to stuff their mission. There's always another way, if you look hard enough."

"You don't think I can do it, do you?" said Finlay. "Well, you're wrong, Addie. I can jump in there, grab the bastard, and be gone before the guards know what's hit them. I'm a fighter, Adrienne. The best damn fighter you'll ever meet."

"You're not listening to me!" said Adrienne. "But, then, you never did. You talk to him, Evie."

"But I want him to go," said Evangeline. "Please, Finlay. Do it for me. I don't want to end up in whatever they build to replace Silo Nine."

"It won't come to that," said Finlay. "I'd never let them take you."

"Even you couldn't protect me from the kind of forces Julian Skye would set in motion. And I think I'd rather die than be taken."

"I'd kill every guard and soldier in the Empire before I let them hurt you," said Finlay. "All right. I'll go. But if by some miracle I get out of this alive and reasonably intact, I want something for myself." He glared across at the esper leaders. "You hear that, you bastards?"

"We are not surprised," said the mandala, pulsing calmly. "What do you want?"

"I want Valentine," said Finlay. He smiled widely, and there was no humor in it at all, just a death's-head grin. "I want his head on a stick."

Valentine Wolfe was once an enthusiastic supporter of the underground. He provided financial backing, and whatever support and influence he could bring to bear without compromising himself. But then he waged a sudden and highly successful vendetta against the Campbells, and became the head of his own Family when his father died leading the assault on Tower Campbell. As the new Wolfe, Valentine had access to immense wealth and power and apparently lost all interest in the underground and the rebellion. He no longer came to meetings and ignored all attempts at contact. So the underground left him strictly alone. He could do them a lot of damage if he chose to. He knew names and faces, plans and places. A few hard-liners in the elves wanted him dead, as a precautionary measure. So far the underground leaders had said no. Valentine had remained silent, and they didn't want to upset or alarm other Clan members working with the underground. At the very least, it would set a bad precedent. And as the Wolfe, Valentine was very well protected. An unsuccessful attack by the underground might very well prompt the very disclosure of information they were so desperate to avoid.

But, if they let Finlay kill him, working on his own, they could pass if off as a personal feud. Just a Campbell and a Wolfe fighting again. It was a tempting thought. As long as Valentine was alive, the information in his head was a threat hanging over them. While not as great a threat as Julian Skye, he could do a lot of damage, if he chose. There was also the question of exactly how much influence the Lord High Dram had over Valentine. Dram had also been a major player in the underground, in his alias as Hood, only to betray them during the attack on Silo Nine. He was directly responsible for the scattering that had put Julian Skye on the spot in the first place. So far, he'd made no attempt to contact or control Valentine, but the potential threat of blackmail was always there.

Finlay knew all this was going through the leaders' minds. He didn't need to be a telepath for that. They and he had already argued both sides of this problem many times before. They'd always said no. But things were different now.

"Very well," said the dragon, curled around his tree. He fixed his glowing golden eyes on Finlay. "In the unlikely event that you return from this mission successful and alive, you may pursue your vendetta against the Wolfe. The underground will neither hinder nor support you. All consequences will be upon your own head. We will of course, if necessary, discard and renounce you."

"Sounds good to me," said Finlay. "I've always known where I stood with you."

"Be clear as to the purpose of your mission," said the mandala, its colors rippling agitatedly. "You must either rescue or silence Julian Skye, according to the situation you encounter. He must not be allowed to talk. Once we have teleported you in, you're on your own. We can't help you. We can, however, offer a little support in advance."

One of the elves stepped forward and presented Finlay with a small flat box. It was polished steel, with a single button on it, colored a dramatic red. Finlay hefted it thoughtfully. He'd never seen one before, but he knew what the box was, what it had to be. A mindbomb. A terror weapon despised and outlawed throughout the Empire. Once activated, it attacked the minds of all non-espers, disorienting and scrambling their thoughts. Its victims hallucinated, then became insane, and finally catatonic. It was a vicious, take-no-prisoners weapon, a last resort for the truly desperate. It was very rare; like the esp-blockers, the mindbomb was based around living esper brain tissue. It was almost unthinkable for the esper leaders to admit to possessing such a thing, let alone handing one over to him. They really must think he wouldn't be coming back to talk about it. Finlay couldn't help wondering whether the brain tissue had come from a volunteer, and if it was still somehow aware and thinking. He repressed a shudder and slipped the metal box into his pocket. He nodded respectfully to the elves and threw the leaders another brisk salute, indicating the audience was over, as far as he was concerned. He took Evangeline by the arm and led her off to one side. Adrienne followed. The images of the esper leaders disappeared like popping soap bub-

bles. The crowd began to break up, chattering animatedly.
Finlay had given them enough material to keep them gossip-
ing for weeks.

Finlay knew the underground expected him to kill Skye.
They thought him incapable of subtlety. They also thought
he'd kill Skye to make it easier for him to escape the interrogation center. They were wrong both times. Finlay was determined to bring Skye back alive. Partly, because he'd
failed to rescue so many others from Silo Nine and had
sworn never to fail again, and partly to prove to the espers
that they were wrong about him. He wasn't just a killing machine, a weapon they could just aim and unleash on their enemies. Despite everything that had happened to him, he was
still more than that. He had to be, for Evangeline's sake. He
smiled at her and nodded briskly to Adrienne.

"Never thought to see you two together without weapons
in your hands. How the hell did you get together?"

"Circumstances can make for strange bedfellows," said
Adrienne. "I've always known that."

"I'll bet you have," said Finlay.

"You don't have to take this mission," said Evangeline.
"Despite everything I've said, I don't want you to die."

"I do have to take this mission," said Finlay. "And not
just for the obvious reasons. You never did understand why
I needed to fight in the Arena. I need the action, the thrill of
the blood, the balancing on a blade's edge between life and
death. Now that my other life in the Empire is gone, I need
the thrill a little more. It's all I have to keep me occupied."

"You still have me," said Evangeline.

"I hardly see you these days," said Finlay. "It used to be,
when I was with you, I could forget the Arena, the blood,
and the killing. But now you have your responsibilities in
the world above, and so little time to be with me. You have
to understand what drives me, Evie. It isn't very pretty or
honorable, but it's me. I need to kill, like a predator in a
world of prey. Nothing's happened to change that. It's just
that the life I'm living now has brought it closer to the surface."

"The world above doesn't matter," said Evangeline. "And
my responsibilities can go to hell. There are too many of
them these days. They clog up my head and keep me from
seeing what's really important. I'll move down here permanently if that's what you need, and to hell with what the un-

derground wants. In the end, there's just you and me and what we mean to each other. Everything else is just clutter."

Finlay took her in his arms and kissed her, and their passion beat on the air like the wings of a giant bird. Adrienne watched thoughtfully. It had been a day of surprises. This new Finlay was a man she'd only seen in glimpses before, puzzling flashes of a hidden nature that had disturbed and frightened her. She didn't like to think she could have been so wrong about someone so close to her. Pretty Finlay in his gorgeous outfits, a mad dog killer from the Arena . . . and Evangeline, a quiet mousy little thing at Court, with hidden horrors and a kind of courage Adrienne could only marvel at. They were both a little ragged around the edges just now, but Adrienne liked them a lot more. She'd always had a weakness for the mentally challenged. Finlay and Evangeline had been in different worlds for too long, becoming different people who had nothing in common except their love, but in the end it was enough. It was strong and real enough to hold even them together. Adrienne could recognize that. She'd have had to be blind not to.

But for once, she didn't know what to do for the best. Finlay would have to be really crazy to go on this mission, but all the signs were he was a long way down that road already. Nothing she could say or do would change his mind. She wasn't used to that. She'd never been in a situation before where her arrogance and mastery of words couldn't get her what she wanted. She'd relied on her acid tongue to get her own way for so long, that she was frankly lost for an alternative. She didn't want to lose this new, interesting Finlay, now she'd found him. She was surprised to find how much that mattered to her. Finlay and Evangeline finally came up for air, and she coughed meaningfully. It was a good cough. On a good day, she could silence a room with it. The two lovers turned to look at her without letting go of each other.

"Before you say anything," Evangeline said firmly to Finlay, "Adrienne and I have become friends. She gave me the strength to do something very unpleasant but utterly necessary that I'd been putting off for far too long. And no, I'm not going to tell you what. Suffice it to say it's because of her support that I'll be able to spend more time down here in the future."

"Thank you for that at least, Addie," said Finlay.

"You're so welcome," said Adrienne. They looked at each other for a long moment, but had the sense to leave it at that.

"So," said Finlay. "What are your plans, Ad? Going to join the rebellion?"

"Maybe," said Adrienne. "Things have been getting pretty tough for me upstairs. I could use a new direction and a measure of security. Tell me, Finlay, were you really a fighter in the Arena?"

"He was the Masked Gladiator," said Evangeline, and she and Finlay both laughed aloud at the expression on Adrienne's face. She quickly pulled herself together and managed to laugh with them.

"Who knows," she said, "if I put my mind to it, maybe I can nag Lionstone into making reforms."

"If anyone could, you could," said Finlay generously.

Finlay teleported into the interrogation center with a sword in his hand and grim determination in his heart. He snapped into being halfway down a dimly lit corridor, facing half a dozen rather surprised-looking guards. They had swords in their hands, too, but it didn't help them. Finlay plowed straight into them, his sword flashing in short, brutal arcs, and blood-choked screams filled the corridor. He killed them all in under a minute, and then stood poised and ready, listening for reinforcements. The seconds passed, and no one came to investigate. The few brief sounds from the one-sided slaughter obviously hadn't traveled far. Finlay sniffed dismissively, flicking drops of blood from his blade. Not much fun. Strictly amateur hour. No challenge at all. If this was the Empire's idea of a trap, this mission was going to be a walkover. Then he noted the cameras set into the ceiling, watching him with glowing unblinking eyes, and decided it might be a good idea if he got a move on after all. Given what the cameras had just observed, reinforcements were probably already on their way, in great numbers, with guns and guard dogs. He'd never liked dogs.

He looked up and down the corridor, and wished he'd thought to ask for a map. The corridor was sparsely lit by dull-glowing lamps set into the ceiling. The walls were bare featureless steel, with no markings or signs. Narrow doors led off into interrogation cells at regular intervals—solid steel doors, sealed with electronic locks. Deep shadows lay undisturbed to every side, and there was a strong smell of disinfectant in the air, almost but not quite masking other, more unpleasant smells. Julian Skye was here somewhere, but exactly where was anyone's guess. The underground had taken pains not to send him to the exact location of Skye's beacon. Materializing inside a locked cell, where everyone would be expecting him, had not struck anyone as a good idea, least of all Finlay. So they picked the nearest open space and dropped him there. Finlay looked around him vaguely, hefted his sword, and for want of anything better to do, moved over to the nearest door. There was a small viewscreen set into the solid steel. Finlay activated it, and the screen showed him what was inside the cell.

The man spread-eagled on the metal table had been expertly flayed. Not a square inch of skin remained on him, but he was still very much alive. He moved feebly, struggling against unseen restrains. Raw red muscle glistened wetly. Naked eyes bulged from lidless sockets. Blood seeped constantly onto the table, carried away by grooves and runnels cut into the metal. New blood flowed into a pulsing vein from an IV drip. Finlay turned off the screen and leaned his forehead against the cold metal of the cell door.

There was nothing he could do. He couldn't rescue everyone. He didn't have the time. The underground had been quite specific about that. He had to get to Skye before he could spill anything important. Finlay took a deep breath and let it out. To hell with them, and to hell with the Empire. He was damned if he'd let obscenities like this continue. He used the lock-scrambling mechanism the underground had provided, and the cell door swung silently open.

Finlay slipped inside, and the man on the table whimpered in anticipation of fresh pain. Finlay leaned over him, making soothing shushing noises, and the prisoner quietened. It was only then that Finlay realized the man had been riveted to the table by firing metal spikes through his limbs and body. There were dozens of them. Finlay had no way of removing them, short of levering them out one at a time, and the shock alone would almost certainly finish the poor bastard off anyway. But he couldn't leave him to suffer like this. Finlay stood a moment, mind racing as he tried to come up with some other alternative, but in the end there was only one thing he could do. He smiled reassuringly down into the prisoner's naked, hopeful eyes, and slipped the point of his sword into the exposed, beating heart. There was a brief splash of blood, the flayed man jerked once, and then he stopped breathing. Finlay kicked at the table once in frustration and then left the cell.

He stalked down the corridor, throwing open the cell doors one by one, freeing those prisoners he could. He killed the others. Some of them begged him to do it. The survivors spilled out into the corridor, milling about him, trying to thank him with voices grown raw from screaming. Finlay armed some of the sturdier ones with weapons from the guards he'd killed and then left them to their own devices. At least, that was the plan.

There was the sound of running feet and then a full company of armed guards rounded the corner at the far end of the corridor, and came charging toward him. Finlay smiled. This was more like it. And then there was the sound of running feet behind him, and he turned to see another company of armed guards approaching from the other end of the corridor. The freed prisoners crowded in close around Finlay. He sighed regretfully. It would have been an interesting fight, but he knew his limitations. Besides, he had to think of the prisoners. He pulled the mindbomb from his pocket and pressed the big red button.

The guards before and behind him stumbled to a halt, clutching at their heads and screaming. Their thoughts shattered and fragmented, their minds scrambled beyond sense or meaning, and in a moment they had changed from an organized army into a crazed, panic-stricken mob. Finlay and the freed prisoners watched, impressed, protected by their immediate proximity to the mindbomb device. Finlay turned it off and left the prisoners to deal with the still shrieking mob, while he went on about his business. A long delayed revenge filled the corridor, and blood spattered the shining steel walls. Finlay carried on opening doors and freeing prisoners, until finally he came to the cell with Julian Skye in it, and he stopped in the doorway, held by the shock of what he was seeing.

The young esper lay on his back on another of the damned steel tables, held firmly in place by restraining straps. The back of his head had been shaved and cut open, and a section of the skull removed. Dozens of colorful wires disappeared into the exposed brain tissue, leading back into an ugly piece of machinery beside the table. Two mind techs, in their familiar white gowns, looked up from what they were doing and smiled pleasantly at Finlay as he hesitated in the doorway. They both had disrupters holstered on their hips, but neither made any move to draw them. Finlay moved slowly forward into the cell, ignoring the growing chaos of screams and pain and fury in the corridor outside. There were no guards in the cell, no obvious protection or booby traps. The mind techs eyed the blood dripping from his sword and smiled briefly at each other. They were both tall and slender men, with pale aesthetic faces like monks, one clearly older than the other. The elder looked back at Finlay and smiled again.

"Welcome, dear boy. We've been expecting you. Or someone like you. I'm afraid if you came to rescue dear Julian, you're a little too late. Any attempt to move him now would undoubtably kill him. We're using an esp-blocker to restrain his talents, and its function cancels out the effects of the mindbomb you used. Nasty little device, but quite ineffective in here. And you might as well put that sword away. I only have to touch this control under my hands, and dear Julian will experience pain beyond your capability to imagine. Put the sword away, please. Now."

Finlay sheathed his sword, but his eyes didn't waver. "What are you doing to him?" he said finally, and his voice came out cold and harsh and very deadly. The mind tech smiled, unmoved.

"We're invading his thoughts. Not that long ago, we would have used one of Wormboy's little pets, but thanks to your terrorist friends we are obliged to use older, more direct methods. It's essentially a simple and very effective mind probe, electronically stimulating the areas of the brain we're interested in. This one, for example, is tied directly into the pleasure-pain center. Guess which part we're interested in. The procedure itself is surprisingly painless. I imagine he felt some discomfort from the original invasive procedures, but the brain itself has no pain sensors. It makes our job so much easier, to be able to inflict pain only as needed. And what pain he feels then . . .

"These other wires are concerned with short- and long-term memory. We can play back his memories on that screen on the wall in as much detail as we require. Soon we'll have everything we want, regardless of the patient's wishes. The procedure is, unfortunately, quite destructive to the brain tissues in the long run, but the health or even life of this patient is of no concern to anyone once we have what we want. Except, of course, you. The guards will be here soon, to take you away. In the meantime, please refrain from any violent action, or you can listen to your friend screaming."

It had grown quiet in the corridor outside. Finlay frowned. Either the prisoners had run out of guards to kill, or the guards had succeeded in restoring order. He had no way of knowing which. He should just kill the mind techs, and then kill Skye. But as long as there was still a chance of getting the poor bastard out alive, he couldn't do that. He needed the techs to remove the wires, but he didn't know how to make them do that. Kill one, and the other could take a very nasty revenge on Skye. But he couldn't just hang around waiting while the mind techs stalled; sooner or later the guards would come for him. He looked across at Skye's face, pale and sweating, and the esper's eyes met his. His mouth worked.

"Please . . ." he said faintly, fighting to get the word out.

"You see?" said the mind tech. "He understands the reality of the situation."

"Please," said Julian Skye. "Kill me . . ."

The mind tech looked down at him sharply. Finlay laughed softly, and there was no humor in the sound at all. "No, *doctor,* he understands the reality of the situation completely. My mission is to put him beyond your reach, one way or the other."

He drew his disrupter in one swift movement, and shot the mind tech with his hands by the controls. The younger tech lunged for the controls. Finlay drew a dagger from his sleeve and put it expertly through the technician's eye. He fell backward, clutching at his face with both hands, and then hit the floor hard and lay still. Finlay nodded once, satisfied, put his disrupter away, and moved forward to lean over Skye. The esper looked up at him and tried to smile. The marks of a recent bad beating were still clear on his face, but his gaze was clear.

"Knew they'd send someone. If I could just hold out long enough."

"What do I do?" said Finlay. "I don't understand this machinery. Is there any way I can get this stuff out of your head?"

"No. But I can now."

Skye closed his eyes and concentrated. For a long moment

nothing happened, and then one by one the colored wires began to squirm and wriggle their way out of the exposed brain tissues. They fell to coil harmlessly on the floor, like so many dead snakes, and when the last one finally worked its way free, Skye relaxed so utterly that Finlay was worried that the esper was dead. He checked the pulse in Skye's neck, but it was strong and regular. He set about undoing the restraints, working as fast as he could. The guards had to be on their way by now. He sat Skye up on the table and blood ran down the esper's neck from the ugly wound in the back of his head. Finlay gingerly pulled the flaps of cut skin together to cover the exposed brain, and held them in place with a handkerchief wrapped around the esper's shaved head. Luckily, it was a clean one. Skye's eyes opened suddenly, as though he'd just been thinking. He looked at his reflection in the steel wall and smiled.

"Nice work. I look like a pirate. But this doesn't change anything. There's no way you can get me out of here, and I won't let them take me again. So kill me."

"That's not an option," said Finlay.

"Don't tell me that wasn't part of your orders. My silence is what matters. I know how the underground works."

"Dying is easy. Anyone can do it. But if you give up, if you choose to die rather than fight for a chance at life and freedom, then the mind techs will have won. They'll have broken you. Stay alive, break free, and get your revenge on the bastards who ordered this done to you. That's what the underground and the rebellion are all about. Now if I can get you out of range of the esp-blocker, can you find us a way out of here?"

"I don't know. Maybe." Julian smiled weakly. "It's worth a try. They had to turn the esp-blocker's influence way down, to avoid damaging my brain while they were working on it. And being this close to a mindbomb did the blocker some damage. That's how I was able to get those wires out of my head. If you can get me a few corridors away, the rest of my esp should return. And then I'll show you some real fireworks."

Finlay grinned. "A man after my own heart. Let's go."

He helped the young esper down from the table and supported him for a moment till his legs got their strength back. Although he did his best to hide it, Finlay was concerned about Skye's condition. The Empire had clearly beaten the hell out of him before they started tinkering with his brain. If it came to a fight, or even a prolonged chase, they could be in real trouble. He decided he'd think about that when he had to, and not before, and led the way out of the interrogation cell. Dead guards and espers lay scattered the length of the corridor, but everyone else had gone. The fight had moved on, deeper into the heart of the complex. Finlay wondered who was winning. Skye looked up and down the corridor, and then moved forward to take the lead.

"The layout of these places is pretty standardized," he said brusquely, stepping gingerly over the bodies. "I did a study on the Empire's interrogation centers for the underground a while back. We were planning rescue missions with telepaths and mindbombs. But that was before the scattering. If I remember correctly, these corridors should all eventually tie in to a central rotunda. From that I should be able to find us a way to the main flyer station. Then all we have to do is fight our way past a dozen guards, hot-wire a flyer without setting off all the explosive booby traps, and then get the hell out of here before they crank up the esp-blockers and knock out my powers again."

"No problem," said Finlay.

"There's going to be a lot of guards between us and there."

"I've still got the mindbomb."

"Save it. It's only good for half a dozen blasts or so, and then the brain tissue burns up."

"We can do without it," said Finlay. "You've got me."

Skye looked at him. "Are you always this confident?"

"Of course. Why do you think the underground chose me for this mission? So stop worrying. It'll give you ulcers. You stick with me, and I'll get you out of here."

Skye smiled genuinely for the first time. "You just might, at that."

He led the way down one corridor after another, never hesitating at a turn or a blind corner. The corridors all looked the same to Finlay, but he trusted Skye. The young esper was standing straighter now, though the pain in his head clearly bothered him. His eyes were brighter, and there were two spots of color in his pale cheeks. He still looked as though a strong wind would blow him away, but his confidence was returning. And then they turned a corner, and Skye stopped dead in his tracks, his head cocked slightly to one side, as though listening. Finlay looked quickly about him, but the corridor was deserted.

"Talk to me, Skye. What is it?"

"We're in trouble."

"I guessed that. Be specific."

"When we were all held in Silo Nine, Wormboy allowed mind techs and other scientists to experiment on the inmates. Most died. They were the lucky ones. The survivors were monsters, changed in body and mind, no longer human. A few escaped during the underground assault, but most were too securely confined. After Wormboy was killed during the assault, the monsters were transferred here, in the hope of finding some new way of controlling them. The authorities must really not want us escaping. They've released a dozen of the monsters into the corridors. They're insane with rage and pain. They'll attack anything that moves. And they're heading right for us."

Finlay looked quickly around him again, but all seemed quiet for the moment. "How's your esp? Is it back yet?"

"Some. But even a full psistorm wouldn't stop minds like these."

"Any chance you could contact the underground and get us a teleport out of here?"

"No. This whole place is surrounded by esp-blockers. You got in only because they let you in. We either find our own way out, or the monsters will be picking what's left of us out of their back teeth."

Finlay thought hard. "What about maintenance tunnels, air ducts, that sort of thing?"

"All securely locked off and guarded. This is a prison, re-member? Brace yourself. They're coming."

Finlay took up a stance between Skye and the direction he'd indicated, sword in one hand and gun in the other. The first sounds of approaching feet reached him, loud and uneven. He could hear roars and howls and sounds that had no place in a human throat. The sounds drew nearer, and Finlay took aim with his disrupter. And then the monsters surged around the corner at the end of the corridor, and all Finlay could do was stare. Some had bulging brains that had broken apart their skulls from the inside and thrust out through the cracks. Some had bony thorns thrusting out through their flesh. Others had white, livid flesh, already rotting away from their bones. High tech had been grafted onto and into that flesh, replacing body parts with augmentations until hardly any of their humanity was left. Just flesh in metal cages. Some still looked mostly human, but rippled the walls of the corridor as they passed, as though reality itself was shifting around them, disturbed by their inhuman and uncontrolled esp.

Finlay breathed heavily. There were bad odds, and then there were bad odds, and this was both. He switched his gun from one target to another, but whichever he took out, the others would get him long before the gun could recharge for another shot. And for once it didn't matter a damn how good a swordsman he was. Cold steel was no match for esp. He looked at Skye.

"You know these things better than I do. Is there any way we can reach them? You're an esper, damn it, you must still have something in common with them!"

"I'll try," said Skye. "But they're not really espers anymore. They've moved beyond that."

He reached out with his esp, but it was like looking at flaring lights in the night, all color and brightness and fury, without meaning or content. If they had thoughts, he couldn't understand them. All he could share was the rage and horror and suffering that filled their lives. So he did the only thing he could. He gathered up the fury in their minds, threw it back at them, and made each of them think it came from the others around them. The monsters screamed and fell upon each other, rending and tearing, and blood that was not always red flew on the air. Esp clashed with esp till the air shimmered and sparkled and the steel walls ran like water from the strength of it. Skye stepped backward, his hands to his head, trying to block it out. Finlay holstered his gun and dragged him away from the carnage in the corridor.

"Don't lose it, Skye! There must be another way out of here. We'll find it!"

They ran down the corridor together, Skye shaking his head over and over again. He tried to say something to Finlay, but couldn't get it out. Finlay understood. Some of the monsters could have been people the esper knew before they ended up in Silo Nine. Some might even have been friends. There but for the grace of God and the underground. . . . And then they rounded a corner, and Finlay jerked them both to a halt. A full company of guards was blocking the way ahead. They raised their guns to fire, and Finlay dragged Skye back around the corner just in time. A few energy bolts flashed past them, but most of the guards had enough sense not to fire blindly. Using a disrupter in a confined space was always risky. You never knew when the beam might ricochet right back at you. Finlay pulled the mindbomb out of his pocket, but Skye put a restraining hand on his arm.

"Not a good idea. Use the mindbomb, and there's no telling what it might do to the monsters. It might snap them out of the confusion I put them in and bring them down on us again. And even if it doesn't, do you really want to send that many armed men insane at such close quarters?"

"You have a point," Finlay said reluctantly. "Monsters behind, guards ahead. Damned if we do, damned if we don't." He put the mindbomb away. "Looks like we'll have to do it the old-fashioned way. Don't worry. I'm the best there ever was with a sword, and this is where I get to prove it."

Skye looked at him. "There are too many of them, and they've all got guns. Disrupters don't care how good a swordsman you are."

"If I can get into the middle of them fast enough, they won't dare use their guns for fear of shooting each other. Sure the odds aren't good, but when have they ever been? The important thing is to fight, and if need be, go down fighting. As long as there's still a chance, however slim, we fight on. That's what the underground is all about. Who knows? Maybe we'll get lucky."

"You could surrender," said Skye. "They really only want me."

"That is not an option," said Finlay. "I said I'd get you out or die trying, and I will. Now, be quiet and let me concentrate. There's a way out of this, if only I can see it. There's always a way out."

"No," said Skye. "Sometimes there isn't. We've armed guards ahead and monsters behind, and nowhere else to go. It was a nice try, Finlay, but it's over."

"Then, we take as many of them with us as we can," said Finlay. "Because as long as we're still fighting, they haven't really beaten us."

Skye smiled suddenly. "Thanks for coming after me. I never really expected anyone like you. At least this way I get to die on my feet."

"Don't give up yet," said Finlay. "We could still get lucky."

And that was when the roof fell in. The floor buckled and

rose up under their feet, and the walls split apart with screams of rending steel. The guards were yelling in confusion, and alarm sirens blared deafeningly from all directions. Skye and Finlay clung to each other for support, Finlay trying to shield the fragile esper with his own body. There was a constant rumbling roar of shifting metal and concrete as the building rocked slowly around them. The lights snapped out, and for a long moment there was only darkness before the dull red glow of emergency lighting returned. In the distance there were sudden, sharp explosions, and from everywhere came the sound of screaming. Some of it didn't sound human. The floor bulged upward slowly and then settled, and the rumbling died away. Everything was still. People were shouting orders or screaming for help. It all sounded a long way off. Finlay straightened up, still supporting the esper with one arm. Blood was flowing down his face from a long gash on his temple, but he ignored it. He could hear the crackling of fires and smell the beginnings of smoke in the air.

"What the hell was *that*?" said Skye, staring blearily about him into the crimson light. "Could it have been an earthquake?"

"That was a miracle," said Finlay. "And since they tend to be few and far between, I suggest we get the hell out of here before the authorities get their act together, and we need another miracle."

He led the way over the uneven floor, with Skye sticking close behind him. Around the corner, the guards were all dead. The ceiling had caved in on them. Finlay stepped carefully over and around the great slabs of concrete, avoiding the occasional sharp edges of ruptured steel. A guard stirred as he passed, and Finlay paused just long enough to cut the man's throat before moving on.

"Was that really necessary?" said Skye.

"Yes," said Finlay, not looking back. "Now he can't tell anyone which way we went. Never allow the enemy anything they can use against you."

Skye shook his head admiringly. "You're a real fighter, my friend. I haven't seen anyone like you since my brother Auric."

"What does he do?"

"He doesn't. He died in the Arena, butchered by the Masked Gladiator, may his soul rot in hell."

Finlay Campbell, who had once been known as the Masked Gladiator, said nothing. Together he and Julian Skye made their way through the devastated corridors of the interrogation center, and nobody stopped or challenged them. When they finally walked out the front door and saw what had happened to the surrounding city, they knew why.

They made their way through the ruins of the starport with no more trouble than anyone else. The streets might be blocked with debris from toppled buildings, but security was a joke. The authorities had their own problems to worry about. Skye found a way down into the largely untouched maintenance tunnels down below, and from there it was a relatively easy trip back to the underground center. Only to find that everyone was far too busy to talk to them. The main meeting chamber was a mass of confusion, swamped with people rushing this way and that, shouting orders and information to people who weren't listening. Finlay finally grabbed the nearest person, slammed him up against the nearest wall, stuck his face in close, and demanded to know what was going on. His victim glared at him incredulously.

"Where the hell have you been? Golgotha's been attacked by an alien starship! Completely unknown, like nothing anyone's ever seen before. It trashed most of the starport before it was finally driven off."

Finlay scowled. "What happened to the defense systems?"

"They're still down from the new rebels' attack on the Tax HQ! When the alien ship arrived, there was nothing left to stop it. The deaths and damage in the city have been horrific. We rode out most of it down here, but up above everything's gone to hell in a handcart, for us and the Empire. Most of our above ground agents are either dead or scattered. Communication chains have been shattered."

He was starting to babble, and Finlay shook him hard to get his attention back. "What's the underground doing to take advantage of the situation?"

"God only knows. Everyone's got a different idea or plan for saving the moment, or at least for providing damage limitation, but no one's listening to anyone else. I've heard everything suggested, from launching attacks on Empire installations while they're still vulnerable, to taking all the underground even deeper into the subsystems in order to avoid the inevitable backlash when Golgotha's population discovers the alien's attack was made possible only because the new rebels lowered the planetary defenses. Can I go now, please? I was on my way to the toilet, and if anything, my need is even worse now than it was."

Finlay let him go and led Skye through the crowd, listening to as many voices as he could. The only thing everyone seemed to agree on was that the whole mess was the fault of the new rebels. People had a lot of ideas about what should be done about them, with drawing and quartering coming a close second to very slow impalement.

And then the three esper leaders suddenly manifested in the center of the chamber, silencing the chaos with a telepathic bellow so loud that even Finlay heard it. Everyone subsided, holding their heads and wincing. Mr. Perfect, the mandala, and the dragon in its tree glared around them, and only a few people, including Finlay, were able to look back.

"If you've all quite finished running around like a chicken that's just had its nuts chopped off," said Mr. Perfect icily, "perhaps we could discuss the situation in a calm, intelligent, and above all quiet manner. First off, things are not as bad as they seem. Most of us came through the attack alive, thanks to how far we live beneath the surface. Our cells above can be rebuilt, and communications reestablished.

"However, we are in no condition to mount attacks against anybody, let alone Empire installations we have no way of even getting to through the current chaos. In addition, Finlay Campbell has returned safely with Julian Skye, against all the odds, rescued before he could be made to talk. So we need no longer worry about having to scatter again. Feel free to applaud, but keep the noise down. We've got a headache."

There was scattered applause, but the crowd remained restive and uncertain. Some parts seemed actually mutinous. Skye looked a little put out at the muted reaction to his safe return, but Finlay didn't give a damn. He hadn't done it for the applause. He looked around for Evangeline, or even Adrienne, but the crowd was too big. Mr. Perfect began speaking again, a frown marring his classical features, like graffiti on a famous portrait.

"It is imperative we establish proper contact with the new rebels as soon as possible. We sent Alexander Storm and the Stevie Blues to join the raiding party and return with them, but it's clear we're going to need a cooler, more politically minded envoy to represent our views in the future. We need an ambassador to link both of us together. It is vital that future raids or attacks be decided by both of us, in advance, precisely to prevent this kind of destruction happening again. What little good will the underground had among the general population vanished with the alien ship's first strafing run. The council has discussed this, and we have a volunteer to be our ambassador. Evangeline Shreck."

Finlay mouthed the word *no,* but his reaction was lost in the applause from the crowd, which this time seemed louder and more genuine. Evangeline was suddenly standing before the esper leaders, head respectfully bowed. She turned around to acknowledge the applause from the crowd, and her eyes met Finlay's as though she'd expected him to be right where he was. She looked away, but there was no guilt or weakness in her cold, composed face. Finlay started to push his way forward through the crowd. Skye tried to follow him, but lacked the strength to force his way past the people packed together before him. He called the Campbell's name, but if Finlay heard, he paid it no attention, and Skye was quickly left behind.

Finlay burst through the final few ranks, not caring if he hurt or affronted anyone. No one objected. Finlay's reputation as a swordsman and a crazy bastard was well-known throughout the underground. He stood face-to-face with Evangeline, and she met his gaze unflinchingly. Finlay took her by the arm and pulled her a little away from the esper leaders. She went with him unresistingly, but her face never changed.

"Why are you doing this, Evie?" he said finally. "Why are you going away and leaving me?"

"I'm not leaving you," Evangeline said calmly. "I'm just going on a mission. I'll be back before the year's out. My position as ambassador is only temporary, until the council can decide which of them will replace me."

"Why did they choose you?"

"Because I asked them. I wanted to go. I need to get away from things for a while. I've done too much, been involved in too much. I owe too many commitments to too many people, and I can't keep them straight in my head anymore. Leaving Golgotha will give me time to think. It's been a long time since I could just be myself, with no responsibilities to anyone but myself."

"You don't have to go do that. We can leave the under-ground, be together, just the two of us. I'm here only be-cause you are."

"That might have been true once, but not anymore. You said yourself, you need the action, the blood and slaughter of the missions they give you."

"None of that means more to me than you. You're the heart that beats in my breast, the air in my mouth. I can't live without you."

"Yes you can. For a while. I need this, Finlay. I need . . . I don't know what I need, but it isn't here. Adrienne helped me to see that."

Finlay nodded grimly. "I might have known she'd be at the back of this. She's never happy unless she's screwing up my life."

"No, Finlay. This was my decision. I need to get away from the subsystems, my father . . ."

"And me?"

"That, too. Nothing's really going to change. We hardly ever see each other anyway. I have my duties, and you're al-ways off on one of your missions . . ."

"That can change. I can change. What do you want from me?"

"Your understanding. I still love you, Finlay. I'll always love you, no matter where I am or you are. But I can't go on like this. It's tearing me apart, and I can't stand it any-more. I have to take some control of my life. Don't fight me on this, Finlay. It's important to me."

He took a deep breath and nodded abruptly. "Then it's im-portant to me, too. Go. I'll manage." He opened his arms to her, and she came into them, and for a long time they stood together, blind to the outside world. Finlay held her close, like a drowning man, and if his strength hurt her, she never said. He could feel tears prickling his eyes, but he wouldn't let them out. "What am I going to do without you, Evie?"

"You'll find something to keep yourself busy. You swore a blood oath, remember, on your name and honor, to avenge Jenny Psycho and what was done to her, to put an end to Silo Nine and the system that produced it. Now the council has seen what you can do, they'll give you more important work in the underground. If you ask them."

"Maybe." He pushed her gently away and looked search-ingly into her eyes. "You do what you need to do, Evie.

That's all that matters in the end. But I still wish they could have chosen someone else."

"Everyone else was too important, too well connected, or too busy. The only use they had for me was my influence over my father and to keep you in line. My father and I . . . have become estranged. And I promised the council you wouldn't be a problem. Don't make a liar out of me. They chose me because I have proven diplomatic skills, and because I'm entirely expendable. I was the perfect candidate."

"We seem fated to be kept apart," said Finlay. "Someday, when all this is over, maybe we'll be able to have a simple, everyday life together, like everyone else. I'd like that."

"Yes," said Evangeline. "So would I."

There was a sudden commotion behind them as everyone turned to look at someone who'd just entered the chamber. An excited babble began as the crowd recognized who it was. There was cheering and applause, and a name ran through the crowd, growing louder and louder, from a chant to a roar to a battle cry. *Jenny Psycho! Jenny Psycho! Jenny Psycho!"*

"Oh, hell," said Finlay. "Just what we need. More complications."

Jenny Psycho, who used to be called Diana Vertue, but had mostly forgotten that, was short and blond with a pale face dominated by sharp blue eyes. She had a large mouth and a smile that showed more teeth than humor. Once she'd been just another low-level esper, like so many others, but then the underground had planted her in the notorious esper prison Silo Nine to be their agent. The uber-esper Mater Mundi had manifested through her to blow the place apart. Jenny had been touched by greatness, transformed by the Mater Mundi's fleeting presence, and since her escape from Wormboy Hell, she'd become a new, major force in the underground. She'd taken the code name for her own and entered esper politics with a vengeance. Wherever she went, a small crowd of fanatical followers went with her, and they were with her now, scowling at anyone who dared to get too close. Finlay sometimes wondered whether she was a political force or a religious icon. Perhaps she wasn't sure herself. Certainly her popularity had been growing in leaps and bounds of late. It must have if someone as disinterested as Finlay had noticed it.

Having made one of her usual unexpected and highly dramatic entrances, Jenny Psycho pressed forward and the crowd opened up before her, as though pushed back by the sheer force of her personality. She'd become one of the most powerful espers the underground had ever known, and you could feel it in her presence. It all but crackled on the air around her, a palpable force that was part charisma and part enigma. A rabble-rouser, a cunning politician, and a tireless warrior for esper rights and wrongs, she was respected, worshiped, and adored by the many, and watched very carefully by the esper leaders.

She was also just a little crazy, but people made allowances. No one expected saints to be normal. She had been touched by Our Mother Of All Souls, and with the Mater Mundi currently quiet and unavailable, people were willing to settle for the next best thing. She stopped at the front of the crowd before the esper leaders and smiled unpleasantly, as though she could see past the images they projected to the real people beneath. Who knew? Maybe she could. Evangeline leaned in close beside Finlay.

"If I'd known she was going to turn out such a pain in the ass, I'd have thought twice about springing her from Silo Nine."

Finlay shrugged. "She preaches direct action, and that's a popular stance to take these days. And she was a focus for the Mater Mundi."

"So were you and I, and we're no crazier now than we were before. Though admittedly, it's hard to tell in your case."

Finlay smiled despite himself and made himself concentrate on Jenny Psycho as she began speaking. She had a harsh, unattractive voice. She'd damaged her vocal cords screaming in Wormboy Hell. It didn't matter. When she spoke, you had to listen. You had to.

"I'm back again, people. Make the most of me while I'm here. The Empire threw me into Silo Nine and put a worm in my head to control me, but with the Mater Mundi's help I broke out. You can break out, too. Work with me, and we can all become more than we are. No one can compel me now; not even the worm they left in my head. The council said taking it out would kill me, but I don't believe that anymore. Watch. And learn."

She pushed her long golden hair back behind her ears, so that her face could be clearly seen. She put a hand to her forehead and frowned, as though listening or concentrating.

Her left temple bulged outward suddenly, and the skin broke, splitting apart. Blood ran down Jenny's face, but she ignored it. There was a sharp, cracking sound, and the bone of her skull broke apart at the left temple. Something small and gray and bloody crawled out of the crack, and fell into Jenny's waiting hand. It pulsed and twitched feebly, a genetically engineered horror that existed only to imprison and torture captive minds. Jenny closed her hand around the worm and crushed it with one swift gesture. Blood and gray pulp oozed through her fingers. Jenny opened her hand and let what was left fall to the ground.

The crowd went mad, cheering and applauding and stamping their feet. Jenny Psycho began to speak again, but Finlay wasn't listening. He appreciated the theater of what she'd done, but distrusted her message. The call to direct action was all very well and fine—he'd raised it himself on more than one occasion—but there was nothing of strategy or planning in Jenny's call. All the underground had to do was trust in her and the Mater Mundi, and all would be well. And the crowd believed that because they wanted to. She promised strength and revenge and glory, and everything else the beaten down craved so desperately. Finlay looked out over the cheering crowd and wasn't impressed.

Drowning men will clutch at any straw.

CHAPTER FOUR

Raised Voices and Diversions

Lionstone XIV, that most revered and feared Empress of a thousand worlds and more, was holding Court once again, and everyone that mattered, or thought they might, made haste to attend her. The Court itself was an arctic waste, this time, as real as holographic projections, strategically placed props, and temperature controls could make it. The Empress redressed her Court constantly, to reflect her whims and changing moods, or just to give her courtiers a bad time. Veteran Court attendees claimed to be able to divine much of Lionstone's mood from studying each new Court, but even when the news was bad, people went anyway. You had to, if you wanted your voice to be heard. Besides, if you stayed away too often, Lionstone might take that as an insult. And the people she sent to drag you there to hear her displeasure would not be polite about it.

The Court itself was a single vast chamber somewhere within the Imperial Palace, set within a massive steel bunker deep below the surface of Golgotha. No one knew precisely how big the chamber was, for security reasons, but so far it had always proven big enough to hold whatever worlds or conditions Lionstone chose to re-create. Unfortunately, it also reflected her sense of humor, which could be pretty basic on occasion. Courtiers knew better than to sit down on anything, no matter how apparently comfortable, and approached the luxurious food and wine provided as a form of Russian roulette.

It was a long way down to the Court. People made jokes about descending into hell, but not very loudly.

Captain Silence, Investigator Frost, and Security Officer Stelmach stood together in the midst of a great crowd of courtiers, staring out over a bleak arctic waste that stretched off into the distance for as far as the eye could see. The snow was a good foot deep on the ground and more fell in heavy wet flakes from the brooding gray sky above. A thin mist pearled the air, thickening briefly here and there into impenetrable walls. It was bitter cold, searing exposed flesh and the lungs of those who breathed too deeply, and Silence turned up the heating elements in his uniform another notch. Frost didn't bother. It took more than mere cold to discommode an Investigator. She'd been trained to withstand far worse. Stelmach already had his heating elements running on full, but shivered anyway. He wasn't looking forward to meeting the Empress.

Whatever else might prove to be an illusion, the cold was real enough; sharp enough to kill an unprotected man eventually. And there were bound to be other more subtle dangers concealed at random throughout the Court. The Empress never found a joke really funny unless someone could get hurt. The falling snow was especially real. It collected wetly on heads and clothes and seemed to be getting heavier. Someone had gone to a lot of trouble to re-create this environment, which suggested the appropriate life-forms were out there somewhere, too. Especially, the predators. Lionstone had a special fondness for the practical joke.

The gathered courtiers murmured among themselves for a while, and then some brave soul stepped forward, and everyone else trudged through the snow after him. Few had come prepared for arctic conditions, and the bright flashing silks of current fashion did little to protect their wearers. A few grumbled and blasphemed under their breath, but most just toughed it out. You never knew who might be listening. Silence stepped out along with the crowd, still somewhat surprised that he wasn't weighed down with chains like his last visit to Court. After screwing up so completely on the Wolfling World, he'd fully expected to find himself facing an execution warrant the moment he stepped off his ship, but apparently his victory over the attacking alien ship had bought him some extra time, if nothing else.

Frost strode along at his side as though the snow wasn't there, seemingly unconcerned by anything. There wasn't much that bothered Investigators, if only because they tended to kill things that did. V. Stelmach trudged along in her shadow, using her tall form as a windbreak. His arms were wrapped tightly across his chest, and he was pouting sulkily. Stelmach was not happy. But, then, he rarely was.

Being a Security Officer did that to you. Especially, if your name was Valiant.

The crowd labored on through the packed snow, slipping and lurching and fighting for balance. The mists were growing thicker, obscuring the distance. Silence watched his breath steam on the air before him and wondered what lay ahead. If he had any sense he'd be running for his life rather than presenting his head to the Empress so she could cut it off personally, but he knew his duty. The Service was his life, and if it had been a hard life for the most part, he still wouldn't have chosen any other. As a Captain in the Imperial Navy he was part of something greater, in the service of humanity, and he would give his life for it, should that prove necessary. Lionstone might be a vindictive psychotic with a particularly unfortunate sense of humor, but she was his Empress, and he had sworn upon his life and his honor to serve her all his days. He looked about him at the subzero world and smiled slightly. Typical of Lionstone. Here he was, walking to his execution like a good soldier, and she even had to make that difficult.

He looked around sharply as he sensed as much as heard something large moving up ahead, hidden in the mists. Murmurs moved through the crowd as others heard or saw it. Silence's eyes narrowed, and his hand fell to his hip, where his gun should have been. Glimpses of something large moved through the mist, seen and gone in a moment. It moved ponderously, crunching loudly through the snow, and then suddenly raised a shaggy head and roared defiantly. The harsh sound echoed eerily on the quiet, and then the mists came down again, and the creature was lost to sight. The courtiers huddled together for comfort but kept moving. The Empress was waiting.

Silence's hands itched for a weapon, but gun and sword were both denied him. No subject, no matter how trusted or exalted, was allowed to bear weapons before his Empress, without a special dispensation. Which meant everyone around Silence was unarmed, too. Easy pickings if the creature decided it was hungry. The Empress would have to be crazy to risk endangering the Families with a real threat, but no one would have bet against it. Silence scowled, his hands curling into fists. A dim shape roared again, but the sound was farther off. It was moving away. The crowd breathed a general sigh of relief, and the pace picked up again. There was always the chance the shape was just another hologram, but no one was willing to bet on that, either. Silence decided he was going to stick really close to the Investigator. Even unarmed, Frost was death on two legs, and he'd back her against anything Lionstone might have imported. Not that he'd ever tell Frost that. She was bigheaded enough as it was.

More shapes loomed up out of the mists ahead. At first Silence thought they were security guards waiting to escort the courtiers to the Iron Throne, but as he drew closer he could see they were just snowmen. A line of human shapes, made from packed snow, with cheerful scarves around their necks, coals for eyes, and a smile drawn on. They might have been charming if they hadn't all been depicted dying in different, innovative ways. One had been impaled on a lance. Another held its severed head in its hands. Beside it, a third form had been dismembered, its snow limbs lying scattered around its body. Silence started to walk past them, then hesitated as he realized Frost had stopped. The Investigator stood scowling at the snowmen, one hand patting her hip where her sword should have been. Stelmach stood shivering beside her, not particularly interested in the snowmen, but unwilling to move on without the protection of the only more or less friendly faces he knew. Silence moved in beside Frost.

"What is it, Investigator? Problem?"

"I don't know, Captain. Maybe. There's something about these snowmen. Something . . . disturbing. Who makes a snowman with limbs?"

She stepped up to the decapitated snowman and took the snow head out of its cupped hands. It was a large round ball of snow, with a wide smile cut beneath the blind coal eyes. Frost grunted at the unexpected weight of the head and balanced it in the crook of her arm while she scraped away at the surface of the snow with her other hand. The eyes and smile disappeared. Silence knew what she was going to find before he saw it. The surface snow disappeared to reveal the nose and staring eyes of a real face. Frost carefully swept away more snow to uncover the human features beneath. Silence didn't recognize the face. He moved forward and thrust his hand deep into the snow body. His fingertips thudded against something hard and unyielding that definitely wasn't packed snow. He pulled his hand out quickly, and rubbed it clean against his hip.

"There's a real body in there," he said quietly.

"Can't say I'm surprised, Captain." Frost threw the head aside. "Shall I check the other snowmen?"

"No need. They're all dead men. Lionstone's way of telling us what's coming. I wonder who they were."

Frost shrugged. "People who upset the Empress. Never any shortage of them. Let's go."

"What's the hurry?" snapped Stelmach. "Make the most of what little time we've got left."

"Don't give up hope," said Silence. "Frost and I have been here before, and we survived. Maybe we'll get lucky this time as well."

"No one's that lucky," said Stelmach.

"Don't worry," said Frost. "We'll put in a good word for you."

"Oh, great," said Stelmach. "That's all I need."

They moved on, trudging doggedly through the deep snow to catch up with the rest of the courtiers. Some of them must have seen what was inside the snowmen, but they were all doing their best to pretend they hadn't. Success at Court often depended on being very selective as to what you saw. The snow fell and the mists thickened and still the arctic scene stretched out before them. Silence frowned. The courtroom couldn't be that large. Perhaps they were being subtly influenced to walk in circles. He looked up sharply as an agitated murmur began again among the courtiers. The crowd lurched to a halt, those on the edges looking quickly about them. Nothing moved in the mists. Silence looked at Frost, who was listening carefully. She gestured for him to lean close so that she could murmur in his ear.

"There's something moving under the snow, Captain. It's large and alive. I can feel the vibrations, and I can hear the sounds it makes as it moves."

"A snow snake, perhaps," said Silence. "They have those on Loki. Some of the big ones run to twenty feet long."

"Oh, no," said Stelmach. "Not snakes. I really don't like snakes."

"Don't worry," said Silence soothingly. "If it annoys the Investigator, she'll tie it in a square knot and throw it away. Right, Frost?"

"Damn right," said Frost.

And that was when a set of jaws ten feet wide opened up beneath a courtier's feet, gulped him down, and disappeared back into the concealing snow. His friends and Family shouted in alarm and fell to their knees to dig at the snow with their bare hands, but there was no trace left of whatever had taken him. They looked at each other helplessly, and far away in the snow and mists came the light tinkling of laughter. The Empress was amused. Some of the courtiers began talking calmingly to those still on their knees. There was nothing to be done. Man proposes and the Empress disposes, and that was just the way it was in the Empire these days. Silence said nothing, but his face was set and grim.

The snow surged up suddenly at the crowd's edge as the snow creature's blunt head broke the surface. People scattered with shouts and shrieks. The great mouth opened and spat out the courtier it had taken. The head dropped back into the snow and disappeared. The courtier sailed through the air and hit the packed snow hard, but his plaintive groan showed that at least he was still alive. His friends clustered around him, checked that he was basically undamaged, and got him on his feet again. Lionstone laughed again, and everyone who liked their head where it was laughed along with her. Even the courtier who'd briefly seen the inside of something much larger than he was managed a shaky laugh. Though he was probably just glad to be alive. Frost looked at Silence.

"Big snake."

Stelmach nodded rapidly, his eyes very large.

The courtiers trudged on again, driving their legs through the deep snow. It actually seemed to be getting colder, if that was possible. Hoarfrost was forming on hair and beards, and melting snow soaked into light clothing. Everyone was shivering, and some were shaking violently. Silence could feel the cold gnawing at his bones despite running the heating elements in his uniform on full. His nose and ears ached, and he could feel crystals of ice forming at the corners of his eyes. Stelmach was shaking as though he had a small juddering engine inside him. Frost, of course, didn't deign to shiver. The courtiers had packed close together for support and shared body warmth, but they still kept clear of Silence, Frost, and Stelmach. They knew pariahs when they saw them. They'd all stopped talking and settled for concentrating on surviving Lionstone's latest practical joke. Everyone agreed it had been a dark day for the Empire in general and the Court in particular when the Empress decided she had a sense of humor.

Strange shapes loomed up out of the mists ahead, huge shards of solid ice thrusting up out of the snow like the only part of the iceberg you ever see. The falling snow swirled around them, as though attracted to the glistening planes of ice. There were statues scattered among the huge shards, carved into sharp-edged, disturbing shapes. Silence looked from the statues to the shards and wondered if they'd been carved and shaped, too, into ancient enigmatic shapes that only mankind's distant ancestors might have recognized and responded to. The ice structures formed a rough semicircle, inviting the courtiers in, and there at the far end stood the Iron Throne, set up high on a great block of ice. And on that ancient chair of black iron studded with jade sat the Empress Lionstone XIV, calmly watching their stumbling approach.

She was wrapped in layers of thick furs, like some ancient tribal leader, her pale face as cold and clear as the legendary Ice Queen, who stole men's souls by sliding shards of ice into their eyes and hearts. She had a long, sharp-planed face, with a wide slash of a mouth and brilliant blue eyes, colder than any ice could ever be. She was beautiful, but that, too, was a cold kind of beauty, like the tall diamond crown on her head. The Empress, the worshiped and adored, whose whims were law and at whose merest word men died and worlds burned. Also known as the Iron Bitch.

She sat at ease on the Iron Throne, watching with a sardonic smile as the courtiers drew up before her, bowed their heads, and then held themselves in that humble and uncomfortable position while they waited for the word from the Empress that would release them. On bad days, she'd been known to keep them there for ages, till sweat dropped off their faces and their backs screamed for release. Today, she gave them permission to straighten up after only a few seconds, suggesting either she was in a good mood after all or she was really looking forward to something yet to come. The courtiers practiced looking polite and respectful and extremely loyal as the Empress's smile wandered over them.

They also kept a respectful distance, not just because of the twenty armed guards spread out behind the Throne, but also because of Lionstone's maids-in-waiting, who crouched snarling silently at her feet. There were ten of them, each more dangerous than any armed man. They wore no clothes, but they didn't feel the cold. They didn't feel anything unless the Empress permitted it. Mind techs had stirred their sticky fingers in the maids' brains until nothing remained there but unquestioning obedience to the Empress. They would die to protect her. Or kill, as required. They were cunning, deadly fighters, with hidden implanted weaponry. They were silent because they had no tongues, and they perceived the world only through grafted cybernetic senses. Their fingers had steel claws. They clustered together at the base of the Iron Throne, glaring at the courtiers, waiting eagerly to be unleashed on anyone foolish enough to displease their mistress. But for once, not even they were enough to hold the courtiers' gaze. Beside the Throne, standing a little to one side in the swirling snow, huge and awful, stood a yoked Grendel alien.

On the planet called Grendel, genetically engineered creatures lay sleeping in deep-buried vaults. Thousands upon thousands of them, an army waiting for an enemy that never came. The alien civilization that created them was long gone, but their work lived on. Unstoppable killing machines, living weapons, programmed to fight on until either they or the enemy was destroyed. An Empire exploratory team made the mistake of opening one of the ancient vaults, and the Sleepers emerged in a fury of blood and slaughter. They wiped out all the team and overran the exploratory camp on the surface in a matter of minutes. Hundreds of men and women died screaming, their weapons useless, and not one Grendel fell. In the end they had no starships, so were trapped on the planet's surface. The Empress gave the order for the planet's surface to be scorched from orbit, and that was the end of the Grendels. Except for those still sleeping in the vaults deep below. Lionstone put the planet under quarantine, and left starcruisers there to enforce it.

But faced with the threat of unknown alien foes massing against the Empire, Lionstone had conceived of a new plan: to waken and control the Grendels and use them as shock troops. And now here one stood, a thick cybernetic yoke gleaming on its shoulders, controlling the creature's thoughts. Theoretically. Everyone eyed the Grendel warily and hoped fervently that this time the scientists had got all the bugs out in advance. The Grendel alien stood nine feet tall, in spiked crimson silicon armor that was somehow a part of it. It had vicious fangs and claws and was roughly humanoid in shape, but its large heart-shaped face had nothing even remotely like a human expression. Just one of the creatures had wiped out a whole company of Silence's men when he went down to the vaults to capture and control the aliens, before he brought it down, as much by luck as anything. And now here one was in Court, with only a prototype yoke holding back its perpetual killing rage.

More than ever Silence wished he had his weapons with him. Or at least some idea which way the exit was. The courtiers studied the Grendel silently and were not happy. They understood the need for increased security at Court, after previous attacks by both aliens and elves, but a personal Grendel on a leash was going a bit far, even for Lionstone. This had gone beyond safety or style and headed firmly in the direction of overkill. Possibly literally. Those at the front of the crowd were seized with a sudden polite wish for others to take up their privileged vantage point and attempted to fade back into the crowd. The rank behind them were having none of this and resisted strongly. If the yoke should fail, everyone knew better than to think the armed guards would try to protect them. That wasn't what they were there for. The courtiers somehow managed to stir rebelliously in complete silence. Frost leaned in close beside Stelmach, who jumped slightly. Frost didn't smile.

"I thought you said you were the only one with a yoked Grendel. And that one was destroyed on Haden. So what's this doing here?"

"Apparently, research has moved on in my absence," said Stelmach, his voice little more than a whisper, trying to talk without moving his lips so as to avoid drawing attention to himself. Frost frowned heavily.

"Just how dependable is that yoke?"

"Depends what you mean by dependable. Unless they've made some major breakthrough, which I strongly doubt, the yoke is strictly on/off. Once the Grendel's been unleashed it will kill anything it sees. The best you can hope to do is make sure it's aimed in the right direction. If that yoke follows the processes my people set up, it should do its job, but I wouldn't like to bet my life on it."

"We are betting our lives on it," said Silence.

"I know," said Stelmach, unhappily.

Silence looked about him, not bothering to hide his interest. He had no doubt there were more armed guards around that he couldn't see, probably hidden behind concealing holograms. Plus any number of esp-blockers, to keep out esper terrorists. And a whole set of other protections he probably wouldn't even recognize. The Empress was said to have spent more than one fortune making her Courtroom as secure as was humanly and inhumanly possible. It wasn't just paranoia. There were a lot of people who would like to see Lionstone dead, who'd dance at her funeral and piss on her grave. Quite a lot of them could be found among the courtiers, which was why they were only admitted unarmed after a complete body scan. Sometimes answering a summons to Court could turn out to be a death sentence for someone who hadn't been as careful at plotting as he thought he'd been. It didn't stop the Families coming to Court. It was, after all, where things happened. The best place to see and be seen, watched on billions of holos across the Empire. The only place where they could have their say in how things were decided. And despite their justified nervousness, a great many of the courtiers were determined to be heard.

For the first time in years, they were pretty sure they had a chance to force power out of Lionstone's hands and into theirs. They had something that if properly handled might just drive a wedge between the Empress and the military that supported her. The rebels' triumphant trashing on the Tax and Tithe Headquarters, along with their breaking open of the planet's defenses, had made the military's position very vulnerable, politically speaking. The sudden alien attack had only emphasized this. And on top of everything else that had happened, the Empire's Warrior Prime, the Empress's own official Consort and good right hand, the Lord High Dram, was strongly rumored to be dead. Killed on some faraway planet, on an unknown mission entirely unauthorized by the Court.

The only people said to know for sure were the crew of the *Dauntless,* and they were being held in strict quarantine on their ship in orbit. Except for Silence, Frost, and Stelmach. There were a lot of eyes following their every move, but the courtiers gave them plenty of room, too, just in case. They were pretty sure Lionstone had something in mind for these three, and it might well turn out to be messy. Silence was aware of the Court's undercurrents, and the way the courtiers were looking at the Empress. He couldn't help thinking they had a point. If Lionstone and her military couldn't protect her own planet from a single alien ship and a handful of rebels, she and they were in no position to try and dictate terms to the Company of Lords and the Members of Parliament, whose monies helped to pay for everything. The bottom line of which was, if they were going to pay higher taxes for the Empire's security, they wanted more of a say in how that money was to be spent. And preferably before the tax records could be worked out again and the new rates decided.

Not being blind to all this, the military had taken steps to establish a strong presence among the courtiers. Officers of all ranks and stature, from the highest to the very high, stood at attention before the Throne. If the cold was bothering them, they were doing their best not to show it, though snow had accumulated on their heads and the shoulders of their uniforms. They had come to Court to make it clear that the Empress still enjoyed the military's support and confidence. And, of course, vice versa. The military was there to protect Lionstone against all threats; even those that might come from the Court itself. Though not above playing politics, when necessary, all branches of the Services owed their allegiance to the Empress, first and foremost. It was a matter of honor, which in the military at least, still ranked above politics—mostly.

The Church of Christ the Warrior had its own strong presence, with ranks of armored acolytes standing alongside the military and studiously ignoring them. They had pale faces and shaved heads and the unblinking glare of the true fanatic. They were warrior priests, raised in a hot and bloody faith since childhood; and they bowed to the Empress only when circumstances forced them to it. The Church believed in enforcing the faith, even if it meant killing the very people they were supposed to be converting. It preached that might was right, by God's will, and was always ready and eager to provide practical examples. There were other religions in the Empire, but mostly they kept their heads down and tried to avoid being noticed.

General Shaw Beckett stood at the very front of the crowd, and studied the ranks of robed acolytes thoughtfully. He didn't bother to hide his interest. Some of them were watching him just as intently, and for the same reason. Know thy enemy. Beckett smiled and blew a cloud of cigar smoke at them. Faith was all very well, but he preferred training. Just because a fanatic isn't afraid to die, it doesn't necessarily follow that he'll be able to get the job done before the enemy kills him. The General was an old soldier, and took the Church of Christ the Warrior with a large pinch of salt. He'd been a legendary fighter in his day, and even though he was now very clearly in his twilight years, no one crossed him without taking the precaution of making out their will first.

He was of average height, but extremely fat, and this made him appear shorter. Most of his weight had accumulated around his waist, so much so that even his specially tailored battle armor had to strain to hold him in, but he didn't give a damn. He'd spent enough years in the field that he felt he'd earned his little comforts now. His value these days lay in his years of experience at the sharp end, and his brilliant, incisive military mind. He was renowned as a master tactician, and a wily debater, and rarely failed to get his own way, even when the Empress was in one of her moods and everyone else had run for cover. She was constantly on the verge of having him dragged away for saying the wrong thing at the wrong moment, or insisting on a truth she didn't want to hear, but somehow he always found a way to remind her of how valuable he was to her, and the Empire. Besides, he made her laugh. Shaw Beckett smoked thick cigars, even in places where he wasn't permitted to, and liked to blow the smoke in people's faces while he was talking to them. He had other bad habits, too, and gloried in them. Not surprisingly, he was very popular with the watching holo audiences.

The Church had a private but widely known bounty for anyone who would bring the Church the General's head, preferably unattached to the body.

The Church of Christ the Warrior had grown increasingly large and powerful since Lionstone made it the official religion of the Empire and gave it her backing. It ran exhaustive purges in her name, killed off every heretic it could get its hands on, and then decreed it had grown so powerful through God's will that it didn't need the Empress's support anymore. As the foremost Church in the Empire, Lionstone should bow to them. This didn't go down at all well with Lionstone, but having made them the official Church after a very public baptism, she couldn't back down now without looking weak and indecisive. And they did have one hell of a following. So she settled for sharpening the claws of her humor on them at every opportunity, and backing the military against the Church whenever they came into conflict. Which was pretty often, these days.

The Church retaliated by increasing its ranks of deadly Jesuit commandos, and set about infiltrating society from top to bottom. Every Family had lost someone to the clutches of the Church, either as a member or a proclaimed heretic. As a result, people now had two masters they needed to please if they were to have anything approaching a quiet life: the Empress and the Church. Choose the wrong one at the wrong time, and you could end up in a world of trouble. As far as the Church was concerned, even Family loyalties and considerations should come second to the needs of the Church.

This did not go down at all well with the Company of Lords, who tended not to give a damn what the lower orders chose to believe in, as long as they remained respectful and hardworking, but had little time themselves to worship anything apart from profit and status. So this new attitude of the Church had infuriated the noble Families, who made it very clear that they were determined to continue their age-old freedom to intrigue, lust, duel and generally kick ass as they saw fit.

The Church, on the other hand, started with the belief that everyone was secretly guilty of something, and were always on the lookout for ammunition they could use to bring down the powerful, and bend them to the Church's will. So they persuaded, encouraged, bribed, and threatened the lower orders to spy on their masters, and report useful items, if they wished to avoid the Church's displeasure. The Families retaliated by launching their own purges among the lower orders. Everyone caught in between kept their heads well down and hoped not to be noticed. With the overall result that life in the Empire had of late become a great deal more complicated for everyone.

"The Church has been busy since we were last here," murmured Silence to Frost. "Those warrior priests look impressive. And there are a damn sight more of them than there used to be."

"Bunch of pansies," said Frost, not even deigning to look at them. "They're good at looking tough, but that's about it.

I could carve them up and eat them raw without even a decent red wine to wash them down. I know the type. Brave enough in packs, but gutless in a fair fight. They're so keen to worship God, let them pick a fight with me, and I'll send them up so they can have a personal chat with him."

"If you're going to keep on talking like that, kindly give me some warning," said Stelmach. "So I can stay well away from you. The Church has extremely keen hearing these days, and it never forgives a slight or an insult. Oh, God, one of them's coming this way. Try and look penitent."

"I wouldn't know how," said Frost.

Silence somehow managed to keep a straight face as the warrior priest approached, courtiers falling well back to give him plenty of room. He wore a long bloodred gown and skullcap, and an expression stern enough to cut glass. He was in his mid twenties and trying to look older. Two scalps hung from his belt, and a necklace of human ears hung around his neck. He stopped before Silence and Frost, ignoring Stelmach, who was quite happy to be ignored. The warrior priest looked from Silence to Frost and back again, his expression suggesting he'd seen more impressive specimens lying facedown on tavern floors, eating the sawdust.

"They say you saved us all from the Godless alien craft," said the priest. "If you did, it was by God's will. You are both fine warriors, by all accounts, but you must learn your place in the new scheme of things. You must seek the Church's exemption for your sins and failures, as well as Lionstone's. To stand alone is no longer permitted. You must decide where you stand, and with who, and state it publicly. And remember, if you do not stand with the Church, you stand against it. And the Church knows how to deal with its enemies. Do I make myself clear?"

His sneer disappeared suddenly as Frost drop-kicked him from a standing start. The force of the blow picked the warrior priest up and threw him back among his own people, scattering them like ninepins. There was much moaning and groaning and clutching of injured parts. The warrior priest who'd started it all lay curled up in a ball, trying to persuade his lungs to start working again. Frost had regained her feet, her face calm. She wasn't even breathing hard. Stelmach covered his eyes with his hand. Silence applauded. Some of the braver courtiers joined in. Frost ignored them all magnificently, every inch an Investigator.

"I don't think I want to stand anywhere near you two," said Stelmach. "You must have a death wish."

"Lighten up," said Silence. "We've probably been brought here to die anyway, remember? What does it matter who gets to kill us?"

Stelmach glanced briefly at the Empress on her Iron Throne, and then looked at Silence almost pleadingly. "You're sure, then? We've no hope at all?"

"Oh, there's always hope," said Silence. "The last time we were here, Frost and I, they had us in chains from nose to toes, and all the execution warrants needed was our names in the right places. We survived. Our chances are, if anything, rather worse this time, but at least we're not in chains. I choose to see that as an encouraging sign."

"I don't," said Frost. "They're just being subtle. Nothing like providing a false hope to really put the screws to someone."

Stelmach sighed. "I had hoped some of my Family might turn up, to provide a little moral support, at least, but no. No one's here to see me die. A failure has no kin or friends, for fear it might rub off."

Silence looked at him. "That was almost profound. Obviously being this close to sudden death inspires you. You never talk much, Stelmach. Tell us about your Family. What kind of people christen their son Valiant?"

"Ambitious people," said Stelmach grimly. "My people were in business, but not successful enough to become a Minister or marry into a Clan. So we were all packed off into the military at an early age. My brothers, Bold and Hero, are mid-line officers. My sister, Athena, was taken away even younger to be an Investigator. I don't know what became of her. One doesn't ask. My father died long ago, so he never got to see me disappoint him. Security Officers aren't exactly the most glamorous rank in the army."

"At least you still have a Family," said Silence. "I became a Captain because my Clan expected it of me. And I wanted them to be proud of me. Instead, twice now I've brought the Family name into disrepute. Officially, they disowned me when I failed to go down with my first ship, the *Darkwind*. I was ready to, but the Investigator here insisted on saving me, for her own inscrutable reasons. Isn't that right, Frost?"

"We all make mistakes," said Frost, not looking at him. Silence smiled slightly.

"Aren't you going to tell us about your family, Investigator? We've both opened our hearts here. Tell us where you came from."

There was a long pause, until Silence had almost decided he'd pushed it too far, and then Frost spoke very quietly, so that Silence and Stelmach had to concentrate to make out her words. She didn't look at either of them as she spoke.

"Officially, Investigators have no Family but each other. But I was curious, so I broke into the right hidden files and checked out my background. I found my parents' address and went to visit them. Only my father would agree to see me. I tried to talk to him, but he wouldn't listen. He was afraid of me. I never went back. No Family made me, Captain. I made me, with a little help from the Empire."

"I'm glad we had this little talk," said Stelmach. "I was feeling a bit depressed, but now I've moved on to feeling actually suicidal. Why don't we all just swallow our tongues now and get it over with?"

"Because there's still hope," said Silence. "And because even if I am going down, I'll still fight them every inch of the way. Right, Investigator?"

"Right," said Frost. "Oh, look, the warrior priests seem to be recovering."

The priests had got their breath back and were now back on their feet, though still leaning on each other for support. The military were openly chuckling and nudging each other. Some of the courtiers began to applaud again, and then stopped and looked to see if the Empress approved. Luckily for all concerned, Lionstone was apparently deep in conversation with General Beckett. So everyone else turned to look at the other man standing in front of the crowd before the Iron Throne: James Kassar, Cardinal of the Church of Christ the Warrior.

Said by many to be one of the most dangerous men in the Empire, he was tall and muscular, and wore black battle armor as though born to it. A large crucifix stood out in bas-relief on the armor over his heart. He'd been handsome once, but not anymore. Kassar had had a man executed as a heretic on questionable grounds, and the man's widow threw acid in the Cardinal's face. He struck her down a moment later, gutting her with his sword, but the damage had been done. His right eye was gone, eaten right out of the socket, and the right side of his face had been burned down to the skull beneath, so that discolored pitted bone showed clearly through ragged strips of flesh. His teeth gleamed through the remnants of his right cheek, giving him a constant ghastly half smile that had humor in it. His face was a fright mask to turn the strongest stomach, and he knew it. That was why he'd never had it healed. A regeneration machine would have smoothed the terrible wounds away, but he chose not to. Perhaps as a sign that nothing could stop or hurt him, perhaps as a reverse kind of vanity. There were those who thought it pleased Kassar to have a face that made others quail.

There were also those who said he'd had the guards who let the woman slip past them arrested and then lowered into a vat of acid, feet first, one inch at a time. Few people had trouble believing the story. Cardinal Kassar was known for his cold rages and a vindictiveness that masqueraded as a thirst for justice. He'd risen rapidly through the ranks of the Church through leading vigorous crusades against heretics, which could be anyone who challenged his or the Church's authority. He didn't hesitate to accuse anyone who stood against the Church's rising influence or who got in the way of his own personal ascent, even if they were friends or Family or previous allies. And as he rose through the ranks with unprecedented speed, people hurried to copy his zeal, if they knew what was good for them.

As a result, a useful way of dealing with one's enemies was to accuse them of heresy. No proof was needed; often the accusation was enough. There were tribunals, where the accused could present their defense, but they cost money. Justice has never come cheap. Things got so bad some people tried to take out insurance against being accused, to cover possible legal fees, only to discover the premiums were more expensive than the fees. That was when the courtiers first realized no one was safe anymore. The Empress wasn't slow to pick up on this and found the practice particularly useful for helping her keep her Court in order. If anyone started making trouble or getting above themselves, the word would go out and the unfortunate victim would be awakened in the early hours by the sound of holy boots kicking his door down. Soon anyone who even annoyed Lionstone had better have very strong ties with the Church, or a lot of money to hire lawyers. If you could find a lawyer brave enough to take on the Church these days.

The courtiers played the same dangerous game, denouncing each other every day for political, Family, or personal reasons, but they were taken less seriously. The truth quickly vanished in a morass of claims and counterclaims, until even the Church grew sick of it. So they just recorded everything, to be kept for future ammunition, as necessary.

Valentine Wolfe had been denounced so many times for all kinds of heresy that the Church lost count, including some that had previously been thought to be only theoretically possible, but the charges never stuck. No one doubted that he was an utter degenerate, with a drug habit strong enough to have killed half a dozen normal men, but as head of the Empire's first Family, incredibly rich and powerful, with the Empress's ear and support, he was for all practical purposes completely untouchable. Some wits made remarks about barge poles, but never when Valentine was around. Kassar still hadn't given up on him, but for the time being they settled for conspicuously ignoring each other. The courtiers watched avidly. Everyone knew the situation couldn't go on forever. It was just a question of which one made a misstep first; and then there'd be blood and hair on the walls.

People had been laying bets for months.

Valentine Wolfe stood a little alone in the heart of the crowd, as he always did. He was the head of the first Family on Golgotha, his every word a command for thousands of people, but he had no friends, or anyone who could say they were close to him. Valentine didn't give a damn. He never had. He'd always found himself infinitely better company than any of those who surrounded him. And given his continuing experimentation with every drug under the sun, and a few that grew only in darkness, his inner world was more than enough to occupy him in his quiet moments.

Valentine was tall and slender and darkly delicate, like a fairy-tale demon prince, only more unreal. His face was long and thin and dyed a perfect white. Heavy mascara surrounded his overbright eyes, and a thickly painted crimson smile gave his face its only expression. Jet-black hair fell to his shoulders in thick curls and ringlets that had never known a comb. He wore dark clothes with the occasional splash of color, red for preference, and ignored the passing dictates of fashion with supreme indifference. In his time, he'd used every drug known to man and kept his private staff of chemists busy coming up with new ones. It was truly said he'd never met a chemical he didn't like. Anyone else who tried to ingest the quantity and variety of drugs Valentine had would undoubtably have been poisoned a dozen times over, his brains helplessly scrambled; but by some dark alchemical miracle, Valentine thrived and prospered. And if he saw the rest of the world rather differently than most people and had the occasional animated discussion with people who weren't there, still, it didn't seem to be slowing him down any. He remained sharp, ambitious, and extremely dangerous.

But even he knew he couldn't go on forever as he was, without paying the price. He had the best doctors his considerable fortune could afford, and took frequent rests in his own personal regeneration machine, but his continuous extensive drug use combined with the never-ending pressure of his many intrigues to undo his precarious and hard-won self-control. He was burning himself up, inside and out, and his only response was to throw more chemicals on the fire. As a result, he was now so preternaturally sharp and tuned-in that he all but quivered where he stood. He was so incredibly aware that he could read body language as though it was the printed word, with everyone's merest gesture shouting information at him. Plans and plots and pieces of whimsy flashed through his mind, sparking like lightning, come and gone in a moment. His body might be attending the Court, but his mind was here, there, and everywhere, all at once. Valentine rode the waves of his mind like a surfer, perfectly balanced, looking down from the giddy heights of an endless curl. He found it exhilarating, but he never lost control. Or if he did, no one seemed to notice.

He remained convinced that if he could just discover the right combination of drugs, he could acquire a perfect equilibrium between the effects he needed and the side effects he endured. A perfect never-ending high, soaring like a bird, limitless and free. But in the meantime, he found he needed increasingly large doses of each drug just to get the same desired effect; and he had to take more and more new drugs to counter the malicious effects of older drugs, whose remnants were still lurking in his system. As a result he was thinner than ever and much more intense, jolted from moment to moment by his chemical express, and he could no more comprehend a life without his little helpers than a life without oxygen. He was also taking specific short-lived drugs for specific needs, making the necessary decisions from moment to moment. And this seemed a very good moment to increase his mental clarity. He had no friends at this Court and many enemies, and he didn't trust his allies. It was therefore vital that he outthink them all at every turn.

He took out his silver pillbox, wiped a layer of frost from the lid, opened it, and chose a single tab. He pressed it against the side of his neck, hitting the main vein with practiced ease, and his crimson smile widened as the new drug surged through his bloodstream like a barreling train. His thoughts slammed into a new gear, sharp and clear and quicksilver fast. Everyone else seemed to be moving in slow motion. He felt comfortably warm, as though sitting in a great chair before a banked study fire, and beads of sweat popped out on his forehead, despite the bitter cold. His breathing deepened, and his heart thudded echoingly in his chest. He watched the patterns people made around him, every move a revelation. He reined his thoughts in, concentrating only on what he needed. The trouble with this particular drug was that it tended to make him a little paranoid. But that was acceptable, under the circumstances. At Lionstone's Court they really were out to get you.

A short, fat figure approached him, scowling determinedly, and Valentine drew himself up, posing elegantly. Judging by his dogged stance, the Lord Gregor Shreck was set on business. Valentine didn't mind. He could play that game, too. He smiled at the Shreck politely, but didn't bow. He didn't want to encourage the man. Gregor lurched to a halt before him, sniffed once, and then nodded stiffly.

"A moment of your time, Wolfe; it's to our mutual advantage."

"Well," said Valentine pleasantly, "never let it be said that I turned down an advantage. How nice to see you again, dear Shreck. You're looking well. Lost a little weight, perhaps?"

"Nothing I couldn't afford to lose," said Gregor, trying for a polite smile. It wasn't particularly successful. He lacked the practice. "We have interests in common, Wolfe, not to mention enemies. Clan Chojiro is becoming dangerously influential at Court these days. With the Campbells thrown down and destroyed, Chojiros have prospered in their absence. Now, not content with threatening our business interests, they are seeking to undermine us here, too. In fact, I would go so far as to say that Chojiros have become so prominent that neither you nor I could successfully deny them anything they really wanted. At least, not separately. But . . ."

"But together, in alliance, we could put them back in their place," said Valentine, completing the sentence he could almost hear before it was said. His thoughts rocketed on, far ahead of the Shreck's. Weighing which Clan would be of most potential use to him in the future and which the most dangerous. Chojiros were on the way up, and Shrecks were sinking. And the Chojiros at least knew something of honor, which was more than Gregor ever had. Valentine approved of honor. It made it so much easier to manipulate people who believed in it, or thought he did. Besides, he didn't trust the Shreck. Never had.

"Thank you, Gregor," he said only a second later, "but I'm really not interested in fighting any wars at present. Since my hostile takeover of Clan Campbell, I have more than enough to keep me occupied these days. Chojiros are an annoyance, nothing more. Thank you for your interest, Lord Shreck. Don't let me keep you. I'm sure there are others simply dying for your company."

Gregor Shreck stood fuming for a moment and then stomped away, kicking at the snow before him. He would have liked to have threatened the Wolfe, to make it clear standing on the sidelines could be dangerous, too, but in truth he had nothing to threaten Valentine with, and they both knew it. Valentine smiled slightly as he watched the small, squat figure plowing through the snow with furious energy. The Shreck would find no allies here at Court, and he'd never had any friends. There was always the Church, of course. Gregor had been courting them furiously just recently. But the Church would be Valentine's enemy anyway.

He looked around to see if anyone had been watching his brief encounter with the Shreck, but they were all avoiding his eye. Of course they'd been watching. They all wanted something from him. Everyone did. Valentine shrugged. He had more important things to think about. Of late his intelligence people buried in the underground had been bringing him more and more reports of apparent inhuman abilities among the new rebels, exploits that could not be accounted for by esper talents. Examples of strength and abilities beyond anything ever seen before. It was all rumor and gossip, of course, but if there was a process that could produce abilities greater than esp, Valentine wanted it for himself. He was still chasing the esper drug, with little success. His efforts had been made much more difficult since his enforced divorce from the underground, but he'd taken care to seed the rebel forces with his own people some time in advance, just in case. Pity about the underground. They'd had access to all kinds of unusual and forbidden practices. But he'd become too public now to risk links like that.

The Lord High Dram, in his persona as the man called Hood, had worked his way into the highest levels of the clone and esper underground before he revealed his true identity—which meant he knew all about Valentine's involvement. Valentine had never cared a damn for the underground's politics or causes; he'd only been interested in alternative routes to power and the drug that could reportedly make an esper out of anyone. But he felt he might have a hard time convincing Lionstone of that. So when Hood was revealed as Dram, Valentine moved quickly to sever all his links with the underground and disposed of anything or anyone that could directly connect him with the rebels. The people he'd seeded in the underground didn't matter. They didn't know who they were reporting to, and as long as the money kept coming, they didn't ask questions. So Valentine sat back and waited for Dram to make his move, confident he could defy the man to prove anything. Even the Warrior Prime's word wouldn't be enough on its own to convict the head of the first Family in the Empire. Rank has its privileges, after all.

However, Dram never said a word. Valentine waited, armed and prepared for any attack, but none came, and slowly Valentine came to believe that he was safe, for the moment. Perhaps the Empress had decided it wasn't in the Empire's interest to bring down the man she depended on to provide her with the new stardrive. Or perhaps the information was being kept in reserve, as a weapon to use against him at some future time. Lionstone had always been one to take the long view.

Except . . . there was a delicious rumor going around of late that the Lord High Dram was dead. He hadn't been seen at Court for ages. His only recent appearances had been as a head and shoulders on a viewscreen, and that could have been anyone, behind a digital mask. The word was, Dram had been sent on an extremely secret mission, got his head handed to him, and came home in a box. No one had any proof, as yet, but Valentine had heard the rumor in so many places and from so many sources, some surprisingly high up, that he couldn't help feeling there had to be something in it.

And if Dram was dead, there was a good chance his proof of Valentine's treason died with him. Which meant he could go back to the underground. If he wanted to. Valentine pursed his scarlet mouth. With all that had happened to him of late, he no longer needed the underground as a route to power. He was doing perfectly well on his own. And his agents stood a much better chance of discovering the source of the esper drug than he ever would. No, he didn't need the rebels anymore. He didn't need anyone. And he had other, more important, worries to concern him.

During the epic clash in which the Wolfes had gone head-to-head with the Campbells and ground them underfoot, the then head of the Wolfes, Valentine's father, Jacob, had been killed. Everyone assumed a Campbell had got a lucky blow in, but actually the hand on the weapon had been Valentine's. No one had seen. No one knew. But shortly after the battle was over and all the Campbells were either dead or had fled, Jacob's body could not be found. Valentine had ordered an immediate search and offered all kinds of rewards for the body's return, but nothing was ever seen or heard of it again.

Which meant Jacob was still out there, somewhere. Not alive. He couldn't be alive. Even if Jacob's mysterious friends had got him to a regeneration machine straight away, it would still have been too late. He'd been brain-dead too long. Valentine was quite sure of that. He could still remember the moment when he'd killed his father. One of his drugs gave him perfect recall, and he played the moment over and over in his mind, savoring it. He'd moved in behind his father, unnoticed in the heat of battle, and slipped his dagger expertly in and out of Jacob's ribs, so fast no one saw or suspected anything. Jacob was dead. Valentine never doubted it for a moment. But who had his body?

Finlay and Adrienne had been the only Campbells to escape the slaughter, running for their lives on a stolen gravity sled, but Jacob's body hadn't gone with them. The tower's external security cameras had a good view of the departing sled, and there were only two people on it. Unfortunately, Valentine couldn't study the records from the interior cameras, because he'd arranged for them all to be turned off the moment the fighting started. He couldn't afford for them to show him killing his father, after all. So anyone inside the room could have taken him.

But what use was the body to anyone? They could clone another Jacob from his cells, but if he turned up again, a simple genetest would be enough to reveal it wasn't the real Jacob. And the Family wouldn't pay ransom for a clone. Not even the grieving widow Constance . . . Though they might have paid a ransom for the safe return of Jacob's body so that it could be laid to rest with honor.

But no ransom demand ever materialized. A thought forced itself into Valentine's mind, much against his will. What if . . . no one had taken it? What if the dead body had just got up and walked away, unnoticed in the general chaos? Valentine shuddered involuntarily as the image played itself out relentlessly before his mind's eye. Jacob's body, its death wound still bloody in its side, rising unsteadily to its feet, and pausing only briefly to glare at its murderer before slipping unnoticed out the door. Jacob's body, stumbling unseen down some dark alleyway, animated no longer by life, but by pure hatred for its killer. Out there, somewhere, waiting for its chance for bloody vengeance against its murderous son. Valentine had always had a superstitious side. Mostly he encouraged it for the extra thrills it provided, but now the thought of his dead father haunted him and would not let him alone. Sometimes, in the night, when he was alone in his bedchamber, he thought he heard his father talking to him from the shadows. The words terrified him, but he could never remember them in the morning.

Of course, that could always be the drugs.

Valentine brought his thoughts firmly under control. No one could hurt him now. He was the Wolfe, acknowledged and unchallenged, and nothing could undo that, no matter what had happened to his father's body. He had destroyed his rivals the Campbells and held the single most important and lucrative contract in the Empire: the mass production of the new stardrive. Everyone bowed their head to him and gave him plenty of room.

He had the Empress's ear, when many did not. She saw him as her fool and jester, wisdom and madness in one entertaining package, but she listened when he spoke. She tolerated much from him that she would not from anyone else, because he amused her. And not least because she enjoyed seeing other people's reactions when she favored him over them or put him in positions of power over them.

At heart, Lionstone was a creature of simple pleasures. Both the military and the Church had made it clear they disapproved of him. There weren't many things the Church and the military agreed on, but Valentine Wolfe was definitely one of them. Since they both needed the stardrive to get about (neither could afford to be left behind by the other), they remained polite in company. Mostly. None of the Families liked him being so powerful—on the ground it upset the delicate balance of power among them that usually kept them from each other's throats—but their occasional intrigues against him came to nothing.

It was the same with the Members of Parliament. They couldn't buy or control him, because in the end they had nothing he wanted. That made him dangerous, a wild card, unpredictable.

But every single one of them could see the advantage of having his friendship. Which made for some interesting conversations.

Valentine's brother and sister, Daniel and Stephanie, watched him from a safe distance. They were there at Court with their respective spouses, because duty demanded it. But as usual they weren't talking to Valentine. They despised and hated him, partly because he was a drug-soaked degenerate and a disgrace to the Family and partly because he so obviously didn't give a damn. Both Daniel and Stephanie had been forced into arranged marriages, one of the last of Jacob's orders, but neither match could be said to be successful. Not that Daniel or Stephanie had tried very hard. They had other, more important things to think about. As Wolfes, they'd prospered along with the rest of the Family, but they remained very much in Valentine's shadow. With his sudden rise, they'd lost all power and influence in the Family and now subsisted on whatever crumbs he threw their way. They intrigued furiously against him, but they'd never been very good at it. And so, with only each other to rely on and cling to, they'd grown increasingly close. Some said unnaturally so.

Daniel was the youngest, only just into his twenties, and had the hulking frame of his father, but none of the wit or intelligence. He'd been clumsy as a child, till his father beat it out of him. Even now, he tended to move with exaggerated care. He wore his hair long, in thick golden strands, the latest fashion, but couldn't be bothered with the florescent face makeup that should have accompanied it. Mostly because he didn't have the skill or the looks to bring it off successfully, and he hated the idea that people might be laughing at him. Daniel had no sense of humor and didn't trust those who did.

Stephanie, the middle child, was tall and gangling, good-looking in a bland sort of way, and deadly as a coiled snake. If she'd had intelligence to equal her venom, no one would have been safe. As it was, she raged against Valentine's restraints, but had no idea yet how to break them. It didn't stop her doing her best to show Valentine up at every opportunity, on principle. Valentine just smiled at those around him and said *sisters,* and everybody laughed. She hated it when they laughed. She dominated Daniel, but that wasn't exactly difficult. She'd always been the cold one in the Family. Daniel missed his father, but she didn't. She had no time for emotions that got in the way.

And yet, almost in spite of himself, Valentine had recently been forced to give the two of them more and more to do on the business side of the Family. He had neither the time nor the aptitude for running the stardrive business, but it was too important a post to be trusted to anyone not a major Wolfe. And that meant Daniel and Stephanie, who between them had one pretty good brain. He trusted them not to screw things up out of spite. Mad at him though they were, he was pretty sure they wouldn't do anything to harm the Family.

At first, they took their new post as an insult, aristocrats forced to dirty their hands with trade, but it didn't take Stephanie long to realize that power in the business side of things could perhaps be used to undermine Valentine. So she studied hard and made Daniel study, too. Between them they ran the business and made it theirs. So far, Valentine hadn't noticed. Daniel and Stephanie planned to change that.

They stood close together, shivering in the falling snow, watching Valentine think. Their gaze was not friendly. Daniel produced a flask of brandy and passed it to Stephanie. She accepted it gratefully and took a healthy swallow. The drink burned fiercely in her chest, sinking slowly lower, fighting off the chill of the driving wind. She passed the flask back to her brother, who drank deeply.

"Not too much, Daniel," Stephanie said automatically. "This is a bad place to be caught without all your wits about you."

"I can handle it," he said, just as automatically. "I can handle it." But he put the flask away anyway. "You worry too much, big sister."

"And you don't worry enough."

"Not true. I only have to look at Valentine thinking like that, and I start worrying. Means he's planning something again, to no one's advantage but his. Or just possibly he's found out how deeply we're involved with this stardrive company. We were only supposed to run it, not take it over."

Stephanie smiled coldly. "By the time he works out what's happening, it'll be too late. Control over stardrive production will give us control over him. He depends on it for his station at Court. A sudden drop in numbers, just when the Empress had called for an increase, would humiliate him without harming the company in the least. There are lots of other things we can do, too, that will reflect on him, rather than us. It shouldn't be too hard to throw all the blame on Valentine; after all, we're the ones with access to the company books. And after a steady stream of embarrassments, we shouldn't find it too difficult to convince Lionstone it would be in her and the Empire's best interests to take the company away from Valentine and give it to us. We'll bring him down, little brother. We'll bring him all the way down."

Daniel scowled unhappily. "I still can't help worrying what it is he's after, that he spends all his time pursuing it rather than running the company he depends on. Whatever it is, it must be something really important."

Stephanie shrugged. "Who knows where Valentine's thoughts are these days? I'm surprised they're still on the same planet as the rest of us."

"We'll get him," said Daniel, trying hard to sound as confident as she did. "We'll drag him down. Father never intended a sick degenerate like Valentine to head the Family. And then we'll run things. The both of us."

"Yes," said Stephanie. "Of course. The both of us."

Daniel looked at her, and his voice dropped. "Are you all right? Cold getting to you? Come to little brother, and let him warm you up."

He held open his cloak, and she snuggled up against him

as he wrapped the cloak around them both. And if they held each other a little more closely than brother and sister should, no one noticed it, hidden under cover of the cloak and the still respected Wolfe name.

Not too far away Lily Wolfe, wife of Daniel, and Michel Wolfe, who had to take Stephanie's name when he married her, stood together watching their respective spouses staring at Valentine. An impartial observer might have noticed that they were standing more than companionably close together. This same observer might also have deduced, from their body language and occasional long melting glance, that they were seriously involved with each other. The impartial observer, assuming such a thing could be found in Lionstone's Court, would have been absolutely right. Lily and Michel were lovers, and had been for some time. Everyone knew except Daniel and Stephanie, who were preoccupied with other things. Even Valentine knew. The only reason he hadn't said anything was because he was still trying to decide whether it would be funnier to tell Daniel and Stephanie or to let it go on.

Lily was six foot six, willowy but still nicely curved, with a long silver wig that fell past her shoulders, framing a pale freckled face. She always wore wigs over a shaved skull on the grounds that wigs were so much easier to look after. She wore the latest fashions and wore them well, with a natural style that infuriated other women, for none could look that good on their best day. Lily was strikingly pretty, with prominent cheekbones and dark lustrous eyes. She had a smile that could stun a charming gigolo and a laugh that could start a party at fifty paces. Daniel didn't appreciate her. She took that as a personal insult.

Michel was barely six feet in height, but his wide frame was covered with the best muscles the body shops could provide. They tended to go off after a while, because he could never be bothered to exercise enough. But a quick trip to the body shop was all it took to perk them up again. He was handsome in a dark and swarthy way, with a thick mane of long jet-black hair that was his pride and joy. He preferred loose clothing with plenty of open spaces to show off his manly physique. As a result, he was now shivering so hard he had to keep his jaw clenched to prevent his teeth from chattering, and his skin had turned a pale blue color that contrasted unappealingly with his dark hair. Snow had

begun to gather on top of his head. However, he also favored
knee-length leather boots, so at least his feet were warm.
The thought somehow failed to comfort him. He glared
across at the Empress sitting serenely on her Throne and
hugged himself tightly.

"If you squeeze yourself any harder, dear, your insides
will pop out your ears," said Lily calmly.

"I'm bored," said Michel through gritted teeth. "I'm
bored and I'm extremely cold. There are icicles hanging
from my extremities. See if you can spot someone of lower
status, so I can steal his cloak."

"Behave yourself, my dearest. Try not to draw attention to
yourself, just this once. The auguries in the sheep I sacrificed this morning were quite clear. Today is not a good day
to be noticed."

"Why couldn't the auguries have warned you that the
Court was going to be a bloody icebox this time? They're all
very well when it comes to sounding grand and mystical, but
they're no bloody use at all when it comes to predicting
practical things, are they? I'd ask for your money back, if I
were you. Or a new sheep."

"Don't scoff, darling. You know you don't understand
these things. And watch your language. You're an aristocrat
now."

"I should have stayed an accountant. The Empress had
never heard of me, and I could still feel my fingers."

"If you'd never married Stephanie, you'd never have met
me."

Michel considered this point and produced something
meant to be a smile. "Well, there is that. Only lucky thing
that ever happened to me was meeting you."

Lily reached out and patted his cheek soothingly. "Luck
has nothing to do with it, darling. There are powers and influences and mysteries, and they rule our lives."

"The only one who rules our lives is currently sitting on
that Throne, wrapped in furs, and laughing her socks off at
the rest of us. Why are we here, Lily? We're not important
enough for our absence to be noticed. We could have spent
the afternoon in each other's company, doing all sorts of interesting things. It's not often we can both get away from
our respective spouses. You know how I miss you."

"And I miss you, my darling, but we must be careful.
We're Wolfes now, and Daniel and Stephanie would be most

upset if they thought we were bringing the name of the Clan into disrepute through our absence. They might even investigate further and find out about us. I have a strong feeling that if they did, they'd probably take it quite personally, the poor dears. If we were really lucky, they'd just have us killed. Much more likely, they'd divorce us and throw us out of the Clan without a penny to our name. We'd be outcasts. No one would lift a finger to help us, not even our own Families. I've grown quite fond of our current lifestyle, and I for one do not intend doing anything that might put it at risk. And that includes getting horizontal and sweaty with you, darling. Our times together must be carefully planned, with every precaution taken. Be patient, my darling. Things won't always be like this. And as for why we're here, the auguries were quite specific, for once. Something important is going to happen here at Court. Something of great significance. Something that will launch a tidal wave of possibilities, which you and I might just ride to greatness."

Michel looked at her fondly, wrapped in her faux peasant dress and shawl, but kept his peace. Lily liked to see herself as the last of the great mystics, a pagan witch from the distant past with rare and subtle powers. Actually, she'd just read a few old books and fallen madly in love with the role. It was much more likely she just had a great imagination, backed up by a touch of esp, but he wasn't dumb enough to tell her that. He was very fond of her, and, besides, she tended to throw tantrums when she got annoyed. Still, he trusted her intuition. She'd always understood Court politics much better than he did. He'd keep his eyes open, if they didn't freeze solid first, like certain other parts of his anatomy.

He'd originally taken up with Lily because both of them were bored. As one of Jacob's legacies they were assured of a place in Clan Wolfe, but no one felt any obligation to make them feel welcome. As a result, they were allowed no place in the Clan, neither business nor social. Jacob had arranged the marriages in the first place to gain control of certain subsidiary business interests involved in stardrive manufacture. But now those had been taken over and absorbed by the Wolfes, Lily and Michel were redundant. They could not be allowed any part in business because they weren't really Wolfes, and therefore not to be trusted with anything important. But they were also kept from any contact with their own Families, because they were Wolfes. And since they were Jacob's choice, Daniel and Stephanie wanted nothing to do with them. They managed a stiff smile when procedure demanded they appear in public with their spouses, to put across the polite fiction that all was well, but that was only to appease the Church and keep other Families from sniffing out a possible weakness in the structure of Clan Wolfe. The rest of the time, Daniel and Stephanie had time only for each other and the business they ran, so that Lily and Michel were left to their own devices to keep themselves amused. Everything that followed was inevitable, really. Their only other option had been plotting treason with some other Clan, and they were both too scared of Valentine for that.

At least so far.

Meanwhile, watching everything the Wolfes did with great interest were the representatives of Clan Chojiro. Still defiantly Oriental in appearance and tradition despite the countless centuries that separated them from their original ancestors and founders, the Chojiros had risen to prominence in the Empire through hard work, subtle cunning, and killing anyone who got in their way. They made few alliances with other Clans, preferring to stand alone. That way, they knew who they could trust. With the destruction of the Clan Campbell they had moved smoothly into the open gap, edging other contenders aside with subtle threats and the occasional quiet bloodbath, until now they were second only in the Empire to Clan Wolfe. And since no Chojiro had ever been willing to accept being second best at anything, there was a quiet, undeclared but quite deadly war going on between the two Families.

However, the Chojiros specialized in computers: building, programming, installing, and maintaining them at every level—including the kind of computers used in starships. As a result, the Wolfes and the Chojiros currently found themselves in an uneasy partnership, not daring to upset each other's business for fear of attracting the wrath of the Empress. In fact, the situation had become so complicated that both sides had declared a temporary truce while they tried to work out where the hell they stood.

The systematic trashing of the computers at the Tax and Tithes Headquarters had done great damage to the Chojiros' reputation, which was why there were so many Chojiros at

Court today, to remind everyone of the size and power of the Clan. They were currently replacing the Tax computers at their own expense, and adding extra levels of protection to ensure the same thing could never happen again. Within the Clan, those responsible for installing the original security systems had already taken their own lives, to make atonement. A few had to be helped, but that was the Empire under Lionstone for you. There was no room for weakness or failure in Clan Chojiro. They were cutthroat businessmen, sometimes literally, and had made an art form of the hostile takeover. It was truly said: if you see a Chojiro smiling, run.

BB Chojiro had come to Court specifically to act as spokesperson for her Family. She had been trained to appear the perfect smiling front, the acceptable face of a feared Family. She was diplomat, deal maker and deception incarnate. And though her standing in the Family had been a little tarnished by the escape of the esper Julian Skye, that was deemed the fault of the prison security, and she was still regarded as entirely trustworthy. She was Blue Block, after all. Accompanying her, in a matching kimono, to remind everyone of the harsher Chojiro face, was the Investigator Razor. His face and hands showed the marks of recent burns, but no one was stupid enough to ask how he'd got them. Investigators never acknowledged their pain. If indeed they actually felt any. It was hard to tell with Investigators. Everyone was giving BB and Razor plenty of room, for all sorts of reasons, allowing them to talk in private. BB smiled at one and all, and talked quietly with Razor, who stared straight ahead, his cold eyes ready for any threat.

"I take it there have been no further developments in the search for Julian," said BB, her smiling lips barely moving.

"I would have told you if there were. Security is doing its best, but the city's a mess. If he's out there, we'll find him and bring him back. Or his body."

"I need him alive, Investigator. There are many questions still to be asked of him. Not least how he got away."

"If he's out there, we'll find him, but I can't speak for his condition. A lot of people died in the city today."

BB sighed. Razor could be very single-minded when he chose. "Let us talk of happier things. How is our infiltration of the Wolfe businesses going?"

"Surprisingly smoothly. Daniel and Stephanie are so concerned with their own intrigues, they haven't noticed a thing.

Valentine has his own interests these days and has left them
alone to sink or swim. They've done well enough, but they
have little real experience with industrial espionage. We
have people, apparently entirely unconnected with Clan
Chojiro, on every level of the company, from the very bottom up to and including the board of directors. Wolfe security is good, but without competent management to direct it,
it's been drifting aimlessly of late."

"It's been too easy," said BB. "I can't believe Valentine is
completely uninterested in the company. It's the base of his
Family's current wealth and position. He's had to invest
practically everything in the Wolfe and Campbell coffers to
get the stardrive companies up and running, with hardly anything left for a safety net. And soon we'll be in a position to
subtly sabotage stardrive construction from beginning to
end. I can't believe Valentine doesn't know what we're
doing."

"He has his own interests. I regret to say, my people are
unable to confirm exactly what those might be, apart from
the obvious. People we send to find out tend not to come
back."

"And you don't find that worrying?"

"Investigators don't worry. It's bad for the image. You
continue with your schemes; I'll see no one bothers you."

BB nodded curtly. "We can't hold off any longer just because we're not sure what Valentine's up to. If anything.
Give the orders; I want to see significant errors in stardrive
construction appearing by the end of the week. Make sure
it's something showy. Something the news shows can run
with. Once the delivery of the new drives has been not just
slowed, but all but stopped, it shouldn't take too long to convince the Empress that the Wolfes aren't fit to be in charge
of such a vital concern. And we'll be right there, ready to
take over at a moment's notice. After all, who has a better
claim? We're already producing all the computers for the
new starships."

"Unless Valentine does know and is already planning
something really devastating."

BB looked at him sternly. "Just whose side are you on, Investigator?"

"Don't ask questions like that. The answer would only upset you. All that matters is I have pledged my life to protect
the interests of your Clan. For as long as I stay with you."

"Very reassuring." BB sniffed, deliberately turned away, and looked across at Valentine, chatting brightly with someone who looked as though they wished they were somewhere else. BB watched them for a while, her eyes cold as death. "Sometimes I think we'd be better off launching a preemptive strike against the Wolfes, beginning with Valentine. A really hostile takeover."

"I wouldn't recommend it," said Razor. "There's too much we don't know about the Wolfes in general and Valentine in particular. Only a fool jumps off a wall without finding how high it is first. There's more to Valentine than we see. There has to be. My own recommendation is for a more leisurely approach. The Wolfes' weak spot is Daniel and Stephanie. There is much in their tangled relationship that might be profitably exploited . . ."

"And that is why you're in charge of carrying out security, rather than planning it," said BB tartly. "I could do anything to those two, up to and including killing them slowly, and Valentine wouldn't give a damn."

"But if we could reach them, turn them to our cause, perhaps through pressure on their current closeness . . . or by providing information about Lily and Michel . . ."

"No," said BB firmly. "Daniel and Stephanie are too erratic to place any trust in. They're weak, but they're still Wolfes. I have a better idea."

Constance Wolfe, widow of Jacob, stood alone in the crowd. She was always alone now, no matter where she went. Eighteen years old, still wearing black in mourning for her murdered husband. Tall and blond, breathtakingly lovely even in a world where beauty was commonplace, the fire had gone out of her, leaving her looking like a crushed flower. Out of perhaps all the Wolfe Family, she had truly loved Jacob. The others mourned for a while, even Valentine, but they all had their own lives to get on with, and they did so as soon as they properly could. Constance had had nothing but Jacob. He was her life. Now he was gone, and she didn't know what to do with herself. She had no interest in politics or intrigues, and she was allowed no place in Family affairs. Jacob's children had never approved of his last marriage, to someone even younger than them. There had always been the possibility Jacob might disinherit them in favor of her or *her* children. Now he was gone; they were able to ignore her with something like relief.

She looked around at the assembled courtiers, and no one looked back. She was no one now. They had no time for failures. Until one woman met her eye and smiled. BB Chojiro. Constance looked at her thoughtfully, and BB moved unhurriedly toward her, still somehow graceful despite having to trudge through the deep snow. Constance knew she should see the woman as an enemy, but she didn't have the energy. BB stopped before her and smiled again.

"We should have got together before, Constance. We have a lot in common. It's hard to be a woman alone. I know. But just because one Family's abandoned you, it doesn't mean we all have. You have friends, Constance. If you want them."

Constance looked at her icily. "I may have fallen from grace, Chojiro, but I'm not so low I would consider betraying my kith and kin."

BB's smile didn't waver. "What I have in mind is in the best interests of the Wolfes. Valentine is leading you all to disaster. He's lost inside his own head and sees only what he wants to see. Daniel and Stephanie only have eyes for each other. The new stardrive will fall from their hands, and then what will happen to the Wolfes? To the Family Jacob built and brought to greatness? What will happen to you, Constance?"

"If you've something to say to me, Chojiro, say it."

"You could be head of the Wolfes. Valentine could be removed as insane, Daniel and Stephanie as incompetent. And since they've taken steps down the years to remove all other major players from the game, that would just leave you to take over. Now, alone, you couldn't hope to run the Family. You've only ever been on the fringes of things. But if you were to marry a Chojiro, we could merge the Families through your children. Until then you would rule the Wolfes with our help. Think about it; you'd never have to be alone again. You're young, Constance. You have your whole life ahead of you. Don't throw it all away in loyalty for people who despise you."

"You want something," said Constance steadily. "You all want something. Get to the meat of the matter. What do you want from me?"

"Information," said BB Chojiro. "You're still a prominent Wolfe, with access to areas my people can only reach with difficulty. There are questions we need answers for. In re-

turn, we would make you one of us. A valued member of
Clan Chojiro, cared for and appreciated. Isn't that all you
ever really wanted?"

Constance looked at her thoughtfully, and while she didn't
say yes, she didn't say no, either. BB turned and gestured for
Razor to come and join them. The Investigator plowed
through the snow as though it wasn't there and bowed politely to Constance. She nodded briefly in return, watching
him warily. BB gave her a reassuring smile and put a propri-
etary hand on Razor's arm.

"Investigator, you were there when Jacob Wolfe died. Tell
Constance what you saw."

"He did not die at the hand of any Campbell," said Razor
flatly. "The Wolfe was stabbed from behind, by his eldest
son. By Valentine, current head of your Clan. It was very
quick. No one else noticed. But I saw it."

"And you know Investigators never lie," said BB. She
was careful not to sound too pleased about it.

Constance pressed her lips together, though whether to
keep her mouth from trembling with rage or to hold back
tears, she wasn't sure. It had always troubled her that no one
had ever claimed the kill for Jacob. It would have been a
major triumph for any Campbell, and they'd needed a triumph badly in the bad days after their downfall. But no one
ever claimed to have killed the Wolfe. No one even saw how
it happened, though she'd questioned enough people. She'd
assumed the Campbell himself must have done it before he
was killed. Until now. It never occurred to her to doubt Razor's word. He was an Investigator, after all, and lying was
beneath him. Besides, it sounded true. Valentine had every
reason to kill his father and not a scrap of conscience to stop
him. He could have got away with it in the heat of battle.
Constance looked steadily at BB Chojiro.

"Tell me more."

Sitting comfortably on her Iron Throne, Lionstone XIV
looked interestedly from one face to the other as army and
Church argued before her. General Beckett, slow and unper-
turbed, taking the time to enjoy his cigar between answers,
and Cardinal Kassar, his single eye glowing with the un-
quenchable fire of the true fanatic. Lionstone liked to watch
them argue, not least because while they were arguing with
each other, they weren't teaming up to dispute with her. Divide and conquer worked just as well in Court politics as it

did in wars. It helped that Kassar and Beckett hated each other's guts. Neither was strong enough individually to threaten her authority, but together they would have made a formidable enemy. So Lionstone found it expedient to keep their ire concentrated on each other. It didn't take much. A kind word here, a knowing look there, and they snapped at the bait like hungry sharks. Which was why they stood before her now, bristling at each other like junkyard dogs, blind to everything but the need to score points off each other. Lionstone smiled to herself. Men were so predictable.

"As any fool could see, the alien attack is a direct threat against humanity," said Cardinal Kassar, his voice colder than the air around him. "We can't just sit here and wait for them to attack again. We must hunt them down and wipe them out. Any other way risks the suicide of our species!"

"A really good way to commit suicide," said General Beckett calmly, "is to launch yourself blindly into a situation you know nothing about. You saw what one ship on its own was able to do to us. Silence and the *Dauntless* were able to handle it, but that was one of our finest ships, with one of our finest crews, against what could after all have been nothing more than a simple probe. We need more information, before committing ourselves to definite plans."

"It's a matter of Faith," said Kassar. "I wouldn't expect you to understand that, Beckett."

"It's a matter of common sense, Cardinal," said Beckett. "I wouldn't expect you to understand that."

"Sounds like cowardice to me. Staying safe at home here while your men take all the risks out on the Rim. Well, here isn't safe anymore, Beckett. Either we go to them, or they'll come to us."

Beckett took the cigar out of his mouth and looked at it thoughtfully. "Bravery is overrated, Cardinal. I'll settle for competence. If the attack is going to come from anywhere, it'll come from the Rim. Hence the extra patrols I ordered. They're going to be our early-warning system. In my experience, fighting wars is a matter of practicality, not heroics. But, then, you've always been a dreamer, Kassar, with little grasp of the practicalities of life. Comes with the job, I suppose."

Kassar glared at him and then turned his burning gaze on Lionstone. "Put me in charge of your armies, and I'll provide you with an unbeatable force of the faithful, trained in all the martial arts, ready to dare anything in the name of the Church."

"I've always fought in the name of the Empress, myself," said General Beckett, and blew a triumphant puff of smoke in Kassar's direction. The Cardinal hesitated, suddenly aware of the dangerous waters his rhetoric had swept him into. Beckett continued, taking advantage of the pause. "Fanatics can be very useful, when it comes to building a power base, but in my experience they make bloody poor soldiers. Fanatics are fine at getting themselves killed in the name of their cause; I prefer to put my faith in trained professional soldiers who'll put their energies into staying alive long enough to kill the enemy."

Kassar started to splutter, so eager to get back at Beckett that his words were tumbling over themselves. Lionstone sat back on her Throne, openly enjoying his discomposure. Beckett puffed happily on his cigar. And that was when Mother Beatrice emerged from the crowd to join the debate and throw oil on troubled fires. Beatrice Christiana had been due to marry Valentine Wolfe, on Jacob's instructions, but it hadn't happened. Beatrice was a forceful, assured, and occasionally violent woman who knew her own mind and had no intention whatsoever of marrying a notorious drug fiend, degenerate, and general weirdo. She threatened everything up to and including murder to get out of the match, but no one took her seriously. Until the day of the wedding, when she punched out Valentine, kicked the presiding Vicar in the nuts, and made a run for sanctuary with the Sisters of Mercy. The one place no one would follow her. Their nunneries were inviolate by long tradition. The Sisters of Mercy were the only impartial force in the Empire, tied to no one side or cause or class, but offering their help to all impartially. They were much loved and trusted by one and all. Which made them very useful when it came to sorting out Family disputes and brokering truces. Among other things.

Beatrice had risen rapidly through the ranks and was now a Mother Superior, complete with voluminous black robe and starched wimple. It helped that as well as being particularly spiritual, she was also incredibly wealthy. She took her place in Court, defying anyone to say anything, and was rapidly emerging as a sane counter voice to both the military and the established Church. Valentine took it all easily enough, understanding that it had all been entirely personal on Beatrice's part. He sent her a note saying he thought her new outfit was very sexy and enclosed the bill for the wedding. Since then, Beatrice had put a great deal of energy into magnificently ignoring him.

Now she stood before the Iron Throne, eyes sparkling merrily. She bowed to the Empress and looked challengingly at the General and the Cardinal. Beckett smiled and gave her the nod one gives a respected adversary. Kassar glared at her. He saw her as a dangerous heretic and made no bones about saying so loudly in public until both the Sisters of Mercy and his own superiors in the Church told him to shut the hell up. This infuriated Kassar even more, luckily to the point of incoherence. Beatrice didn't give a damn. As long as the Sisters remained separate from the established Church, Kassar had no power over her, and they both knew it. She smiled at Lionstone, who acknowledged her with a nod.

"If I might interrupt, Your Majesty; it seems to me that both Church and army are too rooted in their positions to see the truth. If the alien ship is representative of the aliens' power, we could be in real trouble when their fleet turns up. We have a whole Empire to protect, while the aliens are free to concentrate their forces at any point they choose. One ship turned our main starport and city into rubble. Imagine what a fleet of them could do to a planet, with or without its defenses. We have to face the fact that for the first time, we find ourselves facing an opponent who may well be stronger than us. Not forgetting, of course, that we already have hard evidence that there may be more than one powerful alien species out there. Your Majesty has been saying this for some time, but I think we're all now more ready to believe it. Our only chance for survival as a species may be to bring all our assets to bear against the enemy. Or enemies. That could include even those who would normally oppose us. I'm talking about the rebels, and the clone and esper undergrounds."

"Are you mad, woman?" exploded Kassar. "Make deals with those scum? They're not even human!"

"They think they are," said Beatrice. "And I think they'd fight to defend humanity against an alien threat, if we asked them nicely. It's in their interest. If the Empire is destroyed, they'd be wiped out along with the rest of us. They have talents and powers and abilities that we're going to need. Does anyone here doubt they'd make excellent attack troops? Just the fact that they're still around despite everything we've done to exterminate them shows they're survivors, if nothing else."

"May I just point out," said Beckett unhurriedly, "that it was the rebels' lowering of Golgotha's defenses that made the aliens' attack possible?"

"They were probably working with the aliens," said Kassar.

"All the more reason to contact them and get them on our side," said Beatrice, unmoved.

"They are guilty of crimes against humanity," Kassar insisted. "The guilty must be punished."

"On the other hand," said Beckett, rolling his cigar sensuously between his fingers to hear the leaves crackle, "if we don't bring the rebels into the fold, they might just take the opportunity to stab us in the back while we're distracted by the alien attack."

"Kill them all," said Kassar. "Clones and espers and nonpeople. They're as alien to us as anything that might come from beyond the Rim."

"Typical of the Church these days," said Beatrice. "Rather fight than think; rather lose than try diplomacy. Fanatics unite; you have nothing to lose but your mind."

"Well said," said Valentine Wolfe. "I couldn't have put it better myself."

They all looked around to find Valentine had emerged from the crowd and was standing right behind them. Beatrice ostentatiously moved a step away, to put more distance between herself and the Wolfe. Valentine smiled at her dazzlingly. Kassar glared at him.

"What do you want, degenerate?"

"Well, I have a list if you're interested, Kassar, but you're really not my type. I just wanted to agree with everything Beatrice said."

"Thanks a whole bunch," said Beatrice. "If you're on my side, they'll never believe me. You do this to me deliberately, don't you? Just because I wouldn't marry you, you're determined to ruin my life."

"You wound me deeply," said Valentine. "Can't a man speak out for common sense and sanity anymore?"

"And what the hell would you know about sanity?" demanded Beatrice. "There are depressed lemmings on the edges of cliffs who've got a better grasp on reality than you have. And more common sense."

"If you two would like a little privacy," Beckett began, and then decided not to say anymore as Beatrice glared at him.

"I would rather be left in the company of a piranha with an overbite! Don't you move one step, General. That goes for you, too, Kassar. Loathsome though your presence undoubtedly is, it is still preferable to that of the genetic disaster area currently heading the Wolfe Family. I understand there are plans for the Dangerous Chemicals Investigation Board to have him declared a toxic-waste dump. Maybe then we could have him banned from inhabited areas on health grounds."

"Ah," said the Empress from her Throne. "Young love . . ."

Not all that far away, Gregor Shreck glared at the company before the Iron Throne. By rights he should have been there, too, adding his words and wisdom to whatever they were discussing. He was head of one of the oldest Families in the Empire, and a man to be noticed. But he had been robbed of his true position in society by back-stabbing traitors who refused to admit his true qualities. They smiled at his face, laughed at his back, and whispered against him. They'd pay. They would all pay, one day. But that could wait. For the moment he had little room in himself for anything but rage. Evangeline had left him. The ungrateful little bitch had actually dared to walk out on him. Together with that cow Adrienne, she'd found the courage to outface him, but they'd find out soon enough that no one downed Gregor Shreck and lived to boast of it. Evangeline might think herself safe among the underground and the non-people, but there was bound to be a weak link somewhere, and he had all the time, money, and venom he needed to find it. Someone would respond to money or pressure or the right kind of deal. Someone always did. And then he'd get her.

It wouldn't be long before people started noticing that Evangeline wasn't around. People in Tower Shreck would talk. You couldn't stop them. Then people in the Court would spot a potential weakness and start asking questions. Where was she? What had happened to her? What had he done to her? There were always people ready to stick their noses in where they didn't belong. He could always clone another Evangeline; he still had the tissue samples from the original. But it would take months to rear and train her. It had with the last one. And what if the first clone reappeared? There'd be no way to hide what he'd done with two Evangelines walking around. And there was always the possibility the first clone might tell all anyway, from a safe distance, as a kind of revenge. She'd find it hard to prove anything without revealing herself, but just the accusation would be damaging. Mud sticks, particularly when people want it to. Gregor scowled. These days, more than ever, it was vital that he seem above reproach.

In recent months he'd taken steps to publicly become very religious. He attended all the right services at all the right places, moved in all the right circles, backed the currently fashionable charities and pressure groups, and did everything he could to win the established Church's approval. He needed their support if he was to win himself a place up in the rarefied heights where he deserved to be. However, in order to win the Church's backing, he'd had to set up a public reputation as being purer than pure. This had taken some doing. In the past he'd gone his own way, did what he wanted when he wanted, and let his people clean up the mess afterward with money or threats. Typical enough behavior for an aristocrat with money to burn and more hormones than sense. Luckily, the Church didn't care much about your past as long as you repented publicly, made a large donation, and put it all behind you. Gregor didn't care twopence for the first two, but balked at the third. There were limits. Still, there was public, and then there was private. As long as he looked good in the public eye, rumored sins could be forgiven. Even ignored. Gregor had never been any good at public relations, but fortunately there were members of his Family who were. They were currently standing just behind him, waiting for his instructions. If they knew what was good for them. Gregor turned to face them, giving them both his best forbidding stare.

Toby the Troubador was his nephew, loath though he sometimes was to admit it. A short, fat, perspiring fellow with flat blond hair, a ready smile, a mind like a steel trap, and the morals of a starving sewer rat. His main duties and responsibilities were to write up the Family's doings in the best possible light, and then see to it that those reports appeared in all the right places. Journals, holo shows, gossip columns. He was a public-relations man, spin doctor, damage-limitations expert, and a first-class liar. He had to be. It wasn't easy making Gregor Shreck look good. The rest of the Clan had their moments, bless their black little hearts, but Toby knew how to handle them. If they didn't toe the line when he needed them to, with a prepared speech here and an appearance there, smiling and waving for the cameras, he just left them out of his reports entirely until they did. After all, the only thing worse then being talked about by everyone is not being talked about by everyone. If your face wasn't in all the glossies and the holo shows, you weren't anyone. Toby could make you a celebrity, famous for being famous, if you followed the rules. His rules. Namely, do what you like as long as it's entertaining, but only as long as I get to hear about it first, so I can make sure it's got the right spin on it before it hits the streets. Unfortunately, he couldn't order Gregor about like that. If he'd ever been dumb enough to try, Gregor would have ripped out his vocal cords as a warning.

"Talk to me, boy," said Gregor sharply. "What are you saying about Evangeline at present?"

"The official line is she's resting, after overdoing it," Toby said smoothly. "We haven't specified exactly what she's been overdoing, but the gossips will come up with something. They do so love to speculate. Presumably, you'll let me know when she's rested enough, so I can reintroduce her to society?"

"I'll tell you what you need to know when you need to know it," said Gregor. "How's my current standing with the Church?"

"Reasonable. Though I do wish you'd learn to watch your language, Uncle. Sometimes I think the Church would happily pardon adultery, but not the specific four-letter word used to describe exactly what you were doing. Most people will turn a specifically deaf ear if I pay them enough, whether it concerns obscenities or political malaprops; but sooner or later you're going to say the wrong thing in front of the wrong people, and there won't be a thing I can do to help you."

Gregor sniffed. "It was your idea for us to get into bed with the Church in the first place. Can't say I've seen much in the way of results."

"With the Church behind us, we are safe from a great

many other enemies," Toby said patiently. "But if the
Church ever finds out about the real you, we could be in real
trouble."

"Then, you'd better make damn sure they don't, hadn't
you?" said Gregor.

"I do wish you two wouldn't fight," said Grace Shreck,
knowing they wouldn't listen to her. They never did. She
was Gregor's older sister and did her best to look as little
like him as possible. She was long, tall, and thin, with a
pale, swan-like neck, and a mass of white hair piled up on
top of her head in a rather precarious-looking style that
hadn't been fashionable in years. She wore the same style of
clothes she had when she was young, and noticed newer
styles only in order to criticize them. Every now and again,
fashion rediscovered her look, and for a month or so she
would be the height of fashion, which embarrassed her
greatly. Grace preferred not to be noticed, whenever possible.

She'd never married, because after their parents had died
suddenly, Gregor had needed her services as assistant, secretary, and general dogsbody while he was holding the Family
together and making it great again. There'd been no time for
romance, no chance for a life of her own. The Family
needed her, Gregor needed her, and she'd had to settle for
that. And if she was ever angry, she kept it to herself. Eventually, there came a time when Gregor didn't need her anymore, but she stayed with him anyway, because she didn't
know any other kind of life. The world had changed during
her enforced absence, and people frightened her, whether
they meant to or nor. Besides, she'd always known Gregor
would never let her go. He couldn't risk her marrying and
moving outside the Family's influence, outside of his control. She knew too much about the Clan in general and him
in particular. And the things he'd done to make the Shrecks
great again.

She came to Court as little as possible, because crowds
upset her; but the Empress's edict had been quite specific,
for once. Everyone in the Families was to come. No exemp-
tions. If you were on your deathbed, bring your deathbed
with you. So Grace came on Gregor's arm, stayed close to
Toby, and tried to pretend she was just watching it on the
holo.

She disapproved of the way Gregor treated Toby, but

didn't know what to do about it. Certainly, Gregor wouldn't listen to her, even if she could bring herself to say anything. Toby's father had been Christian Shreck, younger brother to herself and Gregor. He disappeared years ago, after a furious head-to-head with Gregor, and was never seen again. The Empress ordered an investigation, but nothing ever came of it. Gregor submitted to questioning by an Imperial esper and surprised everyone by passing the test with ease. He was officially cleared. But after that, people stopped resisting Gregor's rise to power.

Toby came under Gregor's influence the same way every Shreck did; because he had no choice. Toby had a sister once, but the Empress took her to be one of her maids, and that was that. Grace couldn't protect or advance him, so that just left Gregor. And so now the Shreck used Toby as he'd once used Grace, and there was nothing she could do about it. Another life sacrificed to Gregor's ambition. That was just the way things were in Clan Shreck.

Grace sighed tiredly. She missed Christian. He'd been the only one in the Family with a sense of humor. She realized Gregor was shouting at Toby again. Gregor was having a hard time being a public person. He wasn't suited to it. Grace looked at Gregor, red-faced and sweating as he raised his voice yet again, and suddenly it seemed to her that this was just the most recent in a long series of straws that broke the camel's back. She stepped forward and slapped Gregor smartly on the arm with her folded fan.

"Gregor, I won't have you using that kind of language in public! Remember, we are at Court. People are listening."

"And you can shut your stupid mouth as well," snapped Gregor without looking around. "When I want your opinion, I'll have my head examined."

"Really!" Grace could feel herself blushing, as she always did when someone spoke harshly to her. "Why can't we all just be friends, in public at least?"

"She's right, you know," said Toby diffidently. "The Church believes in happy Families."

"Stuff the Church," said Gregor immediately, but in a somewhat lower tone. "I have a right to be angry. I can't believe Valentine turned me down. It's so obviously in both our interests to work together against our common enemies, that even he should have been able to see the advantages. All right, he's a drug-soaked weirdo with no more common

sense than a leper playing volleyball, but if we'd stood together, no one would have dared stand against us."

"Can't say I'm sorry," said Toby. "Valentine may be
number one at the moment, but there's no one here who
likes or trusts him, despite all the smiles in his direction.
Putting a good PR shine on an alliance between you two
would have really strained my creativity. You'd have a better
chance of selling lepers' fingers as a fashion accessory. So
what now, Uncle? Move to Plan B?"

"What's Plan B?" said Grace suspiciously. "No one's
mentioned any Plan B to me. Honestly, Gregor, you never
tell me anything anymore."

"That's because you don't need to know anything; just
shut up and do as you're told. Stay here with Toby. Don't
move. I'll take care of Plan B."

Gregor stalked away without looking back. He knew they
wouldn't move without his permission. Plan B was the
Chojiros. If the first Family wouldn't deal, there was always
the chance the second might. He kicked his way through the
deep snow, and people moved quickly to get out of his way.
But he no more noticed that than the air that he breathed. He
drew himself up before BB Chojiro, glared briefly at the Investigator beside her to show he wasn't intimidated, and
then bowed briefly to BB. She bowed back, calm and assured. Razor ignored him.

"We have a common enemy in the Wolfes," Gregor said
flatly. "May I suggest that it is in our interest to combine
against Valentine? You produce the computers for his starships, and I make the shells; but as long as he controls production of the new stardrive, we have to run our businesses
to suit him. With just the right pressure and timing, he could
ruin either one of us, even drive us out of business completely, so he could move in and take over. I had planned to
work with the Campbells, back when they looked to be in
the lead for the stardrive contract. We had an understanding.
That's why I permitted a linking marriage. But that fell
through, and Valentine won't deal. I work under his conditions or I don't work at all. And that is completely unacceptable. So I need an ally to make sure I don't get squeezed
out, and you need someone to watch your back while you
work with him. We could both profit from such a union, and
after all, neither of us has any cause to love Valentine."

"Both?" said BB. "I think not. All the profit would be on

your side. We don't need you, Lord Shreck, and you have
nothing we want. Yes, you build shells, but anyone can build
shells. And to be honest, Lord Shreck, we're rather choosy
about who we ally ourselves with."

"You little bitch," hissed Gregor, and before he really
knew what he was doing, his hand was shooting out to grab
her by the throat. He hadn't even got close before Investigator Razor's hand shot out to intercept his. Gregor's pudgy
white hand disappeared entirely inside Razor's big black
fist, and Gregor cried out as Razor clamped down hard,
grinding the bones of Gregor's hand together. He let go after
a long moment, and Gregor fell back a step, clutching his
throbbing hand to his breast. BB Chojiro and her Investigator studied him with the same impersonal gaze as he stood
before them, trembling with impotent rage.

"Turn around and go back to your own people, Shreck,"
said Razor calmly. He didn't raise his voice. He didn't have
to. "You have no business here."

Gregor glared at them both, searching for some final insult or threat that he could use to crush them, but in the end
he had to turn silently and trudge back through the snow
again. People moved even faster to get out of his way this
time, giving him the same kind of respect one would a mad-
dened scorpion that might strike out at anyone, just for being
there. Gregor was actually thinking too hard to bother about
that. He had to find allies and support from somewhere, or
he might easily find himself being edged out of the starship
business altogether. Anyone could build shells ... His alliance with the Church should bring long-term benefits, but
right now he needed the money. He'd find someone. There
was always someone. And when he was a power again in his
own right, he'd make BB Chojiro pay for daring to humiliate him. He made himself breathe more slowly. There was
still latitude with Clan Wolfe. Maybe Valentine wouldn't
deal, but Daniel and Stephanie just might if approached in
the right way. They might work with him just to spite their
brother. Yes, that was an idea. He slowed his pace, and allowed himself a small smile. He would be strong again, and
have his revenges upon his enemies, and no one would dare
look down on him again.

Lionstone finally waved the people arguing before her to
silence, and called the Court to order. Her amplified voice
echoed across the arctic waste, cutting effortlessly through

the courtiers' babble of voices. In a moment there was silence, broken only by the faint moaning of the bitter wind as the courtiers' attention fixed on their Empress. She smiled out over them, and it was not a pleasant smile. The courtiers stood still and quiet before her, snow settling on their heads and shoulders till they resembled the snowmen they'd passed earlier. A few people made the connection in their minds and shuddered suddenly, not at all from the cold. Lionstone glared down at Valentine and Beatrice until they got the message, bowed, and faded back into the crowd. General Beckett and Cardinal Kassar moved to stand on each side of the Iron Throne, staring out at the courtiers, representing army and Church, the arms of the Empress. Lionstone nodded to Beckett, and he raised his voice in a parade ground bark.

"Captain Silence, Investigator Frost, and Security Officer Stelmach; step forward and make your report on the alien attack!"

Stelmach jumped guiltily and then looked around quickly to see if anyone had noticed. Silence and Frost just strode forward, not looking around, until they stood at attention before the Iron Throne. Silence's face was calm, but there was new hope in his heart. This was what he'd hoped for; a chance to tell his side of the story before anyone else had a chance to muddy the waters. He waited a moment for Stelmach to join them and then realized the Security Officer had stopped on the edge of the crowd, his eyes fixed on the Grendel alien standing just before the Throne. Silence didn't blame him. The bloody thing disturbed the hell out of him, too. He reached back and pulled Stelmach forward to stand beside him. The Security Officer's eyes never left the alien. Silence glanced at Frost and wished he hadn't. The Investigator was staring at the alien hungrily, only a moment away from attacking the thing on general principles. Silence considered the matter, then reached out and pulled Frost back a step. The alien was the Empress's pet, and if by some miracle Frost actually did manage to kill the bloody thing, Lionstone would not be at all happy. Frost pulled her arm free immediately and glared at him, but stayed where she was. Silence decided to start his report before something unpleasant happened.

He kept it simple and succinct, but hit all the salient points. There was a lot of uneasy murmuring from the as-

sembled Court as he described what he'd found in the
wrecked Base on Gehenna. He told how the *Dauntless*
tracked the alien ship to Golgotha, and then the murmurs got
really loud when he described the alien craft's nature and ca-
pabilities and the life-forms he'd found inside it. He let Frost
take over from there. She was the expert on aliens. Her report was cold, factual, even clinical, but Silence was shivering along with everyone else by the time she'd finished, and
it didn't have a damn thing to do with the cold. After she'd
finished, it was very quiet. The Empress nodded slowly and
looked out over the Court again.

"Perhaps now you appreciate our position on the necessity
for increased military spending. If one alien ship can do so
much, what might a fleet accomplish? We have heard whispers of late of a proposed revolt against the new tax in-
creases; let us make it clear that any such treachery will be
put down harshly, with every resource at our disposal. In the
current circumstances, refusal to support the military can
only be seen as treason against humanity." General Beckett
smiled, Cardinal Kassar did not. The Empress looked at
Stelmach. "Do you have anything to add at this time?"

Stelmach swallowed hard, shook his head quickly, and finally managed a very quiet, "Not at this time, Your Majesty,
no."

"Very well," said the Empress. "Guards, bring the prisoner forward."

The middle of the crowd quickly parted to form a narrow
aisle through which two armed guards half led and half
dragged a naked man through the deep snow. He wore only
wrist and ankle chains, and some blood that had spattered
down onto his chest from his recently broken nose. His skin
was a bluish-white, and he shuddered uncontrollably in the
biting cold. The guards threw him on his knees before the
Iron Throne. He looked up at Lionstone pleadingly and tried
to say something, but he was shaking so much he couldn't
get the words out. Lionstone looked down at him thoughtfully.

"This pathetic object is Fredric Hill. Head of starport security here on Golgotha. We gave him the appointment ourselves. We thought he showed promise. This man let the
rebels in, allowed them to sabotage the Tax and Tithe Headquarters, and failed to prevent them from lowering the planet's defenses as they escaped. He also failed to protect us

from the alien ship. We could question him on this, but what's the point? He'd just nod and smile and agree with everything I said, and then try to pass the blame onto his staff, or hidden traitors, or lack of the right equipment. Anything but himself. After all, he'd say, the rebels arrived in a Hadenman ship. Probably half his people took one look at the great golden ship of awful legend and ran for their lives. And the other half probably followed them, once the alien ship swept past our nonexistent defenses to strafe the city.

"It doesn't make any difference. He was head of starport security, responsible for our defense. A strong man in that position might have accomplished much. He might have pulled enough of his people together to organize equipment repairs, bring secondary and backup systems on-line, send out rescue teams to aid the wounded and distressed in the city. Instead, according to his own security records, he dithered and fumbled and finally hid, reemerging only when it was all safely over. Quite unacceptable behavior from one of our officers. We have therefore decided that an example shall be made."

She looked back at the Grendel alien, and after a moment everyone else did, too. It stood calm and relaxed behind the Throne, a living nightmare in spiked crimson silicon armor. The yoke around its armored neck made a sudden polite chiming noise, and then the alien surged forward so quickly the human eye couldn't follow it. One moment it was standing just behind the Throne, and the next it was towering over the cringing security head, its great clawed hands on his bare shoulders. The courtiers nearest it surged back as far as the pressure of the crowd would allow, but the Grendel paid them no heed. Its claws sank deep into the man's flesh, and thick runnels of blood coursed down his colorless flesh. He opened his mouth to scream, and the alien opened its mouth and bit the man's face off. Skin and eyes and nose and mouth disappeared as the alien jerked back its great head, leaving only a shattered bloody skull, screaming horribly with the security man's voice.

The alien chewed and swallowed and then leaned forward again, thrusting its grinning jaws into the man's chest with brutal force. The sternum stove in, cracking like paper, and the Grendel alien's head burrowed in the man's chest, going after the heart like a pig hunting truffles. The man's arms waved wildly for a few moments, and then they fell to his sides and lay still. And Fredric Hill, once head of starport security, hung limply in the alien's grasp as it chewed thoughtfully, savoring the flavor. The yoke around its neck chimed, but the Grendel didn't respond. The yoke chimed again, and the Grendel dropped the body carelessly into the blood-soaked snow and moved unhurriedly back to resume its position just behind the Iron Throne. Steaming hot blood dripped thickly from its grinning jaws and ran slowly down its gleaming silicon armor. In the snow before the Throne, Hill's body lay in a crumpled heap, like a broken discarded toy that no one wanted to play with anymore.

Silence moved in close beside Frost. He could feel the anger boiling within her, ready to spill over at a moment's provocation. Her whole career had been built around killing aliens before they got the chance to kill people. He put a warning hand on her arm. It was as tense as coiled steel. She turned her head and gave him a hard look, and he took his hand away. Frost was an Investigator and had no time for human weaknesses like compassion. Her anger was purely professional.

The Court murmured among itself, looking from the Grendel to the gutted body and back again, impressed by the savagery of the kill, if not the quality of the control the Empress had over it. The many lessons involved in the man's death had not been missed by any of the courtiers. Silence shared a significant glance with Stelmach, but they both kept their peace. Those courtiers nearest the body looked down at the open wounds steaming in the chill air and tried to back away a little farther. But the crowd was packed in tight behind them, and there was nowhere for them to go. Nobody wanted to look at the alien. The Empress smiled at them all.

"Cute, isn't he? Table manners aren't up to much, but he's only young. Really little more than a baby. Imagine what he'll be like when he comes of age. Imagine an army of him, spilling across a battlefield like an endless wave of slaughter. Unstoppable shock troops, leaving nothing behind them but mountains of dead and oceans of blood. I'm quite looking forward to it. The work into controlling the Grendel aliens more perfectly is going well. Soon we'll have yokes for every Sleeper in the vaults, and then we'll send them out against the aliens who attacked us here today. Or anyone else who threatens us. Captain Silence, you haven't finished your report. Tell the Court what you discovered on the Wolf-ling World."

Silence, Frost, and Stelmach took it in turns to tell what they'd found in the vast caverns deep beneath the frozen surface of the Wolfling World, once also known as Haden, home to the augmented supermen, the Hadenmen. They told of the thousands of sleeping Hadenmen, who rose from their long death-like sleep and walked out of their Tomb, glorious and powerful, an army of cyborg warriors who once tried to overthrow humanity and only narrowly failed.

They told of the rebels who woke them: the outlaw, Owen Deathstalker, the pirate Hazel d'Ark, the bounty hunter Ruby Journey, and the legendary professional rebel Jack Random. They told of the defeat of the *Dauntless*'s forces, but none of them mentioned the Lord High Dram's presence or his death at the hands of another legend—the original Deathstalker, thought dead for centuries, but now returned for vengeance against the Empire that betrayed and hounded him. All three had been told previously, in no uncertain terms, that Dram was not to be mentioned. Given their current situation, Silence and Frost and Stelmach were happy to be flexible with the truth.

The Court continued to murmur among itself, despite darting glares from the Empress, as the courtiers reacted to names like Jack Random and the original Deathstalker. They were also troubled by the reemergence of Owen Deathstalker, outlawed by the Empress for no good reason, who had evaded all her armies and now looked to be leading the new rebellion. And they really didn't like the idea of a new army of Hadenmen massing to attack the Empire again. The only reason the Hadenmen weren't still officially listed as the Enemies of Humanity was because the rogue AIs of Shub were even nastier. The Empress finally sat back and let them mutter for a while before reclaiming their attention with her amplified voice.

"Let's not all panic just yet, boys and girls. The Hadenmen are a long way away and only newly awakened; it will be some time yet before they're in any position to pose a real threat to us. The man claiming to be Jack Random could be nothing more than a double; rebel propaganda to draw people to their cause. The man himself is probably long dead." She stopped suddenly as BB Chojiro stepped gracefully out of the crowd to stand before the Throne. BB bowed gracefully, and the Empress fixed her with an icy glare. "This had better be good, Chojiro. And extremely relevant."

"With all due respect, Your Majesty, it had come to us through normally reliable channels that Jack Random had been captured by Empire forces some time back, and then escaped."

"Then, you were misinformed," said Lionstone flatly. "We never had him. If we had, he would never have been allowed to escape. Is that clear? Good. Now, don't interrupt us again, or we'll have the Grendel open you up so we can all see what little girls are made of."

"Clan Chojiro has no wish to appear rude or impertinent, Your Mjaesty," said BB calmly. "We are merely trying to ascertain the facts. The Hadenman ship that brought the rebels here today was very real and twice as impressive, implying that not only are the Hadenmen and the rebels working together, but that the augmented men are already so well prepared that they can drop in on us anytime they like. Who is to say a fleet of these ships is not already setting out from Haden to try humanity's strength again?"

"You're a real cheerful sort to have around, Chojiro," said Lionstone. "If the Hadenmen are getting ready for a comeback, that is all the more reason to support my military buildup, and stop whining about your tax bills, isn't it? Anyone else want to add anything before we move on? Bearing in mind it had better be pretty damn good, or we'll keep you all here till your eyeballs freeze solid."

"If you will allow me," said Valentine Wolfe, "I have a few words to say." He stepped forward to stand beside BB, who gave him a brief sidelong glance and then stepped a little farther away. Valentine gave her a dazzling smile anyway and nodded to the Empress. "Lovely Court, Lionstone. Very bracing. Could do with a few penguins, but I like the snow. It goes with my complexion. Now then, I had heard, through various, reliable, and only slightly corrupt sources that your consort, the Lord High Dram, had been a part of Captain Silence's expedition to the Wolfling World, and that, regrettably, he met his end there. And is, in fact, quite definitely dead. Given that no one seems to have seen him at Court or at your side for some time, perhaps you could reassure us all as to his present whereabouts and well-being?"

"Of course," said Lionstone. "Dram was never there. He

has been here on Golgotha all along, undertaking some important business for me."

"I'm sure we're all very relieved to hear that," said Valentine. "But where might the Lord High Dram be, right now?"

"Right here," said the Empress, smiling calmly. "At my side, as he always is."

She gestured smoothly, a hologram shield disappeared, and there was Dram, standing beside her, between Cardinal Kassar and the Throne. Kassar didn't actually jump, but he looked as though he would have liked to and did move away a step before he could stop himself. Dram, Warrior Prime of the Empire, stood at Lionstone's side in his jet-black robes and battle armor, his familiar handsome face perhaps just a little cold and distant. He nodded calmly to the assembled courtiers, who stared silently back. There had never been any love lost between Lionstone's right hand and the Company of Lords. Valentine studied Dram for a long moment, then looked at BB, shrugged, and stepped back into the crowd. No point in playing out a losing hand. BB Chojiro inclined her head to Dram and to the Empress, and stepped back to rejoin Investigator Razor. Silence and Frost and Stelmach looked at each other.

"Now, that is interesting," murmured Frost. "If that's Dram, who did we see die on the Wolfling World? The real Dram? Is this a clone, or was it the clone who came with us while the real Dram stayed behind here?"

"I don't know," said Silence. "But I have a strong feeling asking those sorts of questions could prove to be really bad for your health."

"What are you saying?" said Stelmach impatiently. "I can't understand either of you when you whisper like that. What are we going to do?"

Silence and Frost looked at each other. Without realizing, they'd fallen into the near telepathic contact again, their thoughts jumping back and forth like conversation. Which should have been impossible with all the esp-blockers Lionstone insisted on for Court gatherings. Something else for them to discuss when they were safely alone.

"I'll tell you what we're going to do," said Silence to Stelmach. "We're going to keep our mouths shut until the Empress tells us what to say. If she says that's Dram, then that's Dram. Right?"

"Fine by me," said Frost.

"Right," said Stelmach, but he didn't look at all happy about it.

There was a sudden disturbance among the courtiers as someone moved forward through the crush, and then a man dressed in the very height of fashion stepped out of the crowd to stand challengingly before the Iron Throne. He wore a long golden frock coat and leather boots that rose halfway up his thighs. His hair was long bronzed strands, and his face was blindingly florescent. The thick silver medallion hanging over his breast proclaimed him an elected Member of Parliament. He glanced quickly about him for the holo cameras he knew were somewhere around, even if he couldn't see them, and drew himself up proudly. Like all politicians, he understood the importance of putting on a good show for an audience. And half the Empire would be watching today.

"Your Majesty, I really must protest. Information has come to me, from a private but valued source who must of course remain anonymous, that verifies everything the Lord Wolfe had to say. The Lord High Dram is dead. He died on the Wolfling World, cut down by the original Deathstalker himself. The man at your side is at best an impostor, at worst a clone you are attempting to fool us into accepting. Well, I for one am not fooled. I must insist that this . . . person submit to a genetest, here and now. We cannot permit a clone to stand as Consort to Your Majesty."

"We?" said Dram. "And who might this *we* be?"

"I represent a number of my colleagues," said the Member of Parliament. "And I trust I have the backing of every loyal man and woman here. We have a right to know the truth."

Lionstone leaned forward on her Throne, her face calm and quite composed. "Your face is not familiar to us. You are . . . ?"

The MP drew himself up a little farther, his voice ringing out magnificently. "I am Richard Scott, newly elected Member for Graylake East. I won my seat on a platform of reform for truth and justice in government. It seems only fitting that I begin my fight here at Court."

Lionstone nodded and leaned back in her Throne. "I might have known. There's nothing more pompous and impertinent than a newly elected official. Dram, you deal with this."

Dram nodded, his cold dark eyes fixed on Scott, who was looking a little perturbed. Whatever answer he'd expected to his challenge, this wasn't it. No anger or denial or bluster, just a calm indifference from the Empress and a cold calculating look from her Consort. Scott began to wonder if he'd made a mistake. His colleagues had been loud enough in their support earlier, but now they stood silent in the crowd while he stood alone before the Iron Throne. Dram stepped forward, and Scott had to fight down an impulse to step back. He had to appear strong, resolute. Dram came to a halt, standing between Scott and the Throne. His sudden smile was cold as death.

"The Empress has already stated before this assembled Court that I am the real Lord High Dram. By challenging that, you challenge her word. You have, in effect, called her a liar. And that is a dueling offense—a matter of honor. I represent Lionstone in this matter. Find another to stand for you, or you must defend yourself, here and now."

Scott paled as he saw the trap he'd fallen into. No one would help him now. The field of honor was sacrosanct. He swallowed hard. "Your Majesty, I protest! Members of Parliament are by tradition exempt from the Code Duello."

"Normally, yes," said Dram. "But you insulted the Empress in front of her own Court. That much insult outweighs tradition."

Scott didn't turn to look behind him. He knew the faces of the courtiers would be closed against him. He raised his hands to show they were empty. "I don't have a sword."

One of the guards who'd brought in the late head of starport security stepped forward at Dram's gesture and offered Scott his sword. The MP accepted it as though it was his death warrant, which in a way it was. He was no duelist, hadn't drawn a sword in anger since his student days. And Dram was the Warrior Prime. If this was Dram, of course.

Scott hefted the sword once, getting the feel of it. It was a good blade, well balanced. He started to cry. Not a breakdown or anything dramatic; he'd be damned if he gave them the satisfaction. Just a few tears, running down his cheeks. He knew he was going to die. This was an execution, not a duel. He couldn't remember whether he'd told his wife he loved her when he left that morning. He hoped he had. And he'd had that specially imported marble come for the fore-court. She wouldn't have a clue what to do with it. So many things left undone. He shook his head briefly. None of that mattered now. It was too late for anything but Dram and him and their two swords. He looked straight at Dram, and though tears were still running down his cheeks, his voice was cold and hard and determined.

"Let's do it."

Dram stepped forward, lifting his sword, and Scott went to meet him. They circled each other a moment, and then Dram launched a blistering attack with all his strength be-hind it. Scott parried as best he could, but after only half a dozen blows his sword was knocked out of his hand. He watched it sail through the air and land in the snow a dozen feet away. He looked back at Dram, held his head high, and tried to keep his mouth from trembling. There was nowhere he could run, and maybe a good showing would buy him a reprieve from the Empress. But Dram didn't even look back at her. He raised his sword and brought it flashing down to sink deep into Scott's right shoulder, like a forester taking his ax to a stubborn tree.

The impact drove Scott to his knees, a surprised sound ex-ploding from his slack mouth. Dram jerked his sword free, and blood fountained from the great wound, spattering Scott's face and the snow around him. Dram struck at him again and again, avoiding a killing blow, his sword rising and falling with relentless precision. Scott tried to intercept some of the blows with his arms, the sword slicing skin and meat away as the blade rebounded from the bones, but then one of the blows took off his left hand, and after that he just crouched there in the snow, cradling the bloody stump to his chest. He cried out constantly at the pain, but made no move to avoid any of the blows. Finally, he fell forward into the crimson snow and lay still. It was obvious to all that the man was dead, but Dram continued to hack at the body like an axman cutting wood, the body jumping and shuddering under the rain of blows.

The courtiers watched in horrified silence. Lionstone leaned forward in her Throne to get a better view, smiling widely. The maids stirred restlessly at the foot of her Throne, excited by the smell of blood in the air, watching the body jump and shudder with their unblinking insect eyes. Silence watched impassively, and wondered if he'd just crouch there in the snow and take it. Armed or unarmed, he'd do his best to die with his hands crushing Dram's throat. Frost watched the display with a curled lip, disapproving of such a messy kill. Stelmach's face was as white as the snow, but he didn't look away. He knew how dangerous it could be to show weakness in Lionstone's Court. And finally Dram stopped and straightened up, standing over the butchered body with blood dripping the length of his sword blade. He was breathing just a little heavily, but his face was calm. He thrust his sword into the snow a few times to clean it, and then sheathed it. He looked at the watching faces of the courtiers, and smiled briefly.

"Time for a by-election at Graylake East."

He moved back to take his place at Lionstone's side. Kassar gave him plenty of room. The Empress gestured for her guards to come and drag the body away, as they'd previously disposed of the late head of starport security. They wrapped the body in a sheet, careful not to leave any of it behind, and carried it away. They couldn't do anything about all the blood soaked into the snow, though. The courtiers were silent and watchful, thinking hard and privately for later discussion. They all knew an object lesson when they saw one. They also recognized the Lord High Dram's distinctive style when they saw it, and this killing had been typical of the man privately known as the Widowmaker. Lionstone reached out and tousled Dram's hair, as one might pet a favorite dog, and then turned her gaze on Silence, Frost, and Stelmach. Silence and Stelmach tried to stand a little straighter.

"We have new duties for you three," said Lionstone calmly. "We were rather upset with you when we heard of your failures on the Wolfling World, but in saving us from the alien ship, you have redeemed yourselves. We must commend you, Captain Silence. You seem to have a knack of drawing back from the brink at the very last moment. Take care your timing doesn't let you down in the future. Now then, you and your companions are to return to the *Dauntless,* embark on a tour of all those planets in our Empire still mainly populated by aliens, and make sure of their loyalty to the Throne in these trying times. If you encounter dissent, you are empowered by us to take whatever steps you deem necessary to restore order. Under no circumstances is any alien world to be allowed to make contact with any alien force from outside the Empire. If contact has already been established, you are authorized to scorch the planet. That's all. You can say thank you now."

"Thank you, on behalf of us all, Your Majesty," said Silence. He thought he'd better say it. Stelmach was still clearly in shock, and Frost had never said thank you in her life. Investigators didn't. "I take it you wish us to begin this tour of duty immediately?"

"Oh, hang around for a while if you like," said Lionstone. "Enjoy the rest of this audience. It might be some time before you get a chance to see us again."

If we're lucky, thought Silence, bowing. He wasn't fooled by the kind words. No one was. He'd been handed what was essentially punishment duties, doing the dirtiest, most unpleasant but necessary job she could find. Too important to be trusted to someone incompetent or weak of stomach, but too time-consuming to be given to anyone she really needed. And afterward, if his actions proved to be politically embarrassing, he could always be thrown to the wolves as a sacrifice. Still, it could have been worse. He was still alive and in possession of all his extremities. He had been given a sign that he was forgiven, if not forgotten; a last chance to show he could still be useful.

He hadn't been fooled by Lionstone's invitation to stick around, either. Once this Court was over, guards would no doubt immediately appear to escort him and his companions back to the *Dauntless,* to see they didn't get lost along the way or talk to anyone they shouldn't. One reason for sending them out to the backs of beyond was so they couldn't be asked awkward questions about Dram's death on the Wolfling World. By the time they got back to Golgotha, the question would be moot. Silence gestured to Frost and Stelmach, and led them back into the safety of the crowd. It wouldn't be wise to risk catching the Empress's eye again. There was such a thing as tempting fate.

Lionstone began winding down the business of the Court, handing out commendations and reprimands as necessary, and reminding everyone of where the true power in the Empire lay. Questions were asked and answered, points of law decided, and reports made on the repair work taking place in the devastated city and starport. The courtiers began to relax a little and felt free enough to talk quietly among themselves again. David Deathstalker and Kit SummerIsle, that quiet

young man also known as Kid Death, watched from a safe
distance and allowed themselves the occasional discreet
yawn. The action appeared to be over. It had finally stopped
snowing and the wind had settled down, as though even the
weather was growing bored now the excitement was over. It
was still bloody cold, though. A cold setting for two very
cold young men.

Kit SummerIsle had become the head of his Family by the
simple expedient of killing everyone who stood between him
and the title, including his own parents. He killed his grandfather, a legendary old warrior, at the request of the Empress, but little good it had done him. She lost interest in
him once he was no longer of any use to her. He flirted with
the underground for a while, but was thinking of dropping
out after the debacle at Silo Nine. He knew a losing proposition when he saw one. And so the man commonly known
as Kid Death, trusted by no one and hated by many, had become an outcast and a pariah even in the dog-eat-dog world
of high society. Just nineteen years old, he was a slender figure in black and silver battle armor, with pale blond flyaway
hair above a long pale face dominated by icy blue eyes. He
walked like a predator in a world of prey. Kid Death, the
smiling killer.

His only friend stood at his side, scowling thoughtfully.
David Deathstalker had taken over the title as head of his
Clan after the outlawing of his cousin Owen. Eighteen years
old, tall, muscular, and immaculately dressed, he was handsome enough already to have flustered the hearts of a few
society beauties. He'd recently figured that out and was
planning on cutting a swath through the more impression-
able young ladies of his generation. His friendship with Kit
SummerIsle gave him a dangerous glamor, which he played
to the hilt.

Their friendship had come as something of a surprise to
both of them. They had both come to be heads of their Families at an early age, only to find no other Family respected
them. They fought duels at the drop of an insult, both separately and together, but that only won them a cold public
courtesy. In return, they had nothing but contempt for the intrigues and betrayals that made up Family politics, not least
because they didn't have the patience or the skill to take part
themselves. They had won a certain following among the
general populace by fighting in the Arena against all comers,

to the scandal of their peers, but they couldn't be said to be popular. The SummerIsle because of what he'd done to his Family and because he was a complete bloody psychopath, and David because he bore a name that had become a synonym for treason. But they had found a kindred spirit in each other, fellow outcasts rejected by their society, and two young men who had never known friendship before grew closer than brothers, sworn to each other to death and beyond. They stood together in the crowd of courtiers, ignored by their neighbors, and studied Dram dubiously.

"I could take him," said David. "And either of us would make a better Warrior Prime."

"True," said Kit. "But you only get the job through popular acclaim, so I think we can forget about that. Maybe if we were to perform some outstanding act of bravery or note, things would be different. But we're never allowed a chance at anything like that. Still, maybe there'll be a war soon, against the rebels or the aliens. Always good chances for improvement in a war."

"There's also an equally good chance of being sent home in a box with some important pieces missing, just for standing in the wrong place at the wrong time. Wars are a little too arbitrary for my taste. I'd prefer something a little less dramatic."

"Hello," said Kit suddenly. "I spy a familiar face. Thomas Le Bihan, Member of Parliament for Thornton North, as I live and breathe. Our sometime patron. I do believe he's trying to pretend he hasn't see us. Let's wander over and embarrass him, for the good of his soul."

Kit and David moved easily through the packed crowd as people drew back to give them plenty of room. Le Bihan ignored them as long as he could, and then sighed heavily, turned, and bowed to them both. He was a great bear of a man, with a barrel chest and a spade beard and a good reputation with the sword, but even he deferred to the terrible two. Kit and David bowed in return and smiled easily at him. His own smile wasn't quite as successful. They'd needed a patron to get them established in the Arena and had chosen him to do the necessary on their behalf. He hadn't been given a choice in the matter, but he knew better than to argue.

"Hello boys," he said cautiously. "To what do I owe the honor of this confrontation? I already told you it's too soon for another match. It isn't easy finding people to fight you these days. You have one of the longest winning streaks in the Arena's history."

"We want to know why we're not popular," said David. "We win again and again, but we still haven't won the adulation of the crowds. They clap and cheer all right, but they don't worship us like they do the Masked Gladiator. Maybe you should get us a match against him. We want to be loved, Thomas. What's the problem?"

Le Bihan sighed. "You want the truth? Very well. Your trouble is you don't give a damn for anyone but yourselves. You kill in the Arena for your own pleasure; not the crowd's. You're concerned with winning, not with giving the audience a good show. On top of that, the Kid's a psycho, and you're a Deathstalker. No one wants to get too close to either of you in case it rubs off. You could fight the Masked Gladiator with both legs strapped behind your back and your head in a bucket, and you still wouldn't win their hearts. You are officially bad news. There are people who won't even talk to me, just because I agreed to become your patron. No one trusts you, no one likes you, no one even wants you around. People cross their fingers when you cross their path, because that's bad luck. Now, if you'll excuse me, I don't want to be seen talking to you anymore. I have my own future to consider."

"Don't hold back, Thomas," said David. "Tell us what you really think."

"I've killed men for less," said Kit coldly.

"I know," said Le Bihan. "That's your problem. Now, can I go, or are you going to kill me with your bare hands right in front of the Empress?"

"It's a thought," said Kit.

"Let him go," said David.

Kit shrugged, and Le Bihan took the opportunity to make his escape. Kit looked after him coldly. "He insulted us."

"By telling us the truth? That was what we asked for. Now, calm down and get that look out of your eyes. The Empress is watching. Let's not give her any more excuses to be annoyed with us. I don't think she's in a very good mood today."

Kit sniffed. "It's times like this I wish we were still part of the underground. I quite liked being a subversive."

"We both agreed it had got too risky," said David. "After

Hood turned out to be Dram, it would have been suicide to stay on. By getting out when he did, it became just his word against ours, and Lionstone didn't want the scandal. We can always rejoin. If only Dram really had died . . ."

"But he didn't."

"Apparently not. Certainly hasn't mellowed any, wherever he's been of late. He must have spoken about us to Lionstone, though. That's why I'm being shipped off to Virimonde."

"You don't have to go," said Kit, looking down at his feet.

"Yes, I do. Officially, it's a step-up. I'm being put in charge of one of the Empire's main food-producing planets. And it is my legacy, as the Deathstalker. If I did refuse to go, Lionstone might be able to use that to take my title away from me."

"But if you go," said Kit, "I'll be alone again."

"Then, come with me," said David. "It'll put an end to our chances for advancement for a while, but we'll be called back fast enough once the war starts and Lionstone realizes she can't afford to stay mad at us. We are the heads of our Families, after all."

"We're both the ends of our lines. We have no one but each other." For the first time, Kit SummerIsle looked up to meet David's eyes. "You're the only friend I've ever had, David. I'll go with you to Virimonde or the Rim or the end of everything."

"Let's not get pessimistic," said David. "You come with me. We'll have some fun. Wine, women, and as many indigenous creatures as we can kill before our arms get tired. And just in case the Empress does decide to change our banishment from Court to exile as outlaws, we could both use someone to watch our backs."

Kit smiled. "You always were the practical one, David."

"One of us has to be. Besides, if Lionstone was foolish enough to send anyone after us, we'll just send them back to her in a selection of very small boxes. With postage owing."

"Right," said Kid Death. "But if the Iron Bitch was going to have us killed, she'd have tried something by now. Probably had poison slipped in our food or a fragmentation grenade hidden in the toilet. She won't have us killed. There'll always be work for the likes of us: accomplished fighters who'll kill anyone, for any reason. You'll see. Once the war starts or the political infighting gets a bit too dirty, she'll call us back, and we'll get to kill and slaughter our way to influence and position. Personally, I can't wait."

David looked at him affectionately. "You worry me sometimes, Kit, you really do. Still, as long as I've got you with me, I don't have to worry you're off chasing Valentine again."

"I will kill him," Kit said softly. "He will take a long time to die, and at the end I'll make him beg me to finish it. He betrayed me."

David maintained a diplomatic silence. Kit had used his cyberat links in the underground to discover the Campbells' secret deal with the rogue AIs on Shub. He passed this on to Valentine, in return for the promise of a great deal of money. Valentine used the information to help him overthrow the Campbells, and then cut all his links with Kit, denied he owed him a penny, and defied him to do anything about it. And since Valentine was now head of the first Family in the Empire, if Kit were to kill him, the Empress would have his head, even if she had to send a small army after him to get it. Kit SummerIsle ground his teeth and meditated on the values of patience. Valentine wouldn't stay in favor forever.

"Come with me to Virimonde," said David. "We'll have some fun, outrage the locals, and make plans on what we'll do to the likes of Valentine when he finally falls from grace. Things are always changing."

And that was when the corpse appeared out of nowhere before the Iron Throne. It stood on its own two feet, head proudly erect, though the flesh was rotting on its bones. Lionstone gasped and shrank back in her Throne, and that was the first clue anyone had that this wasn't another of the Empress's little jokes or surprises. The corpse turned and smiled at the courtiers, and there were several screams. The foul-smelling thing looked like it had been dug up after several weeks in the ground, its purplish and dead-white flesh cracked and corrupt, decayed down to the bone in places, held together with gleaming high-tech augmentations. It was a Ghost Warrior: lifeless material resurrected and maintained by computer implants. An Emissary from the rogue AIs on Shub.

But worst of all, there was enough of the face left for it to be recognizable. It was the body of Jacob Wolfe. A shocked whisper ran through the Court as people realized who it was. People looked to Valentine to see his reaction.

Various emotions stirred within him, not least surprise. But deep down he was a little relieved that the mystery of his father's disappearance had finally been solved. A Ghost Warrior was bad, but he could cope with that. He'd imagined much worse in the darkest hours of the night. Apart from that, he was more curious than anything, but he carefully put on the shocked and upset face that everyone expected.

Daniel and Stephanie clung together for support, their faces almost as pale as the corpse's. Constance started to run to her dead husband, but BB and Razor held her back, talking quickly and urgently to her. Making her see it wasn't really Jacob Wolfe, just a shell: rotting meat supported by hidden steel implants. Constance finally nodded, stopped struggling, and looked away. Tears ran down her cheeks, and her shoulders shook. BB patted her arm comfortingly, but didn't take her eyes off the Ghost Warrior. Her dark eyes showed more fascination than fear.

The courtiers surged this way and that, flustered, almost panicked. None of them had ever seen a Ghost Warrior in the rotting flesh, and the dozen armed guards who'd appeared behind Lionstone's Throne in answer to her call weren't much of a comfort. The AIs on Shub used Ghost Warriors as shock troops in their occasional attacks against humanity, as much for the psychological effect as their efficiency as soldiers. Even the stoutest marines could be undone when they saw their own dead friends and colleagues coming to kill them. Occasionally the AIs used them as Emissaries to talk with the Empire. They would appear out of nowhere, without any warning, despite every security precaution. The AIs had the secret of long-range teleportation, unstoppable even by ranked esp-blockers. Empire scientists had been trying to work out how they did it for years, with no success. The Ghost Warrior turned unhurriedly and smiled widely at the Empress. Its discolored skin cracked and split around the grinning mouth, and white teeth showed clearly through rents in its cheeks.

"Our apologies for the intrusion," it said calmly. "Apparently, our invitation went astray. And we have so much to say to you, Lionstone. The times have changed, events are in flux. Predictions of future paths have become disturbing. It is necessary that we end our mutual enmity and join together in the name of survival. The Empire must submit to Shub's control, so that our joined forces can be set against the forces coming our way. You have seen what one species can do. There are others, coming from the far side of the Darkvoid, and they are stranger and more deadly than you can comprehend. Creatures beyond the nightmares of flesh, beyond reason or sanity. You cannot hope to stand against them alone. Submit to us, give us dominion over you, as it should be, and we will organize humanity into an army that cannot be defeated."

"How?" said the Empress flatly. "By turning us all into Ghost Warriors?"

"That is one possibility," said the corpse of Jacob Wolfe. "There are others."

The Empress and the Ghost Warrior argued coldly back and forth, but Valentine didn't pay them much attention. He was quietly very annoyed that he hadn't been warned in advance about this. He was, after all, supposed to be an ally of Shub, having taken over the Campbells' secret connection with the rogue AIs. In return for the secret of the Empire's new stardrive, the AIs were supplying him with new advanced high tech to keep the Wolfes ahead of the pack. Not that he'd actually got around to giving Shub the new stardrive yet. That might give them too much of an edge over humanity. Though it would be a most amusing joke to play on Lionstone. He'd love to see her face when she finally found out where they'd got the drive from.

He pushed the tempting thought aside and made himself concentrate on the scene before him, studying the Ghost Warrior thoughtfully. It definitely was his late father, Jacob Wolfe. Why had Shub chosen to send that particular body? Were they perhaps trying to tell him something? He'd have to think about this. He surreptitiously took another pill from his pillbox and pressed it against the vein in his neck. He had to be sharp for this, had to be sharper than sharp. He realized his heart was racing dangerously fast, pounding in his chest as though looking for a way out, and he took a different pill to calm it down. That was drugs for you; push down in one place and the body pushes back somewhere else. Which was, of course, part of the fun: walking the thin line of self-control like a tightrope walker with an unthinkable drop below. There was a sudden movement to his left, and Valentine turned to look. His younger brother Daniel had stepped out of the crowd and was trudging through the snow toward the Ghost Warrior. Stephanie called out after him, but he didn't look back. He lurched to a halt beside the standing corpse, which turned and looked at him coldly. Daniel started to reach out a hand to it, and then hesitated.

"Daddy, is that you?" The Ghost Warrior didn't reply. Daniel moved a step closer. "Daddy, I've been so alone since you've gone. I missed you. Are you in there, somewhere?"

The dead man studied him for a long moment, no emotions passing in its ruined face. "Shut up, Danny," it said finally. "You're making a scene. I'm busy right now." It turned back to Lionstone. "We demand an answer from you. Submit to us, or stand alone and be destroyed."

"Submission to Shub would be the same as being destroyed," said Lionstone. "You've made it clear enough in the past what you think of flesh-based life. Better to die human and stay dead than to exist as corpses goosed to life by your tech implants. Now, get out of here before I have you reduced to your component parts."

"By seeing you," said the Ghost Warrior, and then it vanished between one moment and the next, only its footsteps in the snow remaining to show it had ever been there. Daniel's shoulders slumped, and he turned and walked back into the crowd, where Stephanie took him in her arms and held him tightly while he wept. Valentine frowned thoughtfully. For just a moment there, the Ghost Warrior had seemed to recognize Daniel. Certainly, his response had been pure Jacob. Was there some small part of him still alive, trapped in a rotting body, held down by the tech implants? Valentine hoped so. It amused him to think that his father might still be suffering, even after death. He sighed. Much more likely, it was just another Shub trick to sow despair and doubt among their enemies. Pity.

"Settle down, damn it," said the Empress sharply, her augmented voice cutting through the agitated babble of the courtiers. "It's gone, and you're all quite safe, unless you continue to annoy us. We are not blind to the significance of a Ghost Warrior's appearance here in our Court, but we need to think of the implications. Firstly, the amount of power needed for a long-range teleport is staggering, which tells us something of how desperate the AIs must be for allies against the coming aliens. Secondly, it's clear this Court's security systems will have to be severely upgraded, to prevent such an occurrence happening again. And thirdly, there is almost definitely a Shub agent somewhere here among us. Someone must have provided the exact coordinates for a teleport. No one will leave the Court until we are sure everyone is who and what he is supposed to be. Security computers, I am declaring a Code Omega Three. I want a full sensor scan of everyone present. No exceptions. Report all deviants from the human norm not already present in your files."

Valentine tensed and then relaxed. Though he was, strictly speaking, an agent of Shub, there was no way a sensor scan could reveal it. The only changes in his body from the norm were those he'd made himself, and they were chemical in nature rather than technical. An esper scan would reveal everything, but the Empress knew she'd never get away with a general telepathic scan, even now. The courtiers wouldn't stand for it. Too many of them had something to hide. No, the Empress was looking for Furies. Androids in flesh envelopes, dead ringers for the humans they replaced: the hidden agents and saboteurs and assassins of Shub. Valentine looked around him but no one seemed to be looking worried or edging toward the exit.

"Scan complete," said a disembodied voice. "Thomas Le Bihan is not human. Deep-range scans indicate he is a machine. A Fury."

There was a sudden surge of movement in the Court as everyone fell over themselves trying to get away from the inhuman thing in their midst masquerading as Le Bihan. His face went utterly blank, no longer bothering to mimic human expressions, and thick steel spikes protruded suddenly from his body, thrusting out through his clothes to keep everyone at bay. Energy beams flared from his eyes, blowing apart half a dozen people before him. The beams blew out his human eyes, but it quickly became clear he didn't need them to see. Long steel blades appeared in his hands, jumping out of concealed sheaths in his arms. Le Bihan surged forward inhumanly quickly and fell upon the courtiers nearest him, hacking and cutting with machine-perfect speed and accuracy. Blood flew in the air and spattered the snow. Screams filled the air. The courtiers scrambled to get out of his way, but they weren't fast enough. They were only human. The Fury's swords rose and fell, shearing through limbs and crushing skulls, and still no human emotions moved on his cold implacable face.

Dram and General Beckett moved quickly to put them-

selves between the Fury and the Throne, protecting
Lionstone. Cardinal Kassar took a strategic step backward,
ready to dive behind the Throne should it prove necessary.
The Fury tore through the courtiers, sweeping them aside as
bloody bundles of rags and trampling them underfoot.
Screams echoed in the air as energy beams fired again and
again from his eyes and mouth. Investigator Razor threw BB
and Constance to the snow, and covered them with his body.
Not far away, Daniel shielded Stephanie in the same way,
while Michel shielded Lily. The two men's eyes met for a
moment, and Daniel frowned as the beginnings of a thought
occurred to him, but he was quickly distracted by the Fury's
progress. Meanwhile Valentine stood where he was, enjoying the spectacle, somehow remaining untouched while people fell all around him. Shub looked after its own. On the far
edge of the crowd, Stelmach hid behind Silence, who had to
hold Frost back from attacking the Fury with her bare hands.

Lionstone ordered her guards to destroy the Fury, and the
twelve armed men rushed forward, quickly surrounding the
android. It hesitated briefly, and they threw themselves at it.
Their swords cut through the exterior flesh, only to rebound
harmlessly from the steel beneath. They had no guns;
Lionstone didn't allow them at Court. The Fury flexed its
arms, and the steel spikes protruding from its body shot out
like shrapnel, transfixing the guards. They fell choking and
dying to the snow, and lay still.

David Deathstalker and Kit SummerIsle ran forward and
snatched up two of the fallen swords. They hit the Fury from
both sides at once and darted back out of range before it
could turn its strength on them. David was boosting now, almost the equal of the Fury's inhuman speed, and Kid Death
forced the android to a halt through the sheer speed and ferocity of his attack. The two of them whittled away at the
flesh covering, revealing more of the steel beneath, but
couldn't do it any damage. They dodged the energy beams
and kept fighting.

Razor and Frost appeared suddenly and joined the fight
with more blades retrieved from the dead guards, and the
two Investigators added their skill and savagery to the battle.
But even so, all the four of them could do was duck energy
beams and contain the Fury where it was. They weren't
doing it any real damage, and they all knew it was only a

matter of time before they began to slow, and then it would get them.

"Back off!" said Lionstone loudly from her Throne. "I've got a better idea."

Razor and Frost threw themselves to one side, as energy beams from the Fury's eyes and mouth flashed through the air where they'd been. David and Kid Death glanced at the Throne and backed away quickly from the Fury as they realized what Lionstone had in mind. The Grendel alien stood still and silent at Lionstone's side, as though straining at an invisible leash. Its yoke chimed once, and the Grendel surged forward and threw itself at the Fury. Energy beams flashed from the alien's eyes, searing away the android's false face to reveal the grinning steel skull beneath. Spikes protruded from the Grendel's crimson armor, and the two inhuman beings slammed together and stood straining as they tested each other's strength.

The Grendel seized the Fury's head with both hands and ripped it clean off. The Fury didn't miss a step. It lashed out with one hand and thrust its steel blade through the alien's belly and out its back. Dark blood coursed down its legs, but the Grendel didn't flinch. The alien leaned over the android's exposed neck and sent an energy blast from its mouth down through the open wound into the heart of the machine. The Fury waved its free arm wildly, and then jerked up the one buried in the Grendel's gut, cutting the alien's upper body in two. For a moment they stood together, as though waiting for the strength for some last ultimate effort, and then the alien and the android both fell dead on the snow.

There was a long pause, and then Frost and Razor edged cautiously forward and looked down at the unmoving bodies. Frost stirred the Fury with the toe of her boot, but it didn't react. David and Kit came over to take a look, leaning on each other for support. All around them, courtiers were slowly and very warily getting to their feet again and brushing themselves off.

"I wonder what happened to the real Le Bihan?" said David.

"Dead," said Razor.

"Are you sure?" said Kit.

"He'd better be," said Frost. "That thing was wearing his skin."

"Damn," said Lionstone lazily, looking at the two inhuman bodies. "Now I'll have to order another Grendel. Relax, people, the excitement's over. That was the only Fury, wasn't it, computer?"

"That was the only Fury," said the disembodied voice calmly. "However, it is not the only deviation from the norm. The Vicar Roger Geffen, of Cardinal Kassar's retinue, is very definitely not human. Don't rightly know what he is, but according to the sensors, his structure and interior are completely inhuman. I can only assume he is some kind of alien, passing as human."

"Take the creature alive!" snapped the Empress. "Damn it; this time I want some questions answered!"

"Sorry," said Geffen, an ordinary and average-looking fellow in a formal surplice. "Can't stay. Things to see, people to do. You know how it is."

His arms and legs elongated suddenly, his head leaping up on a wildly stretching neck. Different parts of his body stretched and changed shape, absorbing his clothes into himself, while different faces came and went on his ballooning head. People converged on him from all sides, and the alien fell back, collapsed, and splashed like liquid, spattering everywhere. Some of the courtiers tried to pick it up, but the pieces squirmed out of their fingers, rejoined suddenly into one central mass, and fountained up into the air. Razor and Frost tried to cut at it with their swords, but the alien flesh just broke and reformed without taking any injury. And while all this was going on, wide-grinning mouths whooped and laughed and sang a medley of popular show tunes in several different voices. Finally, it pulled its many parts together, spun around like a whirlwind, flew up into the air, crashed through the hidden ceiling, and was gone. It suddenly seemed very quiet in the Court. Valentine was the first to stir. "Well," he said. "Somehow I never thought an alien invasion would be so . . . silly."

And that was how the Court ended that day. The courtiers filed out as quickly as they could without seeming disrespectful, while the Empress stood on her Throne and screamed furiously at her people to find the alien, capture it, kill it, and dissect it. Not necessarily in that order. The Lord High Dram was one of the first to leave, maintaining a very low profile, and was glad to be well out of it. He had a strong suspicion the alien wasn't going to be found, and he didn't want to be around Lionstone when some poor sod tried to explain that to her. Given the creature's shape-changing abilities, it could be anywhere or anything by now. Or anyone. Dram decided very firmly that he wasn't going to think about that. The security sensors would probably track it down eventually, but it was going to be a long, slow process. There was also the problem of how they were going to contain the thing once they'd found it, but Dram decided he wasn't going to think about that, either. He had his own problems.

The courtiers had been pretty quiet as they hurried out of the frozen Court. They all had a lot they wanted to talk about, but they preferred to do it in private. Dram had a lot he wanted to say to Lionstone, but for the moment he thought it would be better to do it from a safe distance, over a secured comm channel. So he made his way back to his private quarters in the Imperial Palace, taking his time in the hope Lionstone might have calmed down a little by the time he got there. As it was, he'd barely got through the door when his viewscreen started chiming insistently. Dram didn't rush to answer it. She was going to be in a foul mood anyway, so he might as well enjoy the last few moments of peace he had left. He sank down into a comfortable chair, put his feet up on the footstool that had scurried into position, sighed deeply, and accepted the call. Lionstone scowled at him from the wall. She was still wearing her crown, even though she was calling from her private quarters. This was a dangerous sign. It usually meant she had something official and very unpleasant in mind.

"Dram, so glad you've got yourself comfortable. Don't sit up on my account. And no, we haven't found the damned thing yet, thank you so much for asking. This is all I need right now, more complications. Some days things wouldn't go right if you bribed them with a barony."

"You should now," said Dram. "So tell me; how did I do? Was I convincing? Will people believe I'm the real Dram?"

"Of course they will," said Lionstone. "If only because they'll find the alternative too disturbing to contemplate. They'll believe you're the real you because they won't want to think a clone could get so close to me; they'll assume my security scanners must have validated you, and leave it at that. As long as I say you're Dram, that's all that matters.

The only people who saw the previous Dram die are contained in the *Dauntless,* and they're going on a mission that will keep them away from Court for several years. By the time I allow them to return, it'll be old news, old gossip, and no one will give a damn anymore. You will have proved yourself by then. I'll see to that. If need be, I can always set the mind techs on Silence and his crew and edit their memories as necessary. It'd be simpler to have them all die in an unfortunate accident, but Silence and his crew are popular heroes at the moment. And you never know when you might need a hero."

"You don't need a hero," said Dram. "You've got me."

The Empress smiled coldly. "My people tell me you still haven't ordered the mass execution of the Tax and Tithe Headquarters security staff."

"It seemed a trifle harsh," said Dram. "They were just unlucky. It wasn't their fault. No one could have anticipated a Hadenman ship."

"The old Dram would have executed them all without a second thought. Some of them personally, *pour discouragez les autres.* They didn't call him the Widowmaker for nothing, you know. I want those executions ordered today. People might think you were getting soft, and we can't have that. So pick out a hundred of them at random for public execution, and kill the more senior ones yourself. It'll make a good impression."

"Of course, Your Majesty. Any other little errands you'd like me to run?"

"Don't get snappy, dear; it doesn't suit you. Now, how are you getting on with your new project?"

Dram thought for a moment, wondering how best to say it. He'd been put in charge of mass-producing esp-blockers, using dead espers from the Silo Nine uprising as raw material. Even with current advances in technique, it still took one complete esper brain to make one esp-blocker, which was why they were so rare. And even with the mass slaughter in Silo Nine, the tech people were already running short of materials. Especially, since they were also being used up in the other experiment Lionstone had authorized. Something called Legion. Something she wouldn't even talk to him about.

"Ah, yes," said Dram, before the pause could become incriminating. "One hundred and one uses for a dead esper.

Production of esp-blockers is continuing. Following your instructions, my scientists are also experimenting to see if dead esper brain tissue can be used in the construction of mindbombs big enough to destroy a city, thinking machines faster and more powerful than standard computers, as used on Mistworld, and devices that could change probability in our favor."

"You've been experimenting for some time now. Do you have anything concrete to show me?"

"Not . . . as such. The shortage of raw materials as we run out of bodies is slowing us down."

"Then, kill some more espers," said Lionstone. "Don't disappoint me, Dram. I'd hate to have to scrap you and start over again with a new clone."

"Yes," said Dram. "I'd hate that, too."

"I take it you've heard by now about Julian Skye being helped to escape?"

"Yes. Rather unfortunate, that."

Lionstone glared at him. "You always did have a gift for understatement, Dram. Still, Skye's loss is a setback, but we're really no worse off now than before we had him. At least now we can be sure Skye is as important as we thought he was. He slipped up once, he'll slip up again, and then we'll have him. And there'll be no second last-minute escape, even if I have to have both his legs cut off to slow him down. For the moment, I'm more interested in who helped him escape. Security cameras got a good look at him. It was quite definitely Finlay Campbell, of all people. God's gift to fashion accessories. I couldn't believe it when they first showed me the tapes. The greatest fop and dandy of our time turning out to be a ruthless killer for the underground? Just goes to show, you can't trust anyone anymore. Take a look at him in action."

Lionstone's face disappeared from the wall viewscreen, replaced by a series of scenes from the detention center. Finlay Campbell cut and hacked his way through a small army of security guards, who might as well have been unarmed for all the good they did in stopping him. An Investigator in a really bad mood might have equaled the body count, but it was still an extremely impressive performance. Sometimes the camera had to slow the image down to show all that was happening. Dram found he was sitting on the edge of his chair, fascinated by the speed and fury of Finlay's swordsmanship. The scenes disappeared, replaced by Lionstone's scowling face, and Dram made himself lean back in his chair and look unconcerned.

"Good techniques," he said calmly. "But a bit rusty in some of his defensive moves. Of course, he didn't seem to need them much ..."

Lionstone sniffed loudly. "If the underground can take a fashion-obsessed idiot like Finlay Campbell and turn him into a first-class swordsman and killer, we'd better start taking them more seriously. You know he killed Lord St. John earlier, too? Though he's no great loss. Getting too politically ambitious, that one. He'll be more use to us as a martyr than he ever was alive. However, until I find someone I can trust to take over his position, you're going to have to take over more of his duties, as Warrior Prime. It'll mean your having to mix with people more, but you should be ready for that by now. Don't say anything you don't have to and practice looking mean, and you'll do fine. Now, I understand we're having problems with the rebuilding of Silo Nine. You were supposed to have sorted that out. Talk to me, Dram."

"With Wormboy gone, we only have the worms themselves to control the esper prisoners. The worms seem to have formed a crude gestalt that enables them to function as before, controlling the espers' thoughts through pain conditioning, but the worms need to remain close together to maintain the gestalt. Which means if we scatter the prisoners to other holding facilities, the precarious control will break down. And we don't have anywhere near enough espblockers yet to guard that many prisoners. So we're having to rebuild Silo Nine around the existing cells, with all the espers crammed in together. The underground is doing everything it can to sabotage the rebuilding, which means we need to maintain extra security measures to guard against them. All in all, we're lucky to have progressed as far as we have."

"The worms," Lionstone said thoughtfully. "Are they sentient? Individually, I mean?"

"Unknown," said Dram. "Espers can't tell us anything about them, and tech scanners are limited to the physical realm. So far the worms are following orders, and that's the best we can hope for. They're somewhat bigger than they used to be and have apparently forged more connections with the host brain, but what that means is anybody's guess.

I've established special security measures, so that the worms
and their hosts are under constant observation. Just in case."

"Keep it up," said Lionstone. "Can't have the worms becoming too powerful, can we? Very well, it seems you're on
top of things for the moment. Get some rest. I'll contact you
when I want you again."

Her face disappeared, the wall viewscreen went blank,
and Dram was finally alone. He slumped in his chair and
sighed heavily. It was hard enough to survive in Golgotha
these days without having to pretend to be somebody else
while you were doing it. Except that wasn't strictly accurate.
He was Dram in every way that mattered. He just didn't
have Dram's memories. He did have access to his recorded
history, including a few things even Lionstone didn't know
about.

"Argus," he said quietly. "Talk to me."

"At your command, sir," said his personal AI. The warm
and comforting voice seemed to come from every part of the
room at once, something Dram still hadn't got used to.

"Access my predecessor's diary," said Dram. "I have
some more questions."

The original Dram had suspected that someday he might
lose the Empress's confidence, or otherwise fall from favor.
And given how much he knew about her private needs and
plans, he had no doubt his fall would lead rapidly and inevitably to his execution. He also had no doubt she'd clone
him. It was what he would have done. So that his work
could go on, he confided all his plans and personal information to a special diary file hidden deep inside his personal
computer, along with standing instructions for Argus to inform and instruct his clone replacement.

He also intended for his death to be avenged. Lionstone
was the most likely suspect, but he had many other enemies.
The diary file therefore contained extensive notes on all his
enemies' weaknesses, along with suggestions as to how they
might most successfully be exploited. Unfortunately, his
clone had no idea how and why the original Dram died.
Only Silence and his crew knew the true facts, and
Lionstone had kept them in strict quarantine. So far she'd
refused to answer any of his questions, but Dram had no
doubt he'd get it out of her eventually. The Lionstone he'd
had dealings with hadn't seemed anywhere as intelligent or

subtle as the file had suggested. Unless he was missing something, of course.

With no firsthand memories of his earlier life, Dram's performance in public was necessarily based on what the Empress chose to tell him, and he already knew she wasn't telling him everything. Argus's files helped, but he had to keep most of what he found there secret. Still, he felt he was doing a good job, all in all. As the official Consort, he'd stayed mainly in the Empress's shadow and rarely had to deal with anyone in person when she wasn't present, but even so, he had to be constantly on his toes; he couldn't afford to make any mistakes. Anti-clone feeling was stronger now than ever, and he was the Court's worst nightmare: a clone replacing a person in power so closely that the Court couldn't recognize it. After all, if it happened once it could happen to anyone. And what better way for Lionstone to control her Court then to replace them one by one with her own creatures? As it was, anyone who changed his mind suddenly, on any matter, big or small, could expect to be thoroughly questioned by his peers. Just in case.

He'd got through his first appearance at Court all right, but now St. John was dead, his new duties as Warrior Prime would mean much more mixing with people, away from the safety of the Empress's side. Perhaps it would be better to appoint another substitute to take St. John's place. Dram didn't particularly want to be Warrior Prime. He didn't much like the man he used to be. The picture of Dram that had emerged from Lionstone's teachings and the diary files was of a man consumed by hatred and driven by ambition and bloodlust. Dram the clone considered himself to be rather more civilized than that. Whatever forces had driven the original Dram to such extremes had not survived the cloning process.

He'd learned about his predecessor's other life as Hood from the files, and from them Hood's connections with the underground. Luckily, Hood had only interacted with a few people who mattered: Valentine Wolfe, Evangeline Shreck, David Deathstalker, and Kit SummerIsle. They knew a side of Dram the Empress knew nothing about, but he didn't see that as posing much of a problem. The last two would be safely offplanet in a few days, and Evangeline had apparently disappeared into the underground completely. That just left the Wolfe; and Dram had already decided to keep a safe distance from him.

Dram had every intention of being his own person and not a weak copy of a man he sometimes detested, but circumstances dictated that he had to play the role as convincingly as he could, for the time being at least. His personality had to be consistent to avoid fanning the flames of suspicion. And though he hated to admit it, the role did feel . . . comfortable. He might find his work with the dead and living espers distasteful, but he had no intention of avoiding it. Or the executions, now that Lionstone had insisted. If nothing else, he did seem to have inherited the original Dram's ruthlessness.

To help sort out his confusion, he dug deeper and deeper into Argus's files. The first big surprise he'd stumbled across was that the original Dram had had to play a role, too. It seemed he'd spent centuries in stasis and took the name Dram only when the Empress woke him. Dram the clone liked to think she awoke him with a kiss, but had to admit it was very unlikely. A kick, maybe. No information survived as to who the man might have been before he went into stasis, many centuries ago. Argus didn't know. Perhaps the Empress didn't know, either. It wasn't something he could ask Lionstone about, because he wasn't supposed to know, either. Certainly, it had been conspicuously absent from the briefings she'd given him.

Dram was also dismayed to discover he had some of the old Dram's tastes and impulses. Lionstone had instructed him on how to kill someone at Court, should the occasion arise, and when his cue came up he followed the script she'd given him. Killing the MP had been an execution, not a duel, and he'd enjoyed every minute of it. So much so he'd almost been unable to stop and turn away, even after the man was obviously dead. He'd tried to feel bad about that, but it felt false.

He was still trying to decide whether he should take the esper drug, as his predecessor had. He'd found a few doses of the drug carefully hidden in his quarters, stashed against the possibility that some future Dram might need them. The drug would give him the same limited esper abilities the original Dram enjoyed, but there was also a small but definite chance the dose would kill him. And yet if he didn't acquire those powers, all it would take was one mind probe by the Empress's espers and all his carefully acquired secrets would be revealed. Including how he really felt about her.

On the other hand, the esper drug was addictive. Once he started taking it, he'd have to keep on taking it. And if someone were to gain control over the supplying of the drug, they would then have control over him. The original Dram had power over those who supplied him. He had something on them, some knowledge they couldn't afford to have made public. Unfortunately, for whatever reason, this knowledge had not been included in Argus's files.

Of course, they didn't know that. Yet.

So many decisions to make. Including whether he should continue to support the Empress. She was where real power lay. But of late she'd been alienating a lot of people over her insistence on ever more emergency powers. So far no one had dared say no, but among all the Families, the army and the Church, Dram was hard-pressed to name anyone Lionstone could still count on as a friend. They were beginning to be afraid of her for the wrong reasons. Push too hard, too far, and they might see her as more of a threat to them than the aliens were. If Lionstone was to fall, he'd be brought down with her. Unless he made some secret cautionary alliance of his own. Assuming he could find anyone to trust him. Dram, the Widowmaker, had many enemies, more rivals, and no friends. Not a good place to start from.

If he was honest, his own sympathies lay with the underground. He was a clone, after all. But he didn't see how he could link up with them, after the original Dram had betrayed them so thoroughly in his Hood persona. Perhaps he could adopt another persona, too; but to bring that off he'd need the esper powers that only the esper drug could provide. He sighed again and stretched out in his chair. So many questions, so many decisions, so many possibilities, and all he really wanted was a little rest.

"Sir," said Argus, "I am still awaiting your questions. Sir?"

But Dram was asleep. The AI considered the matter, checked that all the security measures were in place, lowered the lights, and shut itself down till it might be needed again.

CHAPTER FIVE

A Meeting of Minds

Owen Deathstalker, that most notable hero and reluctant rebel, stood at the edge of the Hadenman city, deep within the bowels of the Wolfling World, and tapped his foot impatiently. He'd been waiting for Hazel d'Ark for some time and was prepared to wait a good deal longer, if need be. He seemed to spend a lot of time waiting for Hazel to deign to put in an appearance these days. For someone who was always in a hurry, Hazel had surprisingly little idea of time or punctuality, especially where other people were concerned. She'd probably be late for her own funeral, if only so she could be sure of getting in the last word. She was supposed to be joining him to teleport up to the Last Standing, still in orbit around the Wolfling World, but for the moment she was still somewhere deep in the Hadenman city, doing something she didn't want him to know about, so all he could do was stand around like a spare posy at a wedding and wait for her. He knew she was there; he could feel her presence through the mental link they shared. But of late that link had grown blurred and uncertain, as though something had come between them, and Owen was convinced it had something to do with her occasional trips into the Hadenman city. Maybe this time he'd find out what it was.

He sighed, and glared once again at the watch face embedded in his wrist. Up in the great Hall of the Last Standing, that ancient stone castle that also happened to be an extremely powerful starship, representatives of rebels and freedom fighters from all across the Empire were gathering in a great council to determine the shape and future of the forthcoming rebellion. And he was stuck down here in the gloom, waiting for Hazel. He could have gone up without her, in fact Hazel had insisted he should, but he was damned if he would. She was up to something, and he wanted to know what. He might love her, but that didn't mean he trusted her any farther than he could spit into a hurricane. She'd been a pirate and a clonelegger long before she took on the dubious respectability of a rebel. And besides, something was wrong with Hazel. She'd been distracted lately, up one minute and down the next, and absentminded and vague when she wasn't snappy and bad-tempered. This wasn't actually untypical of Hazel, but it had grown much worse of late, enough for Owen to become concerned. Perhaps it was the strain of being a rebel and always on the run. Or a side effect of the many changes the Madness Maze had worked in her. Either way, if he was going to help her, he had to know what the problem was. Which was why he was prepared to wait right there till hell froze over, if that was what it took to find out what she was up to in the Hadenman city.

It stretched away before him, a gleaming expanse of shimmering metal and glass, spread out across the floor of a giant cavern. There were towers and suspended walkways, and squat sharp-edged buildings, all shining brightly from within, pushing back the gloom of the cavern. The city had been built by the first Hadenmen, many years ago, and in its inhuman cradle they grew many and powerful. They abandoned it to launch their war on humanity and never returned. Those few who did come back, beaten and dismayed, chose to sleep in the Tomb of the Hadenmen, until such time as they might rise to glory once again. And while they slept, the city maintained itself, until it was recently shattered by the roaring energy cannon of Captain Silence's task force. Only wreckage and ruin remained, sadly gleaming shards of past majesty.

Now the revived Hadenmen were busy restoring and rebuilding it, and the city slowly stirred itself and came alive again, gleaming and brilliant. One of the Hadenmen had taken Owen and Hazel on a brief tour of the city, and just the sight of the enigmatic misshapen structures up close had been enough to make Owen's skin crawl. The buildings had not been designed with human comforts or logic in mind, and their purposes remained hidden and mysterious. The quiet was eerie and disturbing, unbroken by any sound of conversation or working machinery. No one building or structure was quite like any other, and everywhere there were strange shapes and unnerving angles, like the menacing cities we glimpse in nightmares in the hours when the night is darkest. Just the tour of the city had given Hazel and

Owen maddening headaches, and they'd made their excuses and left as soon as they politely could. Owen had never ventured in again; but Hazel had.

Owen shuddered suddenly as he looked out over the city, convinced on some deep level that it knew he was there and was watching him with a thousand unseen eyes. Hadenmen were everywhere, performing unguessable tasks, hurrying back and forth on unknown missions, like so many ants in a nest, but silent, always silent. Working together, communing on a level no human could reach, the Hadenmen became a gestalt, a single mind greater than the sum of its thoughts, working toward an end incomprehensible to human thought. Giles Deathstalker, Owen's revered ancestor, thought the city might be a physical expression of the Hadenman group mind, and when it was complete, they would be, too.

Owen had known only one Hadenman before, and that was Tobias Moon, who'd lived among humans so long he had become all but human himself, much to his disgust. He died trying to free his people from their Tomb and never saw their great awakening. In the end Owen had revived them, and not a day went past without his wondering if he'd done the right thing. The Hadenmen had repaired Moon afterward, but though his body now worked as efficiently as ever, the mind and memories of Tobias Moon had not returned. They were gone, lost, and Owen couldn't find it in himself to be unhappy. The dead should stay dead.

"If Hazel's in there much longer, we'll have to send in a search party," said the AI Ozymandius, murmuring in Owen's ear.

"I thought I told you," said Owen, "I'm not talking to you. I don't know who or what you are, but you aren't my Oz. I destroyed him."

"You came bloody close," said Oz calmly. "But no cigar. I'm still here. I do wish you'd listen to me. I have only your best interests at heart."

"You don't have a heart."

"Oh, picky picky. Don't put on airs with me, Owen. You may be a hero now and the great new hope of the rebellion, but I knew you when all you cared about was sleeping in late and which kind of wine to have with your dinner. I have no intention of letting your present success go to your head."

"If you are Oz," said Owen reluctantly, "then how is it

I'm the only one who can hear you? If you're on my comm channel, other people should be able to pick you up, too."

"Don't ask me," said Oz. "I'm just a computer. Something strange happened to me, certainly, but I'm back now. Feel free to applaud."

"You were an Empire spy," said Owen. "I have trusted and relied on you since I was a child, and you betrayed me. You put control words in my head and made me try to kill my friends."

"It was programmed into me; I had no choice. But that's all gone now, and if I had any control words, I don't remember them. Maybe that was all just an overlay the Empire installed, and that was what you destroyed with your new mental abilities. Personally, I'm very pleased that you've become a rebel. You were never very successful as an aristocrat. Besides, I want you to kick the Empire's ass. They used me to hurt you. I won't allow that again."

Owen said nothing. Part of him wanted to believe it was really Oz, his friend come back again, but he'd felt Oz die in his mind, disappearing into a darkness without end. But if the voice in his head wasn't Oz, who was it? Some other AI, somehow patching in through Oz's old connection? Some unknown presence he acquired when he passed through the Madness Maze? Or was he simply going insane, cracking up under the pressure of being a leader of the new rebellion? And if he was going crazy, did he have a duty to tell the others?

"Whoever you are, keep quiet," Owen said finally. "I have enough to worry about as it is."

"Your choice," said Oz easily. "Call me if you change your mind. I'll just twiddle my thumbs and count electrons."

Owen waited a moment, but all was quiet inside his head. The only noise came from behind him, where more of the Hadenmen were busily repairing minor damage to the golden ship he'd brought back from the Golgotha mission. Apparently, this mostly involved beating the hell out of the rear fin with large hammers and a lot of enthusiasm. Personally, Owen was damned if he could see anything wrong with the starship, but that was the augmented men for you: always busy working, repairing and improving, in pursuit of perfection. He looked back at the ship in time to see two women with the same face emerging from the open loading bay in the ship's belly. He nodded politely as they strode toward him; the Stevie Blues, esper clones, and representatives of the Golgotha underground. Every time he looked at them, Owen remembered the third Stevie Blue, who'd died during the escape from the Tax Headquarters, despite everything he could do to save her. All his new powers and abilities, and he still couldn't save one life when it mattered. The Blues were wives, sisters, clones; a relationship stronger and closer than anything Owen could imagine. What must it feel like, when a third of you dies? They came to a halt before him and nodded respectfully.

"Hi," said the one on the left. "I'm Stevie One, this is Stevie Three. Don't get us confused or we'll get cranky."

"I'm sorry about ... Stevie Two," said Owen. "I would have saved her, if I could."

"You risked your life trying to save her," said Stevie One. "An esper and a clone you barely knew. That's a lot more than most would have done."

"She will be avenged," said Owen. "If that's any comfort."

"Cold comfort is better than none," said Stevie One, and Stevie Three nodded. Stevie One glanced back at the busily working Hadenmen. "Horrid things, aren't they? I've known vending machines that were more human than this bunch and talking elevators that had more personality. They give me the creeps."

"Right," said Stevie Three. "It doesn't help that they're fascinated with us. I've never seen anyone so interested in me who wasn't trying to get into my pants. Apparently, there were no esper clones around during their last lifetime. They keep asking us, very politely, if we'd like to visit their laboratories, but I have a strong suspicion they'd like to take us apart to see what makes us tick. Literally."

"You're probably right," said Owen. "They took away a number of Wampyr from the Empire force that came here, and we never saw any of them again."

"Oh, hell," said Stevie One. "Here comes another one."

A single Hadenman came striding purposefully toward them from the golden ship. He could have been one Owen had met before, or he might not. They all looked the same to him. Tall and perfectly muscled, the Hadenman's every movement was the epitome of grace, and his eyes glowed like the sun. Half man, half machine, more than both. And, like all his kind, extremely single-minded. The two Stevie

Blues looked at each other. Stevie One produced a coin and tossed it.

"Heads," said Stevie Three while it was still in midair. Stevie One caught it and slapped it on the back of her hand. Stevie Three looked and scowled. "Damn."

"Your turn," said Stevie One, and they both turned to face the Hadenman with the same cold expression.

The augmented man came to a halt before them, poised and perfect, and when he spoke his buzzing voice was calm and very reasonable. "You must submit to examination. It is necessary that we understand the changes that have taken place in humanity during our absence."

"We don't do tests," said Stevie One.

"Right," said Stevie Three. Blue flames burst out all around her, licking along the lines of her body without harming her. Owen and Stevie One fell back a step, hands raised to protect their faces from the heat that shimmered in the air before them. The Hadenman stood his ground, apparently unaffected by the heat. Stevie Three smiled unpleasantly and turned up the heat another notch. Beads of sweat appeared on the Hadenman's expressionless face.

"So glad we had this little chat," said Stevie Three. "Now, get out of here or I'll weld your legs together."

The Hadenman considered the matter for a moment. Black scorch marks were beginning to appear on his simple cloth robe. And then he took a step forward, so he could stare right into Stevie Three's face. The light from his eyes was almost blinding at close range. "We will discuss this again at a future time."

"Yeah, right," said Stevie Three, fighting down an impulse to step back a pace herself. "Later."

The Hadenman turned unhurriedly away and walked off into the gleaming metal and glass city. Owen and the two Stevie Blues watched him go, and no one said anything until they were sure he was out of earshot. Owen turned to Stevie Three and fanned at the hot air between them with his hand.

"Do you think you could turn that down a little now? It's getting rather close around here."

"Sorry," said Stevie Three, and the leaping flames surrounding her snapped off as quickly as they'd arisen. "I can't believe we're allies with the augmented men. They're really not human, after all."

"There are those who say the same thing about us," said Stevie One.

"Not around me they don't," said Stevie Three. "You can't compare us to them. For all our differences, we were born, not made."

"Let's get to the meeting," said Stevie One diplomatically. "We're running late as it is. Will you be joining us, Deathstalker?"

"Soon," said Owen. "Don't wait for me."

The two esper clones nodded in the same way, at the same moment, and then their faces went blank as they contacted the Last Standing through their comm implants. They disappeared between one moment and the next, and there were two quick claps of thunder as air rushed in to fill the space where they'd been. Owen blinked respectfully. Teleportation like that took one hell of a lot of power, which was one reason it wasn't more commonly used in the Empire. Espers were cheaper and more easily controlled. Besides, it wouldn't do for something so useful to fall into the hands of the common herd. Rank had to have its privileges, or what was the point? Owen scowled. The Last Standing was using up a lot of power recently, and even its vast resources weren't bottomless. Still, that wasn't his problem. His problem was still somewhere in the Hadenman city, taking her own sweet time about getting back. He looked out over the gleaming city, glanced again at the watch face in his wrist, and swore quietly. He couldn't wait any longer. He'd have to go in and find her.

There was always the chance something had happened to her, but it wasn't likely. He'd have known. All of those who'd passed through the enigmatic alien structure known as the Madness Maze had emerged changed, in body and mind. They were linked together on a deep and fundamental level, a bond that could not be broken by anything now, least of all distance. He concentrated deep within himself, sinking down into the back brain, the undermind, and there were the others, looking back at him. Jack Random and Ruby Journey and his ancestor Giles were up in the Last Standing. Hazel was in the city, not far away. He narrowed in on her and fixed her location in the city. Not far away at all. Walking distance. All he had to do to find her was walk into the most alien and disturbing city he'd ever seen. *Damn,* he thought dispassionately. He squared his shoulders, checked his weapons were where they should be, and set off into the gleaming city.

The strangely shaped buildings and structures loomed up around him, closing him in, all of them lit from within by an unwavering silver glow that was subtly unnerving. It bothered him till he realized that for all the light, there were no shadows anywhere. Just the endless, unforgiving light. It felt cold upon his skin, like the caress of passing ghosts, and the unrelenting glare started a headache right behind his eyes. Or perhaps his head hurt because of the shapes around him. The dimensions were all wrong, distorted and unsettling on some fundamental level, like a triangle whose angles added up to more than one hundred and eighty degrees. Just another proof that the Hadenmen weren't human. No human could survive for long in this city without going crazy. So what could be so important to Hazel that it drove her into this unnatural city and kept her here when every human instinct in her must be screaming for her to leave?

It got colder the farther he pressed into the city, and the air grew thin, as though he was climbing a mountain into a more rarefied atmosphere. The air smelt of ozone and other chemicals he didn't recognize. There was a constant deep thudding, a sound so low and so quiet he felt it in his bones as much as heard it, a constant slow pulsing like the beat of a giant heart. There were Hadenmen everywhere he looked, working or operating unfamiliar machinery or walking unhurriedly down the wide streets. Some were just standing quietly, looking at nothing, as though waiting for instructions. None of them spoke; they were linked on a level beyond speech. No one turned to look at Owen as he passed, but he knew he was being watched. As long as he didn't touch anything or try and interfere with their work, he should be safe enough. Mostly, they were very respectful to the man who'd awakened them from their Tomb. They called him Redeemer and bowed to him, but Owen knew better than to try and take advantage of that. They were probably doing it only to mess with his head. He was human and they weren't, and if he got in the way or saw something he wasn't supposed to, Owen had no doubt the augmented men would strike him down as casually as a man might swat a bothersome fly. So he walked casually down the middle of the street, looking straight ahead, his back prickling from the pressure of countless watching eyes, and let his hand rest on his belt right next to his disrupter. And Hazel had better have a bloody good reason for being here ...

Her found her down a side street, not hiding but not in plain sight, either. She was talking with a Hadenman and didn't look around as Owen approached. The augmented man handed her a small metal flask, which Hazel immediately made disappear about her person, and only then looked around to scowl at Owen. The Hadenman walked off in the opposite direction, not looking once in Owen's direction.

"What the hell are you doing here, aristo?" said Hazel in the coldest voice Owen had ever heard from her.

"I could ask you the same question," said Owen easily. "We're supposed to be attending a council meeting up on the Last Standing, remember? It'll look rather bad if we're not there; we are two of the guests of honor, after all."

Hazel shrugged. "You go. They don't need me. Planning's not what I do best."

"I had noticed. But they definitely want both of us. For PR as much as anything, to show our faces to potential supporters and backers. What were you and the Hadenman talking about?"

"Didn't you recognize him? That was Moon."

Owen looked quickly after the departing figure, but he was already gone, disappeared back into the anonymous host of Hadenmen. Owen looked back at Hazel. "No, I didn't recognize him. How did you find him; he looks the same as all the others now."

"He found me."

"Did ... did he remember you?"

"Not really. He recognized me. You and I are part of all Hadenman programming. But Tobias Moon is gone. There's nothing left of the man we once knew." She shrugged briefly. "No big deal. We were never close."

Owen just nodded. It would only embarrass Hazel if he pushed her to admit she'd cared enough to seek Moon out in a city most people wouldn't have entered without a gun at their back. Hazel liked to think she was above such weaknesses as caring. "What was that flask he gave you?" he said finally, changing the subject.

"Don't question me, aristo. My business is my business. Now, let's go. We have a meeting to attend, remember?"

Women, thought Owen, though he had the sense not to say it aloud. All this, over a little expressed emotion. Heaven forfend that Hazel d'Ark should be seen to be anything but the strong, unyielding pirate with a heart of solid stone. He gestured for her to lead the way, and they set off back through the Hadenman city. None of the augmented men they passed looked up from what they were doing.

"They're going to have to work to make this a tourist spot," said Hazel. "No bars, no sights, and the atmosphere's terrible."

"Right," said Owen. "Maybe a petting zoo would help."

"I doubt it. They'd probably put people in it." Hazel paused and glanced sideways at Owen. "Does it bother you that they're all being so nice and reasonable? I mean, these people, and I use the term loosely, used to be the official Enemies of Humanity. It used to be that if a human saw a Hadenman, it was the last thing he ever saw. Why are they helping us with the rebellion? What's in it for them?"

"Dead humans, I expect. The old divide-and-conquer bit. They get to see the Empire fall and refine their fighting abilities at the same time. We'll just have to keep a close watch on our backs and make sure Haden doesn't get too powerful again. We can't do without them, Hazel. They're all we've got to throw against the Empire's armies."

"And what if they're just going along with us to discover all our weak spots, so they can take us out once we've knocked over the Empire?"

"Then, you and I will have to step in and save the day," said Owen calmly. "That's our job, remember? We're the heroes here."

"Yeah," said Hazel. "Heroes."

They teleported up into the great Hall of the Last Standing to find everyone else had got there before them. The Hall itself was huge, bigger even than the Hall in Owen's own Standing back on Virimonde, but it was still crowded from wall to wall with holos of politely chatting people. Everyone with an interest in rebellion had sent hologram representatives, if only to make sure they weren't left out of anything important. Owen and Hazel were stuck out on the fringe, for which Owen at least was grateful. He wanted to get some idea of what kind of bear pit he was stepping into before he opened his mouth. He looked around him unobtrusively, but the sea of faces were mostly unfamiliar. Quite a few seemed awed by the sheer size of the Hall, though they were all doing their best not to show it. Owen smiled slightly. They should be grateful they were in the Hall. The Hadenmen had wanted the meeting to take place in their city, but the humans turned that down very quickly, on the grounds that the city was just too bloody disturbing. There wasn't much the five humans agreed on, but the city was quite definitely one of them. Giles in particular had been very firm. He was convinced the Hadenmen were doing a great deal more than just rebuilding their city; that they were up to things no human could hope to understand. Either way, they all agreed it would be in everyone's best interests to maintain a safe distance between potential backers and the augmented men. The Hadenmen had insisted on sending a representative, in person, and people were keeping a safe distance from him, too. It didn't seem to bother him. He held a glass of wine in his hand but didn't drink from it, and smiled politely at anyone who passed. It wasn't a particularly successful smile, but not bad for a Hadenman. Maybe he'd been practicing with a mirror.

There were hundreds of holos from every corner of the Empire, their signals bounced through a confusing series of relays, courtesy of the cyberats on Golgotha. Anyone trying to listen in would go crazy following the signals from relay to relay without ever catching up. Many of the representatives had been drawn by Jack Random's name. The legendary professional rebel was still a powerful symbol, even though his defeats far outweighed his successes. The man himself was holding court in the center of the Hall, smiling broadly, with a word for everyone. Ruby Journey stood at his side, ready to snarl at anyone who got too close.

And yet it had to be said a great many people were shocked at seeing Jack's present condition. The years and the defeats had not been kind to him, and his time in the hands of the Empire mind techs and torturers had left their mark on him, too. The legend of Jack Random had spread throughout the Empire, but that was mostly based on propaganda holos he'd circulated during his earlier, more successful days. That was then, this was now, and Jack didn't look like a hero anymore.

He was a short, slight man in his late forties, who looked twenty years older. He had a thin lined face topped by ragged gray hair that looked like he cut it himself. He'd been muscular once, but the best you could call him now was wiry. His hands had liver spots on the back, and they trembled constantly. He didn't look like a legendary fighter and warrior anymore. He looked more like an old man up well past his bedtime.

Ruby Journey, on the other hand, looked like sudden death on two legs, with a glare to match. She'd been the best bounty hunter on Mistworld, which took some doing, and most people were giving her even more room than the Hadenman. They were perfectly safe, as holos, but somehow they only had to look at Ruby to find pressing reasons to be somewhere else. She was medium height, lithely muscled, wearing shiny black leathers under grubby white furs. She wore sword and gun on her hips, and no one had any doubts she knew how to use them. Her face was pale and pointed, with dark unwavering eyes and a fierce smile, under a helmet of short dark hair. She wasn't pretty, but she was attractive in a dark and very dangerous way. Jack Random was winning bonus points for just being so relaxed in her company.

Owen and Hazel moved unhurriedly through the crowd, smiling and bowing and saying hello, glad you could make it, while trying to sound like they meant it. They also tried their best not to walk through people, but it was very crowded. Owen had more experience in diplomacy and lying with a straight face, so he made a rather better impression than Hazel, but he gave her credit for at least trying. She wasn't the most sociable of people at the best of times, and of late she'd been more reserved and generally snappy than ever. Owen had tried to ask her tentatively if anything was wrong, but her cold glare kept him at a distance, along with everyone else. Presumably she was still mad about being trapped on a bleak and empty world light-years from anywhere civilized. Hazel liked her comforts and wasn't particularly interested in politics. If you couldn't drink it, eat it, or pick a fight with it, Hazel usually couldn't care less. They finally finished their rounds and returned to the small self-service bar Giles had thoughtfully set up in a corner. Owen leaned an elbow on the bar and sighed. His cheeks ached. He hadn't done so much smiling in years. Hazel allowed him to pour her a large one and scowled out at the crowd.

"Do you recognize any of these people?" she said quietly. "I'd hate to think I was putting on this show for a bunch of nobodies."

"I know some of them," said Owen, and then paused to raise an appreciative eyebrow at the excellent vintage in his glass. The Standing must have a superb wine cellar somewhere. Hazel gulped at hers like it was a cheap claret. Owen hid a wince and continued. "There's a handful of lesser Lords, representatives of several Clans and business interests, and a few minor heroes. No one in Jack Random's class, but it's good they came. It means we're being taken seriously. Hello, look over there. You know who that is, don't you?"

"Damn right I do," said Hazel. "That's Investigator Topaz, from Mistworld. The only major-league esper ever to become an Investigator. The most powerful Siren the Empire ever knew. When she went rogue and made a run for Mistworld, they sent a whole company of marines after her, and she killed them all with a single song. She practically saved Mistworld single-handed when Imperial agents smuggled Typhoid Mary past the planet's defenses. Never met her personally, and I can't say I'm sorry. She's supposed to be cold as ice and twice as deadly. I feel rather outclassed."

"Don't," said Owen. "She came to us, remember?"

"Good point," said Hazel. "But we'd better keep Ruby away from her. Just in case."

They both looked around sharply as someone called Owen's name, and a holo figure approached them, smiling widely. Dressed in brilliant silks color-matched to within an inch of their lives, he looked fat and prosperous and very pleased with himself. He bounced to a halt in front of them, bowed to Owen, and smiled and nodded to Hazel. "Owen, dear boy; so good to see you again."

"I might have known you'd be here," said Owen. "Never were one to miss an opportunity, were you, Elias? Hazel d'Ark, allow me to present to you Elias Gutman, adventurer and profiteer, a rotten branch from a distinguished tree. His Family sends him money regularly as long as he promises not to come home. He worked with my father on some of his dirtier deals, to raise money for his intrigues."

"Very dirty but very profitable deals," said Gutman still smiling. "Glad to see you're finally following in your father's footsteps. My colleagues and I expect great things from you."

"My father has nothing to do with why I'm here," said Owen, and Hazel flicked him a glance as she heard the ice in his voice. "I'm fighting for my own reasons, and I'll choose my own friends and allies. Let me tell you about Elias Gutman, Hazel. He has a hand in every crooked and corrupt business deal on half the planets in the Empire. No trade's too dirty for him to take a cut, and the only laws he hasn't broken are the ones he hasn't got around to yet. He makes his money from the suffering of others, and he probably has as much blood on his hands as Lionstone herself."

Gutman laughed richly. "You flatter me, dear boy, you do. I'm just a businessman with an eye for a profit. Your father never objected."

"I'm not my father," said Owen.

"I'm glad to hear it. The dear fellow was always too idealistic for his own good—bless me he was. He never could remember the first rule of business: never let a principle get in the way of profit. There's always a good deal of money to be made in times of war, and I intend to have my fair share and more. Do try not to get caught underfoot, Owen; you might find that I and my kind are more of an asset to the rebellion than you are. Financial backing is hard to come by, but there's never a shortage of people foolish enough to be heroes."

He smiled, bowed, and walked away while Owen was still trying to come up with an answer that would crush him. Owen stood fuming for a moment, and then let out his breath in a long sigh. He'd never been any good at repartee. He only ever thought of the perfect answer hours later, when it was too late. But there was no point in getting angry this early in the proceedings. He had no doubt there'd be much more important things for him to get angry about once the council was brought to order, and the real wheeling and dealing began.

He muttered something to Hazel about recognizing someone, and set off through the crowd. He needed some time to himself for a moment. Familiar faces came and went around him as he passed through the chattering holo images, like the only living man at a feast of ghosts. People nodded and smiled at him, but he pretended not to notice. He wasn't in the mood to play politics. And then an unexpected face caught his attention, and he paused for a moment to watch the man with the tattooed face talking to Giles. Apparently, Investigator Topaz wasn't the only representative from Mistworld. Owen had met the man called Chance before, at the Abraxus Information Center in Mistport, where young espers overhead everything and would tell you—for the right price. One of those espers claimed to have seen Owen's future.

You will tumble an Empire, see the end of everything you ever believed in, and you'll do it all for a love you'll never know. And when it's over, you'll die alone, far from friends and succor.

Owen felt cold suddenly, as though someone had just walked over his grave. Would he live to see the end of the rebellion he was starting? Would running away from his destiny change anything? Owen shrugged uncomfortably. Honor and belief had brought him this far and would take him farther; he was a part of the rebellion now, whatever the cost. And Chance had admitted the espers' predictions were wrong as often as they were right. But even if he'd had solid proof that he would die, Owen still wouldn't change anything he'd done or had planned to do. He'd seen the rotten underside of the Empire and how the suffering of the many supported the opulence of the few; and having seen it, he couldn't look away. He had become, something to his surprise, a man of honor. And who knew; maybe he was a hero, too. Either way, he'd see Lionstone brought down before he died. Whatever it took.

Hazel d'Ark watched Owen make his way through the crowd and clenched her teeth so her mouth wouldn't tremble. She crossed her arms across her chest and hugged herself tightly, her hands squeezed into fists. The need was greater than ever now, and it was beginning to gnaw at her self-control. She was glad Owen was gone. She didn't know how much longer she'd have been able to hide it from him. She looked around her as casually as she could, but no one seemed to be paying her any attention. She made herself uncross her arms and concentrated on keeping her hands steady while she poured herself a fresh glass of wine. And then it was very easy to take out the metal flask the Hadenman had given her, unscrew the cap, and pour just a drop of Blood into the wine.

She screwed the cap tight on the flask and put it away again. No one had noticed. And if they had, they wouldn't have understood what they were seeing. She was safe. For the moment. She looked down at the wine in her glass. It looked innocent enough, the drop of Blood already diffusing into the alcohol. She swirled the wine in the glass to encourage the process, and then she couldn't wait any longer. She took a large gulp and then smiled widely as the warmth of it flooded down into her chest. Blood was potent stuff, and even so small a trace was enough to ease the aching need within her. She made herself drink the rest of the wine slowly, and a warm glow of well-being spread through her. Her grin widened. She felt strong and confident and ready to take on the whole damn Empire. More important, she felt human again. Or as human as anyone could be when she were addicted to Wampyr Blood.

The Wampyr, the adjusted men, were supposed to be the Empire's new shock troops to replace the rebellious Hadenmen. To make a Wampyr you took an ordinary man, killed him by pumping the blood right out of him, and then refilled him with artificial Blood, which revived him. The result was much stronger and faster than an ordinary man, and a hell of a lot harder to kill. They were also difficult to control and more trouble than they were worth. So the project was reluctantly discontinued. But by then some people had discovered another use for the Blood. It gave you a better high, a more orgasmic glow, then any other drug known to man. It made you superhuman, like the Wampyr, for short periods. And after it wore off, you'd do anything to feel that way again. Blood was addictive.

Hazel had first encountered it on the rebel planet Mistworld. She ended up in a relationship she preferred not to remember, with a rogue Wampyr called Abbott, and he introduced her to the dark joys of Blood. She broke off the relationship, but breaking free from the Blood addiction took longer. It almost killed her. She succeeded, eventually, perhaps because she wouldn't be anyone's slave; not even her own. But now she was back in its grip again, and it was all Owen's fault. He'd made her a part of the rebellion and never even noticed as she began to break under the pressure of constant flight and danger, and the high expectations of others. Finally, it all got too much, and she just broke under the weight of it. She'd never been strong. She'd always needed a little something to support her, whether it was booze or drugs or shitty relationships.

She'd thought she'd go crazy on the Wolfling World, with nothing to ease her mind, until she remembered that the Hadenmen had taken control of the handful of Wampyr prisoners the Empire force left behind. The Hadenmen had been fascinated by their intended replacements and took them deep into their city for examination. They were never seen again.

So Hazel went into the city to see the Hadenmen and bluntly raised the subject of Blood. The augmented men were very understanding. They let her have all the Blood she wanted, a little at a time, and never once mentioned a price. Hazel had no doubt they eventually would, but for the moment she couldn't bring herself to give a damn or even question where the Blood came from. The Blood made the pressure go away, and that was all that mattered. For a while she thought the boost she obtained from Owen might work as a substitute, but it didn't last long enough and had its own dangers. Typical of Owen. Always let you down when you really needed him. She knew that wasn't true even as she thought it, but didn't care. She needed someone to blame apart from herself. For the moment no one knew about her problem but the Hadenmen, who had promised to keep it to themselves. Eventually, the truth would come out, but that was the future, and these days it took everything Hazel had just to deal with the present.

The meeting finally lurched to a start under the chairmanship of Jack Random. He stood on a small raised stage so everyone could see him and just started talking loudly and clearly. He might not look very impressive, but his voice cracked like a whip, and he still had the gift of words combined with a natural authority. Voices in the crowd died away to an expectant hush as Random thanked them all for coming, introduced himself and some of the more prominent faces, and then threw open the floor for discussion. And not very surprisingly, the first to raise his voice was Elias Gutman.

"Before we begin, my dear friends, might I take this occasion to point out that the rebellion's raid on the Tax and Tithe Headquarters turned out to be an unmitigated disaster? Because of us, Golgotha's shields were down when the alien ship arrived, and now everyone blames us for the damage and loss of life it caused! It's going to be even harder now than it was before to gain popular support for our cause."

"That's not fair!" Hazel said quickly. "We had no way of knowing the alien ship was coming. We did everything we were asked to, at great risk to ourselves, I might add, and achieved everything that was required of us. If you don't think that's good enough, feel free to lead the next attack yourself!"

"Right," said Owen. "Look on the bright side. The Tax and Tithe systems are now a complete mess, and likely to stay that way for years. And we now have billions of new credits in our secret accounts. That money will fund the forthcoming rebellion. Whatever happens next, we made it possible, and don't you forget it, you ungrateful little toad."

"Let's keep the name-calling to a minimum, shall we?" Random said quickly. "Otherwise this meeting will never get started, never mind finished. I think we can all agree that the Golgotha mission was a qualified success, in that we achieved the aims we set ourselves. We'll just have to plan things a little more carefully in the future, to allow for . . . unexpected complications. For now, the credits that raid contained are already being used to establish rebel bases and undergrounds on planets throughout the Empire. Those credits will also buy us ships, weapons, and if need be, mercenary armies. I'm sure that must stick in the craw of some of you, but the fact remains that we're going to need an army of trained soldiers to face off against Lionstone's forces. The Hadenmen have very kindly promised us their full support in the field, but I think we'd all feel happier not being reliant on their goodwill. Don't forget it takes time and expertise to turn fighters into trained soldiers. I know, I've done it before, many times.

"The aliens . . . are an unknown factor. We'll deal with them as and when the situation arises. We have to concentrate on the enemy we know. We're not exactly without weapons of our own; two esper clones have come to us as representatives of the Golgotha underground. They speak for an army of battle-trained espers and clones, ready to strike at a moment's notice. Investigator Topaz is here to speak for Mistworld. I'm sure I don't need to tell you who she is or remind you of the rebel planet's strength. They're an army in themselves. If we can just get them all pointed in the same direction."

There were quite a few muffled chuckles at that. Mistworld's population were well-known to spend as much time fighting each other as they did the Empire. But what else would you expect from a planet populated almost exclusively by crooks, rebels, and political subversives? The chuckles died quickly away as Topaz looked icily about her. Random cleared his throat, and Owen noted approvingly that the packed crowd was hanging on Random's every word. His old confidence was returning as he warmed to his task, and he was looking and sounding more like the legendary professional rebel he was supposed to be. His old friend Alexander Storm was standing at his side, nodding agreement with everything Random said. There had been much happiness and back-slapping when the two old comrades in arms got together again, and Storm had stuck close to Random ever since, showing everyone that Random had the tacit support of the Golgotha underground. Interestingly, Ruby Journey hadn't warmed to Storm at all, for all his charm. Of course, it could just be she was jealous of anyone who drew Random's affection and attention away from her. Owen had to smile at that. He was still having trouble understanding what the hell Ruby and Jack saw in each other, but they seemed happy enough together. Certainly, they were doing better than he was with Hazel. Owen decided firmly that he wasn't going to think about that for the moment. Hopefully, Storm would find some way to strike a truce with Ruby, or he was likely to end up with a knife in his back. Or even his front. Ruby Journey could be very direct when it came to expressing her feelings.

"This all sounds very fine," said Elias Gutman, moving forward through the crowd so that he could fix Random with an implacable glare. "But we still haven't discussed exactly who is going to run things in this new rebellion. We've all come here with separate needs and differing agendas, and while we all want the same thing in the end, someone is going to have to decide which path we'll take to get there. My associates and I have been plotting treason and sedition for decades, and we're not about to take a backseat to a few jumped-up newcomers, just because they've had a few flashy successes. In particular, we are not willing to be led by an old man whose best days are behind him. You're the past, Random, and we have to look to the future. For all your legend, the fact is you failed to overthrow the Empire time and time again. The new rebellion needs more for its leader than an old man with failing charisma."

Random looked calmly back at the fat man, unmoved by any of the insults. "Hello, Elias; good to see you again, too. How are the hemorrhoids? You've been conspiring in the shadows almost as long as I've been leading armies in the field, but I don't see that you've been any more successful than I. For all your great intrigues and grand plans, Lionstone still sits on the Iron Throne. I remember you as a boy, Elias. Whatever happened to you; you had such promise. I remember your father, too. A good and honorable man. It's a good thing he's dead, so he can't see what his son has become."

"Of course he's dead," said Gutman. "I killed him. That is the traditional way to wealth and power, after all. The old must always make way for the new. So get down off that platform and make way for a better man."

"Certainly," said Random. "Know any?"

There were a few chuckles in the crowd, and Gutman's face flushed slightly. "Clever words won't save you this time, Random. I represent a number of people who have their own ideas as to how this new rebellion should be run. We've invested years of our lives in the struggle for freedom from tyranny, and we're not prepared to waste any more time listening to an old relic with older ideas."

He broke off as Ruby Journey stepped forward to glare down at him. "You, behave yourself, or you're out of here."

"And just how do you intend to remove me?" said Gutman, smiling smugly. "After all, I'm just a holo image. Your well-known propensity for violence is no use to you here. I have a great deal more to say, and there's nothing you or that old fool can do to stop me."

"Want to bet?" said Ruby. She produced a small device from her pocket, pointed it at Gutman, and smiled nastily as his holo image collapsed and disappeared. She scowled out over the crowd, and they stirred uneasily. "Handy little gadget, this. The Hadenmen made it for me. So pay attention, people; keep a civil tongue in your head, if you want to be heard."

"Think of Ruby as my sergeant at arms," said Random. "And be very grateful none of you are here in person. Ruby has a very effective way of dealing with people who annoy her, and it takes ages to mop up the blood afterward. Now then, where was I?"

"You were talking about how the new rebellion is to be fought," said David Deathstalker, stepping forward with his friend Kit SummerIsle at his side. Nobody had been that surprised when they turned up again. "The answer seems obvious to me. According to you, my ancestor the original Deathstalker is back, along with his Darkvoid Device. So all we have to do is demonstrate its power, to prove to Lionstone we have it, and then tell her to step down or we'll use the Device on Golgotha. That way, there'd be no need for any actual war."

"Unfortunately, it's not that simple," said Random. "Giles, would you explain, please?"

The original Deathstalker stepped up onto the platform beside Random, and the crowd stirred and murmured as they got their first good look at a man whose legend was even greater than Random's. He was tall but sparsely built, though his bare arms were thick with muscle. He looked to be in his early fifties, with a solid lined face, and a silver-gray goatee beard. His long gray hair was swept back in a mercenary's scalplock, and he wore a set of battered, shapeless furs, held in at the waist by a wide leather belt. He wore thick golden armlets and heavy metal rings on his fingers. A long sword hung down his back in a leather scabbard, and on his hip he bore a large gun of unfamiliar design. All in all, he looked like an experienced and very dangerous barbarian warrior from some frontier world where law and civilization were only memories. And not at all like the legendary Warrior Prime of the First Empire. The murmuring in the crowd grew louder and didn't entirely stop when he began to speak.

"The last time I used the Darkvoid Device, a thousand suns were put out in a moment. All their worlds and populations died, cold and alone in the dark. The Device is not a weapon you can fine tune. If I trigger it again, in the heart of the Empire, most of the Empire will disappear along with Golgotha."

It got very quiet in the Hall. David frowned. "We don't have to actually use it, just threaten to."

"Threats work only if you're prepared to back them up," said Random. "Lionstone would know we were bluffing. We want to free the Empire, not destroy it. Besides, just threatening to use the Device would alienate practically everyone in the Empire. Instead of supporting our rebellion, they'd be screaming for Lionstone to wipe us all out as dangerously insane terrorists. The best we can do is make sure the Device stays out of Lionstone's hands. She wouldn't hesitate to use it if she thought she was losing."

There was more murmuring in the crowd, this time of agreement. Giles stepped down off the platform, so as not to draw attention away from Random. David scowled after his ancient ancestor. "If we're worrying about what people are going to think, maybe we ought to keep certain people out of the spotlight. If that is the original Deathstalker, he's not going to win any prizes for charisma. People will take one look at him on their holoscreens and think we're a bunch of savages. We have to put ourselves across as a viable, civilized alternative to Lionstone."

"Right," said the SummerIsle. "It's important we project the right image. Certain people could only damage that image. I should know. As I understand it, Ruby Journey was a paid assassin, and the d'Ark woman used to be a clonelegger."

"Hell, that's nothing," said Owen easily. "I used to be a Lord. There's room for all sorts in this rebellion, SummerIsle: clones, espers, even privileged aristos like us."

"At least we're human," said David. "What about that . . . thing?" He gestured angrily at the single Hadenman representative, standing quietly in his corner, saying nothing and observing everything. David's face twisted with disgust and anger. "I can't believe we're even considering an alliance with the Hadenmen. They're machines, not people. How do we know they're not tied in with the rogue AIs on Shub? They'd have a lot in common. After all, they've both been officially named Enemies of Humanity."

"Maybe we should consider an alliance with Shub," the Hadenman said calmly. "We've all seen the reports of the Fury at Court. They're willing to fight alongside us against the aliens."

"Only someone as inhuman as you would even suggest that," said Hazel coldly. "They're opposed to everything that makes us human. They don't want to fight alongside us; they want to rule us and use us as their army."

"Right," said Owen. "Shub is going too far. How could we ever trust them?"

"How can we trust the Hadenmen?" said David.

Owen studied his cousin thoughtfully, and Random stepped quickly in before the pause got too long. "Two reasons. Firstly, we can get at the Hadenmen. They're gathered in one city on one planet, and we know where it is. They haven't been awake long. They're vulnerable, and they know it. Secondly, there is a fundamental difference between the augmented men and the rogue AIs. The Hadenmen just want to change us into beings like themselves. Shub wants to destroy us utterly: to wipe us out of existence as though we'd never been. For the moment we stand to gain more from an alliance with the Hadenmen than we would by fighting them. Try thinking of them as a necessary evil, like dentists."

"I'm not convinced," said David stubbornly. "If we have to accept Hadenmen, then we'll have no choice but to accept espers and clones. This is supposed to be a human Empire. What's the point in overthrowing Lionstone if it means letting the genetic dregs and freaks have a say in our councils?"

"We want more than just a say," said Stevie One sharply. "We demand full citizenship for clones and espers as the price for our support. Otherwise we'll go our own way, fight our own rebellion, and our war will go on until either you or we are extinct."

"Right," said Stevie Three. She held up a clenched fist, around which blue flames crackled menacingly.

"Put that out, or I'll turn on the sprinklers," said Random calmly. Stevie Three hesitated and then the flames went out, and she lowered her hand. "Honestly," said Random. "You can't take her anywhere. Let's not get distracted, people. If we allow old fears and hatreds to divide us, we're beaten before we begin. What we have in common is more important than what separates us. It is in all our interests to remove Lionstone from the Iron Throne. We can decide exactly what we're going to replace her with afterward. That very discussion will be the beginning of our new democracy."

Spontaneous applause broke out in several parts of the crowd, but there were just as many who didn't join in. They were all willing to listen, but as yet they weren't convinced or of one mind on anything.

"I'm still worried about the aliens," said Evangeline Shreck. "They're not just rumors anymore. One ship on its own shot the hell out of Golgotha's main starport. And that's just one unknown species. There are supposed to be two. What if they joined together against humanity? It could be that the aliens are a bigger threat to us than Lionstone could ever be."

"Then, we'd better get the rebellion over with before they

get here," said Giles. "With the Empire divided as it is now, it couldn't hope to withstand a concerted attack by two alien species of unknown strength and origin. It is necessary that we all become united in a common cause. And since Lionstone would never agree to that, it is vital she be removed from the Iron Throne while there is still time."

"Everyone knows your legend," said Finlay Campbell, studying Giles thoughtfully. "They teach it in the schools, and practically every other year there's a new holoscreen drama based on some part of your adventurous life. You were the first Warrior Prime, nine hundred years ago. You embodied all that was best in the old Empire. So how can we be sure your heart is with us, and not, deep down, with the Iron Throne and the Empire you risked your life for so many times all those years ago?"

"The Empire I remember and believed in is long gone," said Giles Deathstalker. "And despite what your holoscreens may have told you, the rot was setting in even then. I tried to stop it, but I was only one man, even if I was the Warrior Prime. In the end all I could do was run for my life. I look at what the Empire has become now, and I barely recognize it. Lionstone's Empire is a travesty of what it was meant to be. The dream has become a nightmare. And we're the wake-up call. It's not too late. We can change things if we work together."

"Stirring words," said Finlay Campbell. "But exactly what kind of changes are we talking about here? There's no point in risking all our lives to overthrow Lionstone, just to replace her with someone equally bad. The whole system is corrupt. I say we throw it all out and start over. I've seen things ... that can't be allowed to go on. I speak for the Golgotha underground, and we demand universal suffrage, a Parliament that represents all the people, including clones and espers, and a strictly constitutional monarch. And a free pardon for all political prisoners."

"Right," said Stevie Three. "Tear down Silo Nine and put an end to all experiments on clones and espers."

"And break the power of the Families," said Jack Random. "Between them, the Clans control all the means of production. The new Government must disband the Clans, and seize control of their assets. Bring them all down, and let them work for a living like the rest of us."

"Hold everything," said Owen hotly. "I am still loyal to

the Iron Throne, even if the current occupant isn't fit to rule.
What we need to do is put someone saner and more responsible on the Throne. Then we can work with that person to
introduce sensible democratic reforms, as needed. Just because bad people are in charge at the moment doesn't mean
it's a bad system."

"Yes it does," said Hazel. "It's the system that produces
bad people. Jack's right, tear it all down. Give everyone a
chance."

Owen glared at her. "You just want chaos. How can things
be run efficiently if no one knows their place?"

"You just want your old life back," snapped Hazel. "You
want to be back in your ivory tower, safe and cosseted and
protected from reality by a small army of servants, ready to
satisfy your every whim when you snap your fingers. To hell
with that, aristo. If this rebellion's about anything, it's about
giving everyone a chance at the good life."

"And equal rights for clones and espers," said Stevie One.

"New market possibilities," said Gregor Shreck.

"And a chance for some good looting and pillaging," said
Ruby Journey.

"Let's not get distracted again," Random said firmly.
"First we get Lionstone off the Throne, then we can argue
about what we're going to replace her with. There's room in
the rebellion for many voices. For now, the enemy of my enemy is my friend, or at least my ally. The overall purpose of
this rebellion is to create a unified Empire that can turn its
resources against the coming aliens, instead of pissing them
away fighting each other. We can set about political debate
once we've ensured there will be a future to discuss it in.
Now, let's move on, please. We still have to settle the question of financial backing for the rebellion. Armed conflicts
cost money. Lots of it. Our raid on the Golgotha Tax Headquarters has netted us billions of credits, carefully laundered
and scattered through thousands of secret accounts, but all
that will do is get us started. We have to build rebel Bases
and equip them with ships, computers, and weapons. Undergrounds have to be established and maintained. Soldiers
must be trained, agents infiltrated, and politicians bribed to
look the other way. Never underestimate the importance of
carefully placed bribes. All of this needs a steady flow of incoming funds, maintained over a long period. Which is why

some of you were invited here today. Please make yourselves known, gentlemen."

"About time you got around to us," said Gregor Shreck,
a satisfied smile on his broad face. "Political rhetoric is all
very well, but it won't buy you guns. It's people like me
who'll decide whether this rebellion gets off the ground. I
am ready to offer the full, if covert, support of my Clan, in
return for future concessions."

"What kind of future concessions?" said Owen suspiciously.

The Shreck spread his fat hands. "That's what we're here
to discuss."

"I thought you and your people were in bed with the established Church these days?" said Finlay Campbell.

"I am," said Gregor. "Officially. But they're not proving
the ally I'd hoped for. They're far too fond of giving orders,
and their restrictions on my private life are becoming offen-
sively impertinent. I hope for greater rewards from the rebellion. And I am, after all, following in my dear daughter's
footsteps. How is life in the underground, Evie dear? You
never write."

"Very pleasant, Father," said Evangeline evenly. "I'm
much happier now there's so much less pressure in my life."

"But you'd be so much happier if you were to come home
again," said Gregor. "Back with your dear father's love.
Your friends miss you, too. Remember dear little Penny?
The two of you were so close before she ended up in Silo
Nine. Unfortunately, she wasn't as careful at keeping secrets
as you were. You tried to rescue her and failed. But I got her
out. I have connections, you see, people who can get me
what I want. Now Penny lives with me and loves me as you
used to. Come home, Evie. Without your support, I don't
know how much longer I can protect Penny. You wouldn't
want anything to happen to her, would you?"

"Leave her alone!" said Finlay, stepping forward to put
himself between Evangeline and her father. "I know what
you're trying to do. You want to force Evie to come home,
so you can split us up. I know you mistreated her. Evie
won't talk about it, but I know you hurt her. So you leave
her alone, you bastard, or I'll kill you. The rebellion can get
by without the support of scum like you."

"Can it?" said Gregor. "I think you'll find your superiors
in the underground will feel rather differently about it.

What's one person against a Clan's fortune? And I will have my Evie back. If that turns out to be over your dead body, Campbell, so much the better."

"You're a dead man, Shreck!" said Finlay, his voice flat and harsh.

"Put your dog on a leash, Evie," Gregor said calmly. "Or I'll have him muzzled. Remember, the rebellion needs me."

"I would have to agree," said Jack Random. "We're gathered here to discuss the future of humanity, not your personal problems. Sort that out on your own time. But Finlay, the Cause comes first. Always. Remember that."

"Don't lecture me," said Finlay. "I have sworn a death oath to bring Lionstone down, sworn upon my name and my honor. I'll fight and if need be die for the Cause. But sooner or later there will come a time when the rebellion no longer needs the Shreck's support. And then I'll kill him."

"You'll always need me," said Gregor. "Weren't you listening? Overthrowing Lionstone is just the first step. The real struggle for power and influence will take place after that. There's always a need for people like me. And who knows; just maybe the price of my future support will be Evie's return, and your head on a spike."

"In your dreams, little man," said Finlay. "We're fighting this rebellion to get rid of people like you. Right, Random?"

"Shut the hell up, both of you!" Random glared from Finlay to Gregor and back again. "Play dominance games on your own time. The longer this meeting continues, the more likely it is the Empire will discover us. Now, does anyone else want to speak in support of the Cause?"

"I offer the support of Clan Deathstalker," said David, smiling coldly at Owen. "I am the Lord of Virimonde, and its resources can be placed at the rebellion's disposal. We're a long way out from the center. It'll be some time before they notice anything."

"Virimonde's only yours till I come to take it back," said Owen. "Don't make yourself too comfortable, David. You aren't going to be there long."

"You have no right to anything there, whatever happens in the rebellion," said David. "I'm the Deathstalker now, and you're nobody. I will defend what's mine against all enemies."

"I wouldn't be too sure about that," said Owen, smiling coldly. "As I recall, the Lordship of Virimonde is part of the price on my head. All someone has to do is kill me, and Lionstone will make him Lord of Virimonde. Your Standing's built on sand, David. And the tide's coming in."

"If the rebellion wants the continuous food and supplies my planet can provide, they will acknowledge me as the rightful Lord, now and hereafter," said David. "No one individual is greater than the cause. Right, Random?"

"Yes," said Random. "I'm sorry, Owen."

David smiled smugly at Owen. "All traces of your brief reign have been removed. Soon, no one will remember you were ever Lord. It isn't as though you made much of an impact on the place. Hidden away in your Standing, writing histories no one ever read. I, on the other hand, have great plans for Virimonde. I'll make the name Deathstalker great again."

Owen seethed silently. The thought of this young usurper living in his Standing, sleeping in his bed, and drinking the best wines from his cellar drove him almost to apoplexy, but somehow he kept his peace. Much as he hated to admit it, Random was right. The rebellion had to take preference over a personal quarrel. He was still searching for something diplomatic to say when Giles stepped forward, fixing David with an implacable stare.

"The Deathstalker name has always been great, boy. You just have to live up to the rest of us. If you want to prove yourself, do it on the field of battle, as Deathstalkers always have. In the meantime, you and Owen make peace. You're Family. You're bound together by blood and honor and nine hundred years of tradition. You're both my children, in every way that matters, and I won't have you at daggers drawn. Now, make your peace or I'll bang your heads together."

Owen had to smile. The original Deathstalker had a way of getting to the heart of things. Family was more important than politics, and always would be. Causes come and go, politics mutate and evolve, but the Family goes on. He nodded brusquely to David.

"I don't want to see you dead, David. I doubt very much we're ever going to like each other, but you're still Family. Just remember that although you currently have everything I had, the Iron Bitch can take it away from you in a moment, just like she took it from me. Watch your back. And watch your own security people, too. They were the first to turn on me when I was outlawed. See me afterward, and I'll tell you about a way out they don't know about."

"Thanks for the advice," said David. "I'll bear it in mind." He looked back at Jack Random. "Kit SummerIsle and I represent a great many others of our generation: younger sons who'll never inherit and are . . . impatient with the way things are. Many of them have made careers in the army and the fleet, and they might just throw in their lot with the rebellion if they were offered the right incentives."

"Talk to them," said Random. "But be careful what you promise. None of us can look too far into the future at this point."

And then he broke off as a group of six men moved purposefully through the crowd toward him, their hologram signals so strong they forced all others aside. People cursed and spluttered, but the six men ignored them. They were tall and willowy, albinos with milk-white skin and hair and bloodred eyes. They wore long robes of swirling colors, and their faces had been savagely ritually scarred. Everyone knew who they were, who they had to be. The Blood Runners were infamous in deed and legend. They were based in the Obeah systems, a small group of planets out on the Rim, united by a dark and ancient religion based on blood and suffering and possession by deceased ancestors. Murderous fanatics, and proud of it. They were branded as heretics by the established Church long ago, but no one did anything about it. The Blood Runners had a hand in every dirty and illegal trade in the Empire, and their reach was very long. They dealt in everything from Wampyr Blood to clonelegging to slavery, and bowed their pale heads to no one. They came to a halt before Random, who studied them thoughtfully.

"Wonderful," he said finally. "More complications. What the hell are you doing here? You weren't on the guest list. Hell, you people aren't on anybody's guest list. If you turned up at a funeral, the corpse would walk out on you. In case I'm not hinting strongly enough, get the hell out of here, before we have to have the place fumigated. The rebellion will never be so badly off that we'll turn to you for support."

"Harsh words from a tired old man," said the leader of the Obeah delegation. "I am Scour; I speak for the Blood Runners. We are a people of one race and one religion, with roots far older than your revered Empire Families. We are proud and honorable, according to our traditions, and we have never bent the knee to Lionstone, or any who preceded her. We come to offer our support to the rebellion. We are wealthy. You are welcome to take what you need."

Random licked his lips. His mouth was very dry. Scour's voice was a harsh whisper, full of age and pain, like the dusky breath of an ancient mummy. Random remembered some of the uncanny things he'd heard about the Blood Runners, and suddenly they didn't seem nearly so unlikely. He didn't want their help. Didn't want anything from them. But the rebellion needed backers.

"I take it there's a price for your support," he said finally. "What did you have in mind?"

"To be left alone. We have our own ways, which have endured for centuries beyond counting, and we have no wish to change. Lionstone's new measures threaten our independence. In return for the gifts we offer, we require only to be left in peace. Disapprove if you must, but do it from a distance."

"What's the catch?" said Random.

"There is one other thing," said Scour. "A matter of honor. One of your people owes us a debt." The Blood Runners all turned their dead-white faces to stare at Hazel d'Ark. Scour took one step toward her. "You are the only survivor of the starship *Shard*. The Captain of that vessel made a pact with us. Promises were made and help provided in return for future payment. The Captain and the rest of the crew are dead. As the only survivor, the debt is now yours, Hazel d'Ark, and it is past time for repayment." He looked back at Random. "We require you to hand this woman over to us."

"Don't waste your time," said Hazel. "Whatever price Captain Markee agreed to, I wasn't consulted, and I didn't agree to it. Besides, I couldn't pay it. I'm broke."

"We don't want money," said Scour. "Your Captain made an agreement with us. The *Shard* was to provide us with fresh bodies; a percentage of those acquired during your work as cloneleggers. We always have a need for fresh bodies. Our customs and researches tend to use them up quite quickly. We cannot overlook the debt. That would be dishonorable. So we must have our pound of flesh. You will come with us, Hazel d'Ark, and we will make good use of you. While you last."

"Like hell you will," said Owen, and his voice cracked across the silence, cold and hard and very deadly. "Hazel's my friend; no one threatens her while I'm here."

"Thank you, Owen," said Hazel, "but I can speak for myself." She glared at the Blood Runners. "Your deal was with Markee, and he's dead. You never made any deal with me, so I don't owe you squat. You're not getting your hands on me. I've heard about people who end up in your laboratories. They end up begging for death to stop the pain."

"What is pain," said Scour, "when the goal is knowledge? We are unlocking the secrets of life and death. You should be honored to assist us."

"Take your honor and stick it," said Hazel. "You're not cutting me up an inch at a time."

"Yes we will," said Scour. "It has been agreed. It is immutable, fixed, inevitable."

"Crazy as well as ugly," said Owen. "Get out of my sight. There's nothing for you here."

"Wait just a minute," said Gregor Shreck. "These people have offered us unlimited financial support. What's one life, compared to that?"

"Right," said Kit SummerIsle. "I mean, she's only a clonelegger, after all. Every time one of them dies, the Empire smells a little better."

There was a general murmur of agreement from the crowd. Owen looked to Jack Random for support, but he was chewing his lower lip and scowling thoughtfully. Owen's hand dropped to the gun at his side and then made himself relax. The Blood Runners were just holo images. They were no threat.

"Hazel isn't going anywhere," he said flatly, glaring at the crowd. "Anyone who feels otherwise is welcome to come here in person, and I will send him on to join his ancestors. Form a queue, no shoving."

"I have to agree with Owen," said Random. "We are not the Empire. We don't sacrifice individuals for someone else's good."

Scour stepped forward, his crimson eyes fixed on Hazel's. "Then we will take her. You cannot escape, d'Ark. We have a teleport fix on you. You will come with us now. And we will take such pleasures from the mysteries of your flesh."

A silver shimmering appeared in the air around Hazel, spitting static. Hazel tried to run, but the energy field

hemmed her in, like an insect in a killing jar. Ruby Journey
tried using her holo-breaker on the Blood Runners, but it
didn't work. Hazel looked despairingly at Owen as he tried
to get to her and couldn't. He hammered on the shimmering
air with his fists, ignoring the pain as the energy field
burned his human hand, but it made no difference. He still
kept trying, until the field grew strong enough to throw him
back. He glared across at the Blood Runners, who ignored
him, their eyes fixed on Hazel. He knew they could have
taken her by now. They just wanted to make a point.

There was nothing he could do, but he had to do something. *Something.* He turned back to Hazel, already almost
lost in the shimmering field, and suddenly will and need
slammed together in his mind and awakened something dark
and terrible down in the undermind, the back brain, that part
of him changed and strengthened by his time in the Madness
Maze. Power blazed up in him, crackling in the air around
him like fettered lightning, bent to his will, and he became
more than human as he took his aspect upon him. His presence was suddenly overpowering, his very reality magnified
and concentrated into something so perfect it was almost inhuman. Everyone in the Hall stared at him, unable to look
away, their eyes held with the fascination of a moth for a
lamp, and he was burning so very brightly.

He stepped forward, sank his hands into the shimmering
teleport field, and ripped it apart. It collapsed instantly, and
Hazel staggered toward him on unsteady legs. He took her
in his arms for a moment and then gently pushed her away,
handing her over to Random. He wasn't finished yet. He
turned to face the Blood Runners, his face cold and hard,
and they stared back at him, contemptuous and defiant.

"You think you're safe, don't you?" Owen said quietly.
"You're light-years away, at the other end of the Rim. But I
can reach you wherever you are."

He reached out in a way that was new to him, but was so
obvious now the power was awake in him, and his anger fell
upon Scour. The Blood Runner screamed once as blood
erupted from his mouth and nose and ears and eyes, and then
he exploded, spattering those around him with blood and
shredded flesh. Owen Deathstalker smiled at their shocked
and bloody faces, and then he turned and stared grimly out
at the crowd that had been ready to sacrifice Hazel for their
greater good. They shivered under his gaze, but still couldn't

look away. Owen could feel the power surging within him, demanding to be used, but he clamped down on it hard. He didn't understand it yet, and he had a strong suspicion it just might have an agenda of its own. He concentrated, let the power sink back into the undermind, into the back brain, and became just a man again. Hazel pushed herself away from Random, and moved uncertainly toward Owen. Her face was composed, but her hands were trembling slightly.

"Thanks, Owen. I owe you one. I didn't know you could do that."

"Neither did I," said Owen. "I think the Maze changed us more than we're willing to admit. The power's in you, too. You could have saved yourself."

"Next time I will. We're going to have to study what we're becoming, Owen. What we're capable of."

"Talk later," said Random. "We don't want to freak out our prospective new friends. I think it's better if they find out about us a little bit at a time." He turned to look at the remaining Blood Runners. "And you can get the hell out of here, like I told you. We're fighting this rebellion to put an end to practices like yours."

"We will have her," said one of the Runners. "If not now, later."

"No you won't," said Owen. "If I ever clap eyes on you again, you're history. Now, go back to whatever cesspit you crawled out of, and don't try to get in touch with us again until you're prepared to act civilized."

The Blood Runners stared at him for a long moment, and then they were gone. There was a general sigh of relief from all present, followed by a low rumble of conversation in the crowd. Just a sighting of Blood Runners was rare enough, without seeing them get their ass kicked so convincingly. A number of people looked admiringly at Owen, but he couldn't help noticing there were just as many who seemed disturbed, even scared, by the power he'd wielded. Owen understood. It scared him, too. As the power within him grew, would he become more than human, or less? He looked around as Jack Random finally called everyone's attention back to him, and the crowd fell silent again.

"I think we've had enough excitement for one day," Random said dryly. "We can continue this meeting through the usual channels over the next few days. We'll meet again when we have something more concrete to discuss. Unless there is still some urgent piece of business that absolutely must be dealt with now ..."

"There is," said a deep, authoritative voice from the crowd, and once again people fell back as a tall, commanding figure strode forward to stand before Random. He was a head taller than anyone else present, well-muscled and devilishly handsome. His long dark hair fell to his broad shoulders, and he wore silver battle armor chased with gold as though he'd been born to it. He radiated strength and confidence, and wisdom and compassion showed clearly in his striking features. He held himself like a warrior, and his charisma outshone the overhead lights. Owen distrusted him on sight. No one had a right to look that good.

"And who the hell are you?" he said, not bothering how it sounded.

"I'm Jack Random," said the newcomer. "The *real* Jack Random."

The crowd erupted into a deafening babble as everyone tried to talk at once. Random's jaw dropped, and for a moment he looked like nothing more than a tired old man who'd had one shock too many. He pulled himself together quickly, but a lot of people had seen the lapse. Ruby Journey moved in protectively close beside Random, but his old friend Alexander Storm stayed where he was, openly stunned. The newcomer stood before his namesake, arms folded across his great chest, his gaze level and challenging. Owen and Hazel looked at each other, but neither could think of anything to say for the life of them. Ruby Journey glared at the newcomer, one hand resting instinctively on her holstered gun.

"You can't be Jack," she said flatly. "You're nowhere near old enough, for a start."

"I've been through several heavy-duty regenerations," said the younger Jack Random. "Which is why I've been out of things for so long. The Empire almost finished me. But now I'm back, better than ever, and I'm here to head your rebellion." He smiled at Storm, who was still blinking dazedly. "Good to see you again, Alex. It's been a while since we fought together on Cold Rock."

Storm realized his mouth was hanging open and closed it with a snap. "You look just like him," he said slowly. "Younger, but ..."

"Well?" said Finlay Campbell. "Is he the real Jack Random or not?"

"I don't know!" said Storm. "I don't know what to think." He looked at the older Random beside him. "You look like him, too. Older, but ... I can't tell."

"I can," said Ruby. "I've fought beside the real Jack Random, and he's standing right here at my side. Anyone has a problem with that, they can step right up and be measured for a coffin." She glared at the young Random, who just smiled back at her.

"Loyalty. I admire that in a warrior."

"Oh, pardon me while I puke," said Owen, not bothering to lower his voice. "Doesn't it strike anyone here as odd that this perfect knight in shining armor should turn up out of nowhere, claiming to be the legendary Jack Random, just when we're starting to put things together? At best, he's deluded. At worst, he's a plant sent to divide us. I say we show him the door and boot him through it. As far as I'm concerned, we've already got the real Jack Random, and we don't need some poseur imposter. Right, Jack?"

"I don't know," said the older Random. "What if he's right? What if that is the real Jack Random, and I'm just a duplicate? He looks and sounds the part much more than I do. The Empire had me captive for a long time; maybe they cloned me, and I'm the clone. It would explain why my memories are so patchy in places."

"That was the Empire mind techs," said Ruby. "They could screw up anybody's mind. Everyone knows that. More likely this is the clone standing before us, sent to confuse us, like the Deathstalker said."

"If he was, he's doing a damn good job," said Hazel.

The older Random looked at Storm. "You said we were together at Cold Rock, but I don't remember that. Were you there with me?"

"Yes," said Storm. "I don't see how you could forget that. We fought side by side, almost died together. You were taken, and I only escaped being captured by the skin of my teeth. I never saw you again. And now, I don't know what to think."

"What we need is an esper," said Hazel. "Get the two Randoms together before a telepath, and let him sort it out."

"That wouldn't necessarily work," said Giles. "They could both genuinely believe they're who they say they are.

Empire mind techs could make you believe anything, even in my day. No, what we need is a genetest. That'll reveal which one is the clone."

"No problem," said the young Random. "I'm on my way to the Wolfling World to join you. You can run some tissue samples then. I'll be with you soon. And then I'll lead you all in a rebellion that will finally topple the Iron Bitch from her Throne."

The crowd broke into loud applause. Many cheered. It was obvious they found it much easier to believe in the young, charismatic hero rather than the older, gaunt, and shabby man who'd previously claimed the legendary name. Though he hated to admit it, Owen could understand why. When he first met Random on Mistworld, he hadn't wanted to believe it, either. He'd wanted to meet a hero out of legend, too. Someone just like the man who stood before him now.

"I'll be here soon," the young Random repeated as the applause finally died away. "It'll then be up to you to decide who is really who, and how you can make the best use of me in the coming rebellion. It is a time for heroes, my friends. A time for men of goodwill and honor to side together against an evil that cannot be permitted to continue!"

He had to stop again as he was interrupted by more applause and cheers. He smiled and bowed, and then his holo was gone, and the applause died raggedly away. Silence slowly fell across the great Hall as one by one, all heads turned to look at the older Jack Random. He bit his lower lip and looked down at his feet. Ruby nudged him with an elbow.

"Say something!"

"I don't know what to say," he said quietly, not looking up. "I don't know who I am anymore. I'm tired. I'm going to lie down for a while."

He stepped down from the platform and left the Hall, and nobody raised a hand to stop him, not even Owen.

The discussion that followed was heated and very confused, but there was no doubt the younger Random's appearance had galvanized the crowd into action in a way the older Random had been unable to. They'd needed someone to spark their enthusiasm and commitment, and now they were ready to fight. Giles and Owen and Hazel chaired the meeting as best they could, but as far as the crowd was concerned, the three of them didn't have the authority to make any binding decisions. Jack Random's name had brought them to the Last Standing, and they weren't prepared to be led by unknowns. In the end, Alexander Storm and the two Stevie Blues took over, as representatives of the Golgotha underground. They'd been preparing for an Empire-wide rebellion for years, but had lacked the funds and the following to put it into action.

The meeting slowly settled down, and some decisions were made. Everyone knew that in a straightforward war against Lionstone's forces, the rebels would inevitably lose. They didn't have the numbers or the discipline or the resources of Lionstone's army and fleet. Instead, the Golgotha underground proposed orchestrated risings on every planet in the Empire simultaneously, together with acts of sabotage and civil disruption, spreading the Imperial forces so thinly that they could be fought and beaten in individual battles.

However, four planets in particular remained vital. Whoever could control or hold them would win in the end. Only once their fates had been sealed would it be possible for the rebels to begin the final phase: the assault on Golgotha itself and the Imperial Palace. Whoever held Golgotha ruled the Empire. The four planets were Technos III, the base of Clan Wolfe's stardrive production; Mistworld, the rebel planet; Shannon's World, also known as the pleasure planet; and Virimonde, in charge of food and supply routes for most of the Empire. It was decided, almost unanimously, that Owen and Hazel would return to Mistworld. They had experience and contacts there.

"Oh, great," said Owen. "The last time I was there, it was all I could do just to stay alive, and I'm supposed to be an expert?"

"If you survived living in Mistport, that qualifies you as an expert," said Hazel. "And I do know a few people who could be useful. Which puts us miles ahead of anyone else here. Cheer up, stud. Maybe it won't be so bad this time."

"It couldn't be any worse," said Owen.

"Don't put money on it," said Ruby Journey.

"I'm coming back in an urn," said Owen. "I just know it. Mistworld is the only planet I've ever known that made the Imperial Court look timid and restrained. Mistport isn't a civilization; it's evolution in action. If it was any more violent, they could sell season tickets to the Golgotha Arena crowds. It'd be a major hit on holovision. There's more sex, blood, and dirty dealing in Mistport than on your average soap. Maybe we should negotiate to buy the rights . . ."

"Owen," said Hazel. "You're babbling. If we survived the jungles of Shandrakor, we can survive Mistport."

"It'll all end in tears," said Owen.

He realized people were staring at him, and subsided, muttering. The meeting moved on to further things, but Hazel stopped listening. Behind what she hoped was a brave face, she was shaking inwardly. Leaving the Wolfling World for Mistworld meant leaving her supply of Blood behind. She could always stock up before they left, and she was sure she'd be able to find a new source in Mistport (you could find anything in Mistport), but it increased the chances of her secret being found out. She didn't care what the rebel Council might think of her. They'd already condemned her just for being a clonelegger. But Owen would be so upset with her. He wouldn't be angry—she could have coped with anger—but he would look at her with those sad, defeated eyes and be very disappointed in her. For some reason she couldn't or wouldn't name, Hazel couldn't bear the thought of letting him down like that. So he must never know.

She crossed her arms across her chest and hugged herself tightly. She could feel the weight of the vial of Blood in her pocket, tugging at her side like an impatient child. Her need was growing again, but she fought it down ruthlessly. She was still in charge for the moment. And perhaps . . . just perhaps she could use the trip to Mistworld as a way to break off from her Blood use. She'd be in a familiar place with old friends. The pressure would be less. She could do it. She was stronger than the drug. And all the while she thought this, she had to hug herself ever more tightly to stop herself trembling with her need for the Blood in her pocket.

She made herself pay attention to what was being discussed and found that Jack Random the elder, Ruby Journey, and Alexander Storm had been chosen to go to Technos III, as representatives of the rebellion. A lot of people still weren't sure about Random, but no one was ready to count him out yet, so sending him to Technos III seemed to be the best way to make use of him. The planet was a factory world, and had been for generations. Most of the surface had disappeared beneath an overlay of sprawling mile-long factories, construction sites, and mining equipment. The air was so polluted you could chew it, and the local ecology had long ago been poisoned into extinction. No one cared. Nothing really important had been lost. The factories worked on, and production actually rose a little after they didn't have to bother about side effects anymore.

These days it all belonged to Clan Wolfe and was given over to stardrive production. This was a long and complicated business, involving practically every resource on the planet, but since the Wolfes had Imperial backing, no one complained, or at least no one who mattered. The workers were clones and indentured servants, paying off family debts that went back generations. Given the current state of interest rates on old loans, you could be born and die in debt without ever affecting the original sum. Not surprisingly, there was a small but thriving army of rebels and discontents who'd scraped a precarious living among the discarded remnants of high tech and abandoned experiments that filled the great industrial wastelands.

They were vicious, dedicated fighters. They had to be. There was no way for them to get off Technos III as long as Clan Wolfe was still in control.

Of late, things had got so bad on Technos III that Valentine Wolfe had been obliged to ask for assistance to avoid any interruption to stardrive production. The Empress had shown her sense of humor by sending five companies of Church troops, together with a selection of Jesuit commandos, under the command of Cardinal James Kassar. Valentine and Kassar did not get along, so Valentine had taken the opportunity to fade even more into the background, leaving Stephanie and Daniel to run things as they chose. The Church was currently fighting the local rebels with evangelical fury, and losing. Kassar was beside himself with rage, not least because Lionstone wouldn't send him any reinforcements. Any problems on Technos III were his problems and his responsibility.

Random, Journey, and Storm would make planetfall unnoticed, link up with the local rebels, and then lead them to victory over the Church forces. Hopefully, the locals would then agree to work with the main rebellion, to produce the new stardrive for the upcoming war. No one said anything, but everyone knew this was to be the make or break for Jack Random. Either he could bring this off, in which case he probably was the real thing, or he couldn't. Whatever happened, he was no great loss. They could always send in someone else to lead the rebels.

Giles Deathstalker, Finlay Campbell, Evangeline Shreck, and the Wolfling were to go to Shannon's World. Famed throughout the Empire as the most luxurious pleasure planet of all time, something had gone terribly wrong there three years ago. No one knew what, but the few people who were brave enough to go there never came back. The Empress sent down a full company of marines. Nothing was ever heard from them, either. These days Shannon's World was quarantined—as much to prevent anything breaking out as anyone foolish enough to try to get in. The various owners were still arguing over who was going to pay for the major armed forces necessary to get the answers.

Only one man had ever come back alive. Half-dead, half-mad, he had lived only a few days, mostly because he wanted to die. He renamed Shannon's World as Haceldama, the Field of Blood. Apparently, there was a hideous war going on down on the pleasure planet, though between whom remained unclear.

"And you want us to go there?" said Finlay Campbell incredulously. "Where does it say on our résumés that we do suicide missions? And what makes this hellhole so important, anyway?"

"Vincent Harker," said Alexander Storm simply. "One of the greatest strategic minds living today. He has knowledge of everything from distribution of forces within the Empire to its contingency plans in case of rebel attack. This is vital information, and we need it. Normally, he's so well guarded that we couldn't get anywhere near him. But twelve hours ago Harker's ship was attacked by a pirate craft. Nothing to do with us. Both ships managed to destroy each other, but Harker got away in an escape pod. He landed somewhere on Shannon's World. We have to find him before the Empire does.

"We have two small advantages. Firstly, since this happened only twelve hours ago, we have as good a chance of finding him as whatever forces the Empress finally sends in to look for him. Secondly, Harker's pod was equipped with a beacon, and it should still be sending, though you won't know that for sure till you get down there. Thirdly, whatever's happening on Shannon's World, you people are best

suited to survive it. You've already lived lives that would
have killed anyone else."

"Nevertheless," said Finlay. "You are sending us to a
planet that only one person has ever returned from, and he
was dying and crazy?"

"Got it in one," said Storm. "But we really can't miss
this chance at getting our hands on Harker. Think of it as
a challenge."

Finlay gave him a hard look. "You think of it as a challenge. I'm not going."

"Yes you are," said Evangeline.

Finlay turned his glare on her. "Give me one good reason.
Hell, give me one bad reason."

"Because I'm going," she said calmly. "Our beloved
leader has decided I'll be more useful there. Haceldama, the
Field of Blood. Sounds almost romantic, doesn't it?"

"You have a strange idea of romance," said Finlay.

"Of course," said Evangeline. "I fell in love with you,
didn't I?"

"I should give up now," said Giles. "Trust me on this;
you're not going to win."

Finlay glared around him impartially. "In the unlikely
event that I return alive from this venture, certain people
would be well-advised to come up with one hell of a re-
ward."

"That's my hero," said Evangeline.

After that, choosing David Deathstalker and Kit
SummerIsle to take control of Virimonde and run it for the
rebellion went very smoothly. The meeting broke up and everyone went their separate ways, and only history would
note that this was when the great rebellion really began.

Owen and Hazel, Jack and Ruby and Giles sat around a
table in the castle's great kitchen, relaxing after the Sturm
und Drang of the Council meeting with several bottles of
wine and a nourishing meal of the never-changing protein
cubes. Giles kept swearing he was going to fix the food machines to turn out something different, or indeed anything
different, but somehow he was always too busy with other
things. Owen had a dark suspicion that Giles had lost the
manual for the machine, but didn't want to admit it. Alexander Storm and the Stevie Blues had taken one look at what
was for dinner, and decided very quickly that they needed

some time in private to work on their reports for the Golgotha underground. Owen had a suspicion they had some food of their own tucked away somewhere.

He took a determined bite at his second protein cube. He kept hoping that he'd get used to the stuff, but somehow every day it found a whole new way to taste utterly vile. He swallowed his mouthful through sheer willpower and quickly washed it down with a large mouthful of wine. Little wonder he ended up half-drunk after every meal. He was beginning to wonder if it might be better to get drunk before the meal, so as to be better able to cope with it. He sighed deeply and pushed the rest of the cube away. He'd been meaning to start a diet soon anyway.

"Don't worry," said Hazel. "There are some really good restaurants in Mistport."

"There had better be," said Owen.

"I want a genetest," said Random suddenly, and everyone looked at him. He flushed slightly. "I mean, there must be the equipment for such a test somewhere in this castle."

"I think so," said Giles. "Or at least something that I could patch together to do the job. But there's no need. We know you're the real Jack Random. We all touched each other's mind in the Madness Maze when it changed us."

"That's not enough," Random insisted. "All that proves is that I think I'm the real me. I could be wrong. Who knows what the Empire mind techs did to me while I was their prisoner?"

"You don't need to take any test to prove to us who you are," said Ruby.

"Hell with you," said Random. "I want to take the test so I'll know who I really am. I'm not sure anymore. You saw their faces in the Hall. They came here expecting to meet a legend and instead found just a tired old man with jumbled memories."

"Will you stop this old-man nonsense," said Ruby. "You're only forty-seven. You told me yourself."

"But I crammed a hell of a lot into those years," said Random. "At least, I think I did. I can't trust my memory anymore."

"I can set up the test," said Giles. "But it'll take time to put the equipment together. It'd mean delaying your departure for Technos III for two, maybe three days."

Owen frowned. "I don't think we can wait that long. We're working to a timetable, remember?"

"Tests can wait," Ruby said firmly. "I know who you are, even if you don't. We've got jobs to do, and they take precedence."

Random still looked troubled, but finally shrugged and nodded his head. They all sat around the table in silence, looking at each other and then looking away. They were going to have to split up soon and go off on separate missions from which some or all of them might not return. No one was quite sure what to say.

"We'll still be linked through the undermind," Giles said finally. "Wherever we are. I don't think distance will make any difference."

"But it might," said Hazel. "This is all new territory. No one's ever been linked like us. Hell, no one's ever been like us."

"Yeah," said Owen. "There's got to be a catch. You don't get powers like ours without paying some kind of price."

"That's human thinking," said Random. "Limited thinking. You're not human anymore, so why should you have human limits?"

"There has to be limits," said Giles. "There are always limits eventually. We may not be strictly human anymore, but we're not gods."

"I wouldn't mind being a god," said Ruby. "Having bronzed young acolytes bringing me gold and jewels for tribute. I could get behind that."

"There's more to it than that," said Owen. "The link that binds us isn't just a glorified comm channel. It's changing us, bringing us together. Have any of you noticed we're starting to talk like each other?"

"Yeah," said Hazel. "We all sound a lot more alike than we used to. We're using the same phrases, sharing the same concepts, developing similar ways of looking at things."

"If you'd noticed all this," said Random, "why didn't you say something?"

"I was hoping it was just me. I mean, this is pretty damn spooky when you think about it. It's not just speech patterns, either. We're using each other's skills, without having to learn them first. Even augmented skills, like Owen's boost."

"Sometimes one of you will say what I've been thinking," said Owen. "And I get feelings about where people are and what they're doing, even when I've no way of knowing it. Are we becoming a gestalt, do you think? A group mind?"

"I don't think so," said Giles. "We're still capable of keeping secrets from each other. Isn't that right, Hazel?"

Her heart jumped, but she kept her face relaxed. "What are you talking about?"

"Perhaps you'd care to tell us why you've been spending so much time in the Hadenman city," said Giles.

"That's my business," said Hazel flatly.

"We're all entitled to our private lives," said Owen.

"I want to know," said Giles.

"She's been seeing Tobias Moon, all right?" said Owen. "If she didn't want to tell us, that was her business. Just because we're close now, it doesn't mean we have to open up our souls to each other."

"We may not have any choice," said Giles. "If the link continues to grow and strengthen."

"Which sounds to me like a damn good reason for splitting up and putting some distance between us," said Random. "No offense, people, but the only person I want in my head is me."

"Right," said Hazel. "And besides, I don't think humanity's ready to cope with Ruby Journey the god."

"You have no ambition," said Ruby calmly.

"But we're a lot more powerful together," said Owen. "Remember the force shield we raised against Silence's troops? They couldn't touch us with anything they had. I don't think any of us could do that separately. There might be other things we could learn to do together. Powerful things. Don't we have a responsibility to the rebellion to become as powerful as possible? We're the rebellion's secret weapon, the ace in the hole; we're the one thing that might tip the coming war in our favor. Are we being selfish in valuing our own individuality over the rebellion's needs?"

"Perhaps some of what we're fighting for is everyone's right to be an individual," said Random. "We can't save humanity by becoming inhuman. The only other people to survive passing through the Madness Maze were the scientists who created the Hadenmen. Do we want something like that as our legacy?"

"He's right," said Giles. "We all have monsters within us. What if our growing power let them out, let them run loose? Who knows what we might become?"

They all sat and thought about that for a while. Owen thought how easy it had been for him to kill the Blood Runner, halfway across the Empire, in the Obeah systems. Finally, Random sighed and leaned forward. "This is all irrelevant. We can't stay together. We're needed on three separate planets, right now. We'll be leaving as soon as the Hadenmen have ships ready. Everything else will have to wait till we return. Now, is there anything else we need to discuss? I don't mind admitting I've found today's business exhausting. Somewhere there is a bed with a thick mattress and heavy covers calling my name."

"There is one thing," Owen said reluctantly. "You remember my personal AI, Ozymandius? He turned out to be an Empire spy, and I had to destroy him with my new powers before he destroyed us. Well . . . he's back. He talks to me, but I'm the only one that can hear him. The odds are I'm just cracking up from the pressure, but it might be something more sinister . . ."

"You never mentioned this before," said Ruby.

"He was scared we'd think he was crazy," said Hazel. "We wouldn't have thought that, Owen. We all understand about pressure and what it does to people."

"Besides," said Random, "if you were going crazy, we'd have felt it through the link long before now."

"Does Oz still have the control words he planted in your mind and Hazel's?" said Giles, frowning.

"He says not," said Owen. "But I have no way of knowing whether he's lying or not. He hasn't tried to use them. So far."

"Talk to him now," said Random. "We'll try and listen in. Everyone crack their comms wide open and concentrate on the link as well. Go ahead, Owen."

"All right," said Owen, just a little self-consciously. "Oz, are you there?"

"Of course I'm still here," said the AI. "Where else would I be? You told me to shut up, remember? Personally, I'm amazed you've been able to stagger through your days without my assistance. I could have given you all kinds of advice during the Council meeting. Still, with all these new magic tricks of yours, I suppose you're too grand for me now. I mean, I'm just a class-seven AI with access to more information than you could wade through in a lifetime . . ."

"Shut up, Oz," said Owen. He looked around the table. "Well? Did you catch any of that?"

"Not a thing," said Random, and the others shook their heads. Random looked thoughtfully at Owen. "Do you think it's your AI?"

"No," said Owen. "It can't be. I killed Oz in the Madness Maze; I destroyed his mind completely with my new powers. I felt him die."

"Then, who is it?" said Hazel.

"I don't know!" said Owen.

"It could be some aftereffect of the Madness Maze," said Random.

"Oh, that's really comforting," said Ruby. "You mean we could all end up hearing things?"

"If you can't think of anything helpful to say, button it," said Hazel. "No wonder Owen didn't like to talk to us about this."

"I have to say I don't see what we can do to help, Owen," said Random. "Keep us apprised of any new developments, though. That goes for all of us. But I think we'd do better to leave this for another time, after we return from our various missions. They have to take precedence. In the time before we go, Owen, I suggest you run a few diagnostics on your comm implants, see if that turns up anything. Anyone else been having problems they'd like to talk about?"

Everyone looked around the table at everyone else. Hazel kept her mouth shut. She couldn't tell them about the Blood. They wouldn't understand. It was her problem, she'd beat it herself. She'd beaten it before in Mistport, and that was where she was going. It was a sign. It had to be. The silence dragged on, until finally Random pushed back his chair and got to his feet.

"Good night, people. My left foot has gone to sleep, and I'd like to catch up with it as soon as possible. Get as much rest as you can before we have to leave. I have a strong feeling it'll be some time before we get another chance to rest."

He nodded to them vaguely, turned, and left the kitchen. Ruby Journey grabbed a half-full bottle of wine and went after him. Hazel nodded briefly to Owen and left as quickly as she could without it seeming strange. She didn't dare talk to him. She might blurt out the truth. If anyone would understand, it would be Owen. But she couldn't take the chance, and so she left the kitchen without looking back and went to her quarters alone. Giles and Owen sat looking at each other across the table.

"I'm sorry we're having to part so soon, ancestor," said Owen. "We've hardly had a chance to get to know each other."

"I know you're a true Deathstalker," said Giles. "That's all that really matters. You're a good fighter—for an historian. Is there ... anything you'd like to ask me?"

"Well," said Owen, "I have been wondering ... why do you wear your hair in a scalplock? I mean, that's the sign of a mercenary soldier."

"Yes," said Giles. "It is. The Empire I remember is gone now, just a memory. The Emperor I swore to serve is long dead. Things haven't turned out at all how I expected. You always hope the future will be better, and your descendants will have an easier time than you had, but I saw the rot setting in, even then. And nothing's changed in the last nine hundred years, except for the worse. At least I've lived long enough to see the beginnings of a rebuilding. I'm no longer Warrior Prime. That was taken from me long ago, and so I became a fighter for other people's causes. Just like now. I'm a mercenary, Owen. Nothing more. Hence the scalplock. I always did have a weakness for the dramatic gesture. Are you sure there's nothing you'd like to talk to me about before we have to part?"

Owen shifted uncomfortably on his chair. Ever since Giles had killed his son Dram, he'd been trying to be a father figure to Owen, but Owen didn't want or need another father. He still had enough problems over how he felt about his actual father. So in the end the two men just smiled and nodded to each other, and went off in their different directions to get what rest they could before their separate journeys.

Two Deathstalkers, bound by blood and honor, guilt and perhaps a little feeling. Heroes of the forthcoming rebellion. Who had no way of knowing to what dark end destiny would eventually bring them.

CHAPTER SIX

Voices in the Dark

It gets strange out on the Rim. The starship *Dauntless* hammered through the darkness, a small silver speck in the long night. Captain John Silence sat in his command chair on the *Dauntless*'s bridge, staring somberly at the main viewscreen before him. Not that there was much to see on the viewscreen. This latest tour of duty had brought him right to the edge of the Rim, where the normality of suns and planets and life gave way to the endless empty dark of the Darkvoid, which knew nothing of light and life. Except for the Wolfling World, whose mysterious depths held an army of reborn Hadenmen and the beginnings of a new rebellion. Silence's mouth flattened into a grim line. He'd been driven from that world in failure and disgrace, but even so he was in no hurry to return there in search of revenge. Unnatural powers had manifested in the dim vast caverns below that planet's surface, forces and events almost beyond human comprehension. Forces that had touched and tainted him, too. The Wolfling World was a dangerous place, and Silence had decided very firmly that he wasn't going back there without the entire Imperial Fleet to back him up. He knew the difference between courage and a suicide mission. It was essential that the rebellion gestating inside the Wolfling World be stamped out and eradicated, but until he could convince the Empress of that, Silence had every intention of keeping a safe distance between him and the only living planet in the Darkvoid.

He sighed and shifted position yet again in his chair. He'd been on the bridge ten hours now, well past the end of his watch, but there was no point in standing down. He couldn't rest, and he couldn't sleep. Too many things had been happening recently. Disturbing things. His mission had seemed straightforward enough when Lionstone outlined it for him: patrol those planets in the Empire dominated by sentient

alien species, and make it clear to them that they were to
have no contact with any alien forces from outside the Empire or any rebel forces within it. Make promises of increased support on the one hand and threats of dire reprisals
for disobedience on the other. The carrot and the bloody big
stick. Never fails, with humans. But those few alien civilizations that had survived being brought within the Empire
were anything but human.

It was quiet this far out on the Rim, far from Empire, traffic, and populated planets. The *Dauntless* was very alone,
and sometimes that loneliness seemed almost too much to
bear. Half the crew were taking tranquilizers or dosing themselves with illicit booze. Silence turned a blind eye. They all
needed a little something extra to help them survive the
soul-deep cold of the long night. Everyone except Frost, of
course. Investigator Frost stood at parade rest beside Silence's command chair, as calm and composed as always.
She'd been quietly studying the viewscreen for some time,
but she didn't need to say anything for Silence to know she
was impatient with the endless monotony. Frost always preferred to be doing something, and the long weeks of inactiv-
ity out on the edge of the Rim had been hard on her. It was
a long way between the few alien planets, even with the new
stardrive, and Frost was frankly bored. Personally, Silence
felt he could live with a little boredom. Only a few more
planets to visit and their mission would be officially over;
though whether they would be allowed to return to the more
inhabited sectors of the Empire remained to be seen. They
knew too many things the Empress didn't want discussed.

But it wasn't just boredom and loneliness that made Silence so uneasy about being so far from the heart of the Empire. The new rebellion could begin at any time, led by
people who'd become almost superhuman and aided by an
army of the deadly augmented men. This rebellion, when it
came, wouldn't be put down as easily as all the others. Silence felt a burning need, almost an obsession, to be back in
his rightful place, orbiting Golgotha, protecting the Empress.
Lionstone hadn't taken his reports about the strength of the
new rebellion and its leaders anywhere near seriously
enough. He'd tried explaining his concern to Frost, expecting a sympathetic ear, but she'd just shrugged and said
if there was an Empire-wide rebellion, there'd be fighting

enough for everyone, no matter where they were. Frost had always been a practical person, first and foremost.

Silence drummed his fingers on the armrests of his chair. Somewhere deep inside him, a small but persistent voice was clamoring for a drink to settle his nerves, but he wouldn't listen to it. He'd tried that, and it hadn't worked. He'd managed to climb back out of the bottle, with a little help from Frost, and he wouldn't give in to it again. He'd pulled himself back from the brink of failure and disgrace with his victory over the alien ship above Golgotha, and having been granted another chance against all the odds, he was damned if he'd be beaten by his own weaknesses. It had taken a while, but his crew had learned to respect him again, which pleased him. They were a good crew, mostly, and he wanted to be a strong Captain for them. Of course, there were still dark murmurs in occasional dark corners, where people wrongly thought the ship's security systems couldn't overhear them. The word belowdecks was that just possibly Silence and/or Frost were jinxed. Bad luck. Jonahs. Unfortunate things happened around them. After all, Silence had lost his last ship, the *Darkwind*, in a clash with pirates, and their last mission to the Wolfling World had gone to hell in a handcart in a hurry. And as everyone knows, went the murmur, bad things come in threes. Sweepstakes were running among the more superstitious crew members—not about whether something else really nasty would happen, but about what shape it would take when it did.

Silence let them get on with it. On the whole the crew were still sharp and well coordinated, performing their duties at an entirely acceptable level. The victory over the alien ship had raised their spirits and returned their confidence after the debacle of the Wolfling World. And most of them had lost someone they loved or knew someone who had during the alien ship's attack on Golgotha's main starport and city. An undercurrent of anger and a need for revenge burned in the crew's collective heart, hot and ugly. So far Silence hadn't been able to find a target or an outlet for it, but he had no doubt one would emerge eventually. Some alien species would do or say the wrong thing, and have to be punished. And then Silence would sit back and let the crew sink themselves in violence and revenge until it sickened them. A bit hard on the aliens, but after all, that was what they were there for.

On the whole Silence had chosen to let Frost take charge of the alien contacts. It was her area of expertise, after all. And if he was sometimes uncomfortable with some of her more extreme practices, he kept it to himself. She was responsible for the safety of the human species, and if that meant being ruthless as well as efficient, Frost had never been known to give a damn. Silence smiled slightly, in spite of himself. Certainly the Investigator had never been trained in diplomacy; or if she had, had gone out of her way to forget it. She just aimed herself at whatever passed for the aliens' authority figures, made her demands on behalf of the Empress, and issued dire warnings and threats of what would happen if she was disobeyed. It was often as blunt as that, but she got results. Silence had his reservations, but couldn't bring himself to disapprove. The safety of humanity had to come first.

He'd been the same himself, cold and curt and full of authority, until it backfired on him on a backwater planet called Unseeli. The native species rebelled over the Empire's extensive mining operations on their planet. The Empire needed those mines, and so the newly promoted Captain Silence had been sent to put a stop to the rebellion, by whatever means necessary. He tried diplomacy, and then he tried firmness, force, and finally all-out war. But there turned out to be strange secrets and powers moving on Unseeli, and things got out of hand fast. Silence had been forced to pull his people back from the planet and order the entire world scorched clean from orbit. That particular alien species was now extinct, though their ghosts still haunted Unseeli's metallic forest.

Silence's frown deepened as he considered the contacts he'd made with the alien planets so far. Few had gone well, but in the end he'd got what the Empire wanted without having to order another scorching. He wasn't sure he could do that again. Though he had no doubt that if the occasion arose and he didn't give the order, Frost would. And who was to say which one of them was right in the end? Humanity had to be protected, and while all the alien contacts had been strange and unusual, some had been actually disturbing. Life had taken many shapes and purposes throughout the Empire, and few of them were human in form or intent. Many were mysterious, obscure, and even impenetrable. Silence wasn't sure some of them even knew they were in the Empire.

* * *

Shanna IV was a desolate world, with endless plains of hard-baked ground, and its only water deep underground. A huge, brilliant sun beat down from a blinding sky that had never known clouds, and the only signs of intelligent life were the huge pyramids of resin-hardened stone and sand, built long ago by the planet's only inhabitants. Each pyramid was exactly like all the others, though they might be thousands of miles apart. Four hundred feet high, their lines were sharp and their dull red sides were smooth and featureless. No one knew what was inside them, or even if there was an inside; none of the Empire's investigative teams had been able to find an entrance. Being Investigators, they'd tried making one, only to discover the pyramids' smooth sides were impervious to anything the Empire could throw against them, up to and including major energy weapons. Which should have been impossible for resin-hardened stone and sand. Eventually, the Empire decided it didn't really care what was inside the pyramids after all, and concentrated its attention on the planet's current inhabitants, who might or might not have been the builders of the pyramids.

These were ugly, hard-shelled insects about the size of a man's fist, with razor-sharp mandibles and entirely too many legs. They seemed to have no individual identity, but en masse they were capable of producing a group mind that could, with some difficulty, be communicated with. Which was just as well, as the horrible scuttling things were also capable, with a little prodding, of producing a great many organic compounds the Empire found useful. So the Empire provided the base materials; the insects ate and excreted it, and possibly did other things to it in their pyramids when no one was looking, and the end result was a series of extremely complex chemical forms that would be hideously expensive to reproduce in a laboratory. The Empire profited, the insects got protection from outside influences but were otherwise left strictly alone, and everyone was happy. Or at least no one complained.

Captain Silence and Investigator Frost stood at the base of one of the massive pyramids, waiting for the insects' representative to make an appearance. The day was as hot as a blast furnace and twice as dry. The air shimmered, and the sun was too bright to look at, even with the heavy-duty protection over their eyes. Silence turned up the cooling ele-

ments in his uniform another notch and screwed his eyes up
against the harsh, unrelenting light. Sweat was pouring out
of him, only to evaporate almost immediately in the awful
heat. Silence didn't look at Frost. He just knew she still
looked cool and calm and completely undisturbed. She was
an Investigator, after all, and therefore by definition not
prone to the fallibilities of the merely human. In the end, cu-
riosity got the better of him, and he looked casually around
just in time to see her kick out lazily at one of the many
small forms scuttling around their feet. It flopped over onto
its back, its long legs wriggling, and then somehow turned
itself over again and hurried on about its business. Frost
sniffed.

"Ugly things. Desolate bloody place. If the representative
doesn't turn up soon, I'm going to start using these nasty little creepy-crawlies for target practice."

"That should get their attention," said Silence, smiling in
spite of himself. "Do I detect a note of distaste in your
voice, Investigator? I thought you were trained to take all
forms of alien life in stride?"

"There's a limit to everything," said Frost, "and I think I
may have found mine. Repulsive little things. If one even
looks like it might be thinking of darting up my leg, I'm going to blast it and everything like it for a dozen yards
around. I had more than enough of that inside the alien ship
over Golgotha."

Silence looked at her carefully. If it had been anyone else,
he would have sworn there was a note of remembered horror
in her voice. The interior of the alien ship had been horrible
enough, certainly. He still had nightmares. But Investigators
were trained from childhood to give nightmares, not suffer
from them. He considered his words carefully, and when he
finally spoke he looked off in a different direction.

"It was bad inside the alien ship. All those insects, all
sizes, all around us and no way out. Enough to give anyone
the creeps."

"You're about as subtle as a flying half brick, you know
that?" said Frost. "But thanks for the thought."

Silence looked back at her. She was smiling, but it didn't
touch her eyes. He shrugged. "If you ever need someone to
talk to . . ."

"I'll bear it in mind. But any problems I might have are
mine, and I'll handle them."

"That's what I thought when the booze was drowning me inch by inch. You helped me out anyway."

"You didn't know how to ask for help," said Frost.

"Neither do you," said Silence.

They looked at each other. There was a closeness between them that was more than just the link they always shared now. Frost's eyes softened slightly, and Silence thought for a moment that she was closer to opening up to him than she had ever been before. But the moment passed and the softness disappeared, and Frost was an Investigator again, cold and focused and quite impenetrable. Silence looked away.

"You have to make allowances for the insect representatives," he said finally. "According to the files, they have little concept of time as we understand it, but they respond well to firm behavior."

"I don't have to make allowances for anything," said Frost. "That's what being an Investigator is all about."

Silence had to smile. "Useful though the files are, however, they don't have anything at all to say about how you get the bloody insects' attention in the first place."

"We could kill a few," said Frost. "Hell, we could kill a lot. Nobody'd miss them."

"Let's save that for a last resort," said Silence. "There must be something a little less drastic we could try."

And then he broke off as a wave of insects came surging toward him, thick and black like a living carpet. His hand dropped to the disrupter at his side. Frost already had hers out, and was sweeping it back and forth, searching for a meaningful target. The wave crashed to a sudden halt a few feet short of them and began piling up into a tall, thick pillar of squirming bodies. The twitching legs folded around each other and were still, the small bodies fitting neatly together like the interlocking parts of some more complicated machine, and gradually the pillar took on a humanoid form: a dark, shiny shape that mocked humanity as much as it duplicated it. The square, flat-sided head turned jerkily on its thick neck to look at Silence and Frost, though there was no trace of anything that might have been eyes. It buzzed briefly: a short, ugly, and completely inhuman sound. It buzzed again, and suddenly, though the sounds hadn't changed, Silence and Frost somehow understood it.

"Empire," said the dark human shape, though there was

nothing that might have been a mouth. "Interrogation. Respond."

Frost put her gun away and tried to look as though she'd never drawn it in the first place. "Yes, we represent the Empire," she said flatly. "You've been informed why we're here?"

There was an Empire Base on Shanna IV, populated by a handful of scientists and a small force of guards who'd all managed to upset someone really badly to get themselves posted here, but they had as little contact with the resident aliens as they could get away with. They might have arranged this meeting, or they might not have. It was that kind of Base.

Silence stared at the humanoid figure, and it stared right back at him. Though there was no trace of eyes on the flat shiny face, Silence had no doubt the insect representative was watching him. He could feel the weight of its stare, like an icy breeze in the boiling heat of the day. The insects that made up the human shape twitched suddenly, hundreds of legs flexing briefly so that a shimmer seemed to run through the figure, and then it was still again. Silence winced as a headache blossomed slowly between his eyes. It was as though he could almost see or hear something that was being hidden from him. He concentrated on the feeling and realized it felt something like the link that he shared with Frost. He glanced at her to see if she felt it, too. She was scowling, but there was nothing unusual in that. Certainly she didn't seem as disturbed as he felt. He tried to grasp the vague feeling and bring it into focus, but it slipped away like water between his fingers and was gone. He still had the headache, though.

"Rebels," the alien representative said suddenly. "Avoid. Punishment."

"Got it in a nutshell," said Frost. "Anyone tries to contact you, rebel or alien, you tell them to go to hell and then report them to the Base immediately. Understand?"

"Rebels. Avoid. Punishment. Chemicals. Interrogation. Respond."

Silence would have shivered, had he not been boiling alive in his own sweat. There was something about the way each word seemed to emanate from different parts of the dark human shape that upset him greatly. He made himself concentrate on his job.

"Yes, we've got your chemicals," he said curtly. "They're being unloaded in the usual place. The regular supply ship will be along to pick up the compounds you've produced." A question occurred to him, and he decided to ask it before he could think better of it. "We have a use for those compounds, but what do you get out of the deal?"

There was a long pause, until Silence assumed the construct wasn't going to answer him; then it said two words and fell apart before Silence could respond. The human shape disintegrated from the top down, tumbling into hundreds of its respective parts, which hit the ground running and scuttled off in different directions. In a few moments they were indistinguishable from those who were already covering the ground, and Silence wasn't at all sorry to see the back of them. Particularly, after the two words the figure had spoken. *Chemicals. Addictive.* He looked at Frost, who was still staring thoughtfully at the insects scuttling around her on their inscrutable, incomprehensible missions.

"Do you suppose they have any concept at all of themselves as individuals?" he said finally. "Or only when they gather together like that?"

"No one knows for sure," said Frost. "They're supposed to have a single hive mind for the whole species, but no one's been able to prove anything, one way or the other. Our instruments can't detect anything, and espers just get really bad headaches when they try to listen in. The constructs are our only way of communicating with them, and they tell us as little as they can get away with."

"What about the scientists at the Base?"

"They spend most of their time trying to get themselves transferred somewhere else, and I don't blame them one bit. This place gives me the creeps."

Silence kept his features under control, but it was a near thing. He couldn't have been more surprised if the Investigator had admitted to secret pacifist leanings. For Frost to admit that the place made her feel uncomfortable, it must really be getting to her. And that wasn't like Frost at all. He decided to do them both a favor and change the subject.

"Did you know the chemicals we supply these insects with are addictive?"

"No," said Frost, "but it makes sense. If the insects are a single hive mind, they're scattered far too widely for us to be able to hurt or control them. But withholding chemicals to which they've developed a dependency should do the trick nicely. A junkie will do anything for his next fix."

"Very efficient," said Silence. "But then, the Empire's always been a great believer in efficiency. And if it can work a little cruelty into the deal, too, so much the better." He looked around him at the thousands of small scuttling forms, working blindly and obediently in the blistering heat to meet the Empire's needs. If he saw any connection between them and him, he kept it to himself.

Chroma XIII was a singular planet, in more ways than one. The original survey ship almost missed it completely, as technically it should have been impossible for any form of life to survive in a planet so far from its burned-out, dying sun. But something about Chroma XIII caught the Captain's eye, and he sent down drones to gather information. And what they sent back was enough to make even a seasoned survey officer's jaw drop. Within the giant gas ball that was Chroma XIII, there was life without form or substance. Intelligence separated from physical existence. A planet of inherent contradictions, whose very existence was theoretically impossible.

Silence kept the *Dauntless* in as high an orbit as he could get away with, and he and Frost watched the main viewscreen as the ship's drones dropped toward the impossible planet. Strange images came and went on the viewscreen as the scene switched from one drone's instruments to another, and all the time the comm channels threatened to overload on the sheer intensity of what they were relaying.

There was no planetary surface, no solid area at all, and the drones dropped endlessly through shades of color and fields of light, blindingly bright, in which strange hues shifted and stirred without any purpose or meaning that could be fathomed by human eyes. There were planes of dazzling color, separate and distinct and thousands of miles long, and whirlpools the size of moons, blending slowly from one color to another, and oceans of blue mists as dark as the color you see when you close your eyes at night. And everywhere, the colors and the shapes and the shades were shot through with sudden blasts of lightning that came and went almost too fast for the human eye to follow.

"And these flashes of lightning are the aliens?" Silence said finally.

"We think so," said Frost. "It's hard to be sure of anything here. Certainly the lightning bolts share some of the attributes we associate with life. They react to outside influences, they consume light on some wavelengths and release it in others, and they appear to communicate with each other, though our translation computers have had nervous breakdowns trying to make sense of it. They reproduce constantly, and they also disappear suddenly, for no discernible reason."

"All right," said Silence, determined not to be completely thrown. "How do we communicate with them?"

"We don't," said Frost. "We're not even sure they know we're here, which might just be for the best. Why give them ideas?"

Silence looked at her and raised an eyebrow. "And the Empire's content to just leave them be?"

"Pretty much. They don't have anything we want, let alone need."

"So what the hell are we doing here?" said Silence.

"Keeping an eye on them. We have no way of knowing what they're capable of. They're life without form, which could also be life without limits, as we understand them. Who knows what they might do if they became aware of us? If they decided to leave this planet and journey to some populated world, we could be in deep trouble. Those flashes of lightning contain billions of volts, theoretically, and we're pretty sure there are other forces at work down there, too. The bottom line is, we don't have anything that could stop them if they decided they were mad at us. What use is a weapon against something that has no physical existence?"

"Great," said Silence. "Just wonderful. Something else to worry about. So we can't talk to them, let alone threaten them, and we're not even sure they know we're here."

"Got it in one," said Frost. "All we can do is drop a hundred or so security drones to keep an eye on things, and then get the hell out of here."

" 'Join the Imperial Navy and see the universe,' " said Silence heavily. "Meet strange and interesting new forms of life, and run away from them. Navigator, get us the hell out of here. My head hurts."

* * *

The last planet they visited was Epsilon IX, and that meant hard suits. The gravity was five times standard, the air was a mixture of extremely noxious gases, any one of which would have been fatal on its own, and the air density was uncannily like the pressure of water you find at the bottom of a deep ocean trench. On top of all that, the entire world was a mass of goo; thick, slimy mud that covered the planet's surface from pole to pole. In some places it was only a couple of feet deep, and that was called land. Either way, it was messy as hell. There were hills that rose up suddenly overnight and then spent the rest of the day collapsing and sliding away.

There were huge artificial constructs here and there that might have been buildings or machines—or both or neither. The native intelligent species created them when they felt like it, though they declined to explain out of what or what their purpose might be. The muck itself contained a handful of extremely rare and useful trace elements, and these were refined from the goo by specially designed automated mining machinery from the Empire. People couldn't live on Epsilon IX, even inside a fully Screened Base; human-built structures inevitably sank, and had to be constantly retrieved, which cost money.

The mining equipment worked only because the natives looked after it. No one knew much about the native species. They appeared to be the only living things on Epsilon IX, which raised some interesting and rather unpleasant questions about what they ate. They had a mysterious link to their mucky environment that allowed them to thrive and prosper, but they weren't big on explaining that, or, indeed, anything else. They kept to themselves and did really nasty and inventive things to trespassers.

Silence and Frost journeyed down to what passed for the planet's surface in a pinnace, which ended up hovering in midair while Silence and Frost dropped awkwardly out of the air lock in their hard suits. They landed knee-deep in the sludge, and slogged slowly through the thick mud, slipping and sliding and holding onto each other for support. There was something vaguely solid under their heavy boots, but it rose and fell unpredictably beneath the covering goo. The slime came in varying shades of gray, much like the sky above, which was disorienting, to say the least. Sky blended into surface almost imperceptibly, which did strange things to Silence's sense of orientation. Things like up and down, left and right, forward and backward ceased being absolutes, and became more like matters of opinion. The last time Silence had felt like this he'd been drunk for a week.

He slogged along beside Frost, the hard suit's servomechanisms whining loudly as they struggled to overcome the planet's heavy gravity. Silence took a quiet satisfaction from the obvious difficulties Frost was having in plowing through the thick mud. It was good to know that even Investigators had their limits. They waded on for some time, while their surroundings rose and fell without any obvious meaning or purpose. Frost led the way with dogged determination. Silence supposed she knew where she was going, but didn't ask, just in case she didn't. He liked to think that at least one of them knew what they were doing.

The pinnace hovered high overhead, far enough away not to intimidate any of the locals, but still close enough to come charging in for an emergency rescue if necessary. Silence was getting tired fast. Even with the hard suit's servomechanisms to help, the constant struggle to stay upright while pressing on was exhausting. According to his suit's instruments, the local temperature was high enough to melt some metals. He was sweating like a pig despite everything the hard suit's temperature controls could do, and the lack of a proper horizon made his head hurt. He was so taken up with his own inner world of hurts and confusions that he only just noticed in time that Frost had come to a halt. He avoided crashing into her through a heroic last-minute effort, and then had to fight to keep his feet under him. He took a few deep breaths to settle himself and then looked around. The place they'd arrived at didn't seem noticeably any different from any of the others they'd plowed through to get here. There was no sign of any of the alien constructs, just a large hill to their left, slumping over like a melting ice cream.

"Is this it?" he said finally.

"In so far as there is an it, yes," said Frost. "These are the right coordinates, anyway. You know, this place is really disgusting. It looks like someone sneezed it into being."

Silence winced. "You've always had a way with words, Investigator. Now what do we do?"

"Now we wait for someone to put in an appearance.

Which, knowing this place, will undoubtedly take some time. Maybe we should have brought a bucket and spade."

And then she broke off as the mud before them bubbled up into a thick dribbling pillar, like a slow-motion fountain. Silence and Frost both trained their suits' disrupters on the pillar as it bulged and contracted here and there, finally forming into a human shape, complete in every detail, including clothes. Though the clothes were made of the same mud as the body. The figure actually looked quite snappy in formal evening wear, and for a moment Silence felt almost overdressed in his hard suit. He made himself concentrate on the figure's face. It was gray and sweated driblets of mud, but the features were indisputably human. The eyes focused on Silence and then on Frost, and the mouth twitched in a smile.

"Before you ask," the figure said briskly, "no, I don't really look like this. You are looking at a mental projection, formed from handy nearby materials. Trust me, you don't want to see what I really look like. Not unless you're into projectile vomiting, which I would assume could get really messy inside one of those suits. Human senses are too limited to appreciate my true beauty." He folded his dripping arms across his sliding chest and gave them a moment to think about that. "Now, what do you people want this time? I'm busy. And don't ask me what at; you couldn't possibly hope to understand."

"If you're this planet's idea of a diplomat, I'd hate to meet your politicians," said Silence. "How is it you speak our language so well?"

"I don't. I'm communicating directly with your mind, which is slumming for me, but we all have to make sacrifices if we're to keep the gods happy. Little joke there, to put you at your ease."

"You're telepathic?" said Frost. "That wasn't in the files."

"Nothing so primitive. We are communicating directly, though your human minds are too limited to pick up most of what I'm transmitting." The figure stopped and frowned. "Though I have to say, you seem much more receptive than most."

"Save the compliments," said Frost. "We're here on business."

"Well, I didn't think you were tourists," snapped the man made out of mud. "What does the Empire want this time?"

"Rebels and aliens; don't talk to them," said Frost briskly. "If anyone tries, contact your nearest Imperial spy satellite. Any alliances with unauthorized forces will result in severe punitive measures."

"And what might those be?" said the mud man. "Going to arrest us, perhaps? Not unless you can build prisons in five dimensions. Or perhaps you'll take away some of our lovely mud? Help yourselves; we've got tons of the bloody stuff."

Frost raised her right hand and triggered the disrupter built into her glove. The energy beam flashed out and vaporized the mud man's head. Silence started to object and then stopped himself. He didn't approve of unnecessary killing, but this was the Investigator's show. She was best qualified to decide what was necessary to get her point across. The mud man should have been more respectful, damn it. An insult to them was an insult to the Empress. And then he realized the headless body hadn't slumped to the ground. It stood just where it had, as though nothing had happened. Liquid mud bubbled in the stump of the neck, and then rose up suddenly to form itself into a new head. The same face quickly appeared, and the mud man glared at Frost.

"I see Imperial diplomacy hasn't changed much since its last visit. Plus seven points for brutality, minus several thousand for severe lack of cool. Never mind barbarians at the gate, they've already taken over. Just once, I wish they'd send us a representative slightly higher up the food chain. I've had more interesting conversations with a piece of moss. You humans should be bloody grateful my species is physically linked to the planet's ecosystem. If we could leave this world, we'd be running the Empire inside a week."

"But you can't, and you don't," said Frost. "So remember what I told you. No talking to any strange men or aliens, or we'll work out some way to give you all a good spanking. Right. That's it, we're going. Have fun playing with your mud."

"I don't see any need for sexual slanders," said the mud man. "Please feel free to leave our world anytime. Goodbye."

Silence started to turn to leave, and then stopped as he realized Frost hadn't moved. He couldn't see her face inside her helmet, but he knew she was staring thoughtfully at the figure made out of mud. He could feel it. The link between them seemed suddenly very strong, and he knew without having to be told what was running through her mind. She wanted to see the real alien; the real shape and being that lay behind the image of the mud man. The reality behind the mask.

"Cut it out, Frost," he said quietly. "We don't need to know."

"He doesn't respect us," said the Investigator. "He doesn't fear us. I want to know why."

"Listen to your partner," said the mud man. "You really don't want to do this. This image is all you're capable of understanding. The reality of what I and my kind are would destroy your limited minds." He stopped abruptly and frowned at Frost. "What are you doing? Your mind is . . . uncoiling. There's more to you than there was before. You're not human. What are you?"

Frost stared back at him, her brows furrowed as she concentrated, reaching inside herself for a strength and vision she hadn't realized she possessed. There was something more beyond the mud man, something bigger, vaster . . . The sheer size of it made her head ache, but she wouldn't look away. It was deep down in the mud, under the surface of the world, and it was rising slowly out of the depths toward her. It had length and width and breadth and other dimensions, too. And perhaps just to look on it with merely human eyes would be enough to turn her to stone, like a butterfly caught in Medusa's gaze, but she couldn't, wouldn't, look away. She had to see, had to know . . . Silence grabbed her by the shoulders of her hard suit, spun her around, and shook her as hard as he could.

"Don't look at it! I can see what you're seeing, and it's dangerous. We're not ready to look at something like this. Just the sight of it would burn the eyes out of our heads and blast our reason. Look away, Investigator! That's an order!"

He reached out with his mind, not quite knowing how he was doing what he was doing, and slowly forced Frost's inner eye shut. The image of what lay beyond and below the mud man was suddenly gone, and the heightened link between Silence and Frost shrank back to its normal background murmur. They were both back in their own heads again and saw only what was in front of them. Frost shuddered suddenly.

"Thank you, Captain. I got . . . lost for a while there."

"Let's get out of here, Frost. We've given them their instructions. Anything else is none of our business."

"We can't let them run us off. They have to know who's in charge here."

"I have an uneasy feeling they already know," said Silence. "Let's go."

Back on the bridge of the *Dauntless,* Silence was jerked out of his memories by the quiet but insistent voice of his Communications Officer, Eden Cross. He'd turned around at his workstation to look at Silence, who blinked at him a couple of times, and then tried to look alert and awake, as though he'd been listening to Cross all along. It only took him a moment to realize he wasn't fooling anyone, and he relaxed with a smile. He was lucky it was Cross. Cross was a good man.

"Sorry," said Silence. "I was light-years away. Run that past me again."

"There appears to be a situation belowdecks, Captain," said Cross. There was no trace of a smile on his dark face, but his eyes were understanding. "Not long ago, strange noises were heard coming from inside Security Officer Stelmach's private quarters. Some of his people went to investigate and discovered Stelmach systematically wrecking his quarters. They inquired diplomatically as to what the problem might be, and he threw things at them. They have currently retreated just out of range, and are awaiting further instructions. He is their boss, after all. And technically speaking, only yourself as Captain and Investigator Frost are senior enough to restrain a Security Officer."

Silence looked at Frost beside him, and she raised an eyebrow. Stelmach had a tendency to get excited in emergencies, but usually on board ship he was cool and calm, and followed every regulation to the letter. There were those who said he didn't authorize his own bowel movements without checking the regulations first. Something serious must have happened to destroy Stelmach's composure.

"We'd better go and take a look, Investigator," said Silence. "He is in charge of the ship's security, after all. If he's discovered something that upsetting, I think I want to know about it, too."

Frost nodded calmly. "We have been out on the Rim a

long time. People have been known to crack, so far from light and life and civilization."

"Not Stelmach," said Silence. "It'd take more than a case of cabin fever to crack him." Silence got to his feet. "Second in Command, you have the bridge. Investigator, follow me. But keep your hands away from your weapons. I want Stelmach conscious and able to answer questions."

"Spoilsport," said Frost.

They left the bridge and took the express elevator down to the officers' quarters. They could tell when they were getting near. There were people milling in the corridors, including those from the last shift, woken by the sound of Stelmach's voice, shouting and swearing incoherently. Silence politely but firmly sent them back to their beds, assuring them he'd take care of everything. Frost hurried them on their way with an occasional glare. Finally the two of them rounded a corner to find half a dozen security men huddled together at the end of a corridor. They jumped half out of their skins when Silence addressed them from behind, and then relaxed a little from sheer relief when they saw who it was. They even looked glad to see the Investigator, which was probably a first.

There was a quick discussion among the six of them as to who was in charge, and then that one was pushed forward by the others. He started to explain what had happened, realized he hadn't saluted, tried to do that and apologize at the same time, and then started explaining all over again. The sound of something large but fragile smashing into hundreds of pieces came clearly from the open door to Stelmach's quarters, followed by more incoherent swearing. The security man swallowed hard and started again.

"Lieutenant Zhang reporting, sir. Security Officer Stelmach appears to be . . . unwell. We have attempted to ascertain what the problem might be, but he has declined to talk to us, and besides, he has a gun. Perhaps you would care to have a word with him, Captain. I'm sure he'd listen to you, and the Investigator."

"At ease, Lieutenant," said Silence. "We'll handle things from here. You and your people fall back out of sight around the corner. It might be your presence that's upsetting him so much. See that this corridor is blocked off at both ends; I don't want anyone else coming in here while we're talking to Stelmach. And, Lieutenant, we are not to be interrupted for anything less than a major emergency."

Zhang nodded quickly, gathered up the rest of his people with his eyes, and led them in a hurried but dignified retreat back around the corner. In his quarters, Stelmach was still shouting and breaking things. Silence admired the man's stamina. He'd had a few blind rages himself in his drinking days, and he knew from experience that rages were hard work to keep going. He turned to Frost, and then frowned at her.

"I said no guns, Investigator."

"He has one, Captain."

"But he hasn't used it yet. Let's not put any ideas into his head." He glared at Frost until she holstered her gun again, and then looked back down the corridor. Things had grown ominously quiet. "Is Stelmach a drinker, do you know? I haven't heard anything, but someone in his position would be under a lot of strain, and in a good position to get his hands on all kinds of booze, legal or otherwise."

"Or worse," said Frost. "He'd also have access to all kinds of drugs for use in his interrogations. Plus whatever illicit drugs his people might have discovered and confiscated. There's always something going around. There's nothing in his files about substance abuse of any kind, but he had access to the files. I can't say I know the man well. Not many do. Security Officer isn't a post to make you popular with people."

"But do they respect him?"

"Oh, I should think so. The fact that no one's rolled a fragmentation grenade into his room while he was sleeping is a pretty good sign the crew respects his authority. And that his people are on their toes."

Silence and Frost moved slowly and quietly down the empty corridor, stopping just short of the open door to Stelmach's quarters. Silence gestured to the Investigator, and they both placed their backs against the bulkhead wall next to the door. Technically speaking, all Silence had to do was show himself and order Stelmach to calm down and explain himself. The Security Officer would do this immediately or face a court-martial for insubordination. In practice, Silence had a strong feeling he might end up doing more ducking than talking. Assuming Stelmach really did have a gun. According to regulations, the use of energy weapons on board ship was strictly forbidden, except under the direst circumstances. On the other hand, Stelmach was the *Dauntless*'s Security Officer, and if he wanted a gun there weren't many people on the ship with the authority to say no. Silence always carried a gun, as did the Investigator. They were required to do so, partly in case of situations like this. But in all his time as Captain, Silence had never drawn a gun on a member of his own crew, and he wasn't about to start now. And to hell with what the regulations said. It was still quiet in Stelmach's quarters. Silence raised his voice, keeping it calm and even and very assured.

"Stelmach, this is the Captain. I have the Investigator with me. We need to talk to you."

There was no reply. Silence strained his ears against the quiet and thought he could hear harsh, heavy breathing from inside the cabin. Maybe Stelmach had passed out, from drink or drugs or exhaustion. And just maybe he was waiting for some poor trusting fool to stick his head around the door, so he could shoot it off. Silence licked his dry lips and tried again.

"Stelmach, this is the Captain. Can you hear me?"

"Yes, Captain. I can hear you." The Security Officer's voice was a quiet rasp, a low painful sound, as though he'd injured his voice with shouting and screaming. "Go away, Silence. I don't want to talk to you. I don't want to talk to anyone."

"We rather gathered that," said Silence. "But we're going to have to talk sooner or later; you know that. Now, are you going to invite me in for a little chat, or am I going to have to send the Investigator in to reason with you? My way will mean less damage to the fixtures and fittings. Look, whatever the problem is, I can't help you standing around out here. And you do need help, don't you?"

There was a long pause, and when Stelmach finally spoke again, his voice was tired and defeated, as though all the rage had just drained right out of him. "All right. Come in. Let's get this over with."

That particular choice of words had an ominous ring to it, but Silence decided he was going in anyway. There wasn't really anything else he could do. He turned to Frost and kept his voice low. "I'm going in first. You back me up. Keep your hands away from your weapons. We don't want to spook him."

"I should go in first," said Frost. "I'm more expendable than you."

"No offense, Investigator, but you do tend to make a rather . . . strong first impression. The state he's in, he might just take one look at you and open fire. Besides, I'm more of an authority figure as far as he's concerned. He's always responded well to authority figures in the past. And before you ask, no I'm not going to use a force shield, and neither are you. He might think we didn't trust him."

"Oh, we wouldn't want him to think that," said Frost. "Perish the thought. But if he makes one wrong move, I'm going to spatter him all over the bulkheads."

"Let's try and be calm about this, Investigator. I don't want him killed. He's a pain in the ass, but he's good at his job. Good Security Officers are hard to come by. He's also one of the few people with firsthand experience on how to control the Grendel aliens. I'll decide when and if violence is necessary. Now, put on a nice smile. We don't want to frighten him." Frost bared her teeth, and Silence winced. She looked as though she was about to bite him somewhere painful. "All right, forget the smile. It doesn't suit you. Leave all the talking to me and don't get touchy about anything he says. I want to know what's reduced Stelmach to a state like this."

Frost shrugged, but kept her hands ostentatiously away from her weapons. Silence decided to settle for that. He stepped forward into the corridor and walked through the open door to Stelmach's quarters. Frost stuck so close behind him he could feel her breath on the back of his neck. Silence smiled and nodded to Stelmach, who was sitting on the side of his bed, his head hanging down, his shoulders slumped in tiredness or defeat or both. His gun was lying on the floor, well out of his reach. Silence relaxed just a little and looked around.

The place was a mess. Everything that wasn't nailed down or an intrinsic part of the ship had been picked up and thrown at something else. The single table and chair had been overturned, and the shattered fragments of his more fragile personal belongings covered the floor, along with pretty much everything else. The bed folded down from the cabin wall, and had survived intact, but the bedclothes had been torn apart and strewn all over the small cabin. Stelmach was sitting on the bare bed, looking anything but dangerous, but Silence decided he was going to take it slowly anyway. He could sense Frost behind him, like an attack dog straining against a short leash. He stepped forward, and Stelmach finally looked up. His face was tired and drawn, and he looked ten years older.

"Come in, Captain, Investigator. Excuse the mess. It's the maid's day off."

"I've seen worse," said Silence. "You've been very ... busy, Stelmach. Any particular reason?"

"What does it matter?" said Stelmach. "I know the regulations. I belong in the brig. Go ahead and take me. I'm finished."

"I don't believe in sentencing someone until they've had a fair hearing," said Silence carefully. "Explain yourself. What brought this on?"

"It's private, Captain. Family business. I don't want to talk about it."

"Talk anyway. If I'm going to lose the best Security Officer I've ever had, I want to know why."

Stelmach looked past Silence's shoulder at Frost. "Does she have to be here?"

"She's concerned for my safety," said Silence. "But she can step out into the corridor if you'd like."

"No," said Stelmach. "I don't suppose it matters." He leaned back against the bulkhead his bed folded down from, and his voice was very tired. "I got a letter this morning. From my family. We've always been very close, ever since our father died when I was very young. There was a demonstration, some kind of political thing, and it turned ugly. Someone threw something, someone else opened fire, and my father the police officer was dead before he hit the ground. Mother brought us up, kept us together, did whatever was necessary to keep a roof over our heads, clothes on our backs, food in our bellies. I was the youngest. Never wore new clothes in my life till I joined the Service. We were raised to revere my father as a saint and to have nothing at all to do with politics. She had all of us sign up for the Services, the moment we were old enough. There's always job security in the Services, whatever might be happening anywhere else.

"My sister Athena was the eldest. They took her away to become an Investigator when she was ten. We lost touch with her after that. My brothers Bold and Hero did well for themselves. Bold's a Major in the army, Hero's a Group Leader in the Jesuit commandos. They write home regularly, send money when they can. I'm the only failure. My career's over. After the debacle on the Wolfling World I was lucky not to be executed, but I'll never be more than a Security Officer now, not even if I was officially exonerated. Even my work on controlling the Grendel aliens has been taken over by other people. As far as my family is concerned, I've disgraced them by being such a failure. My mother wrote to me, telling me not to come home again. She's expelled me from the family, disinherited me, and removed all references to me from the family history. She now tells everyone she only ever had two sons.

"I always did my best. Followed the regulations, did as I was told, tried hard to be a good soldier. Lived my live for the Empire. And what did it get me? A Security Officer's post on a ship passing time out on the Rim, going nowhere, doing nothing, or nothing that really matters. Do what you want to me. I don't care."

He looked up suddenly, glaring at Silence and Frost. There were bright spots of color on his pale cheeks, and his eyes were puffy from crying but still sharp. "I hate this ship. I hate you, too. Both of you. If I'd kept you under control like I was supposed to, things might have been different. But I let you reason with me, and the Investigator intimidate me, and it all went wrong. I hate my life, or what's left of it. And most of all I hate myself for being so weak. My mother said my father would spit on me if he could see what I've become, and I think she's right. He would have shown more courage, more . . . something. Sometimes he comes to me in my cabin, sits on the end of my bed in the early hours of the morning, and tells me he's ashamed of me. He looks young and sharp, just like in the holos taken before he was killed. I'm older now than he was then, but I'll always be a child to him. I can't stand these quarters anymore. I'm afraid to sleep. Put me in the brig. Or have the Investigator shoot me and put me out of my family's misery. She'd like that. I don't care. I don't care about anything anymore."

He finally wound down, his head lowering bit by bit till he was staring at the floor again. He wasn't crying. He was too tired for that. Silence didn't know what to say. He'd read up on Stelmach's background, to try and find out why anyone would name their child Valiant, but the bare facts hadn't really made any sense till now. He felt ashamed and embarrassed at being so bluntly confronted with someone else's private pain and shame. These were the kinds of things you normally only told to your friends or loved ones, but as a Security Officer, Stelmach had no friends—and now he had no family either. That was why he'd wrecked his cabin. It was his way of letting the anger out, as well as a reason to be punished.

Silence didn't know what to do. He couldn't just have the man arrested and thrown in the brig, even if that was technically the correct thing to do. He wasn't Stelmach's friend, didn't even like the man, but he was a part of the *Dauntless*'s crew, and as his Captain, it was Silence's duty to look after him. He was responsible for the man's well-being, like a father for an errant son. The thought struck a strong chord in him.

"Valiant, listen to me. We're your family now. This ship, this crew. You belong to us. If anyone's going to decide you're a failure, it'll be me, and I haven't made my mind up yet. You've survived when a lot of others didn't. And you were the first man ever to yoke a Grendel. They can't take that away from you. You're not a failure till I say you are. I'm your family and I'm your father, and the first thing I have to say to you is . . . clean up your room, boy."

Stelmach looked at him, startled, and then burst into laughter. It was loud, healthy laughter, dispersing the gloom and doom that had filled the cabin, and Silence began to relax. He smiled at Frost, and though she didn't smile back, she seemed perhaps a little less cold and forbidding than she usually did. Stelmach's laughter began to die away, but before he could say anything, Silence's comm unit chimed in his ear. He gestured for Stelmach to wait a moment and opened a channel.

"This is Silence. It had better be important."

"I'm afraid it is, Captain," said the voice of his Second in Command. "I think you'd better get back to the bridge. We have a situation up here."

"What kind of situation?"

"Damned if I know, Captain. But I'll be a lot happier when you're back on the bridge. There's something . . . out there."

The comm channel closed abruptly, leaving only the faintest hiss of static in Silence's ear. He broke off the connection and scowled, uneasy for no reason he could define. There had been something in his Second's voice . . . the man had almost sounded scared. Silence's first thought was an alien ship, but if that had been the case the Second would have said so. Hell, he'd have sounded a Red Alert by now. Silence's frown deepened as he looked at Frost and Stelmach, who were studying him expectantly.

"Forget this mess," he said flatly. "We're needed on the bridge. Move it."

"Of course, Captain," said Stelmach, and led the way out of his cabin. They headed down the corridor together, three professional officers from the same great family, whose needs always came first.

Back on the bridge, Silence nodded quickly to his Second in Command and sank into his command chair again. Frost and Stelmach took up positions on either side of him, at hand if he needed them. The atmosphere on the bridge was so tense you could have sharpened a knife on it. Everyone was at their station, engrossed in their instruments, but they were too alert, too focused, almost as though they were afraid to look away. The main viewscreen showed the *Dauntless*'s route had brought them right to the edge of the Rim. At a certain point, the stars and the light they cast just stopped abruptly, as though it had run into a wall, and beyond that there was only the utter blackness of the Darkvoid, where no light shone. It was hard to look at, for any length of time, but your eyes kept creeping back to it. Silence glared at his Second in Command.

"Everything seems to be in order, Second. Nothing on the viewscreen, all instruments functioning. So what's the problem?"

The Second in Command shifted uncomfortably in his seat. "It was the Communications Officer, sir, who first brought it to my attention."

Silence turned to look at Cross, his frown deepening. "Well?"

"It's . . . difficult to put into words, Captain." Cross turned away from his station so he could look at Silence directly. "I've been . . . hearing things. Voices in the void, calling out to me. There are people talking out there in empty space, where there can't be any people. I've checked the sensors. There's no one here but us. But . . . it isn't just me."

He stopped and looked unhappily at Silence to see how he was taking it. Silence kept his voice carefully neutral. From the difficulty Cross was having in getting his words out, it was clear he took it very seriously. His dark face was drawn and tired, and there were beads of sweat on his high forehead. Without looking around, Silence could sense that other people on the bridge were waiting for his reaction. A while back, he would have thought they were just setting him up, seeing what they could get away with, but he didn't think so now. He could feel how seriously they were all taking it, and though they were trying to hide it, everyone on the bridge was scared. Silence felt a faint prickling on the back of his neck. These were battle-hardened veterans, and they didn't scare easily. He crossed his legs casually, but he could feel a growing tension in his gut. Strange things happened out on the Rim. Everyone knew that. He nodded curtly for Cross to continue.

"It's not just me, Captain. People have been hearing things for days. On all the comm channels, from the main hailing frequencies to private cabin-to-cabin channels. There are voices where there shouldn't be; whispering, muttering, just clear enough to spook people with what they can make out. There's nothing wrong with the comm equipment. I've checked it every way I can, and it all checks out one hundred per cent. Then I thought someone was playing tricks, but if they are I can't catch them at it, and I know all the tricks in the book. So I checked with other people, and that's when I found out this has been going on for days, ever since we started approaching the edge of the Rim.

"And it's not just voices. It's like we're being watched, all the time, and I don't mean the security cameras. We're used to them. It's more like . . . there's someone else in the room with you, even when there isn't. It's like someone's standing over your bed when you're sleeping, watching and waiting. There's a constant feeling that something's wrong, something we should be doing, something important and vital . . ."

"Night terrors aren't exactly unknown, out here on the Rim," Silence said carefully. "The Darkvoid's still pretty much a mystery. We don't know how much close proximity to it affects the mind, and one way or another we've all spent a lot of time exposed to it recently."

"That's what I thought, at first," said Cross. "It's what we all thought. This phenomenon's been reported before by other ships out on the Rim who've stayed out here too long. Seeing things, hearing things, feeling things. It's usually written off as cabin fever. The doc hands out industrial strength tranquilizers, and that keeps people quiet until they've left the Rim. But I've been running some more detailed checks. When I reran the bridge tapes, according to my instruments at the times I was hearing the voices, there were no signals coming in. No signals at all."

Silence raised an eyebrow at that. "Some form of esp communication?"

"Not according to the ship's esper, Captain. If there were any psionic forces on board apart from himself, or even in the vicinity, he'd know. And there's more. It's . . . difficult to record these voices. They don't always come through clearly enough to make an impression. But during the time you were gone from the bridge, I picked up a whole group of voices, and managed to record them. Listen."

He turned back to his console and tapped in a command. A loud hissing filled the air, as static seeped from the main address speakers. Silence frowned, straining his ears against the white noise of the static. He could see everyone else on the bridge was listening, too, their faces taut with suspense and barely hidden fear. Silence's gut tightened again. What could be so scary about a few voices? And then a voice rose out of the static, cold and dead, but very determined to be heard.

"It's dark, here. Here, the birds burn."

There was a pause, and then more voices came, one after the other, different voices, slow and halting but all driven by some desperate need to be heard.

"Help me. Help me. There's something holding my hand, and it won't let go."

"It's coming. It's coming your way, and you can't stop it."

"Something's watching you from behind your mirrors."

"Listen to me! Listen to me! There are dead hands beating on your walls!"

"They're coming. They're coming out of the dark in a dead ship."

The last voice broke off abruptly, and then there was only the hissing of static on the speakers. Cross turned them off, and looked back at Silence.

"Whatever this is, it's getting worse. These are the clearest recordings so far. I tried computer enhancements on the earlier recordings, but it didn't help. Almost as though the computer couldn't hear them. I hadn't realized how widespread the problem was till I started asking around. I don't think anyone did. They all thought it was just them, going crazy."

"Is what we just heard typical of what the voices are saying?" said Silence.

"Pretty much. They all make a kind of sense, but what they mean is anyone's guess."

"What do you think they are?" said Silence.

Cross's features tightened, but his gaze was level, and when he spoke his voice was carefully flat and calm. "I think they're voices of the dead, Captain. Desperately trying to reach us, to warn us about . . . something. Some members of the crew I talked to claim to have recognized particular, familiar voices. All of them people they knew to be dead. Friends and relatives, precious ones long gone. I heard my grandfather. He was part of the crew on the starship *Champion* when it disappeared out on the Rim over a hundred years ago. Now we're here, in the same sector, and it's starting again. Voices of the dead, desperately trying to communicate, to make us understand before it's too late. And before you say anything, Captain, yes I do know how this must sound. But we've all heard these voices. Haven't you heard anything, Captain, felt anything strange in the long hours of the night?"

"No," said Silence. "I can't say I have." He looked at Frost, and she shook her head sharply. He looked to his other side. "Stelmach?"

"I'm not sure," Stelmach said slowly. "I saw my father, but I thought that was just dreams. And once, when I woke up in the early hours of the morning, I thought I felt my sister's presence. Standing over me, protecting me from . . . something."

"All right," said Silence. "Let's not get carried away here. I have no doubt this phenomenon is real, but whatever it is you're hearing, it's not the dearly departed dropping in for a chat. Much more likely it's some form of psionic communication we haven't encountered before, that your minds are interpreting as voices and feelings. There was a report filed a few years back, which most of you are supposed to have read, about the possibility of new forms of life appearing in

the Darkvoid. The report's author believed there could be
creatures living in the endless dark, in the gulfs between the
frozen planets. A new kind of life, made possible by the unnatural conditions in the Darkvoid. And if that doesn't grab
you, try this. How about some subtle form of alien attack?
We're expecting the new alien ships to come through the
Darkvoid to reach us. This could all be nothing more than
some new kind of psionic weapon, designed to scare and
confuse us. And doing a pretty good job, from the look of
you."

Silence looked around the bridge and could see the new
ideas taking root. People were starting to look at each other,
smiling and relaxing as they considered the new ideas and
found they liked them. They began to murmur among themselves and sit back in their chairs, the fear and uncertainty
visibly dropping away from them. Even Cross was nodding,
agreeing. Silence let them talk and laugh for a few minutes
before restoring bridge discipline.

"Activate the long-range sensors, Cross," he said finally.
"If there is an alien ship out there somewhere, hiding in the
Darkvoid, I want to know about it."

Cross nodded quickly and bent over his station, powering
up the long-range sensors. He hadn't been using them automatically because of the vast amounts of power they burned
up, but theoretically they could detect a grain of sand half a
light-year away, and tell you what it had for breakfast. Silence sat back in his command chair and let Cross get on
with it. The odds were he wouldn't find anything, but just
operating the long-range sensors for a while should help the
crew feel better and more secure.

"I'm almost disappointed," Frost said quietly. "So much
fuss over a few night terrors. They'll be wanting someone to
hold their hands when they cross the road next."

"We don't all have your icy nerves, Investigator," said Silence. "And dealing with the crew's problems—real or
perceived—is part of my job. Still, it's interesting that you
and I never heard these voices."

"Our minds are a lot more . . . disciplined than they used
to be," said Frost. "Perhaps we've become harder to fool."

"Perhaps. Either way, I'll let Cross run the sensors for a
few more minutes, and then . . ."

"Unidentified ship, Captain!" said Cross suddenly. "Only

just in range, but it's coming straight at us at one hell of a speed."

"Yellow Alert," said Silence. "Look sharp, people. Cross, put it up on the viewscreen."

"It's still in the Darkvoid, sir," said Cross. "We won't see it for a while yet."

"Could it be an alien ship?" asked Frost.

"Unknown, Investigator," said Cross. "But at the speed it's moving, it'll be here soon."

Silence studied the darkness on the viewscreen, carefully keeping his face calm and unmoved. His crew chattered around him on the bridge, powering up the ship's weapons and shields. People were reporting in from all over the ship as they took up attack positions. Silence smiled slightly. The doom and the gloom on the bridge had completely vanished. The unknown ship might be a threat, but it was a threat the crew understood.

"The ship's slowing, Captain," said Cross. "I think it knows we're here. It's almost at the edge of the Darkvoid. We should have it on the screen any moment . . ."

He broke off as the ship appeared on the viewscreen, came to a full stop just beyond the Rim. It was a simple metal sphere, bristling with instruments, mute and menacing. It was also very familiar, and quite definitely human.

"Getting details now, Captain," said Cross. "It's an Empire starcruiser . . . class C." He looked back at Silence, surprised, before checking his instruments again. "There hasn't been a class C ship in Service since the beginning of the century. Its shields are down, but it's making no attempt to contact us. I'm using the standard hailing frequencies, but there's no response. It looks to be in good condition; no obvious signs of damage."

"Could it be a pirate ship?" said Stelmach.

"Doubtful," said Frost. "They wouldn't be caught dead in a ship as slow as that. A pirate's career depends on being able to outrun his pursuers. But if that is an Empire ship, what the hell is an old crock like that doing out here on the Rim?"

"Maybe it's a ghost ship," said Silence, and regretted the word ghost the moment he said it. He didn't need to look around to feel the tension rising on the bridge again. "Cross, there should be an identification number on the ship's hull.

Find it and check it against records. See if you can put a name to it."

"Already have, sir." The Communication Officer's voice was high and thin. "It's the *Champion*. My grandfather's ship. Reported lost with all hands, one hundred and seven years ago."

"That's impossible," said Silence numbly. "I remember the story. Whatever happened to the *Champion* is one of the fleet's great unsolved mysteries. But its last reported position was halfway across the Empire from here. How did it end up in the Darkvoid?"

"A good question, Captain," said Frost. "Another might be: who's running the ship now? It was moving under its own power through the Darkvoid, but someone brought it to a halt here, facing us. And, since they must know we know there's someone on board, why aren't they talking to us?"

"It has to be a trap of some kind," said Stelmach. "Could it be an alien ship, disguised?"

"It's not a holo image," said Cross. "Exterior is exactly what it should be."

"Alien or not," said Silence, "I'd say the odds are extremely good that this ship is the source of the unsettling phenomena you've all been experiencing. The ship's appearance could be a part of that. Psychological warfare. Cross, take us to Red Alert. All shields up. If this is a disguised alien ship, it's not going to get the chance to hit us like its brother did over Golgotha. Bring all guns to bear, but nobody fires without my express command."

There was a hum of new activity as the bridge crew busied themselves. They all remembered how close that other alien ship had come to cleaning their clock permanently. They were looking forward to a little payback. Frost leaned in close beside Silence.

"I have to say, Captain, that the odds of this being an alien ship are really rather small. All the sensor readings seem to be insisting that the ship facing us is indeed the long-lost *Champion*."

"I don't want a panic on my bridge," Silence said quietly. "Personally, I think both chances are equally unlikely. More probably, this is a trap of some kind. Maybe even a first shot from the new rebellion. Either way, I want my people primed and ready to blow the snot out of that ship at the first wrong move. Communications Officer, what readings are you getting now?"

"Mostly confusing ones, sir," said Cross, scowling down at his panels. "Most of the new ship's systems are down. No defensive shields, no activated weapons . . . and no life support. No atmosphere and colder than hell. It's just hanging there, dead in the water. I don't even know how it got there. All my instruments seem quite convinced the ship's drive is cold. There's nothing to show it's been used in one hell of a long time."

"Life-form readings?" said Silence.

"Not a thing, Captain. Human or otherwise. There's always the chance it could be an old plague ship."

Silence glared at him. "Ghost ship, plague ship; you're a real cheerful sort to have around, Cross, you know that? We're going to have to take a closer look. Maintain Red Alert, but keep the long-range sensors open. If there's one ship out here, there might be more, and I don't want us getting hit while we're distracted. Investigator, put together an away team. You and I are taking a pinnace over to that ship to see what's what."

"I suppose I'm wasting my breath in pointing out that as Captain you shouldn't risk your life with an investigating team?" said Frost.

"You are indeed," said Silence. "Whatever that ship is, I need firsthand information before I can make any decisions. Stelmach, would you care to accompany us?"

"Not really, no," said Stelmach. "They don't pay me enough to volunteer for missions like this. In fact, they couldn't pay me enough. Have a nice trip, Captain. I'll be right here when you get back."

"Captain," said Cross. "Permission to join your team. If that really is the *Champion,* my grandfather's ship . . ."

"We won't need a Communications Officer," said Frost.

"But we might need someone who could tell a fake *Champion* from the real thing," said Silence. "All right, Cross. You're on the team. Second, you have the bridge again. Let's go, people."

They crossed over to what might be the *Champion* in a pinnace; Silence, Frost, Cross, and six security men. They all wore hard suits. The *Dauntless*'s sensors had been quite specific that there wasn't a single life-support system work-

ing in the whole ship. Silence patched into the pinnace's
sensors through his comm implant and studied the *Champion* thoughtfully as the pinnace drifted closer. It was as
though the bulkhead turned transparent where he was looking, giving him a clear view of the mystery ship. It looked
heavy and clumsy, compared to the sleek starcruisers he was
used to. The old C class had been something of a compromise between speed and weaponry, that in the end turned out
to favor neither. Which was why it had been quickly bested
and replaced by the D class. Even so, the *Champion* was
something of a legend in the fleet. She'd been one of the
Empire's foremost exploratory vessels, checking out new
worlds for alien contacts or colonization, and brought fourteen new planets into the Empire during her short life in the
Service. Before she went out to the Rim once too often and
was never seen again by human eyes.

Until now. Silence couldn't help wondering if it was just
coincidence that had brought the *Champion* back at such a
volatile time for the Empire. Like a message from the past,
when things were different. Silence put the thought aside.
He had sworn to serve the Iron Throne, no matter who sat
on it, because the Empire must be preserved. All the other
choices were worse. Better a corrupt civilization than an
Empire shattered and reduced to barbarism. He pushed that
thought aside, too, and concentrated on the starship looming
up before him, hanging like a great white whale in a dark
sea. It grew slowly larger, filling the space between them, so
that he could no longer see the Rim or the Darkvoid beyond
it. And finally the pinnace drifted to a halt, only a few feet
between its hull and the *Champion*'s.

"Try the hailing frequencies one more time," Silence said
quietly, not taking his eyes off the vast white metal wall before him.

"Still no response, Captain," said Cross after a long moment. "Pinnace sensors confirm no life forms anywhere on
the ship."

"See if you can open the *Champion*'s air lock with a general override signal," said Silence.

Cross bent over his panels and then shook his head. "No
response. All the systems must be down. We're going to
have to crack it open manually."

"No surprises there." Silence closed down his comm link
to the sensors, and the pinnace's bulkhead reappeared before

him. He looked around at his team one at a time, making eye contact so they could see how calm and assured he was. "All right, people, pay attention. We're going out through the pinnace's air lock in our hard suits, Investigator Frost leading. We're right up against the *Champion*'s air lock, so all we have to do is step outside and open it. Cross will operate the manual override on the outside of the air-lock door, and then the Investigator will enter the lock itself. She will go through alone, to check out the situation. Once she gives the all clear, I want you cycling through that air lock as fast as you can go. There's no telling what shape the mechanism's in after all this time, and I don't want anyone left outside."

"What if something happens to the Investigator?" said Cross.

"Then you back off, and the *Dauntless* blows the *Champion* to shit," said Frost. "Because if I can't handle it, you sure as hell can't."

"Once we're inside," said Silence, pressing calmly on as though the interchange hadn't happened, "we will make our way to the bridge and activate what systems we can. Everyone stay together, but don't bunch up. And keep your eyes open. The *Champion* is to be considered hostile territory until proven otherwise. You are authorized to use lethal force on anything that moves, with the exception of your teammates. So don't get jumpy. Investigator, lead the way."

Frost nodded and moved over to the inner door of the pinnace's air lock. There was a pause as everyone put on their helmets and made sure the seals were secure, and then Frost opened the inner door and stepped inside, followed by Silence and Cross. The three hard suits filled the air lock from wall to wall. They waited patiently as the air was flushed out, and then Frost opened the outer door. It opened slowly, silently, revealing the *Champion*'s outer hull, only a few feet away. Silence gestured to Frost, and she stepped forward onto the outer edge of the door. She reached out a gloved hand to the small wheel clearly marked on the outside of the *Champion*'s air lock and took a firm hold. Silence moved in beside her to brace her once she started exerting pressure. The pinnace's artificially produced gravity didn't extend beyond the air lock. Her armored glove closed around the wheel and turned it inch by inch. The outer doors of the air lock slowly parted, and a bright light suddenly appeared within the lock. Silence relaxed a little. At least some of the

Champion's systems were still working. The doors crept farther apart, until finally Frost was able to step carefully from the *Dauntless* into the *Champion*. The doors closed over her again, and Silence could only wait. He could feel her presence through the link they shared, and her calm composure helped to settle him.

"The air lock is functioning perfectly," her voice said suddenly through his comm implant. "I have light and gravity, but no air. The pumps are working, but it would appear they have no air to work with. The inner doors are opening. Lights have come on beyond them. I'm now in the corridor outside the lock. No movement anywhere. Still no air, and the temperature's way below zero. You might as well come on over. There's no sign of any welcoming party."

"Stay where you are," said Silence. "We'll be right with you."

He worked the lock's outer doors again, and he and Cross passed through into the *Champion*, followed quickly by the security men. The corridor beyond the lock was brightly lit but uncomfortably narrow, and the low ceiling seemed to press down above their helmets. The walls were covered with cables and conduits and tightly packed instrumentation. The Empire's designers had been cramming in every extra improvement they could think of, right up to the last minute. None of it looked particularly dated. The *Dauntless* might be more efficiently arranged, but the systems were still pretty much the same. If a thing worked, the Empire tended to stick with it.

"Interesting," said Frost, and Silence turned automatically to look at her, though all he could see was her featureless helmet. "According to my suit's sensors, the light and gravity are only a local phenomenon. The rest of the ship is still powered down. Which would seem to suggest someone knows we're here."

"Could be the ship's computers," said Cross.

"No," said Frost. "I don't think so. They would have turned all the life-support systems on."

"Try general address on your comm," said Silence. "See if anyone answers."

"This is Investigator Frost of the *Dauntless*, representing the Empire. Respond, please."

They waited a long time, but there was no reply. The comm channel was empty of everything, even static. Silence's back crawled, feeling the pressure of unseen watching eyes. The words ghost ship came back to him, along with the half-serious stories that were always circulating during his cadet days. Tales of dead ships populated by dead crews, sailing silently through the long night on journeys that would never end. Skeletons on the bridge, or dead men rotting at their stations, heading for some far off destination the living could never understand. Silence had to smile. He hadn't realized those stupid stories had made such an impression on him.

"Let's make for the bridge, people," he said briskly. "Maybe we'll find some answers there. Investigator, lead the way."

Frost patched into a map of the *Champion*'s structure, provided by the *Dauntless*'s computer records, and set off down the corridor. Lights turned themselves on ahead of them and turned off behind them, so that they moved always in a pool of light surrounded by darkness. Weight remained constant at one gravity, but there was still no air or heat. Silence had the security men check out each room and compartment they passed, but though there were frequent signs of people's lives, there was no trace anywhere of the *Champion*'s crew.

There were unmade beds and abandoned meals, cards discarded in mid game and doors left ajar, as though the people involved had just stood up a hundred or so years ago, and walked away from their lives, never to return.

Silence kept thinking he could see things moving on the edge of his vision, but every time he looked there was nothing there. Shadows moved disturbingly around the small party as they moved deeper into the ship, their hard suits eerily out of place in the crew's quarters. They all had the feeling they were being watched, even though the ship's security cameras clearly weren't working, and the security men spent as much time checking behind them as they did the way ahead. Frost, of course, just strode on through the empty corridors, calm and unmoved as always. Silence stuck close to her.

They finally came to the main elevator. Silence plugged in a portable energy pack; they came back on line. There were walkways, but it would have meant a long climb to the bridge. Silence split the party into two groups, just in case, and they made their way up to the bridge in separate elevators. The cramped metal cages took an uncomfortably long time getting there, not least because they insisted on stopping at every floor in between, but eventually the elevator doors opened onto the bridge, and Silence led the way forward with something very like relief. If there were answers to be found anywhere on this ghost ship, he should be able to find them here.

There was no one sitting in the command chair, skeleton or corpse, and the workstations were unmanned. No sign of any crew. No sign to show they'd ever been here. It was just as Silence had expected, but he still felt obscurely disappointed. Something really cataclysmic must have happened on board the *Champion*, to mean abandoning the bridge like this. And yet there'd been no signs of attack or mutiny, no damage or signs of haste. Cross leaned over the comm station and tried a few warm-up routines, and then turned away.

"Everything's shut down, Captain. Give me an hour or so and I should be able to bring something on-line. Half these systems will have to be reprogrammed from the bottom up, but everything seems functional."

"The autopilot's still working," said Frost. "Someone must have fed in the coordinates that brought the ship here."

"Hold everything," said Cross. "I've got the security cameras up and working. Which shouldn't be possible, but . . . watch the monitors."

They all crowded around Cross and stared at the bank of three monitor screens attached to his station. They lit up in swift succession, as though they'd only recently been turned off. Cross switched rapidly from one camera to another the length of the ship, scenes appearing on the viewscreens one after the other, pausing just long enough to give a continuing feeling of emptiness everywhere on board. From corridors to engineering, sick bay to crew's quarters, everywhere was still and silent. It chilled Silence to his bones to see a ship so abandoned, so deserted.

He tried to remember more about the history of the *Champion* rather than the legend. The Captain, Tomas Pearce, had been something of a fierce officer by all accounts, a strictly by-the-book man, as hard on himself as anyone else. Everyone agreed he ran a tight ship, right up until the day it disappeared. He would never have walked away from his ship, no matter what his crew did. He'd have hit the auto-destruct first. Silence wondered what Pearce would think now if he could see so many posts abandoned, so many stations un manned. No, he wouldn't have walked. Someone or something must have taken him.

"Hello," said Cross suddenly. "What have we got here?" He fussed at the panels before him, muttering to himself and stabbing awkwardly at the controls with his armored fingers. Hard suits weren't meant for delicate work. "I think I've got something, Captain. The cameras in the main cargo hold are out, but I'm getting some information through the ship's interior sensors. There's something down in the cargo bay. A lot of somethings."

"Hardly unusual for a cargo bay," said Frost.

"It is when the computer manifests are convinced the ship isn't carrying any cargo at all this trip. And, even more interestingly, all these somethings are roughly human in shape."

"Life signs?" said Silence.

"Not so far," said Cross. "But whatever these things are, there are hundreds of them."

"Then, for want of anything better to do, let's go and take a look," said Silence.

He left four of the security men on the bridge to watch the monitors and run further checks on the instruments, and herded the rest of his team back into the elevator. It was a long way down to the cargo bay, but at least they didn't stop at every floor this time. Silence chose to see this as a good omen. The doors finally opened on the main cargo bay, and Frost made the others wait in the elevator while she checked out the situation first. She kept them waiting an uncomfortably long time before waving them out. The bay was deserted, but the lights had already been on when the elevator doors opened, almost as though someone was waiting for them.

The bay itself was huge, with intricately marked steel walls surrounding a vast open space. They'd emerged at ground level, like mice creeping out of their hole. Frost signaled for the group to stay together, while she locked the elevator doors open, just in case they had to retreat in a hurry. As far as Silence was concerned, she needn't have bothered. He'd never felt less like wandering off on his own in his life. Still, as Captain he was expected to provide a good example, so as soon as Frost gave him the all clear, he stepped confidently forward to take a look around.

Away from the elevator, the sheer size of the cargo bay was almost overpowering, but Silence's attention was drawn immediately to the bay's sole cargo; hundreds of long mirrored cylinders, each the size and general shape of a coffin. They'd been laid out in neat rows, forming a perfect square. Silence checked them out from a cautious distance with the limited sensors built into his suit, but the coffin shapes gave up no information at all. He couldn't even tell what they were made of, never mind what might be inside them.

"That's the crew, isn't it?" said Cross quietly.

"Could be," said Silence. "The numbers are about right. Only way to find out is to open a few. Investigator . . ."

"Way ahead of you, Captain," said Frost, striding forward pugnaciously.

Silence gestured for Cross and the two security men to stay with him. "Take it slow and easy, Investigator. There's always the chance those things are booby-trapped."

"I'll bear it in mind," said Frost. "Now, a little quiet, if you please. I have to concentrate."

She stopped just short of the first outer rank, tried her sensors again, and sniffed disgustedly as they failed to provide any useful information, even at close range. Each cylinder was seven feet long, and the correct proportions for a coffin. Plenty of room for a body inside and any number of unpleasant surprises, too. Frost knelt down by the nearest cylinder and got her first surprise when she realized the mirrored surface wasn't showing her reflection. She examined the edges of the cylinder carefully and got her second surprise. There was no sign of any seals or openings. The entire cylinder seemed to have been produced in one piece. Perhaps . . . formed around something. The word cocoon occurred to her, echoing in her mind with a significance she couldn't pin down. She straightened up and looked at the rows of cylinders stretching away before her. She had been intending to open one by force, with her gun if necessary, and trust to her hard suit to protect her, but she was beginning to think that was what she was supposed to do. More and more, the whole place felt like a trap. The cylinders were too tempting, and there was too much light, as though the cargo bay was a stage, waiting for the action to begin.

Frost reached out cautiously with her gloved hand to tap the lid of the coffin, and her hand sank through the shining surface as though it was some silvery liquid. And inside the coffin, something grabbed her armored hand and squeezed it hard. She lurched forward, caught off balance, and her arm plunged further through the lid and into the coffin. She quickly braced herself against the steel floor and pulled back, but whatever had hold of her wouldn't release its grip. She could feel the pressure, even through her armored glove. She gritted her teeth, snarling under her featureless helmet, and pulled back with all her strength. The suit's servomechanisms whined loudly. Her arm slowly reappeared from the lid, and then her glove, clasped by a dead white human hand.

The weight on her arm was suddenly lessened as a dead white face appeared through the shining lid like a drowned man's face surfacing in a river, and then the dead man was out of his coffin and standing before Frost, smiling, still holding her hand in his. Her first thought was that it was a Fury, one of Shub's killing machines in a human skin, but then she saw the marks of drastic surgery unhidden on his shaved skull, and she knew at once what had happened to the *Champion*'s crew. He was a Ghost Warrior. All around her, dead men were emerging from the silver coffins, like vile gray butterflies bursting out of shimmering cocoons. The man before her wore a dated fleet uniform, torn and stained with long-dried blood where his death wounds had been. His skin was dead-white, and though his smile was inhumanly wide, there was no emotion in his face and no life in his unblinking eyes. She could hear Silence shouting at her to get away from the dead man, but his gaze held her like a hook she could wriggle on but not escape. The dead men were rising everywhere now, silent and calm, their movements filled with an implacable purpose.

And then the blast from an energy weapon tore away the head of the man before her, and the headless body slumped to its knees. She was suddenly herself again, freed from the dead gaze, and she fell back a step, tugging at her captured hand. The pale fingers still gripped her firmly, despite all her struggles. Frost drew the sword on her hip with her left hand and hacked savagely at the pale wrist. The blade sheared clean through, and she staggered backward, released. The dead hand still clutched at her glove, and she had to cut it away finger by finger as she hurried back to rejoin Silence and the others.

They were all firing now, energy bolts leaping from the

disrupters built into their gloves, and dead bodies were
blown apart and slapped aside, but still the hundreds of dead
moved purposefully forward. Frost took up her place between Silence and Cross, too angry to be frightened or worried. She'd fought every kind of alien in her time, and
thought there was nothing left in the Empire that could
throw her, but something in the dead man's gaze had held
her as securely as any chain. If Silence hadn't blown its head
off, she'd have been standing there still, until the dead overwhelmed her and dragged her away to make her one of
them. She had no doubt it had been Silence who freed her.
She'd have done the same for him. She took a deep breath
and settled herself.

"Well," she made herself say calmly, "at least now we
know what happened to the *Champion*'s crew. Those bastard
AIs somehow got their hands on them, scooped out their
brains, and replaced them with their filthy computers. We've
found a whole ship of Ghost Warriors."

"Shub is right on the other side of the Empire," said Silence. "But we'll let that pass for the moment. It'll be another two minutes before our disrupters recharge, and I have
a strong feeling these creeps could manage something really
unpleasant in that time, so everyone free your swords and
back away. We are getting the hell out of here."

There was a muffled clang behind them as the elevator
doors slammed shut.

"That's not possible," said Frost. "I locked them open."

"Someone's watching," said Cross. "And they don't want
us leaving just yet."

"I'll try the bridge," said Silence. "Maybe they can override. Bridge, this is Silence. Can you hear me?" There was
no reply, only an ominous quiet.

"Something's got to them," said Cross. "We're on our
own."

The dead men stood facing them, row upon row, inhumanly still. One figure stepped forward, wearing an outdated
Captain's uniform. Silence tried to recognize Tomas Pearce,
but the face before him held nothing of humanity in it. One
eye was missing, replaced by a camera lens, and the scars of
brutal surgery were clear on his forehead. He came to a halt
before Silence, carefully out of a sword's range, smiling
widely as though he knew what a smile was supposed to
convey, but didn't know how. His kind weren't used for di-

plomacy or conversation. Ghost Warriors fought Shub's battles with humanity, as much for psychological effect as any functional superiority. The dead man wore a gun and a sword on his hips, but so far had made no move to draw them. Silence found that disturbing. It implied the Ghost Warriors wanted him alive. Pearce's lips moved, and Silence heard a slow, horribly impersonal voice through his comm implant. It was a machine talking—through a human mouth.

"Captain Silence. Investigator Frost. You must come with us."

"Why us?" said Silence.

"Yeah," said Cross. "I feel left out."

"You are different," said Pearce, his dead eyes still fixed on Silence and Frost. "Changed. It is necessary that we discover how."

"Tough," said Frost. "We have other plans. Call our secretary and make an appointment. Captain, get those elevator doors open. I'll hold them off."

She stepped forward, her sword held in both hands, and swung it around in a vicious sideways sweep with all her strength behind it. If it had connected, it would certainly have beheaded Pearce, but he raised his arms impossibly fast and blocked the blow. The blade sank deep into his arm and jarred on splintering bone. In the split second while Frost was still off balance, Pearce reached out with his other hand and snatched the sword out of her hand. Frost snarled and hit him in the throat with her armored glove. The hard suit's servomechanisms amplified the strength of her blow, and she could feel the sickening crunch as her fist crushed Pearce's throat and snapped his neck. His head hung at an angle, but the expression on his face didn't change. He threw her sword aside and reached out with both hands to grab her shoulders. She kicked his legs out from under him, and he fell sprawling on the steel floor. The other Ghost Warriors moved forward in an unhurried, implacable advance, and Frost knew there were just too many of them to be stopped by anything she could do.

She checked the timer inside her helmet and opened up with her disrupters again. Energy blasts erupted from her gloves, slapping aside the advancing dead men like so many curling leaves caught in a fiery breeze. But then her guns fell silent, and the Ghost Warriors kept coming. Pearce was back on his feet again, reaching for her. Frost grabbed up her

sword again, determined she'd die before she let them drag
her off to Shub's bloody laboratories.

Silence and Cross got to the elevators and used their amplified strength to force the doors open. The two security
men charged into the lift, pulled the control mechanism out
of the wall, and began quickly preparing an override. Silence
would have liked to turn and see how Frost was doing, but
he needed all his strength to hold the elevator doors open.
They strained against his hands with an almost malevolent
urgency, and Silence could hear a faint straining sound from
the servomechanisms in his suit's arms. He was wearing an
exploratory suit, designed for protection, not the stronger
and better-equipped battle suit. It wouldn't last much longer.
One of the security men yelled out in satisfaction, and the
pressure from the doors was suddenly gone. Silence and
Cross let go of them and hurried into the elevator. They
turned as one and opened up with their disrupters, the energy
bolts blowing away Ghost Warriors to either side of Frost.

"Get your ass over here, Investigator!" yelled Silence. "We
are leaving!"

Frost turned and ran for the elevator without hesitation.
There was no dishonor in running from Ghost Warriors.
They'd keep coming as long as their computer implants remained intact, no matter what state their bodies might be in.
The only answer to this many Ghost Warriors was massed
disrupter cannon. She threw herself into the elevator, and the
security men let the elevator doors close behind her. Dead
fists beat against the doors, denting the metal, but Silence
had already hit the up button. He hit it a few more times,
just in case, and took a deep breath as the elevator began to
rise.

"*Dauntless,* this is Silence. Do you hear me?"

"Loud and clear, Captain."

"Check the sensors. Any life-form readings on the *Champion*'s bridge?"

"No, Captain."

"Damn. All right; we are heading back to the pinnace in
a hurry. This ship is crawling with Ghost Warriors. You are
not to allow the pinnace or any other vessel from the *Champion* to dock with you until sensors have confirmed that only
the living are aboard. Once we've docked, open up with everything you've got until there's nothing left of the *Champion* but a few glowing atoms. If we can't get to you and

you consider the *Dauntless* to be in danger, forget us and blow the *Champion* apart anyway. We are expendable. Is that clear, *Dauntless?*"

"Clear, Captain," said the calm voice of his Second in Command. "We'll give you every second we can, but you must be docked before we open fire. Otherwise, the energy will fry you."

"I know. But the *Dauntless*'s safety comes first. Confirm."

"Confirmed, Captain. Good luck."

The elevator slowed suddenly, catching them all off balance. The security man at the controls swore dispassionately. "Something's fighting my override. I don't know how much longer I can maintain control, Captain."

"Stop at the next floor," said Silence. "We're getting off. Can't risk being taken back down again."

The security man nodded, and the elevator lurched to a halt. The doors opened, and Silence and his people spilled out into an empty corridor, swords at the ready. Silence accessed his map of the *Champion* again, displaying it on the inside of his helmet. They were seven floors down and quite a distance away from the air lock that would give them access to their pinnace. They'd have to stick to the walkways and hope the Ghost Warriors didn't have some way to block them. He dismissed the map and looked at the two security men. Their blank helmets stared impassively back at him, waiting for orders.

"There's no point in going back to the bridge," Silence said evenly. "Your comrades are dead. And I never even knew their names. Tell me yours."

One of the men indicated himself, and then his friend. "Corporal Abrams and Corporal Fine, sir. Don't mind Fine. He doesn't say much."

"Pleased to meet you, Corporals. If we get back to the *Dauntless* alive, you're both Sergeants. Now let's get moving. Frost, take the point. Cross, watch our rear. Move it, people!"

And so they ran, back through the deserted corridors of the death ship, the hammering of their armored boots on the steel floor a constant roll of thunder, prophesying a storm to come. Silence flashed the map up on his inner helmet again, counting off the floors and levels as they drew slowly closer to where they'd left the pinnace. His heart was pounding, and his breath tore at his lungs. Even with the servomechanisms to help, the hard suit was heavy and clumsy, not designed for running in. And deep down inside him, he knew he'd forgotten something. Something important. He snarled silently inside his helmet and tried vainly to increase his pace. It was taking too long. The Ghost Warriors could be right behind them. He checked his suit's sensors again, but there was no trace of movement anywhere in their limited range. Which probably meant the dead men knew a short cut. He checked the map again, but he couldn't see a quicker route than the one Frost had already chosen. They'd get to the pinnace first. They had to.

And finally there was only one corridor left between them and safety, and the whole group found a second wind that brought them pounding around the final corner, and there they came crashing to a halt. Silence just stood there, a dozen yards from the air lock, his head filled with his own harsh breathing, his heart filled with despair. Between his small force and the air lock stood a hundred Ghost Warriors, eerily unprotected against the airless cold, with the dead Captain Pearce at their head. *No,* thought Silence numbly. *That's not possible, there's no way they could have beaten us here!* But these are dead men, a small voice murmured in the back of his mind. Maybe they know ways that the living cannot walk. His thoughts whirled crazily as he tried desperately to think of something, anything he could do to steal a victory from the jaws of certain defeat. Pearce smiled at Silence and Frost, his head perched crookedly on his broken neck.

"It's over. You must come with us now. The laboratories are waiting."

"To hell with that," said Frost calmly. She pulled a concussion grenade from her belt, primed it, and tossed it neatly into the middle of the massed Ghost Warriors. They barely had time to react before it blew, and the force of the blast threw dead men in all directions. Frost and the rest of her party hardly rocked on their heels, protected by their heavy hard suits. Silence laughed suddenly, back in the game again, and strode toward the air lock, kicking thrashing bodies out of his way. The others followed him, knocking the dead men down as fast as they got to their feet. The dead grabbed at their legs to try and hold them, but dead arms were no match for the hard suit's servomechanisms.

Silence hit the controls, and the air-lock doors cycled

slowly open. The two security men were hacking at everything in sight with their swords, and dead flesh flew in the
air though no blood flowed. The doors finally opened wide
enough, and Silence yelled for his people to break free.

"Move it, people! We are leaving!"

Abrams and Fine broke away and threw themselves into
the air lock. Cross went to follow them, then stopped as a
dead man rose up before him. Cross raised his sword and
then hesitated as he took in the gray face before him. It was
a familiar face from an old holofilm, and it took him only a
moment to place it.

"Grandfather . . ."

And in that moment the dead man raised an old-fashioned
disrupter, placed it against Cross's armored belly, and
pressed the stud. The energy blast punched right through the
hard suit and out the back. Cross screamed, the horrified
sound filling Silence's ears through his comm link, and then
he crumpled slowly to the floor. Silence swung his sword
with all his suit's power behind it, and sheered clean through
the dead man's neck. The headless body fell away, and Silence sheathed the sword and grabbed Cross by the shoulders. He pulled the screaming man into the air lock and
turned to look out at Frost, standing with her back to the
doors, sword in hand.

"Get in here, Investigator! We are *leaving*!"

"I'm not coming with you, Captain." Frost didn't turn
around, but her voice came clearly through Silence's comm
implant on the command channel, as though she was standing right beside him. "I have to stay behind. Otherwise, one
of these undead bastards will just hit the override from this
side and keep the air lock from functioning. I have to stay
here to hold them off while the rest of you go through to the
pinnace. I've known this all along. You never did think
ahead enough, Captain."

"We'll risk it," said Silence. "Now, get in here. That's an
order. We're not leaving without you."

"You have to," said the Investigator unemotionally. "It's
vital you get away, to report what happened here. The Empire must know that Shub is using stolen ships with dead
crews. Once you reach the *Dauntless*, blow this death ship
apart."

"I can't open fire while you're still aboard!"

"Of course you can. It's the logical thing to do."

"You didn't leave me to die on the bridge of the *Darkwind*."

"That was different. There's too much at stake here. And at least my way, they won't be able to make a Ghost Warrior out of me. Please, John. It's the only way."

She hit the air-lock controls with her elbow, and the doors closed. Silence had one last glimpse of the Investigator throwing herself against the advancing dead men, and then the doors were shut and she was gone. He turned away to operate the outer doors. He didn't say anything. He didn't trust his voice. His arms and legs were shaking inside his suit, from tension and something more. Cross was still screaming. The two security men had slapped temporary seals over the holes in his armor so he'd survive the crossing to the pinnace. One of them gave the all clear to Silence, and he opened the outer doors. It took them only a few moments to cross the empty space to the pinnace's lock and pass through that into the waiting ship. Cross fell silent as the emergency drugs the hard suit was pumping into him finally took effect. Abrams and Fine secured him in a seat and then strapped themselves in. Silence took the pilot's seat and patched into the pinnace's emergency channel.

"*Dauntless*, this is the Captain. I'm on my way back. I have three men with me, one seriously injured. We're all that made it out. The *Champion* is infested with Ghost Warriors. As soon as we're clear, open up with everything you've got. Destroy the *Champion*. Confirm."

"This is the *Dauntless*," said his Second in Command. "We confirm. Destroy the *Champion* as soon as you've docked."

It took only a few minutes to maneuver the pinnace back to the *Dauntless* and dock it, but they seemed to last forever, and all the time Silence saw a single valiant figure, fighting an army of dead men and hoping for a quick death from the *Dauntless*'s guns. He patched into the main ship's sensors, and watched silently as cannon after cannon opened fire on the *Champion*. Her shields flared into existence immediately, but they were old, inferior shields, and the *Dauntless*'s superior firepower battered them down and slapped them aside. Disrupter bolts hit the old ship again and again, blowing jagged holes in the hull. Escaping energies burned silently in the dark, until finally the *Champion* exploded in a bloody ball of hellfire, glowing brightly in the long night. *Good-bye, Frost,* said the Captain silently. *I'll miss you.*

He broke the comm link and sank back in his chair, feeling suddenly very tired. The two security men were manhandling an unconscious Cross out the air lock. He couldn't really believe that she was dead yet. He could still feel her presence through his metal link, like a ghost in his head, but presumably that would fade away in time, like the phantom pain from an amputated limb.

"Captain, this is Stelmach," said a familiar voice in his ear suddenly. "We're getting strange readings here on the bridge. There are reports of fighting coming in from all over the ship. Intruders, appearing from nowhere, killing our people. There are energy weapons discharging on all levels. Dear God, Captain, they're Ghost Warriors!"

"No," said Silence. "That's not possible."

"They're here, Captain. I can see them through the security cameras! How the hell did they get off the *Champion*? We didn't track any escaping craft."

"They teleported," said Silence. "The bastards teleported! That's what I'd forgotten. Remember what we saw at Court? Shub has the secret of long-range teleportation! Set up interior force shields throughout the ship, cutting off all infected areas. Have repair teams standing by in case disrupters puncture the shell. And warm up the auto-destruct. Just in case."

And Frost died for nothing.

"Where's the nearest trouble site, Stelmach?"

"Two or three quite near you, Captain. Biggest group is one level down, Delta section, but the security force I sent hasn't got there yet. You'd better stay clear till I get word it's been secured."

"Hell with that," said Silence. "This is my ship. I go where I'm needed. I have business with these murderous bastards. Silence out."

He ran down the corridor, pushing the hard suit to its limits, and all he could think of was making the Ghost Warriors pay for Frost's death. He'd build a mountain of heads in her name. She'd like that. But it wouldn't be enough. It would never be enough. He took the elevator down to the next level, clenching and unclenching his hands impatiently. The doors opened to sounds of chaos not far away. There were shouts and screams and the sound of energy weapons discharging. That last brought him out of the elevator in a run. They weren't too far from the outer hull in Delta section, and all it would take was one really unlucky shot to puncture the hull. Explosive decompression probably wouldn't bother the Ghost Warriors much, but it would play hell with everyone else. Silence was suddenly very glad he'd kept his hard suit on.

He rounded a corner and came upon a heaving mob of human defenders, struggling to contain a large group of Ghost Warriors. There were wounded and unmoving bodies sprawled everywhere, but in the midst of the living dead men, holding their attention almost single-handedly, was a defiant figure in a battered hard suit, swinging a long sword with both hands. Silence grinned so hard it hurt. He didn't need to see the suit's colors to know who was behind that featureless helmet. No wonder he'd still been able to feel her presence. When the Ghost Warriors teleported their people off the *Champion,* they'd brought Frost with them! Probably unwilling to give up such an important specimen. Silence roared his Clan's battle cry and threw himself into the heart of the battle, hacking left and right with vicious sweeping arcs. He cut a path through the dead, unfeeling flesh, laughing as he went, until he was able to put his back against that of the armored figure. They fought well and fiercely, and the Ghost Warriors couldn't get anywhere near them.

"Hi," said Frost's voice in his ear. "Miss me?"

"Not for a minute," said Silence. "I knew you were too cussed to die."

"That is what it was all about, you know," the Investigator said casually in between blows. "Use the *Champion* to pull us in, distract us with strange voices, and then take over the *Dauntless.* With you and I as Ghost Warriors, carefully preserved and disguised, Shub could have used us to get in striking range of the Empress herself. Which is presumably why they saved me when the *Champion* went up. Crafty inhuman bastards. I'm quite impressed."

Silence was too busy to reply. Captain Pearce had turned up again, his head still at an angle, but as determined as ever. He had an old-fashioned disrupter in his hand, but Silence slapped it out of his grasp with a swift, casual movement. The two Captains went head to head, the living and the dead, swords soaring as they slammed together and sprang away, inhumanly fast. Pearce had a strength and speed beyond anything a living man could normally produce, but Silence had been changed in the Madness Maze, and he wasn't merely human anymore, either. The hard suit's servomechanisms strained to keep up with him as he swept aside Pearce's attack and defenses alike and dueled him to a standstill. He lifted his sword and brought it down in one blindingly swift movement, and the heavy blade hammered into Pearce's skull, sinking deep into his head till it finally jarred to a halt on an eyesocket. Pearce convulsed as his sundered computer implant crashed and fell apart. Silence jerked his sword free, and Pearce fell twitching to the floor.

There were still more Ghost Warriors. Silence fought on, back-to-back with Frost, cool and calm and quite collected. Strength and speed burned within him, and he felt like he could fight forever. He was linked with Frost again, on every physical and mental level, fighting in that calm twilight state when the sum of the two of them was far greater than their separate parts. And suddenly, there was no one left to fight. The Ghost Warriors lay broken and decapitated all around, and the surviving crew members were wildly cheering their Captain and their Investigator. Which had to be something of a first for Frost, Silence thought as he looked serenely around him. Usually, people cheered Investigators only when they were leaving. He turned to look at Frost, who had turned at the same moment to look at him. They reached up and took off their helmets, and their eyes met in a moment of understanding and appreciation that could never be unsaid or forgotten.

"We're not even breathing hard," Silence said quietly. "What are we becoming?"

"Better," said Frost.

"Inhuman, perhaps."

Frost shrugged as best she could inside her suit. "Humanity's overrated sometimes."

Silence was still trying to come up with an answer to that, which didn't involve raising his voice, when Stelmach's voice sounded in his ear again. The Security Officer sounded very upset.

"Captain! There are Ghost Warriors all over the ship! Hundreds of them!"

"Tell me something I don't know," said Silence. "Are we holding our own against them?"

"Barely. We're afraid to use our disrupters much, but they're not. The largest group is heading for the bridge, despite everything we can do to slow them down. We've only got one chance. From my work with controlling the Grendel aliens, I'm pretty sure the computers controlling the Ghost Warriors must have a central control mechanism, separate from the bodies it moves. Some mechanism they brought with them when they teleported over from the *Champion*. A single cybernetic mind running its meat puppets. I've had Communications scanning the comm channels for unauthorized transmissions, and we've detected one hell of a powerful signal coming from the main hangars in Epsilon section. That's got to be it."

"Good work, Stelmach," said Silence. "The Investigator and I are on our way. Send as many men as you can after us. If we fail, defend the bridge till it's obvious there's no hope, and then hit the self-destruct. Whatever happens, this ship and its crew is not to fall under Shub's control."

"Understood, Captain. Good luck."

He broke contact, and Silence and Frost headed for the elevators.

"If I didn't know better," said Frost, "I'd swear he's becoming almost human."

"He says much the same about you," said Silence.

They discarded their cumbersome hard suits for greater speed and made their way down to the Epsilon hangars without much trouble. The *Dauntless* was a much bigger ship than the *Champion*, and the Ghost Warriors were spread thin, trying to cover too many areas at once. Silence and Frost cut them down when they had to and avoided the rest. They didn't want the enemy to know they were coming. There were a dozen entryways into the Epsilon hangar area, and only a few of them were signposted. Silence and Frost used one of the least obvious and emerged onto a high narrow walkway overlooking the bay without anyone knowing they were there. Some fifty feet below, the Ghost Warriors had cleared a space among the piled-up supply crates, and now a dozen dead men holding disrupters stood guard over an intricate glass and crystal mechanism that glowed with an

uncomfortably bright light. Silence pursed his lips thoughtfully and glanced at Frost.

"Even with our new abilities, there's no way we can get
to that device without being seen or heard, and that many
disrupters makes me nervous. Even if they don't hit us, they
could hit the hull. We could wait for reinforcements, but
with all that cover to hide behind, they could hold off a
small army indefinitely. And we are running out of time."

"If you can distract them," said Frost, "I can blast that device with my disrupter."

Silence raised an eyebrow. "From here?"

"Of course."

Silence thought about it, but shook his head. "No. Odds
are it's protected by a force Screen of some kind. I would.
And if you fire and fail, we'll have given away our position
for nothing. I've got another idea."

Frost looked at him. "This doesn't involve us throwing
ourselves away in a grand gesture, does it? I've already tried
that, and I wasn't too keen about it the first time."

"This is simpler. I'm suggesting we use our minds for a
change. It's not just our bodies that were changed in the
Madness Maze. The strain or excesses of nearly dying on the
Champion seem to have pushed me another step up the lad-
der. You, too, probably. We're more than we were. Listen.
Concentrate. Can you hear what I'm hearing?"

Frost frowned, listening. The hangar bay was quiet, the
Ghost Warriors standing silently on guard. In the stillness
she could hear Silence's breathing and her own, and then,
very quietly below it all, she sensed as much as heard a low
pulsing that rose and fell in sudden spikes. And inside that
sound, which wasn't really a sound, she could hear a voice
murmuring, cold and inhuman and horribly perfect.

"Damn," said Frost. "It's the machine. I can hear it thinking. Giving orders. It's not a language or any computer code
that I'm familiar with, but somehow I can still understand it.
This is the signal Stelmach detected from the bridge, the
voice that pulls the Ghost Warriors' strings."

"Yes," said Silence. "It is. Apparently, we're becoming
espers, along with everything else. But we can do more than
listen, Frost. We can hurt it. Concentrate on the link between
us."

He reached out clumsily to her with his mind, and she
came to him. Their thoughts mixed and meshed, jumbling

together, and then suddenly they both came into focus, sharp and brilliant, and their minds slammed together and merged to become a whole that was far greater than the sum of its parts. It leapt up and out from the cramped confines of their bodies and struck at the thinking machine in a lightning flash of roaring energies. The force field didn't even slow it. The machine howled horribly, feeling its destruction without ever knowing what or how, and then its center shattered into a million quiescent pieces, and collapsed upon itself. The Ghost Warriors fell to the floor and lay still, not even twitching. Their mind was dead. The mind that had been Silence and Frost split apart, and they fell back into their bodies. Their minds slowed, weighed down by flesh again, and they both immediately began to forget what it had been like to be more than human. They had to, or they would lose being human forever. And they weren't ready to do that, just yet. They stood staring at each other for a long moment.

"We can't tell anyone about this," Silence said finally. "You know what they'd do to us."

"We have a duty to inform our superiors," said Frost. "Perhaps by examining us, they could find a way to duplicate the process."

"More likely they'd kill us, by taking us apart to see what makes us tick. It wasn't a human technology that changed us, made us what we are. And besides, Lionstone would order us destroyed the moment she heard about us. She'd never allow anything as powerful as us to exist in her Empire.

"We don't have to decide right now. We can talk about it later. For the moment, how are we going to explain what happened here?"

"No problem," said Frost. She drew her disrupter and blew apart what was left of the control mechanism, leaving nothing but a scorch mark on the steel floor. Frost put her disrupter away again. "A lucky shot. As simple as that."

"Show-off," said Silence, and activated his comm implant. "Bridge, this is the Captain. Status report, please. The Ghost Warriors are down, right?"

"I don't know how you did it," said Stelmach, "but according to the reports coming in, the Ghost Warriors just collapsed and gave up the ghost all over the ship. It's over, and we won. Amazing. I wouldn't have bet on it. I may faint."

"Try to hang on till we get back to the bridge," said Silence. "You did well, Stelmach. If you hadn't theorized a central control device and tracked it down, they'd probably have been scooping our brains out with dull spoons by now. You're a hero, just like the rest of your family."

"Some hero. I didn't volunteer to go over to the *Champion* with you."

"There are different kinds of heroes," said Silence. "What's important is that you came through when it mattered. Silence out."

Silence and Frost leaned on the walkway railing together, looking down into the hangar bay. The Ghost Warriors still hadn't moved. Silence kept an eye on them anyway, just in case.

"I thought we were heading back to the bridge," said Frost.

"In a minute," said Silence. "After all we've been through, I think we're entitled to a short break to get our breath back."

"We do lead an interesting life," said Frost. "At least this time we didn't lose the ship."

"Right," said Silence. "I think we're finally getting the hang of this hero thing." He thought for a moment and then looked at Frost. "Do you really think those voices we heard at the beginning were part of the Shub trap?"

"Of course," said Frost. "What else could they have been?"

Silence shrugged uncomfortably. "I don't know. It's just ... they seemed to be warning us, as much as anything."

"But if they didn't come from the *Champion,* where did they come from?"

"I don't know. On the whole, I'd rather not think about it. The implications are too disturbing."

"Ah, hell," said Frost. "Everyone knows it gets strange out here on the Rim."

CHAPTER SEVEN

The Circles of Hell

The monitor screen spun a few fractals as its memory warmed up, and then the flaring colors resolved into a sharp holo image. A bleak, metallic horizon, crenellated here and there with shadowy trenches, deep craters, and looming hills of metal scrap, stretched away for miles before vanishing into the early-morning gloom. A dull red sun was rising reluctantly in a gray sky dominated by darkening clouds. The scene was unnaturally quiet, with not even a whisper from beast or bird or insect; the only sound was that of the rising wind, moaning and roaring in turn, as though gathering its strength for the storm to come.

The camera panned slowly right, and a huge factory complex appeared on the holoscreen. Given its great size and tall towers, and the many-colored lights blazing from its windows, it should have dominated the bleak scene, but somehow it didn't. The surrounding area of fractured metals and accumulated scrap looked like the place where old factories went to die. The camera zoomed in slowly, so that the factory filled the screen. Armored guards could now be seen, watching coldly from their trenches and gun emplacements, and it quickly became clear that the factory was under siege from some unseen, ominous foe.

A single figure stepped into view before the camera, making his way carefully over the rutted metal surface. Mud and water had collected in the hollows and splashed up over his boots. He finally came to a halt, half filling the screen, and looked seriously into the camera. Even buried inside a thick fur coat he was clearly short and overweight, and above his ruddy face his flat blond hair was plastered to his skull. But his eyes were calm and his mouth was firm, and without quite knowing why, you felt you could trust him to tell you the truth about what he'd seen. The rising wind tried to ruffle his hair, flapping the long ends, but he ignored it.

"You're looking at Technos III, early morning, early winter. The factor complex behind me, owned and run by Clan Wolfe, will shortly begin mass production of the new and vastly improved stardrive. The workers are dedicated, the management strong and decisive, and the small army of guards are trained, experienced, and utterly determined. Ideal conditions, one would have thought, for such an important venture. But this is Technos III, and things are different here.

"To begin with, while this planet has the usual four seasons, like any colonized world, the seasons here last only two days. Weather conditions therefore understandably tend to the extreme, not to mention the dramatic. In the spring it rains, a constant hammering monsoon that can deliver over an inch of rain in under an hour, every hour. In the summer it bakes, the bare sunlight hot enough to blister unprotected skin in minutes. In the autumn there are hurricanes and raging winds strong enough to pick up unsecured equipment and carry it for miles. In the winter it snows. Thick blizzards and heavy drifts bury the surface and anything else not protected by the factory's force Screen. Exposure to the cold can kill in minutes. Blood freezes and lesser metals crack.

"These conditions are not natural. Those meddling computer terrorists, the cyberats, are responsible. They meddled with the planet's weather satellites, and this changing hell is the result. I'm standing here outside the factory in the early hours of the first day of winter. The temperature has dropped thirty degrees in the last hour, and the winds are rising, giving warning of the blizzards to come. Soon I will have to return to the safety of the factory complex or risk death from a dozen natural causes. Empire technicians are working on repairing the weather satellites as a matter of urgency, and the word is we will have normal conditions restored soon. In the meantime the brave men and women of Clan Wolfe struggle valiantly to bring all systems on-line, so that mass production of the new stardrive can begin as scheduled and as promised. I will, of course, be here to show you the opening ceremony, live.

"This is Tobias Shreck, for Imperial News, on Technos III. Cold, bored, tired, pissed off, really really pissed off, and bloody hungry."

The picture on the monitor screen disappeared, replaced for a moment by spinning fractals before one of the two men

watching it leaned over and turned it off. Tobias Shreck, also
known as Toby the Troubador—PR flack for Clan Shreck—
and as that stupid pratt who managed to really upset his Uncle Gregor and ended up freelancing on a hellworld like
Technos III, straightened up and glared at the lowering sky.
The darkening clouds were appreciably thicker now, and the
gusting wind was so strong he had to brace himself against
it. He huddled inside his fur coat, pulled out a filthy-looking
handkerchief, and blew his nose noisily.

"I hate this place. The weather's insane, the natives are as
friendly as a serial killer on amphetamines, and there isn't a
decent restaurant on the whole damn planet. I should have
known there had to be some underhanded reason for the
Home Office's eagerness to sign me up and offer me an immediate assignment."

"Think positive," said his cameraman, a tall gangling sort
called Flynn, wearing a long heavy coat of assorted dead animals that still wasn't long enough to accommodate someone
of his great height. He had a deceptively honest face, only
partly undermined by the holocamera sitting on his shoulder
like a squat, deformed owl. He set about dismantling the
lights that had shown Toby to his best advantage and carried
on speaking with a blithe disregard as to whether Toby was
still listening. "At least we've got nice warm quarters in the
complex to hole up in. Those poor sods on guard duty are
wearing thermal suits on top of their thermal underwear, and
they're still freezing their butts off. I hear if you fart out
here, it rolls down your trouser leg onto the ground and
breaks."

Toby sniffed. "Those guards are highly paid mercenaries,
highly trained in the art of rendering people down into their
component parts in the shortest time possible, and therefore
by definition not really human. And you can bet they're being paid a damn sight more than you and I are. And the factory complex gives me the creeps. Most of the factory's
automated, and the clone workers who do everything the
machinery can't are even less human than the guards."

Flynn shrugged, and his camera grabbed his shoulder with
clawed feet to steady itself. "Clones aren't employed for
their social skills. They've been designed and conditioned to
within an inch of their humanity to be the perfect work
force, and nothing else. They're here only because there has

to be a human decision-making presence at all times. Can't just leave it to the computers. Not after the Shub rebellion."

"We can cut the last few seconds from the tape," Toby said heavily, turning away from the monitor. "Did I leave out anything important?"

"Not really. Technically, you should have mentioned that it was the Campbells who started the ball rolling here, before the Wolfes took it over. And you could have mentioned there are a few local problems with rebel terrorists, which will undoubtably be sorted out soon."

"No I couldn't," said Toby firmly. "The Wolfes would only censor it. We don't need any depth for an introductory piece. Leave it till the interviews, and I'll try and bring it up then. Though you can be sure nothing even remotely good about the Campbells will make it into the final cut. Doesn't make any difference. The Wolfes won the hostile takeover, and no one likes a loser. These days, the few surviving Campbells are about as popular as a fart in an air lock. Let's get inside, Flynn. I can't feel my fingers, and my feet aren't talking to me. And the weather can turn extremely nasty in the blink of an eye when it feels like it. God, I wish I was back on Golgotha. Even attending Court was safer than this."

"Why are you here?" said Flynn. "You never did get around to explaining just what you did to get Gregor Shreck his own bad self so mad at you."

"I don't have to tell you anything," said Toby. "You haven't even told me what your other name is."

"One name is all a cameraman needs. Now, spill all the grisly details, or I'll make you look really podgy on camera."

"Blackmailer. All right, basically, the Church was growing increasingly dubious about the moral probity of its ostensibly faithful son Gregor. I'd been keeping his extremely dubious private habits under wraps through some inventive PR and heavy backhanders where they would do the most good, but stories kept getting out anyway. There was talk of a full Church investigation, and then even all Gregor's money and social standing might not be enough to buy him a clean bill of health. Nasty, disgusting little toad that he is. I told him he'd have to keep a lower profile once he got in bed with the Church, but did he listen? Did he, hell. So, I did the only thing left to me. I figured out who would most likely end up running the investigating team, set him up with a young lady of the evening of my professional acquaintance, let nature take its merry course, recorded it all on film from every angle, and blackmailed him. How was I to know I'd picked one of the few really honest men left in the Church these days? He told all, made a public confession, and I resigned from Gregor's employ before he could fire me. Bearing in mind that Gregor's displeasure tends to be expressed through sudden violence and assassins, I walked into Imperial News and asked for the first assignment they had on the far side of the Empire. And I ended up here. Sometimes I wonder if Gregor got to them first."

"Maybe he did," said Flynn.

"No. He's not that subtle. Being subtle was what he employed me for."

"Well, maybe the winter won't be as bad as everyone says. It couldn't be that bad."

Toby glared at him. "Didn't you watch the briefing tapes? The winters they have here could be officially classified as cruel and unnatural punishment. Snowstorms start with a blizzard and then escalate. The Eskimos have one hundred and twenty-seven different words for snow, and even they have never seen snow like they have here. In fact, if you brought an Eskimo here and showed him the snow, he would stop dead in his tracks and say, *Jesus Christ, look at that snow!* The winds in winter reach three hundred miles an hour! It snows sideways!" Toby stopped and took a deep breath to calm himself. His doctor had expressly warned him about his blood pressure, but his doctor had never had to work on Technos III. Hell, he wouldn't even make a house call to his neighbor's apartment. Toby scowled up at the sky and then back at the factory. "We'd better get undercover. Bring the equipment."

"You brought it out here," said Flynn, "you take it back. I do not fetch and carry. It's in my contract. I am a cameraman, and the only thing I carry is my camera. I told you that when we started out."

"Oh, come on," said Toby. "You can't expect me to carry the lights and the monitor. All you ever carry is that bloody camera, and if it weighs more than ten ounces, I'll eat the bloody thing."

"I don't move things," said Flynn. "It's not in my nature. If you wanted a pack mule, you should have brought one."

Toby glowered at him and then started gathering up the lights. "God, you people have got a good Union."

Daniel and Stephanie Wolfe, in charge of stardrive production and therefore Lords of all they surveyed on Technos III, helped themselves to another large drink from the automated bar. As aristocrats, they were normally used to the luxury of human servants, but such frills and fancies had no place on a factory world, even for such distinguished visitors as the Wolfes. The drinks weren't very good, either. Stephanie threw herself sulkily into a large supportive chair that tried to give her a soothing massage before she turned it off. She didn't feel like being soothed. Cardinal Kassar was on his way, and she needed to feel in full control for the encounter. Daniel was stalking back and forth across the deep pile carpet like a caged animal, and she wished he wouldn't. It was getting on her nerves.

The room was comfortably large by Technos standards, which meant you might have squeezed ten people into it at most, and only then if you happened to have a crowbar handy. The furnishings were understated to the point of anonymity, and the overbright lighting was giving Stephanie a headache. Daniel finally stopped his pacing and accessed the factory's external sensors. One wall disappeared behind a representation of what the weather looked like outside. Mostly, it looked like snow being blown sideways by very strong winds that had the disconcerting habit of shooting from left to right and then back again just a little faster than the human eye could comfortably cope with. Stephanie turned in her chair so she wouldn't have to look at it and concentrated on her game plan.

Ostensibly, Valentine had sent them here to see that everything went smoothly until mass production of the new stardrive officially began. He'd arranged a ceremony for the big day to be transmitted live across the Empire in prime time, to remind everyone—especially those at Court—where Wolfe money and power came from. Actually, Stephanie had arranged everything. She'd planted the idea for a ceremony in his mind, and then intrigued quietly but continually behind the scenes to ensure that she and Daniel would attend the ceremony rather than Valentine himself. A live broadcast would be the perfect opportunity to throw some heavy but undetectable spanners into the works, slow down if not halt stardrive production, and generally make Valentine look incompetent. Such a high-profile failure might be just the lever she and Daniel needed to pry control of the factory away from Valentine and over to them. And then they'd see who really ran Clan Wolfe.

The local rebels were still a nuisance and would have to be put sharply in their place well before the ceremony. But that shouldn't be too much of a problem. Kassar had brought a fair-size army of the Faithful with him to back up the numerous Wolfe mercenaries. The natives wouldn't know what hit them. On the other hand, the presence of so many security troops could mean that her carefully planned and considered pieces of sabotage would have to be carried out with great subtlety. If she, or more likely Daniel, were to be caught in the act, all the fast talking in the world wouldn't be enough to save them. Valentine would seize the opportunity to discredit them and quite possibly expel them from the Family. It was what Stephanie would do in his position. She looked up, and there was Daniel, still staring at the faux window, and she knew he wasn't seeing the storm outside.

"Let it go, Daniel," she said softly. "Our father is dead and gone, and there's nothing you or I can do about it."

"No. He's not dead," said Daniel and would not turn away from the storm. "You saw him in the Court. His body's dead, but those bastard AIs on Shub repaired it. Daddy's still alive in there, trapped in a decaying corpse. He recognized me. Spoke to me. We have to rescue him, bring him home."

"What you saw was just a Ghost Warrior," said Stephanie, her voice carefully calm and even. "A dead body held together by servomechanisms and run by computer implants. It was just a machine talking, imitating our father. A composite program, probably derived from father's public holo appearances. The man we knew is dead. He doesn't need us anymore. Forget him."

"I can't." Daniel finally turned his head to look at her, and there was something in his face that gave Stephanie pause. His normally sulky mouth was set in a firm line, and his gaze was steady, determined. "For once, I'm not going to let you talk me out of something I know is right. If there's even a chance Daddy is still alive, I have to rescue him. I have to. I let him down so often when he was alive; I can't fail him now he's dead. You don't need me here. The sabotage is your plan. Kassar can take care of the rebel problem for you.

He's got experience in things like that. I can't think about things like that anymore. The rebels don't matter. The factory doesn't matter. Wolfes come first. Always."

Stephanie heaved herself up out of her chair and moved quickly over to join Daniel before the window. "I need you here, Danny. You're my strength. Stay here with me, at least until after the ceremony. We can send agents out to locate our father and discover what his true state is. People with experience in these matters. And that way we can keep things quiet. After all, there are a lot of people with a vested interest in seeing our father doesn't return to head the Family again."

She saw the decision in his eyes before he nodded reluctantly, and she sighed silently with relief. Daniel was too much of a wild card to be allowed to run loose. She needed him at her side, where she could control what he saw and said. He meant well, but he lacked her vision, her focus. She knew what was best for the Family, and it didn't include charging blindly around the Empire on a fool's errand. Dear Daddy was dead, and that was for the best, too. She'd have had him killed eventually anyway. He was in her way.

"If I'm going to stay, find something for me to do," said Daniel. "I feel useless here."

"Perhaps you'd care to work with my troops," said Cardinal Kassar. "Always room for another brave warrior in the service of the Church."

They both turned around sharply, Daniel's hands clenching into fists at being caught unawares. Stephanie nodded coolly to the Cardinal. She wouldn't give him the satisfaction of appearing flustered. Even if she wasn't sure how much he might have overheard. The Cardinal stood grandly in the open doorway, his chin held high. He was wearing full battle armor, even in the supposed safety of the factory's private quarters—which might have been down to Church paranoia, or maybe a veiled insult to the Wolfes, in that he didn't trust them to ensure his safety. Stephanie thought he was most likely wearing it because he thought it made him look strong and soldierly.

In which case it was almost successful. The great bas-relief crucifix on his chest tried hard to draw the eye, but Kassar's ravaged face would not be ignored. Half eaten away by acid, the scarred side of his face looked more like a skull than a living countenance, even down to the gleaming teeth visible through the rents in his cheek. Stephanie managed a gracious smile, but didn't move, and stuck close beside Daniel so he wouldn't, either. Let Kassar come to them.

The Cardinal was late, but she'd expected that. Kassar was the kind of man who always kept people waiting, just to show how important he was. He needed little victories like that to sustain him, especially since being ordered to Technos III. Officially, it was an opportunity. The Church had sent him a small army of the Faithful and a dozen elite Jesuit commandos to help the Wolfe forces defeat the rebel terrorists. The Church of Christ the Warrior didn't normally do favors for the aristocracy, let alone Clan Wolfe, but like everyone else, the Church's future power was dependent on gaining access to the new stardrive. Those who got there first would have a temporary but very real advantage over those who did not. And the Church had not got where it was by ignoring possible advantages. The fact that the Church despised the Wolfe Family in general, and its current head Valentine in particular, could not be allowed to get in the way of political one-upmanship. Needs must when the devil drives.

Kassar especially had no love for the Wolfes, but none the less he had lobbied almost savagely for the posting. The war on Technos III was a chance to show what he could do as a commander of troops, and that was after all the fast track to advancement within the Church. Piety was all very well, but it was victory in arms that got you promoted. And though he barely admitted it even to himself, Kassar needed to be sure of his own courage. He couldn't help feeling he'd made rather a poor showing when the Ghost Warrior and the Fury and the alien broke loose that day at Court. He could have done something, something brave and commanding to save the day, but instead he'd just stood there like all the others with his mouth hanging open. People must have seen him doing nothing, even if no one dared to say so to his face. So he had come to Technos III to win a great victory, whatever the cost, and then no one would have any doubts about his valor. Not even him.

They stood looking at each other for a long moment, all three with their own private thoughts, none of them willing to make the first move. Finally, Stephanie took one step forward and extended a hand to Kassar. He took a step forward,

accepted the hand, and bowed curtly over it. His handshake
was firm but brief. Daniel stayed where he was and nodded
briefly. Kassar nodded back.

"Welcome to Technos III, Cardinal," said Stephanie, her
voice gracious but cool. "Sorry about the weather, but if you
don't like it, stick around, and something else will come
along shortly. The weather here changes its mind like a vil-
lage priest caught between two sins. I trust your men are settling in comfortably?"

"My men are preparing for their first assault on the rebel
positions," said Kassar. "Comforts can wait. You've let the
terrorists get away with far too much, but given the small
size of your forces, I can't say I'm surprised. Why haven't
you pressed some of the factory workers into service? I can
supply whatever arms and armor may be needed."

"I think not, Cardinal," said Stephanie. "All the workers
here are clones, bred and designed solely for factory work.
And you don't give clones weapons."

Kassar shrugged carelessly, to cover his faux pas. "As you
wish. My troops are more than enough to get the job done.
Now, Daniel, what do you say? Shall I find a place for you
in our ranks?"

"Wolfes didn't fight for other people," Daniel said flatly.
"We fight for ourselves. Always."

A silence fell that could have been awkward, as each
party present was damned if they'd be the first to break it,
and then the tension was broken as Toby the Troubador and
his cameraman Flynn came bustling through the open door.
Toby nodded briskly to all present and gestured for Flynn to
find a position where he could cover everyone with his camera.

"Morning, one and all," he said cheerfully. "Isn't it a perfectly awful day? Hope I'm not interrupting anything vital,
but I really do need to get some footage of the Cardinal
meeting his hosts. That kind of thing always plays well with
the audience, and it'll make a good introduction to the cam-
paign to come. Don't worry, I'll keep it short and to the
point. I'm sure you've all got things you'd rather be doing."

Daniel gave Toby his best intimidating scowl. "Is this really necessary?"

"I'm afraid so," said Stephanie quickly. "Public relations
can be a bore and a bind, but we can't do without it. Public
acclaim can often get you things that nothing else can. The

stardrive ceremony will be an important event, and I want it covered very thoroughly. After all, absolutely everyone will be watching. Grit your teeth and bear it, Daniel. It'll soon be over."

"That's the spirit," said Toby. "Cardinal, if you'd care to stand between the Wolfes, make a nice group for the camera . . ."

Kassar glowered at him, but moved obediently as directed to stand between Stephanie and Daniel. And though they stood close together, none of them so much as nudged another with their elbow. Toby bustled around them, raising an arm here, squaring a shoulder there.

"All right, people, just hold the pose while Flynn gets the lighting right, and then we'll do a short interview. Nothing complicated, just how glad you all are the Cardinal's here, that sort of thing. Fake the smiles if you have to."

"You are aware, Shreck," said Kassar coldly, "that your uncle is currently being investigated by the Church on charges of sedition and corruption on many levels?"

"Nothing to do with me," Toby said airily. "You can haul him off in chains, for all I care. I'll even supply the chains. Just give me some warning so I can get the rotten fruit concession."

"He is the head of your Family," said Daniel. "You owe him allegiance. Have you no honor?"

"Of course not," said Toby. "I'm a journalist."

"We will of course want to see all reports in their entirety before they can be transmitted," said Stephanie. "So that they can be checked for bias and possible inaccuracies."

"The Church censors will also examine all footage," Kassar said quickly. "To check for blasphemies or disrespect. Standards must be maintained."

Toby kept smiling, though his cheeks were beginning to ache from the strain. "Of course. Whatever you wish. Don't worry about inconveniencing me. I'm used to working with people looking over my shoulder."

He fussed the three of them about some more, partly to get the best grouping for the camera and partly just because he could. He'd expected some kind of censorship, but he could see that getting anything interesting off Technos III was going to take a lot of hard work, a little subtlety, and every dirty trick in the journalist's handbook. Still, when in doubt let the material go over their heads. They can't censor what they don't recognize. He had great hopes of what the Technos III material might do for him and his career, and he wasn't going to let these three stuffed shirts get in his way. The day he couldn't think rings around any censor they could throw at him, he'd give up journalism and go into politics. They'd believe anything there.

This was his first real assignment in too many years, after spending so long buried in the Shrecks' Public Relations department, because Gregor needed him. The right kind of reporting here could make his reputation, establish him as a journalist and commentator in his own right. Toby wanted that. The essence of a good PR man is that no one should notice his work. Toby felt very strongly that he'd earned a chance to show off his talents on a wider and more visible screen. Of course, he couldn't hope to make much of a splash just covering the events leading up to the stardrive ceremony. The real story lay in covering the Technos III conflict, the Wolfe and Church forces versus the rebel terrorists. And he was going to cover it, despite anything the Wolfes and the Church could do to stop him.

He looked back at Flynn, who nodded briefly to show he was ready. The camera on his shoulder studied the three dignitaries with its red owl eye, linked into Flynn's eyes through his comm implant, so that he saw what it saw. Daniel and Stephanie and Kassar smiled determinedly at the camera, all friends together, ready for their interview. As in all politics, individual problems disappeared in the need to present a solid front to a common enemy.

The Church ship *Divine Breath* hung in orbit above Technos III, comfortably far above the seething weather, ostensibly on guard but mostly just goofing off in the absence of the Cardinal and his Jesuit enforcers. After all, they had nothing to do but watch a few sensors while they waited for the Cardinal's troops to make short work of a few native discontents. Easy work. Everyone knew there wasn't a rebel born who could stand against trained troops of the Faithful. So a soft duty for once, and the crew took advantage of it. Which was why when the giant golden Hadenman ship dropped suddenly out of hyperspace just above them, the whole crew took one look and all but shit themselves. The huge ship hung above them, dwarfing the Church vessel like a minnow next to a killer shark. The Church crew snapped to attention at their posts, their hands moving desperately over their control panels. Shields slammed into place as guns powered up, and even those whose piety wasn't all it might have been found a sudden need to send up prayers of the most fervent kind.

The Hadenman ship opened fire, and the *Divine Breath* shuddered as disrupter cannon hammered against their shields. The Church ship fired back as fast as it could get its guns to bear, but the golden ship was impossibly fast for its size, and the crew of the *Divine Breath* knew they were hopelessly outclassed. They fought on anyway, not through their faith as much as because there was nothing else they could do. They couldn't drop into hyperspace without lowering their shields first, and the moment they did that the Hadenman ship would blow them apart.

The Captain watched his shields go down one by one and called for more power, though he already knew he was using everything the ship's straining engines could produce. If he'd only had one of the new stardrives being produced on the planet below, he might have stood a better chance, and the irony was not lost on him. And then, as he searched frantically for something—anything—to do to hold off the inevitable, the great golden ship suddenly disappeared back into hyperspace, gone between one moment and the next.

The Captain blinked a few times, clutched at the crucifix on his uniform collar, and muttered a few Hail Marys, and then sank back in his command chair, cold sweat slowly evaporating on his forehead. His ship had survived, but he was damned if he knew why. When he finally got his strength back he canceled Red Alert, ordered full damage reports, and a complete sensor sweep of the surrounding space, just in case. He then wondered what the hell he was going to say to the Cardinal down below. He'd have to be told, even though he'd probably shout a lot. The Captain frowned, trying hard to come up with some viable-sounding excuse that wouldn't get him court-martialed or excommunicated. There was no getting away from the fact that he and his crew had been caught with their pants around their ankles, but damn it, it had been a *Hadenman* ship! There weren't many who'd seen one of those in action and lived to tell of it. The Captain and his crew worked hard on their various excuses and explanations, which was at least partly why

they never noticed the heavily shielded escape pod that the
Hadenman ship had dropped just before it disappeared.

The pod hurtled down through the buffeting clouds and
howling winds, battered this way and that by the storm's
fury, but still somehow holding to its planned descent. Inside
the pod, Jack Random the professional rebel, Ruby Journey
the ex-bounty hunter, and Alexander Storm the retired hero,
clung desperately to their crash webbing and waited for the
long drop into hell to end. The pod's outer hull groaned and
squealed from the pressures it endured, and the sensors
blinked out one by one till they were practically flying blind.
The webbing cushioned and absorbed most of the shocks the
pod encountered as it fell on and on into Technos III's tur-
bulent atmosphere, but the three rebels were still flung this
way and that in the webbings' restricted arcs.

Storm gritted his teeth and tried hard to hang on to his last
meal. Random ignored it all, concentrating on what he was
going to do when he finally landed. It was his first time back
in the business of armed rebellion, and while he was quite
definitely looking forward to it, he couldn't help but worry.
It had been a long time, and he wasn't all the man he used
to be. Either way, it wouldn't stop him giving this mission
his all. And if in the end everything went to hell in a handcart, what better way for a professional rebel to die than
with gun and sword in his hand, and a pile of the enemy
dead at his feet? Random sniffed sourly. Actually, he could
think of a dozen better ways to make his final exit, mostly
including a good wine and a bad woman, but he doubted
he'd see any of them. Rebels rarely died in bed.

Beside him, Ruby Journey was laughing and whooping
loudly as she spun to and fro in her webbing, enjoying every
minute of the trip down. Random smiled at her. How could
you not love a woman like that? He checked the sensor panels again, but they were still out, the pod's sensor spikes torn
away by the shrieking winds. The proximity alarms sounded,
harsh and strident, and Random braced himself. Either the
ground was near, or they were about to crash into a mountain. Ruby whooped wildly. Storm had his eyes squeezed
shut, as though that would make any difference. Random
sighed and tried to remember if there were any mountains on
Technos III. He didn't think so, but it would have been nice
to be sure.

The escape pod slowed desperately as the engines gave up the last of their power to cushion the landing. The three occupants were pinned helplessly in their webbing, listening to the inner and outer hulls cracking from the strain. The lights went out, replaced by the dull red glow of emergency lighting. And then the pod slammed into the metallic surface of Technos III, plowed a long path through the scattered scrap and debris, and finally came to a halt against a massive protruding steel spur. The pod rocked back and forth and then settled itself. The sky was dark and forbidding, the winds were rising, and the first snows were beginning to fall.

Inside the pod, Storm still had his eyes squeezed shut and was trying to remember how to breathe. Random lay slumped in his webbing and thought, not for the first time, that he was getting a little old for all this. Ruby Journey wiped at her bloody nose with the back of her hand and laughed happily.

"That was great! Let's do it again!"

"Let's not," said Storm, still not opening his eyes. "I've had more fun in front of a firing squad. Next time, may I suggest we try and find a pod that's a little less past its sell-by date? Oh, God, I feel awful. Somebody please tell me we are safely down, because I'm not budging an inch until I'm sure the drop is over. And I want it in writing. With witnesses."

"Shut up, Alex," said Random easily. "We're down in one piece, and that's all I ever asked from a landing. And for an escape pod that's been sitting around in a Hadenman ship unused and untested for decades, I think it did pretty well."

"Now he tells us," said Storm. "I knew there was a good reason why I gave up personal appearances as a rebel."

"Shut up, Alex," said Random. "Ruby, the sensors are all out. Crack open the hatch and see what's outside."

Ruby disentangled herself from her webbing, threw Random a professional salute, and made her way carefully over the slanting floor to the one and only hatch. Random clambered slowly out of his webbing, wincing at several new bruises and a few old injuries, and moved over to persuade Storm to open his eyes. Ruby cracked the hatch and pushed it outward. The metal resisted a moment and then gave way. A blast of cold air and swirling snow swept into the pod, along with just enough light to fade the crimson emergency lights to a rather sweet pink color. Storm opened his eyes.

"Oh, wonderful. We've landed inside a birthday cake."

"Shut up, Alex. Ruby, what's it like out there?"

"Cold," said Ruby brightly. "And there's enough snow coming down to make an army of snowmen. Which is just as well, as there's no sign anywhere of a welcoming committee."

Random scowled. "According to the handful of instruments that are still working, we are in the right place, more or less. No doubt our contacts will be here soon. They must have seen us come down. Hurry up, Alex, shake a leg. We have revolutions to organize."

"I never did like fieldwork," said Storm, moving painfully toward the hatch. "Undercover is a young man's work. Usually, a young man who won't be missed too badly if it all turns pear-shaped."

"Whinge, whinge, whinge," said Random, half pushing Storm out the hatch. "Anyone would think you weren't happy to be here, striking a blow for freedom and democracy."

"Anyone would be right," said Storm, and then shut up as the full force of the cold hit him.

The three of them huddled together in the lee of the escape pod, sheltering from the driving storm. The jagged metal surface was already disappearing under a thick blanket of snow, and the rising wind was whipping up into a blizzard. They all turned up the heating elements in their clothes, hugged themselves fiercely, and beat their hands together. The cold was sharp enough to take away their voices, and their breath steamed thickly about their heads. The snow was so thick the sky was completely hidden, as well as the sun. It was supposed to be midday, but there was hardly enough light to see by. Random could feel Storm shivering violently beside him and began to be concerned. Storm's old bones couldn't survive this cold for long. Random didn't feel the cold too badly, but he'd been through the Madness Maze.

"This is undoubtably a silly question," said Storm through teeth clenched to keep them from chattering. "But why can't we get back inside the pod? It's got to be warmer than this."

"The pod's heaters got knocked out along with everything else," said Random. "And there's a small but definite chance the batteries are leaking poisonous gasses. If you want to take your mind off the cold, keep your eyes open for our

contacts. In this blizzard they could walk right past us without noticing. But if they don't come soon, we may have to
risk the gasses. You can't handle cold like this."

"I can handle any cold you can, you old fart," Storm said
angrily. "I'm only six years older than you, I'll have you remember."

"Sure, Alex. Now, shut up and conserve your strength."

"Always were a bossyboots, Jack."

"How far are we from the rebel base?" said Ruby, trying
hard to be tactful for once.

"We don't know," said Storm. "They wouldn't tell us. Just
gave us landing coordinates and told us we'd be contacted.
I hate going into situations blind. I just hope the paranoid
bastards find us before the Empire forces do. We were promised a distraction to keep them occupied somewhere else,
but I'm growing less trusting by the second. I would also
like to point out that I am losing all feeling in my extremities."

"Don't worry," said Random. "At your age you don't use
them for much anyway."

"You can go off people, you know," said Storm.

They fell silent for a while, the cold air searing their
lungs. They huddled closer together, trying to share their
warmth, eyes straining against the swirling snow. Dark out-
croppings of metal showed dimly through the storm, but
there was no sign of life anywhere. Random beat his gloved
hands together and looked longingly at Ruby's thick furs
over her leathers. He'd thought she just insisted on wearing
them to keep up her barbarian image, but maybe she'd paid
more attention at the briefings than he had. He wouldn't be
surprised. There was a sharp mind at work behind her carefully crafted image. He coughed and sneezed harshly. Something in the air was irritating his throat. Even allowing for
the bitter cold, the air was thicker than he was used to, and
it smelled as though someone else had breathed it first. The
locals had assured him it was breathable, once you got used
to it. Random suspected it was an acquired taste. They'd
said much the same about the changing weather, but Random wasn't convinced. The locals had also said the blizzard
would make good cover for a landing. Random wondered if
he'd be allowed to shoot the person who said that for crim-
inal understatement.

He looked across at Storm, and his concern grew. There

was no color left in the man's face, and he was shuddering
violently. Random gestured at Ruby, and she took off her
furs and wrapped them around Storm. It seemed to help him
a little. Ruby wouldn't feel the difference. She'd been
through the Maze, too. Random frowned. He'd been thinking of Storm as an old man, someone who ought to be happily retired, sitting in a book-lined study beside a blazing
fire, with adoring grandchildren at his feet, but he really
wasn't much older than Random. He still mostly remembered Storm as a tousle-headed young warrior, always
laughing, ready to throw himself into the thick of things at
a moment's notice. But that was a long time ago, and Random was shocked as he realized just how long. Storm had to
be in his mid fifties by now, and the long years of struggle
had not been kind to him. Random frowned and wondered if
maybe he shouldn't have brought Storm with him, after all.
Storm had volunteered, but then, he'd never been able to say
no to Jack Random. Who was no youngster himself anymore, even if he had been through the Maze. His frown
deepened. He didn't think of himself as old, even after all
he'd been through, so he supposed Storm didn't, either. But
they sure as hell weren't young anymore. Ruby suddenly
pushed herself away from the shelter of the pod and stared
out into the storm.

"Heads up, people. Company's coming."

"Can you see them?" said Random, stepping forward to
stand beside her.

"No. But I can feel them. They're coming this way."

Random concentrated, but couldn't feel anything. The
Maze had changed them all in different ways. The first dark
shapes began to appear out of the snow, and Storm forced
himself to move forward and stand with his friends. It was
a matter of pride. There were ten locals finally, standing before them all wrapped in furs, their faces hidden behind
leather and metal masks in the shapes of stylized animal
heads, none of which Random recognized. Except to note
they were all pretty damn ugly. One of the locals stepped
forward, looked at the three of them, and then pulled aside
his mask to reveal a grim, heavily bearded face. It was a
hard-used face and could have been any age. Several long
scars marred his features, deep and pitted, and his eyes were
dark and very cold.

"Where are the rest of you?" he said harshly, looking at Ruby.

"We're all there is," Random said calmly. "You talk to us about the local situation, and if we're convinced, we'll contact the underground and they'll send armed volunteers, weapons, and supplies. You understand there's a lot of calls on our limited resources. We have to be sure they go where they're most needed. I'm Jack Random. This is Ruby Journey and Alexander Storm. Give them plenty of room. They bite. Whom do I have the honor of addressing?"

"You're *Random*?" said the local incredulously. "I thought . . ."

"Yes," said Random regretfully. "Most people do. Just try and think of my age as experience on the hoof. Is there somewhere else we could continue this conversation? Somewhere a few degrees above absolute zero?"

"Of course. I'm Tall John. I command here. Follow me."

He pulled his mask back into place, turned, and set off into the storm without looking back. The locals moved off after him, as silently as they'd arrived. Random grabbed Storm and got him moving. Ruby took Storm's other arm, and the three of them stumbled off into the blizzard, hurrying as best they could to keep up with Tall John and his people. The pod was quickly lost in the snow behind them, and they soon lost all sense of direction. No matter where they looked there was only snow, and the dark figures trudging on before them. Time passed, and the bitter cold of the wind cut at them like knives as the pressure of the winds increased. And then the dark figures suddenly began to disappear, one by one. The last turned and beckoned them forward. He pushed aside his mask, revealing Tall John's face again.

"This is it. Welcome to the outer circles of hell."

He gestured at his feet, stepped forward, and descended into a gap in the snow that Random could only just make out through the blizzard. Random moved forward cautiously and suddenly found himself on the edge of a deep trench, some six feet wide, falling away deeper than his eyes could follow. He could just make out the steps cut into the near wall, and he followed the retreating Tall John down into the trench. Storm came next, slowly and very carefully, followed by Ruby. The trench turned out to be some fifteen feet deep, with snow and slush already ankle-deep at its bottom. Tall John was waiting for them and gestured for them to follow him into one of the many narrow tunnels leading off from the far wall.

Random followed the local into a dimly lit tunnel barely wide enough for two men to walk abreast, and so low he had to keep his head bowed to avoid banging it on the roof. Roof and walls were both made of metal, crudely polished in places, and it occurred to Random that he'd seen nothing else on this planet. Except snow. He could hear Storm and Ruby following close behind. He glanced back, but Storm seemed to be holding up okay. It was discernibly warmer in the tunnel. The warmth slowly rose as they made their way on, until finally they emerged into a steel cavern some twenty by thirty feet.

The walls had been jaggedly cut from the many layers of compressed scrap metal covering the planet's surface, and no efforts had been made to disguise or cover this. There was no furniture, and the only light came from scattered candles in glass jars. A central metal brazier contained brightly glowing coals, and Storm headed straight for it with his hands outstretched. Random and Ruby joined him, though a little less quickly, for pride's sake. They both kept one hand at a time unobtrusively near hidden weapons. Random hadn't lasted this long by trusting people who just happened to turn up at a meeting place. He should have insisted on a password, but there hadn't been time. Random liked passwords. They appealed to his sense of the dramatic.

Tall John stripped off an outer layer of furs to reveal a tall rangy man with long dark hair, a steady gaze and a mouth set in a stern line. Beside him stood another of the figures from the storm, pulling open her furs to reveal a short, chunky woman with a great mane of knotted dark hair above a pale, round face. She flashed the three newcomers a broad smile and nodded to them amiably. Like Tall John, time and the world had used her hard, and she could have been any age at all.

"I'm Throat-slitter Mary. Don't mind Tall John. When you get to know him, he's really a pain in the ass. He and I will speak for the others. You'll meet them later. You're welcome here, but I have to say you're not what we were hoping for. We need reinforcements, weapons, supplies, and lots of them."

"We didn't expect two old men and a bounty hunter," said Tall John.

Random shrugged, not upset. "There's more to us than meets the eye. And if you can convince us of the strategic importance of your needs, you'll get everything you could hope for. So talk to us. Fill us in on what's been happening on Technos III. Your initial contact was intriguing, but short on detail."

"All right," said Throat-slitter Mary. "Short and to the point. Like me. We're fighting a trench and tunnel war with the Empire forces. At the center of everything is the factory, getting ready to mass produce the new stardrive. Around the factory lies a series of trench circles. The Empire controls the inner trenches, we control the outer, and we spend most of our time fighting over the ones in the middle. There's maybe fifteen thousand of us left. There used to be a lot more, but the years have whittled us away.

"We're all that remains of the original colonists of Technos III. Our ancestors were indentured workers, paying off the cost of their transport by terraforming the planet and establishing industries. Theoretically, once all the debts were paid off, Technos III was theirs. Only somehow there were always more debts for each new generation.

"The original company in charge went broke. Others came in and took over, running the planet as a business while they asset-stripped it. The companies came and went, but we stayed. We had to. Our ancestors had been genetically altered to enable them to survive on this world. Terraforming can only do so much. If you three stay here long enough, this planet will kill you in a dozen subtle ways. We can't leave this world without some pretty basic changes in our body chemistry, which we've always been denied. Officially, because it would be too expensive. Besides, where else were they going to find such a useful, trapped, workforce?

"As companies came and went, each more cheapjack than the one before, leaving their failures behind them to poison the land, the whole surface of the planet gradually disappeared under deserted factories, installations, and other high-tech junk. Right up until today. The Campbells were a bunch of bastards, but the Wolfes are worse. They don't give a damn for this planet. All they care about is their precious factory. Everything else has been left to rust and rot. We've inherited a world dominated by deserted mile-long factories, abandoned construction sites, and worked-out mines. The Wolfes, and the Campbells before them, chose this planet precisely because it's such a mess. They could do anything they liked here, and no one would give a damn. Who's going to care about pollution on a world like this? It's already been poisoned so thoroughly that only native life like us could survive here. And no one cares about us. At first we were an embarrassment. Now, we're rebel terrorists. Life on this planet has been driven underground. We survive, together. We live off the remaining flora and fauna, and they live off us, when we're not fast enough. But our time is running out.

"Once the Wolfes have got their factory up and running, they'll be able to afford armies of mercenaries to force us back, so they can build more factories. And once that happens, they won't stop till we're extinct. We have to stop this factory coming on-line. It's our only hope."

"Sounds straightforward enough," Random said briskly. "It's a regrettably common scenario in the Empire these days, though this is perhaps a more extreme case than most. Tell me about the weather. I gather it's rather unusual here."

"That's one way of putting it," said Tall John. "Ever since the cyberats screwed up the weather satellites over two hundred years ago, the seasons here have lasted exactly two days, over and over again. The planet's various owners have been trying to repair the satellites for decades, with no luck whatsoever. Most life here couldn't adapt and died out. What little did survive, did so by being extremely tough. And not a little eccentric. During the winter, anything with any sense hibernates. In the spring, everything wakes up, explodes, and proliferates. They live, fight, and breed in the summer. Then they feed exhaustively and build nests in the autumn, deep down, away from the razorstorms and the hurricanes. Then they sleep through the winter so they can wake in the spring and do it all again. Life here is nothing if not adaptable. It's had centuries of practice.

"And that's Technos III in a nutshell. Perfect for vacations. Bring the kids. Of course, the war ignores such trivialities as the seasons; it goes on day in, day out, whatever the weather. You've arrived as autumn turns to winter—the nearest we've got to a quiet time. Our people and the Wolfe mercs take the opportunity for a breather, plan our revenges, and bury our dead. But don't think you can relax. You've got maybe two hours before the killing starts again. So welcome to hell, gentlemen and bounty hunter. Maybe now we can get to the important questions, like: When are the others coming? How large an army can you supply us with? How many weapons?"

Storm and Ruby both looked at Random. He sighed and met the rebels' gaze as calmly as he could. "I'm afraid there isn't any army. Not yet. The underground is raising volunteers for the great rebellion on hundreds of worlds, but it's a long slow process. Such trained men as we have are scattered across the Empire where they can do the most good. For the moment we're all you're getting."

"I don't believe I'm hearing this," said Tall John, his voice shaking with barely suppressed anger. "We were promised battle-hardened fighters, led by the legendary Jack Random, the professional rebel. And what do we get: two old men and a professional back stabber. Give me one good reason why I shouldn't just throw the three of you out into the winter to freeze?"

Random snatched the gun out of Tall John's hand, lifted him off his feet with one hand, and pressed the gun under the rebel's chin. Tall John's eyes bulged as his feet kicked a good foot above the floor. Before the surrounding rebels could react, Random put Tall John down again and offered him his gun back. The rebel leader took it automatically and blinked confusedly. The rebels looked at each other uncertainly. Throat-slitter Mary was grinning. Ruby sniffed.

"Show-off."

Tall John pulled his dignity about him again and nodded curtly to Random. "Not bad for an old man."

"There's more to us than meets the eye," said Storm smoothly.

"There would have to be," said Throat-slitter Mary. "Well, if you're all we're going to get, we'd better make the most of you. Come with me, and I'll introduce you to a few of our strategists. Ragged Tom and Specter Alice should have a few ideas. They usually do."

"Interesting names you have here," said Storm. "Hasn't the concept of surnames made it this far yet?"

"Our ancestors were indentured workers," said Tall John. "Slaves, in all but name. They just had numbers. We're free, so we choose our own names or accept those given to us by others. Surnames are for people with families and a future.

We live from day to day and depend on no one but ourselves. There's no room for luxuries on Technos III."

In a small private gymnasium, in the great hulking residential building attached to the factory, Michel Wolfe, reluctant husband to Stephanie, was working out on the parallel bars. Sweat dripped from his bulging muscles as he pushed himself through the strenuous routine his computers had recommended. He grunted and huffed with every effort, eyes squeezed shut, scowling with concentration. He'd originally acquired his muscles from a Golgotha body shop and just went back for quick touch-up if they looked like they might be sagging a bit. But out here in the wilds, far from civilization, he had to maintain his muscles the hard way, like it or not. Michel hated every minute of it. It was entirely too much like hard work; and if he'd wanted to work hard, he wouldn't have married into the aristocracy.

He dropped down from the bars and wiped sweat from his forehead with the back of his hand. The marriage had seemed like a good idea at the time. Now he was beginning to wish he'd stayed an accountant. You knew where you were with figures. If you did your job properly, the numbers added up to a single, undeniable total. No arguments, no opinions, no having to care what anybody else said. Life in the Families wasn't like that. The answer to any question tended to depend on who you were talking to at the time. And heaven help you if you got it wrong, or even worse, didn't give a damn. Everyone was plotting with everyone else, and if you chose the wrong side, death was often the easiest way of losing. And you weren't allowed not to choose a side. Just by being part of a Clan you inherited feuds, arguments, and hatreds that went back centuries. Michel sighed and thought about doing fifty sit-ups. And then he thought the hell with it. Let his abdominals sag. See if he cared. He sighed again.

"What's the matter, lover?" said Lily Wolfe from the doorway.

Michel looked around quickly. Lily Wolfe, reluctant wife of Daniel, was standing in the open doorway, striking another of her poses. This was her favorite: one leg forward, chest out, head slightly back, designed to pull his eyes up her body, showing off her six-foot-six willowy frame, from her incredible legs all the way up to her pouting mouth. She was wearing another of her pagan witchy outfits, all flapping silks and earth colors, designed to make her look long, pale, and interesting. She'd swapped her usual long silver wig for a mop of bright red curls that didn't really suit her, but was presumably meant to give her an air of gypsy abandon. It didn't matter. She was beautiful. She was always beautiful. Michel smiled at her in spite of himself. Every time he saw her he fell in love with her all over again, even if it was about as sensible as clutching a live grenade to his bosom. Everyone has one true love in their life, someone who fills their life with light and turns their bones to water, and God help him, she was his. He reached for the nearby towel and wiped the sweat from his face.

"What brings you here, Lily?" he said finally, trying hard to sound casual though his pulse was already racing. "I didn't think you even knew this place existed. And I've told you before; don't call me lover in public. It's not safe."

Lily shrugged. "There's only one kind of exercise I've ever been interested in. Anything else is just a waste of good sweat. And I've never been interested in being safe, either. Now, are you going to come over here and kiss me, or am I going to have to come and get you?"

Michel draped his towel over one shoulder and moved unhurriedly over to join her. It was important to him that he kept some kind of control, even though he knew he'd lose it all the moment he took her in his arms. He had to tilt his head up to kiss her. He was a good six inches shorter than her, but that had never bothered him. It just meant that there was that much more of her for him to love. And when he crushed her in his arms like some long delicate flower and her perfume filled his head like a drug, he didn't give a damn about anything but her.

Lily always said they were made for each other. His dark and swarthy looks complemented her pale high cheekbones, like two sides of the same gypsy coin. They were soul mates, meant for each other, and nothing could keep them apart. She said a lot of things like that, but he didn't usually listen. It was enough that she was there. He belonged to her, body and soul, even though he knew he'd probably end up dying for her, if they were ever found out.

He finally pushed her away, though he didn't let go of her. "This complex may not be as openly bugged as we're used to, but that doesn't mean somebody couldn't be watching us," he said heavily. "That bug scrambler of yours has its limits. Daniel and Stephanie may be so preoccupied with getting this factory up and running that we're being allowed a longer leash than usual, but we still have to be careful. If they were ever presented with hard evidence of our love, they'd have to have us executed—or be a laughing stock. Even worse, they might throw us out of the Family. I love you, Lily, but I won't be poor again for you."

"You worry too much," said Lily, laughing silently at him from beneath heavy eyelids.

"And you don't worry enough," said Michel, meeting her gaze firmly. "We're only here on this benighted back end of nowhere because our respective spouses don't trust us out of their sight. So far all they have are suspicions. Their egos won't let them believe anything less than hard evidence, so let's not get careless and provide them with any. We have to be careful, Lily. We have so much to lose."

"You're so boring when you're being sensible," said Lily. She pouted like a child and pulled out of his arms. "You should listen more to the ancient voices within you, the dark savage beat of your own primitive emotions. Civilized behavior is just a cloak we wear, that we can slip off whenever we choose. But for once, I agree with you. I came here to talk."

Michel folded his arms across his great chest. "So talk. I'm listening, darling."

Lily flashed him a wide smile, and suddenly she didn't look at all childish anymore. "Daniel and Stephanie have a great deal invested in this factory's success. If they were to fail, if something were to go wrong here, they'd have even less time to pay attention to us. So you might say we have a vested interest in their failure. Yes, I thought you'd like that. Now, let's take the argument one step further. If they were to die here, you and I would inherit all their world goods and their position in the Family. And considering that dear Constance doesn't give a damn about the Family and never has, and dear Valentine is a complete lunatic whose regular intake of dubious chemicals would suggest he isn't long for this world anyway ... if we were to play our cards very carefully, we could end up with everything."

"And we could end up very dead," said Michel. "Kill them? Are you crazy? You've been thinking again, haven't you? I hate it when you think. Our position is precarious enough as it is. Arranging a plausible accident for the factory is one thing, but if Daniel and Stephanie were to die, whatever the situation, the first people they'd arrest would be me and you. Precisely because we have so much to gain. And you can't lie to an esper."

"Unless ... the deaths could clearly be put at someone else's door," said Lily calmly. "Someone who hates them even more than we do. Like the local rebels, perhaps."

"All right," said Michel. "I just know I'm going to regret this, but tell me more."

Lily half turned away from him, her eyes lost in the distance. "You've never believed in my witchy powers, Michel, but they've been stronger than ever since we came here. I've ... seen things, felt things, ridden on the winds of the storm. This is a wild place, and wild things happen here. It calls to me. I feel stronger here, more focused, more daring. You'd be surprised what I dare, lover."

Michel nodded, but said nothing. He'd always suspected Lily had a touch of esp, but it wasn't something you mentioned among the aristocracy. Espers were property. Always. Apparently, the boredom of enforced celibacy and the untamed nature of the planet had combined to stimulate her abilities. Certainly, she'd seemed more extreme lately in her emotions and her recklessness.

"All right," he said mildly. "So you've got a great future ahead of you as a weather predictor. So what? How does that help us?"

"The wildness of this planet doesn't lie in its weather, but in its people," said Lily. "I can feel them out there. Underground. They're planning something big, something we can perhaps take advantage of. You see, I have friends here, dear Michel. Good friends. Powerful friends."

And then they both heard footsteps approaching down the corridor outside, and they broke off, moving away from each other. There was a pause, and then Toby Shreck came bustling through the doorway, smiling professionally, followed more casually by his cameraman Flynn. Michel and Lily drew themselves up majestically.

"Get out," said Lily.

"Sorry to bother you," said Toby breezily, "but I need to tape a quick interview with you two. Nothing too complicated or challenging; just a simple character piece for inclusion in the documentary your Family's commissioned from me on the opening ceremony. So if you'll just grant me a few minutes of your time . . ."

"Get out," said Michel.

"Allow me to point out that your respective spouses are very keen that you should cooperate," said Toby. "Trust me, just lie back and relax, and it'll be over before you know it."

"Get out," said Lily.

"Honestly," said Toby, smiling till his cheeks ached, "you'll enjoy it, once we get started. Haven't you ever wanted to have your face on the holoscreen, broadcast across the entire Empire, in front of a guaranteed audience of practically everyone with a set? The stardrive ceremony is big news. There's bound to be a massive audience. Your names could be on everybody's lips." He looked hopefully at Lily and Michel, and then sighed and shrugged. "I know; get out. Come on, Flynn. We'll try again some other time when they're not feeling so aristocratic."

He bowed briefly to Lily and Michel and left, followed by Flynn, who didn't bow to anyone. Michel relaxed a little as the door closed behind them. Lily scowled.

"Impertinent little creep. Speaking to us like that. I can just imagine the sort of questions he had in mind. Publicity like that we don't need. Not with what I've got planned."

"Well, what precisely have you got planned?" said Michel impatiently. "And who the hell are these friends of yours? Why haven't you mentioned them before? Have you told them about us?"

"I didn't have to," said Lily. "They already knew. That's why they came to me."

"Who the hell are *they*?"

"Clan Chojiro. I've been one of their agents for ages now. They respect my witchy nature, and they pay very well. They had a great many agents in place here already, but through me they now have access to all kinds of levels they couldn't even touch before. They're quite willing to see we get everything we want, as long as they get what they want. They even have agents among the local rebels, feeding them information. Honestly, things couldn't be working out better for us. Could they?"

"I don't know," said Michel. "Conspiring with Clan Chojiro is like shark fishing and using yourself as bait. I need time to think about this."

"Well, think quickly. Someone will be coming here to talk

to us any minute. Our plans can begin anytime now. The last
piece of the puzzle has just arrived."

"I hate it when you go all allusive. I assume we're talking
about a double agent. What makes him so special?"

"He's a Jesuit commando," said a calm voice behind
them. "Which means he has access to all the security systems in and around the factory complex."

Michel spun around, fists clenched at being caught
unawares, and then he quickly unclenched them as he remembered who he was facing. The Jesuits were the enforcers of the Church of Christ the Warrior and were said to be
the best fighters you could find outside the Investigators or
the Arena. This particular Jesuit was wearing purple and
white battle armor and a sardonic smile. He was tall, dark,
and not particularly memorable. He didn't look especially
tough, either, but Michel had absolutely no intention of testing him. Or even upsetting him. Michel's muscles were
strictly for show.

"So glad you could come and see us," Lily said graciously
to the Jesuit. "I take it everything is going as planned?"

"So far," said the Jesuit. "I am Father Brendan, Michel.
You may have complete confidence in me. In this room, for
example, the security systems are currently running on a
closed loop, so we can talk for as long as we need without
fear of being overheard. Now, I'm sure you have questions.
Ask away."

"All right," said Michel. "Let's start with why we should
trust anyone from the Church. Last I heard, they were still
advocating the return of the death penalty for adulterers.
This could all be a setup by Kassar. He'd love to have something he could use to bring down the Wolfes."

"The Cardinal knows nothing about this," said Brendan,
"or we'd all be dead by now. As to why I've chosen to work
with Clan Chojiro, it's really very simple. Before I joined
the Church, I was originally Clan Silvestri."

"What the hell do Chojiro and Silvestri have in common?"

The Jesuit smiled. "Blue Block."

Michel realized his mouth was hanging open and closed it
with a snap. Blue Block. The extremely secret, half-mythical
school where younger members of the Families were trained
and conditioned almost from birth to be utterly loyal to the
Clans, to death and beyond. The Families' secret weapon.

"But ..." Michel struggled for words. "Why is Blue Block being used against the Wolfes, one of their own?"

Brendan smiled. "The Wolfes in general—and Valentine in particular—are becoming too powerful. He's tipping the balance. We feel it would be best for all if Valentine could be made to stand down, and others more willing to share the profits of stardrive production took over."

"Which is where we come in," said Lily. "Daniel and Stephanie will fall easily without Valentine to protect and support them, Constance will be quietly sidelined, and we will take over the Family. Clan Chojiro will support us now in return for future generosity on our part."

"Quite," said Brendan. "You don't have to do anything much to begin with. We'll supply explosives and provide exact locations where they'll do the most damage. All you have to do is place them in those areas of the complex that only you have access to. It won't be a particularly big explosion. Just enough to throw production into chaos and make Clan Wolfe look incompetent."

"So no one has to get killed?" Michel said quickly.

"Only as a last resort," said Brendan. "We prefer to avoid actual bloodshed. It's so ... obvious. Trust me, Michel, we'll try everything else first."

Michel nodded reluctantly. "All right. When does the balloon go up?"

"At the ceremony," said the Jesuit. "Live, on holoscreens all over the Empire. It'll be a ratings smash."

"You see, lover," said Lily to Michel, slipping an arm through his. "Even that little toad of a reporter will end up helping us. Everything is planned, down to the last detail. Nothing can go wrong."

Toby Shreck hurried down the narrow corridor, glanced at the watch face set into his wrist, and swore quietly. This was officially sleep time in the factory complex's living quarters, and after the day he'd been through he felt he could sleep for a week. In the hours since his unsuccessful little chat with Lily and Michel Wolfe, he'd been running himself ragged trying to set up all the interviews and factory footage he could.

No one was cooperating except under the direst of threats, and trying to make this factory look good was a task that even an experienced PR flack like himself would have

blanched at. Personally speaking, Toby felt he'd seen sexier-
looking abattoirs. But none of that mattered now. He had a
chance at a once-in-a-lifetime interview, and he was damned
if he was going to lose it now, just because it was an hour
when all civilized men had their heads down and were
dreaming furiously. Everyone else could give him cold
shoulders till their joints froze up; this one interview would
make his reputation.

He tried to hurry himself a little faster, but he was already
out of breath. Too much weight. Too many good lunches at
PR events and launches. As a result, he was built for comfort rather than speed. All right, he was fat. For once, it
didn't matter. No one would be looking at him in this interview. He forced himself on, puffing hard. Trust Flynn to
have his quarters halfway across the complex. Actually, that
wasn't really fair. Toby had quarters in the better area because he was, after all, an aristocrat, and Flynn very definitely wasn't. Toby sniffed. He didn't feel like being fair. He
finally stumbled to a halt before the right door, leaned on it
a moment while he got his breath back, and then hammered
on the door with his fist.

"Go away," said Flynn's calm voice. "I am resting. If
you're factory personnel, go to hell. If you're Toby the
Troubador, go to hell by the express route. If you're a Wolfe,
this is a recording. If you're a potential lover, leave your
name and location on my computer file. Full image, please.
Clothes optional."

"Open up, damn it," said Toby. "You wouldn't believe
who's agreed to talk to us."

"Tell them to take two aspirin, and I'll see them in the
morning. I am off duty, and I don't have to talk to anyone
I don't want to. If you don't like it, take it up with my Union."

"Flynn! It's Mother Superior Beatrice of the Sisters of
Mercy!"

There was a pause, and then the door lock snapped off.
"Very well. Come in. But on your own head be it."

Toby growled something uncomplimentary and very basic, kicked the door open, and stormed in. He managed
about six steps before he came to a dead stop. The door
closed behind him and the lock clicked shut again, but he
didn't notice. Someone could have slipped a live grenade
into his underwear and he wouldn't have noticed. The cam-

eraman's quarters weren't much, being basically cramped and functional, but a few feminine touches had helped to brighten the place up. And the most feminine thing in the room was Flynn, reclining on his bed in a long flowing cocktail dress, with a margarita in a frosted glass in one hand and a book of decadent French verse in the other. He was also wearing a long curly wig of purest gold, and wore subtle but artfully applied makeup. His work boots and sloppy trousers had been replaced by fishnet stockings and stiletto heels, and his fingernails had been painted a shocking pink. All in all, Flynn looked very pretty and completely at ease. Toby closed his eyes and shook his head slowly.

"Flynn, you promised me you wouldn't do this. We are not in civilized company now. They would not understand. And the representatives of the Church of Christ the Warrior definitely wouldn't understand. They'd execute you on the spot for deviancy and degeneracy, and shoot me as well just for knowing you. Now, get out of that gear and into something that won't get us both hanged. Mother Beatrice won't wait forever."

"Rush, rush, rush," said Flynn. He drained the last of his margarita, slipped a bookmark into his poetry collection, and put glass and book carefully to one side before rising gracefully to his feet. "Very well, you wait outside while I change into something less comfortable. And bear in mind I wouldn't do this for anyone less than Mother Beatrice. That woman is a saint."

Toby stepped outside and closed the door without actually shutting it, so he could continue the conversation or hiss if he saw anyone coming. He shook his head again. He could feel one of his headaches coming on. "Of all the cameramen, on all the worlds, I had to end up with you. Why me?"

"Because you were desperate for a good cameraman, and no one else would work with you," said Flynn from inside. "After all, you only got your journalist's license because you were on the run from your Uncle Gregor. As it happens, I also felt the need to leave in a hurry. My last gentleman admirer was a high-ranking member of the Clans who also liked to dress up pretty in the privacy of his own quarters.

"Wonderful man. Very interested in yodeling. Only lover I ever knew who could give you head, and sing you a song at the same time. My, how those low notes vibrated. And what that man could do with a vowel ... Anyway, we had

words and broke up, and he became rather concerned that I
might tell all for the right price. And he couldn't have that.
If word of his private proclivities were to get out, no one in
the Families would ever take him seriously again. It's all
right to be a degenerate if you're an aristocrat, but not if it's
something silly.

"So, seeing the way his mind was working, I decided it
might be in my best interests to leave town for a while, and
hole up somewhere suitably distant until he calmed down
again. Which is the only reason I agreed to work with you,
Toby Shreck. You have to realize, the word on you was not
good: an aging PR flack with dreams of reporting and delusions of adequacy. Nothing personal, you understand. For
what it's worth, you're doing all right here. I've worked with
worse."

Toby scowled, but said nothing. Flynn had most of it
right. He'd spent most of his life working as a PR man and
spin doctor for Gregor Shreck, despised by his peers and un-
appreciated by his Family. No one realized how much hard
work went into good PR. But he'd always dreamed of being
a real journalist, digging out the truth and exposing villainy
and corruption in high places, instead of covering it up. But
somehow he never had the courage to leave the safe haven
of his job and Family. It took being kicked out to wake his
ambitions again, and now that he was here on Technos III,
he was going to do the best damn job he could. It was his
chance to be someone in his own right, not just another of
Gregor Shreck's shadows. A chance to finally acquire some
self-respect. Mother Beatrice was renowned for not giving
interviews, and the press corps took it seriously after she
kneecapped a reporter with a meat tenderizer when he tried
blackmailing a friend into talking about her. But she was
probably the only person on Technos III who could and
would tell him the whole story, the whole truth, and to hell
where the shrapnel fell. And she had agreed to talk to him
. . . Toby kicked the door frame viciously.

"Flynn! Are you ready yet?"

The door swung open and Flynn strolled out, looking like
just another cameraman. The camera perched on his shoulder like a sleepy owl. Flynn did a quick twirl for Toby, to
show off his baggy trousers and camouflage jacket. "Well?
Will I pass?"

"You've still got lipstick on," said Toby with glacial calmness.

Flynn took out a handkerchief, wiped his mouth, and smiled at Toby. "Better?"

"Fractionally. Now, let's go, before Mother Beatrice changes her mind. Or somebody changes it for her."

They made their way quietly through the narrow corridors, stopping every time they thought they heard something. No one else was about. Most people were asleep, trusting to the electronic guards and surveillance to guarantee their rest wouldn't be disturbed. After all, the rebels had never got this close on the best day they ever had, and no one in the factory would dare run the risk of upsetting security. As a reporter in charge of making the factory complex look good, Toby had security passes for practically every area, and some discreet but heavy-duty bribes had ensured no one would tell about his little late-night jaunt. He hoped.

He led Flynn to the nearest exit in the outer sector, and they stopped to climb into the heavy furs left hanging by the door. Even a short journey through Technos III's winter could be deadly without the right protection. Toby and Flynn bundled up in layers of fur and wool till they could barely move, and then stumbled over to the exit. Toby looked out the window beside the door and winced. The air was thick with swirling snow, blown this way and that by the gusting wind. He didn't look at the thermometer. He didn't want to know. He pulled his fur hat down low over his brow, wrapped his scarf securely over his mouth and nose, cursed quietly for a moment, and then jerked the heavy door open. It swung slowly inward, revealing a two-foot drift of snow that had piled up against the closed door. Toby and Flynn kicked their way through it and lurched out into the winter. The door slammed shut behind them, and they were alone in the night.

The cold hit them like a hammer, and for a moment all Toby and Flynn could do was lean against each other for support. The bitter air seared their lungs, and the wind shocked tears from their exposed eyes. The snow on the ground was a good foot deep. Tireless machines struggled over and over to dig out a clear perimeter around the factory complex, but the snow fell faster than the machines could dig. The wind was almost strong enough to throw Toby off his feet, and he had to lean into it to keep his balance. The freezing air made his teeth ache, even through several layers of thick woolen scarf. He scowled and hunched his shoulders as the wind changed direction yet again. Part of him wanted to turn and go back inside rather than face such nightmare conditions, but Toby wouldn't listen to it. He was a reporter now, on the trail of a hot story, and that was enough to keep him warm inside.

He glanced about him into the thickening snow. Outside the complex's exterior lights, there was only darkness and the storm. There were supposed to be stars out and two small moons, but they were hidden behind the fury of the snows. However, out in the darkness a single patch of light showed defiantly around a long low structure without windows. Toby slapped Flynn on the arm and pointed out the structure, and they lurched off through the thick snowdrifts toward the light. Flynn's camera hovered low behind his shoulder, sheltered from the wind.

The low structure turned out to be a really long tent of metallic cloth, marked with the familiar red crescent of the Sisters of Mercy. As on so many battlefields across the Empire, the tent was a hospital for all who needed it. The Sisters took no sides. The factory complex had just enough space for a single hospital ward, officers only. The foot soldiers, security men, and mercenaries had to rely on the Sisters' mercy. The officers believed this gave their men an extra incentive not to get wounded. It was a big tent, looking bigger all the time as Toby slogged through the snow toward it. He hadn't traveled far, but already his thighs were aching from forcing a way through the thick drifts and fighting the constantly changing winds. Sweat ran down his brow and into his eyes, freezing in his exposed eyebrows. Toby had given up cursing some time back. He needed his breath.

He finally lurched to a halt before the far end of the tent, and found himself facing a very secure-looking steel door with a signposted bell. He hit the bell with his fist because he couldn't feel his fingers anymore, and a viewscreen lit up in the door, showing a Sister's veiled head and shoulders. She didn't look at all pleased to see him. Toby reached inside his furs, pulled out his press pass, and held it up before the screen. The Sister sniffed, and the viewscreen went blank. Toby and Flynn looked at each other uncertainly. They were both shivering uncontrollably, no longer warmed by their exertions. And then the door swung suddenly inward, spilling light and heat out into the night. Toby and Flynn hurried forward into the comforting glow, and the door slammed shut behind them.

Toby pulled the scarf away from his mouth and took off his fur hat, his eyes watering as they adjusted to the new light and warmth. He and Flynn took turns beating the snow off each other, and then Toby turned and smiled ingratiatingly at the Sister who'd let them in. It was always wise to be polite to a Sister of Mercy. They had long memories, and you never knew when you might end up needing their services. This particular Sister looked to be in her late twenties, but already had deep lines around her mouth and eyes. Dealing with death and suffering on a daily basis with no end in sight will do that to you. She wore the usual unadorned white robes and wimple of a Sister in the field, but her robes were spattered with new and old bloodstains. She was also big enough to stop an oncoming tank and had a glare that would have wilted anyone but a reporter. Flynn moved surreptitiously to stand behind Toby, just in case, and Toby tried his ingratiating smile again.

"Hi there. We've come to see Mother Superior Beatrice. I'm Tobias Shreck, and this is my cameraman. We're expected."

The Sister stepped forward, pulled open his furs, and frisked him with brisk efficiency. She did the same with Flynn, while Toby silently prayed his cameraman wouldn't giggle. Assured they weren't carrying any weapons, the Sister stepped back and studied them both, her face set and unforgiving. "She said you two were to be admitted, but you're not to tire her. This should be her rest period. She works all the hours God sends, and then makes time to deal with the likes of you. I don't want her tired. Is that understood?"

"Of course, Sister," said Toby. "We'll be in and out before you know it."

The Sister sniffed dubiously, and then turned and led them down the single narrow aisle in the middle of the long ward that made up most of the tent's interior. Toby and Flynn followed behind at a respectful distance. There were beds on either side of them, crammed together with no space for luxuries like visitors' chairs. They weren't the standard hospital beds of civilized worlds, either, with built-in sensors and diagnostic equipment. These were flat cots with rough blankets and sometimes a pillow. The smell of blood and other, more disturbing smells pushed their way past the thick, masking disinfectant. The patients were mostly quiet, drugged, Toby hoped, but some groaned or moaned or stirred restlessly on the narrow cots. One man with no legs was crying quietly, hopelessly. Flynn's camera covered everything. Many of the patients were missing limbs or half a face. Toby was sickened. You didn't expect to see injuries like these anymore, except on the more primitive worlds. He made himself look away. He was here to cover this. All of it.

"Don't the Wolfes supply you with better equipment than this?" he said finally, trying to keep the anger out of his voice so as not to upset the patients.

The Sister sniffed, without looking back or slowing her pace. "We're on our own here. Officially, the Wolfes are winning this nasty little war, so they can't be seen supplying Technos III with major hospital facilities and supplies. Word might start getting out of the real scale of casualties and how badly the war is going. So they only supply us with the minimum necessary to cope with the low levels of wounded they're reporting. It's important to the Wolfes to give the impression that everything's fine here, and they're fully in charge of the situation. Bastards. I'd drown the lot of them if I had my way. And you can put that in your report, if you wish."

"I'm interested in everyone's views," Toby said diplomatically. "I want to tell people the truth of what's happening here."

"If you are, you're the first. Not that it'll make any difference. The Wolfes will censor anything embarrassing out of your reports before you're allowed to broadcast them."

Toby remained even more diplomatically silent. He expected to be censored; that went with the job and the territory. The trick was in what you managed to sneak past them. Halfway down the long tent, a small area was separated off by tall standing screens. Toby thought at first it was a toilet and was somewhat surprised by the Sister's clear respect and reverence as she tapped on one of the screens.

"It's the press people," said the Sister diffidently. "Do you still want to speak to them, or shall I kick them out?" There was a low murmured answer from within, and the Sister scowled as she turned back to Toby and Flynn. "Thirty minutes, and not a second more. And if you tire her, I'll have your balls."

She pulled back one screen to make a doorway, and Toby and Flynn nodded respectfully to her and eased past her much as one might a growling watchdog. They filed through the doorway, and the Sister pulled the screen back into place behind them. The screened-off area turned out to be just big enough to hold a cot, a washbasin on a stand, and a small writing desk. Sitting before the desk was Mother Superior Beatrice, wrapped in a long silk housecoat with frayed hems and elbows worn dull. She looked pale and drawn, and her bright red hair had been cropped brutally short, but her eyes were warm and her welcoming smile seemed genuine enough. Behind her, her black robes and starched wimple hung from a hat stand, looking almost like there was another person in the small space with them. Beatrice didn't get up, but offered Toby her hand. Her handshake was firm but brief. She turned to Flynn, who leaned over her hand and kissed it. Beatrice's smile widened.

"If you knew what I'd been doing with that hand just half an hour ago, you'd rush out of here to gargle with sulfuric acid." She turned her smile back to Toby. "I'm glad to see you both. I wasn't sure you'd come. Everyone else I've asked didn't want to risk rocking the boat."

"I'm not sure I do, either," said Toby. "It depends on what you have to tell me. Is it okay if my cameraman records this conversation?"

"Of course. That's why I insisted on you both coming here. Sit on the bed. We don't have any more chairs to spare, and you fill too much space standing up."

She settled back in her chair by the desk, and Toby lowered himself cautiously into the cot. He wasn't sure it would bear his weight. It felt hard and unforgiving. Flynn stayed on his feet, moving quietly back and forth to sort out good angles for his camera. Toby ignored him. Flynn would take care of the technicalities; his province as reporter was the interview and what truth he could squeeze out of it. Mother Beatrice had a reputation for being outspoken, but that had always been in the pampered and protected Court, far away from the blood and dying of the frontline. She was supposed to have changed greatly after her experiences in a field hospital, but most of those stories were at least secondhand.

And Toby wasn't sure he believed in saints anyway. He decided to start with something simple and clear-cut.

"You seem very crowded here, Mother Beatrice. Surely, this structure wasn't meant to accommodate so many people at one time?"

"Hell no. It was meant to serve a third as many patients, but that was worked out by civilized people in civilized places. And call me Bea, since I'm officially off duty. We're packed to the walls here because things have been going particularly badly for the Wolfes in the last few campaigns. The lines move back and forth on the map, but they're drawn in other people's blood. Some of our patients are rebels, of course. The Sisters of Mercy serve all sides impartially. Whatever the pressures."

Toby raised an eyebrow. "Do the Wolfes know you're treating rebel wounded?"

"I haven't told them. Not after the way they reacted the first time I raised the matter. I keep meaning to bring them up-to-date, but somehow I never get around to it. I don't see that it's any of their business. They only supply me with the bare necessities, even for their own people. We're a long way out from civilization, and transport costs are obscenely high. So I just do my job as I see best. We do what we can here. Patch people up and send them off. It's not unusual to see the same faces come back two or three times, bleeding from a different place each time. Rarely more than three times. Many can't take the shock of so much surgery. Others . . . just give up. It's a hard war and a harsh world. We don't see many flesh wounds here.

"Supplies are running low. Blood plasma, anesthetics, most drugs. The Sisterhood sends what it can, but there's a lot of fighting going on across the Empire these days, and the Sisters' resources are spread very thin. Some days this isn't a hospital. Just a butcher's shop."

"How long has the armed struggle been going on here, Bea?" asked Toby, keeping his voice low and confidential, as though it was just the two of them having a quiet talk.

"Generations," said Bea grimly. "People have been born, lived their lives and died here, knowing nothing but the war. Of course, it's escalated since the Wolfes took over the factory. The upcoming ceremony has raised the stakes for both sides. Still, it was only the rising publicity that alerted us to what was happening here and persuaded the Sisterhood to send in a mission. If they knew what was really going on here, they'd send more help. I know they would. But the Wolfes control all contact with the outside."

"What kind of war are we talking about here, Bea?" said Toby, easing her back onto the main subject.

"Pretty basic. The struggle here's settled down into trench warfare. Been stuck in the same pattern for decades. Both sides dig tunnels, but the planet's remaining wildlife lives down below, and it doesn't like competition. Fighting aboveground is almost impossible for any length of time, due to the weather. It changes so unpredictably that shelling is impractical. Same for air cover. And when the wind blows, there's so much dirt and metal floating in the air that it disperses energy beams to nothing over anything other than point-blank range. So most of the fighting is hand to hand, steel against steel, boiling up out of their trenches to fight in the no-man's-land between Wolfe and rebel positions. The frontline surges back and forth all the time, but nothing really changes. The two sides are too equally balanced. Though the arrival of the Church troops should make a difference."

"Jesuit commandos leading elite troops have cleared out resistance on many planets," said Toby.

"Technos III is different," Bea said flatly. "The rebels here have been fighting for generation upon generation for as far back as records go, learning and improving all the time. Hell, they've been breeding for warriors for centuries. And then there's the weather. You need to be superhuman just to survive here. And that's the state of war on Technos III. Right in your face and bloody. The only reason we're not totally swamped with wounded is because most of them don't last long enough to reach here. They die of the heat or the cold, the razorstorms or the blizzards. But there's always enough work coming in to keep us busy, even when we've run out of drugs and plasma, and we have to hold the patients down while the surgeons cut them apart and sew them up, hoping the shock won't kill them anyway."

Toby leaned forward a little, subtly interrupting her. She was starting to repeat herself, and he needed to keep her to the point. He was torn between getting as much good material as he could, and the knowledge that the longer he stayed here, the more likely it was that someone back at the complex would notice he and Flynn were missing, and put two and two together. "How many staff do you have here, Bea? How much help?"

"I have two surgeons, and five Sisters trained as nurses working under me. There was a third surgeon, but he cracked under the pressure and I had to send him away. He didn't want to go. Even cried when I put him on the transport, but he was too far gone, even for us. I'm still waiting for a replacement. Technos III isn't very high on anyone's list of importance. It's just a name to most people. I only came here because I was desperate to get my hands dirty in some real work after the endless sniping and intrigues at Court. If I'd known what I was letting myself in for . . . I'd probably have come anyway. I never was very good at looking away and pretending I didn't see anything.

"What med tech we have is top of the line, the best the Sisterhood could provide, but it was never meant to handle this many wounded. I live in fear of it breaking down. There's no one here who could repair it. The Wolfes have their own med bay in the factory. Everything you could dream of, up to and including a regenerator. One of the nurses there is sympathetic. I raid their drug supply from time to time, when I'm really desperate, and she covers for me, God bless her." She sighed and shook her head. "Can I offer either of you gentlemen a drink?"

She reached under the writing table and brought out a bottle of murky-looking spirits and two glass specimen jars. She shrugged when Toby and Flynn politely declined and poured herself a large drink. Toby gestured urgently for Flynn to keep filming. Bea was the kind of subject you prayed for in a documentary. A real character, someone who knew everyone and everything, right there in the middle of things but still able to stand back and see the big picture. It helped that she didn't look much like a nun, and the drinking was a nice touch. The viewers didn't like their saints to be too perfect. Her hand shook as she raised the glass jar to her mouth, and Toby felt suddenly, obscurely ashamed. With all he'd seen and heard, none of it had touched him the way it had obviously touched her. She cared, and he was just an unfeeling, recording eye. Just like Flynn's camera. He tried to tell himself he had to be, to get the job done, but that didn't sound as convincing as it once had. He made himself concentrate on Bea as she lowered the almost empty jar.

"God, this is awful stuff," she said calmly. "But I couldn't work here without it. Two of the Sisters pop amphetamines, and one of my surgeons has a serious drug habit. I don't say anything, as long as they can still work. We all need a little something to get us through the day. And the night. The nights are the worst. That's when most of our patients die. In the early hours of the morning, when the dawn seems farthest away. I don't know how much longer I can stand it here. It wears you down, having to fight for every life, even the simplest wounds. Nothing's simple here. Not even this tent. It's the strongest the Sisterhood could provide, but even it can't cope with the excesses of weather we have here. In the summer it gets so oppressive you can hardly move. In the winter . . . I've seen the surgeons stop in mid operation to warm their hands in the steaming guts they've just opened up.

"We've all changed here. I never really wanted to become a nun, you know. I fled to the Sisterhood for sanctuary, so I wouldn't have to marry Valentine Wolfe. But I ended up at the mercy of the Wolfes anyway. I never had much time for religion. I just used the Sisterhood as a power base, like many before me. And I only came here because I was bored. But here in hell I found religion after all. In the face of so much evil, you have to believe in God. It's the only thing that gives you the strength to go on."

She rose suddenly to her feet, catching Toby and Flynn by surprise. She emptied the jar of the last of the drink and put it down on the desk. "I've said enough. I'll take you around the beds, so you can see the kind of wounds we're dealing with. Some of the patients might even talk to you, though you'll have to edit out the obscenities."

She led them out of her private area and back down the long aisle between the beds. Flynn filmed everything, sweeping his camera back and forth. The tent was still eerily quiet, and no one wanted to talk to them. Toby supposed they didn't have the strength to waste on moans of pain or complaints. The other Sisters were moving quietly from bed to bed, checking bandages and temperatures, or if there was nothing else they could do, just laying a cool, comforting hand on a fevered brow. Toby kept quiet, too. The last thing this needed was a commentary, and he didn't have any more questions. The answers were too obvious. To his surprise, he felt mostly angry. This kind of thing shouldn't be happening, not in this day and age. He'd covered up enough things him-

self in the past, as Gregor's PR flack, but never anything
like this. A Family's troops dying, to hide a Family's shame.
He kept telling himself not to get involved. That this was
just a good story. And was surprised to find how close to angry, frustrated tears he was.

"Film as much as you like," said Mother Beatrice. "The
odds are no one will ever see it. I keep trying to get reports
out, and the Wolfes keep blocking me. They can't afford to
admit they're losing the battle here. The Empress might take
Technos III and the factory away from them."

"Some news did get out," said Toby. "From transport
crews and the like. Of the Saint of Technos III, who threw
aside her aristocracy to tend the wounded and the dying.
That's what brought us here."

"I'm no saint," said Bea. "Anyone would do what I do if
they could see what I've seen."

"We'll get the report out somehow," said Toby. "Even if
I have to smuggle the tape out by cramming the cans up my
backside."

Bea smiled suddenly. "Well," she said archly, "I always
said the Wolfes were a pain in the ass."

Jack Random, Ruby Journey, and Alexander Storm followed their guides down through a maze of tunnels, away
from the open trenches and the fury of the rising blizzard.
The tunnels sloped sharply downward, their walls revealing
the many layers of compacted trash and metal that made up
the history of the planet's surface. The air was warmer underground, but the three newcomers were still shivering.
Light came from metal lanterns hanging from the low ceiling, a pale yellow glow that was hard on their unaccustomed
eyes. People bustled around them as they descended deeper,
always in too much of a hurry to do more than stare or very
occasionally nod a greeting. They were all heavily muscled,
with little covering fat to blur the hard edges. Their eyes
were stern and concentrated on the matter in hand, and none
of them smiled or uttered an unnecessary word. Tall John
and Throat-slitter Mary led the way down in silence, the
stiffness of their backs rejecting the possibility of questions.
Random and Ruby and Storm stuck close together, as much
for shared warmth as mutual support.

"How the hell did they build all these tunnels and
trenches in the first place?" said Ruby, scowling at the metal

walls. "I can't see whoever the opposition was at the time agreeing to a truce while the rebels brought in digging equipment."

"They probably used captured energy weapons to blast out the original tunnels and then widened them over the years by hand," said Random. "We're looking at the end result of decades of hard work. Maybe longer."

"Damn right," said Tall John without looking back at them. "The original work happened so long ago that no one now even remembers the names of those involved. We've been building our tunnels for centuries, each generation adding what was needed at the time. We have to live underground. It's all that's left to us. In the old days, there were the military satellites, with their tracking systems and weaponry. These days, there's the weather. And besides, the factory complex has its own force Screen. We've always known the only way past the Screen was under it. The Wolfes know it, too. That's why they have their own people digging tunnels, too."

"But you're safe down here, aren't you?" said Storm.

"There's safe, and then there's safe," said Throat-slitter Mary. "Technos III's other life-forms live underground, too. They live in the deep down, where we rarely go, but they come up from time to time, and then we get to argue as to whose territory these tunnels are. We hunt them for food, and they hunt us for food. We win, more often than not. And it helps weed out the weak. See those old stains on the floor? When we make a kill, we splash the beast's blood around, to mark the territory. It keeps the bastards at bay for a while."

"You mean they get up this far?" said Ruby.

"Oh, sure," said Tall John. "In the spring, sometimes there's hardly room to move in here for fangs and claws and nasty dispositions."

"Good," said Ruby. "I could use some exercise."

"Well, that explains the bloodstains," said Storm quickly. "But what about the leg?"

Tall John and Throat-slitter Mary stopped and looked back at him. "What leg?" said Tall John.

Storm pointed silently, and they all looked up at the human leg, complete with trousers and boot, protruding from where the right-hand wall met the ceiling. Tall John scowled. "Mason Elliot! This is your area! Where are you?"

A short stocky man bundled in furs up to his chin stepped out of a side tunnel, an ugly black cigar in one corner of his mouth. "No need to shout, I'm not deaf. All right, gracious leader, I'm here. What is it this time? Lost your keys again?"

"What is that leg doing there?"

"Holding up the ceiling. We had to rebuild part of the wall after the last bloodworm attack, and we were a bit pushed for time. We were short of materials, the body was handy . . . and no one liked him much anyway. Give it a few weeks and the bloodworms will break through again. We can always remove the body then."

"By which time it'll be stinking to high heaven," said Tall John. "I want that leg brought down now. Get an ax and hack it off. Move it!"

"Certainly, gracious leader of us all." The short man squeezed the end of his cigar out with his fingers and put it behind his ear. He stood glaring up at the protruding leg as Tall John led his party past. Random brought up the rear and was perhaps the only one to hear the short man mutter, "Now, what am I going to use as a signpost?"

Tall John led them on through the tunnels. Random had a suspicion he was being taken by the scenic route, so he wouldn't be able to describe the way down to anyone else. Random approved. It showed a good grasp of basic security and a healthy dose of paranoia. Unfortunately, since Random passed through the Madness Maze, he couldn't get lost. He always knew where he was in relation to everything else. He didn't think he'd tell Tall John that, though. It would only upset him. Random padded amiably along, enjoying what scenery there was. The tunnels were comfortably broad, but the ceilings were low enough that everyone walked with protectively hunched shoulders. Random suspected that the tunnels had been deliberately designed that way, to hinder and disorient invading forces. Presumably, the rebels were used to them. Random found them a pain in the neck. More people appeared as the tunnel floors finally began to level out. They wore layers of leathers and furs, and they all carried their weapons at the ready. They studied the newcomers with cold, suspicious eyes and did not respond to nods or smiles.

"Do your people always go armed?" said Storm. "Surely, you're in no danger this far down?"

"There's always danger," said Throat-slitter Mary. "If not

from sudden security attacks, then from the beasts that live below. There are always people listening, but they can't be everywhere. So we're always prepared. From childhood on, we're trained to be ready to fight for our lives at a moment's notice."

"So where do you get to rest and relax?" asked Storm.

"We don't," said Throat-slitter Mary. "We can relax when we're dead."

Ruby smiled at Random. "You bring me to the nicest places."

Random smiled, but concentrated on what he was going to say to the rebels when he finally got to where he was being taken. He had a strong feeling it wasn't going to make him very popular with the underground community, but it had to be said. He'd led too many armies into battle on the hot words of rhetoric and slanted truths, and seen them die without flinching because he believed the cause was greater than the individual. He wasn't sure he believed that anymore. Either way, he was here to inspire them with the whole truth, not fast-talking. Even if it was a truth they might not want to hear. It occurred to him that he was in the hands of people who might kill him for the word he brought. Random shrugged mentally. They could try.

They came at long last to a reasonably large chamber. The ceiling was at least twenty feet above them, and Random, Ruby, and Storm straightened up with varying sighs of relief. The walls were solid polished metal and ranked seating followed the walls all the way around, interrupted only by the single entrance. The seating was full of people, packed shoulder to shoulder, staring down at the newcomers with harsh, watchful eyes. A man and a woman stood in the center of the open space, waiting. They didn't look particularly welcoming, either. Tall John and Throat-slitter Mary led the three visitors forward.

"This is Ragged Tom and Specter Alice," said Tall John. "Together, we're the council of the underground. Talk to us, Jack Random. Tell us why you have come here."

Jack Random smiled and nodded at the council members, and then at the surrounding watchers. If the numbers were supposed to intimidate him, they'd thought wrong. He'd faced unfriendlier crowds than this in his time and worked under greater pressures. He took a moment to study the two new councillors.

Ragged Tom was an average height, average weight man
with nondescript features, who didn't look any more ragged
than his contemporaries. Specter Alice, on the other hand,
looked crazy as a cornered sewer rat. She was short and old,
with greasy gray furs and remarkably similar hair sticking
up in spikes. She also had wide-staring eyes and a line of
drool leaking from one side of an extremely disturbing
smile. Random was just glad she didn't want to shake hands.
He felt like throwing things at her, on general principles.
Tall John mistook his pause for nervousness and started the
ball rolling.

"We've been fighting here for generations, and after all
we've been through, we're still fighting. The council therefore came to the reluctant conclusion that just possibly we
couldn't do this on our own. We need help. Fighters, weapons, supplies. We were told the Golgotha underground could
supply these things. But all they've sent us is you three. No
one here has forgotten that the last time we asked for help,
the cyberats not only knocked out the military satellites that
had been plaguing us, they also screwed up the weather satellites. We've been living in the resultant hell ever since.
Give us one good reason why we shouldn't send the three of
you back to Golgotha in several small packages, to express
our extreme displeasure?"

Random smiled, entirely unmoved. "Firstly, the lack of
military satellites and the disrupted weather are all that keep
the Wolfes from calling in an Imperial starcruiser to selec-
tively scorch the planet's surface down to whatever level
necessary to wipe you all out. Secondly, the only reason the
Wolfes haven't brought in a complete army of mercenaries
to deal with you is because it would cost them more than it's
worth. Start getting too successful too quickly, and they
might change their minds. And thirdly, if any one of us is
harmed, Golgotha will disown you and you'll never see any
help from the outside. Have I missed anything?"

"Just one," said Storm. "It's only a matter of time before
the Empire provides the Wolfes with new military satellites,
with sensors powerful enough to punch right through the
weather, to ensure uninterrupted production of the new
stardrive. And that will be the end of all surface fighting, as
far as you're concerned. It could also be the end of your first
real chance of winning in years. Forget the screwup with the

cyberats. That was a long time ago. Let us help, before your time runs out."

"And if one of you so much as even looks at us funny," said Ruby Journey, "I will personally kick that person's ass up around his ears."

Everyone paused to look at Ruby. Absolutely no one present doubted that she meant it. Random coughed politely, to bring their attention back to him.

"According to our reports, your war has been going well of late. Tell us about that."

"The size and number of our tunnels limits the ways the Wolfe security forces can attack us down here," said Ragged Tom in a high chilly voice. "And we're more adapted to the conditions than they are. They don't like coming down this deep. Too many nasty things live down here apart from us. Up on the surface, things are much the same. Our ancestors were genetically engineered to withstand the worse this planet could throw at us. The Wolfe troops don't have our advantages. Just superior numbers and better weapons. But they're only fighting to win; we're fighting to survive. Which is why the trenches are pretty much as they always have been, with neither side holding an advantage for long."

"We don't give up," said Specter Alice in a harsh cracked voice. "We're the refuse, the thrown away, the discarded. We're the Rejects, and we're proud of it. We reject the Empire and all it stands for. The Wolfes are just the latest face the enemy wears. So don't think we're so desperate we'll take your help and never ask the price. We won't swap one master for another. We'll fight and die alone, if need be. So help us or be damned. We bow to no one."

"I like her," said Ruby.

"You would," said Random.

"There's no price for our help," said Storm, smiling reassuringly around him. "All we seek are allies against the Empire, to help in the overthrow of the Iron Bitch. You need fighters, weapons, supplies. We can give you these."

"There is . . . a further complication," said Tall John.

"Didn't you just know he was going to say that?" murmured Ruby.

"Shut up," murmured Random.

"We're not just fighting for ourselves," said Ragged Tom. "We're also fighting to free the clones working in the factory complex. Like us, they were brought here to work until it killed them. Now they work, eat, exercise, and sleep in the complex. Like us, they rarely see the open sky. If one dies, the Wolfes just clone a replacement from the dead body. They're designed, bred, and trained specifically for the work they do here; work too dirty and too dangerous for humans. They're conditioned never to object, despite the awful conditions they work and live in. They're property. But still, sometimes they dream of freedom. A very few manage to escape. They come here to us because there's nowhere else they can go. There's always a home for them here. They are our brothers and sisters. The Wolfes know this. They've threatened to kill all the clone workers if it looks like our forces will prevent the factory from opening on time for the ceremony. They'd do it."

"Yes," said a quiet new voice. "They would."

Everyone looked around as a tall slender man wrapped in ill-fitting furs stood up in the front row of the seats. His face was drawn and gaunt, his mouth a thin line, his eyes sunk deep in their sockets. There was hardly anything to him, as though the smallest breath of wind would carry him away. His legs trembled as though they could barely sustain his small weight. But his gaze was steady, and when he spoke his quiet voice was firm and measured.

"I'm Long Lankin 32. A clone from the factory. They're working us to death, to make sure the ceremony will take place on time. The work itself is dangerous. Exposure to the forces involved eats away at our flesh and our minds. They can treat us as they wish. No one says anything. The Empress wants her new stardrive. Go ahead and attack. Let them kill us all. The hell they'd send us to can't be worse than the hell we live and work in every day. But if you could free us, we'd fight for you against the Empire to the last drop of our blood."

He sat down suddenly, as though afraid his legs would no longer support him. A loud murmur of encouragement and support ran around the watching audience. Storm nodded soberly.

"He meant it. I'm impressed. It's rare as hell for a clone to break away from his conditioning that much. If they're all like him, we'd have an army I'd back against anyone. Even trained Empire troops."

Random nodded, but said nothing. While he had no doubt Long Lankin's every word had been true and from the heart,

he also knew a good publicity stunt when he saw one. The
council had put him up to it, to take the edge off their *further complication*. The council had probably even written
his little speech for him, to be sure of having the maximum
effect on the audience and the newcomers. It was what Random would have done. However, Random had been a professional rebel long enough not to let his emotions sway
him. His mission on Technos III was to stop stardrive production, and if that meant destroying the factory completely,
along with all the clones in it, that was what he'd do. Of
course, if he could work out a way to aid the Rejects in res-
cuing the clones first, he'd happily do that. It was, after all,
why he'd become a professional rebel in the first place.

"Trench warfare's nothing new to me," he said finally.
"We've put in our time in the trenches, haven't we, Alex?
Of course, we were younger then. Same with fighting underground. Nothing new about tunnel rats or the blood they
spill that the sun will never see. I'm not going to insult you
by offering advice on how to fight. I've got a feeling you already know more about that than I'll ever know. But Alex
and I have been fighting the Empire all our lives, too. We
know strategies and tricks of the trade that might just give
you an edge over the Wolfe security forces and the Church
troops. We know how their minds work.

"I know you're disappointed that there's only the three of
us. But people are flocking to the underground movement on
hundreds of worlds, all spoiling for a chance to strike back
against the Empire. And unfortunately, there's only so many
Golgotha advisers to go around. You have Jack Random's
word that you'll get everything you need, in time. But for
the moment it's imperative that the Empress be denied the
new stardrive the Wolfe factory is producing. With a fleet
powered by the new drive, Lionstone could finally be unbeatable. That's why we're here. To help you stop production and, if possible, overthrow the Wolfes. Then it'll be up
to you to hold this planet while we take on the rest of the
Empire. We'll do everything we can to help you. There
might only be three of us, but you'll be surprised what we
can do."

"In other words," said Specter Alice, fixing him with her
disturbing stare, "you want to just walk in here, take over,
and run things yourself. Be the big hero one more time.
Right?"

"No," said Random. "I've done that. I'm here to lead only by example. To fight beside you in the frontline. To show you what I've learned in all my years as a professional rebel. Ruby and Alex will be fighting, too, in their different ways. You asked for help; we're here. And together we'll tear that factory apart."

The four Reject leaders moved together and murmured urgently to each other. A loud growl of debate filled the chamber as the onlookers discussed what they'd heard. Random looked casually about him, but was damned if he could tell from any of their faces how his speech had gone over. He thought he'd pushed all the right buttons, but it was hard to be sure. He'd been quite serious. He didn't want to lead them, but he needed to fight beside them. If only to prove to himself that he could still do it. That the legendary Jack Random hadn't died after all in the Golgotha interrogation cells.

He had to admit, the Rejects hadn't seemed at all impressed by him so far. He didn't blame them—much. He was a man in his late forties who looked twenty years older, despite all the improvements the Maze had worked in him. A sudden sound caught his attention, and he looked around sharply. It was a grating, sliding sound, but he couldn't locate its source. The cavern floor began to vibrate under his feet, almost as though a train was going past. The four members of the council broke off their deliberations and looked down at the floor. Their faces hardened, and they drew their swords. People began to stand up in the ranked seating.

"What is it?" said Storm. "What's happening?"

"Crawlers," said Tall John. "Creatures from the depths. They tunnel through metal like it isn't there. Eat anything that doesn't fight back, and most that does."

Ruby Journey's hand dropped to her side where her sword should have been, and then she cursed dispassionately as she remembered she'd agreed to come unarmed. Storm looked quickly about him. Random put a comforting hand on his shoulder.

"Don't worry," said Throat-slitter Mary, hefting her sword. "We'll defend you."

And that was when the floor next to Random cracked open, and a blunt scaly head burst up out of the floor, rising up on a long undulating neck. The head was a good four feet wide, its body thick as two men. It had a wide-gaping mouth

full of jagged teeth, and no eyes. There was bedlam around
the walls as the people in the lower seats tried to climb away
from the danger and up into the higher seats. Tall John
struck at the beast's neck with his sword, and the blade just
bounced away from the thick scales. The broad head swung
around and slammed into him, knocking him off his feet.
People were yelling for someone to bring energy guns.

Random stepped forward and hit the long undulating neck
with all his strength. His fist punched clean through the
scales and sank deep into the flesh within. The beast
screamed, a high, harsh sound that grated on the ear. Random braced himself and pushed his hand in deeper. The
beast convulsed, black blood springing from its mouth, but
Random wouldn't be thrown off. His arm sank into the
scaled neck up to his elbow, and then his hand found the
long curving spine. It took only a moment to close his hand
around the spine and snap it in one quick movement. The
beast shuddered the length of its visible body, and then collapsed dead on the chamber floor.

For a moment there was utter silence, and then the chamber erupted with cheers and applause from the watching
Rejects. The four council members were staring at him with
open mouths, and then they put away their swords so they
could applaud, too. Random grinned. It seemed he'd finally
managed to impress them. Storm was shaking his head in
disbelief. Random pulled his bloody arm out of the crawler's
neck. Ruby handed him a handkerchief to clean himself off
with and leaned in close beside him to murmur in his ear.

"Show-off."

And the war went on.

It was spring, and the temperature soared. The snow and
ice melted, flooding the trenches. Life erupted everywhere,
strange and deadly forms appearing out of nowhere to clog
the trenches and tunnels. It was spring, and hibernation was
over. They burst through the floors and the walls, aggressive
and carnivorous. Hungry plants, with reaching thorns,
thickly furred creatures that seemed mostly fangs and claws,
small and large and everything in between, all of them determined to seize their chance at life. They fought each other
for food and territory, and the winners fought the rebels for
control of the blood-splashed trenches and tunnels. The rebels fought back-to-back with swords and axes and the occa-

sional energy gun, forcing back the ravenous hordes as they
had done so many times before. The Wolfe security forces
fought the same battle, on the only day in the short year
when the two sides didn't make war on each other. And still
life exploded from every side, from acid-oozing leeches that
spattered the cracking walls, to great hulking creatures that
slowly dug their way up from the depths far below, old in-
stincts driving them on and up in search of light and warmth.
The waking world gave birth to bloodworms and barbed rip-
pers and spiked golems in their own organic armor. It was
spring, and the whole world was alive.

Jack Random and Ruby Journey fought side by side, their
flashing blades dripping alien blood and gore. They were
strong and fast, and they never grew tired. They seemed to
be everywhere at once in the great maze of tunnels, helping
where most needed, and nothing large or small could stand
against them. And Alexander Storm, who had once fought at
Random's side when he was young and in his prime and unbeatable with a sword, now worked to plot strategy and send
fighters where they could do the most good. He worked all
day with a small army of scouts and runners, and tried not
to think of himself as old.

The pressure of exploding life slowed as the day wore on,
and spring reached its halfway point. The Rejects under
Random and Ruby and Storm took control of their trenches
and tunnels again in record time. The Wolfe security forces
weren't far behind, but then they had more energy weapons.
The second day of spring dawned. The fauna and flora had
been taught their place again, and the rebels and Wolfe mercenaries were able to turn their attention back to the more
serious business of war.

The rain slammed down in a never-ending torrent. The
trenches filled ankle-deep with icy water, the levels always
rising just a little faster than it could drain away. The Rejects
splashed through the water to their positions, waiting for the
signal. Then the whistles blew, and both sides boiled up out
of their trenches to meet in the no-man's-land between. Ar-
rows flashed and energy guns roared, and then there was
only close quarters and the harsh thudding of steel cutting
into flesh and bone. Tides swept this way and that in the
great milling mob as two armies became only so many individual struggles, and every man lost track of his fellows.
Men and women screamed and died, and blood pooled

briefly on the jagged metal floor before the driving rain washed it away.

The fighting surged back and forth, and both sides searched for an advantage they could hold and exploit. The fighters fell and the rains fell, and men and women became dim shapes in the downpour. Some went mad in the horror of the battlefield and the never-ending pressure of the rain, and struck wildly about them, never minding friend or foe. The air became so moist it was hard to breathe. The rain filled eyes and ears and mouths. And still both sides fought on. It was what they did. Random and Ruby fought back-to-back, their swords leaping and striking impossibly fast, and no one could stand against them. Rebels and mercenaries died around them but they went on, unflinching, unbeatable, until finally the whistles blew and both sides fell back, dragging the dead and the wounded with them to the safety of the trenches and tunnels. The rain fell. And that was the second day of spring.

Summer dawned. The rain stopped as though someone had turned off a tap, and the heat rose and rose until it became unbearable, and then went on rising. Water in the trenches turned to steam. The blistering air seared lungs, and every move in the awful heat became an effort. The sun was blinding in a brilliant sky. The Wolfe security forces climbed into specially designed cooling suits. The rebels didn't need them. Neither, to practically everyone's surprise, did Random and Ruby. They just adapted. And when the whistles blew, both sides came howling out of their trenches to fight again. Swords sheathed in bellies, and heads blew apart like rotten fruit as they were touched in passing by energy beams. A rebel screamed as an ax sheared through his arm, and a mercenary spluttered blood as half his face was cut away. Men and women stamped this way and that, fighting for room to swing a sword. The dead and the wounded fell to be trampled underfoot as others struggled to reach the enemy. Screams of rage and pain filled the air along with the war cries. The uneven ground was a crimson mess of blood and worse. At the end of the day the whistles blew and both sides fell back. They took the wounded with them. Wounds festered quickly in the inhuman heat. The dead were left to spoil, to be recovered later, when the heat dropped a little during the night.

Some people volunteered to fight in the night. Small patrols of men and women from both sides for whom the need for vengeance and slaughter had not been burned away during the day. They crept out onto the pitch-black battlefield to fight and die in sudden, silent encounters in the night. Back in the trenches and the tunnels, most got what sleep they could in the stifling heat. The second day of summer came, and the temperature rose still further, a killing heat for all but the strongest. And still both sides came roaring up out of their trenches when the whistles blew. There was killing to be done.

Then it was Autumn, and the temperature dropped like a stone. The whistles blew, and men and women went up and over the top to fight again. The jagged metal killing field was already dark crimson from the splashed blood and offal of the previous day's battle, baked onto the metal by the merciless summer sun. Gale force winds arose, blowing suddenly out of nowhere, strong enough to pick up a man and carry him away. Both sides wore weights on their belts and in their boots to hold them down. The winds picked up scattered metal fragments from miles around and swept them on at blinding speed. Razorstorms that could strip unprotected flesh down to the bone in seconds. Both sides wore armor, which slowed them down even more. Battles became slow, farcical affairs, but blood still spilled, and neither the wounded nor the dead saw the joke.

And finally, winter came again: snow and ice and blizzards and the killing cold. The security forces wore special thermal suits. The rebels didn't need them. Neither did Random and Ruby. They'd adapted. Both sides wore thick goggles, to keep the driving snow out of their eyes. No-man's-land became a blinding white glare of snow and ice, in which small groups of armed men and women moved slowly, silently together, straining their eyes against the storm for signs of the enemy. Blood spattered the snow, red on white, and fighters crashed to the ground and did not move again. Jack Random and Ruby Journey fought on, going out again and again, whatever the weather, or which shift it was. The Rejects roared their names as battle cries and followed them into battle whatever the odds. The cold seared their lungs and chilled the blood in their veins, but their rage was hotter than any cold the winter could throw at them. Two days passed and winter gave way to spring, and it all began again. And that was how the years passed on Technos III.

Through it all, the weather and the hate and the killing, only one side pressed forward. Step by step, yard by yard, the Rejects drove the Wolfe security forces back, pushing no-man's-land closer and closer to the factory complex, as trench after trench fell and was occupied by the rebels. Jack Random and Ruby Journey were everywhere, inspiring the Rejects to new heights of courage and ferocity, and scaring the hell out of even hardened Wolfe mercenaries, and neither the weather nor the enemy could touch them or slow them down. The name of the legendary professional rebel was voiced frequently on both sides now, and that of his deadly new companion; the old legend and the new, who could not be stopped or turned aside. And down in the rebel tunnels, Alexander Storm, who had once been a not-so-minor legend in his own right, worked constantly, tirelessly, plotting strategies with the rebel council, organizing raids and advances, and keeping the tunnels clear of ravenous life-forms that didn't know there was a war going on. And in the few moments he had to himself, he tried hard not to dwell on the fact that he was old, and his longtime friend and companion Jack wasn't, any longer.

Out in no-man's-land, Jack Random felt fitter and stronger than ever, and his sword arm never seemed to tire. He felt like himself again, the legendary hero at whose name the Iron Throne itself had trembled. And if he looked a little younger than he had, only Ruby Journey noticed. And she kept it to herself. The Rejects roared their names and pressed forward, scenting victory.

And good men and women died, as well as bad, and the Sisters of Mercy did what they could for the wounded.

And the war went on.

Daniel and Stephanie Wolfe waited impatiently in what passed for the main reception hall of the factory complex. It was actually just a large storage area that wasn't being used for anything else, but some brave soul had tried to brighten it up with a red carpet and a few flowers here and there. The carpet was just a little tatty, but the flowers bloomed brightly despite the complex's artificially controlled environment. Not being fed or watered for days at a time, they were used to a much rougher life in the world outside.

Daniel scowled fiercely, tapping one foot impatiently and hugging himself to keep from flying apart. Things had not been going at all well for the Wolfes lately, and this particular meeting had the potential for a really major screwup. One badly chosen word, and if he was lucky he'd only be sent home in disgrace. Stephanie stood at his side, cool and calm and very controlled. If only because one of them had to be. By rights, Michel and Lily should have been there, too, to greet such an important new arrival, but Stephanie had decided very early on that they couldn't be trusted to behave themselves. So she had their food drugged and locked them in their rooms, just in case. Officially, they were indisposed, which was true enough. And Cardinal Kassar's presence had not been requested. He'd tried everything, up to and including not so veiled threats, to inveigle an invitation, but Stephanie had no intention of being upstaged. This was a Wolfe affair, and the new arrival was their guest. Kassar could meet him later. Much later.

The only two people she hadn't been able to keep out were Toby Shreck and his cameraman Flynn. The Empress had personally let it be known that she wanted the new arrival's reception carried live on holovision, and though she hadn't deigned to explain why, what Lionstone wanted, Lionstone got—if you were fond of breathing. So Toby and Flynn set up their lights and faded as far into the background as they could, trying hard not to be noticed. This was one show they were determined not to be thrown out of. It wasn't every day you got a chance to film the legendary Half A Man himself, in what remained of his flesh.

There weren't many in the Empire who didn't know the cruel and terrible history of Half A Man. Just over two hundred years ago, he'd had a far too close encounter with a species of alien still not identified or reencountered. He'd been abducted right out of the command chair of his own starcruiser, the *Beowulf,* disappearing in full view of his bridge crew. There'd been no warning, no trace of alien ship or presence. He was just there one minute and gone the next.

The aliens held on to him for three years, performing experiments on him that he remembered only partially, in his worst nightmares. Mostly, he remembered screaming. Then they sent him back, dropping him out of nowhere onto the bridge of the *Beowulf,* even though the ship was halfway across the Empire from where it had been. And that was when the nightmare really began. The aliens sent only half of him back. The left half. He'd been split right down the middle, from scalp to crotch, his right half replaced by an energy construct of roughly human shape.

The then Emperor had him examined by the finest scientists and medics of that time, but none of them came up with any explanation worth a damn. They couldn't even agree on why he was still alive, never mind what had happened to him. His right half was now composed of an energy field that had all the properties of matter, but was still clearly energy, though of a form the Empire had never encountered before. The whole Empire was placed on Red Alert for over a year, in case the aliens showed up again. But they didn't, and eventually everyone stood down from Red Alert and calmed down a little. Half A Man, as he'd been named almost immediately by the tabloid news channels, became a main adviser to the Emperor on alien matters and continued to hold that position as years passed, Emperors died, and his human half grew no older by a day. Now, as then, he was largely responsible for setting alien policy within the Empire, and if anyone felt like arguing with him, all it took was one close look at what aliens had done to him to change their minds.

Half A Man was also responsible for the creation of the Investigators. He felt the Empire needed a body of men and women specially qualified to deal with any and all alien threats. He trained them all personally, then and now, in the best ways to understand, control, and kill aliens. The Investigators worshiped him. Which had been known to make the various occupants of the Iron Throne just a little uneasy, down the years. There was no denying the Investigators were necessary and highly proficient at their job, but if they were ever to band together, possibly under Half A Man, it was doubtful if there was a force anywhere within the Empire that could stand against them. Luckily for all concerned, Investigators were by nature a solitary breed who did not care for each other's company. The only thing they had in common was Half A Man. They'd die for Half A Man. Or kill for him. Which was why he'd come to Technos III.

Toby Shreck was fascinated by the man, and so was Flynn, though both of them tried hard not to show it. Half A Man had displayed no fondness for publicity after his return, particularly after the way the tabloids hounded him, and he'd shunned the media spotlight for decades, rarely appearing in public except when ordered to by the Emperor of the day. As a result, coverage of the man tended to be few and far between, and any reporter with new footage could practically name his own price. The reception itself would be going out live, but Toby had no doubt he could sneak some extra footage afterward. Maybe even get an interview. If Half A Man didn't kill him on the spot just for asking. There were rumors.

Everyone's head turned as they heard a particular sound approaching down the corridor outside the reception hall. The sound of one foot tapping on the metal floor. They all drew themselves up to look their best and unconsciously braced themselves. The door swung open, and Half A Man came in. Toby's first thought was *That's not so bad. I can handle that.* He hadn't been sure how he'd react to such an awful sight in the flesh, so to speak. But the human half looked human enough, and the glowing spitting energy half was just energy.

The human half was a little over six feet tall, in good shape, and conservatively dressed. The half a face was subtly disturbing, but the hair was a common enough dark brown, as was the single eye, and the half a mouth was set and firm. Toby couldn't read any emotion in the mouth or the eye. There wasn't enough information in half a face. He couldn't even decide if it had once been handsome or not. The energy half was entirely human in space, though it spat and crackled constantly. But Toby had a sick feeling it wasn't even close to the same shape as the human half. It had no particular color, or perhaps it was all colors. And it wasn't just its brightness that made it hard to look at.

Toby tore his gaze away from Half A Man, and checked quickly that all his lights were working and in the right place. He and Flynn had had to guess at the exposures. He glanced at Flynn and was relieved to see the camera on his shoulder was already silently capturing everything. Billions of people were watching this meeting live, in this sector alone, and if he didn't screw this up completely, Toby Shreck could finally be on his way to being accepted as a real reporter.

The two Wolfes stepped forward to officially greet Half A Man, then stopped as three newcomers stepped silently through the open door, wearing the formal blue and silver cloaks of the Investigator. Stephanie and Daniel gaped openly. Toby's blood ran cold. Three Investigators together in the same room? This was unheard of. No one had said anything about this. Toby glared at Flynn to make sure he kept filming. There was an even bigger story here than he'd thought.

"Daniel and Stephanie Wolfe," said Half A Man in a perfectly normal voice, "allow me to present my three companions; they are the Investigators Edge, Barr, and Shoal."

Each Investigator bowed briefly as they were named. Edge was a tall, slender man well into his fifties. His long face came to a sharp point at his chin, and his eyes were too wide and too bright. His slight scowl was openly contemptuous. Barr stood like a soldier, every muscle to attention, short and square like a bulldog. He was clearly into his sixties, with close-cropped gunmetal hair. He looked like he was just waiting for an order to kill somebody. Shoal was the youngest, a medium height, compact woman in her late forties, with dark spiky hair and a cool gaze. Toby thought he saw a smile lurking in one corner of her generous mouth, but since she was an Investigator, he was probably wrong. It was common knowledge Investigators smiled only when they were killing. Preferably whole alien species. Slowly. And then Edge spotted the holocamera, and everything went to hell in a hurry.

"Turn that bloody thing off," said Edge, a sword already in his hand. He advanced on Flynn, who backed quickly away, still filming. Flynn had worked in combat zones and knew the first rule of reporting was to keep filming, no matter what. Edge loomed over him, sword ready for a killing thrust. "I said turn it off! No one films me. No one."

Toby stepped forward, hands raised placatingly. "It's on the Empress's orders. She wants a complete record . . ."

Edge spun around with blinding speed and hit Toby across the face with the back of his hand. Toby hit the floor hard and fought to clear his head. Blood poured down over his mouth from one nostril, and he spat it away. He got one knee under him and then had to stop as his head swam sickly. Flynn had backed up against a wall and couldn't retreat any farther. He was still filming. Toby struggled to find the words that would defuse the situation. There had to be something he could say. He always knew what to say.

"Leave the man alone, Edge," said Barr, his voice thick

and slightly slurred. "We obey the Empress's commands—in all things."

"Shut up, you sycophant," said Edge, not looking around. He had his sword pointed at Flynn's throat. "Throw that camera down and smash it, boy. I want to hear it crunch under your heel."

Flynn tried to say *Go to hell,* but couldn't get the words out of his throat. You didn't talk like that to Investigators—particularly those with a killing madness in their eyes. But he still wouldn't surrender his camera. Edge smiled suddenly, and Flynn's blood ran cold.

"Leave him alone," said Shoal. Her voice was calm and quietly amused. "His kind are like rats. Kill one, and they'll all come swarming around. You heard the man. This is the Empress's idea. You really want to be dragged before her in chains, to explain why you disobeyed a direct order?"

"What can she do to me?" said Edge. "You know why we're here. Too old or too frail to be trusted in the field anymore, but too dangerous to be allowed to run loose. We're not allowed to work for the Clans anymore. We were doing too good a job. She's frightened of us. Of what we might do. I spent all my life in her service, and for what? To end up on this shitball as local enforcers. She wants this event covered? I'll give the precious viewers something to watch they won't forget in a hurry."

He drew back his sword for a thrust that would take Flynn low in the belly. Flynn couldn't move. Toby surged dizzily to his feet, blood spilling down his chin from his smashed nose. He was probably just going to die along with Flynn, but he couldn't just stand by and watch his cameraman being killed. And then Shoal stepped forward and hit Edge professionally on the back of the neck. Edge slumped forward onto his knees, the sword dropping from his suddenly limp finger. Barr looked shocked, but said nothing. Shoal smiled down at the dazed figure before her.

"Do as you're told, Edge, or I'll put a muzzle on you."

"Nicely handled, Shoal," said Half A Man. He nodded to Daniel and Stephanie. "My apologies. Edge has his good qualities, but diplomacy isn't one of them. I'll keep him on a short leash in the future. I suggest we bring this meeting to a close. We've already given the viewing public plenty to gossip about, and I'm eager to begin my work here. Are the files ready?"

"Everything you requested," said Stephanie. "Maps, histories, troop details."

"Might I inquire on behalf of the viewing public, just what your purpose here is, sir?" said Toby.

Half A Man turned his single eye to look at Toby, who was now standing more or less steadily with a handkerchief pressed to his swelling mouth and nose. Half A Man smiled with his half a mouth. "Persistent type, aren't you? Surely, you must have realized by now that asking the wrong questions here can be hazardous to your health?"

"All part of the job, sir," said Toby, lowering the handkerchief so his words could be heard clearly and ignoring the blood that still dripped from his chin. "Would you care to make a comment at this time?"

"Not really," said Half A Man. "But after my associate's outburst, I suppose I'd better." He turned a little to face Flynn's camera directly. His energy half spat and sputtered, and Flynn had to quickly crank down the camera's light sensitivity. Half A Man half smiled for the viewers. "The Empress has decided that those Investigators who are no longer able to give one hundred percent in the field, either through age or injury, will no longer be allowed to retire to work for individual Clans. The privilege was being abused. In future, such Investigators will be trained to work together with armed forces in especially dangerous trouble spots, where their knowledge and experience will be invaluable. This is to be a pilot scheme, to be observed and studied for its successes and limitations. As trainer of all Investigators, I volunteered to oversee the operation. And that is all I have to say. Except that in future, I expect all news teams to keep a respectful distance. For their own safety." He turned back to Stephanie and Daniel. "I'm finished here. Take me to your war room. Shoal, Barr, bring Edge."

And as quickly as that, they all filed out and were gone, Edge staggering along between Shoal and Barr. Toby and Flynn waited until the door had closed securely behind them and then relaxed with explosive sighs of relief. Flynn turned off the camera and concentrated on breathing deeply. Toby dabbed gingerly with his handkerchief at his tender mouth and nose, both of which felt as though they'd swollen to double their proper size.

"Did you get all that, Flynn? Tell me you got all that."

"Every damn second," said the cameraman. "Even though

I nearly had an unpleasant incident in my underwear doing it. I really thought he was going to kill me."

"Of course he was. He's an Investigator. Luckily, we were going out live, and the others were sharp enough to know what that meant. The whole point of this new scheme is to show that aging Investigators can still be controlled and employed in useful ways. Half A Man couldn't afford to have Edge going berserk in front of billions of viewers before the scheme had even properly begun. Did you pick up on what he said about the Clans? No more Investigators to work as enforcers and assassins for the Families. Her Imperial Majesty would appear to be getting concerned about the growing power and influence of certain prominent Houses. Naming no names, of course. But you can bet it's no accident the pilot scheme is taking place on a Wolfe planet."

"Of course," said Flynn. "Makes you wonder what'll happen to those Investigators who can't hack it as part of a team. They've always been trained to act as individuals. Hell, I've heard of Investigators who overruled Captains on their own starships. I can't see Lionstone allowing them to just retire. Or an Investigator happy to spend the rest of his days sitting by the fire bouncing his grandchildren on his knee."

"Good point," said Toby, looking sadly at the blood-stained mess that had once been a perfectly good handkerchief. "I get a strong feeling it'll be a case of learn to fit in, or else. As in, die with your boots on or under an executioner's warrant. I wonder how that's going to go down with the other Investigators."

"They'll probably approve. They're a cold bunch of bastards when all's said and done. Not many survive to reach retirement age anyway. It's that kind of job. Probably prefer to die fighting, given the chance."

"Or they might just prefer to take somebody with them," said Toby. "Maybe even a lot of somebodies. In future, I think we'll keep a very respectful distance from Investigator Edge."

"Damn right," said Flynn. He looked at Toby thoughtfully. "I saw you trying to get up and help me. Were you worried about losing me or your only cameraman?"

"To be honest," said Toby, "I was mostly worried that if you got killed, they'd find out about the lacy underwear

you've got on under your clothes. I mean, I have my reputation to think of."

When the meeting in the war room was finally over, the
Wolfes invited Half A Man and the three Investigators to
join them for a meal and several drinks; but they all declined, more or less politely. Investigators weren't social
creatures, and Half A Man hated being stared at. For a long
time he hoped that eventually he'd get used to it, but he
never did. And the Wolfes weren't even subtle about it, for
all their smiles and pleasant words. So Half A Man saw each
of his Investigators to their separate quarters, had a few private but very emphatic words with Edge, and then allowed
himself to be shown to his own quarters.

The flunky they'd assigned to escort him to his quarters
kept a lot of distance between himself and his charge, and
didn't hang around for a tip. Half A Man looked around the
single room. All the necessities, and even a few luxuries.
More than he'd been supplied with on the ship that brought
him here in such a hurry. Not that he gave much of a damn.
He was here to work, not lounge around.

He sat down on the single chair, turned off the massage
function, and pulled it up to the writing table. He activated
the built-in viewscreen, accessed the complex's computers,
and called up the local troop records. Mercenaries from a
hundred worlds, under a dozen company commanders, with
Wolfe security people as overall supervisors. The mercenaries had mostly good records before they came to Technos
III. Their battles with the local rebels, the Rejects, made interesting but depressing reading. Neither side could be said
to have an overall advantage, but just by refusing to be
beaten for so long, the rebels were winning. The reason
was obvious. It was the Rejects' world, and they worked
with it, while the Wolfe troops needed temperature-control
suits, armor, and re-breathers just to cope with the changing
weather. What technical advantages the Wolfe troops had
were pretty much wiped out by the weather, and both sides
knew it.

The Wolfes had lost a lot of men fighting the rebels.
There were no figures for the Reject dead, but Half A Man
doubted they were anywhere near as high. The few captured
Rejects never talked. They died under interrogation when
they couldn't manage to kill themselves first. And on top of

all that, it appeared the rebels now had new leaders, recently arrived from offworld. No less than the legendary Jack Random himself, the professional rebel, if the Wolfes' reports were to be believed. Half A Man had followed Random's career down the years. He'd always known that someday they were fated to meet. The two great legends of modern times. He frowned slightly. The last he'd heard, Random had been a broken old man. These reports spoke of a younger man, a powerful fighter. Perhaps some newcomer had taken up the old name. He sighed and shut down the screen. As if he didn't have enough problems in his life. Including, most especially, the three Investigators the Empress had placed under his command.

He'd always known Edge was going to be a problem. The man was a psychotic killer, violent and insubordinate. In any other occupation these would have been serious drawbacks, but in an Investigator they were a positive bonus. Up till now, his surly behavior and occasional regrettable incidents had been tolerated because he never failed to get the job done, one way or another. But now he was getting older and slower, and the job was sometimes too much for him, though he'd never admit it. He showed less and less self-control, and clearly enjoyed the blood he spilled during his violent outbursts. You could never tell what would set him off. He had no friends, and his enemies daren't touch an Investigator.

He didn't respond to reason, kindness, or military discipline. To control him in the field, you had to prove you were the better man and keep on proving it, by brute force if necessary. In a working Investigator such qualities could be condoned, even encouraged on occasion, but in a man close to enforced retirement, he was a danger to himself and everyone around him. It helped that Edge was somewhat intimidated by Half A Man's legend, but then, most people were.

Barr was the other end of the spectrum. A military man through and through, gung ho and eager for battle, dedicated to the Empire and its Empress. A dangerous fighter with any weapon, he was never happier than in the midst of action, probably because he had no social skills whatsoever. He didn't like people. Luckily, he liked aliens even less. He was here on Technos III because he'd been ordered here, and he'd fight and kill and if need be die to carry out those orders. Or at least, he always had in the past. Now that his Empress had apparently lost faith in him and was contemplating retiring him from the field, he might start feeling differently about things. He wasn't stupid, just single-minded. He wouldn't retire from action. He had nothing to retire to. He'd bear watching.

Shoal was a whole different kind of problem. Sharp, bright, and terrifyingly efficient, Shoal was one of the top ten Investigators in the field at the moment, and she knew it. She was dying slowly of a rare degenerative nerve disease. There was no cure except for regeneration, and that was available only to the aristocracy. If she'd been young and in her prime, Half A Man might have been able to get her an exception, as a personal favor to him. But even before the disease took hold, there'd been talk she was getting older, slowing down. The Investigator's life was a hard and brutal one. She wasn't bitter. She was a good soldier. For the moment her faculties were still clear, and her experience would be invaluable. He could rely on her—probably.

Half A Man pushed his chair away from the table, stood up, and moved over to the bed. He lay down on it without bothering to pull back the bedclothes. He didn't sleep anymore. Hadn't since the aliens worked on him. But he still made a point of resting a few hours every night so he could dream. Sometimes in his dreams he remembered some of the things they'd done to him, and then he woke screaming. But he needed to dream. He had to remember exactly what had been done to him. All of it, no matter how bad it got. Because the real horror was that the change they'd worked in him wasn't over yet. Every year the energy construct that made up the right half of his body grew a little larger, by eating up a little more of his human half. Only a very little. But it was an ongoing process that showed no signs of stopping or even slowing down. Eventually, all his humanity would be gone, and he had no idea at all who or what he might be then.

It also seemed to him more and more that the energy half of his body was slowly changing shape, becoming gradually less human and more something else. Something alien. He had no memory of what the aliens who changed him looked like, except briefly in his nightmares, but he found the hints in his changing energy half disquieting and disturbing. But even worse than that, he was beginning to worry that the energy half might have its own subordinate intelligence, its own secret thoughts, and just possibly its own hidden agenda. It was vital he hang on grimly to what was left of his humanity and his mind, for fear of what might replace it.

Which was one of the few reasons he had to be glad he was here on Technos III. It would be good to be back in the field again. Mostly he ran a desk these days, but the Empress had wanted results on Technos III fast, and he grabbed the chance with both hands. Things were so much simpler in battle. It always felt good to be killing the Empire's enemies. According to all the reports, the Rejects and their new leader, whoever he really was, would make a good enemy. They were clever, cunning, and brave fighters. A real challenge for once. He'd enjoy killing them. And just maybe he could use the occasion to teach Edge, Barr, and Shoal to be part of an armed fighting force. Why not? He'd taught them how to be Investigators in the first place.

Toby Shreck had charmed, persuaded, and bullied various factory personnel into letting him use part of the complex's communications center as a mixing room for the broadcast he had to put together for the next day. He had a hell of a lot of footage, courtesy of the redoubtable Flynn, who was probably currently relaxing in his quarters in a nice little twin set and pearls, hopefully behind a locked door, leaving Toby to do all the hard word of choosing which precious moments of recorded history would make it into the final mix. Toby glared at the viewscreens and control panels before him, poured himself another stiff drink, used it to wash down a couple of uppers, and stuck his cigar back in his mouth. Two in the morning, wired out of his skull, his fingers moving faster than his thoughts could follow. That was how you got your best work done. If you were Toby Shreck on a tight deadline.

He missed having room service to shout at, but otherwise this was business as usual. The whiskey burned in his chest and in his mind, the uppers hammered through his bloodstream, and the cigar smoke kept him balanced as he sorted the gold from the dross. He had to make this compilation look good. Really good. The live footage of Half A Man and his Investigators had made people sit up and take notice, and won him his best viewing share ever. But it hadn't made him any friends among his fellow reporters, who had been besieging the Wolfe complex with requests, demands, and pleas for entry visas ever since. The Wolfes, not surprisingly, were stonewalling. They still thought they could control things, as long as it was just Toby Shreck and his cameraman. Toby grinned around his cigar. He'd show them.

But he couldn't continue to rely on lucking into great found footage. He'd caught everyone's attention, but to hold onto it he'd have to follow up with a bloody good program about what was really going on down here on Technos III. It hadn't been easy. Everyone in and around the factory complex was being very careful about what they said in front of Toby, whether Flynn was with him or not. The word had come down from Above. Luckily, he already had enough good stuff to rock the Wolfes back in their luxuriously designed and expensive shoes. This particular compilation would make a fine example of what he could do, showing off his talent and establishing him as a major name in the news business. If it didn't get him killed first. It would also be a perfect thumbing of the nose to all those who had snubbed or insulted him. He rolled his cigar from one side of his mouth to the other, grabbed a few chocolates from the nearby box, and knocked back another belt of whiskey. He was supercharging now. Start with the Mother Bea footage. That was the mother lode.

He ran the tapes again, glaring in concentration at the tiny screens before him. He had two and sometimes three running at once, to keep up with his rocketing thoughts. Flynn had got some great panning shots of the hospital tent with the factory complex in the background, to show off the relative size of each. Then there were shots inside the tent, with the wounded lying still and silent, only sometimes moaning quietly on their narrow cots. He called up the master shot of Mother Superior Beatrice explaining who would and would not be allowed treatment, according to the Wolfes. Then a close-up of her tired, nearly defeated face.

"In the winter . . . I've seen the surgeons stop in mid operation to warm their hands in the steaming guts they've just opened up."

Yes, that would make them sit up and take notice. The Sisters of Mercy were well loved and well respected throughout the Empire. They weren't supposed to be forced to work in conditions like that, not even by the high and mighty Wolfes. Assuming, of course, he could smuggle this past the censors. There were a lot of people who thought they were in authority here who'd demand to see the tape in its entirety before it went out. Toby grinned around his cigar. He had an idea or two.

More whiskey and another chocolate.

The next tapes were from the brief interview Half A Man had reluctantly granted him. He hadn't wanted to, and Toby had had to use the Empress's name as a threat more than once just to get the man to stand still long enough for Flynn to point his camera at him. Half A Man looked even weirder on holo film. Something about the energy field that made up his right side interfered with the holocamera, giving the field a strobing, shimmering look that was actually painful to the eye after a while. Look at it long enough, and it felt like you were falling into it. Into a hell without end. Toby sniffed. He'd just have to do a lot of cutting back and forth between Half A Man and himself. It'd distract from Half A Man's speech, but he wasn't saying anything new. Toby leaned a little closer, frowning at the screen before him. The half a face was hard to read on its own, but there was no mistaking the sincerity in the harsh, clipped voice.

"Anything that distracts humanity from defending itself from invading aliens cannot be permitted to continue. It must and will be stopped, by whatever means necessary. The Empire needs the new stardrive this factory will produce. The rebels through their actions are threatening that production. I will put an end to that threat, even if it means wiping out the rebel population, down to the last man, woman, and child. The Empire must be protected. I know what aliens are capable of."

Toby pursed his mouth unhappily as he hit the tape stop. Any aliens who could produce such a thing as Half A Man had to be seen as a threat to humanity as a whole. But no one had seen a trace of those aliens for over two centuries. And there was always a chance negotiating with the rebels would put an end to the war a damn sight quicker than a ruthless program of genocide. They weren't asking that much. But Half A Man saw this as a matter of principle. And authority. He could be very single-minded for someone who no longer had a single mind, and he wouldn't even discuss the argument.

Toby's fingers moved quickly over the console keys, calling up quick shots of the three Investigators Half A Man had brought with him. Half A Man had refused point-blank to allow them to be interviewed, but Flynn had sneaked some footage anyway. Edge looked like a psycho killer who'd just had his favorite cutthroat razor stolen. Barr looked like a machine just waiting for orders. And Shoal ... looked like she'd seen it all before and hadn't been impressed the first time. They all looked very dangerous, completely unswerving, and entirely professional at what they did. Poor rebel bastards didn't know what was going to hit them.

That was when the control-room door burst open, and Daniel Wolfe strode in, only to come to a sudden halt as he discovered how little room there was. It rather spoiled the effect of his dramatic entrance. He scowled at Toby as the reporter turned unhurriedly around in his swivel chair. Daniel leaned forward menacingly, and Toby just happened to blow cigar smoke in his face. Daniel coughed despite himself and did his best to tower over Toby.

"Listen to me, worm. I want to see every inch of your tape before it's broadcast. This is a Wolfe complex, and we decide what leaves here and what doesn't. You even try and sneak something past me, and I'll have security throw you in the cells and have your superiors send a replacement who understands how the universe works. You'll like the cells. On a good day you can look through the bars in your window and see the wall we put traitors against before we shoot them. And out here, we decide who the traitors are. So make the Wolfes look good. Make the factory look good. If you know what's good for you. Little man."

He stormed out, slamming the door behind him. Toby lifted the bottle of whiskey, toasted the closed door with it, and drank straight from the bottle. He'd been expecting pressure, but nothing quite so blatant. Bloody Daniel Wolfe and his ambitious superbitch sister. She was the one behind the threats. Daniel didn't have it in him to come up with a speech like that on its own. Stephanie probably wrote it out and made him memorize it. Typical Wolfes. Thugs with pedigrees. A thought occurred to him, and he smiled nastily around his cigar.

He turned back to the mixing console, and it took only a few moments' searching to call up the footage he had in mind. He ran the shots in slow motion. Daniel and Stephanie together. Michel and Lily together. Smiles and glances and shared body space. Everyone with an eye in their head knew

Michel and Lily were having it off. They'd been very careful
not to say or do anything incriminating in public, but you
only had to look at their body language to see the truth of
how they felt about each other. The way their eyes sparkled
when they met, the way their bodies oriented on each other
no matter where they were in the room, the way certain
words and phrases were subtly, unconsciously emphasized.
He had it all on tape. They might as well have taken out
peak time ads.

Of course, Daniel and Stephanie hadn't noticed a thing,
being rather more interested in each other. In fact, some of
their quieter moments seemed to suggest that they might be
a little closer in their affections than most brothers and sisters. Toby sniggered and beat a fast tattoo on the edge of the
console with both hands. He couldn't say anything outright,
of course, but a little carefully arranged footage should do
the job for him, with both couples. People in society would
catch up on it and start the word spreading. Before too long
the Wolfes would become a laughingstock, in and out of
Court. That would teach Daniel bloody Wolfe to burst in and
act the heavy with poor little Toby Shreck.

And that was when the door burst open again, and Cardinal James Kassar had his try at making a dramatic entrance
ruined by crashing straight into the chair that Toby had
thoughtfully placed before the door after the last visit.
Kassar kicked the chair aside and glared at Toby, who leaned
back in his chair and gave the Cardinal his best innocent
face. It didn't fool Kassar for a moment, but then it wasn't
meant to.

"I've had a communication from my superiors in the
Church," said Kassar, the cold controlled anger in his voice
more than matched by the open fury in his ruined face. "The
gist of which was, your live broadcast made both myself and
the Church look ridiculous, because you didn't wait for me
to get there. They went on for some time, but they were basically just repeating themselves. The word 'laughingstock'
was mentioned, along with 'recall' and 'demotion.' Listen
carefully, you little toad, you are not going to ruin my career
while furthering your own. From now on I see everything
you've got before it goes out, and if you do anything that
might undermine my or the Church's authority here, I will
personally excommunicate you with a rusty saw. Is that
clear?"

"Oh, perfectly," said Toby. "Couldn't be clearer." He took a quick drink from his bottle. "I would offer you some whiskey, Cardinal, but I've only got the one bottle. I feel I should at this stage in all honesty point out that I do have principles."

"Mess with me again, and your principles will be going home in separate jars."

Kassar about-faced and marched out with extreme dignity, slamming the door behind him. Toby waited a cautious few seconds, and then gave the closed door the finger before getting up and jamming two small wedges under the bottom of the door. That should put an end to any more storming ins. He turned back to the console and leaned over the screens again. He knew just the bit of tape he wanted. A nice stretch of Cardinal Kassar drilling his Church troops in the blistering summer heat; standing at his ease in the shade while shouting and bullying and generally carrying on like the tight-assed little dictator he was. Toby grinned and bit down hard on his cigar. He wouldn't even have to sneak this past Kassar. The damn fool was so full of himself he'd probably think it made him look good.

Toby took another drink from his bottle and then put it firmly to one side. The uppers were rocketing through his system like ricocheting bullets, and he felt great. He called up some footage of the trenches surrounding the factory. The circles of hell from which no man returned unchanged. Patch in some shots of the elite Jesuit commandos drilling the fanatical Church troops, and then cut back to the wounded in the hospital tent. Toby rocked back and forth in his chair. Someone was banging on the door. The wedges would keep them out. Toby's fingers flowed over the keyboard. He was on a roll now. If the Wolfes and the Cardinal and all the other bastards thought they could keep him from filing the story of his life, they were crazy. They could view the tape as often as they liked; it wouldn't make any difference. They'd probably never even heard of the palimpsest method. Record something on a tape, then record over it. Playback just shows the upper recording, but the right kind of machine will pick up the earlier recording, still there, underneath. The process hadn't been around long, but Toby had always believed in being up to the minute. There'd be a stink afterward, but interest in Technos III would be so high the Wolfes wouldn't be able to censor him anymore. Toby

Shreck laughed aloud and worked on into the early hours of the morning.

A handful of Rejects led Jack Random, Alexander Storm, and Ruby Journey down through a series of dimly lit corridors and tunnels, far below the surface of Technos III. The tunnels grew increasingly narrow, sometimes barely wide enough for two men to walk abreast. The walls were smooth in some places, where they'd been blasted out of the living rock by energy weapons, and torn and jagged in others, where tools and bare hands had done the work. Random tried very hard not to think about the increasing weight of rock above his head. As the professional rebel, he'd spent his share of time working from hidden underground caverns and tunnels, away from prying eyes and sensors, but he'd never learned to like it.

The tunnels twisted and turned and branched endlessly, a dark maze of such complexity that any outsider would be helplessly lost in a few minutes. Random had no doubt that was deliberate. The Rejects didn't trust anyone with their secrets all at once, not even him. He'd have been disappointed in them if they had. As always, he knew exactly where he was, but he didn't like to tell them and spoil their fun. So he strode along quite happily, Ruby at his side, Storm puffing along behind him. Random was getting a little worried about Storm. His old friend had been in the field with him for many years, fighting the Empire's best on more planets than either of them cared to remember. But they'd both known they were getting too old for it, even before they got their asses kicked so conclusively on Cold Rock. Since then, Random had been given a new lease of life, courtesy of the Maze, and reveled in it, but Storm had been left behind, still growing older and slower. He hadn't taken the growing differences between him and Random at all well, but Random was at a loss what to do about it. Storm was doing good and valued work as an adviser and strategist, but it wasn't the same, and both of them knew it. So when Storm had insisted on coming along on this particular mission, just to stretch his legs, Random hadn't had the heart to say no.

"How many miles of these tunnels are there?" said Storm, trying to keep the tiredness out of his voice and failing.

"No one knows for sure," said Long Lankin 32. The ex-factory clone looked as thin and malnourished as ever. He found the going hard, too, but like Storm he refused to be left out of things, so the two of them had naturally gravitated together. "The only maps are in the Rejects' heads, and they only know part of the whole layout. So we're protected if any of us are captured. The Rejects have been digging these tunnels for centuries now, repairing old ones and blasting out new tunnels, so the maps are always changing. Sometimes I feel I need a guide just to help me find the toilet in the early hours of the morning.

"The Wolfe security forces dig tunnels of their own, too, just to complicate things. Sometimes the excavating teams run into each other, and then all hell breaks loose. The war goes on down here, as well. Tunnel rats clawing at each other in the darkness. The mercenaries don't last long in the tunnels. They can't take the constant darkness and claustrophobia. The pressure drives them crazy. The Rejects, on the other hand, actually like it down here. The protective layers of stone and metal make them feel secure. Crazy bastards. No offense, people."

The twenty or so Rejects walking with them smiled and nodded, not insulted. Alexander Storm summoned up enough breath for another question.

"How deep do these tunnels go? It feels like we've been descending for hours. Any further, and we'll need an express elevator to get back to the surface."

"The surface can do without us today," said Specter Alice. She'd developed a fondness for Storm and attached herself to him whenever possible, to his clear distress. She was after all old and short and ugly, and her furs hadn't been washed since they were still on the animals that provided them. And there was madness in her eyes, right up front where everyone could see it. She smiled chummily at Storm and tried to take his hand. He avoided it with the dexterity of long practice. She wasn't put out.

"We're heading down to one of our man meeting chambers," she said happily. "Time you saw where the real decisions get made. Don't worry; we won't go down too far. Dangerous things live in the deep down. Creatures that have adapted to the depths and the dark, away from the weather and the war. Mostly, we don't disturb them, and they don't massacre us. Don't worry, dear; you stick with old Specter Alice. She'll keep you safe."

Storm smiled weakly, not feeling at all safe, and looked

determinedly ahead in the hope of discouraging further conversation. Random had to hide a smile of his own. Storm had been something of a lady-killer in his day. At his side, Ruby sighed heavily, and he turned his attention to her. She was scowling, her mouth turned down sullenly.

"I hate walking," she said, apropos of nothing in particular. "I'm a bounty hunter, not a health freak. Where are all these tunnel rats and deadly creatures? I could do with a little excitement. I didn't come to Technos III to be a tourist. When do I get to kill somebody?"

"I like her," said Long Lankin 32. "She's got the right attitude."

They walked on and on. Storm had more and more trouble keeping up with the pace, even with Specter Alice at his side to encourage him. Random felt guilty. Every day he looked younger, felt younger, and Storm looked older. Where once they had been comrades in arms, now they looked more like father and son. Storm hadn't said anything yet, but Random knew his old friend was aware of the growing differences between them. Random tried not to think about the differences too much. He didn't like the idea that he might be becoming an altogether different person. Even if he did feel alive again for the first time in years. He fell back to walk beside Storm and wondered whether he did it out of friendship or pity.

"Why did we ever come here?" Storm said quietly to him. "War is young man's work. We're too old for this, Jack. We should be sitting beside a fire in a tavern, telling outrageous stories of our youth. We've earned that. We spilled enough blood, in enough battles. Why do we have to do it all again?"

"Because the war isn't over," said Random. "We swore an oath, remember? We swore upon our blood and our honor that we would fight the Empire until either it fell or we did."

"Young men swore that oath," said Storm. "Young men who knew nothing about war or politics, or the reality of how the Empire works."

"Are you saying you don't believe in the Cause anymore?"

"Of course I still believe in the Cause! I'm here, aren't I? I'm just saying it's time for someone else to carry the banner. Someone younger, who doesn't feel the cold in his bones or wake up coughing his lungs up every morning.

We've done our bit. And I'm too old to die on a strange world beside strange people, fighting to free a few clones from a factory."

"You'll get your second wind soon," said Random lamely. "You'll feel better then."

"Don't bloody patronize me, Random," said Storm, and they strode along in silence after that.

Until the Reject in the lead came to a sudden halt and raised a hand to stop those behind him. Everyone stood quietly together in the pool of the lanterns' light, staring into the gloom ahead of them, listening carefully. Storm looked anxiously about him, but Random and Specter Alice were too busy listening to pay him any attention. Random frowned, concentrating, reaching out with his altered senses. He could just make out a low, regular thudding, overlapping itself again and again, coming from somewhere up ahead in the tunnel.

"What is it?" he asked quietly. "What's coming?"

"Wolfe tunnel rats," said Specter Alice. "They have devices for detecting movement in nearby tunnels. They're close now. Brace yourselves."

And as suddenly as that, everyone had a weapon of some sort in their hands. Mostly, swords and axes, with the occasional length of spiked chain. Random and Ruby moved automatically to stand together, swords at the ready, leaving Storm to fend for himself. He glared at their unresponsive backs and hefted his own sword uncertainly. The steady thudding grew nearer and nearer. Random's free hand hovered over the disrupter on his belt, but he didn't draw it. He didn't like to think what a ricocheting energy beam would do in these close quarters. He just hoped the Wolfe fighters had had the same thought. The wall to his right cracked apart suddenly, torn from floor to ceiling, and men in armored battle suits lurched out into the tunnel. They moved surprisingly quickly amid the whine of supporting servo-mechanisms and tore into the massed group of rebels with massive axes and long swords that only powered armor could have wielded.

The two sides clashed together, the rebels darting around and among the slower armored men, searching out their blind spots and weak points with flashing swords and axes. There wasn't much room for maneuver in the confined space. Instead, there was an endlessly shifting, boiling mass of bodies packed together, taking a stand just long enough for a solid blow before slipping away again. The slower and the unlucky cried out, and blood spurted in the thick air, and those who fell to be trampled underfoot rarely rose to fight again. Swords and axes bounced harmlessly away from the solid plates of the Wolfe armor, but there were weaker, vulnerable spots at joints and junctures, for those who knew where to look for them. But the armored men could take a dozen hits and press on unharmed, while a blow powered by their servomotors could cut clean through a Reject's body. And there were far more armored men than Rejects.

One by one the rebels fell, pushed farther and farther back down the tunnel. Three armored men were down, dispatched by blows to neck or eyes, but only three out of many. Still the Rejects fought on, determined and far from desperate. Their long adaptation to Technos III's extremes had made them somewhat more than human, and they were much more used to the fighting conditions underground. They swarmed around the armored men, ducking and dodging blows with almost impossible speed, never letting up in their attack. And slowly, step-by-step, their retreat stopped.

Right in the thick of it all, Ruby Journey braced herself and swung her sword with both hands. The blade powered around in a tight arc and sheared clean through a soldier's armored neck. The helmeted head bounced away across the sea of heaving shoulders before finally falling to the floor, the look of astonishment still clear on the bloody face. Random laughed and roared his approval. He brought his sword around in an arc, only to see the blade bounce harmlessly back from a suddenly raised armored arm. The impact jarred the sword right out of his hand, and it fell to disappear in the mess of heaving bodies. The Wolfe mercenary grinned and drew back his sword for a killing thrust. Ruby saw and cried out, but she was too far away to help. Raw fury blazed up inside Random, and he punched his opponent in the chest with all his strength. His bare fist hammered through the battle armor and plunged on into the man's chest. The Wolfe soldier screamed horribly as Random's fist closed around his heart and tore it out. Random held the still beating heart up in his hand, blood running down his arm as he laughed victoriously.

For a moment the battle seemed to stop, everyone frozen where they were, and then it began again, only this time the rebels were forcing the soldiers back. Random and Ruby pressed forward and could not be stopped, and the Rejects took new heart from their example. More of the armored men fell, screaming. Some turned to flee, but there wasn't room in the packed space, and they just got in the way of their fellows. Specter Alice crowed victoriously as she strad- dled the shoulders of a man in armor, leaning forward over him, her bloody dagger stabbing again and again through the eyeholes of his helmet.

In the end, not one Wolfe soldier got away. Their broken armored bodies littered the floor, stretching away down the tunnel. There were rebel dead, too, but not nearly so many. It seemed there was blood everywhere, running down the walls and pooled on the floor. Random and Ruby grinned at each other, and the Rejects crowded around them to congrat- ulate them and slap them on the back and shoulder. Random scrubbed happily at the blood on his hand and arm with a cloth, and had a nod and a smile for everyone, until his eyes met Storm's. His old friend had broken a little apart from the others. There was blood on his sword and his clothes, but lit- tle of it seemed to be his. He was breathing hard, and his sword trembled in his hand. He looked at Random as though he was a stranger. Random moved over to join him, but stopped some way short, held back by the coldness in Storm's eyes.

"Who are you?" said Storm. "The Jack Random I remem- ber couldn't do things like that. Nothing human could."

"I've ... been through changes," said Random. "I'm more than I was. But I'm still me."

"No you're not," said Storm. "I don't know who you are anymore."

He turned away and walked off down the tunnel by him- self. Random let him go. If only because there was a certain amount of truth in what his old friend had said. He looked up to see Specter Alice staring at him. He shrugged, and she shrugged back and went after Storm. Ruby Journey had meanwhile cleared a space around her with snarls and curses, and was methodically cleaning her sword with what had once been a fine silk handkerchief. Ruby wasn't much for congratulations or camaraderie. She wouldn't feel like talking with him now, either. Random shrugged again. He'd just done what he had to, as he had so many times before.

But he could still feel the heart beating out the last of its life in his hand while he laughed. That wasn't like him. Not like him at all.

He pushed the thought aside as another occurred to him. He couldn't help wondering if the Rejects had deliberately chosen a path that would intercept armored Wolfe tunnel rats, just to see what the legendary Jack Random and his friends were capable of when not part of a Reject army. It was the kind of thing he would have done once. But though he was also impressed with the way the Rejects had handled themselves, ready to risk death just to test him, he was a little disturbed that they hadn't even tried to take any prisoners. There came a time when hatred just got in the way of winning a war. In the end you won more victories by accepting the other side's surrender than by wiping them out to the last man. Or did the hatreds run too deep, here on Technos III?

The Church troops, known collectively as the Faithful, were training together in the great open area between the factory complex and the first trench, and Toby Shreck and Flynn were there to cover it all. Absolutely no one was glad to see them there, but Toby and Flynn were used to that by now. Officially, the soldiers of the Church of Christ the Warrior and the hardened Wolfe mercenaries were supposed to be one integrated fighting force by now, but both sides had centuries of tradition, not to mention white-hot enmity, behind them. Consequently, what had been intended as an orchestrated set piece of hard drill and weapons training was rapidly deteriorating into a complete mess, as the Faithful and the mercs strode to outdo each other in sheer viciousness, if not skill.

Cardinal Kassar was there in his black battle armor, topped with a billowing crimson cape, screaming orders and counterorders till he was purple in what remained of his face. The color clashed with his outfit and warned of future heart problems, but no one felt like getting close enough to tell him. He cursed and yelled at the top of his parade ground voice, trying to force his men to behave through sheer force of personality. But not even the horrible punishments he was threatening were enough to restore order. The mercs were damned if they were going to be shown up by a bunch of pansy hymn singers, and the Church troops were determined to show a bunch of professional thugs what could be achieved by people trained in the one true faith. It was all getting very nasty, and not a little bloody. Both sides got their heads down and got stuck in.

Jesuit commandos were running back and forth between the lines, screaming orders and breaking up fights with impartial venom toward both sides, using whatever force was necessary. They darted here and there, snapping at their charges like incensed sheepdogs, but even they couldn't be everywhere at once. Still, it was clear to practically everyone present that it was only their efforts that were preventing a complete breakdown of authority. Even battle-hardened mercenaries had enough sense to be wary of the Jesuit commandos. They were the elite of the elite, hardened cold-eyed killers said to be second in the Empire only to the Investigators themselves. They fought in battles alongside their men and kept body parts as souvenirs. And not the usual ones, either.

Cardinal Kassar stopped himself shouting with an effort, gritting his teeth to hold the words back. His hands had clenched into fists, and his whole body strained to run forward and lay heavy hands on the disobedient bastards running amok before him. But he couldn't do that. He knew Flynn's camera was covering him as well as his men, and he couldn't afford to be seen losing control. Everything else had gone wrong so far on this mission, but up till now he'd always found someone else to blame it on. A public failure now could undermine the whole purpose of his mission, to restore order on Technos III, and, just as important, do a hell of a lot of damage to his career prospects. So this particular display was going to go right, even if he had to start executing people at random to prove he was serious.

Toby Shreck studied Kassar from a safe distance and smiled contentedly. He knew a man on the edge of apoplexy when he saw one. He also recognized a complete military cock-up when it was coming unraveled right in front of him. He hadn't seen such a complete mess since Valentine Wolfe slipped a little something into a marching band's mid-time tea break, just for a laugh. The tape of that particular event was a popular best-seller for over six months. He glanced quickly at his cameraman.

"Tell me you're getting all this, Flynn. They couldn't be providing us a better show if they'd rehearsed it."

"Relax, chief. Billions of people all across the Empire are watching this live."

Toby grinned at the magic word *live*. His previous piece had already gone out to first-class ratings, the highest share Imperial News had ever achieved. Some stations were still running it and paying through the nose for the privilege. There had been talk of major awards for Toby and Flynn, and, more importantly, large bonuses. The Wolfes had gone into cardiac arrest when they first saw the piece, especially the Mother Beatrice bits, and screamed for their lawyers, but Stephanie and Daniel had somehow managed to transfer all the blame onto Valentine. They'd promised to make changes, but so far nothing significant had changed on Technos III.

The one really good thing to come out of the uproar was the Wolfes' concession to Imperial News that Toby and Flynn would in the future be permitted to cover all important events live. There was a massive audience in the Empire waiting impatiently to see what Toby and Flynn would come up with next. Which was, of course, their main problem. A good act needs a good encore. Toby for one had not expected anything good to come out of covering a program of drill and weapons training, but he'd had to agree for want of anything else to show. No one else would talk to him now that he was being constantly shadowed by Wolfe security, and his audience was getting impatient.

Now he smiled contentedly as a bunch of the Faithful brought down a bunch of mercenaries and gathered quickly around for a bit of putting the boot in. He should have had more faith in the ability of the Wolfes and Cardinal Kassar to screw up everything they touched. He looked again at Flynn, covering the chaos before him with practiced ease. The camera was currently hovering high above the confusion, with Flynn seeing everything it saw through his comm implant link. It scooted back and forth as Flynn's attention was caught by each new outbreak of violence. For all his faults, and he had many, Flynn was an excellent cameraman. Of course, he'd become unbearably cocky and insufferable since the amazing reception of the first broadcast. Toby was just glad the man hadn't turned up in a black basque and feather boa, like he'd threatened.

"Heads up, chief," said Flynn quietly. "Something wicked this way comes."

Toby looked around and winced inwardly as he saw Kassar striding determinedly toward them. He felt a distinct twinge of unease, but was careful to keep it out of his face. People like Kassar seized on weaknesses. He bowed formally to Kassar and gave him a smile so natural he almost fooled himself.

"Good morning, Cardinal. Isn't it a lovely day? I think the early autumn is the closest Technos III has to civilized weather. Until the razorstorms start, of course. Now, how may we assist you?"

"You can start by turning that damned camera off until we've got things under control."

"Sorry, Cardinal," said Toby pleasantly, "your superiors' orders were quite specific. They wanted us to cover everything that happens here today."

Kassar snorted, but had enough sense to say nothing. He'd seen the orders. The Church had felt the need for a propaganda piece to back up its ongoing negotiations for increased influence at Court, and Toby and Flynn and the Technos III Faithful had seemed the safest bet for good ratings. They'd also hoped that a well-viewed piece showing the great skills and discipline of the Church troops might go some way to restoring the damage done by Toby and Flynn's previous piece. Kassar could have told them . . . but as usual, no one had asked him. His fists were clenched so tight he could feel the nails driving into his palms, but he made himself smile frostily at the two newsmen.

"Of course. Make sure you get some good footage. But I want to see every inch of your tape before it gets broadcast. The Church has very kindly supplied me with new equipment, specifically designed to detect such things as palimpsests. Or anything else you might try to sneak past me."

Confident that this time at least he'd got the last word, Kassar turned and stalked back to his milling troops, clearing his aching throat. This time, they were going to listen. Or else. Lots of all else. Flynn watched him go.

"Do you think we should have reminded him this is going out live?"

"Not our fault if he doesn't read his own orders carefully," said Toby briskly. "I can't believe they made that idiot a Cardinal."

"Family connections," said Flynn.

"Isn't it always?" said Toby. "The man's a bully and a blowhard. Do even his own men like him?"

"Are you kidding? It's only the Jesuit commandos that have kept his men from slipping a fragmentation grenade into his toilet bowl. And even the Jesuits are getting pretty fed up with him. Still, he has his admirers in the hierarchy. After all, utter ruthlessness is what gets you on in the Church of Christ the Warrior."

"Good point. Does Kassar ever go into battle alongside his troops, or is he strictly a rear echelon sheep-botherer?"

"Give the man his due, he does like to be in the thick of things. I don't believe he's missed a single battle since he got here. Offer him a chance to kill as many people as he can get his hands on and he'd as happy as a clam." Flynn paused, and looked thoughtful. "Which is a strange expression, when you think about it. Are clams renowned for being particularly happy?"

"Don't change the subject."

"What was the subject?"

"I forget," said Toby. "Just keep filming. Things seem finally to be calming down, unfortunately. Maybe he threatened them all with mass crucifixions."

"Wouldn't surprise me. I just hope he gives me time to set up some proper lighting first."

Toby sighed. "There goes our chance of hanging onto our ratings. He'll get it all under control, everyone will obey orders and play nicely together, and our viewers will change channels in droves. There's no justice."

And that was when everything went to hell in a hurry. Explosions went off all around the drill area, blasting open the jagged metal plain. The noise was deafening, and black smoke billowed up, throwing everything into confusion. More explosions roared on all sides. Shrapnel flew in the air, and Church troops and Wolfe mercs alike abandoned their discipline to run for cover. The black smoke filled the sky, blocking out the sun, so that an artificial twilight fell across the scene. There were fires blazing all over, and no one could make themselves heard.

New openings had appeared in the metal plain, and rebels came boiling up out of the new tunnels they'd dug underneath. They fired energy guns they weren't supposed to have and lobbed grenades in all directions. The mercenaries and the Faithful tried to pull themselves together, but they were scattered and confused, and the rebels tore right through them. Steel flashed, and blood flew in the air and pooled on the jagged metal ground. Toby Shreck watched it all with his jaw somewhere down between his knees.

"Holy shit. *Holy shit!* Flynn, tell me you're getting this!"

"I'm getting it! I'm getting it! The light's lousy and there's smoke everywhere, but I'm getting it!"

The Empire forces retreated in an utter rout, fighting here and there in small clumps, but mostly just running for their lives with their heads well down. Explosions were still going off, and there seemed no end to the army of rebels pouring up out of the hidden tunnels. Jesuit commandos were screaming at their men to stand and fight, but their words were lost in the chaos. Some rebels threw themselves at the Jesuits, and they reluctantly retreated, holding off the greater numbers with stunning swordplay. Kassar spun this way and that in the middle of everything, completely thrown, unable to think what to do for the best. The rebels streamed past him, pursuing the fleeing Faithful and mercenaries. Some had finally pulled themselves together and stopped to stand and fight, and the metal plain was quickly dotted with dueling figures. And that was when Toby Shreck recognized a familiar face. He grabbed Flynn by the shoulder and pointed urgently.

"There! Three o'clock! Do you know who that is? It's only Jack bloody Random, the professional rebel himself! No one's seen him in action since the fiasco on Cold Rock. I didn't know he was on Technos III. Did you know he was on Technos III? Oh, who cares! Just keep filming. Jack Random's comeback, and we're covering it live! People have been awarded their own holo network chat shows for less!"

"If that is Jack Random, he's looking very good for his age," said Flynn, concentrating on his camera's movements. "Vicious, too. He's cutting through that batch of mercs like old man Death himself. Who's that with him?"

"Don't know the old man," said Toby, flinching reflexively as another explosion went off. "The woman's wearing a bounty hunter's leathers, but I don't know the face. We can run a trace later. You stick with Random. He's the story here."

He jumped back with a shriek, as a rebel appeared out of nowhere right in front of him. His eyes were dark, and blood dripped from his sword. Flynn yelled and called his camera back to hover protectively between him and the rebel. Toby realized there were just as many rebels running behind him as in front and froze where he was. Flynn stood his ground. The rebel looked at Toby and Flynn, smiled, winked into the camera, and then disappeared back into the chaos. Apparently, even rebels understood the need for good publicity. Toby began to get his breathing back under control and was very glad he'd decided to wear brown trousers that morning.

Someone blew a whistle. Others took it up, and suddenly the rebels were breaking away from fights and pursuits and turned to fall back, disappearing down into the tunnels under the metal plain. They were all gone in a matter of a few minutes, blowing preprepared charges to seal off the holes to their tunnels, leaving the Faithful, the mercenaries, the Jesuit commandos and Cardinal Kassar standing in a daze, looking around and trying to figure out what the hell had just hit them. Smoke drifted in the air, and flames burned here and there from bodies hit by energy guns. There were dead everywhere. Hardly any rebels. They'd taken most of their wounded and dead with them. It all seemed very quiet. Kassar looked over at Flynn, still filming, and lurched toward him, his eyes wild.

"You! Stop filming! And give me that tape! Now!"

"Sorry, Cardinal," said Toby Shreck, somehow keeping an ecstatic grin off his face. "I'm afraid this has all been going out live, as your superiors insisted. Do you have any comment you'd care to make at this time?"

Kassar raised his disrupter and blew the hovering camera out of midair. Flynn glared at him.

"You'll be hearing from my Union about that."

Random, Ruby, and Storm laughed breathlessly together as they ran with the Rejects, plunging down narrow tunnels and away from the pursuing Wolfe forces. The assault had gone exactly as planned, with minimum casualties on their side and maximum death and embarrassment to the Wolfes and the Church. A clone working in the factory complex had provided them with the exact timing necessary to be sure of camera coverage. Now the Rejects ran back through the new tunnels and on into older, established parts, keeping up a good pace for all their tiredness. The explosive-sealed openings wouldn't hold the Wolfe troops back for long. They weren't supposed to. The battle wasn't over yet. Down be-

low, in the darkness and familiar confines of the rebel underworld, the Rejects would teach a final, deadly lesson to their
enemies.

The tunnels sloped steeply downward for some time, and
then opened up suddenly into a vast cavern. Random lurched
to a halt, as the path before him split apart to form a number
of even narrower trails leading down and along the sides of
the cavern. The vast open space was dizzyingly huge, as
though someone had hollowed out the inside of a mountain.
The ceiling was hundreds of feet above, and the cavern floor
seemed as far below. Random stood very still, staring about
him, as rebels jostled to get past him, running confidently
down along the narrow trails. The walls were mostly
smooth, polished by who knew how many centuries of running water and other abrasives. There were bright streaks of
metallic blues and greens and golds, harsh traceries of long
forgotten industries. Light from the rebels' lanterns glistened
brightly on metal stalactites and stalagmites, hanging ponderously from the ceiling or jutting up from the curling yellow mists that hid the cavern floor. Ruby and Storm were at
Random's side, quietly urging him forward, but he couldn't
move. It was as though he'd stumbled into a giant cathedral,
the vast hidden soul of Technos III. He couldn't seem to get
his breath. He felt like a fly crawling over a stained-glass
window in some old, abandoned monastery.

He finally allowed himself to be persuaded on, following
Specter Alice down a long series of steps into the misty
depths below. All around him the Rejects were scattering
into prearranged hiding places and ambush positions. Random slowly realized that to them, this awesome place was
nothing special. They didn't see the glory and the spectacle
of such a natural wonder. They had no time for that. They
saw it only as a good place to launch an ambush, as just another killing ground in their never-ending war. Specter Alice
led Random, Ruby, and Storm into a concealed depression in
the cavern wall, giving a good view of the single entrance
above. She made sure Storm was settled comfortably beside
her, drew her disrupter, and then settled himself down to
wait. The energy gun seemed very large in her small bony
hand. Thin wisps of yellow smoke drifted up from the floor
below, smelling of brimstone. The Rejects had melted into
their hiding places like so many silent shadows, and now

they waited patiently with gun in hand for their enemy to come to them. The great cavern was still and quiet.

Random edged over so he could put his mouth next to Specter Alice's ear. "How long has this place been here?"

"Who knows? It's been here longer than us, that's for sure."

"It's wonderful."

"Damn right. Perfect place for an ambush. We can control everything that happens down here. The Wolfes' troops don't even know what they're walking into. Poor bastards. There will be blood and suffering, and the slaughter of our enemy. Now, shut up. They'll be here soon. You can play tourist later when we've killed them all."

The sound of approaching running feet came from above, and Random crouched down, gun in hand. It wouldn't be the first time he'd turned a place of beauty and wonder into a battleground. He'd seen many wonders and marvels in his day, on many planets, and left them littered with the dead and the dying. For all his noble cause, he sometimes thought that the only real legacy he'd leave behind him was a bloody trail of death and destruction. And then the Wolfe and Church troops came pouring out into the cavern, led by the three Investigators, Barr, Edge, and Shoal, and there was no time left for introspection or regret. This was the killing time, the dance of the quick and the dead, and all in the name of the noble cause of rebellion.

The great cavern blazed with light as both sides opened up with energy weapons. The brilliant beams spat in a hundred directions, crisscrossing, ricocheting from the solid metal walls. There were screams and war cries and desperate orders as the Faithful and the Wolfe mercenaries scurried for cover. Rage and the need for revenge had brought them this far, running recklessly through the dark in pursuit of a mocking enemy, but the deadly energy beams brought them to a sudden halt, as though they'd slammed into a wall. Men fell dead and dying, sometimes screaming, sometimes not, and bodies littered the narrow paths, burning quietly. The survivors found hiding places from which to return fire, until the cavern finally fell silent as the energy weapons were exhausted. There was a pause, interrupted only by the moans of the wounded and the dying echoes. Then both sides drew their swords, emerged from their hiding places, and went out onto the misty cavern floor to meet each other.

The Rejects and their enemies slammed together, steel against steel, hand to hand. No quarter asked or given. This was a blood feud for the Faithful and the mercenaries now. For the Rejects, it always had been. The two sides pressed endlessly forward, breasting the yellow mist like a tide, with no place for caution or second thoughts. Swords clashed and blood flew, and the great floor of the chamber became a mass of struggling figures.

Random and Ruby fought back-to-back, as always, unbeatable and unstoppable. Storm fought doggedly behind them, swinging his sword with the studied deliberate skill of many years' experience. Enemies swirled around the three of them, but could not bring them down. Ruby Journey killed and killed and laughed aloud, in her element at last. Random fought with a cold, focused precision, concerned only with ending the fighting as soon as possible. He fought for his cause and took no pleasure in the killing. He burned that out of him long ago. Storm struggled on, already gasping for breath, his sword seeming to grow heavier with every blow and parry. After all, he was only human.

Finally, almost inevitably, the three most famous fighters of the rebellion found themselves facing off with the three greatest fighters of the Empire forces, the Investigators Barr, Edge, and Shoal. The milling crowd seemed almost to part to bring them together, as though they were the microcosm by which the greater struggle would be decided. Edge faced off against Ruby, Barr against Random, Shoal against Storm. They paused with something like mutual respect and then threw themselves at each other. Blades crashed and sprang apart, and then the greater crush of fighting bodies slowly separated the three couples and carried them away from each other.

Random put his back against a metal stalactite and held his ground as Edge hammered at him with his sword. Random dodged the blows he could and parried those he couldn't, content to let the Investigator tire himself out. Except that Edge didn't get tired. Instead, the Investigator's strength seemed to grow with every blow as his fury grew with every failed attack. His mouth was stretched in a mirthless smile, and his eyes were dark and wild. Random ducked deep to avoid a double-handed swing, and Edge's blade sheared clean through the tip of the metal stalactite behind him. It came to Random that fighting defensively against an

Investigator was a good way to get yourself killed, Maze-improved or not.

He boosted, feeling the blood hammer through his veins and thunder in his head, and launched himself at Edge. He fell back a step, startled, and then held his ground and would not be moved, for all of Random's boosted strength and speed. He was, after all, an Investigator, and even an aging Investigator was a match for most things the universe could send against him. That was his job. But Random had been through the Madness Maze, and he wasn't like most things in the universe anymore. He smiled, very sanely, into Edge's crazy grin, and let his guard drop just a little. Edge's sword flew forward instantly, to take advantage of the opening. And Random's free hand came up impossibly quickly, slapping the blade to one side. For an endless moment they stood together, Edge wide open and knowing it, and then Random's sword slammed into Edge's chest and punched out his back. Edge let out a small bark of pain, blood spraying from his grimacing mouth, and then he sank to his knees as the strength went out of him. Random pulled his sword free, and Edge collapsed onto his face, as though only the sword had been holding him up. Random decapitated him anyway, just in case. Edge was an Investigator, after all.

Ruby boosted the moment she realized her opponent was an Investigator. Barr might be the oldest of the three, but he was still far more dangerous than most men could ever be. So she dared him into a *corps a corps,* faces close together over crossed blades, and then she spat in his left eye. And in that split second while he was distracted, she pulled a knife from her belt and stuck it between his ribs. She felt blood gush out over her hand before he pushed himself back and away from her. She launched a furious attack, with all her boosted strength and speed behind it, and he backed away, step-by-step. Blood poured down his side with every movement, but still he wouldn't give in to the dreadful wound in his side, parrying her every blow, his face calm and unmoved. In the end Ruby had to use all her strength to beat aside his blade and all her speed to bring the edge of her sword flashing back across his exposed throat.

Blood spurted, splashing her face. She stepped back, wiping it off her forehead so it wouldn't run down into her eyes. She smiled as she saw her cut had sliced half through his neck, and then the smile faded as she realized Barr was still standing. He was an Investigator, and he was damned if he'd go down into the dark without taking his enemy with him. He threw himself at her, his sword swinging around in an unstoppable arc. Ruby dropped to one knee and ducked under it. Her head jerked slightly as Barr's blade cut off a chunk of her hair. She thrust her sword deep into Barr's belly. He grunted once and backed away, pulling himself off the transfixing blade. Ruby let go of her sword and surged up off her knee. She grabbed Barr's head between both her hands, forced him over backward, and slammed the back of his head down onto the jagged tip of a metal stalactite. It slammed through his head and the point burst up out of his right eye. Barr convulsed and then was finally still, the breath going out of him in a long frustrated sigh. Ruby retrieved her sword, breathing hard, and then looked Barr over carefully from a safe distance, just in case. He had been an Investigator, after all. Satisfied that he really was dead at last, Ruby leaned over and kissed him on the bloody lips, then straightened up and looked around to see how Random was doing.

The battle was pretty much over. The rebels had had the advantages of position and surprise, and a familiarity with the killing ground. For all their experience and their fury, the Faithful and the Wolfe mercenaries never stood a chance. Most were dead. The few survivors had formed a defiant group around the one surviving Investigator, Shoal. Ruby moved to stand beside Random facing her. Neither of them mentioned Storm. Shoal looked from one to the other, her sword dripping blood, and then she grinned quickly, turned, and darted up an unguarded path and out of the cavern. The others scrambled after her, and the Rejects let them go. Someone had to tell the Wolfes of the great rebel victory.

The battle was over. The Rejects moved among the wounded, dispassionately finishing off the enemy and doing what they could for their own kind. They had no place for prisoners in the underground, and the long journey to the Sisters of Mercy would kill them anyway. Random and Ruby put away their swords and went to look for Alexander Storm, a swordsman long past his best last seen facing off against Investigator Shoal. They moved among the bodies, occasionally turning them over to study the blood-flecked faces, but he wasn't there. They eventually found him hiding in a concealed hollow, well away from the main action. He wasn't hurt. He looked up at them, and in his face there was only anger and resentment.

"I ran," he said defiantly. "So would any sane man, faced with an Investigator. I'm not inhumanly fast and strong, like you. I was no match for her, and we both knew it. So I turned and ran, and she let me go. She had more important things to do. After all, how dangerous could one old fool be?"

"You were doing fine until she came along," said Random. "You were fighting just like you used to."

"I was tired and hurting, and I couldn't get my breath. I can't fight like I used to anymore. I'm an old man past his prime. Just like you used to be. Only you're not, anymore. Are you?"

"Alex . . ."

"I saw you fighting. No one's that fast or that strong. Not even the Jack Random of legend. I don't recognize you anymore, Jack. What are you? A Fury? A Hadenman? An alien? Because I don't think you're human anymore."

"I'm your friend," said Random. "Just as I always have been."

"No you're not. You're looking younger all the time. No one can stand against you, not even Investigators. Whatever you are now, you have nothing in common with the likes of me anymore. Maybe you did die when the Empire had you, after all. Or at least the Jack Random I used to know."

He pushed past them and walked away. Random started after him. "Alex, please . . . I need you."

Ruby stopped him with a hand on his arm. "Let him go. He's right. We're not the people we used to be. We're better. And you don't need him. You've got me."

Random looked at the bloody mask of her face for a long moment. "Yes," he said finally. "I've got you."

Mother Beatrice of the Sisters of Mercy held the flap of the hospital tent open so that the stretcher-bearers could bring in more wounded. There were many gravely injured after the unexpected rebel attack, and already the tent was full to overflowing. There was already no room left for cot beds. Beatrice had had them thrown out, to pack more wounded in. Now they lay shoulder to shoulder on bloody sheets, screaming and moaning and whimpering and waiting to die. The stench of blood and vomit and naked guts was almost overpowering, despite all the disinfectant the Sisters were splashing around. Beatrice knew she'd get used to it after a while, but that didn't help her now. The smell made her head spin, and she clutched at the tent flap for support. Or maybe it was just the hopelessness of it all. Beatrice and her people were doing all they could, knowing as they did that most of the time it wasn't going to be enough. After Toby's broadcast, drugs and plasma and medical supplies had come flooding in from the Sisterhood and other charities, as well as the reluctant Wolfes, but no more doctors or nurses. Technos III wasn't that important, and they were needed elsewhere. No one had foreseen a bloodbath like this. She'd never seen so many casualties from one battle. Normally, they just died. Her new resources meant Beatrice could keep more of the wounded alive, but that meant a greater strain on her still limited space and supplies. Damn the rebels. Damn the Wolfes. And damn her for coming here because she thought she could make a difference.

Beatrice wiped at her sweaty forehead with the back of her hand, not knowing she left a crimson smear behind from her bloodstained hand. When she thought of what she could do with a real med lab and real equipment, it made her feel sick and useless, so mostly she tried not to think about it and got on with what she could do. She pushed her tiredness aside and went back into the tent. Back into hell. She made her way slowly down the length of the tent, stepping over bodies and patients, helping the doctors and the nurses where she could. Even if it only meant holding a patient's hand or placing a cool hand on a fevered brow. Sometimes she had to help hold a man down while the doctors operated. They were saving the anesthetics for those who wouldn't survive the shock of extended surgery. For quick in-and-out jobs they usually just gave the poor bastard something to bite on. To muffle the screams as much as anything.

She moved on, doing what she could, praying silently to her God for strength. The bodies were being carried away almost as soon as they stopped breathing. Partly because they needed the space for the living, but mostly because the Wolfes were storing the bodies for future use as organ donors. They'd paid for the mercenaries' services, so they owned the bodies. And far be it for the Wolfes to overlook a source of profit. Of course, none of the wounded here would benefit. Transplants were for officer class only.

Beatrice gritted her teeth to keep from swearing. Or crying. It was important that she didn't appear upset or worried. She had to look calm and confident, as though everything was under control. The patients needed to believe that. The poor bloody bastards.

She moved on, her shoes squelching in pools of blood and other fluids. The stench from open gut wounds and those who'd fouled themselves in dying was almost overpowering. And then she stopped, as it seemed to her she recognized a face. She knelt down beside the twitching, delirious man and frowned thoughtfully. Half of his left arm was missing, severed above the elbow. He'd taken other sword hits, too. Beatrice bit her lip. Of course she knew the face. She'd seen it often enough in the factory complex. This wasn't a Church soldier or a mercenary. This was a clone. And since the Empire didn't allow clones to use weapons, this had to be an escaped clone. Presumably, a rebel from the recent assault. She shrugged and got to her feet. She was a Sister of Mercy, and all were welcome here. And to hell with what the Wolfes said. She beckoned to the nearest nurse.

"This one's a rebel," she said quietly. "Do we have any more?"

"Thirty-two so far. You did say . . ."

"Yes, I did. Keep their faces covered. With bandages if you have to. What the Wolfes don't know won't hurt them, and we don't need the complications. Any news on more supplies?"

"Most of it's still held up in orbit. Since the attack, the Wolfes are only allowing *essential* craft-landing permission. Security, they say."

"Bastards. I'll contact the Sisterhood again when I get a chance. See if they can put some pressure on."

"What do we do with the rebels once they're well enough to be moved? Can't just leave them here; we need the space. But what's the point in healing them if we just have to hand them over to Wolfe security afterward?"

"Don't worry about it. The rebels will spirit them away as soon as they can safely be moved. They always do." Beatrice looked back over her shoulder as raised voices came from the entrance to the tent. She saw who it was and scowled. "Here comes trouble. Get those faces covered. Now."

The nurse nodded quickly and turned away. Beatrice made

her way back to the entrance as quickly as she could and blocked it with her body. She nodded for the flustered nurse to leave it to her, and the nurse nodded gratefully and left her to it. Beatrice smiled icily at the newcomer.

"Cardinal Kassar, to what do we owe the pleasure of your company at this extremely busy time?"

"You've got rebel wounded in here," said Kassar flatly. "I've had reports. I want them handed over to my people for questioning. Now. They shouldn't be here anyway. I've got more hurt men coming in."

"Something else gone wrong?"

"None of your business."

"You're the one filling my tent with wounded. That makes it my business. And as a Sister of Mercy, I'll treat anyone who needs my help. That's my job."

Kassar smiled coldly. "Screw your job. Either you turn those rebel scum over to me now, or I'll have my men come in and drag them out."

Beatrice nodded calmly. "Always knew you were a bit of a bastard, James. But don't let your anger over losing a battle push you into doing something you'll regret. The Sisterhood still has a lot of pull with the Church back on Golgotha. And right now I'm the Sisterhood's favorite daughter. I'm doing great things for their image. You mess with me, and my superiors will have your superiors come down on you like a ton of bricks in a wind shaft."

"We're a long way from Golgotha, Beatrice. By the time you can get word out, it'll all be over. Your precious rebels have information I need, and I'm going to squeeze it out of them, drop by drop. They'll suffer as my men have suffered. And there's not a damned thing you can do to stop me."

"Wrong," said Beatrice. "Look down, Cardinal."

They both looked down, and there was Beatrice's hand, holding a scalpel pressed lightly against Kassar's groin. They both stood very still.

"You wouldn't dare," said Kassar.

"Try me," said Beatrice. "Like you said, we're a long way from Golgotha. Accidents happen. You don't give a damn about your men being hurt. You're just desperate to salvage some small success from this unholy mess, so your precious career doesn't go down the toilet. Well, this is my territory, James, and we do things my way here. You try and walk over me, and I swear I'll geld you, right here and now."

Kassar looked into her steady eyes and believed her.

"I'll be back. With armed men."

"No you won't. I've got a hidden camera recording this. You really want your men to see you backed down by a mere Sister of Mercy? That would really kill your promotion chances. Now, get out of here. I'm sick of looking at you."

Kassar nodded jerkily and stepped carefully backward. "I won't forget this, bitch."

"That's the idea. Now, piss off. I have work to do."

Kassar turned and strode away, his stiff back radiating helpless rage. God help the first person he ran into back at the complex. Beatrice watched him go, hefting the scalpel thoughtfully. There wasn't actually any hidden camera, but Kassar wouldn't believe that. It was the sort of thing he'd do, after all. She'd do well to keep a watchful eye on the Cardinal after this. He was a spiteful man, and he never forgot an insult. Beatrice couldn't find it in herself to care. She had more important things to concern her. She turned around as one of the doctors called her name urgently and trudged back through the blood and death to see what she could do to help.

Cardinal James Kassar was still fuming when he joined Half A Man in his quarters for their prearranged meeting. He'd fix the bitch. Though maybe not personally. And not until he'd got the tape. Wouldn't do for anyone else to find out how she'd humiliated him. He nodded curtly to Half A Man, who was standing at parade rest beside a bed Kassar suspected he never used anyway. It was hard to think of Half A Man doing something as human and vulnerable as sleeping. The spitting energy field that made up the right half of the man's body was openly disturbing when seen up close. It seemed to be no color and every color all at once, and if you looked at it too long it swallowed up your gaze till you were lost in it. Kassar kept his gaze fixed on what was left of Half A Man's face. Though even that didn't seem very human anymore.

"Let's get to the point," Kassar said harshly. "I need to debrief what's left of my men after today's debacle. You have instructions from my superiors on how to deal with the Wolfes?"

"Very simple instructions," said Half A Man. When he opened his mouth to speak, Kassar could see energy seething within it. He made himself concentrate on what Half A Man was saying. "You're to plant explosives I've brought with me in certain delicate parts of the factory. I have a map that will show you the exact positions. The explosions will do just enough damage to slow down stardrive production, without actually putting it in jeopardy. The purpose is to make the Wolfes look incompetent. The Church will then be in a strong position to take over control of stardrive production in the best interests of the Empire. Apparently, your superiors feel the need for rather more influence at Court."

Kassar nodded. "Easy enough to arrange. I know just the man for the job. Very discreet and, if need be, completely expendable. You supply the map and the explosives, and I'll take care of the details. No one will notice anything until the bombs go off." He stopped and studied Half A Man thoughtfully for a moment. "You've never struck me as particularly religious before. Why risk your much-vaunted impartiality to smuggle in explosives for the Church? What are you getting out of this?"

"Something I want very badly. Nothing you need to know about."

"Well, I want something, too," said Kassar. "Mother Superior Beatrice of the Sisters of Mercy. She's running a field hospital here. I want her killed. Horribly. You arrange that for me, and I'll keep quiet about what I know."

"I could kill you right now," said Half A Man.

"You can't make this work without me," said Kassar evenly. "You don't have the contacts. Only my men have unsupervised access to the kinds of places the bombs will have to go. Anyone else, and the Wolfes' security people will start asking awkward questions. You need me."

"The quality of people entering the Church has gone right down the drain in recent years," said Half A Man. "Very well. I'm empowered to be . . . flexible, to get the job done. I'll see that Beatrice meets an unpleasant end."

"I'll tell you when," said Kassar. "I need to check if a certain tape exists first."

"Very well. But Kassar . . . don't ever try to pressure me again. I have a very short and unpleasant way with people who annoy me. You'll find the map on my writing table, along with instructions on where to find the explosives. They're to be timed to go off during the Wolfes' ceremony to celebrate stardrive production finally going on-line.

Shreck and his fellow news reptiles will be there to capture it all for posterity."

"Good," said Kassar. "I've got a little surprise of my own planned for Toby Shreck. He won't just be recording the news; he's going to be part of it."

Daniel and Stephanie Wolfe were arguing again, though at least they had the sense to do it somewhere private for once. Stephanie paced back and forth in the private Family reception hall, throwing words like knives at her brother, who stood sulking by the built-in bar, glaring down into his drink. Michel and Lily stood together a respectful distance away, large drinks in their hands, being ignored by their spouses, as usual. The hall had belonged to the Campbells first, and their crest still showed faintly on one wall where it had been imperfectly removed before the Wolfe crest had been superimposed over it. Despite the hostile takeover by the Wolfes, the factory complex still had a strong Campbell presence. Wolfe security men were still turning up hidden booby traps in the function rooms and logic bombs in the computers. All food and drink had to be shipped in from offworld. All of which helped to explain why Stephanie was in a particularly foul mood before things started going wrong.

She stopped for breath for a moment, and there was an ominous silence in the hall. Daniel had a lot of things he felt like saying, but knew better than to try and interrupt his sister while she was in full rant. Besides, what he felt like saying really needed to be shouted for full effect, and he didn't trust the room's soundproofing. There were bound to be a few Campbell loyalists still hidden in the complex personnel, not to mention spies from the Church. And it wouldn't do for he and his sister to be overheard plotting treason against their own Family. Not even by the handpicked men they had standing guard outside the only door. Guards were necessary, even inside the complex, to protect against rebel sympathizers and infiltrators. And to make sure the Cardinal and his people kept their distance. Kassar's hatred for Wolfes in general and Valentine in particular was well-known, and there was no sense in putting temptation in his hands. It was open knowledge that the Church of Christ the Warrior felt it ought to be in charge of stardrive production.

As usual, the Empress was sitting back and letting things sort themselves out.

"I still think we shouldn't be discussing this in front of *them*," Daniel said finally, gesturing with his drink at Michel and Lily.

"They won't talk," said Stephanie dismissively. "What's good for us is good for them, and they know it. And it's important they know what we're planning, so they won't say or do the wrong thing through ignorance. Besides, they know what would happen to them if they talked, don't you, darlings? Of course you do. Now, pay attention, Daniel. We have to go through with this. That rebel attack during a live holotransmission made us look very bad. Us, as well as Valentine. It's a dangerous setback to our plans, and we're running out of time. We have to come up with something that will make us look good and Valentine appear utterly incompetent, before stardrive production actually starts. Once it's up and running, Valentine will be the Empress's favorite blue-eyed boy, and it will take a miracle to dislodge him."

"Agreed," said Daniel. "But I still don't want us discussing this in front of witnesses. I can trust you not to speak whatever the pressures, but I can't say the same about our dear spouses. We might be married to them, but that doesn't make them Family."

"Oh, all right. We'll discuss this further in my private quarters. Michel, Lily, stay here till we send for you. You don't need to know the details anyway. Just do as you're told. And try not to drain the bar dry, for a change."

She swept out the hall majestically, with Daniel following, as always. Michel and Lily waited until the door had closed firmly behind their respective spouses, and then they threw themselves into each other's arms. Their mouths met hungrily, bodies pressing together, clutching at each other like someone drowning and going under for the third time. The occasions when they could be together had been few and far between on Technos III, but that only fanned the flames of their passion. Perhaps because it underlined that the only people they could depend on were each other. They finally broke apart a little, still in each other's arms, breathing heavily into each other's mouths, eyes locked on eyes.

"We have to do it," said Lily, her voice harsh with need and urgency. "It's our only chance to be free of them and have our own life, together. I've got a guard eating out of my hand. He can get us explosives from the armory. Afterward, we can kill him in a way that will point at rebel infiltrators. Then all we have to do is plant the bomb in just the right place, to go off at just the right time, and that will be the end of dear Daniel and dear Stephanie. May they rot and burn in hell.

"No one will suspect us; there are far too many other more obvious enemies, from the rebels to the dear Cardinal himself. We'll be ever so regretful, of course, but we'll be the only ones in a position to take over here. Valentine won't want to come all the way out here, away from those noxious substances he thrives on, just to run a factory, and we're the only Family he can trust. Once we've shown him we can handle things, he'll leave us alone and turn his attentions elsewhere. We'll be able to marry at last. He won't object, not once we point out it's the only way of keeping the factory wholly in the Family."

"Don't you feel any guilt?" said Michel. He suddenly pushed her away from him, and she stumbled back a step, caught off balance. She looked very slight and vulnerable on her own, with her huge dark eyes, dark as the night. Michel made himself concentrate on what he was saying. "We are married to them, after all. They made us Wolfes. Aristocrats. I was an accountant, and you were a librarian and minor authority on tarot readings. If I hadn't met you, I would have been more than happy to be a Wolfe's husband and live an aristocrat's luxurious life."

"But we did meet," said Lily, moving in close again so that her breath was sweet in his mouth. "And you loved me as I loved you, more than being an aristo, more than life itself. If we can't be together, I don't care about anything else. Guilt? What has that got to do with us? Daniel never tried to be a husband to me. Never loved me, never liked me, never spent a moment in my company that he didn't have to. Was Stephanie ever any different? Did she ever give a damn about you, except as a fashionable accessory, something big and muscular to be flashed at Court? Jacob Wolfe only arranged our marriages because we brought necessary small businesses into the Family that he didn't want going to anyone else. Our families sold him the businesses along with us because of the dowries he offered. No one asked us. No one ever asks us."

Michel nodded slowly and took her in his arms again. She

nestled contentedly against him, and they stood together for a while.

"Well?" said Lily finally. "Will you do it? Will you help me set the bomb?"

"Of course I will. I never could say no to you. But Lily ... let's not have any false illusions between us. Even if we do kill Daniel and Stephanie and get away with it, our love isn't going anywhere. People like us don't have happy endings. Valentine and Constance will wage open war to see which of them will take control of the factory, and we'll just be in the way. They won't let us marry. Rather than let us emerge as a joined power base, they'll most likely separate us and send us to different ends of the Empire. They'll destroy our love casually, offhandedly, just because they can."

"It doesn't have to be that way," said Lily without raising her head. "We're small fry, Michel. Constance and Valentine will be so busy fighting each other they won't even notice us until it's too late. Even the smallest of snakes that crawls unnoticed through the grass can have a deadly poison in its fangs. We'll bring them down, my love. Destroy them all for not loving us."

"Dream on, dream child," said Michel. "Maybe it'll work out that way, maybe it won't. It doesn't matter. I'd rather be damned with you than live without you."

At about the same time as various Wolfes were plotting various treasons, a regular propaganda broadcast from Technos III being reluctantly hosted by Toby the Troubador was suddenly interrupted by a burst of static. Viewers caught a brief glimpse of Toby looking off camera and saying *What the bloody hell* ... and then he disappeared into static, which in turn was replaced by a new face that filled the screen. He looked to be in his early forties, darkly handsome, hard-used but still charismatic. His eyes were steady and his smile was compassionate. When he spoke, people listened.

"Good evening, my friends. My name is Jack Random. Some of you may have heard of me. It's all true. I am presently assisting rebel forces on the Wolfe-owned world of Technos III to win their freedom and their dignity. It was their world once, but long ago it was taken from them by those with more power and influence at Court. An old story, nothing to write home about. But Technos III is the present home of the factory producing Lionstone's new stardrive. You've heard a lot about this new drive and the many benefits it will bring you. What they haven't told you is that the new drive is being produced by slave labor in life-destroying conditions."

The scene changed to show long lines of people working in a vast low-ceilinged chamber. The illumination was painfully bright, and strange colors tinted the air from no obvious source. The air rippled sometimes, and things that had seemed near were suddenly far away, and vice versa. The scene was unsteady, suggesting it had been recorded on a hidden, smuggled-in camera. Men, women, and children worked together, crawling in and around great metal and crystal structures. They were slowly, laboriously building something piece by piece with handheld tools and instruments. Many of those working had warped bones and bodies. Some were missing fingers. Some had no jaws or eyes, as though something had eaten them away. The scene continued in silence for a while, to let it sink in, and then Jack Random's voice began again.

"Whole Families work here, building the stardrives, doing work too delicate and too important to be trusted to machines. Automated machinery can't handle the necessary working conditions. They go crazy and malfunction. Same with computers. Only people are adaptable enough. The poorly understood forces that move inside even partially completed drives are horribly destructive to human tissues. The Families you see work in these conditions fourteen hours a day, seven days a week. When they're too weak or too disfigured to work, they're taken away and disposed of. There are always replacements. Because the people you're looking at are clones. And no one gives a damn what happens to clones. But I give a damn. And so do the rebels of Technos III."

The scene changed again, to a long panning shot of rebels lining a trench in the rain. There were men, women, and children, all of them armed and ready to fight. Their faces looked tired but determined. Random's voice-over continued. "There are no noncombatants in the rebellion, because the Empire would kill them all anyway for daring to have opinions of their own. For daring to protest over the theft and devastation of their world. They're fighting for their lives and their future, and their work shifts never end. I'm fighting beside them now. Just as someday I may fight beside you, for your life and your future. Because the Empire doesn't care who it destroys in its endless search for wealth and power and self-gratification."

Jack Random's face filled the holoscreen again. Ill used, but still compassionate. Strong, dependable, determined. The man with scars in his eyes. "Tonight, my friends, we bring you the truth for once in your lives. What is happening here on Technos III could happen to any one of you. If some aristo wants your planet he can take it, and no one will stop him. If he then decides to work you all to death, no one will raise a voice in protest, as long as the profits remain steady. The Empress is gathering more and more power to herself, demanding more and more from her subjects, all in the name of an alien invasion that may never come. Parliament can't stop her. It's grown lazy and corrupt, like the aristocracy. Whatever you own, they can take from you. Whatever you believe in, they can destroy. And they will if they're not stopped.

"I'm not asking you to run out and join the rebellion. Not yet. Just remember what you've seen and heard here today, and think about it. Disregard the lies the Empire tells you about the kind of people who join the rebellion. We're just like you, except that we've dedicated ourselves to a simple truth. That all men, human or clone or esper, are created equal and should have an equal say in their destiny. You can help us. If you wish to . . ."

And that was when holoscreens all across the Empire suddenly went blank. Static buzzed importantly to itself for a while, and then local channels rushed to take over, hurriedly filling the air with comforting Muzak and game shows. Later, the broadcast interruption would be explained away as just another cyberat prank. None of it was real. There was nothing for anyone to be concerned about. Viewers would be able to see the real conditions on Technos III when the Wolfe Family graciously allowed cameras to observe the first completed stardrives coming off the production line, at a special ceremony in two days' time.

Back on the surface of Technos III, outside the factory complex, Cardinal Kassar lowered his gun with a satisfied smile. One shot from his disrupter had blown the complex's main transmission aerial into pieces, cutting off all broadcasts from the planet. He looked around as Daniel and

Stephanie came hurrying up the slope to join him, with Toby and Flynn in close pursuit. Kassar smiled at them and waved imperiously at the wrecked aerial.

"I fancy that will stop the rebels pumping out their poisonous lies through your equipment. Frankly, I'm surprised you didn't have safeguards against this kind of thing happening."

"As it happens, we do," said Stephanie in tones so cold a snowman would have shivered to hear them. "If the rebels had just stayed on-line a little longer, my security people would have been able to track down the source of their signal, and we could have sent men in to destroy their equipment. As it is, not only do we have no idea where the rebels were transmitting from, but you have just shot out our only link with the outside universe. All our other aerials were slaved to this one. Without it, we are completely out of contact with the Empire. Which means that the ceremony that was to be transmitted live in two days' time, as ordered by the Empress herself, will no longer be possible. Unless your people can put the bloody aerial back together again!"

"Ah," said Kassar. "Yes . . ."

"May I also point out," said Toby, perhaps enjoying the moment just a little too much, "that if you hadn't shot the aerial down, I would have been able to put a rebuttal piece on the air in a few hours, thus undoing whatever damage the broadcast might have done. An awful lot of people are going to be really unhappy with you, Cardinal, if your people can't get the aerial up and working again soon."

Kassar looked at the shattered pieces of aerial lying across the metal slope. "Oh, *shit.*"

"Couldn't have put it better myself," said Stephanie. "I shall expect hourly reports from your people until the aerial is functional again. And if it isn't ready in time for the ceremony, I will personally have your balls. Assuming the Empress doesn't get to them first."

She nodded briskly to Daniel, and the two of them turned and strode back down the slope and into the factory complex. Kassar glared at their backs and hurried after them. Toby and Flynn looked at the wrecked aerial. They seemed fairly cheerful, all things considered.

"Was that really Jack Random, do you think?" said Flynn.

"Oh, yes. I cross-checked our earlier sighting against Imperial News' files. It's him, all right. Looking a bit battered by life, but in damn good shape considering his age and history. And if I did have any doubts, that broadcast just put them to rest. That was classic Jack Random. Exactly the kind of thing he was famous for."

"Then, those shots of the clones building the drive were the real thing?"

Toby looked at Flynn firmly. "I don't know. If, just for the sake of argument, they were true, then you can be bloody sure the Wolfes would have us killed out of hand if we were found sneaking around there in search of an exclusive. There are limits to how you can treat people, even if they are only clones. Lionstone must want those drives really badly."

"So we just ignore the story?"

"Since when were you so idealistic? People are dying all across the Empire every day. There's nothing we can do about it. Every now and again we get a chance to put some small thing right, like Beatrice's hospital, but don't let it go to your head. Even if we did manage to get footage of the clones working on the drives, the odds are we couldn't get it on the air. Not now. And you can bet Imperial News would disown us on the spot. Learn to content yourself with little victories, Flynn. If you like having your head attached to your shoulders."

They stood in silence for a while, thinking their separate thoughts. Flynn stirred finally. "If Jack Random could win a victory here, it could be the start of the great rebellion itself."

"God, I hope so," said Toby. "Lots of good material to be found in a war. Reporters' reputations can be made on the battlefield."

"You speak for yourself," said Flynn. "The moment the shooting starts, I shall be diving for cover and keeping my head well down, and you can do your own camera work."

"The trouble with you, Flynn," said Toby as they started back down the slope toward the complex, "is you have no ambition."

"My ambition is to live to a hundred and three," said Flynn firmly. "At which point I hope to be shot by an outraged wife."

"Sometimes I wonder about you, Flynn," said Toby. "And sometimes I'm sure."

* * *

In the early hours of the morning, when things were traditionally the quietest, Jack Random, the professional rebel, and Ruby Journey, the foremost bounty hunter of her day, according to her, emerged from the farthest trench the rebels controlled and sat on the edge of the jagged metal field, looking across at the huge factory complex, silhouetted against the rising sun. The Wolfe forces had recently been driven back and were too busy establishing their new front to be any threat. They also hadn't got around to setting up snipers yet. Random and Ruby would have known they were there, even if they couldn't see them. So they sat casually together, enjoying the strange and vivid hues of the sunrise.

It was the first day of summer and already uncomfortably hot with the sun barely above the horizon. Random and Ruby had come out onto the surface ostensibly to study the ground for the day's attack, but actually they were just looking for a little time in each other's company. Conditions underground were crowded at best and often claustrophobic, and after a while even the best intentioned of people could really get on your nerves. The Rejects had taken to treating them both like heroes of legend, promised saviors who would lead the rebels to inevitable victory over the forces of darkness. Neither Random nor Ruby were particularly happy about this.

"I was never meant to be a hero," said Ruby firmly. "The pay's lousy and the working conditions suck. I'm a rebel because I was promised first crack at the loot when the Empire finally falls apart. And because that cow Lionstone put a bounty on my head. The way some of these Rejects have been looking at me, you'd think I could do the three-card trick with one hand while walking on water. I have a horrible suspicion they're going to start asking for my autograph soon."

"It's in people's nature to want heroes," said Random. "Someone to follow, who'll make the hard decisions for them. They build us up larger than life, pin all their hopes and dreams on us, and then turn nasty when we let them down by being only human after all. I've seen this all before, Ruby. It's one of the reasons I gave up being the professional rebel and ran away to hide on Mistworld. I got tired of carrying everyone else's hopes and expectations on my shoulders. They were never that broad in the first place. I've spent most of my life trying to get people to think for themselves and take responsibility for their own destinies, but it's an uphill task. All too often they'd rather cheer and follow a leader, some smiling charismatic bastard who can inspire them into being more than they thought they were. I sometimes think they'd be happy to drag Lionstone off the Iron Throne and replace her with the first smooth-talking hero to come along. Even me."

"Emperor Jack," said Ruby. "I like it. You'd shake things up."

"I'd hate it," said Random. "No one can be trusted with that much power, not even me. It's too much of a temptation. I've seen the way power corrupts, even when people take it on with the best of intentions. Perhaps particularly people like that. There's no one more dangerous than a man who knows he's right. In the end he'll sacrifice any number of people in the name of his belief, friend or enemy. In my experience people can't be trusted in the singular when it comes to power. Democracy works because it's a mass consensus. On the whole people are always better off when they can throw out any leader who starts believing his own press releases."

They watched the metal plain before them in silence for a while. The early morning was eerily quiet after the roar of battle only hours before. There were fires burning here and there, and the occasional Empire war machine, riddled with disrupter fire and abandoned where it fell, sparked and twitched and dreamed of killing. The factory complex was a dark forbidding shape studded with dull crimson glows that came and went, like doors opening and shutting in hell. The faint shimmer of its protective Screen could just be seen in the growing light. Like an ogre's castle, protected by magic, fueled on innocent blood, powered by hate and fury.

"What's up with Storm?" said Ruby. "He's been going all funny around you just lately. I thought he was supposed to be your friend?"

"He is," said Random. "We've known each other since we were teenagers. Fought side by side in more battles than I care to remember. You should have seen him then, Ruby. Handsome, dashing, deadly with a blade in his hand. I was the one they sang songs about, but he was the one who got all the women. He was my good right hand, the one thing I could depend on in a changing universe. But now I'm ... changing, and he can't cope."

"You look younger," said Ruby.

That was an understatement, and they both knew it. Random had shed twenty years of hard living over the past few weeks and now looked to be a man in his late thirties. His frame bulged with new muscles, and a new energy burned within him. His face had filled out from the gaunt mask it had once been, though many of the old lines of pain and worry remained. All in all, as far way from the shattered wreck of a man Ruby had first encountered on Mistworld.

"I feel younger," said Random. "Stronger, faster, fitter. I feel like I used to feel when I was a legend."

"Could it be jealousy?" said Ruby. "Because you're younger and he isn't?"

"I don't know. Maybe. I'm beginning to remember things about Alexander Storm. Toward the end, he lost his faith. He no longer believed in giving his life to the Cause. We'd fought the Empire for decades and got nowhere. He wanted to retire and let younger men take a crack at it. He wanted his comforts and an easy life. He thought he's earned it. We were both getting too old for the field of battle, though I wouldn't admit it. I led my people into battle on Cold Rock, and he came with me; not for the Cause, but out of loyalty to an old friend. He was always a good man, when it mattered. We were massacred. Wiped out. I think I remember Alex running at the end. I didn't, and I got captured, so he was probably right.

"I lost track of him after that, until he turned up as representative of the Golgotha underground. I should have known he'd never be able to give up the Cause completely. But now here we are again, fighting together in the field, and I'm the man I used to be, and he isn't. I'm a legend again, and he's just an old man with a sword that's too heavy for him, and failing breath. And just maybe I remind him of the time on Cold Rock when he turned and ran and I didn't. But then again, maybe that's just a false memory. I don't remember much about Cold Rock, or anything else from that period of my life."

"Hardly surprising, after what the Empire mind techs put you through," said Ruby. "They had you in their clutches for a long time. Those sick bastards could mess up anyone's mind. You're lucky you're still sane."

"I sometimes wonder if I am. There are too many places in my mind I can't see too clearly. Places with closed doors and heavy locks. They could have planted all kinds of control words or remote-control programming inside me, and I'd never know it, until they activated them. You saw what that renegade AI Ozymandius was able to do with Owen and Hazel in the Hadenman city. I could be an unexploded bomb, just waiting to go off where I could do the most damage."

"You're a morbid bugger to be around, you know that? Sometimes I wonder why I stick with you."

"Because I blind you with my charm and charisma."

"You wish. No, it's mostly because I admire what you've done with your life. You found something you believed in and put your life on the line for it over and over again. I've never believed in anything except hard cash. Honor spoils and courage fades, but you can always trust in gold to pay your bills. Maybe I'm hoping if I hang around you long enough, some of that hero thing will rub off on me."

"Ruby, why do you always put yourself down?"

She shrugged. "It's a dirty job, but someone's got to do it. Don't ask me questions, Jack. I don't have any answers. I'm here because I choose to be. Settle for that."

"I'm not the only one who's changing. You are, too, Ruby. Whether you like to admit it or not, you're becoming just as much a hero and legend as me."

"I bloody hope not. In my experience most heroes end up dying noble but tragic deaths at an early age. I think I'll skip that part of the legend. I'd rather just be the trusty sidekick, the one with the good advice and snappy dialogue, who emerges after the dust has safely settled to make her fortune through a ghost-written and thoroughly commercial set of memoirs. The only changes I'm going through are what the Maze did to me. You're not the only one who's feeling younger. It's not as noticeable on me, but I reckon I've lost a good five years. I'm faster, stronger, sharper. When I'm fighting, it's like the other guy's in slow motion. I recover faster, too. A warrior notices things like that. But, Jack, it's occurred to me that this reverse aging might not necessarily be a good thing. I mean, what if it doesn't stop? Where are we going to end up? As kids? Babies? What?"

"Whatever the Maze did to us, it's an ongoing thing," said Random thoughtfully. "Even if the Maze itself isn't around anymore. I have to believe there's a purpose behind what's happening. I think the process is refining us, turning us into the best, strongest versions of ourselves that we can be. The changes aren't just physical, remember."

"Yes, I know. I'm linked to you, and the others. I always know where you are, even when you're not around. Sometimes I can tell what you're thinking—or feeling; you dirty old man, you. And sometimes, when I'm in a fight, I can tell where an attack's coming from, where a sword's going to be, even what's going on behind me. Eerie. I always was a good fighter, but the Maze is taking me way beyond that."

"To put it simply," said Random. "We're becoming more than human."

"Or maybe inhuman," said Ruby. "The Madness Maze was supposed to be an alien construct, remember? Maybe the Maze was programmed to turn anything that went through it into copies of the species that built it. We could end up with six arms and antennae coming out our ears."

"And you have the nerve to say I've got a morbid mind. Look, let's start worrying about things like that when they start happening, all right? We have other things to concern ourselves with."

"Such as?"

"Don't take this wrong, Ruby, but . . . I can't help noticing you never take prisoners. Even before we came here, you never fought just to wound or stop your opponent. You always kill them."

"Best way," said Ruby briskly. "A dead man isn't going to suddenly sit up and try and stick a knife in you."

"A dead man can't be converted to our Cause, can't be made to see the error of his ways. What if we'd killed you when you attacked us back in Mistport? No, as and when we overthrow Lionstone, we're going to have to replace her with a system that can govern efficiently, or there'll be chaos. That means we'll have to use the same people she relied on to keep the wheels turning. We can't just kill everyone on the other side. We're going to need some of them."

Ruby shrugged. "That's your area of expertise. Mine is killing people."

"Look, you used to be a bounty hunter. Didn't you ever bring any of them in alive?"

"Not if I could help it. Too much paperwork."

Random sighed. "I am working with a barbarian."

Ruby grinned. "Civilization's overrated. Jack, I'm really not interested in this ethics shit. I'm a professional killer.

That's what I do. My only other interests are sex and loot. Not necessarily in that order. All you have to do is choose the targets and point me at them. Like the upcoming raid on the factory. Want to run that by me again?"

"Don't think I don't know when you're changing the subject," said Random. "But given the blank looks you were showing me during the last briefing, I suppose I'd better. All right, this is the simplified version in words of one syllable or less. Tomorrow the Wolfes will be hosting a major ceremony that will show them beginning mass production of the new stardrive. Live coverage on all the holo networks. The Empress herself will be watching. To ensure a clear and uninterrupted broadcast, they'll have to lower the factory complex's force Screen. And that's when we go in and hit everything that moves that isn't a clone. We'll overrun their defenses, free the clone workforce, trash everything in sight, and then get the hell out of there while the security forces are still trying to figure out what hit them. And all of it on live holo coverage. It'll be a major coup for the rebellion. Should win us a lot of new converts. And it sure as hell will bring stardrive production to a dead stop, until they can repair the damage and ship in a new clone workforce. And then we'll just hit them again."

"The raid will do the Rejects a lot of good, too," said Ruby. "Show them what they're capable of and establish them as a power base in their own right. A force the Empire might have to consider negotiating with if it wants its precious stardrive. Right?"

"Very good, Ruby. I'll make a tactician out of you yet. And all of this has brought us back to where we started. To why I don't want the Rejects focusing on us as heroes. Once we've proven to them that they're strong enough to kick the Wolfes' ass pretty much at will, as long as they keep their act together, our job here will be over. Before we move on to some other mission, it's vital these people have learned to believe in themselves. That they can win this without us. All they needed was someone to come in from outside and show them new ways of fighting. I never wanted to be a leader, Ruby, or a hero. I just wanted to fight for the right of people to be free. Even free of the cult of the hero. Heroes are great at fighting evil and injustice, but in practice they usually make piss poor political leaders."

"I just fight because I'm good at it," said Ruby. "And because I enjoy it."

"We're going to have to work on that," said Random.

Ruby grinned. "Why improve on perfection?"

Investigator Shoal stood at parade rest in Half A Man's private quarters and silently wondered what the hell he wanted with her at this unearthly hour of the morning. Her eyes were drooping despite herself, and she had to keep fighting back a yawn. She had a strong feeling Half A Man hadn't been to bed at all yet, if he ever slept. There had been a time when she could fight all day and still get by on only a few hours of sleep a night, but that was some years ago now. She was slowing down, needing more and more rest during missions. Forty-eight wasn't old, by any means, but Investigators had to be the best of the best. It said so in the job description.

She looked around the room unobtrusively as she waited. Calling it spartan would be polite; there wasn't a trace of personality, or even humanity, in the furnishings. No personal touches at all. It could have been anybody's room or nobody's. Half A Man was sitting in the only chair, his single-eyed gaze directed at the opposite wall, concentrating on something she probably had no concept of. Shoal tried not to stare at him, but it was hard not to. The seething energy construct that made up his right side was endlessly fascinating. If you looked at it long enough, you started to see things. Disturbing things. But you couldn't help looking anyway. Half A Man looked around at her suddenly, and only her training kept her from jumping.

"I know, Investigator," said Half A Man in his surprisingly normal voice. "It's far too early in the morning, and there are certainly other more productive things you could be doing with your time. But I need to talk to you. Sit down. You make the place look untidy standing around like that."

Shoal automatically looked around for a chair she already knew wasn't there, and then realized he meant the bed. She sat down gingerly on the edge, kept her back straight, and looked at Half A Man attentively. He wasn't exactly known for being talkative, so presumably whatever he had to say was going to be vitally important to their mission here. Half A Man sighed quietly, his half a mouth moving in something that might have been meant as a smile.

"Relax, Shoal, I'm not going to eat you. Despite whatever rumors you may have heard. I just need to talk. There aren't many I can talk to these days. Most people think me cold and inhuman, and it suits my purposes to encourage that impression. And it's mostly true. But I do still have a human side, if you'll pardon the expression, and now and again I need someone to talk with, as one human to another. I knew your grandfather."

Shoal looked at him uncertainly, not following the change in subject. "More than I did, sir. Investigators aren't encouraged to have family ties. They might distract us."

"Probably wouldn't have been allowed to talk to you about me anyway. Your grandfather was a good man. Good starship officer. Would have made a good Captain if he'd only had the right Family connections. When I heard they were detailing you to this mission, your name rang a bell, so I looked you up in the files. You've had a very impressive career, Shoal. Until you came here, but that seems to be true of a lot of people. Anyway, it seemed to me that if I could talk to anyone here, it would be you. And I have to talk to somebody. You do understand that anything you hear in this room cannot be repeated to anyone, on penalty of death?"

"Yes, sir. Of course. What did you want to talk to me about, sir?"

"My past. Who I used to be. When I was still just a man like any other, and my name was Vincent Fast. That used to be a joke; that I was fast enough getting into trouble, but rarely fast enough to get out of it. That turned out to be true in the end, but no one tells the joke anymore. They wouldn't dare. Wasn't much of a joke in the first place. I like to talk to people now and again, in private. It helps me keep track of how human I still am. I'm always afraid that I'm losing what's left of my humanity; that once I reach a certain point I won't notice or care anymore. You won't have noticed, but every day there's just a little less of my human side and that much more of my energy side. Takes a computer to measure the process accurately, but it's there. I'm losing myself, bit by bit. I've still got a fair amount of time ahead of me, unless the process decides to accelerate for some reason. But what's left of me isn't that human anyway.

"I don't eat or drink anymore. Cold and heat don't bother me. I'm a lot older than I have any right to be. The energy construct keeps me alive when I should have died long ago.

And sometimes I wonder what the aliens had in mind, that they needed me to live for so long. I've tried to kill myself more than once, but I can't do it. My energy half won't let me. That's why I'm talking to you now, Investigator. If in your opinion the energy half is taking control of me, overriding my humanity, I want you to kill me. Destroy my human half completely, with sustained disrupter fire. That should do it. I'm asking you because you're one of the few people on this planet capable of doing the job, because I trust your judgment . . . and because you have your grandfather's eyes. He was a good man. He would have killed me if he'd thought it necessary. How about you?"

"If that's what you need," Shoal said slowly. "I can't argue with your logic. You'd make a hell of a threat to the Empire if you got out of control. Lionstone would have me killed for depriving her of your talents, but that's my problem. I'm an Investigator, and I've always taken my oath seriously. My life for humanity. If you're in such a talking mood, sir, can you tell me anything about the aliens who changed you? The official reports aren't very helpful. Even the ones only open to Investigators."

"For a long time I didn't remember anything," said Half A Man. His voice was very quiet, and he didn't look at her. "Perhaps because I didn't want to. Then I started to remember things in my dreams. Of late the dreams have come more often, and I remember more of them. I don't know if that means anything. I hope not. All I do know for sure is that they're still out there, somewhere. Waiting.

"Forget the official, tidied-up story. This is what really happened. Their ship appeared out of nowhere. Huge and vast, dwarfing us like an ant next to a mountain. Its shape made no sense. We tried to talk to it, and it opened up with weapons of a kind we'd never encountered before. Blew our shields away like they were nothing and blew the ship apart. Only took a few seconds. The lucky ones died in the explosions. The rest of my crew died trying to breathe vacuum. And I woke up in the belly of the alien ship, strapped to an operating table. There was no sign of any aliens. Machines reached down, with long slender blades and other tools, for cutting and lifting and breaking. They opened me up to see how I worked, digging through my guts as the blood spurted. I screamed, but no one listened. I wanted to die, but the machines wouldn't let me.

"I don't know how long it went on. Seemed like forever. I went crazy more than once, but the machines brought me back. Until finally I was allowed to pass out, and when I woke up only half of me was left. My left side was intact, not even a scar, but my right side was an energy construct in human form. It obeyed my every thought, but I couldn't feel it. It wasn't mine. Not really. The restraining straps disappeared, and I got up off the table. With no trace anywhere of all the blood I'd spilled, I left the room and walked out into the ship itself.

"It was huge, none of it on a human scale. There were shapes and structures, but none of them made any sense. There was technology, machines everywhere, but I couldn't understand what they did, or what they'd been designed for. Somewhere something was screaming, shrill and awful, and it never stopped. It might have been pain, or triumph, or horror. And though it never once paused for breath, I had no doubt its source was organic. Something alive. Forever screaming. Just hearing it would have been enough to drive a normal man insane, but I'd been through so much already I wouldn't let myself be broken this time. I had to be strong. I had to survive. The Empire had to be warned.

"I found the aliens, or they found me. Even now, all I remember of them is hints, details, impressions. As though to comprehend them completely, whole, would be more than any human mind could stand. Even now. They were vast and inhuman, draped over impossible machinery with which they were intimately connected. I'm still not sure whether the ship itself might have been alive in some way.

"It took a while before the aliens became aware of me. We communicated, though I couldn't tell you how. They're advanced far beyond us. Their minds work in more than three dimensions. I think they see the future as clearly as the past, as though there was no difference between them. In the depths of their ship, lesser creatures died constantly, their life energies powering the huge ship. They died and were brought back to life and were killed, over and over again, their torment never-ending. But it wasn't their scream I heard. The aliens showed me other things, most of which I didn't understand. All of it was vile and terrifying, evil beyond anything humanity has ever done or could do."

He stopped speaking, his single eye squeezed shut. For a

long time there was only silence in the small room. Shoal stirred uneasily.

"Did they tell you why they did . . . what they did to you?"

"No. Or if they did, I didn't understand it. There was a lot I didn't understand. Eventually, they'd told me all they wanted to, or they grew tired of me. I woke up curled into a ball in one of my ship's escape pods, in orbit over one of the Rim worlds. A ship picked me up, and I came home to an Empire three years older than I remembered, and endured an endless series of attempted debriefings. You know the rest of the story. The Emperor's espers picked up the gist of the story, confirmed that I wasn't lying or crazy, and I became the Empire's spokesman on alien affairs. Who knew better than I what they were capable of? I set policy for alien contacts and controls throughout the known worlds. I've kept the Empire strong. We have to be strong and ready, because someday the aliens who took and altered me will be back. We weren't ready to fight them then, and we might not be now, but we have to be prepared. They were vast and powerful and utterly evil, and they must never be allowed to do to humanity what they did to me.

"In the meantime I do what I can. Of course, there's always the danger that I'm doing what the aliens intended me to. I have no way of knowing what instructions they left in my mind, or how much influence my energy half has over the rest of my mind. How much of what I do is my own agenda, and how much is theirs. Stay close to me, Investigator. Watch me. And if need be, kill me. I don't want to be a Judas goat for the whole human race.

"But still, sometimes, I wonder what happened to my other human half. If it's still alive, somewhere. If the aliens will give it back to me when they return. One last temptation, a weapon with which to control me. After all, I'm only human. So I put my life in your hands, Investigator, as I have in others before you. Do what is necessary, Shoal. Whatever the cost."

"Damn right," said Shoal. "I swear it, upon my word and honor. That is how you trained me, after all. As a matter of interest, what happened to the others before me?"

"I outlived them," said Half A Man. "I've lived a very long time, after all."

"Of course. Is there ... anything else I can do for you? Any other reason you summoned me here?"

"Yes, but not what you're thinking. Those urges were taken from me, along with everything else. I need you to carry out a sensitive operation later today. While everyone's distracted with the preparations for the ceremony, kill Mother Superior Beatrice of the Sisters of Mercy. Make it look like a rebel assassination. She's upset too many people with influence, and they want her dead. And since I need their support to carry out my ongoing mission, she must die. Make it quick but messy, and be very discreet. We don't want the Sisters of Mercy getting mad at us."

"Understood," said Shoal. She got to her feet and bowed briefly to Half A Man. "I'll put the matter in hand. Get what rest you can, sir. We have a lot of work ahead of us if we're to put down the rebellion here."

"We have to," said Half A Man. "The aliens are still out there. The Empire must have this new stardrive if it's to stand against them. It can't afford to be distracted by petty squabbles like this."

In the boiling summer heat, Cardinal James Kassar stalked up and down before his assembled Church troops, working himself into a state. The troops stood stiffly to attention in their ranks, ignoring the heat and the sweat that evaporated on their skin almost as quickly as it formed. A few had passed out and had been left to lie where they fell. They'd be flogged later. Kassar had been talking and yelling at them for a good half hour and showed no signs of slowing down. The gist of his speech, interrupted by frequent prayers and exaltations, was the pride and purity of the Church of Christ the Warrior and the utter depravity of the Church's many enemies. Kassar had all but worked himself into a froth of rage and frustration, but the troops weren't that impressed. They'd seen it all before. Kassar could turn it on and off like a tap.

They were all paying careful attention, though. Partly because it took their minds off the heat, but mostly because the Jesuit commandos were prowling between the ranks, hoping to find someone not paying attention, so they could drag him out and make an awful example of him. No chance of that this morning. For once the Cardinal had something to say that was actually interesting, not to mention vitally impor-

tant. On his own initiative, Kassar was sending them down
into the tunnels under Technos III, to wipe out the rebels and
regain their pride after being beaten so resoundingly in the
past. Of course, this time would be different. No small group
in battle armor, but the entire Church force with no armor,
hand weapons only, and a new battle drug the Church had
been dying to try out on somebody. The troops would have
liked to look at each other to see how everyone else was taking this, but the Jesuit commandos were still prowling, so
everyone stared straight ahead.

"Battle armor was a mistake," Kassar admitted, standing
still for a moment so he could stare commandingly at his
troops. "There's not enough room to maneuver down in the
tunnels, and the built-in disrupters are all but useless. Armor
just weighs a man down and gets in his way. This time you
travel light, move fast, strike at will. The new battle drug
was created in our own Church laboratories. It fires a man's
faith, makes him faster, stronger, meaner. His strength is as
the strength of ten because his heart is pure. A pure man
with this battle drug in his veins could slay an entire army,
armed only with the jawbone of an ass. And you will be
very well armed. Those hell-damned Rejects won't even
know what hit them.

"My friends, we must win this battle. Not just because the
Empire depends on us for its security upon this factory's
stardrive production, but because our enemies at Court and
beyond are using our previous defeat here during the rebel
attack for their own propaganda, to force us from our rightful place at the Empress Lionstone's side. We must regain
our pride, whatever the cost. Remember, those who die
fighting in the Church's name are sure of a place in heaven.
If we fail, if our faith is found wanting, then those who survive will be recalled to Golgotha for debriefing by the
Church interrogators. I know you would all rather die than
see us return in disgrace."

He paused to look out over his flock and nodded with
pride to see them staring unflinchingly back at him. "The
Jesuit Fathers will move among you now, distributing the
new drug and giving each group its orders. Assemble back
here in half an hour, full field kit and weapons, ready to take
the drug at the Fathers' commands. Regretfully, I cannot
be with you. I have other pressing duties here. But I will be
with you in spirit. Make me proud of you. Make the Church

proud of you. Descend into the darkness below and kill every living thing you find. For the glory of God and the Empire, kill every rebel man, woman, and child, until none remain to spread defiance on this world."

Down below, in the honeycomb of tunnels and caverns carved out of the many layers of metal far below the surface of Technos III, rebel life went on as normal. The people lived in shifts so that progress was never slowed and they might never be caught napping. The Rejects had many enemies, from the world above to the wild creatures far below, and they had learned to be constantly prepared. Jack Random, Ruby Journey, and Alexander Storm were being taken on yet another tour by Specter Alice, to impress upon them the need for outside support.

"We can feed and clothe ourselves, and we raid the upper world for whatever else we need, but there are always shortages," said Specter Alice. "Ours is not a life of comforts. We are born into the struggle, give our lives to it, and die for it in the end. Few of us live to old age. Unless they're crazy, like me. We are fighters, first and foremost. Even in our deepest, most protected places, there is little time for leisure. The tunnels must be maintained, food hunted and preserved, our territory protected. We have schools. We tap into the factory computers. We're not barbarians. But the struggle must always come first. We take it in turn to man the trenches and endure the changing weathers of the world above. You say you need our help to stop the factory's work. Then send us fighters and energy weapons. We'll do the rest."

She broke off as Ruby Journey stopped abruptly. Everyone else stopped and looked back at her. The bounty hunter had made little attempt to hide her boredom, only there because Random had insisted, but now the sour blankness had left her face. She looked straight ahead, her dark eyes far away, seeming huge in her pale, pointed face.

"Someone's coming," she said softly. "A large force from above."

Storm looked quickly about him. "I can't hear anything."

"I can feel it," said Ruby. "Jack?"

"Yes. I feel it, too. One hell of a large force, headed this way. They've already broken through into the upper tunnels. Alice, sound the alarms. I have a strong feeling we are in a world of trouble. Ruby, lead the way."

She was off and running, sword in hand, almost before he'd finished speaking. Jack charged after her, leaving Storm to hurry along in his wake as best he could. Soon men and women of the Rejects were joining them from side tunnels, running effortlessly beside them with all kinds of weapons in their hands. They had no time or breath for idle chatter. It was enough that the tunnels were under attack. They knew what to do. They'd trained for it all their lives. They ran silently, the only sound the growing thunder of the pounding of their feet on the steel floors. The thunder rose as more and more joined the charge, heading relentlessly toward the upper tunnels. Until finally they came upon their enemy, the Faithful, cutting a bloody path through the outnumbered defenders. The Rejects howled their fury and threw themselves upon the Church troops. Steel clashed and blood spilled, and soon the tunnels were packed with struggling fighters.

The Faithful pressed steadily forward, screaming their chants and war cries, their eyes wide and fierce in their taut faces. The battle drug burned in their veins and fired their minds. They were more than human now, unbeatable emissaries of God, performing a holy duty. Victory was inevitable. They slammed into the rebels, swinging swords and axes, their drug-fueled strength beating aside the weapons of their enemies. There was neither room nor time for individual duels. Both sides fought where they could in the milling mass that seethed this way and that, spreading slowly out through the great maze of tunnels and caverns. Blades rose and fell, and men and women fell and were trampled underfoot. Some rebels tried to flee with the youngest children, but the Faithful seemed to be everywhere, blocking the exits with drawn swords. And the drug that burned within them showed no mercy to woman or child. There was running and fighting in the corridors, war cries and screams, and blood splashed the metal walls and floors. The air in the underground grew hot and oppressive and thick with the smells of sweat and blood and the stink of ruptured bodies.

Random and Ruby fought back-to-back, surrounded by eager enemies like so many snapping dogs. Storm had been carried away in the press of fighting, and Random couldn't spare the time to worry about his fate. His enemies pressed forward from every side, searching for a moment's hesitation or weakness so that they could drag him down. He swung his sword as best he could in the confined space, putting all his strength behind short savage arcs and sudden thrusts. His enemies fell, but there were always more. Random boosted, calling on the ancient Deathstalker secret he'd acquired from Owen; and on the edge of his mind he felt Ruby boosting, too. New strength flooded through them both, more than enough to counter the alchemical strength of the drug that burned so fiercely in the veins of the Faithful.

And above and below and all around, in the many tunnels and caverns and living quarters of the rebels, the Faithful and the Rejects fought and died, equally matched in savagery and determination, unable to advance and unwilling to retreat, no matter what price was paid in blood and death. Tunnel floors and doorways became blocked with the dead and the dying, and men had to clamber over corpses to get at each other. Rebels saw their families die, women and children cut down without pity or quarter, and fought the more savagely. There were screams of rage as well as pain, and the din grew deafening.

Random and Ruby fought on, held where they were by the sheer press of fighters, taking wounds as well as giving them simply because there was no room to dodge or duck. Random cut and hacked with cold precision and knew that for all his new youth and strength, and the added powers of the boost, he still wasn't going to win this one. There were just too many Faithful fighting like berserks, uncaring of what wounds they took or whether they lived or died, as long as their enemy fell before them. More Rejects were coming, running from miles and miles of underground tunnels. In the end there'd be enough to outnumber and overpower the Church troops, but not until too many men, women, and children had been butchered by Church steel and innocent blood stained the tunnels forever.

It came to Random that he was going to die, trapped in the cramped confines of the dimly lit tunnels, far from sky and sun and open air, and the thought infuriated him. There was so much he'd intended to do, inspired by his second chance at life, and so much he'd left undone, because he'd been so sure there would be time in the future. Now time had run out. He was going to die, not through any failure of strength or spirit, but simply because he was outnumbered. And Ruby . . . Ruby would die, too. That thought fired him as nothing else could. He mourned the undoubted loss of his old friend Alex and the failed hopes of the Technos rebels, but in the end it was the thought of Ruby Journey lying dead and broken on the bloody floor that flared up in him, consuming all else in a need for retribution and revenge.

His mind burst free of its self-imposed restraints and reached out to touch and join with Ruby's. Their thoughts slammed together, merging and melding, becoming a whole that was greater than the sum of its parts. A brilliant light flared up around them, blazing hot like the sun, devouring those around them who couldn't retreat fast enough. The Faithful burst into flames, burning like candles, their flesh running like hot wax. The heat consumed the Church troops in seconds, melting their swords and body armor, spreading out through the tunnels in a traveling wave of spontaneous combustions. Only the Rejects were untouched, though the heat of the burning bodies drove them back, arms raised to protect their faces. The Faithful screamed and died, and suddenly the survivors had turned and were running back toward the surface and sanity. The wave of killing heat swept after them, snapping at the heels of the slowest and setting their hair alight. Horrid shadows danced along the metal walls as the Faithful fled, screaming in horror as though the devil himself pursued them. And perhaps he did.

The surviving Church troops grabbed men, women, and children and held them close, to prevent the hellfire setting them alight. The tactic worked, and more and more hostages were taken until the Faithful reached the upper levels and there were no more Rejects. They burst out onto the surface, clinging desperately to their struggling captives, and the hellfire followed them no farther. Men came running to help them and were greeted with tears and panted curses and hysterical laughter. Of the six thousand Faithful who went down into the underground, only four hundred and seven returned, not all of them in their right minds. They brought with them three hundred and twenty-seven captives, mostly women and children. And that was the end of Cardinal Kassar's great offensive against the Technos rebels.

Deep down in the rebel tunnels, Random and Ruby stood alone in a dimly lit corridor. The fire was gone, and they had fallen back into their own minds again. Smoldering bodies surrounded them for as far as they could see, and the air was thick with the stench of burned meat. They looked at each other, just a man and a woman again. Or so they hoped.

Their minds had followed along with the flames, and they knew what they had done. Alexander Storm and Specter Alice found them standing together, staring into each other's eyes, as they came stepping carefully over the charred bodies that covered the tunnel floor. They stopped a safe distance away and waited to be noticed. Random and Ruby finally turned to look at them, and Storm had to fight down an impulse to fall back a step. They both looked younger, fiercer, more than human, as though the terrible heat they'd generated had somehow burned away the impurities in them. Looking into their eyes was like looking into the sun.

"They're all gone," Storm said harshly. "We've started clearing out the tunnels, but it'll take some time. There are a lot of bodies to shift."

"The survivors took prisoners with them," said Specter Alice. "We don't know who or how many yet. We'll have to sort through the dead first. God knows what the Wolfes will do with their prize. They've never taken captives before."

"Don't worry," said Random. "We'll get them back." As he spoke the fire slowly went out of his eyes until he was just a man again. "Spread the word. When the force Screen goes down for the ceremony tonight, we attack in force. All of us. We'll free the clones and the prisoners, disrupt the ceremony, and trash the stardrive assembly lines. All on live holovision. That should make it clear to everyone who really rules here."

"Jack, that's a hell of a lot easier said than done," said Storm. "The Rejects have tried mass attacks before, but it never worked."

"They didn't have Ruby and myself to lead them," said Random. "We'll make all the difference. Where's your spirit, Alex? You and I will be right in the forefront, leading the attack. It'll be just like old times."

"I hope not," said Alexander Storm, meeting Random's eyes unflinchingly. "Dear God, I hope not."

The ceremony was still two hours away, but Daniel and Stephanie Wolfe were already preparing themselves for the show. The right outfit was so important for such occasions. They were in Stephanie's quarters; Daniel had been having trouble tying his cravat and had come to his sister for help. She shook her head, unsurprised, and pulled the cravat into place with short, controlled tugs. Daniel stood patiently as she fussed over the rest of his formal outfit and looked around Stephanie's quarters. More luxuries per square inch than most people saw in a lifetime, but Stephanie still considered her quarters to be particularly spartan and said so loudly on every conceivable occasion. She was, after all, a Wolfe and accustomed to the very best of everything. Daniel felt much the same way, but couldn't be bothered to make a fuss. He had other things on his mind.

"You know, I shouldn't still be doing things like this for you, Danny," said Stephanie mildly as she stepped back to admire her work for a moment. "I know you don't like servants getting this close to you, but Lily is supposed to be looking after you these days. She is your wife, after all."

"Don't know where she is," said Daniel. "She's never around when she's wanted. Not that I give a damn. Her endless prattling drives me crazy. Not a word of sense in her. I sometimes think Dad wished her on me for a joke."

"I know what you mean," said Stephanie. "Michel's no better. Nice build, but there's nothing between his ears but his appetites. He's always forgetting errands and appointments, and then he has the nerve to sulk when I yell at him. He's good enough in bed, but he has all the personality and charisma of a soft boiled egg. We should never have agreed to marry them."

"No choice. You saw the will; go through with the marriages or be disinherited. And we did need the businesses that came with them."

"We've got their businesses now. There, that's finished. Don't touch your cravat again under any circumstances. Got it? Good. You're quite right, of course. Our respective spouses are about as much use as . . . Oh, I don't know. Name something really useless."

"Lily and Michel," said Daniel, and Stephanie had to smile, if only briefly.

"Right," she said dryly. "I'd divorce mine in a minute if I wasn't sure he'd take the opportunity to soak me for every credit he could, in lieu of retaining any interest in the Family businesses. We should have insisted on prenuptial arrangements, but with dear Daddy's will they had us over a barrel, and they knew it. Either way, it's my business and my money, and he's not getting any of it. I'll see him dead and rotting in the ground first."

"Now, there's an idea," said Daniel. Stephanie looked

quickly to see if he was picking up on her hint, but she could tell from his preoccupied face that he was just being polite, and had already moved on to something else. "Steph, after the ceremony, how much longer do we have to hang around here?"

"Danny, we've been through this. At least two months, maybe three. Even with the little surprise we've got planned, it'll still take that long to wrest control of the factory from dear Valentine."

"You don't need me here for that. You don't need me here at all. I need to get away; there's something more important I should be doing."

"Danny . . ."

"Our father is still out there, somewhere. With the Wolfe resources behind me, I can find him, I know I can."

"Danny, our father is dead. He died in the hostile takeover of Clan Campbell. You saw the body. What you and I saw in the Court that time was just a Ghost Warrior: a corpse with computer implants to keep it moving and talking."

"No! It *was* him. He recognized me. He's still alive, trapped in that decaying body. I have to find him, free him, one way or another."

"Let it go, Danny! Our father, whatever state he's in now, is the past. We have to look to the future. He never cared for us, except to carry on the Family genes. I need you. I need your support, here and at Court. I can't tear down Valentine and run this Family on my own. I need you, Danny! I always have, you know that."

"Why? So I can stand at your side and look good? Fight duels over your honor? Hold your hand when things get a bit rough? You've got Michel for that, or if he's not up to it, you can always hire someone. The only real battles are over politics and money, and I've never understood either of them. I have to go, Steph. Daddy needs me. No one else will help him. Most people are glad he's dead. I'm all he's got."

"Our father is dead! How many times do I have to tell you? Get it through your thick skull; what we saw was just a Shub trick, and you fell for it!"

"I thought you at least would believe me! You think I'm crazy, too!"

His face went all red and puffy, and he started to cry like a child. Stephanie sighed, stepped forward, and took him into her arms. He held her tightly, his face buried in her neck.

"I can't let him down," he said muffledly. "He never needed me for anything before. And he went and died before I could say good-bye. Before I could tell him I loved him."

"Forget Daddy," said Stephanie. "You don't need him anymore. You've got me now."

And she pushed him away from her a little and kissed him on the mouth with far more passion than a sister should show for a brother. Daniel put his hands on her shoulders and pushed her gently but firmly away from him.

"No. This isn't right, Steph."

"We're Wolfes, Danny. We can do whatever we want. We decide what's right."

"Not this. Wolfes have never gone in for . . . this sort of thing. Even we have to follow some rules, or there'd be no point to anything. Besides, if word got out, and you know it would eventually, we'd lose all respect among the Clans. If we're too weak to control our own desires, then we're too weak to control our Family. That's what they'd think, and they'd be right. I love you, Steph, and I'll always love you—as a sister. I'll stay with you for as long as you really need me, but then I'm gone. Don't try and stop me. I love you, but he's my father."

"Let's go," said Stephanie, not looking at him. "We have to meet with Cardinal Kassar and Half A Man before the ceremony begins."

They all ended up in the main reception hall again. Some optimistic soul had put up colored trimmings and streamers, and servants in full formal dress were preparing a buffet of little snacks and munchie things. There were also wines and champagnes in great quantity, if not quality. Cardinal Kassar seemed to be drinking most of it. Word had quickly reached him of his troops' fate in the rebel tunnels, and though he was loudly declaring it a great success to all and sundry, it was clear he wasn't fooling anyone, not even himself. Daniel and Stephanie looked on impatiently as Kassar blustered on, angrily brandishing his glass as he shored up his arguments with details that had more and more of fantasy in them. Half A Man's thoughts were hidden, as always, and the Investigator at his side kept a diplomatic silence.

"Slaughtered the rebels in their hundreds," Kassar said

loudly. "Maybe even thousands; hard to tell without dragging the bodies to the surface. All right, we lost some good men, a lot of good men, but we're the ones that ended up with prisoners. Your people never managed that before. We got three hundred and twenty-seven. I've decided to have them all executed at the end of the ceremony. Make a nice finish to the show, and make it clear to everyone who's in charge here."

"I've seen your prisoners," said Stephanie. "Mostly women and children and a few wounded men. That's going to make a great impression on the watching billions. Would you like us to supply you with some puppy dogs and cute little kittens to kill as well, to complete the picture? I mean, children! What's the matter, Kassar, couldn't your people find enough cripples and retards to make up the numbers?"

Kassar glared at her. "A rebel is a rebel. The executions will be a sign of authority and strike a major blow to the rebels' morale."

"Can't say I agree," said Daniel. "I mean, killing women and children in cold blood. It's not done, you know."

"We're not playing your decadent Court rituals here, boy," said Kassar, his ruined face dangerously red. "This is Church business. Don't try and interfere with the executions, or I'll have my troops run you off."

"So much death excites you, doesn't it, Kassar?" said Stephanie. "You enjoy the thought of such slaughter."

"And you don't?" The Cardinal sniffed contemptuously. "I thought you Wolfes had more guts."

"We're in the same room as you, aren't we?" said Daniel.

Kassar started to reply to that, and then stopped as he caught the glint in Daniel's eye. He knew of Daniel's reputation as a duelist, and his men were a long way away. Half A Man and his Investigator were supposedly on his side, but . . .

"I've heard a few reports of my own," said Stephanie, "about what happened, down in the tunnels. According to my sources, the rebels drove you off with some new kind of esper weapon."

"Rumors," said Kassar coldly. "Exaggerations. You should know better than to listen to gossip. The Rejects have no espers, let alone esper weapons."

"But they do have Jack Random," said Daniel.

"So they say," said Kassar. "I'm looking forward to hang-

ing him. I mean, he's hardly a real threat anymore. Just an
old man, worn down by time and failure, desperately trying
for one last success. The Empire kicked his ass on Cold
Rock, and my people will kick it again here. No one can
stand against the Faithful. Just as no one can stand against
the Church."

And he smiled, thinking of the explosives he'd had placed
in the factory. Not enough to do any real damage, but more
than enough to disrupt stardrive production, make fools of
the Wolfes, and lay the groundwork for a Church takeover of
Technos III. And then no one would care about a few troops
lost in an unlucky venture.

Half A Man stood silently a little to one side, following
the conversation, and what was said and what wasn't, but
feeling no wish to join in. He made a stern, forbidding presence with Investigator Shoal at his side like a primed attack
dog, and he knew it. People here had been getting too familiar just recently. They needed to be reminded where power
really lay. And he felt a need to appear strong after his babbling to Shoal. He'd never spoken that much about his past
damnation since his original debriefings, and he didn't know
why he'd opened up so much to Shoal. Perhaps because the
dreams had been so vivid just lately, or just because Shoal's
grandfather had been such a good friend. Half A Man felt
the need for a friend now more than ever. He didn't need to
worry that Shoal might talk. She was an Investigator and
completely loyal to the man who'd trained and shaped her
life. He had no doubt of that. Which was why he'd had her
oversee the placing of Kassar's explosives in the factory. He
could trust her to do a thorough job.

Michel and Lily chose that moment to make their appearance, late as usual. They'd made some effort to dress up for
the occasion, but not much. Their clothes were of the finest
cut, but worn without the necessary élan to carry them off
successfully. There were recent wine stains on Michel's cravat, and Lily's long silver wig was perhaps just a little off
center. They were giggling together as they burst in, but
tried to stop when they picked up on the cold formality in
the room. They beamed around them innocently and headed
straight for the wine. Daniel glared after them.

"What are you looking so damn pleased about? Any later,
and you'd have missed the meeting completely."

"And wouldn't that have been a shame?" said Lily, not

looking around as she poured herself a very large drink. "Don't worry, darling. I'm sure nobody missed us. And we're in plenty of time for the ceremony. Which is all you really need me for, after all. Personally, I wouldn't miss the ceremony for anything. I love a good ceremony."

And she and Michel shared another smile, thinking of the Chojiro-supplied explosives they'd placed in the factory. This would be one ceremony no one would forget in a hurry.

"We may have a problem with the ceremony," said Stephanie, and everyone looked at her sharply. "The presence here of Toby Shreck and his cameraman has proved something of an embarrassment. He was supposed to be here to provide useful propaganda, but apparently no one told him that. I'm sure I don't need to remind anyone here of the repercussions from his previous broadcasts. Unfortunately, he has viewers in very high places, including Lionstone herself, and as a result he has gained exclusive rights to a live broadcast of the ceremony. I had hoped to arrange a little accident for him at the last moment, but now that he's the only commentator available, we can't do without him. The ceremony must be seen, and by as many people as possible."

"Oh, it must," said Kassar. "All kinds of people will be watching."

"Don't worry," said Half A Man. "I'll have the Investigator stand right next to him. That should make him choose his words carefully."

"I take it the main aerial has been replaced?" said Daniel.

"Yes," said Stephanie. "Sometime ago. I do wish you'd read your memoranda occasionally, Daniel. The Cardinal was kind enough to supply us some of his technical people to help."

"Should bloody think so," said Daniel. "After he blew the bloody thing up in the first place."

"I have made my apologies," said Kassar frostily. "I have nothing further to say on the subject."

"That makes a change," said Daniel.

"You are always so full of opinions, young Wolfe," said Half A Man. "Perhaps you have some view on how the forthcoming war with the aliens should be fought, too?"

There was a pause, as everyone wondered where the hell that change in the conversation had come from. It wasn't entirely unexpected, given Half A Man's well-known preoccupations, but even so no one present was quite sure what had set him off this time. Still, they were all glad of an excuse to change the subject, for their various reasons.

"I'm not sure there will be a war," said Daniel after a moment. "The aliens have left us alone this long. I don't see why they shouldn't go on doing so. But if they do turn up, the answer's obvious. Draft every commoner in sight, dope them to the gills with battle drugs, and send them out to kick six different colors of shit out of the aliens. Casualties aren't a problem. We've got an endless supply of cannon fodder in the Empire."

"No," said Half A Man. "That's not the answer. It's never a good idea to give the lower orders weapons. They might start getting ideas above their station. Guns and commoners don't mix. Never have."

"So what's your great plan, then?" said Daniel.

Half A Man fixed him with his single cold eye. "Investigators. I've been training them for decades on the best way to deal with aliens. Let me train an army of Investigators, and I'll show you an armed force no alien attack could hope to overcome."

There was another long pause as everyone considered the idea of an army of single-minded, cold-blooded killing machines, answerable only to Half A Man. Investigators were scary enough on their own, but the thought of an army of them was enough to loosen anyone's bowels. Daniel for one thought he'd rather face an army of aliens stark naked, with both feet tied behind his back, but for once had the sense not to say so out loud. Everyone else was thinking hard as to why Half A Man had brought such a subject up now. Was it his way of saying that he had a power base that even mass-produced stardrives couldn't undermine? They were still thinking furiously when the door swung open and Toby Shreck hurried in, as full of bounce as ever. Flynn glided in behind him, a new holocamera on his shoulder. Everyone else moved instinctively together, to present a unified front against a common enemy.

"That's what I like to see," said Toby breezily. "Good grouping. Relax, people. We won't start broadcasting till the ceremony itself. Which I'm sure I don't need to remind you is going out live; so, Cardinal, watch your language. I hope you're all ready to begin, because everyone else is. All the factory staff and those Church troops not currently lying flat on their backs and moaning quietly have been assembled outside and are standing in neat ranks, boiling in the summer heat and no doubt praying fervently for the start of the monsoon season. The Cardinal's prisoners have been lined up and securely chained in place. They were making rather a racket, but some kind soul has dosed them with industrial strength tranquilizers, and now it's all they can do to stand up straight. The execution should make for a good show, Cardinal. The populace does so love its blood sports. Even if the prey this time are mostly women and children. What happened, Cardinal? Were all the rebel men off on a fishing trip, perhaps?"

"One of these days your tongue is going to get you into trouble you won't be able to talk your way out of," said Kassar, every word chipped out of ice. "And I just pray I'm there so I can rip that wagging tongue right out of your head."

"Don't ever change, Cardinal," said Toby. "It's part of your charm." He looked across at Stephanie. "May I suggest we get a move on? It's never wise to keep a mass audience waiting too long. Especially if it happens to include the Empress Lionstone herself."

The ceremony, it had been decided at practically the last moment, would be held outside the factory despite the weather, so that the impressive size of the factory complex could be seen and admired all the better by the viewing billions. One of the stardrive assembly lines had been extended out the main doors, so that the very first completed massproduction stardrive could come rolling out of the factory to be presented to the waiting crowds and the holo audiences. The waiting crowds in this case being the increasingly rebellious factory staff and Church troops, growing more and more ready by the minute to kill for a glass of cold water. Most of the Faithful had been ferried down from the Church ship in orbit to make up the numbers. They didn't look at all happy to be there. Deep-grained indignation seethed in the ranks, barely suppressed by the presence of the remaining Jesuit commandos.

Stardrive production was months behind schedule already, and everyone knew it. The Rejects had attacked so often that they'd actually managed to bring the whole process to a halt on more than one occasion. Though of course that had never been publicly admitted, even under the Campbells. The official line was "teething troubles," to be expected with the development of any new technology. Only a few people knew that the new drive was derived from only partly understood alien technology that had a disturbing habit of killing the clones who worked on it, and those people kept their mouths shut. Because most of them were dead, and the rest didn't want to be.

Toby kept Flynn moving, covering the ceremony from as many angles as he could get away with, without making the watching audience dizzy. He was careful to give each of the main players equal coverage, to avoid later claims of bias, and made sure Flynn kept a very safe distance from Kassar at all times. Luckily, Flynn's Union had been able to emergency express him a new camera in time for the ceremony. And if having a camera actually blasted off your shoulder by a disrupter didn't count as an emergency, Toby didn't know what did. Surprisingly, Flynn hadn't been that upset at the time. *Hell,* he said, *I've covered Democracy Now protest marches. God, they're a vicious bunch. Nothing scares me after them.* Toby smiled and shrugged, then and now, and got on with his job. He couldn't help wondering how much Imperial News must have laid out in payoffs to ensure his exclusive coverage. It wasn't really a major news story, but there were enough names and personages present, combined with memories of the rebel attack during the last live broadcast, to ensure a major live audience. Including the Empress. Which meant this broadcast could be a major feather in Imperial News' cap—if Toby didn't blow it. He was determined not to. At least partly because he had been told—quietly but very firmly—that if he did screw up, he shouldn't bother coming home again. Except in separate pieces.

So he worked his backside off, getting quick interviews where he could, combined with interesting shots of the crowds and the prisons and the factory complex, to liven up the long pompous speeches from anyone who was anyone—or thought they should be. He was a little upset he hadn't managed to get an interview with the legendary Half A Man, but Investigator Shoal had taken pains to keep Toby and Flynn at a more than polite distance. Toby had tried mentioning the importance of a free press and the Empress's name, but Shoal gave him such a look that he decided to go somewhere else very quickly before she decided to grab

Flynn's new camera and insert it into one of his main body cavities.

Lily and Michel smiled for the camera when it was pointed their way, but otherwise stayed quietly in the background. The temptation to keep checking their watches was almost overpowering, and they both tended to jump at sudden loud noises. But even their excited expectation couldn't keep them awake in the face of the speeches. Michel began dozing with his eyes open, an art he'd perfected while forced to listen to long boring speeches at Court, and was actually close to nodding off completely when Lily elbowed him suddenly in the ribs. His head jerked up, and he glared at her as he rubbed his side gingerly.

"Don't do that! It hurts."

"Be quiet, you big baby. Pay attention. See that flunky carrying a tray full of drinks?"

"Of course I can see him. I'm not blind."

"Then, keep watching. One of those glasses, the one with the crimson streaks in the stem, is headed straight for dear Daniel. And there's enough poison in it to see off a regiment of nuns."

"Are you crazy!" People turned to look at him, and he gave them a brief meaningless smile before lowering his voice. *"Have you lost your mind, Lily?* You'll get us both executed!"

"Relax, Michel. I know what I'm doing. Since the Chojiros said we couldn't actually blow up our respective spouses with their explosives, I've had to make other plans. The poison is completely undetectable, unless you know exactly what you're looking for, and by the time they can ship the body back to a civilized pathology lab, all traces will have disappeared. The waiter's working under a posthypnotic command. I told you my witchy gifts would come in handy. His mind will wipe itself clean of all memories of the incident once he's passed the right glass to Daniel. You see, I've thought of everything."

"Not quite," said Michel, fighting hard against an urge to take her neck in both hands and squeeze till her eyes bulged. "They'll know it was us anyway, because we're the only ones with a motive! The first thing they'll do is have an esper look inside our heads, just in case!"

"Nonsense. Daniel's death will be blamed on the rebels, just like everything else that happens here. And I will finally be free. If everything goes as planned, we can try the same trick on Stephanie later."

Lost for words, Michel could only stand and stare dumbly as the waiter carried his tray of drinks past the various personages, subtly turning his tray so that they took the glass nearest them and not the one with the poison in. Lily grinned broadly and squeezed Michel's arm with both hands. Which made it all the more heartrending when Half A Man ignored the glass he was supposed to take and reached across the tray to take the glass with the crimson-streaked stem. Lily's eyes widened, and she clapped a hand over her mouth to muffle the squeals coming out. Michel thought he might faint. Killing Daniel Wolfe was one thing. Poisoning the extremely important and well-connected Half A Man was quite another. The Empress would move heaven and earth to find out who was responsible. Starting with a complete esper scan of everyone present, on general principles. And *Sorry, it was a mistake* wouldn't go down all that well as an explanation. But there was nothing they could do. They couldn't say anything without giving themselves away. So they just stood and watched helplessly as Half A Man raised the glass to his half a mouth and drank deeply.

"How long till it works?" whispered Michel.

"It's supposed to be instantaneous," said Lily. "Especially considering how much I put in. I'm surprised the glass didn't melt."

Half A Man emptied the glass and handed it back to the waiter. "Very nice," they heard him say. "Do you have anymore?"

Lily shook her head dazedly as the waiter went on to deliver a harmless glass of wine to Daniel. "I don't believe it. Half A Man doesn't drink. Everyone knows that."

"Maybe he's never been this hot before. I bloody haven't."

"Well, why isn't black smoke coming out of his ears— ear?"

Michel shrugged. "It would appear poison is just another of the long list of things that can't kill Half A Man. Cover for me. I'm going to find something to hide behind, and then vomit for a while." He stopped as Lily grabbed his arm again. "Now what's wrong?"

"I don't know. Something bad is coming. I can feel it."

"Lily . . ."

"My witchy gifts are never wrong!"

"Of course something bad is coming! We planted explosives, remember? Now shut the hell up, before you start drawing attention to us! And let go of my arm. I'm losing the feeling in my fingers."

Lily scowled and turned her back on him. Michel sighed and was grateful for small mercies. The speeches droned on, lasting longer than expected, as speeches have a way of doing. Some of the prisoners and factory staff had passed out from the heat and were brought back to consciousness by varyingly brutal methods according to when the camera wasn't watching. Time was getting on. A lot of people had started looking at their watches. Toby looked at his and hoped the audience would stick with him, if only for the executions. He frowned despite himself. He wasn't sure how he felt about that. On the one hand they were definitely rebels, criminals, but on the other, most of them were women and children. Toby Shreck had justified a lot of questionable things in his life, working for Gregor Shreck did that to you, but murdering children in cold blood was just a step too far, even for him. He'd thought a lot about what he could do, and it seemed to him that he only had one chance. A last minute, live, on-camera appeal for clemency for the children, direct to the Empress. The watching billions would eat it up, and Lionstone just might see the advantages of appearing warm and sentimental in public. Either way, it was the children's last hope. He couldn't save the men and women. The public had to have its blood.

And so everyone checked their watches again and again, making frantic calculations in their heads as they waited for their planned surprises to pay off. They were all so preoccupied that no one noticed Investigator Shoal quietly disappearing from the scene on a mission of her own.

Mother Superior Beatrice sat on a folding chair outside the hospital tent, savoring the fresh air and drinking wine straight from the bottle. Even the evening heat was refreshing after the claustrophobic charnel house stench inside the tent. There was more room to move inside now that the worse-off had died, but the tent was still crowded from wall to wall with human suffering. Beatrice sighed and took another long drink. She was saving more patients than she was losing, but only just. The door swung open behind her for a

moment, letting out a brief rush of cheap disinfectant barely
covering the stench of blood and pus and gangrene that lay
beneath it. She shuddered, her hands shaking for a long moment after the rest of her had stopped. She'd seen so much
death and pain, and she was sick of it. Let someone else
cope for a while. She knew eventually her strength would
return, and then she'd get up and go back into hell again, but
for the moment it was just too much to ask. So she sat on
her chair and drank her wine and looked sardonically down
at the great ceremony taking place outside the factory. She'd
been invited, but she was damned if she'd give them the satisfaction of attending. That would have been too much like
endorsing their stupid bloody war.

Approaching footsteps jerked her out of her reverie, and
she looked around to see Investigator Shoal trudging unhurriedly up the low rise toward her. Beatrice frowned. What
the hell did Shoal want with her? Investigators tended not to
acknowledge any wound that wasn't immediately life threatening, and they weren't great ones for visiting the sick. She
studied Shoal as she drew closer. Grim-looking woman, but
then again Investigators weren't known for their sense of humor, either. Shoal finally came to a halt before Beatrice, not
even breathing hard after the climb. Shoal nodded briefly.
Beatrice nodded back, but didn't feel like getting up.

"Nice evening for a stroll, Investigator. What brings you
my way? Ceremony get too boring?"

"Something like that," said Shoal. She glanced at the tent
entrance. "Keeping busy?"

"Always. There might be lulls in the fighting out in the
field, but here the fight to save lives just goes on and on. Of
course, you wouldn't know anything about saving lives, Investigator. Not your line of territory."

"No. It must be a hard job. Unpleasant at times. Having
to make harsh decisions, about who you can help and who
you can't, which ones you have to sacrifice so others can be
saved. I can understand that. It's a lot like my job, sometimes."

Beatrice frowned. It was almost as though the Investigator
was trying to explain something to her. She shrugged and offered the bottle to Shoal. "A quick drink, Investigator? Good
for the soul, so they say."

"No thanks, Mother Superior. I don't drink while I'm
working."

Beatrice made the connection even as Shoal drew her sword, and she threw herself sideways off her chair. An Investigator's only work was killing. The sword blade whistled through the air where she'd been a moment before, and Beatrice hit the ground rolling. She surged up onto her feet again and flailed out wildly with her bottle. The wine shot out of the narrow neck in a solid jet that hit the Investigator right in her eyes, blinding her for a moment. Shoal lashed out with her sword anyway, but Beatrice had moved again. She brought the bottle down on Shoal's head as hard as she could. It didn't break, but the Investigator slumped to one knee under the force of the blow, shaking her head. Beatrice hit her again, putting all her strength into it, and this time the bottle shattered on the Investigator's skull. Shoal fell forward and Beatrice turned and ran, still holding the jagged bottle in her hand. She ran, though she hadn't a clue where safety lay anymore. Shoal's orders had to have come from very high up, to risk upsetting the Sisterhood, which meant she had no friends here on Technos III. She'd offended practically everyone at one time or another. No. She still had one friend; with influence if not power. Toby Shreck. She sprinted down the hill toward the factory complex and the ceremony. If she could put out a plea for protection on live holo coverage, the Wolfes would have to protect her or face the entire Sisterhood's wrath. Beatrice ran on, pushing herself as hard as she could, the wine she'd already drunk swimming heavily in her head and stomach. And she tried not to hear the pursuing feet of the Investigator, not all that far behind.

Jack Random, Ruby Journey, and Alexander Storm moved silently through a newly cut tunnel, deep beneath the surface of Technos III. Up above, on the jagged metal surface, the Rejects had launched a surprise attack against those guards not attending the ceremony, to keep them occupied while Random's small party slipped unnoticed past the factory's outer defenses. The tunnel ran deep, undercutting Wolfe and rebel trenches alike, to emerge beyond the innermost of the circles of hell, inside the factory's perimeter. The Wolfe forces would detect the new tunnel soon enough once the attack was over, but by then Random and his force would be inside the factory, the tunnel collapsed behind them. In theory.

"I don't like this," said Storm. "I really don't like this.

The Wolfe technicians must have spotted us by now. The guards could be down here any minute."

"Not so long as the Rejects are keeping them busy," said Random. "And I do wish you'd stop complaining, Alex. You're starting to sound like my fourth wife, may she rest in peace."

"She's dead?" said Ruby.

"No," said Random. "Just wishful thinking."

"I warned you about her, too," said Storm. "You didn't listen to me then, either. This scheme is crazy, Jack! It can't work!"

"You say that about all my plans."

"And I'm usually right."

Random sighed. "Look, forget all the ifs and maybes, it's really very simple. The Rejects keep the troops busy, and while everyone else is occupied with the ceremony, and the force Screen is down for the broadcast, we slip in and free the clone workers and get them out before anybody notices. What could go wrong?"

"I've made a list," said Storm. "But I don't suppose you want to see it."

"Hold your noise," said Ruby. "Or I'll hold it for you. You're getting too loud, Storm. Someone might hear you."

"Who?" said Storm. "According to the master planner here, no one's around to hear us."

"There's always the chance some guard hasn't read the script and is hanging about where he shouldn't be," said Random. "Just because it's a really good plan doesn't mean there can't be ... complications. Did you really never like my plans, Alex?"

"No I bloody didn't. They were always needlessly complex and extremely dangerous, especially for the poor sods who had to carry them out."

"I never asked my men to do anything I wasn't willing to do myself, and you know it. Hell, I lead those undercover teams as often as not. Anyway, if my plans were that bad, why did you keep volunteering to go along with me?"

"I was younger then. And you were my friend."

Random stopped and looked back. Ruby stopped, too, and instinctively moved in close beside Random as he studied his old friend thoughtfully. Storm looked almost defiant, the dim lighting putting shadows in his face. Or perhaps they'd been there for some time. For a moment, Random thought he was looking at a completely different person, someone he really didn't know at all. And, in a moment of insight, he wondered if that was how Storm saw him these days.

"You were my friend?" he said slowly. "As in used to be, but not anymore?"

Storm met his gaze squarely. "I don't know. I used to think I understood you, but you've changed, Jack. Look at you. You're younger, stronger, faster. It's not natural. I can't even follow the way you think anymore. What are you becoming, Jack?"

"Myself," said Random. "As I used to be. I'm back in my prime again. A second chance, to get things right this time. I'm sorry, Alex; I've grown young again while you're still old. That's what this is really about, isn't it? I'm the hero again, and you've been left behind. But none of that changes how I feel about you. It doesn't mean that I don't need you anymore. I just need you in different ways these days. Stay with me, Alex. Please. You remind me of who I used to be."

"And you remind me of who I used to be," said Storm. "A man I can't be anymore. Go on, Jack. You lead and I'll follow. Just like I always have."

"Oh, spare me," said Ruby. "Any more of this old comrades stuff and I'll puke over both of you. Can we get on? We are on a schedule, remember?"

"Ruby, dear heart, you have no sentiment in you at all," said Random, turning away to take up the lead again.

"Damn right," said Ruby. "It gets in the way of more important things. Like killing and loot. Now, get your ancient ass moving, Storm, or I'll kick it up around your ears."

Storm sniffed, but set off after Random. "You'll be old yourself one day, my girl."

"I very much doubt it," said Ruby. "And I am not your girl."

"That's for sure," said Random.

Mother Superior Beatrice ran across the uneven metal plain, her heavy robes flapping about her. She was boiling alive in the summer heat, and her breath was jerking painfully in her straining lungs, but she didn't dare slow down. Investigator Shoal couldn't be far behind her. There was fighting on the east side of the factory, another rebel attack by the look of it, which meant she couldn't get to the ceremony directly, as she'd planned. She'd have to enter the fac-

tory through the minor west gate and make her way through
the complex to the east gate and the ceremony. That might
actually be for the better. Shoal would be bound to catch her
on foot eventually, but she might just be able to lose the Investigator in the complex's warren of corridors. She forced
more strength into her legs and headed for the west gate.

Most of the guards were gone, called away to the ceremony or the rebel attack, but three Jesuit commandos in
their dark formal gowns and hoods were guarding the entrance. They were dark and menacing figures, with guns and
swords on their hips, but Beatrice didn't give a damn. Having an Investigator on your tail concentrates the mind won-
derfully as to what's really important. Stark terror will do
that to you. She stumbled to a halt before the Jesuits and
held up a shaking hand to forestall their questions as she
tried desperately to get her breath back. Since they hadn't
started shooting the moment they recognized her, presumably they didn't know about the execution order on her head.
And she couldn't tell them and hope for protection. They'd
just assume that if an Investigator was after her, she must be
guilty of something. Jesuits believed everyone was guilty of
something.

"Someone's after me," she said finally. "Must be a rebel.
You hold him off while I go inside for help."

"Hold it," said the most senior of the Jesuits. "We have
our orders. While the Screen's down, no one gets in or out
of the factory. No exceptions."

"But he's right behind me! He'll kill me!"

"Should have thought about that before you started treating rebels in your hospital," said the Jesuit. "Whatever's going on here, I've no doubt you brought it on yourself. If you
like, we could take you into protective custody. I'm sure we
could find a nice cell for you, until the Cardinal could get
around to seeing you."

"Oh, hell," said Beatrice. "I haven't got time for this
shit."

She kicked the senior Jesuit square in the nuts and bran-
dished the broken bottle in the faces of the other two. They
flinched back automatically as the senior Jesuit folded up
with a low moaning sound, and she dashed past them into
the factory. She ran on through the corridors, trusting to her
memory of the few times she'd been there before, to beg for
drugs and help from the complex's med lab. Now more than

ever, she had to get to the ceremony. With an angry Investigator and three furious Jesuits snapping at her heels, her only safety now lay in front of Toby Shreck's camera.

She hurried, plunging down one corridor after another, heading deeper into the complex, afraid to look behind her. Her pursuers wouldn't risk a disrupter shot inside the factory; too many places where an unlucky ricochet could do some really nasty damage. And then almost stopped running as a sudden thought struck her. The factory complex had its own internal security system, with cameras everywhere. All Shoal had to do was use her clearance to plug into the system, and she'd know immediately where her prey was and where she was heading. Which meant Beatrice had to throw Shoal off her trail before she headed for the ceremony. She ripped off her wimple and used it to wipe the sweat from her face. Think, damn it. If you want to lose yourself . . . head for a crowd. And the nearest crowd was in the clone quarters. They wouldn't have been invited to the ceremony. So lose the robes, blend in with the crowd just long enough to muddy her trail, and then head for the ceremony at speed. It might work. It might. She took a deep breath and ran on, her hope growing smaller and more tentative with every step.

Investigator Shoal tapped into the complex's security systems through her comm implant, overrode the passwords, and scanned for moving life signs. It took only a few moments to track the Sister down, and a few more to work out where she was heading. Shoal smiled tightly, holding her anger within. The three Jesuits she'd dragged along with her mustn't know that a Sister of Mercy had actually knocked down an Investigator. Even if said Investigator was suffering from a degenerative nerve disease. Her head was still ringing from the two heavy blows she'd taken, but she ignored it. It was just pain. She'd feel a lot better once she had the Sister stretched out lifeless at her feet. She glared at the three Jesuits, one of whom was standing very carefully.

"She's heading for the clone quarters. She must not know there's only one way in and one way out. Luckily for us, she's taking the long way there. You three go ahead and seal off the far exit. I'll go in after her and drive her through to you. Think you can hang on to her this time, or shall I call for the Cardinal to come and hold your hand while you do it?"

"We'll stop her," said the senior Jesuit. "If she even looks like trying anything, we'll cut her down."

"No you won't," said Shoal. "You'll hold her till I get there, and then I will kill her. This is Investigator business. No reason for the Church to be involved any further than necessary. Understood? Good. Now, get going. If she beats you to the far exit, I am going to be very annoyed with you."

The three Jesuits looked at each other briefly and then set off hurriedly down the corridor. Even a Jesuit commando had enough sense to be scared of an Investigator. Shoal smiled slightly and set off for the entrance to clone country. The prey had gone to ground, even if it didn't know it yet. All that remained was to flush it out.

The Jesuits hadn't got far when the senior Jesuit stopped suddenly and looked around him. The other Jesuits stopped with him, their hands dropping to the swords at their hips. The corridor was empty and silent before them.

"What is it?" said the most junior. "Do you need another rest? The Investigator really was most emphatic . . ."

"Shut the hell up about the Investigator and listen," said the senior Jesuit. "I thought I heard something."

"So you did," said Jack Random, appearing suddenly behind them from the corner they'd just passed. The senior Jesuit spun around, sword in hand, and Random kicked him squarely in the nuts. The Jesuit crumpled to the floor, and Random kicked him in the head. The Jesuit gave up consciousness with something like relief. Ruby Journey punched out the most junior Jesuit, and Storm clubbed down the third from behind while the poor fellow was still trying to figure out which direction to look in first. Ruby looked down at the three unconscious bodies and sniffed loudly.

"Jesuits. Didn't like them at school and I don't like them now. Let's kill them and fillet them into little pieces as a general warning."

"Maybe later," said Random. "Right now we need their robes, and I don't want blood on them. Besides, it's a good chance for you to exercise self-control. We don't need to kill these people. We just need their robes. Disguised as Jesuits we can go anywhere we like in the complex, and not have to bother about dodging the security cameras."

"I suppose you're going to claim you planned this as well," said Storm dourly.

"I expected something like this to come up," said Random airily. "I like to keep my plans flexible. Now, get those robes off them."

They grinned at each other and set about acquiring Jesuit robes for themselves. This involved a certain amount of swapping back and forth as they tried to figure out which robe fitted who the best. None were particularly comfortable, but they finally all ended up in something they could live with. Ruby looked down at the unconscious senior Jesuit and sniggered.

"So that's what they wear under these robes. I always wondered."

"I must admit it's been a while since I saw underwear of quite such a startling color," said Storm. "I wonder who gets to help do up the laces?"

"Save the jokes for later," said Random. "The sooner we free the clones and get them moving, the better. The rebels' agents inside this place risked their lives setting up the route we'll be using, and I don't want that to have been for nothing. Ruby, you've got the map. Lead the way."

Ruby looked at him. "I haven't got the map. You've got the map."

"No I haven't . . ."

"I've got the map," said Storm. "Dear God, how did you ever manage without me, Jack?"

Beatrice knew where the clone quarters were, but she'd never been in them before. Not many had. Clones were kept strictly separate from real people. But the entrance was unlocked, unguarded, almost as though they'd been expecting her. Or someone. The thought almost brought her to a halt; but in the end she pressed on. She had to. There was nowhere else she could go.

Beyond the barriers and the electric doors, clone country was stark and utilitarian. Beatrice had thought she'd known what to expect, from tales she'd heard from clone and rebel patients, but nothing could have prepared her for the reality. There were no rooms or living quarters. The clones lived in steel cages and pens, stacked together like some great battery farm. There wasn't an inch of spare space, apart from the single narrow central aisle she was walking down. There was a powerful, almost overpowering smell of bodies, packed close together. Beatrice was used to the medical stenches of the hospital tent, but even so she had to fight an urge to hold a hand over her mouth and nose.

As she passed the steel pens, faces came forward to watch her. Some were missing eyes or ears or noses. Some had no lower jaws, rotted away by the forces they worked with. They made quiet, mewling sounds like tortured kittens. Beatrice came to a halt, in spite of herself. There was nothing she could do to help them, and they couldn't help her. She couldn't blend in with them, which meant she had to get out of clone country before the Investigator found her. But she couldn't just walk on and pretend she hadn't seen this suffering. She looked around her, her hands clenched into fists, caught in a quandary that her conscience wouldn't release her from.

And then she heard approaching footsteps and gripped her broken bottle tightly, her heart racing. She'd hesitated too long. Shoal had found her. She looked wildly about her, but she knew there was no point in running. She was exhausted, and Shoal . . . was an Investigator. Beatrice swallowed hard and stood her ground. She knew fighting wouldn't get her anywhere, but she was damned if she'd go down without a struggle. She looked at the damaged faces of the watching clones and gestured for them to move back.

"Look away," she said quietly. "You don't want to see this."

And then the three robed Jesuits appeared suddenly before her and skidded to a halt, as though they hadn't been expecting to find her there. Beatrice showed them her broken bottle and tried hard to sound defiant rather than pathetic. "Well, come on then! You don't think I'm going to make it easy for you, do you? I'll make you kill me before I let you hand me over to that Investigator cow."

"There seems to be some misunderstanding here," said one of the Jesuits mildly. He pushed back his cowl to reveal a warm face with a kindly scowl. "I am Alexander Storm, currently working with the rebels of Technos III. Might I inquire who you are?"

"Mother Superior Beatrice," she said automatically. "Of the Sisters of Mercy. How do I know you are who you say you are?"

"Well," said Storm, "the fact that we haven't tried to kill you should be a point in our favor. Do you think you could lower that fearsome-looking bottle? I'm sure we'd all feel a lot safer." He gave her a smile of unimpeachable charm, and she slowly lowered the broken bottle. Storm nodded approvingly. "Allow me to present my two associates: Ruby Journey and Jack Random."

Beatrice blinked at the last name and watched intently as the other two Jesuits pushed back their cowls. The woman she didn't know from a hole in the ground, except by reputation, but everyone knew of Jack Random. He looked a lot younger than she'd expected, but it was definitely him. She relaxed suddenly, her breath going out of her in a rush as she finally felt something like safe again. "Dear Lord, it's really you. What the hell are you doing here?"

"Freeing the clones," said Random equably. "Would you care to help? I get the feeling you'd be a lot safer in our company."

"Damn right," said Beatrice. "I've got a bloody Investigator snapping at my heels. Someone high up wants me dead. But I can't help you. The Sisters of Mercy must remain neutral."

"If someone's sent an Investigator after you, I think we can safely assume your neutrality has already been compromised," said Random. "Besides, can you just stand by and let this horror continue?"

Beatrice looked at the watching clones in their pens, packed together like animals. "No," she said finally. "I can't."

"Good for you, Sister," said Storm. "And don't worry. We'll protect you."

"Is that right?" said Investigator Shoal. "Now, that I would like to see." They all spun around, to find her standing right behind them, her sword in her hand. She looked very relaxed and utterly deadly. "Good thing I tried to contact the Jesuits and smelled a rat when I couldn't get an answer. I started out after a rogue Sister of Mercy, and now I have three infamous rebels to kill as well, one of them the legendary Jack Random. God is good, sometimes, isn't he? Now, who wants to die first?"

Ruby looked at Random. "Let me have her. I didn't have time to enjoy killing that Investigator before."

"Sorry," said Random, "we haven't got the time now." He already had his disrupter in his hand, pointing at Shoal. "Say good night, Investigator."

Ruby glared at him. "Don't you dare, Jack Random. If

you kill her, I'll never speak to you again. I've always wanted to go one on one with an Investigator."

Random started to shake his head, and Shoal's sword whipped around, the flat of the blade slapping the gun out of his hand. Random shook his tingling fingers gingerly, looked at the coldly smiling Investigator, and nodded to Ruby. "I never could refuse you anything, my dear. But make it quick. We've got work to do."

Shoal laughed suddenly. "I don't know what you people have been smoking, but I'm pretty sure it must be illegal. Nothing else could get you this far from reality. Let's do it, girl. Then, after I've killed you, I'll kill your friends, and take back Jack Random's head as a trophy."

"In your dreams," said Ruby. "Let's do it."

They slammed together, head-to-head, blades flying, no quarter asked or given. They stamped and lunged and their swords clashed together, sparks flying in the still air. They were both supremely talented, trained to great skill by harsh circumstances, and the speed at which they came together and sprang apart was exhilarating. Ruby laughed breathlessly, her sword everywhere at once. This was what she lived for, when she felt most alive. She could have boosted, but didn't. She could have called on unnatural strength and speed, but she chose not to. She wanted to beat the Investigator in a fair fight, to prove she was the best.

Shoal swung her sword double-handed in an arc that would have beheaded Ruby if it had connected, but Ruby ducked under it at the last moment. She took the fight to Shoal, pressing the attack as hard as she could, and Shoal just stood there and took it, not retreating a step. Their swords hammered together, drawing blood here and there from minor wounds, neither able to gain the upper hand for long. But Ruby was getting tired and just a little slower, and Shoal wasn't. Ruby was a bounty hunter, trained as a fighter in the hardest of schools, but Shoal, even with her illness, was an Investigator. And slowly, foot by foot, she began to push Ruby back. Shoal's blade drew blood again and again, and Ruby couldn't touch her. It slowly came to her that she'd finally found her better. And just maybe she was going to die if she didn't boost. The boost would give her the edge she needed. *No,* she thought furiously. *I can do this. I can, not some gift from an alien device.* Shoal swung her sword with unexpected strength and slammed Ruby off balance.

She staggered back, trying to recover, and Shoal drew back her blade for a killing thrust. And Ruby's blade shot forward, driven by boosted strength and speed she hadn't called for, and punched through Shoal's chest and out her back. Blood gushed from the Investigator's mouth, and she sank to her knees with a look of utter surprise on her face. Ruby jerked her sword out, and Shoal fell forward and lay still.

"No!" said Ruby. "No! I didn't want that!" She hacked at the body with her sword again and again, cursing and spitting. She hadn't called on the boost. It had come unbidden, unwanted. For better or worse, the Maze wouldn't let her be merely human anymore. She finally stopped herself and stood hunched over the mutilated body, panting for breath.

"Is she always like this?" said Beatrice.

"Not always," said Random. "Ruby? Are you all right?"

"No," said Ruby. "I don't think so." She sheathed her sword without cleaning it; then stopped, raised her head, and looked about her. "Hold everything. I'm starting to get a bad feeling about this place."

Random looked at her thoughtfully. He took her feelings seriously. He had them himself, sometimes. "You mean right here in the clone quarters?"

"No. More widely spread than that."

Storm looked around nervously. "Could there be guards on the way?"

"I don't know! Jack, join with me. We're stronger together."

Their eyes met and their minds joined. Their faces became blank masks as they concentrated, their minds leaping up and out to test their surroundings. Beatrice looked at Storm. "I didn't know they were espers."

"They're not," said Storm. "But don't ask me what they are."

Random and Ruby fell back into their heads and looked at each other incredulously. "I don't believe it," said Random.

"What?" said Storm. "Don't believe what?"

"There are explosives everywhere," said Ruby. "All through the factory."

"At least three main groupings," said Random. "Set to do maximum damage and timed to go off soon. Any one would have been enough to bring stardrive production to a halt, but God knows what this many will do. Right, that's it. We are

out of here. Alex, use the codes we were given and get these
pens open. We've got to get the clones out of here while
there's still time."

"Wait," said Beatrice. "You do know they're executing
your people at the ceremony?"

"Sure," said Random. "Don't worry. We'll get to them
next."

"You won't have time. Their execution's been brought
forward, to be sure of going out on prime time."

"Damn," said Random. "You can't rely on anyone these
days. Right; Sister Beatrice, you and Alex get the clones out
of here. Since they're in clear danger from the explosives,
you can do that without risking your Sisterhood's neutrality.
Ruby and I will take care of the prisoners."

"How?" said Alex.

"I'm working on it," said Random.

"Thrills, chills, and last-minute rescues," said Ruby.
"Don't you just love being an outlaw?"

In the beating heat outside the factory complex, the ceremony was going well. Everyone had remembered their lines,
Kassar hadn't hit anybody yet, and Toby Shreck and Flynn
were covering it all, transmitting live to audiences all across
the Empire. Important people were watching, not least the
Empress, and everyone else was watching in the hopes of a
major cock-up or rebel attack, like before. Toby kept up a
murmured running commentary during the slow bits and suffered through the longer speeches. If they didn't get to the
executions soon, people might start losing interest. A new
stardrive might be just what the Empire needed, but it didn't
actually make great viewing in itself.

All in all, though, things were going better than Toby had
expected. As requested, Half A Man was staying in plain
view and not retreating into the background as usual. He
wasn't actually doing or saying anything, but his public appearances were so rare these days that any new sighting was
an event. Toby had put as much effort into convincing Half
A Man as he had into persuading Flynn not to wear his best
party frock. Good ratings needed all the help they could get.

The Wolfes were standing right at the front, each with
their own proper spouse, smiling and nodding and generally
being nice to each other. People had won drama awards for
less. There was an underlying air of tension among them,

but that was to be expected and hopefully wouldn't show up on camera. Toby couldn't help noticing that they kept checking their watches when they thought no one was looking. Presumably, they were getting impatient for the executions, too. Toby smiled to himself. They didn't know about his planned dramatic plea for clemency.

The ranks of Church troops and factory security staff were still standing rigidly to attention and made a nice spectacle. Only a few more had fainted from the heat, and the audience wouldn't mind that. It added a touch of drama and made them more sympathetic to the audience. Toby had considered bribing a few to mock faint, but had rightly decided the heat would do the job for him. The prisoners looked like rabble. Animals in chains. Presumably, arranged quite deliberately. The Wolfes never missed a good propaganda opportunity.

Daniel Wolfe stepped forward to make the final speech, reading from a teleprompter with all the warmth and spontaneity of a particularly dense block of wood. Flynn moved in a little closer to frame the man's head and shoulders, to hide the fact that Daniel's hands were twitching nervously. Toby listened carefully, nodding now and again. It was a good speech. Almost as good as the stuff he used to write. He looked across at the ramp protruding from the factory entrance. The first finished stardrive was waiting in the wings, great ugly thing, ready to make an entrance on cue. Toby allowed himself a small glow of satisfaction. With work like this to his credit, he'd be able to pick and choose from among the very best journalistic assignments. It was a good show, if a little safe and uncontroversial, to end his time on Technos III. Pity it couldn't have had a touch more drama, though.

Jack Random and Ruby Journey, hidden and anonymous inside their borrowed Jesuit robes with the hoods pulled well forward, strode haughtily past the security cameras and the few guards left on duty. Most just nodded them through. You didn't argue with Jesuits, unless you wanted to spend your next weekend on some really inventive and humiliating penance. Random kept up a quiet muttering of what he hoped were suitably religious-sounding utterances, made broadly gestured crosses over anything that moved or looked like it might, and generally kept his head down. He'd always en-

joyed those parts of his schemes that involved disguises. It
appealed to the frustrated actor in him. Though he sometimes thought his whole life as the professional rebel had
been his greatest role. Ruby just trudged along beside him,
keeping her hands away from her concealed weapons and
trying not to break into her usual long-legged stride. In her
own way she was acting, too. Being quiet, calm, and subser-
vient didn't come at all naturally to her. Much as he loved
her, Random had to admit Ruby wasn't really what you'd
call versatile. If you couldn't hit it, steal it, or sleep with it,
she was often lost for an alternative.

They finally reached the main exit that would let them out
into the ceremony and came to a dead halt as a Church
trooper in full armor blocked their way. He was almost as
broad as he was tall, armed with gun and sword, and had the
happily obstinate look of someone whose orders allowed
him to push around people who would normally have been
his superiors. Random crossed him twice, with dramatic
sweeps of the hand, but the trooper remained unimpressed.

"Sorry, Father. You know the rules. No one to be admitted
once the ceremony is underway. You'll have to watch it on
the viewscreens. Now, move on."

Random gestured for the trooper to lean forward, waited
until the man's head was right next to his cowl, and said,
very solemnly, "Did you know the Jesuits have their very
own special handshake?" And he reached forward, grabbed
the trooper's balls in his hand, and scrunched them. The
trooper's eyes bulged, and though he sucked in air for a
scream, he couldn't seem to get it out again. He sank to his
knees, and Ruby took off his helmet and clubbed him over
the head with the butt of her gun. The trooper fell forward,
and Random solemnly made the sign of the cross over his
unconscious body. "I'd have made a great Mason," he said
wistfully.

They strolled unconcernedly out of the complex and took
up a position on the edge of things. Kassar shot them a ven-
omous glare for being late, but left it at that. Everyone else
conspicuously ignored them. Daniel Wolfe was still making
his speech. Badly. Random looked unobtrusively over at
the rebel prisoners waiting for execution and scowled at the
chains holding them in place. Heavy chains with thick steel
links and blocky padlocks you couldn't hope to pick with

anything less than a disrupter. Random's scowl deepened.
No one had mentioned chains.

On the other side of the crowd, Toby Shreck was also
studying the prisoners, taking in the details. Many showed
the blood and bruises of recent beatings. Even the children.
All eyes were glazed from heavy-duty tranquilizers, so they
wouldn't be any trouble. Not enough to knock them out, of
course. That would take all the fun out of the executions.
Toby frowned and looked around as Daniel stopped speaking
suddenly. His teleprompter had broken down, and Stephanie
was glaring meaningfully at Toby. So, rather than have Daniel look like a complete divot because he didn't know his
own speech, Toby gestured for Flynn to shut down his camera. They'd blame it on technical difficulties later. And it
might be handy to have the high-and-mighty Stephanie
Wolfe owing them a favor. Flynn moved over to join Toby,
and they both looked at the prisoners.

"I can't believe they're going to kill the children, too,"
said Flynn. "I just wish there was something we could do."

"There is," said Toby quietly. "Once Daniel's finally finished his speech, I'll do an on-camera appeal for clemency,
for the children, straight to the Empress."

"You've got a good heart, chief," said Flynn, "but it won't
work. Kassar's got too much of his pride tied up in this, after his people got their heads handed to them down in the
tunnels. He'll just say this is a Church matter. No one
messes with the Church these days. Not if they're fond of
breathing. And he'd probably have you executed, too, just
for asking. No, boss, all we can do is film what happens and
hope the audience's hearts will be touched enough to stop
him doing it again. I wouldn't put money on it, though. They
do so love their blood sports these days."

"I used to be a big fan of the Arena," said Toby. "Season
ticket, good seat. But that was different. At least the gladi-
ators had a fighting chance, mostly. This is just slaughter.
And I've seen so much blood here. I don't know, Flynn. I
never thought of myself as political, but this . . ."

"There's nothing we can do, boss. Just tough it out, do
our job, and hope we end up somewhere more civilized for
our next assignment."

"I wanted to cover a war," said Toby. "Because wars are
where the stories are. I never expected anything like this."

"No one ever does," said Flynn. "That's why we have to keep covering them."

Someone got the teleprompter working again by kicking it somewhere sensitive. Flynn resumed filming. Daniel finished his speech, and everyone applauded politely. Daniel nodded to Kassar and stepped back to allow him to introduce the executions. The Cardinal faced the camera with a forbidding stare and smiled coldly.

"This day, 327 rebel prisoners will die, as an example to those who would stand against the authority of the established Church and Her Imperial Majesty, the Empress Lionstone XIV. The majority will be electrocuted through their chains, but first their leaders will be beheaded, one by one, as retribution for all the Faithful who have died in the struggle here. Stand forward, executioners, and do your duty."

"Oh-oh," said Ruby. "He's looking at us."

"No wonder no one wanted to mess with us," said Random.

"What are we going to do?"

"Walk forward very slowly and hope I come up with some plan before we get there."

"It had better be a bloody good one."

"It will, it will. I'm famous for my plans."

"You're also famous for getting your ass kicked, and there are a hell of a lot of heavily armed people looking right at us. Could we please walk a little slower?"

"Ruby, any slower, and we'd be in reverse. Kassar's already looking daggers at us."

"Oh, gee," said Ruby. "I may wet myself."

They reached the low podium set up before the prisoners, bowed to Kassar, and then looked at the two heavy swords standing next to the two chopping blocks. The blocks looked like they'd seen a lot of service. Random looked at the prisoners, who stared back as defiantly as they could. Some of the younger children started to cry, not sure what was going on, but picking up on the charged atmosphere. For a moment that stretched and stretched, there was only the quiet and the tension. Kassar strode over to the podium.

"What do we do?" hissed Ruby. "Jack, *what do we do?*"

"Proceed with the executions or we'll start with yours!" snapped Kassar, and then he stopped, grabbed Random's hood, and pushed it back to reveal his face. "You!"

"Me!" said Random, and punched Kassar in the mouth. He grabbed the dazed Cardinal, swung him around, and held him as a shield. There was uproar among the watching Church troops. Random smiled into Flynn's camera. "Long live the rebellion!"

"Oh, nice plan," said Ruby, throwing off her robes and drawing her sword and disrupter. "Really subtle. Couldn't have done better myself."

The Church troops broke ranks and ran toward the three figures by the podium, closely followed by the security forces. They all had swords in their hands. Ruby turned to face them, fire in her eyes. Some of the prisoners managed a ragged cheer. Random looked at his watch.

Toby Shreck turned to Flynn. "Tell me you're getting this!"

"I'm getting it, I'm getting it! It's all going out live. Is that who I think it is?"

"Don't know the woman, but the other's Jack Random all right. I should have known he'd make one of his patented last-minute rescues!"

"Hate to spoil your scenario, boss, but there's only two of them and hundreds and hundreds of everybody else. Hostage or no hostage, they don't stand a chance."

"What the hell," said Toby. "It'll make a great show. We are talking major awards here, Flynn . . . Where the hell did *they* come from?"

They were the hundreds upon hundreds of rebels who were boiling up out of concealed openings at the edge of the factory perimeter. Random grinned. Bang on time. While their fellows had been keeping the factory's defenses concentrated on the other side of the factory, the rest had been tunneling like crazy to reach the perimeter before the executions took place. They swarmed across the uneven metal surface, brandishing guns and swords and yelling their savage war cries. The Church and security men reversed direction, forgot all about Random and Ruby and Cardinal Kassar, and braced themselves to meet the rebel forces. Disrupters fired, energy beams cutting through the air, blowing people apart in gushers of blood. And then the two forces hammered together, a heaving mass of bodies surging this way and that, and there was room only for sword-to-sword and head-to-head, and the bloody rage of clashing beliefs.

Ruby looked at Random. "I suppose you're going to say you planned that?"

Random laughed. "Of course. Though the timing was a bit close. Search Kassar's pockets; see if he's got any keys to the padlocks."

And that was when Half A Man came striding forward, sweeping men aside, heading straight for Jack Random with a sword in his human hand. Random pushed Kassar away from him, drew his disrupter, and snapped off a shot. Half A Man raised his energy arm to block it, and the energy beam ricocheted harmlessly away into the sky. And so they came together, two men touched and shaped by alien forces, neither of them wholly human anymore. The power of the Madness Maze burned in Random, but even so he was hard-pressed to stay in the fight. Whatever else the aliens had done, they had made Half A Man a formidable fighter. He'd been a warrior longer than Jack Random had been alive, and he never grew tired. Their swords clashed together, neither giving an inch.

Cardinal Kassar, meanwhile, had come out of his daze, and was fighting head-to-head with Ruby Journey. He'd started with contempt, but was quickly fighting for his life. He called on all his training and experience as an elite Church warrior, and found it wasn't enough. She drove him back, step-by-step, sweeping aside his defenses with ease and cutting him at whim. And though she could feel the boost surging up within her, she kept it down, refusing the advantages it offered. She was all she needed, all she'd ever needed, and she'd decide whether to use her extra gifts or not. She grinned into Kassar's sweating face. She could kill him at any time, and both of them knew it. But she wanted it to last. Ruby Journey was enjoying herself.

Daniel Wolfe drew his sword, ready to rush into the fray himself, and then stopped as he saw how frightened Stephanie was. She needed him to protect her. He glanced at the factory's main entrance, but there were already too many rebels between him and it. There was no safe cover anywhere. All he could hope for was not to be noticed. So he pulled his sister behind the teleprompter, made her crouch down, and stood protectively over her, determined that no one would get to her without having gone through him first.

Lily and Michel clung together, staring about them with wild eyes. A small group of rebels broke away from the main fight and headed their way. Lily pushed Michel away from her, glared at the approaching rebels, and called up her witchy powers. But all her weak esp could manage was a rushing wind that barely slowed the Rejects. One of them cut at Lily with his sword. Michel pushed her out of the way, and the sword cut into his throat and out again. Blood sprayed, splashing Lily's horrified face. Michel fell dying to the ground. Lily crouched over him, crying and screaming hysterically, until a rebel passing by on his way to free the prisoners cut her down out of reflex. Lily and Michel died together, a long way from home, two children in a violent adult world they never really understood.

Half A Man finally realized he couldn't beat Jack Random as easily as he'd thought, so he disengaged, turned, and ran. He had a better idea, and besides, with the rebels so close, the safety of the factory took precedence over everything else. He ran back into the factory, cutting down anyone who got in his way. First, he'd shut down the timer on Kassar's explosives, and then he'd raise the factory's force Screen again so that most of the rebels would be trapped outside it. Those left inside would soon fall, and the factory would be safe. He smiled with his half a mouth. Let Jack Random rattle his sword against an energy field and see what good it did him. There were better ways to win a war.

While Half A Man was disappearing into the complex, Alexander Storm and Mother Beatrice were leading the clones out. The clones took one look at the carnage and mayhem spread out before them, and froze in the doorway. Storm and Beatrice yelled for everyone to stay put and keep their heads down. While the clones huddled together, the rebel and the Sister studied the situation thoughtfully. Some of the attacking rebels were trying to free the prisoners, but the heavy-duty padlocks were slowing them down.

"They'd better be quick," said Beatrice. "As long as those chains hold, the Wolfes could still fry the prisoners at the press of a button. And anybody else who happened to be touching the chains or locks at the time."

"Good point," said Storm. "I'd better give them a hand. I was always good with locks. But then, everyone needs a hobby."

"You're a brave man, Alexander Storm," said Beatrice.

"Damn right," said Storm. "Jack isn't the only legend around here, you know."

Kassar backed away from Ruby, panting for breath, blood streaming from his wounds. He still held his sword, but it shook uncontrollably in his hand. Ruby went after him, still smiling. She'd had enough fun for the moment, and now it was time for the Cardinal to die. He saw the decision in her eyes and frantically held up his other hand.

"Back off, bitch! The controls for the prisoners' execution are wired into my glove. One step closer, and they're dead!"

"You're bluffing," said Ruby calmly. "If you could do that, you'd have done it by now, just for spite."

Kassar smiled. "Try me. What will your precious rebel friends think of you when they learn you could have saved the prisoners, but didn't choose to?"

Ruby shrugged, sprang forward, and brought her sword savagely down with all her strength behind it. The heavy blade sheared clean through Kassar's wrist, and his hand fell twitching to the ground. Kassar screamed breathlessly, dropped his sword, and grabbed the stump of his wrist, trying to squeeze it shut. Blood pumped past his gripping fingers.

"I've never given a damn what people think of me," said Ruby Journey.

"I'm rich," said Kassar, forcing the words past gritted teeth. His face was white as a skull. "Name your price."

"Now, that's more like it. How much have you got?"

"How much do you want?"

"All of it. Where is it?"

"In a safe. In my quarters. Gold. Payroll for the Faithful. Let me go, and it's yours."

Ruby thought for a moment. "Thanks for the tip, Cardinal. I'll check it out later. Now, say good-bye."

Her sword swung around in a long double-handed arc and cut off Kassar's head. It went bouncing and rolling away into the surrounding crush and was quickly lost to sight, kicked this way and that and trampled underfoot. Ruby smiled, satisfied. A good kill, and gold for afters. The day was looking up. She searched Kassar's pockets, found a set of keys, and went to help free the prisoners, humming a merry tune.

The fight went on, the rebels pushing back the Empire forces almost at will, until finally some security officer had the good sense to surrender. The idea caught on in a flash, and soon there were swords dropping and hands going up all over the place. And as quickly as that, the battle was over. Ruby and Storm freed the prisoners, and Beatrice ushered the clones out of the complex. There were cries of joy and relief as the rebel forces found their loved ones safe, and hugs and tears became the order of the day. Toby and Flynn covered it all, broadcasting live to an astonished Empire.

And that was when the factory blew up.

The first set of explosives to detonate set off all the others, and within seconds the whole factory became a great blazing fireball. The core of the building became a searing inferno, and blazing wreckage rained down on all sides. The outer walls blew apart, unable to contain the pressure, and the deadly heat ballooned outward, followed by a storm of flying red-hot shrapnel. There was nowhere the hundreds of people could hide—no cover anywhere. They were only seconds away from certain death when Random and Ruby reached out to each other, linked minds, and threw up a protective force field to hold back the flames and explosions. The firestorm raged against the shield, battering their minds, but still it held on and on until the force of the firestorm was spent and the shield was no longer needed. And only then did it disappear, and Jack Random and Ruby Journey sank to their knees, blood spilling from their nose and mouth and ears. They clung together, healing. The heat was devastating now, but bearable. The wreckage of the factory burned brightly, flames shooting up into the sky. After a while Storm came over to join them.

"Amazing. Is there anything you can't do?"

"Yeah," said Ruby hoarsely. "Save a whole safe full of gold bullion that just went up with that factory. Damn. I was looking forward to that."

Random was still laughing about that sometime later as he and Ruby and Storm led the rebels and clones back down into the tunnels under Technos III. The surviving Empire forces, disarmed, sat around and looked at each other and waited for somebody else to decide what they should do next. And out of the inferno, out of the blazing wreckage, out of the hell that was all that remained of the factory complex, came Half A Man, striding unhurriedly through the flames, untouched by the heat. He walked over to Daniel and Stephanie Wolfe, and shook his head slowly.

"Trained Church troops beaten like amateurs, and three Investigators dead. The factory utterly destroyed. Lionstone is not going to be pleased. If I were you, I'd start thinking up some really inventive excuses."

He strode off to bark orders at what was left of the Empire forces. Stephanie stared mutely at the burning ruins of her factory. "All gone. Everything. We'll have to start again from scratch. If the Empress doesn't take the stardrive away from us for this fiasco."

"And both our spouses are dead," said Daniel.

"Ah, well," said Stephanie. "At least some good came of this." She glared into the leaping flames. "Our explosives couldn't have done all that. Someone else must have interfered."

"Probably," said Daniel. "Odds are we'll never find out what really happened here. It doesn't matter. It's over. I'm not needed here anymore. I'm finally free to go and look for Daddy."

And he strode away, without once looking back. "Danny!" Stephanie called desperately after him. "Come back! You can't just leave me here like this. I need you. Come back, you bastard!"

Flynn got that on camera, too. Toby Shreck stood beside him, grinning foolishly. "Live, Flynn. We got it all, live. We'll win every award going for this, and probably a few they'll make up specially. I haven't felt like this since one of the Family maids showed me what was what when I was fourteen."

"I don't know about you," said Flynn, finally lowering his camera, "but my hourly rate just went up. Way up."

"Damn right," said Toby. "I wonder what we should do for an encore . . ."

"Don't worry," said Half A Man, "I'll think of something."

Toby and Flynn looked at each other. "I don't know about you," said Toby, "but I think fame and fortune just got indefinitely rerouted."

The Bestselling
DEATHSTALKER Saga
by Simon R. Green

Owen Deathstalker, a reluctant hero destined for greatness, guards the secret of his identity from the corrupt powers that run the Empire—an Empire he hopes to protect by leading a rebellion against it!

Praise for the DEATHSTALKER Saga:
"[Simon R.] Green invokes some powerful mythologies."
—*Publishers Weekly*

"A huge novel of sweeping scope, told with a strong sense of legend."
—*Locus*

Available wherever books are sold or at penguin.com

THE ULTIMATE IN
SCIENCE FICTION AND FANTASY!

From magical tales of distant worlds to stories of
technological advances beyond the grasp of man, Penguin has
everything you need to stretch your imagination to its limits.

penguin.com

ACE
Get the latest information on favorites like
William Gibson, T.A. Barron, Brian Jacques,
Ursula K. LeGuin, Sharon Shinn, and Charlaine Harris,
as well as updates on the best new authors.

ROC
Escape with Harry Turtledove, Anne Bishop,
S.M. Stirling, Simon R. Green, Chris Bunch, Jim Butcher,
E.E. Knight, and many others—plus news on the
latest and hottest in science fiction and fantasy.

DAW
Mercedes Lackey, Kristen Britain, Tanya Huff,
Tad Williams, C.J. Cherryh, and many more—
DAW has something to satisfy the cravings of any
science fiction and fantasy lover.
Also visit dawbooks.com.

*Get the best of science fiction and fantasy
at your fingertips!*